Fifty Stories

BOOKS BY KAY BOYLE

Novels

THE UNDERGROUND WOMAN
GENERATION WITHOUT FARE-
    WELL
THE SEAGULL ON THE STEP
HIS HUMAN MAJESTY
"1939"
A FRENCHMAN MUST DIE
AVALANCHE

PRIMER FOR COMBAT
MONDAY NIGHT
DEATH OF A MAN
MY NEXT BRIDE
GENTLEMEN, I ADDRESS YOU
    PRIVATELY
YEAR BEFORE LAST
PLAGUED BY THE NIGHTINGALE

Stories and Novelettes

NOTHING EVER BREAKS EXCEPT
    THE HEART
THREE SHORT NOVELS
THE SMOKING MOUNTAIN

THE CRAZY HUNTER
THE WHITE HORSES OF VIENNA
THE FIRST LOVER
WEDDING DAY

THIRTY STORIES

Poetry

TESTAMENT FOR MY STUDENTS
COLLECTED POEMS

A GLAD DAY
AMERICAN CITIZEN

For Children

THE YOUNGEST CAMEL
PINKY IN PERSIA

PINKY, THE CAT WHO LIKED TO
    SLEEP

Memoirs

THE AUTOBIOGRAPHY OF
    EMANUEL CARNEVALI
Compiled and Edited
by Kay Boyle

BEING GENIUSES TOGETHER
Revised and Supplemented
by Kay Boyle

Fifty Stories

KAY BOYLE

1980
DOUBLEDAY & COMPANY, INC.
GARDEN CITY, NEW YORK

Library of Congress Catalog Card Number 78-22151
ISBN: 0-385-14996-4

ACKNOWLEDGMENTS

From *The New Yorker:* "Security," "Winter Night," "Army of Occupation," "Evening at Home," "Summer Evening," "The Criminal," "Fife's House," and "Adam's Death," copyright 1936, 1946, 1947, 1949, by The New Yorker Magazine, Inc.

From *Tomorrow:* "French Harvest," "Cabaret," and "The Lost," copyright 1948, 1951, by Garrett Publications, Inc.

From *The Nation:* "The Lovers of Gain," copyright 1950 by The Nation Associates, Inc.

From *The Spectator:* "Rondo at Carraroe."

From *Harper's Magazine:* "Aufwiedersehen Abend," copyright 1951 by Harper & Bros. "Dear Mr. Walrus," copyright 1936 by Harcourt, Brace and Company.

Thirty Stories acknowledgments: for "Episode in the Life of an Ancestor," originally published in the volume *Wedding Day and Other Stories*, to Jonathan Cape and Harrison Smith, Inc.; for "Wedding Day," originally published in the volume *Wedding Day and Other Stories*, to Jonathan Cape and Harrison Smith, Inc.; for "Rest Cure," published in *Story Magazine*, April–May 1931, and in the volume *The First Lover and Other Stories*, to Story Magazine, Inc., and to Harrison Smith and Robert Haas, Inc.; for "Ben," published in *The New Yorker*, December 24, 1938, to the F-R Publishing Corporation; for "Kroy Wen," published in *The New Yorker*, July 25, 1931, and in the volume *The First Lover and Other Stories*, to the F-R Publishing Corporation and to Harrison Smith and Robert Haas, Inc.; for "Black Boy," published in *The New Yorker*, May 14, 1932, and in the volume *The First Lover and Other Stories*, to the F-R Publishing Corporation and to Harrison Smith and Robert Haas, Inc.; for "Friend of the Family," published in *Harper's Magazine*, September 1932, and in the volume *The First Lover and Other Stories* to Harper's Magazine and to Harrison Smith and Robert Haas, Inc.; for "White as Snow," published in *The New Yorker*, August 5, 1933, and in the volume *The White Horses of Vienna*, to the F-R Publishing Corporation and to Harcourt, Brace and Company, Inc.; for "Keep Your Pity," published in *The Brooklyn Daily Eagle* and in the volume *The White Horses of Vienna*, to The Brooklyn Daily Eagle and to Harcourt, Brace and Company, Inc.; for "Natives Don't Cry," published in *The American Mercury*, March 1934, and in the volume *The White Horses of Vienna*, to The American Mercury and to Harcourt, Brace and Company, Inc.; for "Maiden, Maiden," published in *Harper's Bazaar*, December 1934, and in the volume *The White Horses of Vienna*, to Harper's Bazaar and Hearst Magazines, Inc., and to Harcourt, Brace and Company, Inc.; for "The White Horses of Vienna," published in *Harper's Magazine*, April 1936, and in the volume *The White Horses of Vienna*, to Harper's Magazine and to Harcourt, Brace and Company, Inc.; for "Count Lothar's Heart," published in *Harper's Bazaar*, May 1935, and in the volume *The White Horses of Vienna*, to Harper's Bazaar and Hearst Magazines, Inc., and to Harcourt, Brace and Company, Inc.; for "Major Alshuster," published in *Harper's Magazine*, December 1935, and in the volume *The White Horses of Vienna*, to Harper's Magazine, and to Harcourt, Brace and Company, Inc.; for "How Bridie's Girl Was Won," published in *Harper's Magazine*, March 1936, to *Harper's Magazine*; for "The Herring Piece," published in *The New Yorker*, April 10, 1937, to the F-R Publishing Corporation; for "Your Body Is a Jewel

Box," published in *Caravel*, and in the volume *The White Horses of Vienna*, to *Caravel* and to Harcourt, Brace and Company, Inc.; for "Major Engagement in Paris," published in *The American Mercury*, August 1940, to *The American Mercury*; for "Effigy of War," published in *The New Yorker*, May 25, 1940, to the F-R Publishing Corporation; for "Diplomat's Wife," published in *Harper's Bazaar*, February 1940, to *Harper's Bazaar* and Hearst Magazines, Inc.; for "Men," published in *Harper's Bazaar*, February 1941, to *Harper's Bazaar* and Hearst Magazines, Inc.; for "They Weren't Going to Die," published in *The New Yorker*, October 12, 1940, to the F-R Publishing Corporation; for "Defeat," published in *The New Yorker*, May 17, 1941, to the F-R Publishing Corporation; for "Let There Be Honour," published in *The Saturday Evening Post*, November 8, 1941, to *The Saturday Evening Post* and the Curtis Publishing Company; for "This They Took with Them," published in *Harper's Bazaar*, October 1942, to *Harper's Bazaar* and Hearst Magazines, Inc.; for "Their Name Is Macaroni," published in *The New Yorker*, January 3, 1941, to the F-R Publishing Corporation; for "The Canals of Mars," published in *Harper's Bazaar*, February 1943, to *Harper's Bazaar* and Hearst Magazines, Inc.; for "The Loneliest Man in the U. S. Army," published in *The Woman's Home Companion*, July 1943, to *The Woman's Home Companion* and the Crowell-Collier Publishing Company; for "Winter Night," published in *The New Yorker*, January 19, 1946, to the F-R Publishing Corporation.

Contents

8   *Contents*

Introduction

The short story is in some respects the most testing prose form for the literary artist. The writer cannot here compensate for a lack of significant pattern or of imaginative vitality by loquacity, variety, or picturesqueness. He cannot immerse himself in his material and allow the sheer abundance and flow of events to build up a picture of life. On the other hand, because of the necessity of disposing his material in brief compass, he is constantly tempted to rely entirely on neatness and adroitness, on the contrived situation or the trick ending. Or again, aware of the extremes which he must avoid, he may employ the sophisticated deadpan, assembling an insignificant collocation of actions and dialogue and stopping abruptly when the insignificance has been made manifest in the hope that the very abruptness of the conclusion, at a point where no obvious conclusion seemed warranted, would force the reader into believing that some subtle pattern of meaning—too subtle for any obvious formal rendering—had been worked out. This kind of short story represents the last infirmity of noble minds, and many talented modern writers have practiced it. But neither it nor the story that uses the trick ending meets the real challenge of the short story, which is to invest a brief sequence of events with reverberating human significance by means of style, selection and ordering of detail, and—most important of all—to present the whole action in such a way that it is at once a parable and a slice of life, at once symbolic and real, both a valid picture of some phase of experience and a sudden illumination of one of the perennial moral and psychological paradoxes which lie at the heart of *la condition humaine.*

Neither curiosity nor compassion nor narrative skill nor the camera eye nor psychological understanding can in itself produce a great short story. What is required above all is the literary imagination working searchingly on human material that it really knows (and knows with a deep inward knowledge, not merely as a journalist) together with a sense of form and of language that will combine to crystallize the workings of that imagination in a way that achieves both density and sharp clarity of outline. The short-story writer must "load every rift with ore," because he is aiming at effect through concentration, but at the same time the shape of the whole must stand out brilliantly. Above all, the short-story writer, if he is to get the most out of his small-scale art, must concentrate his moral feeling. All prose fiction of any significance is concerned directly or obliquely with moral feeling, but in the novel this can be deliberately diluted or introduced indirectly as a by-product, almost, of the cumulative movement of life which it displays. The short-story writer, on the other hand, if he is to be more than an entertainer or an exhibitionist, cannot prevaricate about the moral meaning—in the fullest sense of that phrase—of art. The tightly organized picture of life which he shows us must speak to our sense of man as a moral being moving continually in disturbing predicaments if it is to justify its organization.

All this is perhaps a cumbersome way of pointing to the merits of Kay Boyle's short stories. But it seems to me to be necessary to understand both how hard it is to write a good short story and what is the true justification of the short story as an art form. The short story is concerned with texture and quality of living, and quality of living of course involves moral feeling at some level. The conflict or the relation between sensibility and habit, between the articulate surface of life and the silent reality below, between true and false dignity, between vitality and prudence, between different kinds of egotism, between love and fear, between spontaneity and feeling and the claims of tradition and society—these are all themes, reverberating with haunting overtones, which Kay Boyle handles in the earliest of the four groups of stories in this collection. Not that these stories pose these questions as questions or specifically single out opposing feelings or attitudes with a view to a dramatic confrontation. The drama is never the drama of simple conflict. For all the sharp lines of the stories the situations they project are as teasing and complex as life itself. Order is imposed, but the selection of significant detail which creates the order is so cunningly done that, while we see and are moved by the pattern, we know that it is a symbol of life's complexity rather than a schematization of life's problems. Of course art is not life, but its function is to illuminate life in its own unique way. Too much modern criticism shies away from "life" as a bad word. No one who reads these stories can doubt that the primary impulse behind them was the expression of some kind of *interest* in life, and that the virtuosity that enabled their author to find an effective way of communicating these kinds of interest existed from the beginning in the closest contact with—and indeed was in important respects determined by—the nature of the interest. It is time that it was roundly asserted that the first duty of a story is to be interesting. And the first duty of an artist is to relate his craftsmanship to his interests, to allow his sense of his medium to intermesh with his sense of life. That, indeed, is how he becomes an artist.

"Sense of life" is a vague phrase. Perhaps it can best be illustrated by examples—the brilliant combination of gaiety and pathos (and the sheer virtuosity of the gaiety) in "Friends of the Family"; the shrewd handling of incident which achieves the counterpointing of irony, comedy and pity in "Keep Your Pity"; the devastatingly realized detail of "Your Body Is a Jewel Box." Kay Boyle's stories wring from us a startled assent. We are both surprised and convinced, as in the ending of "Black Boy." The element of surprise keeps them continually lively, while the element of conviction keeps directing our imagination to the true centers of experience.

In the early group of stories there is sometimes a technical exuberance, an exultation in the potentialities of the medium, which shows the writer almost exhibitionistically relishing her own power. We see this in "Wedding Day." Nevertheless, what compelling use of incident Kay Boyle makes in this story! Consider the episode of the brother and sister on the lake. It is almost too much in its realized particularization of the moment, flanked on both sides by inconsequentialities of action and the haunting repetitions in the language ("The sun was an imposition, an imposition . . ."). But the zest for life is there, the controlled excitement, the fascinated and sympathetic curiosity about the different kinds of texture which experience can wear. It is this which gives a special kind of joy to Kay Boyle's stories. The incidents take on symbolic meanings by their very surface inconsequentiality, which compels and surprises, and also by a use of language that is both incantatory and most concretely spelled out in its imagistic detail. We are drawn right in, immersed, to savour the combination of mystery and prosaic detail which is a central paradox of experience. Other stories, such as "Kroy Wen," "Black Boy," "White as Snow," show less exuberance, and the line of meaning is more strictly controlled; though the theme has a stronger impact as a result, we miss some of the sheer wonder, the relish of the very *quality* of experience. In "Friend of the Family" craft and insight are effectively welded and exuberance is given its defined correlative (and corrective!) in the story.

The later stories show the progressive impact of experience (as determined both by Kay Boyle's own life and by modern European history) on Kay Boyle's art. "Maiden, Maiden" takes a simple romantic plot but by the precisely realized mountain setting (with continuously echoing symbolic overtones in the use of scenery and in the characters' relation to the mountains as well as to each other) and the selection and ordering of detail enriches it to a point of tragic irony that illuminates a whole area of human hope, fear, pride, love, self-delusion and pity. "The White Horses of Vienna" uses a background of political material counterpointed against a foreground of individual relationships in a mountain setting to evoke the subtlest problems of the moral personality. The quiet control and skilful balancing of generalization with minute descriptive detail, combining elements of folklore, poetic symbolization, and an almost clinical psychological realism, give "Count Lothar's Heart" a strange power of its own. Of the English group, "Major Alshuster" seems to me to show most effectively Kay Boyle's characteristic control of detail, her mingling of the fully realized scene and provocatively suggested meanings.

The French group shows how personally involved Kay Boyle's own emotions were in the fall of France in 1940 and in the whole impact of the Second World War on Europe. The material here is sometimes almost (but never quite) too much for her. Events as powerful as these were hard to subdue to the artist's complex and subtle intentions. The bitter "Effigy of War" and "Defeat" are in a sense documentaries, possessing a strength that, for many contemporary readers at least, derives as much from the sadness of historical truth as from their illumination of some of the moral paradoxes at the center of experience. "Diplomat's Wife," in some ways rather like "Maiden, Maiden," manages to make admirable use of the atmosphere of modern European history by employing it as climax in a carefully controlled and cogently imagined story; the theme, which is almost a folk-theme in essence, is given complexity and significance by the use of symbolic detail in the handling of both incident and setting. The American group similarly shows Kay Boyle reacting to the emotional pressure of contemporary history. The note of compassion and of personal implication rises steadily through the stories of the French and American groups. But this does not mean that art has given way before autobiography or propaganda. The most remarkable thing about the best of these stories is that they combine accurate reporting of the "feel" of a historical situation with all those overtones of meaning, those probings into the center of man's moral and emotional experience, which we demand of the true literary artist.

Yet formal statements of this kind fail to account for the power and the appeal of these stories. One emerges from reading the stories in the French and American groups with one's imagination held and haunted by the human implications of the moments in modern history which they are designed to illuminate. They read as though they have been *lived through,* reminding us of Whitman's "I am the man, I suffered, I was there." But they are far from being merely "on the spot" reporting, nor are they "war stories" in the conventional sense. Their object is not to describe either horror or heroism, but to explore the core of human meaning in these desperate situations. I find "Defeat" almost unbearable in its quiet and controlled projection of the implications of the fall of France; but that, I know, is partly because I am still emotionally involved in the events of 1940 and can never forget the shock of hearing of the abject French collapse in the face of Hitler's armies. I must not give the impression, however, that the power of these stories derives only from the way in which they recapture poignant moments from the past. They exist in their own right as *stories*, works of the literary imagination in which the skill of the artist has devised the proper patterning of incidents and prompted at each point the appropriate handling of language so as to achieve a special kind of permanence, even finality. We can point to a story and say, "There! Within these bounds is contained a true vision of some aspect of the human situation." Man's behavior has been linked to man's fate, and history has been employed as a means, not as an end.

Compassionate without being sentimental, moral without being didactic, contemporary without being ephemeral, *engagés* without being simply autobiographical or hortatory, these stories show one of the finest short-story writers of our time counterpointing imagination and experience in different ways as experience took on new forms and imagination shifted its role and scope to meet it.

DAVID DAICHES

▲▲▲▲▲▲▲▲▲▲▲▲▲▲▲▲▲▲▲▲▲▲▲▲▲▲▲▲▲▲▲▲▲

Early Group

1927–1934

▼▼▼▼▼▼▼▼▼▼▼▼▼▼▼▼▼▼▼▼▼▼▼▼▼▼▼▼▼▼▼

Episode in the Life of an Ancestor

What a gold mine it was to come into the stable on an early morning that sparkled with rain and to start the horses tossing their manes on their shoulders, stamping and lashing with fury because she passed by them. Even more active was the one she would slap under the belly and throw the saddle over. She would stand close to him, whichever one he was, tapping him on the ribs with her knuckles until he blasted what breath he had in him straight out and drew his waist in tapering and fine. At the moment she passed his head with the single bit in her hand he would stand quiet, venturing to crane out his head and nibble with his soft loose lips at her shoulder.

The smallest horse was the favorite, and when he saw her he lifted his trim hind legs and shot them at the sides of the stall. His delicate hoofs ran like a regiment over the blackened timber. He kicked in a frenzy, but his eyes were precisely on every move she was making, and his teeth, small and sweet and unlike a horse's teeth, were ready to smile. Even with his ears flat as a rabbit's as he kicked, there was a flicker of knowledge in the tips of them that waited patiently for her decision of whether she would fling the saddle over him or whether she would go on to another stall, leaving him ready to cry with impatience.

Her father was proud of the feminine ways there were in her, and especially of the choir voice she used in church. It was no pride to him to hear it turned hard and thin in her mouth to quiet a horse's ears when some fright had set them to fluttering on the beak of its head. But at a time when the Indian fires made a wall that blossomed and faded at night on three sides of the sky, this grandmother was known as one of the best horsewomen in Kansas.

They were used to seeing her riding with a sunbonnet on her head—not in pants, but with wide skirts hullabalooing out behind her in the wind. At this time of the century nobody was very particular about the great length of the distances covered, and a day's ride from one town to another was like nothing at all. Kansas was like any other place on the map to them, and there was nothing strange about it to their minds. The horses that grew up there were simple enough not to shy away from skirts that slapped at their sides, and reserved their skittishness for lightning or for the occasion of the moon rising suddenly at night out of the dust of the highway. Trains were no trouble to them, for they could see them only in the distance on an edge they never approached, but for cows, that they knew capable of ripping open their sides, they had no antics, only ungarnished cowardice. Smoke, like the railway, was another thing too remote to be taken into account. They were used to seeing it along the edge of the prairie, twisting up from the Indian encampments and becoming a part of the wind woven of many odors that blew through the long tunnels of their noses but never interfered.

To her father it was a real sorrow that a needle and thread were rarely seen in her fingers. His wife was dead and it seemed to him that he must set flowing in his daughter the streams of gentleness and love that cooled the blood of true women. The idea was that she be sweetened by the honey of the ambitions he had for her. There was this irritation in him that could not be quieted: her indifference to the things that were his, his house, or the color and strength of his beard, and her interest in the sumac trees at the time they were ripe, or the sky with the crows flying across it in search of the shortest distance between two points (and finding it with a dignity and patience that was a shame to mankind).

Her father would listen for her to come down the hill from the stable, for she would often be singing aloud as she came around the side of it. It was he who had first taught her to ride, and even in the first months before year after year in the saddle had

rubbed any tenderness out of her flesh, he had seen her way
with horses. What she had no pity for, but a kind of arrogance
instead, was for the melting eyes, the rich false chocolate drops
of despair in a horse's head. But a horse's eye rolled in the socket
back at her in fear over his foaming shoulder, tied fast with its
own bloody veins, was a treasure. Rather than see this fact in
her, her father preferred to lower his gaze and contemplate the
patent tips of his boots.

One day as she was coming down from the stable he heard
this miracle: she was singing and her voice struck some hollow
in the opposite hill and curved and warbled there like the voice
of a second singer. For a full minute he stood listening while the
two voices sang together, her own voice deep and voluptuous
and full like that of an older woman, and the other voice fresh
and thin, singing always a note or two behind the other. Once
she rounded the side of the barn there was nothing more to it,
and she came down singing, and not suspecting that the other
hill had taken the notes out of her mouth and piped them back
at her father.

To please him maybe, but he was never sure enough if it were
for that, she'd do the things that were to be done in the kitchen.
She could stuff a cod very nicely, stitch up its belly, and see that
it baked. From the French side she had learned to put fresh
mackerel in kegs with white wine and lemon peel and a bouquet
of spice. But on these occasions her beautiful red hair would be
pulled back from her face, tight into a net at the back of her
head, as naturally as if it had of itself recoiled in distaste from
the monotony of the tasks performed before it.

There was a special flavor to the snuffle that a mount splattered out of his nose on the wind and back onto the face and
mouth. What a feast of splatters when she would come out
from a long time in the kitchen and walk in upon the beasts who
were stamping and sick with impatience for her in the barn! She
would find them in fury at every hole in the stallboards, and at
the hay fleas jumping through the fodder in the manger, and at
the soft balls of manure packed solid in their hoofs. An ovation
of splatters would shower out before her. It was early fall and
black as a pocket when she came out from a whole day in the

house and saddled the smallest horse and rode him out the door.
Her father saw her riding off alone this way and he sat home
thinking of the things that might become of his daughter. He sat
away from the window, thinking that the sight of the darkness
outside was no help to him and that with his paper down on his
knees and his eyes closed he was better off. Outside she was riding away, any way, hammering off through the dark with nobody knowing what was going on inside her or what she was
filled with, the hoofs of the horse hammering tack tracks in the
blackness that was maybe the road, or the dust, or the prairie,
that blew richly from side to side. Her father was thinking that
someday she might go off and be married, and he was willing for
her to marry a gentleman someday, but these were not the feminine ways he thought of stirring in her. He was more concerned
with the cooking and the sewing ways that would be a comfort
to him and keep him to his own satisfaction.

The thought of her marrying made him think of the schoolmaster who was the only gentleman in the countryside. Her father sat with the points of the fingers of his two hands together
and with his elbows resting on the arms of his rocking chair. He
sat rocking gently back and forth with his thoughts, and then it
came to him that early in the evening he had seen the young
schoolmaster walking out as well onto the prairie. He had sat
by the window, watching the small strong figure of the schoolmaster making his way up the road over the prairie, and he
began wondering how it would be to have the schoolmaster in
the family, married to his daughter and living with them there
every day in the house. This was a quiet enough thought to him
and it kept him rocking gently back and forth for a while.

But with his daughter off in the night this way he became restless, and presently he started up and found himself at the window, looking out for her. He was surprised to find that in the little time he had been sitting in his chair the moon had come up
and was lighting up all the country around. He could see very
clearly the softly flowering goldenrod, white as flax under the
moon, and the deep valleys and gulfs of the whole blossoming
prairie. All along the edge of it were the Indian fires burning as
hard and bright as peonies.

He asked himself what in the world his daughter could be doing out at this time of the night. It was such a strange thing that he crossed the room and went up the stairs that had a narrow ribbon of carpet running down the middle of them like a spine. He opened the door of her room and looked in, but it was empty. Only with the lamp in his hand he saw something that caught his eye. It was the corner of a volume sticking out from under her folded quilt. Maybe she had intended to hide it away in her quilt, but the old man took it out by the end and turned its face up to the light. Poetry it was, he saw, with pictures engraved through it of a kind that brought the blood flying to his face. His fingers trembled on the flyleaf and there he saw the name of the schoolmaster inscribed in the young man's long leaning hand, while the book itself had been left open at the picture entitled *The Creation of Eve*. Under it he read the words the poet had written:

> *. . . To the Nuptial Bowre*
> *I led her blushing like the Morn: all Heav'n*
> *And happie Constellations on that houre*
> *Shed thir selectest influence; the Earth*
> *Gave sign of gratulation, and each Hill;*
> *Joyous the Birds; fresh Gales and gentle Aires*
> *Whisper'd it to the Woods, and from thir wings*
> *Flung Rose, flung Odours from the spicie Shrub,*
> *Disporting, till the amorous Bird of Night*
> *Sung Spousal, and bid haste the Evening Starr*
> *On his Hill top, to light the bridal Lamp.*

You fine example to the young, screamed the father's mind. You creeping out into the night to do what harm you can, creeping out and doing God knows what harm, God knows. He went quivering down the stairs, his mind in a fury. The low educated fellow forgetting his precious learning and out after the poor girl after dark on the prairie, he was thinking. Very clearly in his rage he could see the meeting of the eyebrows over the schoolmaster's nose, so hateful had he become to him, seeing them in detail, the black sprinkling of hairs that grew down between the schoolmaster's eyes. In his mind he thought of every part of the

young man's face, and especially of the pores in the wings of his
nose, and he began to walk back and forth in a fury in the house.

The horse on which the grandmother was riding had come to
some kind of incline in the ground, and there he slowed his pace
and began feeling his way with great delicacy through the
bushes that flowed back over his thin knees. The grandmother's
hands let the rein ride loose on his neck, and he flicked his ears
forward and back in the dark for some sound from her. He kept
chewing with his teeth at the bit in his mouth and tossing the
rings of the mouthpiece so that they rang aloud. There was no
movement even in her legs that hung down around his belly, and
with the interest of selecting his own way absorbing him, without any display of fear he watched the moon coming up, straining his ears almost out of his head as he followed it edging up
ahead of him through the prairie grass.

It was at this moment that he was startled by a faint stir in the
bushes, and to quiet his heart's beating he drew several long cool
blasts into his lungs the better to listen for what was to come. No
help was given him by the grandmother who had never before
abandoned him to his own wits, and trying to keep his head
clear and away from fright he was left to discover all by himself
that the wind had risen with the moon.

After the first moment it went out of his head to make a scene
about the wind and he went on, pointing his ears to the sound of
it in the grass and clicking his heels sharply on every stone he
passed over. The wind was lifting off the bunches of white
feather from the milkweed pods that had burst dry and floury in
the September night. It was taking the ripe milkweed seeds with
the cotton crowning them and blowing them over the crust of
the prairie. First it was this, a simple rising and falling of the
breath as the tufted seeds went, and then as fold of the wind
opened on fold, out they came in a tide, leaving the empty
husks rattling and hissing like snakes behind them.

Presently the milkweed blow had strengthened so that it was
sweeping across the whole upper reaches of the prairie. To the
eye it seemed knee-deep and ravenous, but it came only to the
crests of the little horse's hoofs and there washed delicately
about them. He gave many humorous leaps and cavorts in the

blowing tide, spraying it with splutter from his nose and sidling prettily up to the moon. Only when he ventured a sharp glance out over any distance did the terror of the enormous shifting plain, seething as it was with the milkweed blow, disturb him.

This was tame idle sport, suited to ladies, this romping in the milkweed cotton across the miles of piecrust. Suddenly he felt this anger in the grandmother's knees and it caught and swung him about in the wind. Without any regard for him at all, so that he was in a quiver of admiration and love for her, she jerked him up and back, rearing his wild head high, his front hoofs left clawing at the space that yapped under them. To such a frenzy of kicking she urged him that he was ready to faint with delight. Even had she wished to now she could never have calmed him, and she started putting him over bushes and barriers, setting his head to them and stretching him thin as a string to save the smooth nut of his belly from scraping, reeling him so close to the few pine trunks that streamed up like torrents that he leaped sideways to save his fair coat from ripping open on their spikes. It was a long way to travel back, but he never stopped until his hoofs thundered into the barn that had shrunk too small for him. There he stood in the darkness, wet and throbbing like a heart cut out of the body.

The leap of the grandmother down off his back startled him afresh into such terror that he sprang off as light as a frog across the boards of the floor. The leather of the saddle was steaming with his sweat, and after she had stripped him she brushed him down quickly and slapped him into his stall.

In the parlor of the house the father was sitting quite still at the table. He was asking himself in great self-pity how he was to know what had become of her during the night. A great many things that had nothing to do with it went through his mind, and one thing was that it was sad to have no one of his own time to talk to. When she came into the room she was there in front of him in the same way that the roses on the floor were woven straight across the rug. Where have you been to, he wanted to say to her, but he could not bring himself to speak. With someone of his own years, maybe, speech would already have been running nimble between them. He was ready to say right out that he had seen the schoolmaster walking out early in the evening up on the road that led nowhere except out onto the prairie. Well, now, what have you been up to with the schoolmaster, he was ready to say.

But the grandmother in anger had seen her book and picked it up from the table, and put it close to her under her arm. In his sorrow for himself the father turned his head away from the sight of her. With this woman in the room with him he was beginning to see the poor little schoolmaster, the poor squat little periwinkle with his long nose always thrust away in a book. He began to remember that the horse his daughter had been out riding all night had once backed up on just such a little whippersnapper as was the schoolmaster and kicked his skull into a cocked hat. He began to worry for the sake of the schoolmaster who was such a timid little fellow and not used to Kansas, who might get into harm's way.

The father kept turning his head away from the sight of this woman. She stood by the table with her eyes staring like a hawk's eyes straight into the oil lamp's blaze. The farm and the prairie, he thought in anger, and the sky with the moon in it would only be remembered because this woman would carry them off in her own hard heart. They would not be remembered for anything else at all.

"What have you done to the schoolmaster?" he wanted to say to her. The words were right there in his mouth but he couldn't get them out.

Wedding Day

The red carpet that was to spurt like a hemorrhage from pillar to post was stacked in the corner. The mother was shouting down the stairway that the wedding cake be held aloft and not bowed like a venerable into the servants' entrance. Oh, the wedding cake. No one paid any attention to the three magnificent tiers of it. It passed into the pantry, tied in festoons of waxed paper, with its beard lying white as hoarfrost on its bosom.

This was the last lunch and they came in with their button-holes drooping with violets and sat sadly down, sat down to eat. They sat at the table in such a way that she flew into a rage and asked them to sit up please to sit up as if they were eating at the same table as if they were of the same flesh and blood not odd people at a lunch counter. Every bouquet that arrived, blossoming forth from its gilded or from its pure white basket, softened the sharp edge of her tongue.

"Have you decided to give your daughter the copper sauce-pans?" he said.

At this the mother collapsed. She deflated in her chair and pecked feebly at the limp portions of strawberries that remained on her plate. But a drop too much of that black arrogance she had inherited and could not down said No, a thousand times on every note of the scale. NO, she said. The pride of the kitchen to be scratched, burned, buttered, and dimmed. At the thought of them her heart swelled in an agony of sorrow. She was an old woman, fine arrogant old lady that she was, and the saucepans hung in the kitchen like six bull's-eyes coldly reflecting her thin face with its faded topknot of hair. Not a bite had been cooked in them for twenty years. NO swelled in her heart, brimmed in her eyes, until the two could have killed her in her chair.

"Don't cry," he said to her. He pointed his finger directly at her nose so that when she looked at him with dignity her eyes wavered and crossed. She sat looking proudly at him, erect as a needle staring through its one open eye.

"Don't," he said.

A thunderous NO now stormed at them, a bitter, hard, a child-ish no. A whimpering no. Your father prized them highly. Your father, he prized them highly, she said.

Suddenly she turned upon her daughter.

"Your brother is looking for some trouble to make," she said grimly. "You see that, don't you? Don't you see that he is trying to make trouble between you and your young man?"

The three of them stared into one another's faces, and a look of bewilderment came upon the old lady's face. Why she was bewildered, she did not know. She knew quite well what she was about, but her son looked at her even more sharply, and he said:

"Who was it that wanted this wedding?"

"Certainly not I," said the old lady, and these words echoed what was in each one's mouth.

"I certainly did not want this wedding," the old lady repeated with emphasis, when she saw she had not been contradicted. "Your sister's choice has appalled me."

"Enough!" shouted her son. "No one can question that, my sister's choice!"

The roast beef made them kin again, and they sat watching the mother almost lovingly as she sliced the thin scarlet ribbons of it into the platter. It was a beautiful roast, and it had scarcely been cooked at all. The son kept snatching bits of it away, and she heaped their plates full of them.

"I'm carvin' and carvin'," she was whimpering, "and I don't get anything to eat myself. Haven't ye had enough?" she said. She looked plaintively at them, her lip trembling as she looked into their faces.

"I'm going to take it under the table," said her son, "and snarl at anyone who comes near."

At this the brother and sister burst into laughter which rocked them back and forth and flushed them to the roots of their light hair. At the end he tossed his napkin over the glass bells of the chandelier and his sister followed him out of the room. Out they went to face the spring before the wedding, and their mother stood at the window praying that this occasion at least pass off with dignity, with her heart not in her mouth but beating away in peace in its own bosom.

Here then was April holding them up, stabbing their hearts with hawthorn, scalping them with a flexible blade of wind. Here went their yellow manes up in the air, turning them shaggy as lions. The Seine had turned around in the wind and in tufts and scallops was leaping directly away from Saint-Cloud. The clouds were cracking and splitting up like a glacier; down the sky were they shifting and sliding, and the two with their heads bare were walking straight into the heart of the floe.

"It isn't too late," he said. "I mean it isn't too late."

The sun was an imposition, an imposition, for they were another race stamping an easy trail through the wilderness of Paris, possessed of the same people, but of themselves like another race. No one else could by lifting of the head only be starting life over again, and it was a wonder the whole city of Paris did not hold its breath for them, for if anyone could have begun a new race, it was these two. Therefore, in their young days they should have been saddled and strapped with necessity so that they could not have escaped. Paris was their responsibility. No one else had the same delight, no one else put foot to pavement in such a way. With their yellow heads back they were stamping a new trail, but in such ignorance, for they had no idea of it.

And who was there to tell them, for the trees they had come to in the woods gave them no sign. They were alone in the little train that ran on rails through the dead brush under the boughs and snapped around corners so smartly that it flicked them from side to side.

"It isn't too late yet, you know," he said.

At this moment they laughed. Here were their teeth alike in size as well as the arrogance that had put the proud arch in their noses. Wallop and wallop went the little train through the woods, cracking like castanets the knuckles of their behinds.

When the train stopped, these two descended, stroked the sleek pussy willows, scratched them between the ears and watched the seals awhile skipping and leaping for ripples of fish in the spring light. "What I mean is," he said, "that I don't, I don't consider it too late."

Into a little boat they got and in a minute he had rowed her out to the middle of the pond. She sat buttoned up very tightly in her white furs. The brisk little wind was spanking the waters back and forth and the end of her nose was turning pink. But he, on the contrary, had thrown off his coat, thrown it to the bottom of the boat with his feet on it, and as he rowed he pressed the fresh mud of the spring that had clustered on his soles into every seam and pocket of it. Back and forth went his arms, back and forth, with the little yellow hairs on them standing up in the wind.

"What a day for a wedding," he said.

As he spoke there was a sudden disturbance among the birds on the bank, and the swans streamed out after them in steady pursuit, necking and bowing after the boat with their smooth coats ruffling up in the wind. Around the boat gathered the swans, peering curiously at the new race, lifting their flat heads at an angle to fix the beaks of the new race in their scarlet eyes.

Down, down could the brother and sister see into the very depths of the pond. Down under the tough black paddling feet of the swans and below their slick wet bellies could be seen the caverns of the pond with flowers blooming under the water. Every reed was podded with clear bright bubbles of light closely strung, and the fish were waving under them like little flags, deep but clear in the water. Over them was the sky set like a tomb, the strange unearthly sky that might at any moment crack into spring.

"It isn't too late," he said.

A slow rain had begun to fall, and the fruit blossoms on the banks were immediately bruised black with it. The rain was falling, it was running steadily down their cheeks, and they looked with glowing eyes at each other's faces. Everywhere, everywhere there were other countries to go to. And how were they to get from the boat with the chains that were on them, how uproot the willowing trees from their hearts, how strike the irons of spring that shackled them? What shame and shame that scorched a burning pathway to their dressing rooms! Their hearts were mourning for every Paris night and its half-hours before lunch when two straws crossed on the round table top on the marble anywhere meant I had a drink here and went on.

"What a day for a wedding," he said as they came wearily, wearily up the street, dragging their feet through the spring afternoon.

They found their mother upon her knees in the hallway, tying white satin bows under the chins of the potted plants. As they passed she was staring a cactus grimly in the eye. Before she turned to them she let fall one last reproving look upon the silver platter by the entry door. Once she had turned her back, her son kicked it smartly down the hall, and without a word of protest she pursued it. She was convinced as she halted it and stepped firmly on the silver tray that this outburst presaged a thousand mishaps that were yet to come.

But in peace the guests arrived, one after another and two by two, leaving their cards upon the platter and hastening forward to press their hostess' hand. The army was handsomely represented, and finally down the drawing room came the bride on the arm of her brother who was giving her away to the groom. With such a gesture he gave her away, and it was evident that she had no thought for her satin dress, nor for the fine lace that was hanging down the back of it. Not a thought for the music did she have, nor a word for the reverend except yes and no. This was the end, the end, they thought. She turned her face to her brother and suddenly their hearts fled together and sobbed like ringdoves in their bosoms. This was the end, the end, the end, this was the end.

Down the room their feet fled in various ways, seeking an escape. To the edge of the carpet fled her feet, returned and followed reluctantly upon her brother's heels. Every piped note of the organ insisted that she go on. It isn't too late, he said. Too late, too late. The ring was given, the book was closed. The desolate, the barren sky continued to fling down dripping handfuls of fresh rain.

Like a Continental gentleman he slapped his thighs, exchanged jokes with the other gentlemen, and in his bitterest moments his eyes traversed the heads of the company and exchanged salute with hers. Her feet were fleeing in a hundred ways throughout the rooms, fluttering from the punch bowl to her bedroom and back again, and her powder puff fell from her bosom and was kicked by the dancers like a chrysanthemum around the floor. Over the rooms she danced, paused at the punch table, her feet like white butterflies escaping by a miracle the destructive feet of whatever partner held her in his arms.

The punch it was that daintily and unerringly picked out her brother's steps and made him dance, that took his joints and swung and limbered them, divined the presence of his antagonism and sent him jigging. He danced with the silver platter of cards held high and perilous, and as he danced from room to room he scattered the cards about him—a handful of army officers here, a handful of deep-bosomed matrons strewn across one shoulder. The greater part of the American colony fluttered behind the piano as the mother, in triumph on the arm of the General, danced lightly by. Her face was averted from the mesh of his entangling beard, but in her heart she was rejoicing. If this were all she had to fear, she hummed: the cards could be gathered up, no glass had yet been broken. Up and down the winding roads, over the black cascades and the fountains, over the decks of the sardine boats that were barging quietly in the hemp of the Chinese rugs she danced. The punch had turned her veins to water and she felt her knee rapping sharply against the General's as she skipped. In triumph in his elderly arms, she sped away. What a real success, what a *real* success! Over the Oriental prayer rugs, through the Persian forests of hemp, away and away.

Rest Cure

He sat in the sun with the blanket about him, considering, with his hands lying out like emaciated strangers before him, that today the sun would endure a little longer. Certainly it would survive until the trees below the terrace effaced it, toward four o'clock, like opened parasols. A crime it had been, the invalid thought, turning his head this way and that, to have ever built up one house before another in such a way that one man's habitation cast a shadow upon another's. The whole sloping coast should have been left a wilderness with no order to it, stalked and leafed with the great strong trunks and foliage of these parts. Cactus plants with petals a yard wide and yucca tongues as thick as elephant trunks were sullenly and viciously flourishing all about the house. Upon the terrace had a further attempt at nicety and precision been made: there his wife had seen to it that geraniums were potted into the wooden boxes that stood along the wall.

From his lounging chair he could reach out and, with no effort beyond that of raising the skeleton of his hand, finger the parched stems of the geraniums. The south, and the Mediterranean wind, had blistered them past all belief. They bore their rosy topknots or their soiled white flowers balanced upon their thick Italian heads. There they were, within his reach, a row of weary washerwomen leaning back from the villainous descent of the coast. What parched scions had thrust forth from their stems now served to obliterate in part the vision of the sun. With arms akimbo they surrounded him: thin burned Italian women with their meager bundles of dirty linen on their heads. One after another, with a flicker of irritation for his wife lighting his eye, he fingered them at the waist a moment, and then snapped off each stem. One after another he broke their stalks in two and dropped them away onto the pavings beneath his lounging chair. When he had finished off what plants grew within his reach, he lay back exhausted, sank, thin as an archer's bow, into the depths of his cushions.

"They kept the sun off me," he was thinking in absolution.

In spite of the garden and its vegetation, he would have the last drops of sun. He had closed his eyes, and there he lay looking straight ahead of him into the fathomless black pits of his lids. Even here, in the south, in the sun even, the coal mines remained. His nostrils were sick with the smell of them and on his cheeks he felt lingering the slipping mantle of the English fog. He had not seen the mines since he was a young man, but nothing he had ever done between would alter them. There he sat in the sun with his eyes closed, looking into their depths.

Because his father had been a miner, he was thinking, the black of the pits had put some kind of blasphemy on his own blood. He sat with his eyes closed looking directly into the blank awful mines. Against their obscurity he set the icicles of one winter when the war was on, when he had spent his twilights seeking for pine cones under the tall trees in the woods behind the house. In Cornwall. What a vision! How beautiful that year, and many other years, might have been had it not been for the sour thought of war. Every time his heart had lifted for a hillside or a wave, or for the wind blowing, the thought of the turmoil going on had beset and stricken him. It had lain like a burden on his

conscience every morning when he was coming awake. The first
light moments of day coming had warned him that despite the
blood rising in his body, it was no time to rejoice. The war. Ah,
yes, the war. After the mines, it had been the war. Whenever
he had believed for half a minute in man, then he had remembered that the war was going on.

For a little while one February, it had seemed that the
colors set out in Monte Carlo, facing the Casino, would obliterate forever the angry memories his heart had stored away. The
great mauve, white, and deep royal bouquets had thrived a week
or more, as if rooted in his eyes. Such banks and beds of richly
petaled flowers, set thick as thieves or thicker on the cultivated
lawns, conveyed the wish. Their artificial physiognomies masked
the earth as well as he would have wished his own features to
stand guard before his spirit. The invalid lifted his hand and
touched his beard. His mouth and chin, he thought with cunning
satisfaction, were marvelously concealed.

The sound of his wife's voice speaking in the room that
opened behind him onto the terrace roused him a little as he sat
pondering in the sun. She seemed to be moving from one long
window to another, arranging flowers in the vases, for her voice
would come across the pavings, now strong and close, now distant as if turned away, and she was talking to their guest about
some sort of shrub or fern. A special kind, the like of which she
could find nowhere on the Riviera. It thrived in the cool brisk
fogs of their own land, she was saying. Her voice had turned toward him again and was ringing clearly across the terrace.

"Those are beautiful ones you have there now," said the voice
of the gentleman.

"Ah, take care!" cried out his wife's voice, somewhat dimmed
as though she had again turned toward the room. "I was afraid
you had pierced your hand," she said in a moment.

When the invalid opened his eyes, he saw that the sun was
even now beginning to glimmer through the upper branches of
the trees, was lolling along the prosperous dark upper boughs as
if in preparation for descent. Not yet, he thought, not yet. He
raised himself on his elbows and scanned the sky. Scarcely three-

thirty, surely, he was thinking. The sun can't be going down at once.

"The sun can't be going down yet awhile, can it?" he called out to the house.

He heard the gravel of the pathway sparkling and spitting out from under the soles of their feet as they crossed it, and then his wife's heels and the boots of the guest struck and advanced across the paving stones.

"Oh, oh, the geraniums——" said his wife suddenly by his side.

The guest had raised his head and stood squinting up at the sun.

"I should say it were going down," he said after a moment.

He had deliberately stepped before the rays of it and stood leaning back against the terrace wall. His solid gray head had served to cork the sunlight. Like a wooden stopper, thought the invalid, painted to resemble a man. With the nose of a wooden stopper. And the sightless eyes. And the creases when he speaks or smiles.

"But think what it must be like in Paris now," said the gentleman. "I don't know how you feel, but I can't find words to say how grateful I am for being here." The guest, thought the invalid as he surveyed him, was very conscious of being a guest—of accepting meals, bed, tea, society—and his smile was permanently set beneath his nose.

"Of course you don't know how I feel," said the invalid. He lay looking sourly up at his guest. "Would you mind moving out of the sun?" As the visiting gentleman skipped out of the way, the invalid cleared his throat, dissolved the little pellet of phlegm which had leaped to being on his tongue so as not to spit before them, and sank back into his chair.

"The advantage—or rather *one* of the advantages—of being a writer," said the visiting gentleman with a smile, "is that he can settle down wherever the fancy takes him. Now, a publisher——"

"Why be a publisher?" said the invalid in irritation. He was staring again into the black blank mines.

His wife was squatting and stooping about his chair, gathering up in her dress the butchered geraniums. She said not a word, but crouched there picking them carefully up, one by one. By her side had appeared a little covered basket, and within it rattled a pair of castanets.

"I am sure I can very easily turn these into slips," she said gently, as if speaking to herself. "A little snip in the right place and they'll be as good as new."

"You can make soup out of them," said the invalid bitterly. "What's in the basket," he said, "making a noise?" ·

"Oh, a *langouste!*" cried out his wife. She had just remembered. "We bought you a *langouste*, alive, at the Beausoleil market. It's as lively as a rig!"

The visiting gentleman burst into laughter. The invalid could hear him gasping with enjoyment by his side.

"I can't bear them alive," said the invalid testily. He lay listening curiously to the animal rattling his jaws and clawing under the basket's lid.

"Oh, but with mayonnaise!" cried his wife. "Tomorrow!"

"Why doesn't Mr. What-do-you-call-him answer the question I put him?" asked the invalid sourly. His mind was possessed with the thought of the visiting man. "I asked him why he was a publisher," said the invalid. What a viper, what a felon, he was thinking, to come and live on me and not give me the satisfaction of a quarrel! He was not a young man, thought the invalid, with his little remains of graying hair, but he had all the endurance and patience of a younger man in the presence of a master. All the smiling and bowing, thought the invalid with contempt, and all the obsequious ways. The man was standing so near to his chair that he could hear his breath whistling through his nostrils. Maybe his eyes were on him, the invalid was thinking. It gave him a turn to think that he was lying there exposed in the sun where the visitor could examine him pore by pore. Hair by hair could the visitor take him in and record him.

"Oh, I beg your pardon," said the gentleman. "I'm afraid I owe you an apology. You see, I'm not accustomed to it."

"To what?" said the invalid sharply. He had flashed his eyes open and looked suspiciously into the publisher's face.

"To seeing you flat on your back," said the gentleman promptly.

"You covered that over very nicely," said the invalid. He

clasped his hands across his sunken bosom. "You meant to say something else. You meant to say *death*," said the invalid calmly. "I heard the first letter of it on your tongue."

He lay back in his chair again with his lids fallen. He could distinctly smell the foul fumes of the pits.

"Elsa," he said, as he lay twitching in the light, "I would like some champagne. *Just because*," he said, sitting up abruptly, "I've written a few books doesn't mean that you have to keep the truth about me to yourself."

His wife went off across the terrace, leaving the two men together.

"Don't make a mistake," said the invalid, smiling grimly. "Don't make any mistake. I'm not quite finished. Not *quite*. I still have a little more to write about," he said. "Don't you fool yourself, my dear."

"Oh, I flatter myself that I don't," said the gentleman agreeably. "I'm convinced there's an unlimited amount still to come. And I hope to have the honor of publishing some of it. I'm counting on that, you know." He ended on a playful note and looked coyly at the invalid. But every spark of life had suddenly expired in the ill man's face.

"I didn't know the sun would be off the terrace so soon," he said.

His wife had returned and was opening the bottle, carefully and without error, with the end of her pliant thumb. The invalid turned on his side and regarded her: a great strong woman whom he would never forget, never, nor the surprisingly slim crescent of her flexible thumb. All of her fingers, he lay thinking as he watched her, were soft as skeins of silk, and tied in the joints and knuckles by invisible satin bands of faintest rose. And there was the visiting gentleman hovering about her, with his oh-let-me-please-Mrs.-oh-do-let-me-now. But her grip on the neck of the bottle was as tenacious as a snake's. She lifted her head, smiled, and shook it at their guest.

"Oh, no," she said, "I'm doing beautifully."

Just as she spoke the cork flew out and hit the gentleman square in the forehead. After it streamed a geyser of purest gold.

"Oh, oh, oh," cried the invalid. He held out his hands to the golden spray. "Oh, pour it here!" he cried. "Oh, buckets of it going! Oh, pour it over me, Elsa!"

The color had flown into Elsa's face and she was laughing. Softly and breathlessly she ran from glass to glass. There in the stems played the clear living liquid, like a fountain springing upward. Ah, that, ah, that, in the innards of a man, thought the invalid joyfully! Ah, that, springing again and again in the belly and heart! There in the glass it ran, cascaded in needlepoints the length of his throat, went whistling to his pulses.

The invalid set down his empty glass.

"Elsa," he said gently, "could I have a little more champagne?"

His wife had risen with the bottle in her hand, but she looked doubtfully at him.

"Do you really think you should?" she asked.

"Yes," said the invalid. He watched the unbelievably pure stuff flowing out all over his glass. "Yes," he said. "Of course. Of course, I should."

A sweet shy look of love had begun to arch in his eyes.

"I'd love to see the *langouste*," he said gently. "Do you think you could let him out and let me see him run around?"

Elsa set down her glass and stooped to lift the cover of the basket. There was the green armored beast lifting its eyes, as if on hinges, to examine the light. Such an expression he had seen before, thought the invalid immediately. There was a startling likeness in those small audacious eyes. Such a look had there been in his father's eyes: that look, and the long smooth mustaches drooping across the wee clefted chin, gave the *langouste* such a look of his father that he exclaimed aloud.

"Be careful," said Elsa. "His claws are tied, but still——"

"I must have him out," said the invalid. He gripped the *langouste* firmly about the hips. He looks like my father, he was thinking. I must have him out where I can see.

In spite of its shackles, the animal contrived to wave his wide pinions in the air as the invalid lifted him up and set him on the rug across his knees. There was the same line of sparkling dewlike substance pearling the *langouste*'s lip, the same weak disappointed lip, like the eagle's lip, and the bold suspicious eye.

Across the sloping shoulders of the beast lay a sprinkling of brilliant dust, as black as coal dust and quite as luminous. Just as his father had looked coming home at night, with the coal dust showered across his shoulders like a deadly mantle. Just such a deadly cloak of quartz and mica and the rooted roots of fern. Even the queer blue toothless look of his father about the jaws. The invalid took another deep swallow of champagne and let it seep quietly through his flesh and blood. Then he lifted his hand and stroked the *langouste* gently. You've never counted, he was thinking mildly. I've led my life very well without you in it. You better go back to the mines where you belong.

When he lifted up the *langouste* to peer into his face, the arms of the beast fell ludicrously open as if he were seeking to embrace the ailing man. He could see his father very well in him, coming home with the coal dirt all over him in the evening, standing by the door that opened in by halves, opening first the upper half and then the lower, swaying a little as he felt for the latch of the lower half of the door. With the beer he had been drinking, or the dew of the Welsh mist shining on his long mustaches. The invalid gave him a gentle shake and set him down again.

I got on very well without you, he was thinking. He sipped at his champagne and regarded the animal upon his knees. As far as I was concerned you need never have been my father at all. Slowly and warily the wondrous eyes and the feelers of the beast moved in distrust across the invalid's lap and bosom. A lot of good you ever did me, he was thinking, as he watched the *langouste* groping about as if in darkness; he began to think of the glowing miner's lamp his father had worn strapped upon his brow. Feeling about in the dark and choking to death underground, he was thinking impatiently. I might have been anybody's son. The strong shelly odor of the *langouste* was seasoning the air.

"I've got on very well without you," he was thinking bitterly. From his wife's face he gathered that he had spoken aloud. The visiting gentleman looked into the depths of his glass of champagne.

"Don't misunderstand me," said the guest with a forbearing

'm quite aware of the fact that, long before you met me, you had one of the greatest publics and following of any living writer——"

The invalid looked in bewilderment at his wife's face and at the face of the visiting man. If they scold me, he thought, I am going to cry. He felt his underlip quivering. Scold me! he thought suddenly in indignation. A man with a beard! His hand fled to his chin for confirmation. A man with a beard, he thought with a cunning evil gleam narrowing his eye.

"You haven't answered my question," he said aggressively to the visitor. "You haven't answered it yet, have you?"

His hand had fallen against the hard brittle armor of the *langouste*'s hide. There were the eyes raised to his and the canny feelers lifted. His fingers closed for comfort about the *langouste*'s unwieldy paw. Father, he said in his heart, Father, help me. Father, Father, he said. I don't want to die.

Ben

Ben was a black man who pushed rolling chairs on the boardwalk once, but before the war even he wanted to belong to Puss, and in 1917 he gave himself to Puss forever. Puss was my little grandfather, and he bought Ben a dark-green jacket with dull buttons on it, and three alpaca aprons so that he could change often and keep looking smart. He learned how to wait at table and do the shoes and tend the furnace and use the vacuum cleaner. He was so big he had to stoop as he passed under every doorway in the house; he stooped down from his height and stooped in reverence as he took the little white man's orders. He could have stood Puss up on the palm of his hand and snapped him in two like a white-headed weed, but his voice instead was hushed with awe when he spoke to the saucy little man. All the time he harked to what Puss said, his head hung low and his full slack heavy lip hung down, in shame for his height and in shame for his strength and for having gone bald too soon.

Every room in the place became theirs in a while, theirs to go into, the four flights up and down. Through the furnace room and the cellar where the shower baths stood with bathing suits and old caps hanging in them, past the laundry and up the stairs into the library and the dining room. Through the halls and in and out of the conservatory they went on their journeys of perquisition: the little white man first in his silk skullcap and his doeskin slippers, and the black man big as a giant in his jacket and apron following behind. Through the pantry, the kitchen, and up the back way to the bathrooms they went, picking up, collecting.

"Here, just catch hold of that, Ben," Puss said, and the black man answered:

"Yes suh, yes suh, I got it right heah in my apron."

Into the guests' rooms and the bedrooms after the friends and family had left them, their marvelous excursions into tidiness took place. Here they redeemed a glove without its mate dropped on the top of a bookcase, here the top of a fountain pen, and somewhere else a postcard from the Poconos. Stray toothbrushes, balls of wool, schoolbooks, odd knitting needles, bracelets or rings removed to wash the hands and forgotten next to the soap, all these lay within their province of impeccability.

"Here, just pick that up, Ben," my little grandfather said, and Ben answered:

"Yes suh, yes suh, I got it right heah, suh."

Any time of day you could go up to Puss's door and knock, and he cleared his throat before pronouncing distinctly:

"Come in." And when he saw it was a child he added: "Come in, come in, whoever you are! Come in!"

Inside, his room was furnished like a business executive's: a glass-topped desk, a swivel chair, and standing alphabetic files. On the desk stood a green glass-shaded chromium office lamp, and there were two wire wastepaper baskets placed on either side of his chair with never more than a single slightly crumpled sheet of paper dropped in the bottom of one. His room was at the top of the house and through its windows you could see the roofs of the other Atlantic City houses and the vast sea moving quietly beyond.

You could say, "Puss, I've lost a doll's shoe," and he pinched his glasses on his nose and reached out for the card file and slid the box to him across the desk. His well-manicured, small fingers ran rapidly through the alphabet to "S," through the long list of variously described scissors they had retrieved to "Shaving: one brush (boar's hair), 6 Gillette blades," down to "Shoes," and paused there.

"Shoes," he read out, clearing his throat. "Gumshoes, Kate's silver slippers (tarnished), Madge's low button shoes, one bathing shoe (dark-blue canvas, cord sole), doll's black patent leather with instep strap (one)."

He looked up over his spectacles in inquiry, and if you said yes, that was the one, he rang the electric bell under his desk and Ben came up, coming carefully up the stairs and through the hall and into Puss's room, tiptoeing gingerly as if fearful of disturbing someone's sleep or merely of colliding with the diminutiveness of what was ceiling and wall and house itself around him.

"Number 3 ab, left," Puss said briefly to him, and Ben replied in awe:

"Yes suh, numbah 3 ab, left, suh," and higher even than this fourth floor he went, mounting the final ladder to the attic, his monstrous crouching body carried upwards on his hands and knees.

The attic was kept as clean as wax and stacked neatly with uniform cardboard boxes, for this was how their work went on. All the long winter afternoons, Ben crept across the boards there, too big to stand, sorting and labeling their spoils and closing them away in boxes, while Puss sat at his elegant glass-topped desk below and filled in the lined white file cards with explanation.

"One chile's mitten, suh," Ben would call down through the opening of the trap door in the attic floor, and Puss repeated:

"One child's mitten. Put it in Number 6 fg, right, Ben. What color?"

Ben would wait a minute before he said:

"I cain't tell you that, suh. I couldn't say. I never got to know much about color. I never got that far in school."

I remember Ben, and I remember that year on Christmas morning he came upstairs from stoking the furnace. It was only half-past five, but he saw the light in the hallway from below; and because he had been listening for us he heard us open our doors, and heard us whispering together. Our stockings were filled and pinned up on the velvet hangings where we'd hung them empty the night before. It was while we were unfastening them and holding them crackling wondrously against us that Ben came tiptoeing up the stairs.

"I hung up my stocking too," he whispered across the hall to us. "I sure did. You wait a minute and you'll see."

His mouth was hanging wide open with his joy, and all his teeth showed pure as milk within its cavern. He was dressed already in his jacket and his apron, or maybe it was the way Aunt Madge said, that he never cared about taking his things off at all. Just set the two long human faces of his shoes beside the bed, and laid his green jacket over the chair's back and slept.

"I didn't ask nobody nothing," he said, his voice shaking in his throat with bliss for what would come. "I just hung my stocking up the way you children was doing."

It was lost in the velvet folds of the curtain until he went over and carefully moved the hangings aside, and then we all saw it: the long dark gray woman's stocking with a white seam at the heel, quite new and dangling without life or promise in it. He had hung it up in the dark between where ours had been, but it was empty still because nobody had seen it there.

"I hung up my stocking——" he began, and standing there with his back to us, he lifted one big hand and passed the inside of it over his forehead and the bald part of his head. "I sure hung up my stocking," he said, not understanding and perhaps never getting any nearer to understanding.

We children stood in the lighted hall, holding the still untouched new dolls and the trumpets and the tissue-paper bundles in our arms, and Ben turned slowly around and looked at us in bewilderment. After what seemed a long time, his lips opened and they made no sound, but then he began crying. He did not try to turn his head away, or touch the tears, but let them run unheeded down his face. There was nothing we dared say to him or do, but in a minute we heard a door above us open, and Puss in his doeskin slippers and dressing gown came stepping quickly down the stairs.

"What's this, what's this?" he said, with his white mustaches bristling. "What's up? What's up? Ben, why are you making a spectacle of yourself like this before the children?"

His look darted around the hallway at us, and when he saw what it was he put his hands into the pockets of his dressing gown and said:

"Now, Ben, I'm very much surprised to see you acting like this. Here you are, a man of thirty, crying like a child!"

"Children ain't got no cause to cry," Ben said, and the tears ran down his face still while he looked at the stockings we held. "I wouldn't be crying if I was a chile today," he said.

"What would your father and mother say if they saw you cutting up like this on Christmas morning?" said Puss. He stood with his hands in his pockets, looking boldly and saucily up the black man's height to where the face hung shining with tears. "A great big fellow like you, over six feet tall and strong enough to carry the whole house around on your shoulders! Why, I'm ashamed of you!"

I remember Ben, and how he wiped his hand across his face, drawing the side of it under his wide-nostriled, seemingly boneless nose.

"That old Santa," he began, and Puss interrupted him, moving his hands a little uncomfortably in the pockets of his gown.

"Come, come, Ben," he said. "This is no way to talk. Perhaps your Christmas is coming later. Perhaps old Santy——"

"That's my Christmas," said Ben before he went tiptoeing down the stairs, his shoulders stooped in pain. "There's my Christmas hanging up, still waiting——" And we turned and looked again, holding our toys against us, at the long gray empty cotton stocking that nobody had ever worn.

I remember him, and how he used to make the fire in the living room in the evenings, crossing the fur rug on his hands and knees and reaching the big logs in. The place was dark, and when he put the match to the kindling, the flame ran fast along the edge of paper. Kneeling like this, he took the combs out of his pocket one evening and opened the tissue paper they lay in and showed me what they were. I was sitting up in the armchair, looking, and the fire's reflection streamed bright as oil across his forehead and flanged his nostrils and his naked throat with light.

"I got the ones with the jewels in them because they was the best," he said. They were the kind of tortoise-shell combs a lady wears in her hair, and these had stones set in them: turquoise, and pearl, and some sort of cut pinkish jewels that sparkled as beautifully as glass. "I got to have the best now for everybody I got anything to do with and no mistake about it," he said. "Your grandfather, I learned a lot from him I never thought of knowing. About having a home," he said, "and keeping things neat and right just like anybody ought to. I didn't pick these out just nohow. I kept in mind the different dresses she'd be wearing. They're for my wife," he said without looking up. "They're for my wife," he said, kneeling there and holding them tenderly in the paper.

"When did you get married, Ben?" I asked him, whispering as he did across the darkness. "I never knew you had a wife. I didn't know."

"I got her all picked out," he said. He folded the tissue paper over the combs, his fingers long and broad, and hairless as a savage's would be. "I saw her on the boardwalk once, but I ain't going to be hurried into nothing. I ain't going to be rushed into nothing by nobody," he said. "I'm biding my time for this year, anyway. I'm going to do my courting easy and slow."

That was the year before he died of the Spanish influenza, and after it Puss made his excursions into immaculateness from the cellar up to the foot of the attic's ladder alone. One day in the laundry, behind the bars of washing soap, wrapped in tissue paper still and tied with a tinsel ribbon that had "Yuletide Greetings, Yuletide Greetings, Yuletide Greetings" stamped the length of it in red, Puss found the side combs for a lady's hair. In the afternoon, he sat down at his glass-topped desk and made out their card in the box file for them: "Two celluloid hair combs, new, ornamented with jewels (imitation)." Later he climbed the ladder to the attic, going slowly in his doeskin slippers and wear-

ing his black skullcap, and he put them away in a box labeled
with some number or another and slipped it into its place either
to the left or right of the trap door.

Kroy Wen

The two little Italians looked up the tower of decks to the sight
of Mr. Wurthenberger with his Panama pulled down over his
eyes. Three large birds, balancing on their wings like albatross
and yet as black as crows, had followed them now for the past
two days of quiet weather. There they were when the night
came down, melting away into the tar of it, and in the morning
they were riding the sky like three black crescent moons.
Whether the same kinds of omens were good or bad on the
water as they were on land was something that the two Italians
with their soft Italian faces did not know. But thoughts and men-
aces passed through their heads like a passing breeze, or like a
feather blowing, and they never thought of any one thing for
very long at a time. They had sought out the gentlest corner, and
the farthest on the lower deck of the ship, and there they had
turned about upon imaginary grasses and sat down close to one
another in the sun. She seemed to be making something like a
red hood for her baby to wear. The baby, apparently, was going
to be born in a minute or two.

The Italian woman's steel needles worked and languished in
the wool. The tips of her fingers were better suited to pulling
idly at the curly wool, or to lying still in the Italian's hand. They
sat in the sun on their own warm soft behinds, exchanging looks
at each other, with a cloud passing over their faces whenever
they caught a sight of the three black birds circling after the
ship. Their teeth were shining as they plucked petal after petal
from the fragrant bouquets of their conversation. Garlic was part
of their own breath to them, and their tongues and nostrils re-
pined without it.

Thus could they be seen from the upper deck. The black birds were flying behind them, soiling the purity of the clear blue sky. It was no place for an artist to be, nor for a man who could feel the heart of all humanity beating against his own ribs.

"I could use those two," Mr. Wurthenberger said.

The steward had come along the deck to him, with a special tray in his hand. On it was steaming a cup of broth.

"I've brought a little cup of bouillon, Mr. Wurthenberger," said the steward. "It's quite nice and delicate, sir. I think you'll have no trouble with it."

Mr. Wurthenberger's lifted hand struck the faces of the two Italians below as if he had flashed a mirror upon them, for the sun had caught in the gems of his fingers and swung a blade of fire across their eyes.

"I want to go down into the steerage," was what he said.

He had taken this leisurely broad boat toward Italy to get away from art. Art and humanity were what he was escaping. Tobacco and alcohol were safe behind a resolve not to touch them again until his hand was steady as a metronome. And here was the artist soul and the love of humanity in him betraying him and dispatching the steward to find his secretary.

"There's color," he said. "I needed a few yards of a pregnant woman. God, what an atmosphere!" he said.

Out went his knees like nutcrackers and down the glittering flights he ran. As he passed through the promenade deck, his nerves played the same trick on him: he caught himself spelling backwards the name of the steamer that was lettered out on the life preserver so that in the tail of his eye it was read: "Kroy Wen." This had been the warning his nerves had given him when the specialist had said: "Go away. Six months, a year. You can't keep on as you've been doing. Let the movies take care of themselves."

But it would take more than a wreck of nerves to persuade him that the movies could take care of themselves. He had agreed to rest. He was taking a sea voyage. But who was to blame if art and humanity pursued him, got him by the eyes and the ears and made him act? He knew that he had a way with him, but who would have guessed it now that he had passed fifty and his teeth had turned as yellow as grains of corn? Maybe he had once been a fine-looking fellow with his belly thin and curving into his breeches, but he knew that the reputation he had in every corner of the world was gaudy enough to make a bambino's hood.

"Old, am I?" he thought as he stood in front of the two young Italians. They were sitting on the deck, eying him gently in the sun. "These damned wops with their pretty skins!" he was thinking.

He looked at the little Italian woman shaking the gold hoops in her ears. He had begun to talk to them in his winning way. He had never owned a circus or anything like it, he answered them, but he had a great deal to say in short hard words of all the things he had done. He had even taken a star in his own hands.

"My wife," was what he said to these two gentle little people, "is a star."

They thought of the five sharp points and the brilliance of her.

"Your first baby you're having, is it?" he said. "Your first one, eh?"

They were sailing back to Italy to give birth to their first child. The director had no children, he said. The star had never given birth. From this their minds drifted gently to thoughts of falling stars, and to the arch of daisies which keeps the sky at night from ballooning down like a circus tent. This was a usual enough thought for them, for the Italian had swung on a trapeze for thirteen years.

"I could use you two," the director said.

If the heavens had not wept and the wind slapped the sea so smartly, if entrails had not sought to reach fore and grip the earth forever, he would have photographed them the next morning. For this reason they had sticks of greasepaint in their cabin which they were to put on their faces once the secretary had shown them how. But the Italian woman was so sick that she felt the baby retching and dying in her. With every swell of the waters, nausea washed over her like a tide.

Mr. Wurthenberger came into their cabin in the rain. The stench of it was such that he had to disregard his resolve and light a cigar before he could bear it. There was no porthole, and even in their agony they took the little white bulbs of garlic out of a nosegay of raffia and sliced it raw upon their tough bread.

"You're a couple of kids," said the director with a puff of sweet tobacco. "You're young, eh, to be having a baby?"

Maybe they could start taking the pictures tomorrow, said Mr. Wurthenberger, provided the rain let up.

"Noolas," he read backwards as he passed the saloon. "Dnoces Ssalc."

The three black birds seemed to be carrying on in their beaks the curtain of foul weather. Even the sun was doing its best to torment him, thought Mr. Wurthenberger on the morrow. The rain was continuing to fall. He was in a temper of irritation, thinking of the lights he might have brought with him. He might have brought a lamp or two with him and it would have done his nerves less harm than fretting this way about the rain. But it was not the end of his nerves, for with the rain and the wind spanking the waters for dear life, he had to bide his time. Time he had for reflection upon his own life and all the great things he had done. He sat alone in the drawing room, not daring to call for a drink. Reflection was something that gasped for sustenance in him, like a trout ripped out of its universe into a brutal one that hammered fists of agony against its red-lipped ears. The thought of the weather had made Mr. Wurthenberger bite his nails ragged to the quick.

On the fine day that eventually dawned, he fled down to the steerage, pursued by the fear that a squall might spoil the weather. The Italian woman had fallen fast asleep after the storm. Her hand was lying in repose in the Italian acrobat's short thick hand. "She has hadda pain," her husband said.

Maybe the bambino was going to be born. This was a nicer scene than Mr. Wurthenberger had dared hope for. His heart began to shake in him as if he were standing upon the brink of love. Whatever it was that was going to happen, he knew he could understand it, for every human emotion was as clear to him as the day. He knew the kind of heartbreaking picture this would make and the warm source of tears that it would make spring from the apple of the eye. His hands were shaking so that

he could scarcely get the camera up before the two Italians
where they were sitting in the sun.

He started taking the picture of them as she sat there asleep,
leaning against the acrobat. After a while Mr. Wurthenberger
said:

"I tell you what, Tony. You'd better wake her up. I'm getting
a picture of a woman having a child, see? She's had a couple of
pains and she's feeling pretty bad, see, and maybe the baby is
going to come on the boat because the weather's been rough,
you see, and maybe it's going to come beforehand and not in
Italy as they'd been planning. So they're both feeling pretty bad
about it, see? The doctor on the small boat they're traveling on
isn't so much as a doctor, and they're both feeling pretty sick
about the baby coming on the boat instead of in Italy as they'd
been looking forward to."

Mr. Wurthenberger's knees had gone soft under him with his
tenderness and his love for the thing he was saying. He was
stooping down before them with his hands held tight together.
Beads of anguish were lying like a crown of thorns upon his
head.

"Do you get it, Tony?" he was saying. "Do you get an idea of
the whole thing? Now, you just wake her up a little, Tony, just
gradually, you see, while I start turning the handle."

He skipped lightly back to the camera, scarcely daring to
breathe, and in this way the picture went on. After a little while,
the Italian woman pushed herself up until she was sitting back
against the blisters of dry paint on the side of the deck.

"I feel bad," she said.

She sat very still, holding her two hands under her shawl. A
small white mask of agony had fallen upon her lips but she made
no sign. She sat close to the white blisters of paint on the side of
the ship and closed her eyes. Tears had begun to run slowly
down the face of the Italian acrobat.

Suddenly Mr. Wurthenberger dropped the handle of the camera and walked toward them.

"You're all right, Tony," he said. When he looked at the
woman he had to hold onto himself to keep from shaking her.
"She's got to register something," he said. "I'm taking a woman

in childbirth, you see. She can't just sit there kind of mooning and dozing along. You're getting something in the way of cash out of this, you know. After all, you aren't doing it for the love of the thing. Now look here," he said. "She can make a few movements. She's got to get her hands into play." He squatted patiently down before the two Italians. "Now, look here," he said. "This is a big thing. This is a big human crisis, do you see?" Suddenly he was stricken by the awful futility of any kind of speech with them. He jumped to his feet. "Can't you understand? Can't you get it? Can't you get the big importance of this thing?" He thought he could strike the woman for her obstinance. She sat there in silence, stubbornly pressing the small of her back into the blistered wood.

"Open your eyes, can't you?" he said. His nerves were shaking in him. He was ready to scream aloud. "Listen," he said deliberately. "You got to open your eyes, you understand?"

The Italian woman opened her eyes and looked at him.

"There," he said. "That's fine."

Nervously he skipped back to his camera against the rail.

"That's fine," he said again as he watched her through the lens. "Now hold it. That's it. Keep on looking. Now roll 'em about a bit."

The woman straightened back against the deck.

"I can't," she said. Her face had no expression at all. The woman sat perfectly still. Her eyes were closed.

"Christ!" said Mr. Wurthenberger.

"Maybe it hurts her pretty bad," said the Italian in apology. He wiped his nose on the back of his hand.

Mr. Wurthenberger felt his mind revolving in his skull. He crossed the deck and crouched before them again. "Listen," he said with a cold terrible patience. "Just let your jaw fall open and scream." He turned patiently to the little acrobat. "Does she understand me?" he said. "Just tell her to try and scream. Won't you open your mouth and scream?" he was whispering to her persuasively.

The Italian woman's head was moving from side to side.

"Maybe it hurts her," said the Italian. He didn't know what to do.

Black Boy

At that time, it was the forsaken part, it was the other end of the city, and on early spring mornings there was no one about. By soft words, you could woo the horse into the foam, and ride her with the sea knee-deep around her. The waves came in and out there, as indolent as ladies, gathered up their skirts in their hands and, with a murmur, came tiptoeing in across the velvet sand.

The wooden promenade was high there, and when the wind was up the water came running under it like wild. On such days, you had to content yourself with riding the horse over the deep white drifts of dry sand on the other side of the walks; the horse's hoofs here made no sound and the sparks of sand stung your face in fury. It had no body to it, like the mile or two of sand packed hard that you could open out on once the tide was down.

My little grandfather, Puss, was alive then, with his delicate gait and ankles, and his belly pouting in his dove-gray clothes. When he saw from the window that the tide was sidling out, he put on his pearl fedora and came stepping down the street. For a minute, he put one foot on the sand, but he was not at ease there. On the boardwalk over our heads was some other kind of life in progress. If you looked up, you could see it in motion through the cracks in the timber: rolling chairs, and women in high heels proceeding, if the weather were fair.

"You know," my grandfather said, "I think I might like to have a look at a shop or two along the boardwalk." Or: "I suppose you don't feel like leaving the beach for a minute," or: "If you would go with me, we might take a chair together, and look at the hats and the dresses and roll along in the sun."

He was alive then, taking his pick of the broad easy chairs and the black boys.

"There's a nice skinny boy," he'd say. "He looks as though he might put some action into it. Here you are, sonny. Push me and the little girl down to the Million Dollar Pier and back."

The cushions were red velvet with a sheen of dew over them. And Puss settled back on them and took my hand in his. In his mind there was no hesitation about whether he would look at the shops on one side, or out on the vacant side where there was nothing shining but the sea.

"What's your name, Charlie?" Puss would say without turning his head to the black boy pushing the chair behind our shoulders.

"Charlie's my name, sir," he'd answer with his face dripping down like tar in the sun.

"What's your name, sonny?" Puss would say another time, and the black boy answered:

"Sonny's my name, sir."

"What's your name, Big Boy?"

"Big Boy's my name."

He never wore a smile on his face, the black boy. He was thin as a shadow but darker, and he was pushing and sweating, getting the chair down to the Million Dollar Pier and back again, in and out through the people. If you turned toward the sea for a minute, you could see his face out of the corner of your eye, hanging black as a bat's wing, nodding and nodding like a dark heavy flower.

But in the early morning, he was the only one who came down onto the sand and sat under the beams of the boardwalk, sitting idle there with a languor fallen on every limb. He had long bones. He sat idle there, with his clothes shrunk up from his wrists and his ankles, with his legs drawn up, looking out at the sea.

"I might be a king if I wanted to be," was what he said to me.

Maybe I was twelve years old, or maybe I was ten when we used to sit eating dog biscuits together. Sometimes when you broke them in two, a worm fell out and the black boy lifted his sharp finger and flicked it carelessly from off his knee.

"I seen kings," he said, "with a kind of cloth over they heads, and kind of jewels-like around here and here. They weren't any blacker than me, if as black," he said. "I could be almost any-thing I made up my mind to be."

"King Nebuchadnezzar," I said. "He wasn't a white man."

The wind was off the ocean and was filled with alien smells. It was early in the day, and no human sign was given. Overhead were the green beams of the boardwalk and no wheel or step to sound it.

"If I was a king," said the black boy with his biscuit in his fingers, "I wouldn't put much stock in hanging around here."

Great crystal jelly beasts were quivering in a hundred different colors on the wastes of sand around us. The dogs came, jumping them, and when they saw me still sitting still, they wheeled like gulls and sped back to the sea.

"I'd be traveling around," he said, "here and there. Now here, now there. I'd change most of my habits."

His hair grew all over the top of his head in tight dry rosettes. His neck was longer and more shapely than a white man's neck, and his fingers ran in and out of the sand like the blue feet of a bird.

"I wouldn't have much to do with pushing chairs around under them circumstances," he said. "I might even give up sleep-ing out here on the sand."

Or if you came out when it was starlight, you could see him sitting there in the clear white darkness. I could go and come as I liked, for whenever I went out the door, I had the dogs shoul-dering behind me. At night, they shook the taste of the house out of their coats and came down across the sand. There he was, with his knees up, sitting idle.

"They used to be all kinds of animals come down here to drink in the dark," he said. "They was a kind of a mirage came along and gave that impression. I seen tigers, lions, lambs, deer; I seen ostriches drinking down there side by side with each other. They's the Northern Lights gets crossed some way and switches the wrong picture down."

It may be that the coast has changed there, for even then it was changing. The lighthouse that had once stood far out on the white rocks near the outlet was standing then like a lighted torch in the heart of the town. And the deep currents of the sea may have altered so that the clearest water runs in another direction, and houses may have been built down as far as where the brink used to be. But the brink was so perilous then that every word the black boy spoke seemed to fall into a cavern of beauty.

"I seen camels; I seen zebras," he said. "I might have caught any of one of them if I'd felt inclined."

The street was so still and wide then that when Puss stepped out of the house, I could hear him clearing his throat of the sharp salty air. He had no intention of soiling the soles of his boots, but he came down the street to find me.

"If you feel like going with me," he said, "we'll take a chair and see the fifty-seven varieties changing on the electric sign."

And then he saw the black boy sitting quiet. His voice drew up short on his tongue and he touched his white mustache.

"I shouldn't think it a good idea," he said, and he put his arm through my arm. "I saw another little oak not three inches high in the Jap's window yesterday. We might roll down the boardwalk and have a look at it. You know," said Puss, and he put his kid gloves carefully on his fingers, "that black boy might do you some kind of harm."

"What kind of harm could he do me?" I said.

"Well," said Puss with the garlands of lights hanging around him, "he might steal some money from you. He might knock you down and take your money away."

"How could he do that?" I said. "We just sit and talk there." Puss looked at me sharply.

"What do you find to sit and talk about?" he said.

"I don't know," I said. "I don't remember. It doesn't sound like much to tell it."

The burden of his words was lying there on my heart when I woke up in the morning. I went out by myself to the stable and led the horse to the door and put the saddle on her. If Puss were ill at ease for a day or two, he could look out the window in peace and see me riding high and mighty away. The day after tomorrow, I thought, or the next day, I'll sit down on the beach again and talk to the black boy. But when I rode out, I saw him seated idle there, under the boardwalk, heedless, looking away to the cool wide sea. He had been eating peanuts and the shells lay all around him. The dogs came running at the horse's heels, nipping the foam that lay along the tide.

The horse was as shy as a bird that morning, and when I drew her up beside the black boy, she tossed her head on high. Her mane went back and forth, from one side to the other, and a flight of joy in her limbs sent her forelegs like rockets into the air. The black boy stood up from the cold smooth sand, unsmiling, but a spark of wonder shone in his marble eyes. He put out his arm in the short tight sleeve of his coat and stroked her shivering shoulder.

"I was going to be a jockey once," he said, "but I changed my mind."

I slid down on one side while he climbed up the other.

"I don't know as I can ride him right," he said as I held her head. "The kind of saddle you have, it gives you nothing to grip your heels around. I ride them with their bare skin."

The black boy settled himself on the leather and put his feet in the stirrups. He was quiet and quick with delight, but he had no thought of smiling as he took the reins in his hands.

I stood on the beach with the dogs beside me, looking after the horse as she ambled down to the water. The black boy rode easily and straight, letting the horse stretch out and sneeze and canter. When they reached the jetty, he turned her casually and brought her loping back.

"Some folks licks hell out of their horses," he said. "I'd never raise a hand to one, unless he was to bite me or do something I didn't care for."

He sat in the saddle at ease, as though in a rocker, stroking her shoulder with his hand spread open, and turning in the stirrups to smooth her shining flank.

"Jockeys make a pile of money," I said.

"I wouldn't care for the life they have," said the black boy. "They have to watch their diet so careful."

His fingers ran delicately through her hair and laid her mane back on her neck.

When I was up on the horse again, I turned her toward the boardwalk.

"I'm going to take her over the jetty," I said. "You'll see how she clears it. I'll take her up under the boardwalk to give her a good start."

I struck her shoulder with the end of my crop, and she started toward the tough black beams. She was under it, galloping, when the dogs came down the beach like mad. They had chased a cat out of cover and were after it, screaming as they ran, with a wing of sand blowing wide behind them, and when the horse saw them under her legs, she jumped sidewise in sprightliness and terror and flung herself against an iron arch.

For a long time I heard nothing at all in my head except the melody of someone crying, whether it was my dead mother holding me in comfort, or the soft wind grieving over me where I had fallen. I lay on the sand asleep; I could feel it running with my tears through my fingers. I was rocked in a cradle of love, cradled and rocked in sorrow.

"Oh, my little lamb, my little lamb pie!" Oh, sorrow, sorrow, wailed the wind, or the tide, or my own kin about me. "Oh, lamb, oh, lamb!"

I could feel the long swift fingers of love untying the terrible knot of pain that bound my head. And I put my arms around him and lay close to his heart in comfort.

Puss was alive then, and when he met the black boy carrying me up to the house, he struck him square across the mouth.

Friend of the Family

When they were young they had a theater with men and women, and the shrubbery even, on wires they could shift about. They hung a curtain across half the room and set the stage up on a table in the middle. Thunder was present in a thin piece of cardboard waved till it bellowed out behind the scenes. But the best play was the one in which the glass coffin with the princess visible in it was allowed to fall. "The coffin," said the voice of one of the children, reading behind the stage, "fell and was broken into a-toms." And then the coffin was whisked off on its wire, and bits of white cardboard were cast in from the wings.

At this moment the Baron always burst into applause, clapping and shouting to stamp out the sound of his own laughter, maybe; but even then the curtain was descending, so the storm of his clamor fitted in very well.

"*Bis! Bis!*" shouted the Baron.

They learned the word from his mouth. He stood up from his chair and held his hands up far and high as he applauded. They brought out the players and jerked them at him, and at Mother, and at whoever else might be watching. A minute or two after, the Baron would go to the piano in the other room and sing the "Glowworm" song in German, the words thundering, thundering till the walls of the house fell in, and his voice went soaring away.

He had a big dark voice that filled the spaces of concert halls and made the glass sticks of the chandeliers shudder. Twice they were taken to New York, and there they heard him sing in the opera at night. The first time he wore tights and a doublet and played stormily in the darkness. The second time he looked as they knew him: in an evening suit with a white flower in his lapel. But however he dressed, he remained a foreign young man to them, luxuriant and black as a bear, making all the other young men who came to the house seem white as albinos and as tasteless.

He did not come often, only two or three times in the year maybe; but Mother had her ostrich feather dipped bluer and curled up fresh every time before he came. She bought him neckties and put them away in the drawer for him: as rich in color as she could find, because that was the way he would have chosen them himself. He did not dress like any man they knew. This time he wore a snow-white overcoat of wool, and a heliotrope suit, and white spats over his shiny shoes. He stood on the step of the Pullman car when the train came in and he jumped off shouting before it had so much as halted. His gloves were yellow chamois with black backbones, and he ripped them off when he kissed their cheeks and gave all the flowers to Mother.

"Good God, how are you all?" he said with joy, while they

stood looking speechless, because they had forgotten he was so tall and talked so loud. He was a Bavarian, and the Middle West was as unsuitable as the grave to him. He walked out of the station to the car with Mother's arm in his, and his foreign aspect like a bright cloak all around them.

The Baron sat beside Mother on the cushions, and the two little girls, in their patent-leather hats, sat erect on the side seats with their backs to the others and watched him in the strip of glass.

"I miss my own mother so much," he said, and there in the mirror they could see him kiss Mother's hand inside and out. She shook her blue feather at him, and his dark eyes were shining, and his gold face was filled with alien things.

He changed into white flannels for lunch and walked boldly out onto the terrace. His voice hummed deeply in his throat, and his fingers danced on his open shirt, rapped quick and hard as if striking music from a shapely barrel of sound. He remembered everything that had been there, and what changes they had made.

"Ah, the jump-ups here this year!" he sang out deeply to Mother. "You know, I'll tell you something. I like it much better. What a good idea you had, Mrs. *Mutter*."

Even Mother's dress was changed.

"It's so hot," she said when the children saw it with delight. "It's suddenly so mild," said Mother, "that I slipped this one on."

"But it's *new!*" said the little girls. "It's awfully pretty!"

"Yes," said Mother. "Now let's show the Baron the baby doves."

"But what a beautiful dress!" said the Baron. "I can't quite take my eyes off it." He caught his clean white shoe in a croquet wicket and must put out his hand and touch Mother's arm to get his balance again.

"Did you hurt yourself?" cried Mother softly, and he stood quite still, looking at her.

"Yes," said the Baron in his dark deep voice. "Yes, I have hurt myself for all my life."

He remembered the number of white doves there had been before in the autumn. The gladiola trees were blooming and they now cast a blush and a languor on the air. He remembered the exact proportion of gin and grenadine for Father's cocktail. When he came back to the table on the terrace, he rolled up his sleeves to make it, and the black silk hairs lay quiet on his arms.

"Ah, ah, ah, *ahhhhhh!*" he sang, as though practicing his scales. The silver shaker was frosting in his hands. "Here comes Mr. *Mutter* out of the car! Hello, hello, hello!" he cried. He went striding down the flight of steps in the garden as if welcoming a guest who had come to call. "Hello, hello, Mr. *Mutter!*" he shouted.

"Hello," said Father quietly. Standing beside the Baron, he looked like a small man, and all of a sudden the gray hairs seemed to spring out like magic all over his head. "When did you get here?" said Father. He had come from the office, and he had his dark-blue suit on.

"In time to make a cocktail for you!" the Baron cried out with a burst of laughter.

"You'd make a first-rate butler," said Father, but he did not smile.

When they sat down to lunch, with the little girls sitting quiet and respectful at one end of the table, the Baron began to tell them of what his own mother had meant to him. His teeth shone out like stars and he ate his food with gusto. The sun was on his face binding great wreaths of beauty to his brows.

"When you grow up, little girls," he said, "it does a terrible thing to your mother. It wipes the light right out of her sweet face and puts something else you never thought of there. Br-rr, rr-rr," said the Baron in his own peculiar language, and he shook as if the cold had struck him. "It sometimes keeps me awake at night, the awful things that one year after another put into my mother's eyes. She couldn't get used to me being in the army. She thought she could persuade everyone that I had dressed up like an army officer just for the fun. When I'd come home to her, she'd say: 'Now you will take off the uniform,' as if that would make a little boy of me again!"

The Baron helped himself to the chicken and cream sauce sown with scarlet peppers. But in spite of his interest in this, his thoughts were elsewhere, for he was telling them of the first time he ran away from home.

"Mr. *Mutter,* she looked in all the cafés for two days for me, and she went to every musical revue in town, where she hated to be. She waited outside the opera every night, because she couldn't bear to go inside and see the stairs where my father dropped dead from his heart when he was a young man of thirty-five. Think of that! Dead from singing too loud, and eating too well, and drinking too much wine. Now that's a fine way to pop off, Mr. *Mutter,* what do you know about it? My God, what a wonderful look that man left behind in my poor mother's face!"

The Baron threw aside his knife and fork in his emotion.

"My God, Mr. *Mutter!*" he cried out to Father. "Sometimes I think I could talk for the rest of my life to your children here, saying, 'Be good, be good, be good to that wonderful thing that God gives you for a little while!' Sometimes I think I could go down on my knees," said the Baron, "and ask them that they be good to their wonderful little mother."

Father wiped his lips with his napkin and he sat looking at the Baron.

"You mean because of her resemblance to your own mother?" Father said politely.

"My God, yes!" cried the Baron. But he picked up his knife and fork again as though his taste for the food before him had returned. "Here we are, living men, Mr. *Mutter,*" he said after a moment. "But do you think that either one of us could bring that wonderful look to Mrs. *Mutter* that one dead man gave to my own mother's face?"

"I'm quite sure that, either alive or dead, I couldn't," said Father.

"And all the time she was looking for me, the poor woman," said the Baron, "all the time I was out of the city. I grew up overnight, and I went off with a soubrette into the country. I——"

Father laid down his napkin and pushed his chair back from the table.

"After all," he said, "there are children present whose development may be less precocious than yours was——"

The little girls did not lift their eyes. In a minute their father stood up and said he must be going back to the office. The Baron stood up and bowed a little over the table.

"I don't doubt I'll see you this evening," Father said.

They all watched the limousine turn and saw Father driven down the driveway, the gravel crackling slowly under the soft, elegant tires on the wheels.

"What's a soubrette?" one of the children said.

"It's a kind of a frying pan," said Mother. She looked without smiling at the Baron. "Well, what happened next?" she said. The Baron gave her a cigarette from his case and lighted it for her.

"My God. It was awful," he said.

"I should have thought it would be awfully nice," said Mother.

"Two days in the country with a—with a——" said the Baron.

"With a frying pan," said Mother, smoking. "Do, please, go on."

But the Baron jumped up, as if in anger, and started across the terrace. Suddenly he came back and stood great and broad, towering and mighty over Mother's chair.

"Two days!" he thundered at her. "Two days I kept jumping out of the window to see the trees, or the sky, or the river, or anything that tasted fresh and good!"

"Just like a musical-comedy officer!" said Mother lightly.

"Very well," said the Baron. The color ran up into his golden face. "Very well," he said, and he turned and walked away.

He went the length of the terrace and down the steps, and they could hear his white shoes crunching across the drive. The little girls, having finished their fruit, folded their napkins and followed Mother to the balustrade. There they saw the top of the Baron's head disappearing around the grape arbor's arch.

"It might be almost anywhere," Mother said to them. Her voice was soft and filled with love for them. She stood looking out over the sight of the river and the thick curve of woods above the shining bands of blue. There were no barges or ferries to spoil it just at that moment, and the current seemed swift and clean, although the city lay hidden not far beyond. "It might be almost anywhere, it's so lovely," Mother said, and she took the little girls' hands. "He's such a little child," she said, "we'd better go and see."

They found the Baron on his knees looking for four-leaf clovers; for things went in and out of his head like this, and no anger could fix them there. Mother and the little girls sat down and spread out their skirts on the grasses. They saw Mother's crossed ankles and her little, high-heeled boots, and they saw with shyness their own and each other's bare red knees sprinkled over with yellow hair. They tried to cover their knees, but could not. But the Baron, in any case, was talking about the new roles he was going to sing.

In the afternoon he wrote a one-act opera for them. He sat on the bench in the music room, rippling it out across the keyboard: songs and ballets that charmed them and set them to dancing because they were like so many tunes they had heard before. All afternoon Mother sat in the window, stitching new skirts and cloaks on the puppets. In the end it was an opera filled with humorous songs, written out nimble and fast by the Baron's pen as he played with the other hand, preserved for them in notes with tails and without tails on the glazed, ruled sheets.

Mother accompanied them day after day, and in a little while the children knew it all, could sing out the parts without laughing, and could make the saucepan dance on its strings. "An *opéra-comique* in one act," said the Baron, "entitled: *The Soubrette, the Saucepan, and the Percolator*." He himself sang the coffee percolator's part, striking his broad ringing chest and shouting with joy when they practiced it together. The Soubrette was a frying pan, very shiny and small, and Mother had stuck a piece of her own blue feather over the painted eyes.

On the night of the performance Father sat down in the front row; and when the curtain went up he said:

"The Soubrette looks like Mother."

"How silly!" said Mother from where she was softly playing the opening bars. The children saw her turn her head in the candlelight and smile at the dinner guests who now made up the audience. The scene before them was the top of a kitchen stove, and in a moment the Percolator was jerked onto the stage, and the Baron began to sing his stirring song.

"*Moi, le Percolator,* perka, perka, perk!" sang his rich wondrous voice. The song was taken from the Toreador's, but it did not matter at all. Deeply, widely rang out the bubbling voice of the Baron from behind the tall curtain, while the silver Percolator in a purple cape strutted across the stove. "*Je* perk, *je* perk, *je* perk!" sang the Baron, and now the little Soubrette suddenly leaped upright from where she had been reclining on the coals. Her mouth was painted open for singing, and the children's voices blended and lifted together to give her speech. She uttered one phrase:

"*Quand tu es là, je ne pense qu'à ton percolating!*" and then the Baron again burst into song. His gay mouth opened wide behind the children, and his voice torrented out upon them, so close that it set their hearts to quaking. In his magic throat there swelled a breaking sorrow, a terrible, stirring sorrow that made their spines go cold with joy. Every other time and all other music had been but a preparation for this wild moment. Surely the stones and the beams of the house must fall when his voice arched up as ringing and strong as stone itself, and he called out, as though summoning someone to his side:

"*Soubrette, ma poêle à frire, je t'aime!*"

Everyone in the room burst into instantaneous applause, but in a moment, Father said in a voice that could be heard quite clearly:

"I've always liked my Bizet sung by the Italians or French. The Teutonic interpretation leaves me a little cold."

Then, like a small, passionate choir, the children's voices were softly raised in song. Behind them hummed the Baron's voice, tender, wooing as a cello, shaping them and guiding them toward love. Softly their mother played the breathless bars, and their own frail lungs went wide and piped all their mother's loveliness to beauty for the world to hear. The Frying Pan hastened across the glowing stage to the Percolator's side and melted into his embrace.

Spout to painted mouth, thus it was the Saucepan found them, and by a wonderful feat, steam exploded in fury from under his lid. He sent them clattering apart, the Soubrette's blue feather blowing in agitation. He tossed his tin cover down on the stove and minced his anger out. It was the Baron's voice again that gave vent to a pompous, testy ire; but the Baron's voice turned high in spite, running shallow, and his mouth turned up to smile.

> *Je suis une casserole pleine d'affaires,*
> *Je trouve les arts bien amers.*
> *L'Etat Civil, les Codes, la Loi,*
> *Sont toujours respectés, grâce à moi.*
> *Je n'ai pas le temps de m'amuser*
> *Car je fais la cuisine—c'est la vérité!*
> > *Je n'ai pas le temps pour quoi que ce soit!*
> > *Je suis une casserole!*

The Saucepan began a *pas seul* across the stage, but suddenly Father stood up among all the laughing people.

"What is the matter?" said Mother's soft voice across the dark as she played the music.

"Haven't the time to be amused," said Father. There was a little stir of surprise among the guests.

"Don't be so silly!" Mother cried out, for now the Baron had ceased singing.

"I don't like the part that's been given me," said Father loudly. He had brought the whole performance to an end.

"But you're not the Saucepan!" cried Mother, and everybody laughed. Even the Baron behind the wings stood shaking with laughter. "Ha, ha, ha, ha, ha!" his golden notes rang out.

"My God, Mr. *Mutter!*" he called out in his thundering voice. "You don't even look like a saucepan!"

"I suppose I do!" said Father savagely from the door. "It was just something that hadn't occurred to me before!"

Sometimes at night the children remembered how the Baron looked when he was laughing, or how he threw his head up in the sun, or how his hands spread wide over the keyboard of the piano. That was the last time he ever came to the house, but they remembered him for a long while after he went away, and how Mother had lain on the bed, and how the wind or something else had moaned and sobbed at the window like a woman crying all night.

White as Snow

There is only one history of importance, and it is the history of what you once believed in, and the history of what you came to believe in, and what cities or country you saw, and what trees you remembered. The history of other things comes in one ear and goes out the other, and the history of places you have never been to is as good as a picture, but with no taste or smell. Nor is it enough to speak the name of a city, for if the name of this one were said you might recall things no one else remembers. Easter gave that town a special glamour, not as Rome must have, but different, for it was not a religious place at all. It had no use for Christmas; winter was not its time of year.

Then it had long looped strings of lights hanging from pillar to post along the sea. It had gulls to it the way a wilder place might, but that was not good enough for it; it had put theaters the length of the waterfront as well. It had a thing for every hour of the day and night: ponies to drive on the sand, and a merry-go-round as big as an island, and on days when the rain fell the rolling chairs were made elegant as palaces with lights inside and glass panes set on each side and out before. Riding at night in them, the rain could be heard running swift and shallow at the wheels, and the rain polished as wax would the splinters and the grain of the timber walk that stood the length of the sea.

That was the year Carrie came down as nurse with us instead of the other. She was colored sweet and even like sarsaparilla. And she had never before been near the sea. She was so thin that we took all the best things on the plates to give her, honey and corn and waffles in the morning, because when she was a little girl they had never heard of such things. The family ate in the hotel dining room, but Carrie sat in the Ordinary between us with her hand on the edge of the table shaking with fear of what they might serve her next and whether a spoon or a fork should go beneath it. The first time the artichokes passed, she started laughing soft and high, as if she didn't care for them, but she remembered them forever. She always talked of them in the evening when she sat in the room waiting for the time to eat to come.

"If you children hadn't been talking so loud-mouthed that time, I'd of seen better what they was," she said softly, holding her thin blue hands between her knees in mourning. Or just before lunchtime she would remember. "I could of took hold of them leaves as neat as could be," she said to her own face in the glass, "if I'd had any idea what was passing by."

Carrie would be twenty in a few years, but then she stood thin as a bone in the hall, with her hair slicked back tight and shining. The porters were white men, but they had plenty of time to talk and linger, making little pieces of conversation with her whenever we went out or in. Here inside the house, she had a strong sweet artificial odor on that took all other smells aside, but out on the beach there was nothing left of it. Everything in life there, the high or the low tide or good weather or bad, or whether or not we smiled depended on one thing: it depended on Adamic and if he had come to the shore early that summer or if he wouldn't be coming until July. It was easy to know, for before you were out of the hotel bus you could see the marks of the tennis ball on the wall at the side, and if they were new he was there, and he was not there if they were fading away from the year before. Or you could maybe see Adamic standing, pulled out longer and longer every year, but with his face still like a child's face, the way a flower's head will remain unchanged no matter how tall the stalk may grow. This time when we came he had long trousers on that reached to his tennis shoes, and he was standing knocking the ball back against the wall, standing still with his arm swinging to take the ball square on the racket, however it might come.

No word was ever said to him, but such things were thought

in solitude of him that if the step of the tennis ball was not pacing the wall all summer, then the heart expired in the breast. Under the stone porches of the hotel there was never any word spoken. The chairs with the people sitting on them, one after another, were there, but children went speechless past them. For when people begin to speak their minds out, then something falters. It is easy to talk of one thing or another only when you do not believe any more in the purity and fervor of everyone else alive.

This was the time Carrie came with us; it was raining hard and she had cotton pansies on her hat, and she was afraid to get in the bus from the train and afraid to get out at the hotel for what the rain might do to the pansies' faces. When we stepped down, Carrie opened her handkerchief out and set it on top of her hat, and Adamic was standing under the shelter, hitting the tennis ball back against the wall.

"It might just as well be Philadelphia," Carrie said to the man who took the bags in. "The rain's just as wet as."

We went up to the bedrooms, and in the elevator Carrie took out her powder and did her face light again, beating the flat puff hard with her thin hand. We did not speak about Adamic then, but when we were at the floor we went running away from our delight that he was there, leaping and skipping down the carpeted hall. Carrie came running on her sharp thin legs after, jumping from one design to the next and laughing.

"You look like Eliza on the ice!" I cried out, thinking with joy of Adamic maybe. And Carrie stopped dead in the hall, in the dark, thin and still and faceless against the light that was shining in the ceiling far in back.

"No, I don't," she said. "That's not true."

The white porter was coming with the bags, and we could not tell what her face was, for she was standing black as a paper doll against the little moon of light.

"I ain't anything like Eliza," she said. "I never'd of thought to hear you say it." She saw the porter coming down the hall behind her, and she said: "Why would you want to say a thing like that for, and before the gentleman that way?"

It did not come to an end when we were washed and dressed in white, but went on like a song all evening.

"If I wanted to tell you out, I could tell you out like some colored people as would," she said, and this was the first time she had been in a hotel anywhere, but her sorrow was so great that she could not keep it still. The other nurses were talking among themselves at the table, but whether they heard her or not she could not help it. "I've heard colored people all over the world treating people to names like 'white trash' and other things worse than. To some it comes easy," she said in grief, "and to others it comes hard."

Even when we gave her the three ears of corn it was no comfort to her. She ate them slowly, silently, one after the other, chewing the buttered grains and wiping the grease off her brownish lips. We sat one on each side of her, watching her eat, each with a hand laid on her knees under the table. I said: "I'm sorry, Carrie, I'm sorry." But as soon as the corn was done with her voice began again, mourning and sighing. "You got no reason to care," she said. "Anything gets harmed for you, folks get you a new one. Anything happens to me, it just stays that way. But I got a heart as red as yours, my blood runs the same color, if I was to cut my finger and you cut your finger, nobody'd be able to tell the two of us apart."

But even that was not the end, and she went on with it through the hotel parlors, speaking soft and low and blameful as though she would never be the same. She put on our jackets and we went out on the stone piazza where the people were walking after dinner, and when she saw Adamic standing there in his white trousers, hitting the tennis ball back again, over and over, she stopped at once as if a hand had been laid on her mouth. It may be only for the things not said that youth is remembered so sharply. We stood there a long time watching Adamic. Carrie did not speak any more and we had no thought of speaking; this is the special privilege given before the tongue turns womanly and bold with comment and intention.

The days were fair and long that year and the beach striped with thin blue lagoons. We had Mexican hats and each a tooth out in front, and the afternoons were so hot that the wax beads from Venice melted and changed color on our necks, and Carrie said: "My hair," and when she spoke she stopped digging in the damp sand and smiled. "It seems it might be getting straighter here. It seems the air on the beach, it's known it takes the curl out. I heard that," she said, "I heard it," but she wouldn't say where. "It seems colored people often found the seashore beneficial." Her thin hands turning gave the tunnels their long secret shape. "It seems colored fellows comes here in particular and the sun does what it can to take their coloring away."

She was talking like this when Adamic came walking over the sand, with his head down to make himself a smaller man, and his feet bare, and letting his yellow bathrobe swing. He was not looking at us, nor looking either at the sea, nor watching, and he lay down, as if unknowing, near to us on the clean burning sand. Carrie was saying: "Maybe not as real white as a lily, but white enough so there was no telling," and then she saw Adamic and stopped talking.

The waves came in and out for a little while, and Adamic was lying there on his face with his robe spread under him, lying in his black swimming suit, letting the sun shine on his back and legs.

"What was it I was telling you children?" said Carrie, laughing high and wild. "Can't you tell the truth once? Don't you recall? I was telling you about the place my uncle had and all the servants waiting on him. That's where we was reared," she said, talking higher. "I was telling you. It was near to Boston, where the most of the good families inclines to be."

Resting on the damp sand, her hands seemed scarcely darker, and only under her chin on her throat when she turned her head toward Adamic did any shadow of color seem to be. Her bones were little and breakable under her skin, and her big lids in her sallow face swollen and smooth and blue. Her nose and her cheeks had freckles across them, colorless, like dark scattered drops of rain.

Adamic did not move, but suddenly his voice could be heard across the sand from under his folded arms where his face was hidden.

"I come from Boston," he said slowly.

"Your father, he certainly looks like a real Bostonian," said Carrie, arching and preening.

"I knew colored boys in high school there," said Adamic, looking straight over his arms to her.

"Oh, everywhere," said Carrie, and the sand ran through her fingers, "wherever you go the colored element is bound to be."

We all sat still on our knees, stricken with silence, waiting, with our ears gaping for whatever next he might say.

For three days Carrie did not tell us, and then she told us that Adamic was going with us to the moving pictures. He would not walk out of the hotel with us, but when we got to the moving pictures Adamic would be waiting there. So Carrie stayed in from the beach that morning, doing over the blouse and the little hat, sewing the pansies up as tight as buds for a change, and passing to and fro before the glass, languid and slow. Because she did not go out, we must stay in the room with her, painting pictures until it was time for lunch.

"They should have been in the sun all morning, Carrie," Mother said. And Carrie said:

"I couldn't make them move a step, ma'am. I couldn't do a thing."

"There are runs in their socks, Carrie," Mother said, and Carrie said:

"I know, ma'am, I know. But here I was cooped up with no needle or thread."

When we went out, Adamic was there, waiting with his back to the sea, leaning on the rail in the sunlight, tall as a grown man and smoking a cigarette hasty and short, as if the taste of it were bad. He was watching the crowds passing, his eyes moving quickly over everyone passing, but when we came along he made no sign at all. We could see his face very near as Carrie took us by him, and his eyes were fast on Carrie, on her hat and her smooth hair and the veil that went almost to her mouth. Her color was light with powder now, almost like chalk laid thick upon her skin, and she had put rouge on her cheekbones so that her sad sharp face seemed burning with delight.

"'Afternoon, Mr. Adamic," said Carrie, and she went stepping by him on her high thin legs. But Adamic only threw his cigarette out over the rail and did not speak. We passed so close to him that we could see the invisible golden down that was coming on his chin. His head was everything it had ever been, but the long, lank, uneasy limbs were strangers to us; he might have been a carnival thing, the limber, grotesque members holding a small child's familiar head on high.

He came following down the boardwalk behind us, as if he did not know us even, looking the other way. Only when Adamic was in the sea did his face seem natural and human to us, for the endless body was then lost, swimming out of sight. But when he was out, dressed full length in his good clothes with his watch on his wrist, there was this difference: there was a stranger standing erect inside him, looking bitterly and selfishly out of Adamic's eyes.

"The weather is surely pretty," Carrie said. She kept her head turned a little, like a bird's head, on her shoulder, so that she could keep him in her eye.

"It's not so bad," said Adamic, walking with his head down, swinging uneasy, almost behind. From where he was we knew he could see the holes still running in our socks.

"It might just as well be Philadelphia," said Carrie. She was stepping in her elegant heels over the splintery walk. "The sun shining so strong, Mr. Adamic."

"It might be Boston," said Adamic, smiling with his lip turned up. But still he was laughing, with his head bent, the way he had laughed every other year. "If it wasn't for the sea out there, and the boardwalk, and if it wasn't for the sand——"

"Oh, I've found," said Carrie, speaking high on her shoulder, with her blue veil drawn tight across her eyes, "I've found no matter how wide you travel, things is everywhere mostly similar. Ain't that the way, Mr. Adamic?"

"Oh, yes, that's true," said Adamic, talking slowly as if he must shape the words stronger and more daring in his mouth. "Sure," he said, and his head hung, swinging. "Girls, women——"

Carrie began laughing, quickly, softly, and she pulled her kid gloves over her bracelets to hide the pieces of her arms.

"What do you mean, Mr. Adamic? I'm sure I don't know what you mean," she said.

We were passing by a salt-water-taffy shop, and Adamic turned in the door and left us, and Carrie lingered at the window, seeming to look at all the fancy boxes, but staring straight into her own face reflected there within. She smiled her own small teeth at herself and moved the whites of her eyes in pleasure.

"Looks like I got a good sunburn," she said.

Adamic came out the door, carrying a box with a pink ribbon on it. He turned around quickly as if he was not speaking to Carrie and he put the box in her hands, and he said: "Here, that's for you."

"That surely is kind of your part, Mr. Adamic," said Carrie, and we started down the walk again, Carrie with one of us on each side of her, and Adamic following close, but not quite behind.

"I used to know a gentleman in Pawtucket," said Carrie, speaking over her shoulder to him as she stepped. "He was always making gifts of some kind. It was like a habit with him."

"Sure, I know," said Adamic, his voice low and hoarse. "If you have a lot to do with women you get into that habit. I've been trying to break myself of it for some time now, but what's the use?"

We came to the moving-picture place and Henry Walthall was playing, and Adamic put his hand deep in his pocket and passed in before us. We stood before the posters in the entrance way, looking at the pictures of the people in Southern hats, with dust on their riding boots, holding Carrie's hands.

"It's what they call *The Birth of a Nation*," Carrie said. "It has to do with what colored people there was they treated just like they was slaves."

When Adamic came back to us, a tide of shame had flowed across his face and it was still burning there, and his eyes were shifting from its flame. He had no tickets in his hand, and he said:

"I waited to ask you. They haven't four seats left together. There's one left up in the balcony, if you'd like to take that one yourself," he said. He looked this way and that, but he could not look at Carrie.

"We can go to another moving picture," my sister said.

"I guess it's a crowded afternoon everywhere," said Adamic, looking from one thing to another. "I guess there isn't much use. They might all be that way."

The man in the ticket window was looking through the glass at us, looking down the length of carpet to where we stood. And when Adamic turned, uneasy on his heels, the man in the window shook his head slowly back and forth at him, smiling at him, but shaking his head. Carrie put her hands up to her cheeks, and suddenly she started laughing.

"The kind of sunburn I got," she said, "you couldn't tell one person from another." And she said: "It isn't as if I'd been fixed on seeing that picture. War and fighting all the time would of tired me out."

The man in the window was shaking his head still at Adamic, and Carrie took out her powder puff and beat it hard all over her face.

"We might walk as far as the shoot-the-shoots," said Carrie. "The weather looks so fine."

But Adamic said, not looking at either of us, nor looking at Carrie: "I just remembered something I was supposed to do." He took his Panama hat out folded from his pocket, and he set it on the front of his head. "I'd better get along," he said. "I promised." His hat cast a blind shadow over his eyes, and he looked at the man selling tickets in the window, and the man looked out at him.

"Anyone makes a promise, he better keep it," said Carrie, "or else it might turn out he wasn't a gentleman no more."

"Sure," said Adamic, and we watched him walking off, swinging his arms and his legs, off through the people, holding his child's face small and low.

That might have been the end of it, if Carrie hadn't lain down on the bed in the dark when we got to the hotel. She drew the curtains over the windows and lay there saying nothing at all. There was no reason to light the light, for no word or touch could move her. We sat still on the bed beside her, thinking of things to say.

"There'll be strawberry ice for supper tonight," I said to her.

And my sister said: "There's going to be creamed chicken too." And after a while Carrie spoke, and said to us: "I might just as well stay here in the dark for always, because there ain't going to be any more good things for me."

She lay silent, as if dead and shrouded in the strong artificial flowery scent she wore, cold and speechless with some knowledge we did not share. Her hands were crossed over her breasts, and her pointed feet stood upright at the end of the bed. After a little while she said: "You don't know, children. I'll never tell you what it was. You're too young to know."

But when it was time for dinner, she got up and put the light on, and she went and looked at her face close in the glass. She took the hairbrush off the table and sat there brushing her black hair back, brushing it tight and small.

"I knew all right," she said. "I wasn't fooled. It was the Jim Crow gallery. Colored people goes upstairs, other people goes down." And Mother came in and said:

"But, Carrie, you haven't changed the children's dresses for supper," and Carrie said:

"I know, ma'am, I know. They've been cutting up again. They're getting too much for me. Maybe I'm too young to handle them. They get out from under my control."

Keep Your Pity

Va, garde ta pitié comme ton ironie!—MALLARMÉ

I

Mr. Jefferson was an American, a good and simple man, so he did not see these people as they were: haughty, aloof, almost distasteful in their pride. He did not see them, the two old people, as weird as skeletons jerking down the walk; his eyes swathed them in weakness and frailty, and smoothed out the skin that hung crumpled and soft from their faces. Mr. Jefferson sat on the café terrace and watched them coming down the promenade one morning after another in the sun: colorless in their flesh, with a faint smell of a final spring on them, shaking a little on their limbs as the first pale mimosa flowers quivered on the branch.

It was the sun that brought them forth, making new promises every day to them. He wore a tight-fitting black-and-auburn check, old Mr. Wycherley, and a tan bowler hat, light in color, and he must have been elegant in his time. But now his time was past, or should have been, and there was nothing to be said for the cut of his jacket at the waist, or for the black silk stock that wound glossy around his haggard throat. He was a genteel old man, to the eye, with his wife on his arm, and she with her lids swollen yellow and thin as gauze under her veil, wearing plum velvet and a litter of tiger cats' hides fast on the points of her shoulders.

They had no use for pity, having seen it a common thing in the faces of everyone passing. And there was no need to give it, for they had their own style, their own special wraithlike air amongst the living contemporary people walking by the Mediterranean Sea. No one need have pitied them their transparent hands on their canes, for when they paused to stroke the thin cat near Mr. Jefferson's table they did not speak of its bones or hunger; there was something like mockery or greed in the eye they gave it. They ran their old hands over the links of its spine, touching its knobs curiously, as if for the value of the skin or the real amber in the sockets of its head. Mr. Jefferson witnessed, as a blind man might, this spectacle. He heard their childish, pure voices speaking English, and because they had halted there and stroked the animal, he took for mercy the rapacity of their hearts.

He heard the old lady say in her querulous, pride-bitten way: "It's damnably small, Mr. W."

And the old gentleman answered, quoting in proud, elegant French: "'Va, garde ta pitié comme ton ironie.' Keep it for yourself, Mrs. W. There's no telling but what you may have need of one or the other someday."

Mr. Jefferson had come the week before to Nice, an American sitting there in his good gray suit, with the unfailing credulous

soul of his country lighted in his eye. He was presented by the
French people sitting next at the café table where the Wycher-
leys had paused to speak a moment. They were the Aristocrats,
the high-and-mighty old couple, the seemingly frail and gracious
pair. They gave a great interest and care to their conversations,
and to the conversations of people they exchanged the time of
day with, as if some great ear were gaping in space, spying forever on what they had to say. But they never accepted the invi-
tations to sit down on the café terrace, but halted at one table or
the next, talking with charm but inscrutably to those they knew,
but moving on as if an hour had been fixed elsewhere with someone else who might even now be waiting. Mr. Wycherley held
his hat pressed to his linen vest as he spoke. His thin yellowish-
white hair was parted to one side and smoothed across, lying
listless, as the fingers of a dead man might have lain upon his
skull.

They had simply bowed to Mr. Jefferson, but then, a thun-
derclap to their reason, they felt his hands fall in familiarity
upon their arms. The sun was out, and the air melting and fair,
but the blast of their horror swept them cold. They stood rooted,
their sap standing motionless in their veins and their senses
stilled in fright. Before them the American's face was grimacing
and urging, as though it would be a gift from their hearts to him
if they should bend their brittle knees and take the empty chairs.
He did not know what kept them from sitting; he did not know
if it was for fear of their antique clothes splitting up the seams, or
for fear of what he might do or say.

"You'd be doing me a favor," said Mr. Jefferson gently, "if
you'd have a little glass . . ."

But Mr. Wycherley cried out: "Ah, no, sir, we do not drink!"

His bones seemed to buckle and knock in his skin as he
stepped back in his pumps and gaiters from Mr. Jefferson's table.
His voice ran fast through his smooth shining lips, his head
reared on the cords of his neck, and his wild glance smote the
stranger's viciously in mistrust. He saw the American as many
things, the man sitting there, his eyes a straight unwinking blue
behind his big-hewed features, and a little mat of graying hair
set up on the top of his head.

"Well, if you'd sit down, then, and have a little talk," said Mr. Jefferson, with the slow wistful smile so little matched to the clanging voice. "I'm new to this country. I feel like a fish out of water with all this parley-voo."

So after a while they saw it—through their suspicion for what he might be they saw the accumulated hunger for speech that sucked away at his clean-shaven jaws. He knew no one in the city, he said, and this did not touch them, although they saw his solitude very well. He was famished for kind words to be spoken to him, and there they stood listening, warily, giving nothing from their deceptive silence. He sat talking, with his glass on the table before him, with no thought of rising in respect, though he was still a youngish man, fifty-five or less.

"This is called the city of perfume and flowers," said Mrs. Wycherley in her frail, wincing voice. She spoke breathlessly, in caution to him, as a young woman speaking her marriage vows might do. This was her welcome to Mr. Jefferson, although she smiled little because of the holes in the far sides of her mouth where the teeth were missing.

"That's what I'm here for," said Mr. Jefferson. As he talked they could see the absolute wastes and stretches without beauty that lay behind him. Strange, strange, the undulations of life given so in a few uneasy sentences to them. They stood with their eyes bright and callous before the spectacle of his years running quick over impediments and falls, the narrow, tortuous current of his life passing with difficulty before them, like a stream squeezed hard in its bed. But now the time for rest had come, he said. Now he could sit still, if he liked, and watch the waters of his repose lap in expansion, far, and deep, and wide.

He was from Ohio, and in this way he talked of his home until they saw it, even as much as some details of it, in their cold perverse hearts. The dust lay three inches deep on the roads in the summertime, he said, and in winter there was the cold, and the months of the winter were laid away in the country, sunless and endless.

"And here, sir," said Mr. Wycherley, with his smile in his long old teeth, and his bowler hat pressed over his linen vest, "here, although we are not native sons, we enjoy the native sun!"

Mrs. Wycherley looked slyly at the American and laughed her faint high laughter. But Mr. Jefferson had seemingly not heard, or else not understood. There he sat, thinking of the many years of perseverance that had brought him so far and left him idle there.

"I cleared out of things just in time," he was saying. "I wasn't really hit at all. What I've got put away, I want it to pay me some dividends in real enjoyment now." But there was the wistful, the hopeless longing in his mouth, sorrowing of itself under the hard ringing clamor of his voice. He had worked so hard, gone in the teeth of it for so long, that now there was no place of rest and pleasure left vacant for him any more.

"I built up my business alone," he was saying, not in pride, but in mild complaint to them. "I sold out at a profit this year. Now my time's all my own," he said in sorrow. "All my own." He had no one to share it with. The two old people stood still, eying him with cold, vulturelike, inward eyes.

"Why don't you folks have dinner with me?" Mr. Jefferson said.

Such speech in the mouth of any other man would have sent them off in affront, but this man was speaking out of his own ignorance to them. There was no hesitation in Mr. Wycherley's mind: he knew very well they could never sit down at table with this stranger. He was some kind of court fool, a jester, and they, in their pride, were the royalty in a high, indifferent society of death.

"You're kind indeed, sir," said Mr. Wycherley, bowing. "I'm afraid we shall have to beg off this time," said the old man, smiling down from his perilous height of race and breeding upon Mr. Jefferson. "Mrs. Wycherley and I have guests to dinner . . ."

"Damn it, I'm hungry," said Mrs. Wycherley, and her underlip went wrinkled and small as if she were about to cry.

"As I was saying," said the old gentleman, and he cleared his throat in rebuke at her, "Mrs. Wycherley and I have guests, as it happens . . ."

They had lived twelve years in the apartment, almost without event, it might be said. But when they came home from their talk with the American, a new thing awaited them. There was a blue notice pasted flat on the wood of their handsome ancient door. Surely some warning must have been given, but although they searched the confusion of their thoughts for it, no memory of it lingered. They had done the four flights at length, with the breath running thin in their lungs, and when they paused, gasping, they saw the blue paper fixed fast to the door.

Mr. Wycherley put his glasses on his nose and began reading it aloud: it said because you have not paid, or because you will not pay, or because you cannot pay the rent for the last quarter and this, everything inside will be laid hold of tomorrow morning at nine o'clock. Mr. Wycherley took out his pocket handkerchief and passed it over his face in haste as if to wipe from his features any sign of fear. Then he began to laugh aloud:

"Ha, ha, ha," said Mr. Wycherley. "Here's a fine one! This is a good joke indeed! I'll have to run over and see Jean Medecin!"

Jean Medecin was the mayor of Nice, and although they did not know him, the sound of his name spoken now lifted their long heavy heads rearing, like a bit in the mouth. But the divinity had faded in Mrs. Wycherley's face, and she stood by his side, shaking.

"Preposterous!" cried Mr. Wycherley sternly to her. Together their minds went back, groping through the uneasy darkness of their memories. Had they paid, or had they not, or why had they not? "Take my arm," said Mr. Wycherley. "This is the most preposterous thing!"

Twelve years, they were thinking, twelve years. They stood quiet, groping slowly back through the confusion, feeling for the corners and grooves of something known in the darkness. And then suddenly Mr. Wycherley touched it and drew it forth tentatively, little by little, to the light.

"The proprietor called in a month ago, didn't he, Mrs. W.?" he said. "Didn't he speak of raising the rent?"

The dew on her brow shone strangely out, supernaturally lucent, yet milky, like mother-of-pearl.

"Herriot shall hear of this," said Mr. Wycherley. Herriot was the mayor of Lyons, and with the strength of that name in their ears they unlocked the door and passed through it, arm in arm together. She had no strength left to put out her hand and lift the edge of her velvet, and it rode in silence and majesty over the threshold's stone.

They proceeded to the bedroom together, with such dignity as if the invisible eye were watching, the unseen ear listening still in space. Here was the garden party to which they had been invited: the false Aubusson over the bed, the paper flowers blooming on the chimney, and the two windows with the shutters drawn in combs of sun. Outside the sun was shining hot and bright on the square named after Garibaldi. The gray coat of a goat or two had been stitched together into a square coarse rug, and it might have been a soiled chrysanthemum discarded there and fading on the floor.

"Now, Mrs. W.," said Mr. Wycherley, "you go to bed, my dear." She seemed to be slipping, slipping away in bewilderment, with only the hard active bubbles of her eyes riding to the surface of her confusion. She sat on the side of the bed, thinking that the police should never get the goatskin rug, but there seemed no certainty left in her. There she sat, curved and senseless in her velvets, speechless on the Aubusson greens and blues of the iron bed.

Old Mr. Wycherley went to her and undid the small pearl buttons at her throat. He was very careful with her, unhooking her sleeves to the elbow, carefully, as if her bones were made of glass, lifting her skirt to loosen her garters, his fingers quivering with age. When he laid the lace collar back from her neck, the whalebonings in their frenzy seemed to writhe. Only when he touched the quaking brim of her hat did she stir and say:

"Hold on, Mr. W., I'll keep my hat where it is."

Mr. Wycherley took off his own jacket, folded it, and set it down with his cane and his bowler hat on a chair. His white linen vest covered his braces from sight, but in a moment he took that off and laid it in a drawer with his black silk stock. She could see his face reflected in the glass, the fine-wrinkled jowls hanging, and the wild eyebrows standing forth, white and abundant. There was a strange, a powerful, smile of victory on his mouth.

"Life," he called out, "ah, life, ah, life, the tricks it can conceive to play on one! Inestimable, inestimable, and one must be prepared with a countercheck for every move that's made!"

So he spoke to the memory of his wife left lying on the bed, or to the ear that eavesdropped forever in censure. He doubled his arm up above the elbow. His arm was bony and long, and when he clenched the long, loose hand the shifting ball of muscle rolled up, anchored as it was by the full blue veins under his skin.

"You've got a husband, Mrs. W.," he said, with his vanity getting the best of him at last. "A man to stand between you and the onslaught. Let me to it. There's a man's work to be done."

II

Mr. Wycherley made the tea at seven in the morning and bore it on a tray to the thin little old lady who sat motionless against the pillows. She was sitting quite erect, but her head, with the black lace hat still on it, was drooping forward like a heavy wilting flower. She had no human look in her eye for him; the canny, the wily jet of her eyesight ran here and there at random like shiny beads unstrung.

"When you've had your tea, then you'll dress and go, Mrs. W.," said old Mr. Wycherley, setting the tea down beside her. She was looking through him at the wood of their dark, ancient furniture beyond. Her glance clicked over the glass of the wardrobe that held so many beauties; it might have been a silver screen on which the great dramas of her youth and life were passing.

"There may be harsh words exchanged," Mr. Wycherley was saying, and he watched her hand fall in greed upon the bread by her plate. "I wouldn't want you to hear anything unpleasant, Mrs. W."

"Damned if I'll move a foot," said Mrs. Wycherley. Her eyes had bubbled up from the source of misery again and were turned upon his face. If it had come into her head that this was the first time they had spoken of separation, or had come to things and not passed through them together, she gave no sign of it. Mutely she took down her tea and stepped from the bed while Mr. Wycherley finished his dressing. It was the touch of the goat-hair hide under her bare foot that startled the memory in her. She stooped and seized it up by one corner, and the lace hat quivered in wild agitation on her head.

"Mr. W.," she said, "I'll take the goat rug with me."

When she was dressed in her velvet, she pinned the rug over her shoulders. She moved quietly down the hall, with an aura of dust riding out from behind, and through the parlor in silence. In front of the chimney piece she paused and vaguely plucked a candelabra from the mantelshelf. She went mutely, a ravaged, haggard-eyed queen of sorrow, mutely after Mr. Wycherley into the kitchen, with her plum skirt following elegantly behind. One hand was fast on the handle of her cane, and the candelabra was in the other. When she drifted to a halt at the stove, she saw that Mr. Wycherley was laughing. The laughter was shaking under his linen vest and blowing in dry blasts through his conqueror's nose.

He said: "I've done a most ingenious thing, Mrs. W." He pointed to the sink, and Mrs. Wycherley saw the string and the rubber hosing whipped fast around the faucet. "This runs through the hall," said her husband, "ties up with a sinker and fishing rod over the front door and carries the aqueduct upwards."

He offered her his arm, and they went down the length of the narrow sightless corridor together. It seemed a gay and lavish thing to Mrs. Wycherley, a thing in preparation for a fete, the cord and the hosing winding in and out like a clinging vine above them. Mr. Wycherley was laughing youthfully by her side. "If anyone pulls the bell handle," he said, "a stream of fresh water jerked through the transom will persuade our good friends to think twice before ringing again. . . ."

Slowly, as Mr. Wycherley explained, Mrs. Wycherley began to see it; slowly, revealingly, like a negative emerging, shadow by shadow, from its acid bath. The two old people stood there laughing, their loose jaws fallen open, their limbs shaking with their clamor, snickering in their skins, and their necks stretched for it.

"Once you are safely out, Mrs. W.," said Mr. Wycherley, suddenly clapping into silence his laughter, "I'll fetch the sack of flour on to the doorknob and raise it to the transom. . . ."

When Mrs. Wycherley stepped into the street, the freshness of his lips where he had saluted her was still cool as mint on the back of her hand.

"So he worked all night at that, did he?" said Mr. Jefferson. There he sat at the café table, harking to her under the deepening tides of sun.

But Mrs. Wycherley could not remember. She was sitting as if at ease with the American, with the goat rug fastened with nursery pins across her shoulders, but her face was pure of color, and blue pits of drama and fear were excavated under her bird-bright eyes.

"Perhaps half the week!" she said with spirit. "He's very ingenious, Mr. Jefferson!"

To this man, this absolute stranger, Mrs. Wycherley knew she had said many things. The evil empty glass of port was standing before her in the sun, and she felt its madness in her face: two coals of color burning as if the fever of her fear had smoldered into light.

"But it couldn't have been all the week," said Mr. Jefferson, patiently feeling the way.

"All I know," said Mrs. Wycherley with sudden conviction, "is that when he called my attention to it this morning, damned if I could believe my eyes!"

"Ho, ho, an inventor!" said Mr. Jefferson slowly. "By George, it takes the old guys! Look at Edison. Thomas Edison."

"I don't know who he is," said Mrs. Wycherley, facing him with her hard, sharp, unchanging eyes.

"Well, take Bell," said Mr. Jefferson. "Take Bell . . ."

"Take Mr. Wycherley, damn it," said the old lady sharply. "Eleven o'clock now, and no sign of him." She gave her withered, wincing laugh and looked up slyly and sideways at Mr. Jefferson. "If he had the money to go on with his inventions, he might invent almost anything. He might invent the wireless if he were given any support."

"Yes, it takes his kind of mind to think of such things," said Mr. Jefferson, shaking his head. "Like that flour-and-water invention," he said, trotting his tongue, lost in thought or awe on the other side of the table.

When Mrs. Wycherley stood up, the promenade swept about and made a deep curtsy to her. She put out her hand and lifted the candelabra from the café table and held it forth.

"Mr. Jefferson, I am beginning to feel perturbed about Mr. W.," she said, and the words were strange and cumbrous on her tongue.

"I'll walk along with you, ma'am, if you'll allow," said Mr. Jefferson, rising.

She knew she was in a state of intoxication when she tried to climb the stairs.

"We were expecting unpleasant callers this morning, Mr. Jefferson," she said brightly, and suddenly she put her hand to the side of her face and began to cry.

"Why, Mrs. Wycherley," said the American, taking the candelabra from her, "this is too bad, now, too bad."

"It was the police who were coming," she said, but the sound of the truth was as good as a slap in the face to her. She looked straight into Mr. Jefferson's blue eyes; standing there fierce and straight, with her hand quivering on her cane.

"They're persecuting him because he's a genius, Mr. Jefferson," she said fiercely. "They've accused him of plagiarism. But it isn't so. He was the first, the very first, but they're after him for being clever."

"The police!" said Mr. Jefferson. He whistled softly. "You don't say so, Mrs. Wycherley!"

They started up the stairs, Mr. Jefferson's arm on one side of her, and the cane on the other to bear her up, and the empty candelabra held in Mr. Jefferson's hand.

"The police are all from Corsica here," Mrs. Wycherley was saying wildly. "If they see anyone with force of character, they must track them down. They've been waiting year after year for another leader. They're so envious of the Italians because of Mussolini, whose name we mustn't say here. You must call him Mr. Smith, Mr. Jefferson, whenever you speak of him. Mr. W.

keeps me up on politics. If they've put him in jail, I'll get in touch with someone higher up. Anatole France said if there was ever any trouble we were to let him know."

The breath was shaking for peace in her throat, and at the fourth-floor landing they halted. There was flour and water spilled out on the boards there, and the blue warning was pasted still on the door.

"If Mr. W. had the wherewithal," said the old lady hoarsely, "damned if they'd attack him."

When she lifted her quivering hand and drew the long pin from the lacy crown, her hat went riding sideways on her head. Mr. Jefferson stood by, watching her as she ran the pin under the notice, ripping it up in soft furrows of paper with the flexible length of the pin. Her mouth was drawn up and tied fast like a bowknot under her nose, and her eyes never shed their inscrutable dark veneer. But Mr. Jefferson did not believe in what he saw; old ladies, their hair, their frailty, their querulousness even, struck a chord of puerile gallantry in his heart.

Mrs. Wycherley pulled the rope of the hanging bell and a jet of water sprang out from the transom and fell upon their heads. There they stood quietly waiting, Mrs. Wycherley under the goatskin rug, and the water dripping quietly off the brim of Mr. Jefferson's Panama hat and down the length of his nose; the candelabra in Mr. Jefferson's hand held to the fore, as if to cast light on the landing's darkness.

After a while, Mrs. Wycherley called out: "Benedict! Benedict!" She rapped on the panel of the door with the head of her delicate cane, and they heard the bolts slip on the other side, and then Mr. Wycherley opened the door slightly.

"Mr. Wycherley," the American began at once, "I've been hearing a great deal about your inventions."

They could see him, wedged, tall and overbearing, suspicious still, in the opening, with his yellowish hair parted like wax on his head; uncertain, and fingering the chain on his vest, not quite ready to open to them.

"You're very kind indeed, sir," said Mr. Wycherley, bowing. "Won't you and your wife step inside?"

"My wife?" said Mr. Jefferson, but there was no confusion in the old lady's face. She put her arm through the American's. "This is Mrs. Wycherley!" Mr. Jefferson said.

The old man opened the door to them.

"Ah, yes, I dare say it is," he said wearily. Wearily he led the way into the parlor and indicated the armchairs in the shadow to them. His shoulders, in the great length of his coat, were stooped; even his presence, so schooled, so rigid, seemed drooping on the air. "I haven't seen her for some years," he said.

Mr. Jefferson set the candelabra on the mantelpiece, and Mrs. Wycherley unpinned the goatskin rug from her shoulders and spread it on the floor. When they were seated, the three of them in the dimness of the blinded room, Mr. Jefferson began to speak.

"I'm interested in inventions," he said with respect. "I think I could make it worth your while to go on, Mr. Wycherley."

The old lady lifted her hand to remove the remaining pins from her hat and looked sharply at the American.

"I'd like to donate some money," said Mr. Jefferson, "to the interests of science."

"My good sir," said Mr. Wycherley with his aged, withering charm, "you are very kind, but I could not hear of it."

Mr. Jefferson turned his head and looked at the old lady, and Mrs. Wycherley looked sharply at the American and slowly winked one eye.

"My good sir," said Mr. Wycherley again, "if you are determined to persist upon the realization of inestimably high qualities, it is scarcely my place to forbid you to convert him into whatever exchange you value. But I must say that I consider it an act in very questionable taste, and I insist that it be regarded in the light of a temporary loan."

In the mock twilight of the shuttered room, the three of them sat waiting for what next would be said.

"I could arrange to pay you a percentage," said Mr. Wycherley in a measured tone out of the stillness.

"Yes," said Mr. Jefferson. "That would do very well. A percentage on every invention made."

A week later Mr. Jefferson went back to the States, and they never saw anything more of him except the money and the post-cards he sent.

III

It was the second year after the money began coming to them that Mrs. Wycherley brought the first cats in from the street. Whether they would or whether they wouldn't, she would have them in off the street and into the back room next the kitchen: the men of the race to the one side with a barricade of chicken wire between them and the mothers and young on the other.

She would go over the back fences of the quarter for them, for now that Mr. Wycherley was an inventor, a man who went his own way, his time was taken up and his hours filled for him. When Mrs. Wycherley came in on tiptoe with her latest cat under her arm, she could see him sitting in the parlor, his hands folded on the papers that she had laid neatly on the table before him. The cries of the newest cat caught and held fast in her hands pierced the absolute silence of what Mr. Wycherley was always about to do.

It was as if their status had been altered, for the time was no longer left to them to linger on the promenade at the café tables, speaking with people there they knew. Twice in the week they went out together, but now Mr. Wycherley was a man with a vision, an inventor, and the menace of his career hung over them like a shadow about to fall.

In December the neighbors began speaking of it, began saying that Mr. Wycherley did not come out any more. They spoke to the old lady in the hall, and then they passed on, wondering. The look on her face was strange and high and secret. Only once, when the two women were shaking out their door mats at their thresholds, did the neighbor opposite on the landing speak to Mrs. Wycherley about her husband.

"How is Mr. Wycherley these days?" the Frenchwoman said.

The wave of pride and secrecy went over the old lady's deli-cate crumpled face, rose to the smooth edifice of her brow, submerged feature after feature until only her clear obdurate eyes were left exempt.

"Mr. Wycherley is absorbed in his inventing," she said. She spoke with such equity, such natural contempt, that it put an end at once to the questioning. In a moment she stooped over and shook out the mat in her brittle hand. There was a mauve silk scarf tied around her head to save her hair from dust.

"It is something that will keep flowers from fading," she said to the other woman. The two of them looked strangely at each other across the dusty landing. "It is something to keep the dead from corruption," said Mrs. Wycherley with an evil gleam. "It will make him famous all over the world."

The neighbor watched her drift through her own doorway, move like a sleepwalker into the dark of her own corridor. There was no other word spoken, no sound except the whisper of the old lady's slippers over the tiles, slipping, slipping into the absolute darkness, and then the door closed behind.

In this way they saw her sliding out all through the month of December, moving out as if in a dream to fetch the bread on the Place Garibaldi and the other things the two of them were used to eat. But when on New Year's Eve there was no sign of Mr. Wycherley, then the story began to run from mouth to mouth throughout the house. They began to say that Mr. Wycherley had taken the money out of the bank and run away from his wife. They all knew about the money the rich American had given, and they began saying that it was the number of cats in the apartment that had driven Mr. Wycherley mad. He must have taken his clothes and things with him at night and gone off early in December; a month now since he had gone away.

The story was blowing like a high wind through the place, so after the holidays the proprietor came and asked for Mr. Wycherley. It was the middle of the morning, and Mrs. Wycherley was dressed for her shopping, with her lace collar buttoned up under her ears. There she stood in the piece of the doorway, her hat on, peering up her nose, looking, as if sightless, up into the proprietor's thick, unflickering face. Everyone had a certain respect and homage for this man, and now special concern because his son, an automobile racer, had been killed on the race course in his Bugatti scarcely a week before.

The bereaved father stood at the door dressed in his clothes of mourning. There was a hush and expectancy up and down the halls and stairways of the house. He was dressed in black for the death of his son, but because he was a Niçois there was much of the Italian in him, and behind his solemn mask and sleeping temper there was almost a chuckle waiting in his throat. He took off his broad black hat and spoke gravely to Mrs. Wycherley.

"I'd like to have a word or two with your husband, with Mr. Wycherley," he said.

"Mr. Wycherley is busy with his work," said the old lady, but even as she spoke her spirit faltered and swooned. She was too weary, too old, too worn now to face them alone. She shrank back against the wall and the man pushed his own way in. He went down the dark passage, clearing his throat aloud, attempting to hum a tune in his throat to hearten his dismay. Now he knew, now he knew what it was for certain. He beat his broad black hat against the side of his trousers as he walked. Now he knew, he knew very well. He knew what he was going to see when he opened the parlor door. He took out his handkerchief and covered his nose and mouth with it before he walked into the room.

Mr. Wycherley was sitting fully dressed at the table, but he made no move when the proprietor came in. His hands were laid out on the papers before him and his head had fallen sideways. The old lady came up and stood still in the doorway.

"You see, he's working," she said.

"Yes," said the proprietor, "yes, I see."

He went out into the hall with her and closed the door, and he said: "I'll be back in a little while, Mrs. Wycherley. We'll have to take your husband away."

"No, he'll stay here, damn it," said the old lady sharply. "I won't let him out of the house in the delicate condition he's in."

"We aren't going to hurt him," said the proprietor, putting his hat on. "I'll come back with some friends and we'll take him out for a little drive."

He was not afraid, he had seen death before, and in violent

shapes and ways he had seen it. But he wanted to get quickly down the hall and out of the door. He shook Mrs. Wycherley's breakable hand, and he said:

"A little air won't harm him, Mrs. Wycherley."

She could hear the chuckle lurking in his throat.

"Mr. W.," she said vaguely at the door, "he never cared for driving. You're very kind, I'm sure."

The report ran this way: it said that when the door was broken in there was nothing to be seen in the darkness, but the objects, whatever they were, hanging over the door hit every officer in the face as he passed under. Once they switched on the light they saw it was the old English lady hanging, hung just there in the doorway, with malice, so that her feet caught each one of them, even the proprietor, square in the face as he passed.

And that was not the end of it. After they cut her down and found she was dead, then the cats began running wild from the doors they opened in the backrooms of the apartment. The gendarmes, the short Corsican men, had their clubs in their hands and struck them down like rats. There were over a hundred cats, it was said, flying like demons at the faces of the officers, and the back rooms foul with them. Mr. Jefferson read this in Ohio, but even then he did not believe the truth; he never for a minute saw them as a grasping, sinister old pair.

Security

I'll never forget Puss, the way he looked when he came into a room, dancing sideways, a little old man with a black silk skullcap on his head, I'll never forget the sound of his voice, or his love, or his anger. He wore doe-skin slippers in the house, and good kid gloves when he went into the street, and nothing was ever too good to buy, not silver or gold or diamonds or jade. He bought everything fine that caught his eye or the eye of anyone he loved. He had champagne for dinner every night, because the

sight of it flowing into other people's mouths sent him dancing
and reciting across the room. He never drank, but his love for
other people made him dance faster, laugh louder, talk wilder
than any of the others drinking. He was Puss, my little grandfather. He had the voice of a charmer, as young and sweet as
grass.

Early in my life he said to me I must have a bond, either a
stock or a bond, but he advised a bond for safety. For money,
said Puss, money was the blood of the world. It is not something
you carry in your pocketbook from country to country, from
place to place, but it flows strong as life from hand to hand. It is
the groomed sides of horses, and good ceilings, and clean linen,
and the silver spotless, and the fireplaces thick and fragrant all
the winter with the bodies of dry, monstrous trees. It is everything respected, preserved, enhanced. It is nothing neglected or
rendered useless by abuse. And the sooner you learn this about
money, the better it is, for then you will not be afraid of wanting
money any more. The head in the clouds, the feet on the ground,
said Puss, taking my arm through his as he skipped down the
boardwalk. Oh, I can see him, the dear gay little man, the sweet-
tongued poet of Wall Street with the strangely-hooded wisdom
in his eyes.

The name of my bond was "Union Iron and Steel, Preferred."
That was the melody of the name it bore. It was mine, though I
never knew its color or shape or anything else of it except the
word of it in the paper every evening. But it was there, and the
knowledge of it was a strong, secret power that went up the
beach with me in the rain, and that waited at the window, quiet
with me, watching the smoke from the steamers to see if the
wind was changing when the waves ran up to the door. I could
look up its health in the paper every night, and on days when
there was snow over the sand down to the yellow, quivering
edge of foam, that name and the power it gave me moved my
heart as music might have done. I was ten years old, and the
thought of my bond was stronger than drink to me, and wilder
than the cold Atlantic wind.

It was the year Henry B. Walthall was playing the little Colonel in "The Birth of a Nation," and whatever I did then I did for

Henry B. Walthall to see. In the spring we began our magazine, typing the stories and the poetry on our typewriters, fifty copies each month which we stitched together, and my sister painted the covers on the front. The stories were our own, and the poetry, except for a sonnet sequence to the edelweiss written by Puss' broker who had been to Austria one summer, and except for Puss' story of his education in a Catholic school near London which ran from month to month. He had a stenographer in to take this down for him, and after the first installment appeared, mother would not speak to him. But after a few days he had some flowers and some candied marrons sent her, and then he called upon her on the second floor.

"I was presenting," he said with dignity, "the life of one child to two other children. Would you be so good as to point out to me wherein I have erred?"

"You were making an attack upon the Catholic teachings," said mother, eating a marron. "Of course, that's neither here nor there, but why must you force these poor children to print it? They don't know what you're doing. They don't understand yet that there is propaganda, and that is one thing—and then there is art."

"Good writing," said Puss humbly, "is literature. I take it you concede the truth of that?"

"It doesn't mean anything at all," said mother, putting her powder on before the mirror.

"It means," said Puss, his voice rising, "that if my writing is good, then it is literature. And by the same token, it is art. Good writing," he said, pacing the room with his short, buoyant step, "makes it possible for a man to write interestingly, stirringly, on any subject, any subject in the world. As it happened, I chose my early education. I might just as well have chosen the—the habits of the flea."

"That's where you made your mistake," said mother, and Puss ate half the box of marrons in annoyance.

But in the evening Puss came to this decision: he decided he would "back" our magazine. He would have it printed every month for us, a hundred copies to begin, he told me and my sister; and he would have mimeographed in color the covers that my sister did. He would not be the legal owner of it, he explained, and he would have no say in what the policy would be. But he would be the backer, the security behind it, just as money backed a stock or bond. I held him tight in my arms and I stroked his brow as he liked it stroked, and my heart was shaking for joy inside me. Oh, Puss, my little man, my love, this was what I had hoped and prayed, this is what I had dreamed could be!

The first month of the new magazine was going to press when Puss came in with a manuscript he had dictated the day before.

"I hope you may have room to slip it in," he said, and he cleared his throat. It was a parable, and I remember it very well. America was not in the war yet, and because of the story's timeliness, Puss said he thought it should appear at once. We said yes without looking at the page, and he began talking of the Sheeler photographs we had chosen. Some should be printed in gray tones and some in brown for the magazine, and he wanted our decision on it. Oh, he was a dear good generous man, the way the rich alone can be!

The magazine came out and mother read the parable Puss had written. She was sitting in her room in her blue silk dressing-gown, and her evening-dress was waiting on the bed behind her, shining in the small lamp's light. She took my hand without a word, and we ran downstairs together, and the open magazine was shaking in her fingers. Puss was sitting quietly in the library, eating cheese-straws by the open fire, waiting there for the cocktails to be brought in for other people and for the smell of the white gin to start him dancing on his heels.

"This is an outrage!" said mother's low, shaken voice. She was suffering so that I put my arm strong around her. "Good God, what a coward you are!" she said.

Puss went on nibbling at the cheese-straws, but now his evening was destroyed, the gay, animated prospect of it, by this intense, this highly feminine attack.

"To what," said he courteously, "if I may ask, am I indebted for this outburst?"

"You, reading your *Wall Street Journal,*" said mother, and her hands were quivering, "playing your market, you, the head

of a family—the patriarch!—making two little girls responsible for
your militaristic views!"

"I fail to grasp your meaning," said Puss as he wiped his delicate finger tips in his pure white handkerchief. "I am in no sense
a militarist. You are making a preposterous statement, my dear
Kate."

"Too cowardly," mother went on as if he had not spoken, "to
put your own name to it! Signing it 'Grimm Anderson'! I should
think you would be ashamed!"

Puss reached forward and politely took the magazine from her
agitated hands.

"If you will allow me," he said. He cleared his throat, and in a
distinct, well-modulated voice he read aloud the two paragraphs
of his little story.

"There was once a householder," he read, "living quietly in
his well-ordered household, happy in his simple, humble fashion,
surrounded as he was by his devoted family. But one fine day, a
robber carrying a great club scaled the wall of the householder's
neat little garden, and without warning began belaboring the
wife and children of this worthy man. When the householder
hastened to the assistance of his dear ones, he too fell a victim to
the aggressor's blows.

"Even when neighbors crowded to the wall and witnessed this
spectacle with horror, the robber continued to beat the householder, all the time crying out that he had been grievously
wronged. Some of the neighbors then came loyally to the good
householder's aid, but the strongest and most powerful neighbor
calmly folded his arms and blandly watched the fray. When
questioned upon his attitude, he replied:"—here Puss cleared his
throat, and with a savage twinkle of his eye he looked at mother
and finished—"'There is such a thing as being too proud to
fight!' Now I cannot see," he went on as he laid the magazine
down on the cocktail wagon beside him, "what objection a fair,
unprejudiced mind—"

But mother's low cry of disgust cut short his words.

"What a cad you are!" she said. "What a hypocrite!" Then she
turned to me. "You should keep clear of such issues," she said.
"You shouldn't get into politics in your paper. You don't know

enough about war and peace. You don't know the kind of horror and wholesale death words like these would lead us to! You should keep to the other things—poetry—pictures you like—"

"As backer of this publication," said Puss, selecting a cheese-straw, "I see no reason why undisputable common sense should have no place in its pages—"

"Then," said mother with passion, still addressing me, "you should get rid of him! You should let him have nothing to do with your magazine! Bring it out as you used to, on your own typewriters, paint it with your own brushes! Don't let him print it if he's going to use you as a mouth-piece for his views!"

For three days then, mother had her meals brought to her room, and Puss was closed, silent and wounded, in his study. He could think of no way of annoying her without knocking upon her door, and this he would not do. But the second day he thought of having the carpenter in to change the moldings all around the landing outside mother's room. He had the carpenter come at seven in the morning, and Puss was there in his dressing-gown and his doe-skin slippers to meet him and to talk politics with him while he ripped and hammered and sawed. And all day, with the noise of the tearing wood and the nails struck in so loud that there was no peace anywhere in the house, Puss talked with the carpenter about the possibilities of America going to war, talked without rancor, in a charming, intelligent voice which he knew carried clearly into mother's room.

At the end of that day, I knew it was their affair no longer. It was to the editors of the magazine to move. I went to see Puss in his little room, and I could scarcely speak, for the thing seemed terrible to me. I said we had to be an independent paper or else we had to perish, and my voice was shaking in my mouth. I said:

"We owe you for the publication of this number. I am able to settle it. I wish you would take over to your account my Union Iron and Steel, Preferred."

I knew that the color went from my face as I spoke, and the room was turning so that I held to Puss's table. He sat quiet for a moment, smoking a cigarette, reflecting. And then he lifted his face and he said:

"Very well. It's probable I've made a dollar or two on the deal. If I have, I'll let you know and settle it with you."

"It's all right," I said. "It doesn't matter."

When I left the room my legs were so weak that they scarcely bore me to the stairs, and my heart was numb. I was not a bond-holder any more.

It was my birthday the week after that, and I was eleven. At dinner, Puss cleared his throat and looked at me among the others sitting there. He said:

"I thought you might like to have a bond for your birthday—just for security's sake, as it were. I rang through to my broker this afternoon and picked one up for you—a Union Iron and Steel, Preferred." And he ordered the champagne to be brought in quickly, and when everybody was drinking, Puss began to dance.

Dear Mr. Walrus

It was a great pride to Fanny and Lydia Walrus that their brother was a writer, and when their father and mother died it gave them courage. Stuyvesant had his career before him, untouched and quivering, like a still ungathered flower. He was the writer of the family, the personality: his research, his papers, his time for writing were the pulse that throbbed quiet and unfaltering in their house and gave their life its growth and its maturity. Out of their own humility they spoke of him and his work in quiet voices to the servants. The old people had died, and now it was left to his sisters to protect him. "Mr. Stuyvesant is writing," Fanny would say. "You will have to let the hall go until tomorrow when Mr. Stuyvesant will be at the library." Or even to Dr. Beard who came in to tea at times now that the daily visits to the mother and father were past. "Stuyvesant is having tea in his room," Lydia would say, her voice soft but final with dignity. "He is working." It had such a sound of sanctity: he is At Work, he is Working, he has his Work to do. "You must get that boy out in the fresh air every day all the same," Dr. Beard said to them more than once as they helped him on with his coat as he was leaving. "Work is all very well in itself, but it isn't good for anyone to sit at a desk like that all day." Dr. Beard was a full five years older than either of the girls, and he spoke with authority because Stuyvesant was the youngest of them all. "A walk down to the library twice a week isn't enough to keep that boy fit," he said. "You must see that he takes care of himself. You two," he said, "Fanny and Lydia—" singling them out because they were all that was left now to Stuyvesant.

It was a great pride to them that Stuyvesant was a writer, for they were vaguely aware that many things in life had altered. Friends had died, servants were dearer, and their mother and father had told them that no one had so much money any more. Great fortunes were out of fashion, but the old family house just off Fifth Avenue, and the fine old clothes, and the silver plate, and the bronzes still were theirs. They had learned to give up many things, but they had never been asked for the cameos, or the porcelains, or the small silver stamp boxes, or the portraits and inlaid Chippendale. Whenever they went out into the street they took the ancient, perishing smell of their history with them. It was there in the pleats of their skirts, and in the gaiters and gloves and the mantle of Stuyvesant, there in the October sunlight as they crossed the avenue to Central Park. The leaves were fallen as yellow as corn on the paths and Stuyvesant walked with a light, bounding step between his elder sisters. He was just fifty-seven that autumn and the girls had to hasten their steps to keep apace with his.

The estate was at last settled, and when Stuyvesant had the papers before him, he called Lydia and Fanny into the study that had always been father's. The estate had been settled and they were still in mourning, in the terrible, relentless mourning which bespoke for them the grief of their hearts; and the two women with their long, white faces, their Modigliani hands, and the brother with his skin drawn fine as paper across his sharp, high bones, sat there like creatures of the grave themselves, their lids pale rose, their voices hushed to the uncanny silence of the rooms that stood beneath them: mother's reception-room, the family's dining-room, the hall for dinner parties, the parlor, the library, the ballroom, the butler's pantry, the kitchen, and the servants' hall.

There they sat, the girls a little nervous in father's study, waiting for Stuyvesant to speak to them out of the darkness and mystery of this room which had never been freely allowed them before. The two girls sat as if stricken with humility in the dark leather chairs, waiting for Stuyvesant to speak to them in explanation. He had never discussed his work with them, nor did they ever think of speaking of it. He was writing a book, or books, of life of which they knew nothing; he might be writing of travel, or science, or history, or of men and women of distinction, but they knew nothing of it. He was part of the speech of life, of the articulation; and they were the harkers, saying hush forever on the threshold of the sound he made. They knew that he had met a publisher just after graduating, and the publisher had looked at two of Stuyvesant's articles, and he had spoken well of them; in a letter which Stuyvesant always kept by him, the publisher had said that Stuyvesant's work showed "a certain, self-evident promise." Every word of the letter was known to them—"Dear Mr. Walrus" it began, and the other words the publisher had written were there, as clear as if engraved upon their hearts. These were the words that measured the distance between the two sisters and their brother; they had been written by a stranger to him, and they promised him to the future of an elusive, literary world.

"I have decided," he said at length, "to make a few changes in our way of living now that I know how matters are with us." He sat there before them, the slightly reddish hair standing dry and crimped from his blue-white scalp, his white hand toying with the enameled pen, playing carelessly with it as if this place and the things in it were now indisputably his to touch and alter as he pleased. "I have decided to take mother's and father's bedroom as my own," he said. He cleared his throat and looked fearlessly at them. But how could there be protest or murmur against his will? "Yes," he said. "Then I can have the study here to do my work in. I think this will prove the most satisfactory arrangement."

"Yes, yes," murmured Fanny and Lydia together. "Of course, Stuyvesant, yes, of course."

But still it was a shock to them—Stuyvesant sleeping in mother's and father's bed! For a while the sisters could not look into each other's faces. Stuyvesant working at father's desk! It was almost ludicrous for a moment. Yes, they murmured, but it would take them a time to accustom themselves to it.

"There is little money left for us," said Stuyvesant. "You must try to understand that we shall have to live very economically. I'm sending all but two of the servants off. So we will close the ground floor away. I think you'll agree with me. We'll do very little entertaining now, and the rooms are an expense to heat and a trouble to keep in order." .

This was a relief to them, and they both exclaimed with pleasure. They could feel the breath coming freer into their bodies again. Never to have to take tea again in the parlor where mother had always served it! Never to have to eat again in the big or the smaller dining-hall! What a stroke of genius to close off the entire floor, and never again let the gilt-embellished mirrors catch sight of them passing in furtive haste or presiding uneasily where mother or father had always held the floor. Oh, close it off today, at once, their eagerness besought him, and Lydia said: "I think mother will be happy knowing we've done this. There's no necessity to use her service, either. We can leave it exactly as she would have liked it."

"Of course," Stuyvesant went on, "we'll have to make use of the kitchen. But the girl can use the back stairway to bring the food up to us. There's no reason why we should not continue to use the front door as usual, but the rooms off the main hall below can be all locked away."

The rooms and their memories and the reflections the mirrors held locked off and kept, like violets pressed between the leaves of a book preserved miraculously forever.

"I have also decided," said Stuyvesant, and the two girls drew closer in quivering uncertainty, "that Lydia may now sleep in the yellow guest room."

"Oh, no," cried Lydia with a blush, "I couldn't hear of it—"

"Yes, you have always liked the yellow guest room," said Stuyvesant with decision. "Now I have decided it is to be your room."

"It was only a passing thought—" said Lydia, but her hands had closed fiercely on themselves.

"Now we are the masters of our own destinies," said Stuyvesant, "and you are to take the yellow guest room. When we have guests," he added, "I am sure they will not object to sleeping on the second floor."

"Under the servants' quarters?" exclaimed Fanny in surprise. Stuyvesant nodded slowly.

"Things are not as they used to be," he told them in his cultivated voice. "People do not feel as they used to about such things. There is a general tendency, I have observed, towards indulgence—towards *laisser faire*—"

It was the tenor of his thought, and his words so strangely, so marvelously incomprehensible to them, that fashioned their belief in all he said. So might a musician or a poet have swayed them by the very quality of the confusion his utterance brought them to. He was the creator, and they were the blind material beneath his hand. So Lydia moved at once into the yellow guest room.

The paper on its walls was a facsimile of gold satin ribbon that untwisted, stripe after stripe, from a frieze of golden and white bouquets. Here and there, the ribbons were looped up with garlands of tea-roses and asparagus fern. All the furnishings were of maple, like a young girl's room, and the first night she slept under the yellow satin eiderdown, Lydia made four wishes in the four corners of the virgin room: a wish in the first corner that when Stuyvesant's book was published it would have an outstanding success—the book of the age it should be, she wished, and then she could think of nothing further. So the same wish was spoken to the four corners of the room, and then came the delicious dying in sleep; on that first night the dying of joy in the sheets while the room she loved stood upright in yellow garlands about her. She had waited so long for the room, so many years of girlhood and womanhood. And it had taken the death of mother and father to bring it to her in the end.

Month after month Stuyvesant's work went on just as it had in the years before. It was his Work: not book, nor trilogy, but his endless monumental Work. Two days a week were spent at the library, and back he came in the evening with his notes in his brief-case, and the look of weariness in his eyes. But there was this difference at times: there were days when the Work went well, and there were days when he could not speak, could not come from his room because of the turn the Work had taken. Dr. Beard said to him at tea that he knew of authors who showed their work to the publisher before it was quite completed, and he said:

"Stuyvesant, why don't you show what you've been doing to that publishing man of yours? That book ought to be pretty far advanced by this time. He might let you have some money on it."

"Money?" said Lydia, and she looked from one man to the other with a bewildered little smile. It was the first time they had heard Stuyvesant's Work referred to in this way—as if it were a thing for sale, a commodity.

"Times are hard right now," said Dr. Beard, taking a second piece of buttered bread. "I'm feeling the pinch a little. Railway stocks," he began, and their brother nodded.

"Way down," he said quietly. "Father left everything in railway stocks."

"Patients just don't pay any more," said Dr. Beard, licking the butter from his fingers. "Can't pay. And I'm getting on, you know." He looked sharply at the empty platter. "Not so young any more. Young doctors stepping in. We're all getting on, Stuyvesant," he said, and their bother looked at him with slight irritation, but the girls began to laugh. "If the railway goes smash," he said.

"Perhaps it is the fault of the aeroplanes," said Lydia softly. Almost everyone, she had heard, rode in aeroplanes now.

"I believe there's dishonesty somewhere," said Fanny sharply, and an ugly look suddenly marred her eye. "Perhaps in the managers or at the railway stations themselves. Or even the conductors. And then they put Negroes in responsible positions on the trains," she said bitterly. "Colored porters given free-hand with your baggage, and colored waiters in the dining-cars."

"The owners are suffering from the depression too," said Stuy-vesant in his even, cultivated voice. Perhaps just as many people rode on the trains, and the price of tickets was the same, or even a bit dearer, and yet—

"They're robbed by underlings," said Fanny shortly. "Just what I said."

They had never asked Stuyvesant to sell his Work; the thought had never come to them. But now that Dr. Beard had spoken out before them, Stuyvesant must make the situation clear.

"We're getting along on very little," he said quietly across the tea table. "What comes in now is scarcely enough to heat the house and keep us fed. But we must all of us realize that this state of affairs is only temporary. My work," he said, and he cleared his throat, "I believe, my work should assure us of some-thing rather steady at a not too distant date. I cannot make promises as to when it will be finished—"

"Ah, Stuyvesant!" cried Lydia softly. "You must not speak this way. We are making out very well. Your work must not be hur-ried."

But the two girls talked of the stock market and the railway in Lydia's room, and in the morning they put on their hats and jackets and they went down the cold, abandoned stairway and out the dark hall into the street's brilliant assault. On Fifth Ave-nue they hailed a down-town bus, boarded it, and rode to Forty-second Street. There they descended and walked to Grand Cen-tral Station, and what they were they put aside in the haste of the great, moving crowds. They did not speak to each other, but their hands sought each other's as they were carried on, will-less, from one gate to another, from one ticket window to the next, from wicket to wicket, and as they moved, they glanced at each other with bright, unbewildered eyes. Having no tickets, they never passed onto platforms where people waited or trains slid away, but they descended stairways, passed under painted ceil-ings, moved through long passageways of light.

But now they knew that the talk of the railway going smash was folly. Poor old Dr. Beard, thought Lydia. Because his prac-tice had fallen off he took a sour view of things.

"The old fool!" said Fanny sharply, and although Lydia did

not approve she knew at once of whom her sister was speaking. The mistake was, she thought, that he made no effort. He spoke always like an old and defeated man. He was clean-shaven and he dressed neatly, and had he walked with a surer step and spoken confidently of the future, he might have been quite a dandy even now. He might easily have passed for a man of under sixty, but nothing of modern times ever came into his con- versation—never a reference to aeroplanes or Leonard Merrick or Whistler or Sargent.

"Don't be hard on him, Fanny," said Lydia as they pushed along with the people. "It's just that he doesn't know. He hasn't a feeling for what's happening now, at this instant. He's always back in Germany at medical college—he doesn't understand that he's being pushed aside by people who are alive, not just by younger people. He's failed as a doctor," she said, "and he doesn't want to see other people and other things successful."

Poor old Dr. Beard! Nothing as mighty as this, as prosperous, as active, could be on its way to failure, they now knew. They moved on with these hurrying strangers who were pressing deeply on into the mystery of life, and they saw the priceless marble of the stairs, the invaluable paintings on the soaring vault, and the inlay of the corridors. These things were the truth, and they felt the sense of poverty and depression lifted from them.

They returned to the house on foot, and once inside it they be- came almost hilarious in their content. They cast off their jackets and they spoke aloud from one bedroom to the other, having for- gotten everything except that they were saved. They left their doors standing open, and they called back and forth to each other.

"I think I'll change my blouse," Fanny cried out, and she gave a high, girlish cry of laughter.

"You ought to put on your Irish lace," called Lydia, "as long as Dr. Beard will be dropping in."

"The amount he *eats*," cried Fanny bitterly. "I'm sure he stints himself at lunch on purpose when he knows he's coming here for tea!"

Their spirits were so high that Lydia could not help bursting into laughter, but she said:

"We shouldn't begrudge it to him, Fanny, if he's really in want."

"Want!" shouted Fanny aloud. "It's just his meanness—"

The sound of it was too much for Stuyvesant and he opened the door of the study.

"Isn't it possible for me to have any quiet while I work?" he demanded of the sudden silence. They could not see him from where they stood, each halted in alarm in their separate rooms, but his voice came stern and admonitory to them, like the voice of God speaking from the hall. "I am at work," he said, and their hearts went cold at the knowledge of what they had done. His Work—they had raised their voices while he had been At Work. "It is a very grave time in our lives," came the voice of retribution from the hall. "I have found it necessary to send the second servant away. I don't doubt you girls could find enough in the house to keep you occupied now that there is only one servant here."

Lydia stood looking at herself in gentle agitation in the mirror of the yellow bedroom's dresser. Her mouth was parched and she could never have spoken, but the voice of her sister came sharply across the hall.

"Has the cook gone or the other?" she said, and Stuyvesant cleared his throat.

"I have sent the cook off," he said in a moment. "I did not doubt you girls would be willing to turn out a cold dish for us once or twice a day—"

"You mean we're to do the cooking?" Fanny's voice exclaimed, and it seemed to Lydia that she could sense Stuyvesant lowering his eyes as he stood there alone in the hall.

"I wouldn't put it just that way," he said. "It is only a temporary measure. We must all recognize and meet with fortitude this period of crisis we are passing through."

Even Dr. Beard agreed with Stuyvesant's decision: if they must do practically all their own work, then far better for the girls to have only one floor to care for.

"There are fireplaces in every room on the second floor," said Stuyvesant at tea, "and we could stop lighting the furnace entirely. Of course, this is only a temporary expedient—"

"Good Lord," said Dr. Beard, taking a slice of bread and butter, "if none of us come to any worse than that before this reign
of terror is over, we have nothing much to complain of!"

"Reign of terror?" exclaimed Lydia in dismay.

"He is referring," said Stuyvesant with dignity, "to the present
administration."

Dr. Beard talked to them then about food, and about the
things that were the easiest and quickest to prepare.

"Keep away from green vegetables," said Dr. Beard, taking his
second cup of tea. "I've never touched one since my wife passed
on. Buy them all in the bean, soak them overnight, and cook
them four hours on a small, economical flame."

There was no sense in cooking the meals on the big, old stove
below, he went on, and having the girl carry them up two flights
of stairs. Why not have a kitchenette put in one of the bedrooms? He offered to see a carpenter for them who would make
a corner for a gas-cooker and put in shelves.

Two days were spent making the change from the first floor to
the second, and this move filled the girls with an inexplicable
gayety. Out of the yellow guest room went all Lydia's things,
and because such a time had passed she felt she no longer
minded any more. They moved up into the old guest rooms, just
under the servants' quarters, carrying their hats, and their frocks,
and their pairs of high, laced shoes. When Fanny spilled her
glove box and her box of ribbons, they sat down on the stairs
and gasped with helpless laughter, unable to collect themselves
until Stuyvesant came out of the study below and slowly up the
stairs. He was carrying his books of notes, and his piles of script
neatly clipped together, and he mounted slowly, carefully, with
his face as white as death. He looked in quiet rebuke at the girls,
and Fanny rose and made a dive for her scattered gloves. He
had mounted the stairs with his reference books and his papers
more than a dozen times, and still he was nowhere near the end.

When he passed them so, with his papers, his Work, carried
upright in his arms, it was like the monument to their life being
carried past. The virgin statue of their living was carried by in
his white, priestly hands, and they scarcely dared raise their eyes
in reverence to it. Here was the divine mystery of the future and

the past, the essence of their being, seen in passage for a moment from sanctuary to sanctuary through unpurified air.

The kitchenette and the cookbook Dr. Beard had brought them were a great diversion in those first days when they believed that now they were living cheaply enough. But in a while they found they must get on with one good meal a day; and a little while after that, the one servant must go. Now the two girls did all there was to be done, quietly, willingly, so that nothing should disturb the tenor of his Working. They could still have tea and bread in the morning, but the butter must go, and the milk, and presently Lydia and Fanny took their tea without sugar any more. They soaked their bread in their tea, sitting up in bed in the morning, waiting until the coals shoveled into the fireplaces brought some warmth to the air. For warmth there must be, and the other things they could do without. Stuyvesant must have a warm room in which to do his Work—even if the weather was severe enough to make him sit at his desk with his cloak and his gum shoes on. But food they could take less and less of, the girls found, and they took the habit of serving Stuyvesant in his room. In this way he did not see how little they set down before themselves, or what they gathered up to cook up again into soup for the evening: bits of crust, or a few of the white beans he had not finished, or a potato or two he had scarcely touched.

It was no longer a matter of living cheaply: it was simply that they could not afford to live at all. The truth was, Stuyvesant told Dr. Beard one afternoon when the girls were out, that he did not know where the next money was coming from.

"Of course, I'm finishing my work," he said with dignity. "Once that is completed, it will be a different story. I have some connection with the publishing world," he said, and he cleared his throat. Dr. Beard knew very well that he was referring to the letter he had once received. But it was already tea-time and the girls had not returned, and Dr. Beard's real interest was for some sound of them on the stairs.

"I find by going light on lunch," said Dr. Beard, moving uneasily in his chair, "and eating a slice or two of bread at tea, that it cuts down the daily expenses—"

"It is my intention," Stuyvesant went on, "to use my influence with my publisher to the very last degree. I am aware that the size of my work may prove a drawback on first sight. But there are, as I shall point out, such works as the encyclopedia, for instance, for which there is a continuous demand. A matter of ten concise volumes should scarcely frighten an erudite public off."

Dr. Beard waited in distress until six o'clock, while Stuyvesant spoke gravely to him of these things, but the girls were late in coming home. It was almost seven, and Stuyvesant had left the door of the study open in anxiety; then they returned, and he saw the timorous, hesitant light of joy in their faces as they came up the stairs. Fanny was carrying a paper parcel, and they walked straight into the study, neat and clean in their immaculate black, their still brown side-combs set high in their thinning, smoothly done, gray hair.

"Stuyvesant—Stuyvesant dear," Lydia began, and then Fanny ripped the paper from the parcel she was carrying and cast it aside with something like defiance in her eyes.

"There," she said shortly, and the things that the paper had held spilled out over the orderly desk, and these things were babies, dozens on dozens of cardboard babies, quite naked, with their plump fists doubled up, and dimples in their knees, and their little feet finished off with round, naked toes.

The three lean, long-faced human beings remained motionless by the desk, the bones high in their noses, their hands as thin as an eagle's pale and horny foot. Stuyvesant did not move from his chair, and Fanny and Lydia stood twitching nervously by his side while this mad orphanage of undressed flesh lay heaped in orgy on the chaste, dark wood, the countless eyes rolling to the three Walruses in terrible, infantine appeal.

"What—what is the meaning of this?" Stuyvesant contrived to say at last. But he could not meet his sisters' eyes for the shame of the naked creatures Fanny had flung down.

"We are going to paint them," said Lydia in low, agonized apology. "We saw an advertisement this morning. It's just until your work is finished, Stuyvesant—just to help out a little."

"They pay us twenty cents a dozen," said Fanny arrogantly, and Stuyvesant raised his hand as if to ward off a blow. Supporting himself on the carved wooden arms of his chair, he raised himself, trembling, to his feet.

"Have I deserved this?" he asked them, facing them now, and his proud, white features did not soften. "Is this the way you've chosen to make clear to me that I have failed to provide for you?" Had he been capable of violence he would have swept the mass of indecent infants from his desk, but instead he made a gesture of disdain with his fine hand towards the swollen limbs, the well-nourished cardboard bellies of the dolls. "You will please be good enough to remove these—these—"

"They're little babies, Stuyvesant!" cried Lydia softly. She picked one up from the pile and held it tentatively before his unflickering gaze.

"They are atrocities!" Stuyvesant pronounced, and the girls stepped back in fear at the sound of his voice lifted for once against them. "You will return them at once to whomever gave them to you. I'd like to thrash him for his impudence!"

The sisters' hands moved slowly over the desk, trembling as they collected the babies to their black-clad, withering breasts. And Stuyvesant watched them with rising anger, almost with jealous wrath that their hands should touch that foul and alien flesh, that they should clutch the dolls against them as if in love as they hastened from his sight. He followed them to the door, quivering with his rage, and he called out sharply:

"I don't want them in the house tonight! Not under my roof, do you understand?"

There was then the shame of this to survive, but by morning Stuyvesant's anger had abated and he spoke to them quietly of what they had done.

"You and your sister," he said to Lydia when she brought his lunch tray in, "have lived very sheltered lives and I doubt if you are fully aware of the significance of that innocent act of yours. I will say no more on the subject," he continued as Lydia stood silent by his chair, "but I wish you to realize that these so-called lady-like occupations are rarely what they appear on the surface. Unscrupulous cads," he said distinctly, "make it their business to offer certain inducements to inexperienced women and so lead them into their—into their premises." His voice ceased for an instant, and he looked with blind eyes upon the food before him. "I must add," he went on, "that if it had not been for this disturbance of last evening I had hoped to bring my labors to a conclusion within a day or two—"

"Oh, Stuyvesant," cried Lydia softly. "You mean, you would have finished your work—?"

"It is quite possible," said Stuyvesant. He made a gesture with his hand. "But now all that is changed. I can scarcely get ahead if these interruptions to my peace of mind continue—"

But a week after this Stuyvesant told them that the Work was done. He told them quietly over the tea-table, and Lydia uttered a soft cry of joy. Fanny and Dr. Beard had both reached forward for the last piece of bread at the same instant, but the doctor's hand was the quicker.

"What's that you say, what's that?" said Dr. Beard, avoiding Fanny's eyes.

"Of course," Stuyvesant went on, "there is the polishing up to do, and the rewriting of certain portions throughout. But I believe that possibly another month or two will see it in shape for discussion with my publisher."

He spoke with modesty, turning Dr. Beard's congratulations aside with his pale, lifted hand.

"No, no," he said. "A complete work on the subject would be a much more painstaking affair than mine. I've gone into it superficially; but I've been pressed for time. If things had been going better with us, I could have given to it more what it deserves."

But still the cool gleam of his satisfaction was there, covert in his rosy-lidded eyes. Even now, at this instant, their escape seemed indicated to them: they sensed completely how it would be to pick up a paper and see his picture in it, how it would be to travel with him as conspicuous people—the sisters of the well-known writer, Stuyvesant R. Walrus. But that they might read his book was a thing that never crossed their thoughts. The completing of his Work never meant to them that now they might turn the pages of it familiarly and read what Stuyvesant had written, or come even to the threshold of what his life had been for almost forty years.

"Lydia and Fanny," Stuyvesant remarked to Dr. Beard when the girls had retired to the kitchenette, "have led a very sheltered life. I'm not at all sure—just between you and me, of course —that it would be wisdom to allow any of my work find its way into their hands. Naturally, I shall see that you have a complete set, but there's no reason why the girls," he finished, "should—"

"My boy," said Dr. Beard, leaning forward and laying his hand upon the younger man's, "I am seventy this week, and I may say that I haven't got to where I wanted to in life. You are ten years my junior, and you have worked hard for the success which is now about to come to you."

Stuyvesant seemed to smile as he looked into the dim, old eyes of the doctor whose strong fingers still clutched at his own. But a flame of rage was licking at his heart, a small fire of fury ignited by old Dr. Beard's unheeding words. He saw the frayed cuffs at the doctor's wrists, and the shine that ran like leather from his elbow on the under sleeve. When he glanced down he could see the pink of the doctor's knee through the giving threads of the trouser leg. He had not asked for a reminder of his age from this old man, he thought; he had not asked for pity for all the years that he had worked. He had asked for nothing but gratitude and applause from this old doctor whose practice had dwindled away.

"My publisher," he said, removing his hand from under Dr. Beard's, "will undoubtedly be willing to discuss terms this spring. I believe fall publication is generally conceded the—"

He had not been in the street for many days, but now he was going to walk as far as the avenue with Dr. Beard and see him on the up-town bus.

"Ah, this is the first time I've been out for a fortnight," said Stuyvesant as the two men stepped out the door. The evening air swept through his head like a strong, clear breath of cold from the street, and all that he saw was marvelously defined, seen sharper and more perfect in his giddiness than it could be in reality. His head was light as he walked, and as the air went trembling deep into his soul he said:

"Lydia and Fanny need a change, I think. I hope to be able to take them on a little trip once the proofs are off my mind."

"There's Yellowstone," said Dr. Beard. They had come to the corner and halted before the news-stand there.

"There's Europe," said Stuyvesant, with a look of daring in his eye as he smiled at the old doctor. Dr. Beard threw up his hands and shook his head.

"You Walruses!" he said. "You're ready for anything."

He watched Stuyvesant with admiration, but slyly so that the other would not see how covetously he recognized this purpose and strength; he watched him buy an evening paper and put it folded beneath his arm, and from the window of the up-town bus he watched the erect, lean figure underneath its cloak making its way down the long block towards home. The shoulders were straight as those of a younger man, but the step was wandering and slow.

"He's getting on," said Dr. Beard with satisfaction to himself.

Stuyvesant was tired now that he had climbed the two flights of stairs, and he sat down in the study with his cloak still on and opened the evening paper on his desk. He turned the lamp on by his side, and there he sat reading the paper under the soft flood of light. He read the first page, and the second, and the pages that followed after, sitting there with his mantle on his shoulders still and a pale pink line about his brow where his hat had rested.

Fanny and Lydia were in the kitchenette, preparing the soup, when Stuyvesant walked in. He was wearing his mantle still, and he carried the evening paper in his hand. His face was white, and to Lydia it seemed that his mouth was blue, as if the blood in his lips had been drawn away. He stood looking at them gently, in bewilderment a moment, his long arms fallen by his sides, and then he said:

"Lydia, Fanny, dear, I must go to a funeral tomorrow." His eyes were absolutely painless, yellow and clear as a cat's eyes, and as thin as wine. "My publisher," he said, holding out the paper with a vacant lift of his hand, "my publisher is dead."

It was not quite true that they had no money left, for the next day Stuyvesant bought a great purple wreath at the florist's shop, with a strong, metallic edge of bronze leaves to it, and he had this sent to the publisher's house. In the morning he dressed in his good black things, and he took a train to the suburban place where the funeral was to be, and there in the church he kneeled by the publisher's body as those who were near and dear to the publisher kneeled. The publisher was very old when he died, but in Stuyvesant's breast pocket was the letter the publisher had written him when he was still a young man. "Dear Mr. Walrus," it said. "It was kind of you indeed to give me the opportunity of seeing the enclosed articles. There is no doubt that they bear proof of a certain self-evident promise. Unfortunately, I cannot see my way clear towards making any use of them just at this time."

In the evening he returned to New York, and when he mounted the stairs and came into the kitchenette, the girls were heating up the soup. They did not speak to him of his bereavement, but he said:

"I feel I have every reason to be satisfied with my day. I shook hands with the widow and with his married daughter—a quiet, lovely girl who bears a striking resemblance to her poor father. I had the honor of exchanging a few words with those who had been his constant companions throughout his life."

"It must have been nice for them as well," said Fanny sharply, "to see an old friend of his that way."

When Dr. Beard rang the doorbell a day later just at tea-time, he could get no answer. Nor was there any answer on the following day. He walked down to the end of the street with his cane in his hand, and there he spoke to a policeman. When he walked back to the house, there were two policemen with him, and his heart was shaking as if with the cold within him.

Even the lower hall was filled with the smell of gas, and Dr. Beard found his legs had gone weak beneath him, and he began to whimper as the two policemen made their way upstairs. But it was he, as a friend of the family, who must say the word for the sake of the law, and after the windows had been flung open the policemen helped old Dr. Beard up the stairs and into the kitchenette.

"Yes," he said in a whisper, "yes, those are the Walruses."

Lydia and Fanny and Stuyvesant were lying on the floor in freshly-laundered pajamas, each with a pillow beneath the head.

"Suicide pact," said the policeman who was supporting Dr. Beard.

"I'm a doctor," said the old man, drawing himself up. "I am prepared to sign the death certificate."

"Sure," said the policeman, and they helped him into the study and sat him down, for he was shaking like a leaf in the wind. There he sat at Stuyvesant's desk and he looked in bleak bewilderment about him. In the fireplace were the bits and the ends of a great mass of paper that had been burned.

Rondo at Carraroe

There was a pattern at Carraroe and Rondo was there with a rifle range and a roulette table. It was after the day's work was finished with that he went down the road to Flaherty's house for oil and petrol, and in the darkness that was beginning to fall he saw three or four young men coming towards him, and it was then, so he swore on the Bible in court, that he was stabbed.

"One of these men was swinging his arms around in the dark," said Rondo to His Lordship, "and when he passed me by he swung his arm out to the one side and struck me in the back with what I took to be either his doubled-up fist or a stone. I thought some of my ribs were broken in half, so I put my hand under my vest at the back and there I found blood pouring out of a wound. 'My God, I've been stabbed!' I called out, and then I fell down."

"Here was my client," said Mr. Keeley with a tear in his voice, "left lying there in the center of the road, and these ruffians making for Lettermuckoo and never caring whether they'd left him dead or dying. It's enough to break your heart."

"God knows it's a terrible story," said His Lordship, "and we must get to the truth of it all, come what may. Now, Rondo," His Lordship said, "did you see the face of the man who struck you and would you be able to point him out to the rest of us here?"

"Well, now," said Rondo, smoothing the lick of his hair on his forehead, "I can't say I saw him actually striking me, but I saw him looking back over his shoulder just before it. There was no one but these three or four men passing at the time, and there's no question in my mind anyway. They must have been drinking for what they did to me, and leaving me there with the blood soaking out through my clothes."

His Lordship then called a parade of men they had picked up on the road on Sunday night, and Rondo looked straight into Bartley's face and said:

"Right there's the man that stabbed me."

"Now that's a lie," said Bartley at once, and Mr. Keeley said with scorn:

"Well, then, perhaps you will tell the court, Bartley, where you were last Sunday night."

"There was a pattern at Carraroe," Bartley began, "and I was with friends in a publichouse. We went home by the road about ten in the evening. The first I knew of anything at all was when the guards stopped us at the crossways and showed us Rondo in an ambulance. I couldn't say who had attacked him, but the guards said we were to step over to the barracks. 'What for?' says I. 'Why, you're accused of stabbing Rondo,' they says. 'Sure,' says I, 'put it on me. You've been after me a year now since my brother went off without paying a poteen fine!'"

"Now you're making a serious charge against the guards," said His Lordship sternly. "You're suggesting the guards have brought you into the dock on a charge they know you're innocent of. Now if there's no foundation for these charges you're making against the guards, then we'll have to arrive at the conclusion that you have no regard for the truth."

"You'll never get a story straight from a Lettermuckoo man," said Mr. Keeley, smiling quietly at His Lordship.

"Is this a court of justice?" Bartley cried out, and his eyes were flashing and the curls were wringing wet on his head.

"Order!" His Lordship cried out.

"Now what did you find on the prisoner?" asked Mr. Keeley, turning to the guards.

"He had a cut of tobacco in one pocket and a pipe in the

other," said Sergeant Conroy with a grin. "Now a man won't carry tobacco around without a knife to cut it with. It's certain he felt weak after the stabbing and tossed the knife away."

"Well, now," said Bartley, holding his temper in, "the truth of the matter is that I've never owned a penknife in my life. I've been smoking a pipe for over a year now, but I cut my tobacco at home with my old dad's knife. It's not people like mine that can afford two penknives under the one roof. On Sunday night I got the loan of a knife from a man called Conneely at Carraroe, and I cut my tobacco there."

"Now Conneely's in court," said His Lordship, and he called him to the stand.

"Well, Bartley," said Conneely once they had sworn him in, "had the loan of my penknife on Sunday evening and he cut his tobacco with it after the pattern at Carraroe. He gave it back to me at eight at night, and there was nothing at all like blood on it. I know his brother is wanted by the guards for absconding without paying a poteen fine, and there are some who believes the law has it in for him on this account."

"Keep to your story," His Lordship said, and Conneely went on.

"I came down the road behind Bartley on the Sunday night," he said. "He was walking three yards ahead of me all the way to the crossroads. I never laid eyes on Rondo that night and nothing happened at all. I think the whole thing's a fabrication."

"It's enough to break your heart," said Mr. Keeley, "the way blackguards of the worst description will hang together!"

"Now," said His Lordship, striking the table, "I'm determined to reach the bottom of this terrible affair! If the guards of Carraroe barracks are worth anything, then they're capable of keeping the roads safe at night. Now Patrick Mulligan was coming up from the other side, and it was Mulligan found Rondo lying in the road."

So Mulligan took his oath in court and began to tell his story.

"On Sunday," said he, "there was a pattern at Carraroe, but I couldn't get to it because my wife's brother was sick in Galway and we spent the day there with him. My wife made up her mind to stay the night, and I came home alone and was walking up the road when I heard someone moaning away on the side of the road, and when I went to it, I found Rondo was lying there. It was clear the man had been drinking, the way he was carrying on."

"They've all been bought!" cried out Mr. Keeley. "It's a shame the way the case is turning!"

"I lifted him out of it," Mulligan went on, "and took him in the state he was in to Dr. Lydon's. That was a good mile away. He kept calling out there was blood coming out of his back, and even in the dark it was plain that his clothes were sopping wet. I asked him if he had been carrying a bottle in his pocket to the back, and he started crying that he'd been stabbed in the ribs."

"I suppose he didn't mention seeing snakes?" said Mr. Keeley with fine scorn. "Better make it a good one while you're about it!"

"Snakes never came into it at all," said Mulligan. "The doctor got Rondo's clothes off him, and sure enough, there was a hole in his back as big as the head of a pin," and the court burst into laughter.

"So you're trying to tell us it was for that Dr. Lydon called the ambulance?" said Mr. Keeley with a jeer.

"Now I didn't say that," said Mulligan. "The truth of it is there was no holding Rondo quiet. Dr. Lydon called in his brother and nephew, but the four of us together were like helpless babes in arms. He was in the throes of drink for fair, and the doctor had a sick wife upstairs and the noise was bringing the roof down."

"I examined Rondo," said old Dr. Lydon, "on Sunday night and found him suffering from shock and a slight wound in the lumbar region. From the nature of it, I couldn't say whether it had been done with a penknife or a bit of glass. He was bleeding a little, but his clothes were soaked through with some other liquid. A few bits of broken glass were there in the pocket of his vest in the back, and Rondo said the blackguards had broken to pieces a bottle of scent he was taking home to his wife from the pattern at Carraroe."

"Well, now, there's one thing sure," cried out Mr. Keeley, "and not a soul can deny the truth of it!" His face was livid red with his anger and his legal papers were shaking in his hand. "You all agree that there was a pattern at Carraroe and that my client was there with a rifle range and a roulette table. . . ."

"That he was not!" a woman cried out from the benches. "My husband was home in bed all Sunday with a toothache that never let up till the Monday morning, and his brother went off to the pattern instead. . . ."

"Now this is one of the worst cases I've ever heard of in the whole country," said His Lordship, and he adjourned the trial until the next session of the Court of Galway.

Austrian Group
1933–1938

Natives Don't Cry

We went to Austria that summer. It was the time of the year when hay fever made Father's eyes cry all day, and in the mountains there was no sign of dust, there was almost frost in the evenings, and if he saw any goldenrod growing he could take the long way round across the snow. We went to Austria, driving there from England, and Miss Henley came to us the night before we left. She was not very pleased to come, but it was only for the month, so she came as a gift to us. She did not believe she would like us because of the hotel where we were in London and because of the color of Mother's hair. She did not say these things in these words to us, but she said them in other ways so that we knew. But the first night she came to us there were a Lord and Lady to dinner. They were an Irish Lord and Lady, brother and sister, twins. They were both sixteen. Miss Henley did not say much to them at table, but it was easy to see she was satisfied they were there.

The hotel belonged to Mrs. Lewis, and she stood at the top of the stairway smoking cigarettes, knowing at once when you came in whether she'd like you or whether she wouldn't. There was a picture of the dead King, signed with his name, in her parlor, and she used to sit there talking to Mother about the royalty. She said the dead King's mother had worn a plaster mask on her face when she saw she was getting old; she couldn't bear the sight in the glass of her features falling to pieces. And Francis said:

"What did she do with the mask when she had to laugh at something funny?"

Mrs. Lewis said: "She never saw anything funny, never in all her life."

She was always a little bit drunk when she received at Court, Mrs. Lewis said, and one day they unveiled a statue for her, and the Mother Queen, who was dead a long time now, hiccuped too much to speak the words she had to say, so they had to play the music.

"Ha, ha!" said Mrs. Lewis after everything. "What would your little girls like to see in London?"

"They'd like to see a Lord and a Lady," Mother said.

So Mrs. Lewis invited the Lord and the Lady. Miss Henley came in time to put Francis to bed and then she took us down to dinner. The Lord and Lady were waiting in the hall. The Lady wore a green dress, and she had long straight red hair, and because they both had freckles like our own we could scarcely look into their eyes for sorrow.

"I don't believe they were a Lord and a Lady at all," my sister said when we were in the room, undressing.

"My dear child," said Miss Henley, "as you have doubtless never so much as laid eye on a titled Englishman I daresay you have no reason to believe that these young people were impostors. I thought them very well bred."

"I know they couldn't have been a Lord and a Lady," my sister said. "They had freckles."

"Nevertheless," said Miss Henley, folding our dresses sharply into the open suitcase, "I have no doubt they were, and I daresay I am a better judge of such things than a little girl who has always lived across the water."

Miss Henley had a thin coat and a wide felt hat that almost escaped from her head when we drove. She had to hold it with her two hands, riding in the back between us. She was not dressed for driving, you could feel the bones in her legs shaking, but she was very vain of everything she had. Mother put a fur jacket in the back of the car at Southampton and said:

"If you feel the wind, just put this around you, Miss Henley."

There was a ring of blue around Miss Henley's mouth, and she had no gloves on her hands, but she said:

"Oh, I'm not accustomed to bundling up in season and out! In England we don't take our winter things out quite so early, you know. I would be very glad to know," said Miss Henley, looking severely at Mother, "if it doesn't seem too presumptuous, where we may be going. It's on account of my mail, of course I haven't anything else but my letters," she said, and she looked at us all as if we were strangers to her. "I have nothing else to live for now."

We thought she was fifty because she had no color in her face, and her hair was pinned back in a knot on her neck, and it was gray near the ears. Father took her passport on the French side, and when he came back to the car he said:

"I think you are much too young to be leaving home, Miss Henley."

He had a soft voice, and whenever he smiled he seemed shy and uneasy to us.

"Miss Henley is almost as young as you girls," said Father, and we saw the color run into her cheeks. "She's only twenty-five!"

"How old did you think I was?" she said, and Francis said:

"A hundred."

But he was so young there was nothing to say to him. It was just a number he had heard somewhere.

She had been born in Burma, she was a civil servant's daughter, and she had no patience for the ways of any children except the children she and her brothers had been. In the hotels at night she took their pictures from her bag and set them on the bureau. She spoke of them all, and of the places they had lived, as if these things were clearer seen than any others. And she spoke of them only a little at a time, and not too often, as if they were too good to be given quite away.

She did not say these things or anything like them to Mother, but if Mother was having her hair done in Paris or Strasbourg or Munich, she said them to Father and to us where we were having tea. She looked at Mother in mirrors when Mother was putting a dress on or changing her hat, but she never told her about Rudolpho, although she wrote to him every day. She said to Mother:

"Where would be a safe place to have mail sent to? I have to know about my letters."

And Mother would be looking at the side of her own face, through the hand glass, in the mirror, and she would say:

"Oh, I'm sure the American Express or Thomas Cook would do, aren't you?"

But Mother never said which city because she scarcely ever knew which country she was traveling in. She could not remember the capitals of Europe even. She could only remember people's faces and whether they liked Picasso. So Miss Henley did not say to her:

"When I was a little girl my father never could shave in the morning unless I was curled up on the table where his basin of water stood!" She gave such gasps and whispers of laughter while she spoke of herself to us that sometimes her words were lost forever. Her cheeks squeezed up red and the tears of laughter seemed ready to fall from her eyes. "I always had to hold his brush for him, imagine!" she cried out. "He used to make a mustache for me out of the lather——" She said more after this, but she laughed so wildly that we never made it out.

Her family was dead, even her brothers, so there was no one left to write to, but there was Rudolpho. Every day, he was a name written out very big across an envelope, and Father said:

"If your young man likes to read so much, Miss Henley, I think he must be quite literary."

Whenever we had tea with Father, we had it beside the bar where he sat because he didn't like the drinks in other places. And after a week Miss Henley forgot about tea. She sat at the table with us, but she had a cocktail and potato chips instead.

"Oh, he's not exactly that!" said Miss Henley, laughing. "He's foreign of course, but so many people are these days that one gets accustomed to it. He's been ten years in London, too, so you'd scarcely know. I don't know what he's doing to cheer himself up, poor thing. He must feel like a duck out of water. He wanted me to go, of course, and he told me not to hurry back, but I know perfectly well what's going on inside him."

"You'll probably have mail waiting in Salzburg," said Father. "What about another cocktail?"

"Oh, I scarcely ever drink!" cried Miss Henley.

"But these were small," said Father.

"Yes," said Miss Henley. "That's quite true." She saw Mother

coming in through the swinging door and the smile went sharp
on her lips, and she said:

"Do sit up, girls! Francis, take your spoon out of your cup!
One would never think I'd been with you over a week now. I'd
hoped to see much more improvement."

"Well, anyway, they've learned to say lef-tenant," Father said.

Father went to the post office the first thing in Salzburg. He
took the passports in his hand, and when he came back he was
carrying a great many things. There were letters from America,
and there was Mother's picture playing golf in *The Tatler,* but
there wasn't a single thing, there wasn't even a postcard, for Miss
Henley. She sat quite still on the terrace of the coffeehouse on
the Mozart Place, and the sun was shining for a change. She
looked straight into the sun, past Father, smiling at what he said.
He said:

"There wasn't anything for you today, Miss Henley. Better
luck tomorrow."

Mother opened her letters, and Father opened his, and we did
not look at Miss Henley. No one lifted his eyes, and no one felt
easy in the silence at the table. Miss Henley sat with her cup of
coffee and cream in front of her, and because she did not speak
there was nothing for anyone to say. But Francis said:

"Maybe nobody likes you," and Mother said quickly:

"Would you like to wander around a bit by yourself this afternoon, Miss Henley? There's quite a lot to see here. I'll take the
children out to the Grand Duke's palace to see Elizabeth Dun-
can. You might go see Mozart's skull."

"Mozart's skull!" cried Miss Henley. "How disgusting!"

In the evening we found her in the room still; she was sitting
there in the half-darkness when we came home. She had been
writing a letter by the window and she was putting the name on
the envelope when we came in the door. Father was with us, and
Miss Henley said:

"Where would the best place to change English money be?"

Miss Henley stood, very small and thin, with her hand holding
to the back of the chair. She wore high black shoes, and a
shirtwaist, and a skirt that had no year or season, wide at the

knees and dark. She had never worn anything else but this, no matter how the weather changed.

"Look here," said Father. "If you'd like your salary in advance, you just tell us. I can pay it now or whenever you want it, just as you like."

"Not at all," said Miss Henley. "I had no intention of asking anything in advance. I just happened to find a few shillings in my pocket and I thought I would change them here. I only want to buy a stamp," she said.

She did not like the seeds in the bread, or the cream in the coffee. There wasn't a thing she could eat in the breweries, because of the thickness of the meat and the smell of beer in the place. The way of eating frankfurters in the fingers, and the linen suits the women wore, were things she could never get over. She couldn't believe anyone could have so little care for the kind of figure that he cut.

"Imagine going off on your honeymoon with your husband's head shaved like a convict's!" she said to Father as they had a drink in the Mirabelle garden one afternoon. "I'll never forget these frightful heads if I live to be a hundred!" she said, and she looked around at the German tourists sitting big and heavy at the tables.

"I'm afraid you favor the long-haired, artistic type," said Father. "Let's try their Sidecars."

"Oh, I never drink more than one, if that!" said Miss Henley. "Of course, I've seen some of the funniest photographs of this young man in England I've spoken of before. When he was in the war, they got things, you know, things in their heads, if you can imagine it. They had to shave the entire regiment's heads! But he wouldn't let them touch his beard, and he did look so silly! He had a little bit of beard, he was only twenty-one then——" Miss Henley's voice was lost in her gasps of laughter, and Father, although he had never seen the photograph, opened his mouth and laughed as well as he could. Miss Henley picked up the second cocktail glass, and suddenly she stopped laughing. "I was wondering about something this morning," she said. "I was going to ask you, that is. The next time you do go to the post office, would you mind asking if there are any letters for Mary

Gwendolyn, or for Gwendolyn Henley. My passport has my name down simply Mary Henley. But some of my friends were in the habit of calling me by my middle name, Gwendolyn. This friend I've mentioned to you before always called me that."

At the end of the week we went away, we went up the valley into the mountains, and Miss Henley rode in the back of the car with us. She held Francis on her lap, and she closed her eyes and told us of the places she had been. There were eight natives struck by lightning in the hills in Burma one night in the summer, and she had seen them in the morning when the others carried them down. Their bodies were burned as black as logs in the fire.

"What did you give them to make them stop crying?" Francis asked.

"Natives don't cry," said Miss Henley. "They don't feel things the way other people do."

"Not even lightning?" asked my sister.

"Not even lightning," Miss Henley said.

It was cold climbing, and Father stopped the car for a glass of wine in a country tavern. We all went in and sat down by the stove, and Mother and Father and Miss Henley drank a pitcher of hot red wine.

"How do you like Austria, Miss Henley?" Mother said. "This is Austria, isn't it?"

"Oh, it's very like the country in Burma, you know," said Miss Henley. "I was telling the children, I've a friend who has a little car of his own. He drives it all over England. I told him we would be driving around Salzburg. It would be a joke, wouldn't it, if he suddenly turned up on the road!"

"Perhaps he's going to surprise you by coming right over as soon as he knows where you are," said Father, and Miss Henley's face squeezed up with laughter.

"It would be just like him to!" she said. "I'll never forget the time we were asked to a fancy-dress party. He dressed up the same as two friends of his did, and I never knew until the party was over and everybody unmasked that I'd been dancing with somebody else all evening. He had got tired," said Miss Henley, "and gone home early."

"That was a good joke," said Mother. "That was a very good joke."

Father said: "Have a little more wine."

"Oh, I never take much," said Miss Henley, watching him fill her glass up. "If this friend I was speaking of did happen along the children would have a wonderful time with him. He's like a child himself," she said, and she began to gasp with laughter. "He'd be down on his hands and knees all the time playing with Francis if he were here."

"Francis," said Mother, "please get off your hands and knees, darling."

"If I get off my knees, can I stay on my hands?" said Francis.

Day after day Miss Henley walked us slowly over the hillsides, in the rain even, with our thick boots on, and on cloudy windy days. Mother and Father went up mountains together, escaping the goldenrod and the cut hay lying wet in the fields. Whenever we went back to the hotel, there would be letters on the table, but there would never be anything for Miss Henley.

"Nobody writes to you, Mrs. Hen," Francis said. He was proud because he had two cards one day from people we scarcely knew. He had a card with a cat's head on it, and when you pressed it the cat cried. And the other was of a man in a bathing suit and when you undid the back of his trousers all the views of Venice opened out.

"My dear child," said Miss Henley. " 'Fools' names and fools' faces,' " she said. "As a matter of fact, Francis, if I wanted my letters sent here, I could easily tell people to write to me here, couldn't I? So you see how silly you are."

But we never saw her writing any more letters. She did not even speak of Rudolpho. She would sit reading books that Mother gave her, and she never found any of them very good, not nearly as good as the books she had read somewhere else at some other time.

"Always the same old thing," she said, and she gave them back to Mother. "Always love, love, love, and whether the beautiful girl will, or whether the handsome hero won't, succumb! It's just a bit tiresome, I think, you know."

Mother and Father put their feet out by the fire and Mother

said Miss Henley wasn't a good thing for the children even if she was leaving so soon. She said it was the worst thing to have this for every meal with you, this pall, this bitterness, this dead, unspoken sorrow. What could we give her to take away her silence, and her sharpness, and her grieving face? After a little while Father said:

"What do you think if I should be Rudolpho? He's been an absolute skunk to her. I'd like to give him a piece of my mind. He probably took every penny she made from her, and now that she's down and out he's through with her. Anyway, I could write letters to her. I could typewrite them and sign them Rudolpho. I could tell her how much I miss her. They wouldn't have to be long."

"How could you possibly get them mailed?" said Mother, putting the bright clear red on her fingernails.

"I could have them mailed from Innsbruck," said Father. "I could tell her I couldn't stand England without her. I could tell her I'm going absolutely mad."

"The last statement would be true, at least," said Mother.

In the morning, Father and Mother took us partway up a mountain. We were going to the first hut underneath the glacier, because anything else was too far. We left very early, while it was dark still, and we would be back late, in time for supper. Going up, we would take it very easy, and we would not speak much, for you needed all your breath in your body for climbing. But coming down we could run as we liked and pick gentians and forget-me-nots all the way.

So we climbed quietly, very silent, my sister and I, listening to Mother and Father talking to each other ahead. It was growing light when we reached a plateau where the stream spread out and made soft, marshy ground, and at the far end of this we saw a herd of horses standing. They stood with their heads laid across one another's necks, a great many of them, dark and glossy in the early morning, with their long tails softly brushing across one another's flanks.

They did not move until we were near the center of the field, and then they seemed to see us quickly, and, as if it were a game they were playing, they broke apart and a few of them cried out in high clear voices. The largest horse had started toward us, her head down, her nostrils spread, her tail arched out behind. The others scattered across the end of the field, and then they wheeled and swung to the heels of their leader who was coming fast, pounding over a trail as if toward water, following the smell of it hard to where we stood. Behind her came the others, younger and wilder, shouldering each other and rearing in their haste.

Mother said: "Get behind me, girls. I never heard of such a thing. I never heard at any time in my life about horses acting like this."

Father waved his stick at them, but very gently, as if he really would do them no harm.

"Perhaps they've had an unfortunate experience with humans recently," said Father. "They may be looking for someone in particular."

Mother put her arms down about us and drew us off toward the trees that stood ahead, keeping us close beside her under her arms.

"I'm not in the least afraid of horses," Father said, waving his stick. "I never have been. I was brought up with them. I've ridden all my life."

"I know," Mother called back from where we were. "Neither am I," and her voice was shaking.

But the horses knew very well what to do: when they were almost on us all, they drew their chins in close against their shining necks, as swans might, floating on the water, and they swerved wildly and perfectly in their circle. First the leading horse drew in her head and made the curve, and then the others followed in the tumult of their advance. It might have been some kind of game they had made up out of their loneliness and their boredom on the mountainside. They went off over the deep marshy ground and near the edge they took their place again, their sides blowing fast, their heads shaking the hair on their necks from one side to the other, fitting again into their attitudes of rest.

We came home another way and we did not see them, and when we got to the hotel it was six o'clock and Miss Henley was giving Francis his bath. There was a look of something else in her face, and whatever she said to us she couldn't keep from smiling.

"Did we get any mail?" said Mother.

"Oh, all the mail was for me for a change today," said Miss Henley.

"Oh, how nice!" said Mother.

"It was quite a joke," said Miss Henley, her face squeezed up with laughter. "The porter came staggering up—three telegrams and seven letters! They'd never heard of such a thing here! You can imagine!"

"I hope your young man's well?" said Father.

"Oh, he's awfully well, thank you," said Miss Henley. "He'd put the wrong address on all the letters and they were all returned to him. So that explains how it was, you see. He's awfully excited about the Lindberghs being in England. He's working on a newspaper now and he's been trying to find out where they are so as to get a peep at them and perhaps a word or two for a story."

"Well, we'll get a good bottle of wine tonight," said Father, "and we'll all drink to Rudolpho!"

"Oh, that's so nice of you," said Miss Henley, "but you know how little I drink." She stood up to put the bath towel around Francis, and she said: "The heat in here, you know, it really makes me a bit dizzy."

It wasn't until after the bottle of wine had been drunk and Miss Henley had taken Francis up to bed that Father said anything about it. Then he said to Mother at the table:

"There wasn't any mail today. The bus broke down on the main road and nothing ever came through. The porter told me when we came back this evening. The mailbag was still hanging in the hall."

"I think the girls had better go up to bed," said Mother. "They've been up a mountain and they're awfully tired."

Maiden, Maiden

The guide wore a smart little velvet coat that had been washed many times over. On this evening there was wind, and his jacket hugged his waist fast as a woman's arm might, and on the shoulders it sprang away like new wings. He came in through the door and hung his green felt hat up on a peg in the wainscoting, and then sat down by the fire.

The dining hall was wide, but dark because of the color of the stained wood, and a great stove stood, tiled blue and white, clean and seemingly as cool as wax, in the center. It was past the time for dinner, and the girl and the man who sat drinking hot wine in the corner were apparently going to take dinner as they were, in corduroy breeches, and their climbing things.

The guide saw them at once when he came in; because of the young woman he felt a sudden movement in his blood, but he had no time to talk with one or two people at a time. He was after his living, and the more people there were, the better were his chances for setting off early in the morning. With a rope around the thin part of his being, he guided climbers up the mountains, and guided others down. No one knew what became of him after September. Once he went back to the city, the mountain people knew nothing more of him until the spring.

On the other side of the hall there was an Italian youth sitting, dressed, it would seem, for a dance, jerking his idle, wide trousers on his legs, whistling under his hairless lip, and looking at the young woman who was drinking her wine. Only his mother beside him, old and soft and dark-looking with her mustaches, might be the explanation of why he had come to the mountains. He was there, it might be, because of his mother's constitution, and she crocheting yellow silk in the evening mountain air.

There were as well three maiden ladies from Dresden whom the guide had talked to in the morning: two of them schoolteachers and one a librarian. They had books in paper jackets on their table by their plates, but they did not read them now, but conversed with an air of sprightliness and taste. It was their laughter that seemed startling: so fresh, so loud, and so unbridled, at once obscene and innocent, like children's laughter, mocking every stranger in the hall.

The family of Germans from Berlin were ready at once for speech when the guide turned his back, the small of it and the space of his shoulders, upon the girl and the man drinking wine in the corner and said "God greet you" to them. The Germans had come over the glacier and down that day, and they were taking leave of the Tirol tomorrow. They had strapping, golden-haired limbs with muscles packed monstrously in them: the father with tassels on his pipe, the mother, simple and bold and motionless as a Flemish portrait, the two young men, the sons of the family, with their narrow shaven skulls and their white lashes, were all giving ear to the quick, thin-lipped guide.

It was only when they said they would not be back again that summer that his talk began to ebb from them; that was the necessary end. He had no more light in his eye for the way they had crossed, for they were of no more use to him. Tomorrow they would be gone, and he left—with the dark wrists showing out of his jacket sleeves and his legs in his breeches that tapered down to the cuff of his woolen socks—left with his living to make from the foreigners, from the French, the Italians, the English, whoever they might be.

He turned himself about the dining room for hope: passed the teachers at the table, and the Italian youth with his legs swinging loose for the dance hall. He even walked out of the Gasthaus and onto the road in the vision of the evening's clear blue shell. The daisies lay white and sharp as stars in the grasses, and the air off the snows was better than drink. He passed up and down on the road before the open door, separately seen as objects are at that hour, at that height, carved in the clear, luminous twilight like a fly set in blue glass.

When he came in he nodded at once to Willa and Sarat, because they were the only ones, they were the last thing left to him now.

"God greet you," he said casually, and he loitered over to the corner where the girl and the man were drinking, their legs stretched out in their breeches. "Did you come down by the glacier?" he said in preparation; he was feeling his way with the soft Germanic tongue.

"No, we came over the pass," said Sarat. The guide stood before them, so made for grace that he could stand with his belly slightly out, his loins drawn in, and yet lose nothing of his stature. He was watching their two faces, his eyes dark and quick, and the lashes heavy along the firm thin lids. "We'll go up the glacier tomorrow and down the other side to Heiligenblut," said Sarat. Because the language was unfamiliar to him, he gestured with his hand.

"Why doesn't he sit down and have wine with us, Sarat?" said Willa, speaking English, but dimly, slowly speaking as if she had been roused from sleep, stretching her arms out straight on the table in her jersey sleeves. They had come a long way, and this was the end of it: the languor of the heat and the wine moving down the tongue and stirring, as a dream might stir, the heart and flesh and speech. She did not think of taking her gaze from the guide's small even face; it lay soft and heavy on him, without insinuation, almost without intent.

Sarat's face was one she had known a long time: the broad nose, the eyes shut away behind glasses, and the long pleasant-looking lip. The wind and the sun had altered his complexion for the moment, but there was no real difference in him. He was the doctor, even in the Tirol he had his ceremony. He said, "Do take a seat," to the guide as he might have said it to any patient in any city. The guide suddenly took his hands out of his pockets and sat down.

He sat down beside Sarat, but still he did not turn his face from Willa; he knew English, he could speak quite a little of it, and he knew what she had said. Sarat filled up the three glasses from the pitcher and left the slices of lemon floating, translucent, on the rosy surface.

"The way over changes every year," the guide was saying. He picked up his glass and said, *"Berg Heil!"* to them. When he looked over his glass at Willa a look of shyness came into his eye. "It is bad this year because of the soft snow," he said. "Last

year the ice was straight all the way over. This year you don't
know what you're coming to."

Willa could see the profile of the Italian boy beginning his
soup with his mother, and the dark woman, soft with fat, wiping
her mustaches clean with the edge of her folded napkin. There
was the guide's jaunty shoulder against the dark-stained wood,
and the piece of his neck out of his flannel shirt turned now to
Sarat as he talked, and the wealth of purely uttered German that
lay like a deep mine of ore within his throat and came through
his thin lips to sound. Beyond this was the profile of the Italian
youth having no place whatsoever in the hall, the Italian boy in
his dandy coat and the brilliantine lank of his crown, his face
grotesquely planted with the amorous, monumental nose that
cast a shadow where the chin was not. His spoon was lifted and
his lower lip hung open for it when he turned his look again to
Willa's hair and eyes and gave her an edge of smile.

"If the weather is threatening, we don't intend to go, of
course," said Sarat. Willa was watching the three Dresden ladies
laughing on the other side of the room.

"With a guide you could cross in two hours," the guide was
saying. Here in the warmth, with the hot wine in them, his voice
was making the preparation still, his words coming slowly as if
creeping in stealth on them.

"I think we'd be fools to go without one," said Willa. Her face
with the loose light hair around it, the eyes heavy with wind,
was turned vaguely to the guide.

So, early in the morning, the three of them set out. It was toward the end of August, and at four in the early day there was
still an amount of darkness, a cold, blue twilight, left in the
morning sky. They went through the fields at the start, through
the pasture grasses and the dew-drenched nightly cold on their
heavy boots. Their packs were hung on their backs, and their
breathing smoked out white in the clarity before them. The
woods and the marshes were dark with rot and wet, and birds
were calling in notes as bright and separate as drops of water
falling singly from a branch.

The guide walked a pace or two before them, even when they
began to climb. Because they were paying him for his presence,

he must subdue his gait to theirs. Small flowers of edelweiss and a soft little feather, like the down from the breast of a dove, were stuck through the ribbon at the back of his hat. The colors of cloth and rock were coming slowly out of the morning darkness, and ahead, against the yellowing sky, stood the snow peaks, miraculously clear and still. The guide was carrying his ice ax in his hand, using the point of it in the soft soil as he went; and after him came Dr. Sarat, picking, out of habit, the cleanest places in the sucking mud of the cattle path. When he turned to look at her, Willa felt his gaze come up short against his spectacles, seemingly balked there so that he really never saw beyond.

"If he goes too fast, we can slow him down, you know," said Sarat. But the stream was passing in such wild commotion, leaping in such deep and icy warbling spray that Willa did not hear him speaking. She was watching the water as she climbed: here was the substance of the glacier gushing forth like life from a wound, even this morning cold sapping the glacier in such torrents that one wondered how it might survive another summer's heat.

They had begun to mount the spiral path to the first hut, and Sarat was pleased with the feel of health and vigor the climb stirred in his veins. Every step was a thing of measure and purpose to him. He was already taking the scarf from his neck and folding it carefully into his pocket, for the blood was rising in his body. In a little while he would turn to her and say this was man's true repose, when every limb was struck alive with motion. He halted, and turned with a smile hanging on his open lips, and she knew what he would say.

"This is man's true——" he began, but Willa stuck out her tongue.

"You're abominably rude," said Sarat.

"I wish we could climb a mountain once, just once," said Willa, "without having to hear that it is man's true horse feathers."

Walking is a gift, she thought as she followed the two men up in silence. It is a Christmas present given the body to become lighter until at last it is severed wholly from whatever else there is. That is the explanation for the thick and mindless men and women who climb up and down the Alps. After a little, the body disappears. There is no talk, for the lips are closed to save the breath for better things; and at last the climbing hour after hour becomes the separate silent excursion of deliverance. The days begin in the dark and end when the light ends, not coming to a halt because of any decision or rule, but ending when the end has come. Only when the delivered spirit can endure no more of height and solitude and disembodiment does it return, fawning, to the familiar substances and smells.

The dawn was now soaring up, rising as if from the valley, and casting a strong rosy edge from the highest points of snow. The guide had stopped by a spring that gushed swiftly from the dark bronzed rock, slipped the straps from his shoulders, and set the pack down by his side. They had climbed two hours, and now they would sit in the cold damp hollow by the water and eat their bread and cheese, and drink from the lip of rock.

Sarat sat with his legs spread, eating the thick yellow slab of cheese on his bread. He was chewing slowly and watching the tide of slowly gathering sun lifting in the valley below them, the slowly rising transparent wave of powdery yellow mist that was the true beginning of the day. The guide was kneeling, his cheek and the side of his throat lean, his eye shadowed with his lid and lash, his hand thin and brown with a few black hairs laid sparsely across it, holding his folded hat to the murmuring mouth of stone.

"If we had a house here, it would put an end to our troubles," said Sarat out of his peace and wisdom.

The guide lifted his head and looked down the valley.

"There couldn't be a house here," he said. "In the spring the water carries everything away."

"Have you seen that happen?" said Willa. She rested her elbows on her knees and broke her bread in her two hands, and looked quietly at him.

"I come in June," he said. "The floods are over."

He took his package of cigarettes from his pocket and took one into his lean, lipless mouth.

"I suppose we're about the last of the visitors?" said Sarat genially, but the guide did not understand him.

"Last year," said the guide, "there were three visitors killed in August. There was an avalanche on the other side."

"What do you do in the winter?" said Sarat, and the guide did not answer for a moment. Then he said:

"I go to the city."

"You're in luck to have all these months of it," said Sarat, breathing the air in. "Chaps in my kind of business are lucky if they get a fortnight of it in the year." The guide asked no question, so Sarat gave the explanation without it. "I'm a doctor," he said with a deprecatory smile.

The guide smoked his cigarette in his thin cheeks and looked down over the valley.

"I don't believe in doctors," he said.

For a moment Sarat started in his skin, and then he threw back his head in laughter.

"You're damned right!" he said. He slapped his leg and looked, laughing still, at Willa. "What do you think of that?" he said.

Willa sat silent on her piece of rock, her yellow hair back under her cap and her face set against the two men and their talk. She was watching the far streaming of the moist slopes below that smoked with such radiance that it seemed the sun was emanation from their sweltering flanks. The warm light rose from out the succulent earth. It had not reached yet the glacier's ice ahead.

Suddenly the guide lifted his hand and pointed to the rocks that lay beyond the fresh green pasture of the water's fertile land.

"The weather will keep," he said. "You can see the sheep going high."

There was the scattered flock making their way upward; strong mountain sheep as big as calves, their smooth ebony faces turned to the sight of the people, and the wool on their backs matted and dark like a buffalo's thick shawl. A few whitish ones walked among the others, and under their eyes were shadows of disillusionment and the long powdered cheeks of the old and evil and dissipated. Willa saw the flock passing near, their horns worn low like headdresses, carved and close-fitting, Egyptian-like against the sophisticated cheeks, and their features hard as ivory, with the bland, bilious, lingering look for the humans sitting there. Only the tails behind them had no dignity, as if made for smaller, whiter beasts than these.

Sarat took his binoculars from the case over his shoulder and went up the rocks for a wider view of the valley opening out below. And the sheep, with unaltered faces, fled, bucking, up the steep mountainside in fright before him.

"If the weather was going to change, they wouldn't climb," the guide said to Willa. So the clouds gathering at the start of the gorges had no meaning. Willa and the guide sat quiet a little while by the water, and then he said, "If your husband is ready, we could go on now."

But she did not make any move; she did not even turn her head to him. She said, "Are you married?"

The guide smiled, as if this interest was a pleasant thing to him, and he took another cigarette from his pocket.

"No," he said.

His hat was pulled down to his brows, his thin hand holding the match unshaken, unhurried. Their eyes did not turn to meet each other's but remained leveled in distance, remote and cool on the black island of the far needle trees below.

"Sarat's married," Willa said. "I'm not his wife."

The guide took little puffs of his cigarette, seemingly drawing the smoke along his tongue.

"I've taken the habit of being by myself," he said. "I can go and come as I please. It's better."

They seemed to be scarcely speaking, watching the valley and the sun moving up it, each talking as if to himself with the other merely eavesdropping there. Sarat had gone up on the rocks and they had no thought for him; they did not remember him even, and he did not know they had so much as opened their mouths.

"We go up and down mountains like mad all August," said Willa. "There isn't any sense to it. We keep on climbing so as to get away from each other. There used to be some reason for us being together but there isn't any more."

"I do a certain kind of work that is not very much," the guide said, saying what he had not let Sarat know. "In the winter I am a teacher in a school in the city. I teach the boys who want to learn tennis and swimming and riding on horses. In the summer I come back here. This is my own country," he said. "In Heiligenblut I was born."

They did not know that Sarat had come down until he was standing there between them, and Willa looked up into his face for some grievance in his eyes. But he was occupied with buckling the lid of the leather case over and putting the glasses to sleep again.

"I could see the hotel quite clearly," he said to them, smiling. "Every detail. Even the window of our room."

After the first hut, they were to rope themselves. They had soup and bread at the pine table, served by the mistress of the hut, and the guide was served in the corner alone, eating his soup apart from them. It was eight o'clock in the morning, and the sun was beginning to burn in comfort across the windows. The hutkeeper and the guide talked together in the low brightening room, and when the guide was done eating, he went out alone through the sunlight in the door.

"I've been thinking about life," said Sarat. "These natives, having no grasp of its meaning, take it for granted."

"Careless of them, what?" said Willa. She saw the bewilderment and pain traverse his face, the gaze go stubbornly blinded with his patience to forbear. He was smiling at her, the skin on his nose peeling a little.

"You're upset today, Willa," he said.

"I've been thinking about death," said Willa. "Something rather refreshing about it."

"Oh, I daresay it's unlike anything else," said the doctor in facetious irony. "As far as the limited knowledge of man goes, death is believed to be unique."

"Unique's a pretty poor word," said Willa. "I wouldn't be seen dead with it."

The guide had gone out before them, and while Sarat settled with the hutkeeper's wife, Willa walked out over the short bright grass. The guide was waiting at the side of the hut, his pack on his back, his ice ax in his hand, facing a rocky shelter that had been hollowed in the mountain's side. In the half-light under the rock a statue stood, and the guide, with his hat off, was waiting before it. The statue was life size, cast in bronze, and when Willa came close to the man's side she saw that it was the monument set there in memory of a last embrace. There were two figures: a woman's and a man's. The woman wore the bodiced full-skirted dress of fifty years before, bronze braids hung long across her shoulders, and her bare arms clasped the neck of the mountaineer with edelweiss and medals on his hat. He was kissing her face, but his hand with his tall stick in it was lifted, pointing, to the heights above.

In a moment, when the guide turned his head, he saw Willa and he began to uncoil the rope from his waist. "Johannisöl von Heiligenblut," said the inscription. "1875."

"What happened to him?" said Willa. She spoke quietly to him, but her heart was moved as if in pain. It might have been for this, for this innocent young monument of love that she had climbed so far.

"Him?" said the guide, looking quickly up at the statue. "He was killed when the waters came down that spring. He went up to find some of the sheep that had strayed. His wife came this far to say good-by to him. He was my grandfather," he said. He turned his face down to the work of the rope before him in his hands. "Come here," he said, and when she was near to him he put a length of the rope around her. He stood with his arms around her, knotting it at her waist.

"Who put the statue here?" said Willa. His head was lowered below her, the brim of the felt hat cocked and the medals shining, but still she saw the color that came across his cheek.

"I had it put here," he said, facing her with his sharp dark eyes, and then the look of shyness came on him. They were tied together now and he backed away, unwinding the rope as he went. When Sarat came up he would be secured at the other end. "With married people it was different then," he said. "People stayed together. She had her husband, only for a year, but she belonged to her husband. And she had her child. That was enough for her."

"I've never had anything of my own," said Willa. She saw the guide backing away still, backing as if from the touch of her flesh. "Not even Sarat," she said. "He belongs to his wife and his children every other month of the year."

She lifted her hand to put her yellow hair back under her cap, and she saw that her fingers were shaking.

"I've known him three years," she was saying not quite steadily. "I was eighteen when I met him, so everything he said seemed important. He'd been on a polar expedition, and he knew all about free tariff. But, my God," she said, and suddenly she threw out her hand toward the statue and the tears started up in her eyes, "if you think it's ever been anything like that!" she cried out in pain. "If you think it could ever be spoken of like that——"

"Why don't you tell him," the guide said quietly, winding the rope in his hands, "that you would like to fall in love?"

The little glacier began where the grass left off; almost without preparation or pause the earth turned suddenly from rock to ice with scarcely a step of hesitation between. There were a few deep-sunken prints across the sloping desert land of snow, and the guide set his feet in these and led them, toiling, into the blind white wilderness ahead.

The guide led them, and Sarat, with his pack and his binoculars, was roped behind. She could see the movement of the guide's body as he walked, the ear with the dark point of hair before it, the lip of his flannel collar out of his coat, and the piece of his neck burned brown. But here again was the gift of utter isolation made them. All that bound them as they walked was the vein of tough loose rope between, for each in himself was going separately, and the things of love, or of speech, or of restlessness had perished. Now and again black crows, still blacker against the steep bleached plain, went flapping languorously over, passing close enough to show their yellow feet curled inward and to speak distinctly their harsh single sound. But beyond this, the one thing heard of life was the inhuman cry of the guide from time to time in warning before he took a jump across a fissure in the snow.

It was late afternoon, and they had eaten in the second hut, when the last miles of the great open glacier came to sight. It was there below them as they walked, incredible in its wrinkled

absolute unmotion, held wide between the snowy shaly mountains and the cliffs of grass. It seemed prepared to move, or had
perhaps just ceased in movement. There it lay, locked, halted, in
its stone-bedappled gray hide. There was a gentle thickening visible the length of its broad paralytic spine, and the riblike flanks
curved slightly inward toward the land. For even in slumber it
had not ceased to fatten on the lean pickings at the mountain's
roots where even needle trees could not find sustenance.

A feeling of gaiety came over the three people now. They
were unroped and running free above the bed of the glacier over
the gentian-scattered, short bright grass. Sarat went leaping
heavily from clump to clump, his breath short in his mouth, but
humming as he went, and the guide went darting sideways, skipping down. Beside them the edge dropped away to the silent
rump of the glacier. A bit of the roof of the Franz Josef Haus
could be seen far at the end, waiting around the shoulder of
land. The luminous light of evening had begun to wash deeply
down the grass.

Willa took the last jump behind the guide, and then he halted
and stood looking down upon the motionless torrent of ice. He
had a sort of contempt for it, because there was so little danger
in it.

"It's a nice little tourist walk," he said, "if you come up from
the other side."

They could see the far, matchlike figures of the men and
women in twos and threes who picked their way over the soiled
hide of the immobile beast. Far back at the end, toward the desolate wastes of snow, the ice falls were shining out like marble
steps, sheer and elaborate and palatial in the yellow of the setting sun.

Sarat and Willa slung down their packs in the hall of the
Franz Josef Haus and stamped up the timber stairway, the two
of them following the bare-armed maid to the bedroom floor
above. This seemed a shelter of comfort and elegance with bits
of rug on the floor by the beds, and sheets as well as the starch-
encased eiderdown. The house was filled with talk and movement. It seemed to quiver and shake in every plank from the

power of the voices and laughter in the halls and the stamp of the mountain boots on the stairs.

It was not until they came down again, fresh washed in the warmth, with their rough boots off and their slippers on, that Willa remembered the guide would eat away. He had gone off to himself, withdrawn with the others of his kind, for now his work with the foreigners was finished. Willa saw the timber room beyond with the stack of ice axes upright like cornstalks in the corner, the long, uncovered tables, and the benches against the walls. The air, spiraled and veiled with pipe smoke, was visible. And the guides slouched there, eating from the full steaming platters, drinking and talking, and the older ones dozing, their seats tipped back against the wood. That would be the end of him, thought Willa: Sarat will pay him after dinner and there will be nothing more to say.

"Why should everyone make this difference, Sarat?" she said, and they sat down at table in the big dining hall. "Why should the guides be sent off like servants? All day we share whatever comes with them, but at mealtime something like class distinctions begins to play its part. So comforting to know there is a social standard in the mountains! Bring propriety to a glacier! Beautiful, isn't it, *Herr Doktor?*"

"We can have the fellow in, if it comes to that," said Sarat, beginning his goulash. He was never quite content with the evening meal because soup in these Austrian places was out of the ordinary at night. "I'm sure he'd take it as quite the thing. He's pretty certain of himself."

"We could have him in for the *Salzburger Nockerln* and wine," said Willa, and Sarat fixed his glasses on his nose.

After the goulash and beer, Sarat strolled casually out to the guides' dim, smoke-blued room, drawing his head down as he passed under the low beam in the door. Here in the main dining room people were eating their evening meal and talking with a great deal of clatter and commotion: women and men as stout and hale, as ponderous, as cattle, returned to shelter after the day's sweet, strange excursion of the soul. Here they had come as she and Sarat came, to release their spirits for a day or two of silence in the wilderness. But not for too long, not for too fearful a time. When the night fell they drew them back to fire and food and bade them perish in the flesh, and Willa watched the others as they ate.

In a little while Sarat came back, came slowly through the crowded dining hall, with his hands idly in his pockets in a semblance of ease. A little behind him followed the guide, his head lowered, his soiled boots sounding loud and impersonal upon the pine planks of the floor. There was a clean, blond, shining look in the bespectacled countenance of Sarat coming smiling to the table, and the guide behind him seemed humbled and frail, as if disoriented among these stronger, light-haired people.

But once he had taken the place facing Willa and tasted his wine, the change came over him. He talked with Sarat, but his eyes moved in pride and power over her hands and her arms on the table, dark and secret over her face and her hair.

"You should go up the Gross Glockner," he was saying. "It is too bad to go away without going up. The climb is easy, five hours maybe, over the snow."

The red wine and the soft sugared omelet were divided among them, and Sarat took two cigars from his silver case and gave the guide one.

"The ways down are different," said the guide. "You can come down by the rocks. It makes it more difficult."

"I won't climb any more," said Willa. She sat with her face gone vague and soft, her eyes drugged heavy with wine, or sleep, or love. "I won't climb any more. I'm not a bloody excursionist. I want to stay a long time in these places. By myself, anyway, as long as I stay. I won't go up any more and I won't go down," she said. "I'm going to spend the night finding the peace of mind to stay by myself here or some other good place forever. Or until I'm old, or until I'm ugly as sin. I believe in God, Sarat, in my own God that *Herr Doktors* don't know anything about. Thingumabob here doesn't believe in doctors. Neither do I. I'm going to sit here forever until I find someone who believes in the excursion of the soul."

"You'll probably sit a long time!" said Sarat, laughing. He looked quickly at the guide's face to see what he was making of it all. The guide was sitting quite still, listening.

"I don't mind how long I wait," said Willa. "Fill up the glasses, Sarat. Just because you got me up a mountain doesn't mean you're going to get me down. I'm not going back to England. That's the end of that."

"Look here," said Sarat quickly, and he put out his hand and took her tumbler of wine. "You've had a long pull, Willa, old girl. Why don't you call it a day?"

"We might as well have it out, Sarat," she said. She drew her glass back across the table and drank down the wine. "You can't take people on high places and then expect them to take what's left over after. I'm not having any more rural valleys. I'm going to stay up here. England and the medical profession will just have to muddle along without me."

Sarat put his cigar down in the blue dish, and settled his spectacles on his nose.

"You're being a bit silly, Willa," he said. And then he turned genially to the guide. "What's this about the Gross Glockner?" he inquired.

"We came along across from it today," said the guide. "It's the best climb in the country. If you like to come down by the rocks there's a needle to scale down. That makes it a little more difficult. They call her the Maiden. They call her that," he said, and he smiled, "because not many men have been able to reach her."

Sarat laughed pleasantly at this and said: "You've been one of the lucky ones, I suppose?"

"Yes," said the guide. "I've been twice there. In the day you can see her through the telescope outside. All summer there's a little piece of snow left, like her face, near the top."

Willa lifted her drugged soft eyes and smiled at him.

"Say that again," she said. "Please say it."

The guide looked at her and the color moved slowly up to his clear burned brow.

"Very well," said Sarat shortly. He picked up his cigar again and struck a match for it. For all his calmness, there was a glint of outraged patience in his eye. He could not defy her, not here, not in private, but his mind was stubbornly setting for him and the guide to go off together. They would go up the Glockner, and they would come down the difficult way, by the Maiden, leaving her the rebuke of solitude as if meting out punishment to a willful child. "I don't see why we shouldn't have a try at it to-morrow," said Sarat. "The two of us. My wife has done enough for a day or so."

"If we start at four it will be early enough," said the guide, and Sarat nodded.

"Good," he said. "Have them wake me shortly after three." He stood up and dropped his hand genially on the guide's shoulder. "Well, good night," he said. He looked at Willa, smiling. "I'm turning in, Willa, as long as I'm starting early. You do as you like. Don't worry about me."

They saw him go out into the hall, close the glass-paned door behind him, and mount the flimsy timber of the stairs. When he was out of sight their eyes came back and met. Willa stood up and buttoned her jacket.

"I'm going out to see the glacier, what's-your-name," she said.

She went out through the hall, and through the door at the back, and she stood in the cold, on the threshold. Lying wide and monstrous in the pass below was the dark-scarred glacier, seemingly tossed in iron tumult like a wintry sea. Beyond it were the black mountainsides, and on their heights the glittering crests of snow standing sharp in the cave of nightly blue. The moon was high and delicate in the sky, but its light, bleached as starlight, came from all sides and flooded richly over the entire land. There was no sound of movement or of water falling. The cold and calm expanse annihilated in silence any remembrance of sound.

The guide came out on the stone step, and, with a quick shud-der of cold, he closed the heavy door behind him. It was not yet ten at night, but the house was darkened, and a sense of deep unbroken slumbering had fallen on the solitary, mountain place. For a little while, Willa felt him beside her in the wan icy night, and then the guide put his arms around her and drew her close against him. As if in fear, he kissed her face.

After a long time, he said: "I haven't anything to give you."

Her arms were around him, and she could feel the bones of his shoulders sharp and strong through the arch of his velvet wings.

His mouth was fresh with wild, new kisses, and here on the shelter's step was the heart of warmth and promise, and the dead abandoned world beyond bathed in floods of purest cold.

"We'll have a good life," said Willa softly. In wonder she could feel it coming to life in the falling of warm tears on her face. "Say that we'll have a good life, say it!" she whispered.

"Yes," said the guide, "yes. You know how I want it. Maiden," said the guide, "maiden, maiden, maiden," out of his bewilderment of love.

But even the words of love were lost to them, withered and shed in the utter durability of silent cold. Only their hands and faces opened slowly to each other, touch by touch, like flowers unfolding to a simulation of the sun's pure heat. They did not know how long they stood, left living in the unmoving deathly blast of the glacier's exhalation. It lay below, unseen now in their sight excluded to each other, but awful in its presence, like a body left uncovered in its grave.

It was the voices of the children calling that awoke her. She heard the clear far shaking of the goat bells, and then the voices of the children calling: "*Mägdlein, Mägdlein!*" in the scarcely broken morning. From the narrow bed she could see the first of the goats hesitating on the crests of shale and grass beyond the open window, their chins shifting, their ears shaped in indecision toward the children's call.

"*Mägdlein, Mägdlein!*" the children cried out in high voices, and despite themselves the goats made answer, speaking their small nasal sound. "Come, come, come here!" the children called, wooing the goats down to drain their milk from them. But the goats were new to motherhood, surely this was the first young they had borne, and there was still a sweet rebellion in them. So the children with their pails must climb up the cliffs after the shaking bells and the soft humanlike words of answer. "*Mägdlein, Mägdlein!*" called the children, and the goats lifted their heads, harking, and bleated. But if the hands reached out to touch them, they tossed the ripening horns on their brows and swerved across the grass.

Willa put fresh linen on, made her pack, separating the things of her own from Sarat's things, and the morning went by warm and idle in the sun. She lay, her eyes covered, stretched out on a bench in the heat, without impatience, waiting in indolence for the men's return. In the evening she would say it to Sarat, and once it was said she could take the road with the guide to Heiligenblut. "Holy blood, holy blood," she said in her heart. She felt it moving deep and exultant in her, the wondrous thrust of what was to begin piercing swift and blissful in her flesh.

The keeper of the Franz Josef Haus pointed out the ways to her in the afternoon, and she stood behind the telescope sweeping the long glass eye over the precipices of shale and snow. It was early still, it was hardly four, and the towers of the Gross Glockner each bore a gleaming metal side. After a while she caught one man clearly in the lens: a dark single thing scarcely moving, scarcely descending above the chasms of stone.

Willa called out to the housemaster. "There's one man coming down," she said, but the housemaster shook his head.

"No one does it alone," he said, and he took the solitary eye of vision to him. She saw his face at the glass squint, seek, and alter. "*Ja,* only one. That's so," he said.

It was five o'clock when a party of people appeared on the far edge of the glacier. They themselves had descended the mountain and were making their slow, plodding, seemingly motionless advance over the indifferent flanks of ice. But still they were advancing, the six pack-burdened strangers.

"They may have seen the others," said the housemaster, shifting, adjusting, seeking explanation for the single figure in the blank uncanny eye.

They were a long time coming, they were better than an hour on the glacier, and when they came up the path they were breathless, for they were coming fast. Willa and the housemaster went out to meet them: there were two women and four men and in their faces there was the shock and strain of warning.

Willa stood by the housemaster and listened to the slow absolute German speech. She had no real belief in what they said nor any fear or pain to meet the curious distress they labored under. When they had done talking, she said, "Was it an Englishman you saw?"

But that none of the six could tell. He had been so far, calling separate words through his hands to them; and the one who had been struck down they never saw at all. He was out of sight where he had fallen, and the other one calling down from so far to them to say he was going down to where the man had dropped, and that he would wait there until they sent help back. How was the one dressed? Oh, he had a short jacket on, of course. And glasses? Two of them said he had worn glasses; they had seen them taking the light of the sun. But the women said that it was the guide medals on his hat they saw shining. They agreed that he seemed to have no accent when he called out to them, but it was from such a distance they could not be certain even of that.

"He said the other one had been hit with a falling rock and he was going to him. We were close to this side, and much lower, so it seemed useless to go back. Three of our party are new climbers and it was the most dangerous way to go."

"An Englishman and his guide went up this morning," the housemaster told them, and suddenly Willa's heart went still, as if she had heard the truth at last.

"Who was the guide?" said one of the men.

"Johannisöl of Heiligenblut," the housemaster said.

The guides were well out on the ice with the emergency sledge running sideways behind them, when Willa set out alone on the glacier. She was walking the way they had gone, Sarat and the guide in the early morning, picking her way over the hard riddled crust toward the tall fair figure of the white-faced Maiden, walking, walking, until in a while the gift of deliverance was made and the flesh severed wholly from fear or calculation. Her head, stung clean with air, was floating lightly in abeyance toward the Glockner and its Maiden and the high pale slopes of snow. The men traversing the glacier with their sledge and sticks were fixed in motion, swimming without progression in the slow dying fire of the ebbing light. There seemed to be no advance made, none sought for nor desired. The distance did not lessen or increase between herself and the group dignified by its heroic measure.

The two names, Sarat and Johannisöl, drifted, faceless, on the slow deep flux of musing: one was lying dead or dying in the mountains and one was walking down alive. Whoever had survived was descending over the rocks; through the telescope they had seen him coming. And whichever of the two he was, Willa was going out to meet him, perhaps not believing in death so soon, or believing that the flesh did not move from ecstasy to tragedy with so little respite given. For a moment she had believed that it would be Sarat who was saved, but once the power of walking had quelled the tumult in her, she knew it would be the guide, and that she had never doubted it would be the guide come down alive because of the vision borne in his face of two lives miraculously given to his keeping.

She stopped still on the ice when she heard the guides calling back to her. The dark was beginning, and their voices returned distinct through the chill imperfect light.

"He's coming down, he's coming down! He's on the glacier, your man, your man!" they were crying back, as if in comfort and assurance to her. "The Englishman is on the ice! Your man, your man," they said.

She ran forward, shouting, and the tears fell down her face and into her open mouth. She was talking aloud as she ran, and crying, with her tongue shaken loose and wild in her head.

"Sarat," she said. "Sarat, oh, yes, Sarat, Sarat, Sarat, where's thingumabob, oh, God, where's what's-his-name?"

She heard her own sharp bitter cries, as if witnessing the mad bereavement of a stranger who stumbled past her, crying mercilessly, shaking her grief-stricken empty hands before her as she ran.

"Where's thingumajig?" she cried. "Sarat, you beast, you're a doctor and you left him! Where's what's-his-name?"

Sarat was coming over the ice, past the guides and the sledge, his face sapped thin and bloodless with what had befallen, his mouth white with what had become of the day. He put his arm tight around Willa to halt her shaking.

"It's all right, little girl, it's all right, I'm here," he said. "There was nothing to be done for the poor chap by the time I got there. It was all over. It might have been me, Willa," he said, holding her to keep the teeth from rattling from her head. "It might just as easily have been me," he said.

The White Horses of Vienna

I

The doctor often climbed the mountain at night, climbed up behind his own house hour after hour in the dark, and came back to bed long after his two children were asleep. At the end of June he sprained his knee coming down the mountain late. He wrenched it out of joint making his way down with the other men through the pines. They helped him into the house where his wife was waiting and writing letters by the stove, and the agony that he would not mention was marked upon his face.

His wife bound his leg with fresh, wet cloths all through the night, but in the morning the knee was hot with fever. It might be weeks before he could go about again, and there was nothing to do but write to the hospital in Vienna for a student-doctor to come out and take over his patients for a time.

"I'll lie still for a fortnight or so," said the doctor, and he asked his wife to bring him the bits of green wood that he liked to whittle, and his glazed papers and his fancy tag ends of stuff. He was going to busy himself making new personages for his theater, for he could not stay idle for half an hour. The June sun was strong at that height, and the doctor sat on the *Liegestuhl* with his knee bared to the warm light, working like a well man and looking up now and again to the end of the valley where the mountains stood with the snow shining hard and diamond-bright on their brows.

"You'll never sit still long enough for it to do you any good," said the doctor's wife sharply. She was quite a young, beautiful woman, in spite of her two growing sons, and in spite of her hus-

band's ageless, weathered flesh. She was burned from the wind
and the snow in winter and burned from the sun at other times
of the year; she had straight, long, sunburned limbs, and her
dark hair was cut short and pushed behind her ears. She had her
nurse's degree from Vienna and she helped her husband in whatever there was to do: the broken bones, the deaths, the births.
He even did a bit of dentistry too, when there was need, and she
stood by in her nurse's blouse and mixed the cement and porcelain fillings and kept the instruments clean. Or at night, if they
needed her, she climbed the mountain with him and the other
men, carrying as well a knapsack of candles over her shoulders,
climbing through the twig-broken and mossy silence in the dark.

The doctor had built their house himself with the trees cut
down from their forest. The town lay in the high valley, and the
doctor had built their house above it on the sloping mountainside. There was no real road leading to it: one had to get to him
on foot or else on a horse. It was as if the doctor had chosen this
place to build so that the village might leave him to himself unless the need were very great. He had come back to his own
country after the years as a prisoner of war in Siberia, and after
the years of studying in other countries, and the years of giving
away as a gift his tenderness and knowledge as he went from one
wild place to another. He had studied in cities, but he could not
live for long in them. He had come back and bought a piece of
land in the Tirol with a pine forest sloping down it, and he built
his house there, working throughout the summer months late
into the evening with only his two sons and his wife to help him
lift the squared, varnished beams into place.

Inside the log walls the doctor made a pure white plaster wall
and put his dark-stained bookshelves against it and hung on it
his own paintings of Dalmatia and his drawings of the Siberian
country. Everything was as neat and clean as wax, for the doctor
was a savagely clean man. He had a coarse, reddish, well-
scrubbed skin, and the gold hairs sprang out of his scalp, wavy
and coarse, and out of his forearms and his muscular, heavy
thighs. They would have sprung too around his mouth and along
his jaw had he not shaved himself clean every morning. His face

was as strong as rock, but it had seen so much of suffering that it had the look of being scarred, it seemed to be split in two, with one side of it given to resolve and the other to compassion.

All of the places that he had been before, Paris and Moscow and Munich and Constantinople, had never left an evil mark. None of the grand places or people had ever done to him what they can do. But merely because of his own strong, humble pride in himself his shirt was always a white one, and of fresh, clean linen no matter what sort of work he was doing. In the summer he wore the short, leather trousers of the country, for he had peasants behind him and he liked to remember that it was so. But the woven stockings that ended just above his calves were perfectly white and the nails of his broad, coarse hands were white. They were spotless, like the nails of a woman's hand.

The day the student doctor arrived from Vienna and walked up from the village, the doctor and his wife were both out in the sun before the house. She had been hanging the children's shirts up on the line to dry, and she came around to the timber piazza, drying her hands in her dress. The doctor was hopping around on one leg like a great, golden, wounded bird; he was hopping from one place to another, holding his wrenched leg off the ground, and seeking the bits of paper and stuff and wood and wire that he needed to make his dolls.

"Let me get the things for you!" his wife cried out. "Why must you do everything for yourself? Why can't you let anyone help you?"

The doctor hopped across to the timber table in the sun and picked up the clown's cap he was making and fitted it on the head of the doll he held in his hand. When he turned around he saw the student-doctor coming up the path. He stood still for a moment, with his leg still lifted up behind him, and then his face cleared of whatever was in it, and he nodded.

"God greet you," he said quietly, and the young man stopped too where he was on the path and looked up at them. He was smiling in his long, dark, alien face, but his city shoes were foul with the soft mud of the mountainside after rain, and the sweat was standing out on his brow because he was not accustomed to the climb.

"Good day," he said, as city people said it. The doctor and his wife stood looking down at him, and a little wave of pallor ran under the woman's skin.

The doctor had caught a very young fox in the spring, and it had now grown to live in the house with them without shyness or fear. The sound of their voices and the new human scent on the air brought it forth from the indoor dark of the house. It came out without haste, like a small, gentle dog, with its soft, gray, gently lifted brush and its eyes blinking slowly at the sun. It went daintily down the path toward the stranger, holding its brush just out of the mud of the path, with the black bead of its nose smelling the new smell of this other man who had come.

The young doctor from Vienna leaned over to stroke it, and while his head was down the doctor's wife turned to her husband. She had seen the black, smooth hair on the man's head, and the arch of his nose, and the quality of his skin. She could scarcely believe what she had seen and she must look into her husband's face for confirmation of the truth. But her husband was still looking down the little space toward the stranger. The fox had raised the sharp point of his muzzle and licked the young doctor's hand.

"Is this a dog or a cat?" the young man called up, smiling.

"It's a fox," said the doctor. The young man came up with his hat in his hand and said that his name was Heine and shook hands, and the doctor gave no sign.

"You live quite a way from the village," said the student-doctor, looking back the way he had come.

"You can see the snow mountains from here," said the doctor, and he showed the young man the sight of them at the far end of the valley. "You have to climb this way before you can see them," he said. "They're closed off from the valley."

This was the explanation of why they lived there, and the young man from the city stood looking a moment in silence at the far, gleaming crusts of the everlasting snows. He was still thinking of what he might say in answer when the doctor asked his wife to show Dr. Heine the room that would be his. Then the doctor sat down in the sun again and went on with the work he had been doing.

"What are we going to do?" said his wife's voice in a whisper behind him in a moment.

"What do you mean? About what?" said the doctor, speaking aloud. His crisp-haired head did not lift from his work, and the lines of patience and love were scarred deep in his cheeks as he whittled.

"About *him*," said the doctor's wife in hushed impatience.

"Send one of the boys down for his bag at the station," said the doctor. "Give him a drink of *Apfelsaft* if he's thirsty."

"But don't you see, don't you see what he is?" asked his wife's wild whisper.

"He's Viennese," said the doctor, working.

"Yes, and he's Jewish," said his wife. "They must be mad to have sent him. They know how everyone feels."

"Perhaps they did it intentionally," said the doctor, working carefully with what he had in his hands. "But it wasn't a good thing for the young man's sake. It's harder on him than us. If he works well, I have no reason to send him back. We've waited three days for him. There are people sick in the village."

"Ah," said his wife in anger behind, "we shall have to sit down at table with him!"

"They recommend him highly," said the doctor gently, "and he seems a very amiable young man."

"Ah," said his wife's disgusted whisper, "they all look amiable! Every one of them does!"

Almost at once there was a tooth to be pulled, and the young wife was there in her white frock with the instruments ready for the new young man. She stood very close, casting sharp looks at Dr. Heine, watching his slender, delicate hands at work, seeing the dark, silky hairs that grew on the backs of them and the black hair brushed smooth on his head. So much had she heard about Jews that the joints of his tall, elegant frame seemed oiled with some special, suave lubricant that was evil, as a thing come out of the Orient, to their clean, Nordic hearts. He had a pale skin, unused to the weather of mountain places, and his skull was lighted with bright, quick, ambitious eyes. But at lunch he had talked simply with them, although they were country people and ignorant as peasants for all he knew. He listened to everything the doctor had told him about the way he liked things done; in spite of his modern medical school and his Viennese hospitals, taking it all in with interest and respect.

"The doctor," said the young wife now, "always stands behind the patient to get at teeth like that."

She spoke in an undertone to Dr. Heine so that the peasant sitting there in the dentist chair with the cocaine slowly paralyzing his jaws might not overhear.

"Oh, yes. Thank you so much," said Dr. Heine with a smile, and he stepped behind the patient. "It's quite true. One can get a better grip that way."

But as he passed the doctor's wife, the tail of his white coat brushed through the flame of the little sterilizing lamp on the table. Nobody noticed that Dr. Heine had caught fire until the tooth was out and the smell of burning cloth filled the clean, white room. They looked about for what might be smoldering in the place, and in another moment the doctor's wife saw that Dr. Heine was burning very brightly: the back of the white jacket was eaten nearly out and the coat within it was flaming. He had even begun to feel the heat on his shirt when the doctor's wife picked up the strip of rug from the floor and flung it about him. She held it tightly around him with her bare, strong arms, and the young man looked back over his shoulder at her, and he was laughing.

"Now I shall lose my job," he said. "The doctor will never stand for me setting fire to myself the first day like this!"

"It's my fault," said the doctor's wife, holding him fast still in her arms. "I should have had the lamp out of the way."

She began to beat his back softly with the palm of her hand, and when she carried the rug to the window, Dr. Heine went to the mirror and looked over his shoulder at the sight of his clothes all burned away.

"My new coat!" he said, and he was laughing. But it must have been very hard for him to see the nice, gray flannel coat that he had bought to look presentable for his first place scalloped black to his shoulders where the fire had eaten its covert way.

"I should think I could put a piece in," said the doctor's wife, touching the good cloth that was left. And then she bit her lip suddenly and stood back, as if she had remembered the evil thing that stood between them.

II

When they sat down to supper, the little fox settled himself on the doctor's good foot, for the wool of his stocking was a soft bed where the fox could dream a little while. They had soup and the thick, rosy-meated leg of a pig and salt potatoes, and the children listened to their father and Dr. Heine speaking of music, and painting, and books together. The doctor's wife was cutting the meat and putting it on their plates. It was at the end of the meal that the young doctor began talking of the royal, white horses in Vienna, still royal, he said, without any royalty left to bow their heads to, still shouldering into the arena with spirits a man would give his soul for, bending their knees in homage to the empty, canopied loge where royalty no longer sat. They came in, said Dr. Heine in his rich, eager voice, and danced their statuesque dances, their *pas de deux*, their croupade, their capriole. They were very impatient of the walls around them and the bits in their soft mouths, and very vain of the things they had been taught to do. Whenever the applause broke out around them, said Dr. Heine, their nostrils opened wide as if a wind were blowing. They were actresses, with the deep, snowy breasts of prima donnas, these perfect stallions who knew to a breath the beauty of even their mockery of fright.

"There was a maharaja," said the young doctor, and the children and their father listened, and the young wife sat giving quick, unwilling glances at this man who could have no blood or knowledge of the land behind him; for what was he but a wanderer whose people had wandered from country to country and whose sons must wander, having no land to return to in the end? "There was a maharaja just last year," said Dr. Heine, "who went to the performance and fell in love with one of the horses. He saw it dancing and he wanted to buy it and take it back to India with him. No one else had ever taken a Lippizaner back to his country, and he wanted this special one, the best of them all, whose dance was like an angel flying. So the state agreed that he could buy the horse, but for a tremendous amount of money. They needed the money badly enough, and the maharaja was a very rich man." Oh, yes, thought the young mother bitterly, you would speak about money, you would come here and climb our mountain and poison my sons with the poison of money and greed! "But no matter how high the price was," said Dr. Heine, smiling because all their eyes were on him, "the maharaja agreed to pay it, provided that the man who rode the horse so beautifully came along as well. Yes, the state would allow that too, but the maharaja would have to pay an enormous salary to the rider. He would take him into his employ as the stallion's keeper, and he would have to pay him a salary as big as our own President is paid!" said Dr. Heine, and he ended this with a burst of laughter.

"And what then, what then?" said one of the boys as the student-doctor paused to laugh. The whole family was listening, but the mother was filled with outrage. These things are foreign to us, she was thinking. They belong to more sophisticated people, we do not need them here. The Spanish Riding School, the gentlemen of Vienna, they were as alien as places in another country, and the things they cherished could never be the same.

"So it was arranged that the man who rode the horse so well should go along too," said Dr. Heine. "It was finally arranged for a great deal of money," he said, and the mother gave him a look of fury. "But they had not counted on one thing. They had forgotten all about the little groom who had always cared for this special horse and who loved him better than anything else in the world. Ever since the horse had come from the stud farm in Styria, the little groom had cared for him, and he believed that they would always be together, he believed that he would go wherever the horse went, just as he had always gone to Salzburg with the horse in the summer, and always come back to Vienna with it in the wintertime again."

"And so what, what happened?" asked the other boy.

"Well," said the student-doctor, "the morning before the horse was to leave with the maharaja and the rider, they found that the horse had a deep cut on his leg, just above the hoof in front. Nobody could explain how it had happened, but the horse was so wounded that he could not travel then and the maharaja said that he could go on without him and that the trainer should bring the horse over in a few weeks when the cut had healed. They did not tell the maharaja that it might be that the horse could never dance so beautifully again. They had the money and they weren't going to give it back so easily," said Dr. Heine, and to the mother it seemed that their shrewdness pleased his soul. "But when the cut had healed," he went on, "and the horse seemed well enough to be sent by the next boat, the trainer found the horse had a cut on the other hoof, exactly where the other wound had been. So the journey was postponed again, and again the state said nothing to the maharaja about the horse being so impaired that it was likely he could never again fly like an angel. But in a few days the horse's blood was so poisoned from the wound that they had to destroy him."

They all waited, breathless with pain a moment, and then the doctor's wife said bitterly:

"Even the money couldn't save him, could it?"

"No," said Dr. Heine, a little perplexed by her words. "Of course, it couldn't. And they never knew how the cuts had come there until the little groom committed suicide the same day the horse was destroyed. And then they knew that he had done it himself because he couldn't bear the horse to be taken away."

They were all sitting quietly there at the table, with the dishes and remnants of food still before them, when someone knocked at the outside door. One of the boys went out to open it and he came back with the Heimwehr men following after him, the smooth, little black-and-white cockades lying forward in their caps.

"God greet you," said the doctor quietly when he saw them.

"God greet you," said the Heimwehr men.

"There's a swastika fire burning on the mountain behind you," said the leader of the soldiers. They were not men of the village, but men brought from other parts of the country and billeted there as strangers to subdue the native people. "Show us the fastest way up there so we can see that it's put out."

"I'm afraid I can't do that," said the doctor, smiling. "You see, I have a bad leg."

"You can point out to us which way the path goes!" said the leader sharply.

"He can't move," said the doctor's wife, standing straight by the chair. "You have reports on everything. You must know very well that he is injured and has had a doctor come from Vienna to look after the sick until he can get around again."

"Yes," said the leader, "and we know very well that he wouldn't have been injured if he stayed home instead of climbing mountains himself at night!"

"Look here," said the student-doctor, speaking nervously, and his face gone thin and white. "He can't move a step, you know."

"He'll have to move more than a step if they want him at the *Rathaus* again!" said the Heimwehr leader. "There's never any peace as long as he's not locked up!"

The young doctor said nothing after they had gone, but he sat quiet by the window, watching the fires burning on the mountains in the dark. They were blooming now on all the black, invisible crests, marvelously living flowers of fire springing out of the arid darkness, seemingly higher than any other things could grow. He felt himself sitting defenseless there by the window, surrounded by these strong, long-burning fires of disaster. They were all about him, inexplicable signals given from one mountain to another in some secret gathering of power that cast him and his people out, forever out upon the waters of despair.

The doctor's wife and the children had cleared the table, and the doctor was finishing his grasshopper underneath the light. He was busy wiring its wings to its body, and fastening the long, quivering antennae in. The grasshopper was colored a deep, living green, and under him lay strong, green-glazed haunches for springing with his wires across the puppet stage. He was a monstrous animal in the doctor's hands, with his great, glassy, gold-veined wings lying smooth along his back.

"The whole country is ruined by the situation," said the student-doctor, suddenly angry. "Everything is politics now. One can't meet people, have friends on any other basis. It's impossible to have casual conversations or abstract discussions any more. Who the devil lights these fires?"

"Some people light them because of their belief," said the doctor, working quietly, "and others travel around from place to place and make a living lighting them."

"Politics, politics," said the student-doctor, "and one party as bad as another. You're much wiser to make your puppets, *Herr Doktor*. It takes one's mind off things, just as playing cards does. In Vienna we play cards, always play cards, no matter what is happening."

"There was a time for cards," said the doctor, working quietly with the grasshopper's wings. "I used to play cards in Siberia, waiting to be free. We were always waiting then for things to finish with and be over," he said. "There was nothing to do, so we did that. But now there is something else to do."

He said no more, and in a little while the student-doctor went upstairs to bed. He could hear the doctor's wife and the children still washing the dishes and tidying up, their voices clearly heard through the fresh planks of his new-made floor.

Usually in the evening the doctor played the marionette theater for his wife and children, and for whatever friends wanted to come up the mountainside and see. He had made the theater himself, and now he had the new personages he had fashioned while nursing his twisted knee, and a week or two after the student-doctor had come he told them at supper that he would give them a show that night.

"The *Bürgermeister* is coming up with his wife and their young sons," he said, "and the *Apotheker* and his nephews sent word that they'd drop in as well."

He moved the little fox from where it was sleeping on the wool sock of his foot, and he hopped on his one good leg across the room. Dr. Heine helped him carry the theater to the corner and set it up where the curtains hung, and the doctor hopped, heavy, and clean, and birdlike, from side to side and behind and before to get the look of the light and see how the curtains drew and fell.

By eight o'clock they were all of them there and seated in the darkened room, the doctor's and the *Bürgermeister*'s boys wait-

ing breathless for the curtain to rise, and the *Apotheker*'s nephews smoking in the dark.

"I think it's marvelous, your husband giving plays like this,
keeping the artistic thing uppermost even with times as they
are," said Dr. Heine quietly to the doctor's wife. "One gets so
tired of the same question everywhere, anywhere one happens
to be," he said, and she gave him a long, strange, bitter glance
from the corners of her eyes.

"Yes," she said. "Yes. I suppose you do think a great deal of
art."

"Yes, of course," said Dr. Heine, quite guilelessly. "Art and
science, of course."

"Yes," said the doctor's wife, saying the words slowly and bitterly. "Yes. Art and science. What about people being hungry,
what about this generation of young men who have never had
work in their lives because the factories have never opened since
the war? Where do they come in?"

"Yes, that too——" Dr. Heine began, and the whispered dialogue ended.

The curtain had been jerked aside and a wonderful expectancy lay on the air.

The scene before them was quite a simple one: the monstrously handsome grasshopper was sitting in a field, presumably
a field, for there were white linen-petaled, yellow-hearted daisies
all around him. He was a great, gleaming beauty, and the people watching cried out with pleasure. The doctor's sons could
scarcely wait until the flurry of delight had died and the talking
had begun.

There were only two characters in the play, and they were the
grasshopper and the clown. The clown came out on the stage
and joined him after the grasshopper had done his elegant
dance. The dance in itself was a masterpiece of grace and wit,
with the music of Mozart playing on the gramophone behind.
The children cried with laughter, and Dr. Heine shouted aloud,
and the *Bürgermeister* shook with silent laughter. It lifted its
legs so delicately, and sprang with such precision this way and
that, through the ragged-petaled daisies of the field, that it
seemed to have a life of its own in its limbs, separate from and

more sensitive than that given it by any human hand. Even the little fox sat watching in fascination, his bright, unwild eyes shining like points of fire in the dark.

"*Wunderbar, wunderschön!*" Dr. Heine called out. "It's really marvelous! He's as graceful as the white horses at Vienna, *Herr Doktor!* That step with the forelegs floating! It's extraordinary how you got it without ever seeing it done!"

And then the little clown came out on the stage. He came through the daisies of the field, a small, dwarfed clown with a sword ten times too big for him girded around his waist and tripping him at every step as he came. He was carrying a bunch of paper flowers and smiling, and there was something very *friseur* about him. He had no smell of the really open country or the roots of things, while the grasshopper was a fine, green-armored animal, strong and perfectly equipped for the life he had to lead.

The clown had a round, human face and he spoke in a faltering human voice, and the grasshopper was the superthing, speaking in the doctor's ringing voice. Just the sound of the doctor's compassionate voice released in all its power was enough to make the guilty and the weak shake in their seats as if it were some accusation made them. It was a voice as ready for honest anger as it was for gentleness.

"Why do you carry artificial flowers?" the grasshopper asked, and the clown twisted and turned on his feet, so ridiculous in his stupidity that the children and all the others watching laughed aloud in the timber room. "Why do you carry artificial flowers?" the grasshopper persisted. "Don't you see that the world is full of real ones?"

"Oh, it's better I carry artificial ones," said the clown in the humorous accent of the country boor, and he tripped on his sword as he said it. "I'm on my way to my own funeral, *nicht?* I want the flowers to keep fresh until I get there."

Everyone laughed very loud at this, but after a little, as the conversation continued between the grasshopper and the clown, Dr. Heine found he was not laughing as loudly as before. It was now evident that the grasshopper, for no conceivable reason, was always addressed as "The Leader," and the humorous little clown was called "Chancellor" by the grasshopper for no reason that he could see. The Chancellor was quite the fool of the piece. The only thing he had to support him was a very ludicrous faith in the power of the Church. The Church was a wonderful thing, the clown kept saying, twisting his poor bouquet.

"The cities are full of churches," said the Leader, "but the country is full of God."

The Leader spoke with something entirely different in his voice: he had a wild and stirring power that sent the cold of wonder up and down one's spine. And whatever the argument was, the Chancellor always got the worst of it. The children cried aloud with laughter, for the Chancellor was so absurd, so eternally on his half-witted way to lay his bunch of paper flowers on his own or somebody else's grave, and the Leader was ready to waltz away at any moment with the power of stallion life that was leaping in his limbs.

"I believe in the independence of the individual," the poor humble smiling little clown said, and then he tripped over his sword and fell flat among the daisies. The Leader picked him up with his fragile, lovely forelegs, and set him against the painting of the sky.

"Ow, *mein Gott,* the clouds are giving way!" cried the clown, and the grasshopper replied gently:

"But you are relying upon the heavens to support you. Are you afraid they are not strong enough?"

III

It was one evening in July, and the rain had just drawn off over the mountains. There was still the smell of it on the air, but the moon was shining strongly out. The student-doctor walked out before the house and watched the light bathing the dark valley, rising over the fertile slopes and the pine forests, running clear as milk above the timber line across the bare, bleached rock. The higher one went, the more terrible it became, he thought, and his heart shuddered within him. There were the rocks, seemingly as high as substance could go, but beyond that, even higher, hidden from the sight of the village people but clearly seen from the doctor's house, was the bend of the glacier and beside it were the peaks of everlasting snow. He was lost in this wilderness of cold, lost in a warm month, and the thought turned his blood to ice. He wanted to be indoors, with the warmth of his own people, and the intellect speaking. He had had enough of the bare, northern speech of these others who moved higher and higher as the land moved.

It was then that he saw the little lights moving up from the valley, coming like little beacons of hope carried to him. People were moving up out of the moon-bathed valley, like a little search party come to seek for him in an alien land. He stood watching the slow, flickering movement of their advance, the lights they carried seen far below, a small necklace of men coming to him; and then the utter white-darkness spread unbroken as they entered the wooded places and their lamps were extinguished by the trees.

"Come to me," he was saying within himself, "come to me. I am a young man alone on a mountain. I am a young man alone, as my race is alone, lost here amongst them all."

· The doctor and his wife were sitting at work by the table when Dr. Heine came quickly into the room and said:

"There are some men coming up. They're almost here now. They look to me like the Heimwehr come again."

The doctor's wife stood up and touched the side of the timber wall as if something in it would give her fortitude. Then she went to the door and opened it, and in a moment the Heimwehr men came in.

"God greet you," the doctor said as they gathered around the table.

"God greet you," said the Heimwehr leader. "You're wanted at the *Rathaus*," he said.

"My leg isn't good enough to walk on yet," said the doctor quietly. "How will you get me down?"

"This time we brought a stretcher along," said the Heimwehr leader. "We have it outside the door."

The doctor's wife went off to fetch his white wool jacket and to wake the two boys in their beds. Dr. Heine heard her saying:

"They're taking Father to prison again. Now you must come and kiss him. Neither of you is going to cry."

The men brought the stretcher just within the doorway and the doctor hopped over to it and lay down. He looked very comfortable there under the wool rug that his wife laid over him.

"Look here," said Dr. Heine, "why do you have to come after a person at night like this? Do you think the *Herr Doktor* would try to run away from you? What are you up to? What's it all about?"

The Heimwehr leader looked him full in the eyes.

"They got Dollfuss this afternoon," he said. "They shot him in Vienna. We're rounding them all up tonight. Nobody knows what will happen tomorrow."

"Ah, politics, politics again!" cried Dr. Heine, and he was wringing his hands like a woman about to cry. Suddenly he ran out the door after the stretcher and the men who were bearing the doctor away. He felt for the doctor's hand under the cover and he pressed it in his, and the doctor's hand closed over his in comfort. "What can I do? What can I do to help?" he said, and he was thinking of the pure-white horses of Vienna and of their waltz, like the grasshopper's dance across the stage. The doctor was smiling, his cheeks scarred with the marks of laughter in the light from the hurricane lamps that the men were carrying down.

"You can throw me peaches and chocolate from the street," said the doctor. "My wife will show you where we are. She's not a good shot. Her hand shakes too much when she tries. I missed all the oranges she threw me after the February slaughter."

"What do you like best?" Dr. Heine called down after him, and his own voice sounded small and senseless in the enormous night.

"Peaches," the doctor's voice called back from the stretcher. "We get so thirsty . . ."

"I'll remember!" said Dr. Heine, his voice calling after the descending lights. He was thinking in anguish of the snow-white horses, the Lippizaners, the relics of pride, the still unbroken vestiges of beauty bending their knees to the empty loge of royalty where there was no royalty any more.

Count Lothar's Heart

I

Elsa was twenty-four the year the Count went off to war, and the Count was twenty-two. She remembered very well how he looked the day he left: the light hair brushed back from the point of his forehead, and color high on his cheeks because he had come fast through the chill of the September afternoon. All the manly, bodily things came alive in his blood when he walked and rang aloud until the echo was heard in every woman's heart that he passed. He had broken the black branches from the trees as they walked that day and carried them back to dress up the *Schloss* before he went away. On the other side of the Traunsee stood the mountains Elsa and Count Lothar had climbed all their childhood together, rising almost straight from the water and the crests, unwooded and faintly blue with height.

The *Schloss* had no beauty or comfort to offer, belonging as it did to other centuries and people with a grimness no woman or season could subdue. The flagstones in the entryway were wide enough to mark a grave, and the carpets Count Lothar's mother had set down in the halls and the reception rooms were as good as nothing. There was nothing strong enough to defeat the hard, cold living of the ancestors: their cellars and their earth beneath the house were present in every room, imbuing, invading, destroying with a damp, chill, deathly breath.

The old Countess was sitting with her velvet boots on by the fire, and the old Count reading his newspaper there. It was nearly dark, but the lamps were still unlighted. Everything that came into the house and everything that went out of it was counted so there would never be any want for the people who came after. There was only a little wood in the chimney, burning slowly, scarcely enough to give a heart of warmth to the tall, gray-windowed, sepulchral room.

Elsa and Count Lothar came in through the arch of the door and put down their branches of leaves on the piano. The leaves hung yellow and thin as silk from the ebony stems of the boughs. The old Countess looked up at once at Elsa, and took her hand from the pocket of her gown. It might have been that she had been waiting for them, her thoughts going sharp and lean with venom, gathering her bitterness close to give it to them when they came through the door.

"Here's the ring, Elsa," she said. Her face was set in dry and violent old age against the blast of evening they brought in. "You may as well have it now as long as Lothar has taken it into his head to die."

Lothar stepped toward the fire, smiling, rubbing his fair, strong hands over and over before the wan, fluttering wings of flame.

"I'm not going to die, Mother," he said with patience.

No one said anything about the war, except these other things that were said of it, but in a little while he would be on a train going toward it with a quiver of exaltation in his blood. He was so young that he was in haste to make for himself an unconquerable, a manly past, and come back with the power of that as well in the look that he gave a woman on the street. He squatted there on the hearth on his fine, strong thighs, reaching out with his hands for the fire that was nearer to death than life. And Elsa sat down near the old Count, and opened her coat at the neck.

"There's your engagement ring," said the old Countess sharply, and she leaned forward from the other side and tossed the ring into Elsa's lap.

"Whom am I engaged to?" said Elsa, and she picked it up from her dress and laughed. She sat in her dark suit in the chair, looking with laughter in her eyes at the two old people, and at their son, who did not turn from the flame.

"If Lothar hasn't asked you yet," said the old Countess, lighting a cigarette, "then I'm sorry for you. Love and courtship, thank God, were entirely different when I was young. My husband fought two duels for me in the afternoon and we waltzed the whole night together after he had won me."

The old Count started up gently, as if from sleep, folded his newspaper over, and smoothed out his white soft mustaches with his delicate, shaking hand.

"I forgot about it," said Lothar, without turning on his heels. "It's all right with you, isn't it, Elsa?"

They had known each other so long, the same mountains and lakes, heard the same music, the same words over and over, all since they were children, but there had been no talk of love. But somehow, and without passion, it had been known between them; it had been understood, and Elsa's face was warm and brimming now as she held the fine ring closed inside her hand.

"Yes, Lothar. Yes, it is all right," she said softly, but the old woman cried out: "Kiss her! Kiss her!"

Count Lothar stood up and turned his back to the fireplace and walked to the chair where Elsa sat. She saw his face, clear and youthful, coming closer, bending to her, his eyes confused, his color rising. And suddenly she leaped up laughing.

"No, no, Lothar, not now!" she said. "It's really silly to do it now, isn't it? It doesn't matter! We'll do it some other time," she said.

"I never met 'another time' coming toward me," said the old Countess, and she snapped the end of her cigarette into the scarcely flickering fire. "They were always going the other way and they always will be."

The old Count cleared his throat and took out his watch in the palm of his hand.

"The train goes in half an hour," he said, peering into the face of it in the gathering dark.

"I'm going to the station with you," said Elsa softly, and Count Lothar said: "I'm going to drive the horses myself," and his eyes were glowing.

The old Countess watched her son sharply a moment, and then she stood up and faced him, holding fast to the back of her chair.

"If you come back," she said, "I hope you have some of the rot licked out of you. War has nothing to do with courage. You won't hear me out when I try to tell you. You and your father here, you take every word from the papers. Neither one or the other of you has ever had a thought of his own. When I was a girl there weren't any politics, the men were too good for it. But you were born too late in my life, and you're the worse for it. You kept hemming and hawing around and taking your time, and when I was near forty you made up your mind to appear. War has nothing to do with gentlemen!" she cried out. "Anyone with good blood in him and some sense has better things to do!"

Her hand was shaking on the high, carved head of her chair, and her face was lifted, white and strongly boned, with the skin drawn over it like lace.

"Lothar will be going in five minutes now," said the old Count as if in apology to them all.

"Upstarts!" said the old lady fiercely. "Pot-wallopers like Napoleon! War was good enough for them, just as harlots were good enough for them to marry." She stood with her two hands clasping the head of the chair, the empty folds of her soft cheeks quivering, the beak of her high nose thin as a blade. Her lids were stretched across her marble eyes, like curtains fallen, and she looking mightily and brazenly up from under their frayed hems. And suddenly Lothar crossed the space between them, dropped his head, and with his lips embraced her hands which did not falter. She stood holding to the strong, elaborate carving while Lothar followed the old Count from the room.

"You mustn't worry. It will be all right," said Elsa softly.

And "Worry?" cried out the old lady. The sound of the horses and the carriage could be heard on the drive. "My dear girl," said the old Countess, "you have my sympathy." She stood tall and immobile, staring without emotion beyond the sight of Elsa buttoning her warm coat over. "Your fiancé is a man of no particular talents, neither studious nor musical, gifted nor ambitious. He could never keep a single date of history in his head. He is stubborn as a mule, and I frequently wonder where he gets it from." Elsa pulled on her gloves, and from the hall they could hear the sound of his box being carried down. The old Countess drew her mouth in, close and bloodless in her sagging face. "He has no more idea why he is going to war than those horses out there, tearing the ground up with their feet, know why they're being driven to the station."

Elsa went quickly to the old lady and touched her hand. Her

eyes had filled with tears before the old lady's dry, unswerving gaze.

"Say good-by to him then," she said softly. "Say good-by to him before he goes."

"Good-by won't enlighten him," said the old Countess tartly. She stood quite motionless, her hands holding fast to the chair back as Elsa too went out into the hall. The dark was gathering in the window behind her and blotting out entirely the day.

II

Count Lothar had been gone six years, and now it was the end of the summer again and the war a long time over. The old Countess was dead, and the old Count lived to himself, alone in the castle among the ravaged trees. In the spring of each year since Count Lothar had been gone, the trees had been cut down for fuel, and the *Schloss* was no longer now a place of mystery and darkness. It could be seen clearly from the road and from the water, towering in solitude over the gaps and the destruction where the bitten trunks stood.

No one had thought to see him again, for everything that had to do with his youth had dwindled and dimmed and it was almost certain that he had died as well. The whole country had fallen into poverty, and if he were alive somewhere, why should he return? Elsa wore the ring on her finger still, but she wore it in dignity and resignation, as an old lady might who had known the things of love and sorrow as they came: year after year the births and deaths and the altering of the spirit, the despair and the renunciation. If he comes back, was written in Elsa's face but she never spoke it out, he will come back because there is nowhere else to go.

There had been letters from him from Siberia, where he worked in the prison camp, and letters from China when they wrote him that his mother had died. But no one ever thought to see him back again, for so many of the prisoners had stayed and made a new life where they were, or else they had perished; but Count Lothar came back one day at the tail end of summer. He had only a rucksack to carry on his shoulders, so when he came through the gate at the station he started at once down the road. His boots were heavy and caked with earth and his topcoat was graying with a mist of use and age. He was still a thick-set fairish man with a small nose, fresh color running under his skin, and a look of gravity and willfulness in his eyes. His face was marked with weariness, and in weariness he took the first path into the woods, packed thick with the rotting leaves as it was under foot, and followed it as if from habit.

At the side of the water he halted and watched the boats curving out under their single canvas wings. He thought of his own sloop lying, still belly-up doubtless, as he had left it in the boat shed near the mouth of the stream. The swift, lovely boats were blowing across the Traunsee's shining breast, and he remembered the leap of his own boat's perilous giving and the rope running quick as water through his hands. He stood there a little, watching the single petals of the masts unfurling, now to the right in the wind and now to the left. The mountains on the other side had looked mighty and barren to him when he went away, and he saw with surprise now what had happened to them in his sight: they seemed to have lost their wildness and their power, and they were as pretty and mild as any pastureland.

Near to the town where the moored boats and the little white steamer rode on the water, the swans were floating still as they had floated every summer of his life. He had put his rucksack down on the gravel and with his arms crossed on the railing he watched these things, dimly, dimly, as a man in a dream might see profoundly, yet scarcely see. And, watching so, he saw the swans rise suddenly and of one accord from the water where they drifted and fly in great, strong, eager flight above the lake. Their necks were stretched out hungering and thirsting before them as they went, and the mighty flap of their wings was as good as a clear wind blowing. The blood ran up into Count Lothar's face, and he cried aloud:

"My God, I'd forgotten the swans flying!"

They were not near to him, but still he could feel on his flesh the strength of the pure white pinions stroking the quiet air. They might have passed close to him, so well could he feel the power and love of their bodies as they went. They were not like birds in flight, for the masterful wings seemed to raise strong, stallionlike, white bodies from their natural place and fling them headlong in egression into space. White horses might have flown like this, their vulnerable, soft breasts pressed sweet with flesh upon the current. The sight of the swans in flight across the Traunsee was a thing that made Count Lothar's heart rouse suddenly in anguish.

The birds had settled again on the water, and Count Lothar was standing so by the rail when Elsa came down the walk. Her head was lowered, her face ageless, colorless, and she was walking toward the streets of Gmunden with her shopping bag over her arm. There was nothing of youth left to her, nothihg there that he might remember. She went past him in her high-laced, black shoes, and he looked back at the swans which were drifting at ease far out on the water. How ugly and shabby this woman and all the other women were, he thought, going down the walk past the lake and into the town.

"Your mother was very sorry to go without seeing you again," said the old Count after they had eaten together. He looked from Lothar's face to Elsa's, apologizing because the old Countess had died. "She was very sorry at the end."

"What did she say?" asked Count Lothar, sitting with his legs stretched out and his eye and his heart quite dry.

"She didn't say anything," said the old Count, smoothing in his fingers what was left of his mustaches. "But she turned your photograph around so that it faced her. She had turned it to the wall the day you went away."

In a little while the old Count went out of the room, leaving Count Lothar and Elsa together, and the afternoon light came through the windows and fell on the dust on the floor and the ashes in the fireplace. There was white in Elsa's hair: it ran back from her brow in a dull, wide avenue of resignation, and Count Lothar turned his face from one side to the other. He looked at the rug worn thin on the floor, and at the light in the window. He did not want to see her face or to hear what she would say.

"You'll take a rest for a while, won't you, Lothar?" she said at last.

"What's that?" he said, and he started at the sound of her voice.

"You'll take a rest here," she repeated, "and then I suppose you'll go to Vienna?"

"To Vienna?" said Count Lothar in true surprise.

"There isn't anywhere else to make a living, is there?" said Elsa, and she opened her hands out quietly in her lap.

"Oh, no," said Lothar. "I forgot. That's true."

"What do you think you want to do?" said Elsa gently after a moment.

"Do?" asked Count Lothar, and the look in his face might easily have been taken for stupidity. He had no sharpness and no subterfuge, but all that he felt in his flesh he felt so deeply that it moved him one way or the other of its own accord. All the years were put away behind him in confusion, and he was back amongst his people in confusion. He sat quite still, looking at the rug at his feet and the dust that had gathered on it, his gaze threshing from the table to the window, away from Elsa in despair.

After tea they walked down to the lake and past it out over the pathway of wooden bridges that followed the overflow of the Traunsee where it fell in a fast-running stream. Here the water poured out of the lake and went off down the mountains, and here where they walked above it, it was dammed in a staircase of smooth sliding falls. On the edge of these the swans had gathered; they were standing clear of the falling water on the brink, their webbed feet spread in the fernlike slime that rippled with the current, their legs as black as leather in the startling clarity of the quivering stream.

Count Lothar and Elsa stopped on the bridge, and the birds below them were preening their immaculate breasts and opening their wings out one by one, stretching them stark white against the water.

"How wonderful their necks are!" Count Lothar said, and suddenly a tremor of wonder ran through his blood and he had to steady himself by taking the wooden rail of the bridgeway in his hands.

"Do you remember?" said Elsa softly, holding his arm in hers. "We used to come here so often——"

He saw her face beside him, distasteful as a stranger's face, the lip of it trembling, and the bar of gray like a warning in her hair. And he turned his eyes back, slowly, in dumb confusion to the sight of the birds on the edge of slipping water. Some of them had thrust the long stalks of their throats down into the deeper places before the falls and were seeking for refuse along the bottom. Nothing remained but the soft, flickering, short peaks of their clean rumps and their leathery black elbows with the down blowing soft at the ebony bone. In such ecstasies of beauty were they seeking in the filth of lemon rinds and shells and garbage that had drifted from the town, prodding the leaves and branches apart with their dark, lustful mouths.

"Lothar," said Elsa, and then she stopped speaking. "I thought——" she began again, and suddenly she slipped the ring off her finger and put it in his hand. "I don't want you to feel bound to me, Lothar," she said. "It's been so long. I don't want to hold you to anything you don't want. I know there may be someone else. I understand that very well."

Count Lothar looked at the ring lying in the palm of his hand, and then he gave it back to her.

"No," he said. "There is nobody else. I'll make some money, I'm sure I shall find something to do, and then we can get married."

And then he burst out laughing at what was left of the swans above the water: the white, beautiful rumps wagging and flickering and seeming to hark to the sudden burst of sound. Elsa put the ring back upon her finger and she spoke his name softly, but he was laughing aloud in delight and he did not hear her. He scarcely knew she was there, for he was watching the strong, greedy beaks and the weaving of the swans' necks under water.

So he took the habit of coming to see the swans every afternoon, no matter what the weather. He would come down past the Traunsee and stand on the bridgeway, watching the swans. When the fine mountain rain of the autumn was falling, the great birds would go under the beams, under the rotting pillars of the pier, and he could see them interwinding the long, white vines of their throats, one with the other. He could stand so on the boards over the shallow stream, leaning with his arms crossed on the railing, and watch the swans forever. They were a deep caress to his wandering spirit, they were a soft call in the darkness to his heart. He did not know what he thought of them, but there he stood hour after hour, watching the writhing necks of the white birds uncoiling and bridling suavely in embrace.

"I hope the snow doesn't come early this year," Count Lothar said to his father one afternoon, for he was thinking of what might become of the birds once the cold of the winter set in.

But the old Count said: "Perhaps you'll be in Salzburg by that time."

Count Lothar was thinking of the swans, and for a moment he did not seem to hear. He could not remember well the things of his youth and he did not know any more if the birds stayed here or if they went to warmer places. But suddenly he lifted his head.

"Why should I be in Salzburg?" he said.

The old man had begun to tremble as if in fear of some echo of his dead wife's wrath which might now sound out of his son's mouth. He raised his failing, gentlemanly hand and from where they walked on the road he pointed back through the mutilated trees.

"There's the *Schloss*," he said, and his voice was shaking. "I would like to give it to you when you marry. I would like to see you and Elsa live in it together, while I am still here. Elsa and I have been trying here and there, and there's a bank in Salzburg where they've offered you a place. You could come back here with your wife to the *Schloss* for the summers. It would be nice for your children to grow up here," he said.

"That's true," said Count Lothar, but he spoke as if he had scarcely heard. "Do the swans migrate or do they stay the winter here?" he asked after a little while.

In the night the moon was out and Count Lothar put his coat on after supper. The old Count woke up in his chair where he had been sleeping by the fire, and looked with his small, pink eyes at his son.

"Are you going to see Elsa?" he asked, and his voice was faint with hope on his lips. Count Lothar nodded, and at once the tears sprang from the old man's eyes.

But Count Lothar's heart was as dry as a dead leaf blowing down the driveway. He went past the gleaming edge of the lake, and walked through the town, and so out over the bridges that carried the wooden pathway down the shining stream. The moon was high and perfect in the sky, and the swarming light of it gave the land a single dimension of cold, exalted purity. The waters below him were slipping down the stony bed, warbling and calling softly to each other, hollow and sweet as flute notes sounding. Count Lothar stopped on the bridgeway and looked back at the lake that lay behind: the moon's light was riding, white as ice, on the dark waves that murmured in through the stones.

As the Count stood watching the nightly, muted world, a stirring of life sounded out across the water: it began at the end of the lake that was far from him, and it moved like a wind on the water. It came as strong as a foehn wind over the lake, gathering throb by throb until the sky and the land were filled with the sound of passage. Count Lothar held fast to the rail of the bridge, and the blood was shaking in his body, and his ears and his mouth were filled with music like those of a drowning man. There was no longer any earth on which to stand, no air to breathe, no human sound to hear. The elements had become one in the great wind that filled the rushing heavens, drawing with it, long and slow and mighty, the power of spread, gigantic wings.

"Is it the swans? Is it the swans indeed?" Count Lothar cried out in madness, for it seemed to him that a thousand birds had risen on the current and were passing above him, their necks outstretched, their rich, majestic bodies flowing with the deep, ardent pulsing of their monstrous wings. "Is it the swans?" he cried into the thunder of their flight, and the air itself was passing, lashed fast as pinion feathers to the curved and reaching bone.

As he listened now, he could hear the young Cossacks coming, riding six abreast, the sound of their horses as they galloped. He could see their young faces, as beautiful as women's, and he could hear them singing in wild, high, boyish voices, galloping, with their coats gone white as swans under the falling snow, galloping, galloping, galloping as they crossed the heavens. Elsa had come onto the bridgeway and was standing there beside him, and he seized her arm in his fingers and began calling out to her of what he saw. He could hear the young Cossacks coming, he could see them riding six abreast, coming into the camp as young and rich as stallions.

"Listen to me now, Elsa," he said. "Listen to me."

He saw the women well who came to the prison camp, and were given to the men as rations were given, with no youth or beauty or gusto left in their flesh. He saw their hard, long, riddled faces, and the look of greed they had under the scars left there by hunger and pox and cold. He held Elsa's arm like a man gone mad, and he told her what he saw, telling her these things, talking fast. There were the women offered them, and over the snow rode the Cossacks, galloping, galloping six abreast. They came into the camp, elegant in their good furs, stamping and chattering and dancing like lively women as they warmed their fingers by the stove.

"In some men and women there are conflicting cells," said Count Lothar, talking wildly as they walked. "There are the male and the female cells. We're near the beginning of life still and there is still the conflict of the two physical demands in us. We're near to the worms and the snails, and they are both male and female in themselves."

He saw them laying their coats off, the wide bear coats that went down to their heels. He heard them asking that wine be brought, and the youth in their bodies was thundering, thundering, like the blood that thunders aloud in the ears.

"They never looked at the women," he said. "Some of the women were so strong that they carried wounded men for miles on their backs. And some of the strongest, youngest men turned in loneliness to one another."

He could see their faces clearly, and their eyes turned up like Oriental women's, tilted with lust under their silky brows.

"In some men," Count Lothar was saying wildly, "there are more of the female cells, and only in need they discover this. . . . And in need we turned to one another. . . ."

They had suddenly come to the road, and Elsa was holding fast to him, looking up into his face. At last, at last, was her silence saying softly, at last. He is speaking, and I am to know a little of what became of his youth and what became of the things he had in the years he has been away. At last, at last. . . .

"In Siberia," Count Lothar said, and then his throat seemed to close in despair and he could say no more. Elsa pressed his arm in gentleness.

"Tell me, tell me," she said. "It is very beautiful . . . it is friendship . . . tell me, do."

Count Lothar saw that the road lights were burning at intervals beneath the hanging boughs along the road, and that people were walking back from the *Kino* that was just over in the town.

"There is nothing to tell," he said in a low voice. "No, I have said it all. There is nothing more to tell," he said, and they never spoke of it again, neither in Salzburg, where he worked in the bank in the winter, or in the *Schloss,* where they came every summertime.

▲▲▲▲▲▲▲▲▲▲▲▲▲▲▲▲▲▲▲▲▲▲▲▲▲▲▲▲▲▲▲

English Group
1935–1936

▼▼▼▼▼▼▼▼▼▼▼▼▼▼▼▼▼▼▼▼▼▼▼▼▼▼▼▼▼▼

Major Alshuster

If anyone thinks I saw him only that once, the time he showed me his mother's house in June, that isn't true, for the truth is every time I go out, if I go up the country in the rain or walk on the chalk edge in the evening and watch the swans below, only the two of them, moving down the river's mouth to the rim of salt where the low waves run into the dark fresh water, I meet Major Alshuster. He comes through the drenching grass or along the cliff path, and he puts out his hand at once and says: "I'm sorry I didn't let you have my mother's Dower House." He looks just as he did in June: he is a young man still, he is not quite forty, and if he is on horseback when I meet him he gets down from his horse and we walk along together with the gulls over-head crying like cats through the mist or riding curved in the clear evening light. His head is narrow, unlike a military head, and his hair is black like a Spanish girl's; his shoulders are broad and his waist is thin, and he has a handsome, vain, a slightly be-wildered face, and a loud, unhappy laugh. But there is one thing that has altered in him since the first time we met: it is his eyes that have altered, and he looks at me with courage as if there were nothing of India left to mar his sight.

The first time I heard of him was in June, when they told me in the hotel bar: "If you're looking for a house to let, there's a man up at Needlehay with a house to let," and they said to ask for Major Alshuster where he lived at the Manor House with his mother and sister.

"His sister, you see," said the Scotchwoman who served behind the hotel bar, "his sister, she never married, so as to keep house like for the old mother and for this Major Alshuster." Nor had Major Alshuster ever married, said the Scotchwoman, who was

still unused to the English. "I don't know why he never married," she said, and she looked quickly around the hotel bar to see
how near to the sound of her voice the people were sitting. "Unless it's because every damned one of the English has a heart like
that," she said, and she rapped the wood of the counter. She
opened her newspaper out flat on the bar between us and she
said: "I put five pounds up every time there's a Scotch hearse
running," and a grim smile of love came on her mouth as if there
were more kin between herself and any Scotch horse than between her and the English. "One running tomorrow name of
Bonnie Dundee," she said with the sports page spread out. "You
can put your faith on a Scotch hearse every time."

There was a paper written about the place at Needlehay, and
I sat at the corner of the bar, reading the things about the house
to let. It had boot and knife houses, a tile-floored dairy, and
"practically every window," said the paper they gave me to read,
"is stone-dressed and many have stone mullions with tracery
above filling the pointed arched headings. The drainage has recently received attention; the soil is light topsoil, gravel and sand
subsoil." There was a building on the grounds, it said, "erected
in keeping with the House, with a livery room and a fireplace, a
cobbled wash, and three rooms for the chauffeur. Hidden from
the drive by the yew hedges are a heated span greenhouse, a
peach case, a range of pits, and an open barrow shed. The trees
not only include forest trees," said this document signed with
Major Alshuster's name, "but ornamental ones as well. Splashes
of color are provided by the variety of flowering shrubs planted
in clumps about the grounds. There are an undulating lawn
shaded by oak and coniferous trees, a rambler screen, mown and
rough grass with bulb carpets, a rose garden, strawberry and
asparagus beds." There was a photograph of the Dower House
standing quiet, looking out to sea, and of this the paper said
"there are ribbed stone quoins, mullions, tracery to windows,
cappings to gabled ends and parapet walls, carved masks to
springing of archings, and parts of its elevation clad in a variety
of choice flowering and evergreen creepers."

"If I had any money at all," I said to the picture at the bar,
"this is a place I'd grow old in, and die in its arms," and on Fri-

day I went in curiosity up to Needlehay in the rain and heat, and I met Major Alshuster at the gate of the Dower House, where he said on the telephone he would be. He was touching his short, black mustaches with his fingers, and he could scarcely see me getting out of the car for the hand of blindness that twelve years of India had laid across his eyes. He was wearing breeches and puttees, and his horse was standing at the gate with its bridle drawn through the iron ring.

"We don't really want," was the first thing he said, "that is to say, we never let anyone have the house before. We're not at all keen on having," he said, and he looked away over the fields where the men were scything down the hay. A mile or so off, the gray wing tip of the Manor House could be seen, showing above the trees.

"My mother," said Major Alshuster as we went through the gate, and he winced at the sound of the intimate word as if in saying it he had given too much of his own life away, "she's rather the worse for wear at present, so it's up to me."

He put the key in the lock of the Dower House door, and I saw very close to me the coarsening, thickening side of his face that had carried his features with it from what might have been clear-skinned wonder in youth to this texture of caution and despair. He was as delicately made as a girl, with his black hair nipped close at his ears, and his cheekbones standing high. But here was the thickening, toughening side of his face saying "huntin', shootin', fishin'" to the eye and nothing else besides.

This was the first time we met and he did not speak of other things to me. He did not tell me the names of the different grasses growing thick in the fields, although he knew them very well. He did not say that for a horse's mouth hay should be a year old, smell sweet but not be mow-burned, but instead he went quickly through the reception rooms and through the servants' hall and the kitchen, escaping before one, as though pursued by the person who had come to see.

"This is the study sort of thing," he said, without stopping, and he started in haste to mount the stairs. He was always ahead, with his back turned on this woman or any other. They were none of them going to get the house as long as he was there. "This is a bedroom and so's that," he said, hastening past the doorways. He wanted the place standing empty in its grounds alone, with its Italian garden and its grass tennis court leading almost to the edge of chalk, and below it the sea sucking in and out with a hollow sigh as it left the shore. He did not want strangers asleep in its beds or sitting at ease by its fireplaces. He wanted it empty of life, chambered and clean as an empty nut, with the key of the door in the palm of his own hand to set in the lock when he liked. He did not want strange people in it, speaking what must be a foreign language there, because for foreigners he had no judgment, but only condemnation. Give him an army man, or his wife, and he knew at once, he knew without mistake (unless they happened to be of an army not the British). But give him British army people and he could tell you at a glance, before they opened their mouths he could tell you, but not even British army people did he want living here.

But the thing was that his mother was ill, he had said so as he went through the gate, and now he could use the money that the Dower House might bring. He had made up his mind to let it—to let it furnished with all the old things in it, and if he could not decide for himself, then he looked to the fine old things, to the chests and the solid tables and the strong beds to speak out, to cry aloud if he had opened the door to people he was going to regret for the rest of his life.

He did not speak of horses that day, he did not say that "spirit and ardor are in the temper of a horse what passion is in the mind of man," but on other days he talked of the horse that was standing in the shade by the gate, and he said this horse was bold and generous, quick and active.

"He's bold as brass over rough, blind country," Major Alshuster said to me as we walked along one night. "He has plenty of heart room, and he's a good doer." We stopped to listen to the sea below us murmuring in and out, and Major Alshuster spoke suddenly out of the darkness. "Did you ever do any pigsticking?" he said.

But on this day he hastened past the third lavatory door of the Dower House, and then he reached back and opened it in confusion, and closed it quickly again.

"That's just another thingumabob, a thingumajig," he said in a low voice as he escaped to the second floor. "You saw the one like it just below."

The woman he didn't want in his house came breathless to the landing.

"A what?" she said, looking straight at him up the stairs. She opened the door quite wide and stared at the varnished mahogany-colored seat within, and a blush of shame ran up the Major's neck and ended in his hair.

"Daresay your husband's not an army man?" said Major Alshuster uneasily in the nursery, and the woman said:

"I haven't any husband. I'm quite alone. Except, of course, for my children."

"Oh, yes," said Major Alshuster, staring at the wall.

He saw her counting out the beds, and he touched his black mustache in fear.

"Where," he said, clearing his throat, "where would the children be going to school?"

His eyes moved swiftly to the window in escape. She might say the wrong school, and then what was he going to do about it; in spite of the strength and wisdom of his race he must wait with the meekness of a beast for the words to be said so that he should know.

"School?" said the woman, catching sight of herself with pleasure in the glass. "Oh, yes, school. I'll have to see about a school when I've found a house I like."

Some thought took hold of the Major's mouth and twisted it aside.

"Oh, I daresay," he said, and he shut his teeth on his contempt. "Of course," he said presently, clearing his throat, "here in England we'd go about it the other way. Cart before the horse sort of thing, I daresay," he said in mock humility.

"In my country," said this woman, smiling at the Major, "horses know their place. They wouldn't dream of getting behind a cart."

That was in June, and there were a hundred sheep in the heat on the other side of the garden wall asking for peace of mind all afternoon. We went down the staircase to the hall, and we could hear the hard, high rattle shaking in their mouths, the question shaking unanswered on their pallid tongues. Major Alshuster's delicate shadow ran down the massive stone of the stairs, and my voice came back like a cry from the entrance hall below.

"What do they want?" I said. "What are they asking you for?"

But whether they wanted water or care, or a direction in which to follow, Major Alshuster could not be brought to say. He stood near the gate where his horse was stirring from the flies, and he held the answer in his mouth.

"I daresay my farmer knows what's up," he said, and he did not listen to the sound of the sheep asking for what he did not have to give. He saw a rabbit hurrying down the land and it was of that he began speaking.

"The rabbits are the ruination of this country," he said with bitterness as the little white puff of tail went under the hedge at the end.

"The rabbits!" said the woman, looking brightly at him. "Not the dole then?"

"No, not at all," said the Major shortly. "I daresay you'd scarcely have anyone with you with a gun?"

"No," she said firmly, "I don't believe in guns. I wouldn't let my children have them. I don't believe in war."

"Oh," said the Major, clearing his throat. "Of course, whatcha-call it, civilization sort of thing, naturally we're all out to avoid it if we can."

"Have you managed," said the woman he didn't want in this place at all, "to avoid it?"

"That's neither here nor there," said the Major with sudden briskness, and he stepped ahead as if to speed her on her way. "We'd need someone here to keep the rabbits down, there'd scarcely be any use . . ."

"But I want this house," she said behind him. Out of curiosity she had come this far, out of curiosity saying the things she said. She felt the stones of the gravel through her shoes as she walked, and even in poverty, even alone, she knew this was the house she wanted. There was no money for the wax on its floors, for keeping the grass courts rolled or the dovecots clean, there were no pigskin bags to be carried in the door. But her voice went up the

Major's back and around his neck like a tender arm. "This is the only house I've ever wanted," she said.

The gulls were flying inland over the house and garden, their voices crying, their salt-white breasts firm on the wind. The clouds were breaking now, and shaped clear against them the gulls mewed their sour word over the full-headed trees and the beds of marigold and straight, strong sweet William. For a little while nothing remained of England, with these wild, white birds of the sea crying hunger, hunger, hunger to a land as fresh as moss.

"I'd just like to see the greenhouse," said the woman, and the Major cleared his throat and went over the little step at the end, showing her hastily the way. But once within the greenhouse there arose a languorous, a nearly stifling tide of heat that clasped their limbs in a mute, lingering embrace, and folded close upon their throats; the smell of geranium stopped their nostrils with crimson corks, and the heart cried out in vain for breath. The sun burned strong and white and pitiless on the glass panes above their heads—this sun, coming suddenly after rain, is the fiercest, having waited and gathered vengeance into its pale, swooning light—and through this fecund, slowly expanding world they moved, this woman behind the Major, pressing deeper and deeper into the tropic, suffocating belt of rich, unfolding life.

Here, in this heart of glass, were cactuses besought to grow, wooed from the dark earth and rotting wood until they stood, leather-thick and coarse, with their soft yellow or long, silvery beards upon their bellies, rearing upward like snakes poised to strike. But only in one had the promise been fulfilled, and the bright cactus flower had blossomed on the leather leaf. On one side were the ginger plants in bloom, and mingling with the others on the air the smell of these frail, spidery, yellow ginger flowers; and on the other, ferns uncurling in yards of narrow, deep-green lace, the prongs of fern opening finger by finger from the dark, skeleton hand.

"Here," was the glass above their heads wooing them, "is Spain, Italy, sweet-mouthed islands; nothing to do with pale ale tepid in the glass, with the Cathedral Close, with Cookery

Nooks, or lobster teas upon a stony shore that does not hesitate to
cast the first." Deeper and deeper into the jungle heat of the
greenhouse they went, and here were the tomato plants lifting
their lean, burdened arms, and here the onions in basket trays
drying in their burnished skins, and their blood ran as slow as
honey in their veins.

"England is outside," said the woman, scarcely speaking aloud
in the Italian heat, and the Major turned swiftly around, and his
eyes were burning in dark, impassioned bewilderment. The gar-
dener's broken mirror was hanging to an upright beam, and the
woman walked straight toward Major Alshuster, and stopped
close enough to touch him with her hand as she looked into the
glass. She saw the blue hat on her head, and the pieces of
smooth, light hair drawn back, and the straight, white nose, and
the red put on her mouth, and she said:

"Don't look at me, please. It's not fair to look at any woman
over thirty in the sun."

"I am looking at you," said the Major savagely behind her.
"I've been looking at you for an hour. I don't want to stop looking at you," he said. "I don't want to stop at all."

"Please," she said lazily into the glass, "look at something else
while I fix my lips. And besides, I'm not here. Not a single bit of
me is in England. I'm at Lago di Garda, lying in the sun."

But when she turned around from the bit of mirror there was
nothing left of what the Major had said. He was looking straight
at the tomato plants and it might very well have been someone
else who had spoken, for the fire was extinguished in his eyes.
He had turned a little from her, and there was absolutely nothing left, unless it was the trembling of his hand as he put back
his Spanish hair.

"Do you think," she said, "that if devastation came to this
place, this island, England, I mean, do you think in the fury of
the burning and the flood and the chaos there would be one person, just one person, drunk and dancing, making music of some
kind to die by?"

"The what?" said Major Alshuster in a loud, startled voice and
he stepped back before her.

"I think," said this woman he couldn't stand the sight of,

"there would be people standing still all over the country, standing in groups, misshapen by their own fear, waiting . . ."

The crying of the sheep had grown so strong now that when she stepped out of the greenhouse it was as if a hundred fleshless hands were rattling in desperate supplication before them on the air. They were asking her one thing, the bare knuckles of their anguish asking it of her, and she had no answer to give them but to turn her back on the ague of their speech and make as if she had not heard them. The Major's tethered horse turned his head to look at her as she got into the small, old car.

If anyone thinks it was because I never saw Major Alshuster again that I remember every word we said, it is not true. For even after the letter he wrote me, even after the matter of letting the house or not letting it was finished with, still that was not the end of it. The day after I visited the Dower House, I had a letter from Major Alshuster. He wrote me: "Dear Mrs. Whatchername: Due to unforeseen circumstances, I fear I shall have to forego the pleasure of renting you my mother's Dower House. Thank you for your inquiry. Yours very truly."

I did not see him at once, but I went up to the Half-Way House one wet afternoon in late July, and I was at peace in my heart for all the colors that came alive as soon as the sun was out of sight, for the fresh little furze flowers, and the red sumac beads, and the power of the thick, short grass. That afternoon I met him on the downs, and he was on horseback, and he sprang off, the saddle leather and the leather of his gaiters creaking aloud as sweet as small birds speaking in the bush. He walked along beside me, looking at the ground before his feet, and the reins of his horse were through his fingers, and his horse was following docilely behind. He said, "The way it happened was that everything came at once this year: too much rain at first, and then too much sun, and the time I knew the hay should be cut was the time they should have been shearing the sheep, and not enough hands for it. A late crop," said Major Alshuster, "loses half its value because the seeds fall out. We got the wool off the sheep that night—they were asking it the day you looked at the house." He was saying these things at once to me as if making up for the things he had not said. "We'd had them closed in a day

and a half, thinking we'd make the time. But we did it by lan-
ternlight, and the cattle went unmilked until half-past three in
the morning. They looked as if they'd been struck with the
rickets, the lot of them, by then, with their hind legs falling away
from under them because of the weight of milk."

The hills lying beyond us and beyond Sidmouth were as blue
as pansies, and the heather sprang up fresh and rosy at our feet,
and the Major walked along beside me, talking of many things.
It was as if he had waited a long time, as if he had waited his
life, perhaps, to say them. He talked of his horses, and of this
horse that was following now as soft as music over the sod behind us. He was a pigsticker, he said, with the strong loins, and
thighs, and hocks of a pigsticker, the hard, sound legs and the
good sloping pasterns, and the heart room to spare that a good
doer and a good pigsticker should have.

"A man can see a lot of fun fox hunting," said the Major, and
without any warning given or heard Mrs. Whatchername saw
that the Major had great beauty. He was a wonderful thing, with
his neck fitting well into his shoulders, and his face lifted to the
open embrace of the rain. His throat was strong and bare from
his coat, and to the sides of it the ears sprang up and lay flat and
close to his narrow, perfect skull. "Even on a horse that is neither bold nor generous," the Major said, "a man can see a lot of
fun. But that isn't true for pigsticking. If your horse isn't bold or
free over rough, blind going, and is too cunning and careful to
take you within spearing distance of the pig, then there's no use
wasting time on him. He may be a savage in the stable," said the
Major, and the line of his teeth was white as a tusk under his
ruddy lip and his black mustache, "but if he'll gallop over hairy,
blind country and go blindly up to an angry boar and face a
charge, then you can forgive him for anything else."

"Yes," said Mrs. Whatchername, scarcely breathing. "Yes."

She saw how small and strong were the Major's wrists, and
how the lip of his leather glove turned back showed the skin
burned dark on his hands.

"It's the boar," said the Major, walking up the country over
the smooth, short, wild grass, "that chooses the ground, and
that's the devil of it. When he's hunted he'll take good care to

select a line where the going's as rough and the covert as thick as he can find."

"Yes," said Mrs. Whatchername. "Yes."

Her words were spoken softly, almost without breath, so the Major could scarcely have heard. She was walking beside him in the rain, walking with the sight gone from her eyes, and with the knowledge in her limbs that the Major was shaped in strong, pure movement beside her, walking in step with him toward wherever he was going to go. "Toward what are we going?" she said, scarcely aloud, and the Major said:

"When he finds he's being overhauled, he'll still have lots up his sleeve, the bastard will. He'll suddenly jink sharp right or left, quick as a hare from a greyhound."

"Yes," said Mrs. Whatchername.

"The great thing is to kill your pig with one spear," said the Major. "Only you must never thrust at him, and that's always the thing you want to do. You must just drop the point and hold it steady and let the force of the collision do the rest. If you thrust at him you'll miss him clean, nine times out of ten. Just set your spear and then wait," said the Major with the wet, green bracken slapping at his puttees. "And if your spear is sharp," he said, "it will go in like a hot knife into butter."

The rain was falling on the side of his face, down from the brim of his soft brown hat, and falling sad and pale on the land and sea ahead. And suddenly the Major took savagely hold of Mrs. Whatchername's hand.

"The way women go after a man," he said, speaking quickly, with his fingers biting into her palm. "It's enough to make you sick, choosing their own ground, by God, and keeping to it, day after day, for a lifetime, riding him hard, ready for any turn or ruse, into the jungle and out of it, India, home, following him jink by jink until they think they've got him!"

"They didn't get you," said Mrs. Whatchername proudly, walking the way he walked to whatever destination he had in mind.

"By Gad, they didn't!" said the Major with a snort of laughter. "Moved right into the country to get me, two of them did. One went as far as Calcutta. And this is what," he said. "None of them wanted me, d'y' see? Not a one of the damned bitches. Wanted Needlehay or the name beginning with what it does, or a standing in South Devon, y' understand——"

"They didn't get it, did they?" said Mrs. Whatchername softly. She was walking tall and close beside him, looking ahead, with her mouth red, and her yellow hair pinned back. The Major pulled her roughly against him as they walked.

"Look here," he said. "I like your hair. I like you walking beside me."

And another time it was at Landslip we met, and when he got down from his horse I said:

"I knew two horses once called Prince and Star."

We were near to the place where the cliffs had taken off from the land and slid with their burden of high, ripe wheat onto the rocks and into the quiet sea. The grass here was nibbled short by sheep, and the smooth, sloping firmament underfoot was starred with thistles that lay against the ground. I began telling the story of Prince and Star, taking it word by word from what I remembered and what I knew, and it was the story of Rufus King as well.

Rufus came from the country near Buffalo, where the buffaloes and the horseshoes grow like the shamrock bringing luck to the soil (and the horse Major Alshuster was leading came following, his feet on the earth as soft as music), and Rufus King had photographs taken of himself sitting still in costumes: one as a Spanish bullfighter, and one in a cap and gown. He used to sleep in the washhouse, and his cheeks were run with scarlet threads of blood, and my sister and I were kneeling by the frog pond near the wood buckets when he brought the photographs down. We had sixteen frogs in all and we sat them on canopies of moss and sailed them on rafts in the square, small, moss-hung pond, the beauties, with sunshades over them and buttercups around their necks, for this human homage pleases the vanity of frogs very well. Rufus brought down the photographs and we squatted at the edge with the poison ivy and the wild roses flowering cheek by jowl behind us.

"What college did you graduate from, Rufus?" I said, and Rufus said:

"Oh, I graduated. I graduated all right. You can see me there in my graduating things."

His finger was thick and yellowed by the sun, and the end of it was edged with black. We sat there looking straight at the photographs his finger was pointing out, and in a little while I said:

"What was the name of the college, Rufus?" And he said:

"That was it, sure. That's me. You can see me in my graduating things."

(Major Alshuster's horse came following soft as music over the ground behind us, carrying sneezes in the purse of his velvet nose. And after Rufus had gone I could hear my sister's voice saying to me over the heads of the frogs: "How can you be such a fool? Couldn't you see he had the photographs taken in a place where they let you put things on, like having your picture taken in a cardboard car or driving an aeroplane? . . .")

In the winter the dam was frozen six feet thick, and it was his work to bring Prince and Star down with the sledge on the timber road at the brink, on the corduroy road that crossed the falls. Prince and Star were as black as seals and here they stood in the white unmelting world, the two black horses steaming against the hard, bright, crusted snow. The white boughs of the trees were forked full in the woods around, and the twigs of the underbrush and bushes were tubed in glass the length of the frozen falls. The hired men were standing on the ice, carving it immaculately with saws as long and lithe as eels. Up and down in their hands ran the flexible saws, setting deeper and deeper the small, black teeth into the blue-white, the majestic cake that held the water fast.

It was these great, aquamarine-hearted slabs that were carried across the drifts and loaded upon the sledge behind the sloping rumps of Prince and Star. Then Rufus drove the horses back past the bowling alley and the kitchen to the icehouse out beyond. The sides of this house were of wood that was rotten and black and curved out with the swell of the ice that stood within; and in this house were the richest mosses to be found flourishing upon the rotting, weeping walls, and lichen pale as anemones grew there, and strong, fresh, leathery fungus. We used to climb in summer up to the one opening the icehouse had and step from the hot, bright afternoon into the great, sepulchral shadow of this place that was as moist as the mouth of a spring no matter what the weather. This was the dark and secret world which drew you from the parched afternoon onto a carpet of sawdust drenched with cold; this, set like a deep well in a desert, was there all summer, a slowly, imperceptibly melting glacier night.

Twice a week in the summer Rufus drove Prince and Star to the Quaker Inn twenty miles off, driving the wagon piled up with ice. The road lay around the mountain, and from one side of it the pine forest dropped steeply away, and through the trees the gully could be seen, the rocks of it seen in miniature from the height and the thread of water stringing through it. Twice every week Rufus drove over with the ice to the inn and was back again in the evening.

(There was lemon-meringue pie for supper that night, I said, and Major Alshuster's horse behind us was taking the sounds of my words in the chestnut tents of his ears and sheltering them in quiet. And Rufus didn't come back to supper that night, I said, and the sheep stopped grazing to look at us in wonder as we passed.)

Prince and Star came back at dawn, as weary as bitches in heat. They were harnessed together still with what remained, and the broken shaft hung between them, striking their forelegs as they came. I can see Prince now, with his rusting mane, and Star with the five-pointed mark on his brow. Their bits were gone and their mouths were white, and their knees were cut wide open as if they had kneeled on broken glass. They walked straight to the barn and waited on the earth floor, in the dark, with their heads down, ready to drop with pain. And you could put questions all year to them but they made no answer. You could say Where's Rufus, and What have you done to Rufus, and even if the tears ran down your face there was nothing but the twitch of their shoulders underneath your hand.

(Now, why do you tell me the story of Prince and Star, said Major Alshuster, and the star on his own horse's forehead was shining out white behind us, and some of its light fell on the Major's face. Because they killed Rufus, I said, and I put my arms around Major Alshuster. It was for grief for Rufus that I was crying, and I clung to this man as if to life, and nothing could stop the shuddering of my heart.)

The trees had snapped off like matches where Prince and Star had gone from the road, and the ice had scattered all the way. They must have begun at Castle Loma, maybe skipping a little in fun like hares at night; and then the fright lighted in the eye of one and leaped wildly to the other. They had turned the wagon over on him, they had pierced his eyes with needles from the pines and set slabs of ice to mark the place they left him. ("He was eighteen," I said, and I was crying. I could see very well the face of Rufus King from the country near Buffalo, photographed dressed as a bullfighter. But the Major was thinking of something else. "Mrs. Whatchername," he was saying, "there's never been anyone like you. Blow your nose in my handkerchief. I'm in love with you," he said.)

The next time I saw him was in a few days, but it was in the evening, and it was quite dark when I went up the red cliff at the end of the town. I had been in the common, leather-benched lounge where the ailing and poor and old came in for their beer, and I had been talking there to an old lady with her grandson beside her and her bonnet tied fast to her head.

"He's only three," said the old lady, taking another glass of beer, "but he can use words as long as your arm." This was the third we were having together, and her tongue was not quite clear.

"Give me somethin' to drink, com' on now," snarled the grandson, and the little old lady rocked with laughter and settled her bonnet on her knot of hair.

"Just listen to him!" she gasped with joy, but she gave me a sly look to one side. "Now, swish! He must have heard somebody asking for a drink one time."

"You give me a drink now," he said, and he set his nails hard in her arm. I knew I must look the other way while she lifted the glass up quick and put it to his mouth.

"He's as good as good with his granny," she said when I looked around again, "and with his mommy and pop he's just a terrible boy. They got all kinds of houses and things," she said with her melting eye, "you never saw. Today when he was to the beach and see a great big car, he went over to turn the crank of it. Only three he is! He thought as it was his pop's big car!"

"My pop ain't got no car, never did," said the boy, and the old lady looked narrowly at him over the brim of her glass.

"Just listen to him, will ya?" she said with her loving smile. "I'm sure I don't know where he gets hold of them words as he does. His pop, he's got the finest car in Devon."

"Give me a drink," said the little boy, and the old lady reached slyly under the table and pinched his skin. He gave her a kick with his boot, and the old lady lifted her black bag up to hide from the others the sight of him finishing the beer.

"He minds me like anything," she said. "And with his mommy he's like possessed."

The Scotch lady who served at the hotel bar was passing in the hall, and when she saw me she came in to ask if I'd found a house.

"Did you ever go up to Needlehay that time?" she said, and I said yes. I had been up to Needlehay and looked at the Dower House in June, and now it was August.

"It was too large for what I want," I said, and the Scotch lady said: "What'll you have this time? You have a drink with me."

I said I'd have a gin, and after she had poured it out, she went on speaking to me.

"Did you see Major Alshuster?" she said in a low voice. "Was he still alive when you went there?"

I put down my glass of gin and waited a moment.

"Of course he was alive," I said. I looked right across the bar into her face, and she was shaking her head.

"Well, it must have been right after you were there," she said. "He was killed in June. The end of June."

I knew that there wasn't a word of truth in it, but I sat there quiet, listening to what she said.

"I know it was when they were cutting the hay on his place," she went on, "because the hearse took fright of the mowing machine and reared up, and the Major pulled him over backwards. That's what they told me. The hearse and the Major, the two of them, broke their backs and they were dead in a minute."

I took another gin and then I went out in the dark and along the sea for the length that the walk goes, and up the cliff path; and where the land ceased and the water and space began I could not see. But if I looked to one side the breath came freer, and if I looked to the other it was as if the unseen hand of the land were lifted in silent warning, and I knew from this on which side the sea must lie. Major Alshuster was waiting for me where he always waited, leaning on the piece of railing on the perilous edge that in daylight was like a window onto the water that whispered a mile straight down below.

"Listen, Major Alshuster," I said, and I took hold of the wooden rail beside him. A beautiful mist, sleek as a cat, was moving against my face. "This is the wrong country for me," I said. "I don't belong in this country." I went on talking fast so that I would not cry. "I can't bear it," I said. "I can't bear it. I might as well be dead if I have to go on living the way I'm living here."

The Major pulled me suddenly against him and his mouth closed hard and hot upon my mouth. It was dark, and only our breaths and our hands could seek each other out and cling in love together. There were no words left, there was nothing to say, there was only the swooning touch of one taken wildly from the other.

"To hell with the country," said Major Alshuster after a while, and his voice was so hoarse it was like the voice of a stranger speaking. His hands held fast to my shoulders and he lifted his head to look straight into the darkness which was England stretching invisibly away. "To hell with the country," he said. We stood close on the edge of it together. "You don't belong in this country any more than I or anyone else belongs here. But you belong to me," said Major Alshuster. "I don't happen to believe in death, Mrs. Whatchername," he said.

How Bridie's Girl Was Won

I

There is no sand to this part of the coast, but a shingled beach on which the sea calls deeply, loudly forever. Ah-h-h-h-h, goes the long, deep sighing of the water, and the waveful of stones shudders back into the tide. Ah-h-h-h-h, goes the hollow warble of the sea, withdrawing, and the fishing boats return and their sails fold down at the edge like petals shriveling in the cold. One man, or two, will jump down from them as their heels strike, leaping hip-deep into the white water, and will haul the craft up from the shuddering echo of the stones. Ah-h-h-h-h, goes the murmur of the water, and as it dies the boats ride inward, their guts a-gleam with the light-bellied fish they carry. The fishermen draw them up over the golden ribbons of seaweed to where the sea no longer comes.

"They catch them in June at Shetland," the fisherman with the beaked nose said, "and around October off the North Foreland, and in November at Folkstone, and then to the southward up to the month of February."

This was the news they were waiting for every night in the pub, for it to come by word of mouth, or by letter even, or over the radio to them. Or in the daytime, when the nets were mended and the rain was blowing as usual, the men came into the pub and sat there with their beer, or without it, and talked of the weather and of when the herring would be likely to come. In the summer, the women had time to walk in without hats on for a glass of beer or to watch their husbands drinking, but now that it was winter, there were only the fishermen left, and this one woman with her hair cut short like a man's and wearing riding breeches.

"We'll know suddenly like," the fisherman with the beaked nose told her. He was not a young man any longer, with the texture and brine of sea in the leather of his neck, and a drop on the end of his nose, and his little eyes rimmed with red. "There may be a change in the weather," he said, "and before you can pull your boots on, the herring'll be there."

The woman was standing at the bar with the others, a smart-looking, rich-looking woman lighting her cigarette for herself under the big framed picture of the King. His Majesty was in khaki, his beard tinted almost golden, his cheeks like the petals of roses, and a travesty of Viking strength in his pretty, painted face.

"Look here," said the woman to the fisherman as she slipped her lighter into her pocket. "You have a drink with me, the lot of you."

"All of us? Everyone in the place?" asked the fisherman, speaking in reverence to her.

"Yes, the lot of you," said the woman. "I want to get acquainted."

"Her's giving a drink," he said, and he turned around to the others and spoke their language to them. "What'll it be, then? Her's asking what it'll be."

He turned back to her, rubbing his hands together, and he watched her carefully. His sharp, little, red-rimmed eyes were on her as she called the pubkeeper and ordered what they wanted, watching her as if in fear that a change in her face might say her mind had altered. But there was her unswerving eye, and her good chin, and her closed mouth holding the cigarette unflinchingly. She was not very tall, a woman of thirty, maybe, with a head of her own, and a worldly way that went well with the clothes she was wearing. Once she had opened her purse and paid the pubkeeper over the bar, the fisherman with the beaked nose looked more respectfully at her and he chose his language with care.

"Word ought to be along any day now," he said to her, "and then we'll know whether to steer north or southward for them." He picked up his glass of ale and he looked at her over it with his bright, unhappy eyes. "Cheerio," he said dismally, and all the fishermen in the bar picked up their glasses and said "Cheerio" in voices as melancholy as the weather that fell endlessly against the panes.

And another day in the week, this word came to them: that the herring gulls had left the ports to the north and were traveling southward. They were thick as thieves off Weymouth, the fisherman with the beaked nose was telling her, and the next news might be that the herrings themselves were moving down the coast. The woman stood at the bar beside him, in her riding breeches and her yellow oilskin coat hung down to her heels behind. There were two dogs lying at her feet, two feathery red spaniels with their hair waved dark and drenched by the rain; and save for them and the two people standing, there was no one else in the place.

"My son, he telephoned me last night from Weymouth," said the fisherman to her. "He says the herring gulls is like a snowstorm over there. Did you ever run across my son?" he asked her. "A big, fine-looking man with black eyes and a fine head of hair? A well-set-up-looking fellow when you see him?"

"No," said the woman, hiking up her breeches, "I don't think I ever met anyone like that around here."

There were only the spaniels tenderly licking the cushions of their feet on the boards of the floor, but the fisherman hesitated a moment before speaking.

"He was going to get married," he said then, looking down at the varnished wood where his empty glass was standing. "But everything goes queer with him, someway." His voice passed low between them. "Everything was set for it—the ring and the house. They were going to get married in April or May."

"Look here," said the woman sharply, and the dogs raised their heads at the sound of her voice. "What about having a drink with me?"

"You see," said the fisherman when the pubkeeper had come and gone, "my son's never had a mother to look to him." He wiped his nose on the back of his hand and he leaned on the bar beside her. "My wife, she died, and everything went up in smoke like, and here was this lad. Well, it's always been women," said the fisherman, tasting his beer. "First one and then another. And then he took up with this girl, and she was a nice girl, and I couldn't do enough for them. I gave them the house and I got Bridie his own boat, and he was going to settle down for good and all."

The door of the pub opened in from the rain, and a fisherman with the stench of fish on him and the crablike legs of a sailing man came into the bar and shook the rain from his visored hat. The woman in her riding breeches and the fisherman with the beaked nose turned around and looked at him from the bar.

"Hello, Watrus," said the fisherman standing beside her. He pushed his own hat back from his short, gray fringe of hair. "Here's she as give I and all a drink of beer last week."

"Pleased to meet she," said the fisherman. He stood a little way from them in respect, and he smiled a shy, sweet smile at her under his stained mustaches. "I wasn't here last week, and that's a fact'm. The skipper'll tell you that's so."

"Have a drink now then," said the woman in riding breeches. "My name's Stephens—I call myself Mrs. Stephens."

"Pleased to meet you," said the little old fisherman, taking his hat off. He stood looking at the rouge painted on her lips and the pure-white shirt, and the yellow satin scarf at her neck with the hound dogs patterned on it, brown and white and quick, as if crying after the scent.

"Been telling she about Bridie," said the fisherman with the beaked nose, and the other man shook his head and his eyes shone bright at the sight of the beer set down before him on the counter.

"Bridie's the finest man on the coast," he said. He smoothed back his mustaches with the crooked side of his hand and he lifted his glass up. "Cheerio," he said, and his lips closed eagerly on the bitter at the brim.

"What I was saying was, Bridie's girl, she run off," said Bridie's father in a low voice. "That wasn't any kind of a trick to play on a fine upstanding man like he. Everything was as good as done, and she runs off with some kind of a chap."

"Why didn't he go after her?" asked Mrs. Stephens, smoking. Bridie's father thought of that for a moment, drinking slowly at his beer, and then he said:

"I can't tell you that. Bridie, he never said a word about tracking them down. Maybe it's his pride. He has a lot of pride, has Bridie."

"Oh, has he?" said Mrs. Stephens. She looked down, as if speculating on it, at the clean, light toe of her leather riding shoe.

"He could have fought that man and whipped him, if the fellow had ever come out and said what he wanted," said Bridie's father. "But that fellow, he goes off at night with the girl, and when Bridie goes to fetch her on a Sunday, she's gone since the night before. They run off in the other fellow's car."

"If he's anything like a man, he ought to fight for her," said Mrs. Stephens. She snapped her silver cigarette case open and took one out.

"Bridie's as good as any man in the country," said his father quietly.

"His girl didn't seem to see it that way," said Mrs. Stephens, smoking.

"Her wasn't near good enough for Bridie," said Watrus, and the door from the street opened fast, as if from a gust of wind, and another man came blowing in. He was tall and broad, with his eyes as black as tar in his face, and his fisherman's leather-billed cap set rakishly on his head. The turtleneck of his dark-blue seaman's sweater was rolled up to his ears, and his black oilskin hung careless as a cloak from his shoulders.

"Here, Bridie, when did you get in!" said his father, and Bridie came swinging across the public room with a cigarette in the end of his mouth. He put his hand down flat on the varnished bar, and the sound of money rang out, and he said:

"Everyone present has a drink with me now. The herring's come. I seen them. You," he called out to the pubkeeper, who came in from the dining room, "bring us half a pint of bitter all around. What are you drinking, lady? A pink gin! Ain't you the toff, now? I tell you, I seen the herring," he said, talking fast. He leaned on the bar between Mrs. Stephens and his father, head and shoulders taller than the other man, his cheeks fresh and wet from the rain, his black eyes gay.

"Saw they?" said Watrus with a burst of laughter in his mustaches.

"Thousands of them," said Bridie, flinging his arm out.

"They're getting the boats out now. You drink fast. I seen them resting on the sand at the bottom, thousands on thousands of them, the whole army of them, shedding down their roe. You and Dad'll come with me. My boat's as good as on the water. I seen them this morning, just before sunrise. They rose up like a flock of sheep and started southward."

Mrs. Stephens stood there near to him, smoking her cigarette, and watching him: watching the beer run quickly into his strong, brown throat, watching the manly, dark-haired hand on his glass, and the side of his face, and the quick, bold, flashing eye.

"They'll be up with the rising of the moon tonight," he said. "Bring us another half pint all around." He paid his money out flat on the counter, and the pubkeeper said:

"It's five minutes to closing time."

"Five minutes is four and a half minutes too long for us," said Bridie, talking quickly. "There's a fortune out there, and we're going to bring it in. Come on, drink fast, drink fast, old men," he said. "Drink it up, lady. We're going to sweep the sea clean and pick 'em off like daisies."

"Look here," said the woman in riding breeches. "I think I'll go out there with you."

"Sure," said Bridie, but when he looked at her something altered his eye. "The sea's like glass this afternoon, and it's freshening. From the look of it there won't be rain tonight."

"This is she as give I and all a drink one night last week," said his father, and Bridie's teeth went suddenly white in his face as he looked down into the young woman's face and tilted his hat and smiled.

II

It did not seem as if there were clouds above their heads, but as if this were the somber color of the heavens, this wide, unchanging, ashen tide of sky that flowed without barrier into the wide, unchanging, ashen tide of sea. The air was cold, and in spite of the fact that the rain had ceased, it was wringing wet on the hair and mouth. The fleet of boats went separately out across the water, and the nets were spread and allowed to drift with the movement of the current. And then the action of the men, and of Bridie even, lapsed like a lull in the breeze.

Every plank of Bridie's boat, and every inch of rope was spangled with the silvery dead scales of the fish he had taken the night before and the night before that. They were clinging even to the coats and the boots that Bridie's father and Watrus wore. Mrs. Stephens sat in the tar-stained belly of the yawl with a great fur coat buttoned up to her chin and a cigarette in her fingers. Beyond them rode the other boats, and behind stood the smoke-white cliffs of the coast with the gulls hovering high, in clear, gleaming crescents of light against the heaven's darkness.

The two old fishermen were seated in the stem, and only when they cautiously, now and again, pulled the nets toward the surface was any movement made. Bridie stood not far from Mrs. Stephens, filling his pipe up and looking out to sea, and the boat rocked gently, gently on the water, gentle as a cradle rocking in a quiet, still unlighted room.

"Look here," said Mrs. Stephens suddenly out of the stillness to Bridie. "What's this about your girl turning you down?"

Bridie's face flashed quickly toward her, his eyes gone sharp with wrath.

"Who's been talking?" he said. He stood holding the bowl of his pipe in his brown, bare hand, his oilskins falling loose from his shoulders, and his visored hat set sideways on his short, black, lively hair.

"Look here," said the woman again, and she crossed her legs in their leather boots and stretched them out before her. "I like you. Sit down here a minute. I just got kicked into the middle of next week myself. My husband's divorcing me."

She made a little face at him, and Bridie looked at her, and then he sat slowly down:

"What's over's done with," he said in a moment. "I'm not wasting any time thinking about her."

He put his pipe in the corner of his mouth and he felt for a match in his pockets.

"Here's my lighter," said Mrs. Stephens, and she leaned forward with the little flame held in her hand.

"Only you know how it is," he said, sitting back and smoking. "I've always given women the go-by when I'd had enough, and here this little chit, she up and turns the tables on me."

"Yes," said Mrs. Stephens quietly. "That's how it is."

"She was the Queen of the Carnival this year," said Bridie, and he looked out, his eyes half smiling, half grieving, over the darkening sea. "She had her dress all the way down from London, from a theatrical costumer's. You've never seen anything like the way the fellows went on about her. She had them all knocked silly."

"She's a great beauty, is she?" said Mrs. Stephens a little bitterly, but curiously as well.

"That was the whole trouble," said Bridie. "I never knew where I was with her. I might have known the way things would turn around in the end."

"That's the way I felt about my husband," said Mrs. Stephens. "Women were always after him, damn him. He should never have married anyone. But I went through everything with him—everything—and now *he* has started proceedings! Can you imagine it? *He's* divorcing me!"

"Good riddance to bad rubbish is what I says," said Bridie, folding his arms over.

"I suppose I say that too," said Mrs. Stephens. She gave a little laugh and took another cigarette from the silver case. "Look here," she said. "What do you think you'll do next?"

"Who? Me?" asked Bridie, looking at her in surprise. "Oh, I'll recover. Her going away hasn't made ten minutes' difference in the time I get up in the morning or the time I go to bed. I'm not losing any sleep, or getting any gray hairs either over that bit of fluff, I'll tell you," he said with a little grunt.

"Of course, you have your work to do, you have your fishing to go on with," said Mrs. Stephens. "If I had any work, I might think of it that way too." She looked down at her hands, as if asking help of them. "But my husband and I, we didn't live separate lives, we just lived one life together. Whatever he did, I helped him at it. We were together all day—riding together, walking together, painting together. You see, he did a little painting."

"You mean houses?" asked Bridie.

"No. I mean pictures," said Mrs. Stephens. "He liked the wind and the sun and the rain the way I did," said Mrs. Stephens in a low, pain-tightened voice. "We liked the same things, always, five years of it," she said, "and then this insane thing had to happen." Bridie was looking out over the sea and thinking of the weather, and the boat rocked gently, gently on the softly running tide. "I can't get used to it, to being alone, Bridie," she said, and when he looked back at the sound of her voice, she made another small, wry face at him and laughed. "What am I going to do about it?" she said.

"Well, you just look at me," said Bridie, shifting on the seat and spreading his shoulders wide. "The first few days, I took it pretty hard. I won't make no secret of it. I went blotto, as they says, for five days, but after that I straightened up. They were talking about a ship up at Weymouth, and I went up there to see her. That was a sight, I tell you!" His eyes were on Mrs. Stephens as he talked, black and bold and almost merry. "She'd touched at St. Michael's on her way home and laid three weeks there," said Bridie, "and there the goose barnacles had fastened on her and she was covered thick with them from stem to stern. You could see them all over her, good as armor, it was! Well, do you know, they hadn't been able to make two miles an hour, even with the wind, from the weight of the barnacles on her, and they were putting her up for sale once her cargo was discharged!"

"Yes, I suppose that was a great help at the time," said Mrs. Stephens, looking down at her helpless hands. "But nobody ever brought a barnacled ship along to take my mind off my husband when he went away. Waking or sleeping, night or day, I can't think of anything but him. I want him back, and that's all I can think of now."

The two men at the other end of the boat had got to their feet again and were stooping over in the failing light to raise the nets and peer within them, and Bridie rose uneasily and moved behind Mrs. Stephens and laid hold of the rope hanging into the water from the stern.

"Take it easy, Bridie," his father called in a low voice down the length of the boat to him, and the three men cautiously and in rhythm drew the dripping ends of the cotton nets in and folded them on the timber.

"Not a sign," said Watrus from the stem, and Bridie's father called out: "Let 'er go, Bridie." Hand over hand in rhythm, ·the three men fed out the nets again into the lapping sea. There was the free, sharp taste of salt on the air as Bridie returned and sat down again beside her.

"Sure," he said. "I know how you feel about it. But the worst of it is I can't get it out of my head that this bloke she went off with, he was a toff, and how's that going to end up for her, I'd like to know? She's got the looks all right to carry anything off, but you can't tell me she could step as high as the kind of society he steps out with."

The darkness was deepening now over the water, and the buoys were lighting, single and clear and distant as stars. Far at the end of the land, the pale white wings of the semaphore lifted and fell and lifted. Slowly, like planets rising, the lights began burning below the fading cliffs in the windows of the town.

"I know," said Mrs. Stephens. "I'm sure in a case like that they couldn't be happy together."

He was sitting so close to her, his elbows leaning on his knees, and his oilskins gleaming, that she saw the smile that went suddenly white across his dark-burned face.

"I bet she could carry it off, at that," he said. He might never have known that Mrs. Stephens was there, or that she had spoken. "I bet she could sit down at table with royalty even and nobody'd see any difference in her."

"Look here," said Mrs. Stephens abruptly. "Did you ever think of doing yourself in?"

"Doing myself in?" asked Bridie, starting back. "Who, me?"

"I think about it all the time," said Mrs. Stephens in an unsteady voice. "I take a drink to forget about it, and then I feel more like doing it than ever. If I don't get my husband back, I'm going to do it. I've picked out the cliff. It's right over there," she said and she pointed into the dark.

"You need a change, maybe," said Bridie, uneasily. "You need a change of scene, as the saying has it."

"This is my change of scene," said Mrs. Stephens. "I came down from London to get away from where we'd lived together. I came down here to the coast to think things out and try and square my shoulders." She looked toward him in the darkness, and tried to grin at him. "Well, I don't seem to be squaring them, do I?" she said.

"Sometimes things like this is harder on a woman," said Bridie. Only the whites of his eyes, and his teeth, white as a dog's teeth, were left of him in the gathering dark. "Women don't take things so lightly as men, that is, some women."

"Oh, don't they?" said Mrs. Stephens. "Look here, Bridie," she said. "Kiss me. They can't see from the other end."

"Who cares if they do?" said Bridie, bold and reckless, and he put his arms quickly around her. He kissed her hard and long on the mouth, and the leather bill of his rakish hat struck the top of her head and rolled off down between them.

"You've got beautiful hair," said Mrs. Stephens, drawing away in a minute.

"By God," said Bridie, breathing hard. Mrs. Stephens took a cigarette from her case and put it between her lips.

"Have you a match, Bridie?" she asked. "I'm afraid my lighter has perished."

He took out a box from his pocket and struck one on it, and she saw his hand was shaking as he held the flame from the breeze. With the light of it between them, they looked into each other's faces, and Bridie stooped forward in confusion and picked up his hat from the bottom of the boat and put it back on the side of his head.

"Look here," said Mrs. Stephens, smoking. There was nothing to be seen now but the lights on land and the lights of the buoys moving, and they might have been anywhere, sitting together in darkness, except for the lapping of the cold tongues of sea. "What are you going to do about your girl?" asked Mrs. Stephens. "Aren't you going to put up a fight for her?"

"What's over's through with, like I said," said Bridie's troubled voice. "They say she went over to France or somewheres. I don't know where she went. I'm not one to cry over spilt milk," he said with a short laugh. "Not me."

"No, but if you love someone, you go after them tooth and nail," said Mrs. Stephens. "That's why I came down here to the coast," she said, and lap, lap, went the cold tongues of the sea, lap, lap, at the fishing boat's side. "Look here, you're going to go after that girl of yours, Bridie," said Mrs. Stephens. "You're going to get her and bring her back to her people. And you're going to marry her. You're crazy to ever think you weren't."

"What about the other bloke?" said Bridie. "Maybe they're married now."

"Maybe they're not," said Mrs. Stephens. She sat smoking her cigarette, her voice tight and hard beside him. "Maybe he's already got a wife somewhere."

"I haven't the money to leave the country and go after her," said Bridie, shifting on the seat.

"I'll give you the money," said Mrs. Stephens. "I'll give it to you forever. You don't have to pay it back. And why, do you want to know why?" she said. He had put his arm around her again and his salty hand was as cold as a sea thing in her coat's dark fur. "Because I believe in love," she said. "I believe in it. That's all."

The men were at the nets again, but Bridie did not move from where he was. Her head came almost to his shoulder, unseen, but the hair brushed softly against his chin, and there was the odor of flowers in it.

"Look here," she said in her brief, quick voice. "Don't let them tell you anything else. Nothing matters but love: I know. I'm thirty. I'm old enough to be your mother."

"Hold on, lady," said Bridie, softly, "I'm twenty-six."

"It doesn't matter," said Mrs. Stephens. "Love matters. You're going to go after her and bring her back. You're going to do it. Do I sound hard? Do I sound tough? Do I look like a hard-boiled baby? Well, I am. I'm so damned tough that I'd cut anybody's throat for it—for love, I mean. I'd steal, lie, murder for it. And now you know."

"How do you know I'm going after her?" asked Bridie, and his heart was shaking with wonder within him.

"Because you're going to listen to me," said Mrs. Stephens. "I've got a lot of money, too much money, and I'd give every cent of it for the one thing worth being poor for. Love isn't something you meet on every street corner, Bridie."

"I know that," Bridie said.

"Then don't let it go once you've met with it," said Mrs. Stephens. "Go and tell her, as I've told you, that nothing else matters, not holding me or any other woman, nothing except holding the woman you want in your arms. What good is anything on earth going to do you, Bridie, my love, if you haven't the girl you want to wake up to in the morning and to come home to in the evening when you come home from the sea——"

"Shut up," said Bridie. He jumped to his feet and stood swaying in the darkness, and she knew he was standing there still because of the skirt of his oilskin coat that moved with the motion of the water, now the touch of it on her knee, and then the touch of it gone, like a hand withdrawing from her and then returning in the dark.

"If you're in love, Bridie," she said, "for God's sake go and bring her back to the people she belongs to and the kind of life she'll be happy in. It's for her sake as well as for yours that I'm saying this to you. You can get off tomorrow on the early train."

"Yes, I could do it," said Bridie, scarcely aloud.

"Sit down," said Mrs. Stephens, and Bridie sat down beside her. "I want this so much," she said in a strong, tight voice to him, "that I'm ready to go off the end of this boat if anything interferes with it. I want to see you two married, and I'm not going to stop until it's true. If you looked at her once again the way you looked at me in the pub today, Bridie, she'd leave any man and follow you back from wherever she is, and she'd live and die beside you."

"Do you think so?" asked Bridie, holding her close in his arm. "Do you think that might be true?"

"Yes," said Mrs. Stephens, "I'm telling you. She doesn't belong to him, they have nothing to do with each other. I know it. She belongs to that town back there, and the cliffs, and she ought to be sitting here tonight in your arms the way I'm sitting, and you ought to be kissing her the way you finished kissing me." Her hand reached out as if for help, and it closed with strength on Bridie's. He was sitting there smiling in the dark at the thought of what she said. "You ought to reach Glasgow tomorrow evening at the latest," she said. "You could be in Wick by the following day. From there you can get to the Orkneys in no time."

"The Orkneys!" said Bridie in bewilderment. "What am I going there for?"

"They're at the Ship Inn at Kirkwell," said Mrs. Stephens. "Waiting for his divorce to come up."

"How do you know?" asked Bridie.

"Look here," began Mrs. Stephens, and then the voice of Watrus called out from the other end, deep and sweet, like a song being sung in the darkness.

"Stand by, Bridie," called Bridie's father the length of the boat. "The nets is heavy as stone."

The Herring Piece

I

The woman who owned the Kettle and Anchor was standing behind the zinc when the boy came down the stairs at the back after leaving his suitcase in the room. The sign outside said her name was Angie Flower, and once Arthur was in the bar he could not take his eyes from her serving the men and talking. There was a thin man, a city-looking man, in an overcoat and a hat who stood near to the bar, drinking his ale and talking to Mrs. Flower with the glass in his hand held level with his chin. Around the room, on the benches against the wall, the fishermen were sitting.

"I was at the searchlight with Jellicoe at my elbow," one of them said, and Arthur looked for a moment at this man with the stained mustaches hanging, spidery-haired, bright golden from tobacco and beer, over his lip and the foul dark teeth bitten short in his head. "If he was a-running away he wouldn't have steamed south, would he? He was standing there by I, and us were steaming south all night and us could see the lights of the blasted German fleet like cigar butts going out ahead."

"What'll yours be, sir?" said Mrs. Flower's voice, and Arthur turned in confusion to the scarcely perceptible flutter of her lids.

"I'll have a rough cider, please," he said, and the color ran up to his eyes.

He paid for it at once and as he lifted his glass to drink he looked again at Mrs. Flower, his eyes, like the eyes of a boy looking at good food, going without apology but a little shyly to the powdered flesh held in the tight blue velvet dress, the bare white neck, and the diamond buttons in the immaculately shaped ears. Her hair was not red, nor anywhere near it, but the color of a tangerine, oily and bright, and she stood just under the bulb with the green shade over it, her perfectly white small hands holding to her elbows as she listened to what the thin man in the overcoat said.

"Looks a bit stormy tonight, doesn't it?" said Mrs. Flower after a while, speaking in her carefully uncommon voice to Arthur, watching her accent very well.

"I've heard you have lots of good weather down here," said Arthur so hurriedly that they could scarcely make out what he was saying. At the roots of her hair there was half an inch of dark showing, but this only made her the more exotic to him, the more bizarre. The man in the overcoat and the brown hat nursed the glass of ale in his hand, the fleshless, hairless saddle of his hand almost concealed beneath the hat brim, the end of the pale, obscenely nostriled nose hanging nearly into the glass. On either side of his head the big ears stood out with the brown hat seemingly resting on them.

"That's bad form," said the man in the overcoat before Arthur had even seen his mouth was opening to speak. "They're touchy down here about their climate. Better talk about something else." His voice flat and dry and pared systematically of humor was saying of itself, "You've made a blunder, my boy, a social blunder," his mouth washed out at once with the eternally undrunk or eternally replenished liquid in the glass. The two eyes, neither dark nor light, were clamped on either side of the grief-stricken nose, and the hat brim, very neat and new, stood strictly above and outside, giving decorum to the sneer, the bile, the dyspepsia of what was featured below.

"I suppose you're down here on holiday?" said Mrs. Flower to the boy. She spoke to him with an almost childish sweetness of tone and she gave him for a moment the small priceless pearls of her smile.

"Yes," said Arthur. He stirred in a desperate contortion of ease and finished his cider. "I had the flu, you see, and the doctor told me to take a week off and run down to Devon for some sun."

"Ever hear of it, Mrs. Flower?" asked the thin man in the overcoat and hat. His hand nursed the glass of ale before his mouth. "Species of big round yellow ball generally believed to be overhead for a certain number of hours out of the twenty-four." The glass gyrated slowly under his nose as he spoke. "S-u-n," he spelled out. "Usually found off the coast of Spain and used to dry clothes with."

"There isn't a sign of fog here on the coast," Mrs. Flower said to Arthur. She was over forty maybe, he thought, but so fresh, so white, so scented that she might have been a girl. He stood thinking intimately, sensuously of her as she chose a cigarette out of the pack he held toward her, looking rapt at the peacock-full blue bosom, the velvet's sheen, the soft ballooning of the breasts.

"The fog must be pea soup in London tonight," he said, looking.

"Oh, well," said Mrs. Flower, speaking like a child. "In the city you can always manage to forget about the weather, I think. And then you have all the excitement, of course, and that makes a difference."

"Oh, yes, rather," said Arthur. Thinking of the Duke of Windsor he was filled suddenly with the sense of his own strong implacable male power.

"I couldn't sleep for weeks, I was so excited," said Mrs.

Flower. She held her elbows fast in her two hands and rocked herself on the edge of the counter, the cigarette held tight between her lips.

"As if sleep made any difference," the voice of the man in the overcoat went on behind his glass. "As if I ever got any sleep. I never had any except one night in Madeira once about ten years ago. You stop talking to that young man and get me a drink now, Angie." Mrs. Flower sighed and put down her cigarette and went to the keg of ale behind. Arthur watched her stoop down among the other dark wood kegs with the thin man's glass in her hand. He saw she had light silk stockings on, her flesh quite soft and milky through the mesh, and little rhinestone buttons on her black satin shoes. "Thing about islands is," said the man in the overcoat, "there's water all around them, under them, over them, but that's where Madeira fools you. There isn't any water on top of you in Madeira, none of that nasty invention leaking down all over the roofs and hats of everybody on the island, thing called 'rain.'" Arthur saw Mrs. Flower straighten up and return across the wooden floor. "Holiday," the man in the overcoat and hat was saying, mixing his fresh ale now with the low drowsy mumbling of his talk. "Hole like this for a holiday. I'm in artificial silks," said the voice, the clamped eyes as motionless as wood beneath the brim. "No, not wearing them, traveling for them. That's my line. Salesman for pretties with a sales line that starts going after a couple of pints. I've been supplying Mrs. Flower here for forty-odd years now——"

"Why, Mr. Romsey!" she said, and she slapped at him with her hand.

"I pass through here twice a year," his voice went on, "and there isn't anything about the place I can't tell you. You've made one mistake, young man, this isn't the time of year to come here. You'd better get out before you make another. This is a summer resort, y'see——"

"That'll be fourpence, Mr. Romsey," said Mrs. Flower. Romsey felt for the money in his pocket and paid it out on the counter without turning his head.

"A summer resort," he said, "and this is winter and everything closed except the graveyard, so there's no use hanging around here."

"Rotten luck, I must say," said Arthur. To escape the pressure of Romsey's almost single eye, he pushed his empty glass toward Mrs. Flower. "Let me have another cider, please," he said. And Romsey went right on:

"If I were in your place I'd take a train and go somewhere else. Push on to Land's End. There's a good pub near Mousehole where they'd take care of you. I've got the hours here in my pocket and I'd go as far as the station with you. I've got nothing to do till tomorrow except talk to Mrs. Flower here."

"Maybe he likes fishing," said Mrs. Flower, smoking again and looking at Arthur. "We have very good fishing here. That's what the gentlemen come down for."

"Fishing," said Romsey, the warm bitter mouthfuls of what he drank taken into the narrow-chested, padded-shouldered, bloodless, nearly fleshless frame. "Yes, fishing. You go out after filthy little beasts full of bones, you know." He looked with his barren, clamped and mournful gaze at Arthur and made a wiggling movement with one hand. "Met them here and there of a Friday, I daresay?" said Romsey.

"Oh, rather," said Arthur. He took his purse out and opened it and paid for the second glass of cider.

"I suppose you Londoners feel as bad as we do about it all," said Mrs. Flower. "I can't get over the way he threw it all over for her, an American and twice-divorced and everything like that."

"Oh, quite," said Arthur. He looked into his glass with the thoughts of Mrs. Flower not to be drowned now, but taking monstrous proportions, knowing that he too would have foregone, forsworn, relinquished for anything she promised.

"It was the weather," said Romsey's voice from behind the glass of ale. "They kept it out of the papers, but all Fleet Street was on to it. There'd have been hell to pay if a thing like that broke the press. Edward VIII unable to weather another day of atmosphere which had first been painted a good substantial long-wearing green and then used to wipe the city streets with before being wrung out and hung up to dry in the rain. They had to choose," he said. "It was the royal family or the climate. They weren't going to let the old-school climate down." He began shaking with what, for want of a better name, might be called laughter, jerking and rattling with a convulsion that gave no sign upon his face, and without raising his glass a fraction of an inch or lowering his head he drank. "Look what's happened to the herring industry alone," he said. "All these fisher lads here'll tell you the same thing. Dyeing has killed the kipper and bloater and haddock trade. But that ain't the half of it. How would you feel if you were a fish, Angie, and every time you came up for a breath of air it was raining?"

When Arthur looked at Mrs. Flower he saw she was making a sign to him and his glass of cider stopped in mid-air as he watched the little twirling motion of her hand beside her temple.

"Drunk—he's had a bit too——" He saw her lips shaping it, but she did not say it aloud, and with it she gave Arthur the sweet untroubled innocence of her smile, secret and childlike, like a promise made him. You and I know this, it is something between you and me alone as other things might be some time shared intimately between us. Arthur felt the strength go from his knees.

"Mrs. Flower," he said with his voice hoarse. "Have you ever been in the pictures? I was thinking a little while back you'd be beautiful in the pictures."

"If you're not going to take that train," Romsey's voice went on with it, "you'd better consider fishing. They're going out now, Dawson and a couple of the other boats." His close-set eyes, that might have been a single eye bisected by the nose, were fixed motionless on Arthur. "Once the pub closes down there's nothing else to do, so you'd better face it. The first night I struck this town I went upstairs to what's maybe the same room you're sleeping in tonight and maybe the thing, the same thing you're counting on having happen to you tonight happened to me." Arthur heard Mrs. Flower stir impatiently behind the bar, but he could not bring himself to lift his eyes. "And another time I came here and I was going to commit suicide there in that room upstairs, just to give the place a reputation, a little publicity for poor old Angie here. I'd have done it, too, if it wasn't that everything here's a little bit rottener than any other town on the coast, even the climate, even the women——"

"Mr. Romsey," said Mrs. Flower with dignity, "I'm your hostess for just so long as you——"

"But even the gas here couldn't do me in," the voice went on. "Inferior stuff, inferior like the——"

It might have been that last pure promising look of Mrs. Flower's that had made a man of Arthur at last, for he found himself without surprise taking Romsey's arm and taking him with decision through the door and into the street outside. It was dark, except for the lights from the pub windows and the street light blowing near the beach.

"I'm inviting you to come out fishing with me tonight," said Romsey, walking not quite straight, his hands in the pockets of the rather nattily cut overcoat, the elbows and ears beneath the hat brim protruding against the illumination from the light beyond. The rain had not begun to fall yet, perhaps held off by the wind that moved in from the dark wide invisibility beyond the shingles which was, only because of its smell and the rush of it through the quivering pebbles, the sea. "Not to fish, you understand," said Romsey, "but because there's nothing else to do here. Even the fishermen don't fish. They put in their time going out there and coming back."

"They might go home to bed," said Arthur shortly. Out in the air his strength and pride became as sweet as music to him and he walked toward the beach a step or two behind the other man, thinking of Mrs. Flower. In a minute he would get rid of this drunk, he thought, and because of it he scarcely felt the damp on his face or the wind.

"You wouldn't," said Romsey, walking not quite straight before him. "You wouldn't go home all night if you saw the women they'd married."

"Well, I'm going back to the pub and get to bed now," said Arthur. He began to whistle. It had happened to other men before, men as young as he was, younger.

"Come here," said Romsey, and Arthur saw him turn around. He stood there in the half-darkness of the street light and the night, his hands in his pockets, his hat brim down, very trim in

his overcoat, his ears and elbows out. "Come here," he said, and
when Arthur stopped before him Romsey took his right hand out
of his pocket. Arthur had stopped whistling and he stood there
waiting, his mouth just opened, ready to speak, when Romsey
hit him squarely on the chin.

II

When he awoke there was a lingering moment of confusion, of
shock and pity, in his head. In a while he knew he was lying in
the rocking dark and against his face, as if he tasted it, was the
smell of fish, the gluey substance of what fish were or where fish
had been, the inescapable scales of fish numbing the ends of his
fingers so that the sense of touch and warmth seemed gone from
him forever. After a time he saw there was the coal of a cigarette
glowing above him, almost within reach, and at the farthest point
of darkness a half moon of yellow cupped out of the night,
shaded and swinging like a buoy on the movement of the tide.
"Deep-sea fishing," said Romsey's voice, beginning from behind the spark of the cigarette and coming through the dream of
darkness to him. "How do you like it by this time?" Arthur
stirred below him, dimly aroused by the sense of outrage and
pain. "Don't try to move, don't try sitting up yet," said Romsey's
voice. "That light down there is the nose of the boat, where the
men are." The boat rode slowly, deeply, as if at anchor on the
water, and the rain was still somewhere just beyond sight, just
before falling, perhaps waiting for the dawn before it fell. "I was
telling you," said Romsey, "about Madeira. I was twenty-four
hours there, something like ten years ago, and I've been like a
dead man ever since, talking about it to anybody the way the
dead must talk about life together. I woke up one morning, just
one morning, in Madeira without feeling any shame or guilt, just
once since I was born waking up without cringing from what I'd
see outside the window. . . ."
Arthur lay quiet, listening, comforted slowly by the sound of
this voice he had known a long time somewhere else, listening,

as if his wounded heart lay open-mouthed to the nourishment of this gentle, almost compassionate despair.

"Every time I get on a boat," said Romsey's voice from behind the little ember of light, "my bones start asking for it, but there isn't any answer. I've got a wife and three kids and there's no business to take me toward Madeira again. Take a drink of this," he said, and when he leaned toward him, Arthur made out that Romsey still had his hat on, the ears still spread to hold it in place, and he put his lips around the metal grooves of Romsey's flask and drank the brandy down. "Maybe I'm like a dead man asking women for life," Romsey said, once he had drunk from the flask himself and screwed the cap on. "Not asking every woman, but ones like that, like Angie Flower, asking them to tell me all over again what life was like, so I'll remember. Women with hair that color, out of a bottle, put on with a tooth-brush. . . ." Lying there, without moving his hand, without thinking it even, Arthur knew it was Romsey's overcoat that cov-ered him and knew it was Romsey who had put a sweater under his head as he slept. "I come down here maybe twice or three times in the year, and the rest of the time when I'm not here I don't know what happens, and if I'm in Plymouth or Manchester, to hell with what happens at the Kettle and Anchor. But tonight I wasn't in Manchester. As long as I don't have to see it going on under my nose . . ." Arthur lay listening, quiet and without im-pulse listening to the voice's unfaltering and unaccented lullaby. "I didn't come down all the way from Hanley just to see you and Angie Flower, because I know well enough when she's up to it and I saw tonight——"

"What's that?" said Arthur suddenly out loud, and he raised himself quickly on his elbow, for all around them in the dark now was the movement of wings, the curiously strong threshing and whispering of an army of wings passing over their heads and passing continuously, unseen, bewildering in the night. It might have been all the birds of one land crossing to another, for the twittering tongues could be heard speaking as they swept on in the enormous torrent of flight.

"What's that?" he called out to Romsey in a fearful voice, but Romsey made no answer, and the light of the cigarette was gone.

He heard his own words crying out in the flutter of wings and voices, asking for sense and reason to be given. He felt his heart leaping in his mouth in terror at this unearthly whistling of the night. "Romsey, Romsey!" he called in anguish. The fisherman's voice from the lighted end of the boat sang out:

"Hi, Romsey, there's the Herring Piece passing over," and at once the sound of the wings and the musical speech was gone and there was nothing but the slap of the water against the side.

Romsey struck a match, and the boy in the bottom of the boat held his breath in his teeth still as he watched him set it to the fresh cigarette.

"No rain tonight and full nets by morning then," said Romsey, and he shot the dead match into the sea. "Take a drink of this," said Romsey's voice again, good as a mother's above him. "That's their good omen," he said when Arthur had drunk. "The Herring Piece. To you and me it's redwings saving their souls before the mildew and rot eats them to the bone. They'll be in Madeira by tomorrow, maybe. They'll be sitting on a tree, waiting for Madeira worms to come out of the Madeira ground while they dry their feathers in the Madeira sun. S-u-n." Romsey's voice stopped for a moment as he drank. "Ever hear of it?" he asked then.

"I think you mentioned it in the pub tonight," said Arthur, and he could hear Romsey's teeth shaking with the cold.

Your Body Is a Jewel Box

I

The rain was falling just as it did every day at this time of the year, great handfuls of it flung hard on the windows, and when Olive got out of bed she saw that Mildred was sitting on the roof again, holding her knees in her bare arms and crying in the rain.

"For heaven's sake," said Olive, opening the window, "come in, Mildred. Don't sit there like that. Come in, now, do," she said, reaching her hand out to her sister. The two of them were in their nightgowns still, the dark girl on the roof and the yellow-haired girl standing inside the bedroom. "Come in now, Mildred, and we'll go down to the fire and get dry."

But Mildred only raised her head from her arms and looked in what might have been grief at her sister. But in spite of the tears that ran out of her eyes, it was not grief, for there was no look of sorrow in her face; only the black inhuman look of a wounded beast, even in pain, the small, suspicious, weary eye. Her night-dress was so thin and it clung to her so with the wet that the shape of her breasts and her thighs could be clearly seen. Her short hair was in wringing curls all over her head, and down the lower side of her cheek and jaw sprang a little growth of darkness, as on a youth's still virgin face.

"Come in, now, do," said Olive at the window, and it was as if an evil, black-eyed man were sitting there on the roof, looking distrustingly at the blond young girl in her nightdress as she leaned out into the rain. "You have no right to do like that!" Olive cried out. "If you catch your death, who is it has to nurse you through? You don't think of anyone. I'm cold here, I'm catching cold."

"I'm not cold," said Mildred, and the animal-dark, animal-wounded eyes looked at Olive, and she drew her knees up closer. The shaking of her flesh could be seen, her quivering, dark-haired arms, and the shaking shape of her rain-wet thighs.

"I'm going to call everyone, then," Olive said, hugging herself in her arms for warmth. "I'm going to fetch Dr. Peabody over."

Mildred put her head down on her arms again and she did not answer, and Olive went running downstairs in the little old house. The kitchen was warm, with the fire already red in the kitchener, and Olive ran in and stood shaking in her nightgown with her bare feet on the linoleum floor. The father was eating his breakfast in the kitchen, and the mother was filling the teapot with water from the kettle on the stove.

"Mildred's out on the roof again," she said, rubbing her bare arm in the palms of her hands. Her face was wet from the rain and there were drops of it clinging still in her light, uncombed hair.

"For heaven's sake," said the mother, putting the kettle down, and the two of them ran upstairs after Olive: the mother shaking her short, little hands from her wrists, and the father with egg on his mustaches.

"Come in now, Mildred, do," said the father, standing at the window and looking at his daughter sitting there in the rain. "Come in to us, now, there's a good girl," he said. His hair was gray, but in his mustaches there was still a shade of russet left, like the flash of a fox's tail. He had not put on his collar yet, and there was a brassy collar button holding his striped shirt together at the neck. His eyes, pale and innocently blue, were wide open on his daughter.

"Come in now to your dad," said the mother with her full neck shaking. "Mildred, lovey, this is no way to do."

"I'm going to fetch Dr. Peabody over," Olive shouted out impatiently at the window, but Mildred did not lift her head. Olive put on her stockings, pulling them up over her plump, hairless legs and twisting them savagely above her knees. Downstairs, she put on her Wellingtons and her raincoat and ran down the path to the gate. Every house in the block was the same, and the same little pieces of garden ran from the front doors to identical gates on the narrow, quiet street. Dr. Peabody's house was on the other side, set apart in the grounds, with trees around it. He did not lose a moment, and in spite of his sixty years he hurried as fast as Olive across the street and into the house where Mildred was sitting on the roof overlooking the back yards.

"Now, Mildred," he said, standing among the members of the family at the window, "I know you want to please us, Mildred. I know you want to be a good girl, don't you? So you're going to make us all happy, and you're going to come in out of the rain."

Mildred looked up at the sound of his voice, her head quickly lifted and a little cocked to one side, as a dog might at the sound of a whistle he knew. But still she had no intention of coming to them.

"I like it here, Dr. Peabody," she said with the rain falling over her face. Her neck was strong and short, like a man's, and broad, with the Adam's apple riding thick and slow in it as she spoke. "I'm not cold, whatever you say. Like this I don't get time to think about other things. I feel hot when I'm lying in bed. I don't feel sick out here in the air like I do closed up in a room, Dr. Peabody."

Dr. Peabody, Dr. Peabody, save me, said the eyes in the thwarted, manlike face. *Let there be some words for the fire in me, that it be suffocated, that it expire. Dr. Peabody, Dr. Peabody,* asked the black, mistrusting eyes, and Dr. Peabody answered:

"Look at your mother and father here, Mildred, look how you're worrying them. Why don't you make up your mind you're not going to act like this any more? Think how happy they'd be if you didn't act like this, Mildred. They've got everything they need to make for happiness in this life, and so have you. Health, and work, and a nice home to live in." Dr. Peabody stood at the window, leaning his old hands on the sill and talking in his equable voice of these things to her: of health and happiness, of tranquility and love, as if the sound of these words of the sane would draw her back from the brink of where she was. "Come back, Mildred," he said. "You're freezing to death out there, my dear. You mustn't try to make us think you're not. You mustn't try to deceive us, you know. Now, be a good girl and come along in."

"I'm not trying to deceive you, Dr. Peabody," said Mildred, with her black, hard, animal eye on him in distrust. "I'm not trying to deceive anybody. Only I don't think I'm a girl. I think something's happening to me. I don't think I'm a girl any more."

"Of course, you're a girl," said Dr. Peabody. He looked at the mother's and father's faces and smiled in gentle sympathy as he quietly shook his head. "Enough of this now, Mildred," he said in a brisker tone. "You come right in now and we'll get you warm and dry, and I'll give you a warm drink that'll send you off to sleep for a little while."

"No," said Mildred, putting her head down again on her bare shaking arms. "I want to stay here."

It was as well the time of year for the birds to be flying, and there was a great movement of them now through the rain. There were small black birds of one kind or another passing over the roofs with quick, unswooping strokes of the wing, and these came, as if in curiosity, to settle on the wires that stretched through the back gardens, and now at the windows of the houses behind there were other onlookers gathering. The family could see the shirt sleeves and the aprons of their neighbors moving with guilt behind the curtains of their kitchen or back bedroom windows, watching the sight of Mildred, wearing nothing but a nightgown, sitting on the roof in the rain.

In a little while, the father had to go off to work, and Dr. Peabody left the house to telephone the police station and tell the constables to come. The last time it had been the fire department that came when Mildred set fire to the rug in the dining room. The mother stayed at the window, talking in a low, loving, tremulous voice to her daughter, but Mildred never answered.

"Leave her be, why don't you?" said Olive in anger as she dressed quickly in the bedroom before the constables would come. She put her corsets on over her soft, white, apple flesh, and snapped her stockings fast. "She's just doing it on purpose," she said over her bare shoulder to her mother. She could not bear to think of the neighbors watching the scene on the roof from their houses. "She ought to be ashamed," she said. She was wondering which of the constables would be sent. She combed her hair out quickly and rolled it into a bun at the back of her neck, and then she put on her brown wool dress. Her face was round and sweet-looking in the glass before her, and she put on her brooch with care. "She ought to be ashamed," she said to her mother bitterly, "sitting there showing her legs and everything like that." She looked a good, pure, healthy girl standing there fixing her hair before the mirror, with her backside shaped out broad and soft in her dress.

The mother turned back from the window and looked at Olive with her little eyes.

"I read a thing in the paper last night," she said, and she clasped her swollen little hands together. "Maybe it would bring her to her senses, Olive. You run and get me the paper. I don't know what to do."

She had a blue apron tied around her, and her spectacles were on her nose, and when Olive brought her the paper from the kitchen, she stood pressing herself against the sill of the open window, reading the poem out loud to Mildred on the roof.

"Listen to this, Mildred," she said. "You listen, lovey, to what it says. It goes: 'Your body is a jewel box, Given to you to hold A gift that is more precious Than rubies, pearl, or gold.' That's pretty, isn't it, now, Mildred?" Olive stood with her back to the window, angrily fastening on her low, brown shoes. "'Guard it from marauders,'" the mother's voice went on, reading out loud, "'Let nothing sordid soil it. No smirch of soot or coal. Your body is a jewel box,'" said the mother's shaking voice, and she could see the neighbors watching slyly from their windows. "'The jewel is your soul.'"

The mother put down the paper, and there were tears standing underneath her spectacles. She said:

"That means you oughtn't to let all those strange people look at you, Mildred, lovey. You ought to be too proud to let them see you haven't got anything on."

The breath was coming short in her breast, and suddenly the constable's head moved up beyond the rain gutter. There were his helmet and his face just above the rain gutter, and then the tops of his shoulders in his waterproof could be seen. He was standing on a ladder, waiting to be told what to do. Dr. Peabody and another constable came up the stairs without ringing the doorbell and came into the bedroom. Olive saw it was the young constable, and she looked swiftly at her reflection in the glass.

"Mildred," said Dr. Peabody from the window, but Mildred gave no sign. "I've called some friends of mine here to persuade you to come in and put some clothes on. But I know you're going to come along without making any more fuss about it."

But in a little while there was nothing for the young constable to do but to squeeze himself through the window and start making his way across the roof in the rain to where Mildred was sitting.

"If she makes a jump for the edge, you get her," he called out to the other constable, who was waiting on the ladder. He was holding on to the rain pipe now and he nodded his head. The young constable slid cautiously along toward the seated girl, and as he came close to this dark, strange, inhuman creature, a rush of excitement filled his heart. He could see everything clearly through her thin white nightdress, and even the color of her flesh where the cloth clung fast.

All the neighbors were watching from their back windows quite openly now, and some of them were laughing as the constable moved along the sloping roof until he had come between Mildred and the edge. There was just place for him there to squat down, with his hands holding on to the rain-wet shingles.

"Come on, now, Miss," he said, squatting before her in his raincoat. "You must be cold sitting there like that. You don't want to do a thing like that, you know."

Mildred sat with her face hidden in her arms and the rain falling thick and fast upon her, and in every line of her body, in the naked, dark-haired arms, and the shape of the legs revealed, there was a terrible power that roused and impelled him. And yet he felt that he would be sick if he had to touch her with his hands.

"Just help her up here to the window, Constable, please," said Dr. Peabody, leaning out in the rain. The young constable stood up and moved forward toward Mildred, and put his fingers, a little hesitant, underneath her arm. The skin was cold and wet, and he felt his soul recoil within him, and yet she seemed to him a marvelously strange, marvelously evil thing.

"Come along, now, Miss," he urged with a husky voice, and without a word Mildred rose and went with him back up the roof and in through the open window. She stood in the middle of the bedroom, and *Dr. Peabody,* was her anguish saying, *Dr. Peabody, save me from the down springing up on my face and the heaviness in my groins that I cannot give away.* There was no sign of it in her wary eyes as she stood with the rain dripping from her, looking in distrust from one face to the other, looking at her own mother and at her sister and at the doctor and the constable, as if she could never comprehend them as long as she lived.

II

The rain had drawn off for a little in the afternoon, but Olive and Mildred were wearing their raincoats when they left the house. The doctor's double-seated car was stopped by the curb, with the light-tan top up over it and the isinglass curtains fastened all around, and because the doctor could not get off that afternoon, his nephew was sitting in the driver's seat. Beside him sat his friend, the chemist's son, a responsible young man, whom the doctor had asked to go. As the girls came down the front walk to the little gate, the young constable, wearing plain clothes now, got out from the back seat and opened the door of the car for them.

"Mildred's very glad to be going for a ride this afternoon," said Olive, looking the young constable full in the face. The color ran up from under his collar and into his ears as he helped Olive in. The two young men in the front seat of the car lifted their hats and said good afternoon to her. "We've been telling Mildred how nice it was of you to ask us driving," she said, and she gave a sly, quick glance out the open door to the sight of Mildred standing there with her head averted.

"I don't want to go," said Mildred, scarcely aloud.

"Of course, you want to come," said Olive, and she leaned forward and smiled wisely at the young men. "We're just going for a little ride, Mildred. You know that's all we're going to do."

"You help Mildred in, now, Fogarty," said the doctor's nephew, nodding to the constable. The mother was standing in the sitting-room bay, watching them, with her handkerchief up to the side of her face. She saw the young constable help Mildred in, and then follow her into the car, and close the door behind them. When the car started down the street, she waved her handkerchief and the tears fell down her face, but no one in the doctor's car looked out through the yellowing, misted glass.

"I don't want to go," said Mildred. She had a white felt hat on, and her hair stood out dark and bushy from underneath the brim. Her nose was small and pinched in her face and her cheeks were as white as candles. She was holding her bare hands clenched between her legs.

"You're fine and dandy here now, Mildred," said Olive, looking across her to the young constable in his plain brown suit sitting on the other side. "You know it was nice of these young men to ask us out, now, wasn't it, Mildred?" she said, and her mild, blue, wide-set eyes were on the constable.

"I know where you're taking me," said Mildred. The car took the corner of the street and set out fast on the highway.

"We're taking you for a little drive, Mildred," said the doctor's nephew, looking around from the wheel. "You ought to be tickled to death," he said.

He winked at Olive, and she gave him a broad, quick smile.

"All you have to do is to lean back and stop worrying," said the chemist's son.

"I don't want to go there," said Mildred. She was riding with her hands pressed down between her legs and her eyes fixed on the soiled, worn bit of carpet on the floor. The constable had folded his arms across his chest and he rode with his face turned away from Mildred, his eyes staring straight at the dark isinglass through which nothing could be seen. The air was beginning to fill with the smell of the girls' rubber coats as the five of them rode in the curtained-in, swaying car.

"Everything's going to be all right, you'll just see," said Olive. She looked, half smiling with pleasure, at the two heads and the shoulders of the young men riding before them, and then she glanced at the constable sitting on the other side. "Mildred's being a very good girl, isn't she, Mr. Fogarty?" she said.

"Yes," said the young constable with a start, and then his voice stopped in his throat.

"I don't want to go there," said Mildred, and he could feel her flesh beside him. Their thighs were pressed close in the unwieldy, shaking car, their knees withdrawn, their feet apart, and he sat looking into the strange afternoon of yellow isinglass, his heart stirred by the wild power of her hidden flesh. It might have been the most beautiful woman of all riding there beside him, for the terrible, the unbearable love he had for her as he looked into the isinglass. But when his gaze slid sideways to her face, he saw there was nothing of beauty about her, but only her youth, and something like perversion in her body or mind, and this appetite that was starving in her, and crying for food whenever he turned away.

"We're not taking you anywhere, Mildred," said the doctor's nephew, looking around from the wheel again and smiling at Olive. "You just trust us and there won't be any trouble."

"I think Mildred ought to be very grateful to you for taking the afternoon off like this, Mr. Fogarty," said Olive, looking across her sister to the young constable. Suddenly Mildred turned her head and looked straight at her sister with her small, black, wary eyes.

"Don't take me there, don't take me there," she said quickly. Her two hands were held down tight between her knees. "Don't do it. Don't do it to me," she said. "Don't do it, Olive."

"Come on now, Mildred," said the chemist's son. He turned halfway around in his seat and looked at Mildred. "Look here, we're all good friends of yours," he said. "You know me, and Kingdom and Jim Fogarty riding there beside you. We wouldn't do anything to do you any harm."

"Don't take me there," said Mildred in a low, quick voice. She looked with her small, inhuman eyes at the chemist's son, at the back of the other man at the wheel, and then she turned to the constable, who sat with his arms folded over beside her. "Please don't take me there," she said.

The road was running now along the edge of the lake, and through the glass of the windshield they could see the quiet waters, wide and black and still, as the deep waters of the sea might be. The constable could not bring himself to look into her face, and he sat watching the toes of his shoes on the carpet near the long, black-strapped shoes of the girl who rode beside him in the car. She was so near to him that he thought his heart would burst with his desire, but then when his gaze slid to the side of her face, he saw there was nothing in it to draw a man: there was nothing in the pinched, white nostril, and in the piece of the hard, thick, manlike neck that showed.

They had been an hour driving, and the doctor's nephew turned around from the wheel and nodded wisely at Olive.

"It won't be much longer now," he said.

At the sound of his voice, Mildred started up as if from sleep and her thigh in the raincoat pressed hard against the constable's leg.

"I don't want to go there," she said, and Olive, with her hands folded over in her lap, smiled at the chemist's son.

"Let's have a song," she said. She looked toward the constable. "I'm sure you have a good singing voice, Mr. Fogarty," she said.

"I never sing, I can't sing," said the constable, and the color ran into his neck.

"Oh, I'm sure you're a fine singer, Mr. Fogarty," said Olive, smiling. "I always think a good song makes the time pass quicker, don't you?"

"Well, anyone can sing *Tipperary* or anything like that," said the chemist's son. They had finished the stretch of country now and were coming into a town.

"Here's Sloughcombe," said the doctor's nephew, and Mildred said:

"Don't do it. Don't do it to me, Olive."

The darkness was beginning to come, and here and there along the city street a few of the windows were lighted.

"Getting ready for Christmas," said the doctor's nephew above the sound of the car rattling over the cobbles. There were festoons of green and red paper, and strings of tinsel, strung across a stationer's and a toyshop's glass. In a moment they were out of the town and mounting the hill on the other side, and Mildred said:

"Please don't do this to me."

Her voice came out of the dark to them, small and cold, without entreaty or despair. The doctor's nephew leaned forward and turned on the headlights of the car, and on one side of the road the hedges stood up, as green as if flooded with sunlight.

"We're coming to it now," said the chemist's son under his breath, and the doctor's nephew slowed down the car to take the curve at the gateway. As they drove up the private road of the grounds, they could see the lighted windows of a building hidden in the darkness and trees before them, and Olive took a pair of gloves out of her raincoat pocket and drew them over her hands.

"Put your hat on straight," she said quickly to Mildred.

The car came to a stop at the steps of the building. There were bars at the windows, and an attendant in a white coat opened the door to let them in.

III

It was seven o'clock at night by the time they had settled everything for Mildred. They left her sitting on a chair in the big hall, and they went out and got in the car again and drove away.

"Well, it all went off without any trouble, after all," said the doctor's nephew at the wheel.

"She was meek as a lamb, wasn't she?" said Olive. She was sitting in the back seat alone with the constable now. He sat far from her, in the other corner, and she could just make out the shape of him, sitting erect, with his arms folded over, swaying with the motion of the car.

"We ought to be thankful it passed off the way it did," said the chemist's son. "The time I went there with Weston's brother, it took four of us to hold him down. You never knew what he was going to do next. But that was shell shock. That wasn't the same thing."

"You ought to be glad she's where she's off your hands," said the doctor's nephew, driving. "She'll be better off there than anywhere else. When they're like that, it's all the same to them. They don't know if they're home or where they are. They're living on another plane, you know." He said this easily and with authority, for he was studying to be a doctor himself. "You only have to look at her eyes to know she's not like everybody else," he said, watching the road before him. "There's no use trying to reason with them when they're that way."

The lights of the town were coming up before them, and just within the paved street the chemist's son said:

"Why don't we stop and have a drink?"

"That's just what I need," said the doctor's nephew.

Olive glanced at the constable as the car drew up at the curb before the public house. She could see his profile outlined clearly against the dim, glowing curtain of isinglass. His nose was short, like an Irishman's nose, and his lip was long, and his under-jaw was square and firm. Under his brows there was a fringe, and this was the curving brush of his lashes thrusting thick and ferny against the yellow light.

"Come in and have a drink, Olive," said the chemist's son, opening the door of the car. But Olive shook her head.

"I'll wait here," she said, smiling at them. The young constable made no move to get out of the car.

"You drink, Fogarty?" asked the doctor's nephew.

"No," said the constable, shifting a little. "I don't care about having a drink."

"Don't you think you ought to have one after a ride like this?" said Olive, looking toward his corner.

"No, thank you," said the constable, uneasily. Olive watched the other two go through the door to the public bar.

"I thought the weather was going to clear," said Olive, turning her head again toward Fogarty. "The radio said last night it was going to clear."

"It looks as if it might rain now," said the constable, looking into the isinglass. He cleared his throat, and recrossed his legs. Olive smoothed the front of her raincoat out.

"Well, it passed off very well, didn't it?" she said in a moment.

"Yes," said the constable, starting as he spoke.

"It was the first time I was ever inside an asylum," said Olive, looking toward him brightly. "I suppose it was the first time you were ever inside an asylum, Mr. Fogarty? I think it was a very interesting experience to have."

The two young men came out of the public house and climbed into the car again.

"It certainly sets you up to have a drink like that," said the doctor's nephew. "Fogarty, you and Olive would feel better if you had. We've a long way to go and we won't get home till late."

"You see, I don't like going in," said Fogarty.

"Oh, you're all right without your uniform, aren't you?" said the chemist's son. "Look," he said as the motor started, "I'll run in and get you each a drink. What'll it be, Fogarty?" He opened the front door of the car again and jumped down into the street. "I don't mind having another myself," he said. "What'll it be, Olive?"

"Oh, I'll just have a little whisky," said Olive, "with a splash of soda in it."

"I'll have the same thing," said the constable from the corner of the car.

"Nobody's going to get ahead of me," said the doctor's nephew. He turned the motor off and followed the other man into the bar. Olive and Fogarty sat waiting for their drinks to come.

"They're a pair, the two of them!" said Olive, laughing. But the constable was thinking that if he were a man with a wife there would not be this fear and trembling in him. He was scared of his life that Olive would sit nearer to him, or that she would reach out and touch him with her hand. "I feel as if a weight had been lifted off me," Olive was saying. "We've been talking for months now about taking Mildred to the asylum, and Dr. Peabody has been urging us to do it. Of course, Mom and the rest of us were against it all the time. But I know it's all for the best, and she'll be in good hands there."

The constable sat erect in the corner of the car, with his arms folded over, not daring to turn his head to her, to speak, not daring to see her, for fear that she stir him as Mildred had done. But even as he took down his drink, and the car started off, even then he could feel her turned toward him in the dark. He could see her face, wide and peach-colored under her felt hat, the yellow hair rolled up from her neck in back, and her lips half open.

"I'm sure we've done the right thing for Mildred," she was saying, and the doctor's nephew looked back from the wheel and said:

"Oh, you don't have to worry about that." He talked with authority to her over his shoulder. "They've got good men there," he said. "The kind of methods they put into operation ought to bring anyone around if there's any hope for them. I wouldn't be surprised to see Mildred walk out of there as sane as you and me at the end of a couple of years."

"I know," said Olive, looking toward the constable in the dark.

"Look, there's a pub along here in a minute," said the chemist's son. "What do you say we all pop in and have a drink?"

"That's a good idea," said the doctor's nephew.

This time the four of them went in, and the constable stood a little apart from the others, tall and clean-looking in his plain brown suit, drinking his whisky quickly down. They had two drinks each, and Olive stood at the bar, laughing, with the two young men. The constable saw her pure-white throat, laughing and bare in the collar of her coat, and the color that was shining on her face. He watched the chemist's son put his arm around her as they went out the door. When they got to the car, he said:

"Say, I'm going to join you two in back, Olive. I think you need a chaperon."

"Ha, ha, ha," laughed Olive, getting into the car, as she sat down, gasping with laughter, between Fogarty and the chemist's son. As the doctor's nephew took his place at the wheel and started the motor she began singing: *I'm in the Mood for Love.*

"It's a shame I've got to drive this car," said the doctor's nephew, looking around at her. The chemist's son put his arm around her again.

"You watch the road, Kingdom!" he called out. "You've got enough to keep you busy driving in this rain."

Fogarty could feel Olive's body close to him on the seat. He could feel the pressing of her heavy thigh in the raincoat beside him, and the seeking of her legs for his while she lay in the other man's arms. She was trying to sing, with her head pulled away from the other man in the corner, and he could feel her eyes, and her legs, and her body turning toward him and seeking him out.

But, as if riding in the car with them, there was Mildred as well: the figure bowed double in the raincoat, the hat that was not white any longer, and the voice saying, the voice repeating. He could see the side of the nostril, the down dark on the jawbone, and the manlike neck descending, bone by bone, to where the small breasts sprang. In a moment, he saw that they had stopped again, and the light from another public house was blurring the yellow isinglass.

"Get us a drink, you, Fogarty," said the chemist's son. "I'm not moving from where I am."

"Come along in with me, Fogarty," said the doctor's nephew. "We'll bring those two their drinks outside."

The constable walked into the bar behind Kingdom and began drinking very fast. He drank three whiskies, and then he carried the two glasses out to Olive and the man in the car. He stood on the sidewalk, waiting while they drank, not looking in at them, but lifting his face like a blind man to the fine, fast-falling rain. Kingdom was still drinking when he went back into the bar with the empty glasses, and Fogarty had another glass with him. When he climbed into the back seat of the car again he was thinking of Mildred and how they had left her sitting in the insane-asylum hall.

"Don't, don't, please, don't," came Olive's voice out of the darkness.

"Some chaps have all the luck," said Kingdom from the front seat, jerking his head toward the chemist's son. "You better come up for air, Geoffrey," he said as he started the motor.

"Mind your own business, Kingdom," said the chemist's son in a muffled, tight voice from the depths of the seat of the car.

"I'll call a policeman if you try anything like that," said Olive, laughing. She drew away from him and closer to Fogarty.

"Come on, now, come on," wooed the chemist's son. He was trying to draw her down again into the darkness of the seat. "Come on, come on, now," came his soft whispering, wooing voice as the car went rattling, racing on through the dark and the falling rain.

Fogarty sat upright in the corner, holding his hands fast under his folded arms. Olive's legs were feeling for his, softly, yearningly closing on his as she pulled away from Geoffrey. And if he had a wife, Fogarty was thinking, if he had a wife of his own the fire would not be burning like this in his body. Deeper and deeper, and wilder and wilder burned his blood until he felt that his bones themselves were utterly burned away.

"Say, you chaps back there," said the doctor's nephew with a whine, "you've got all the luck. Who wants to drive this car and let me have a chance?"

"Come on back," Olive called out. "There's always room for one more!"

Suddenly she turned around on the seat and faced the constable in the corner. His leg was running to wax against her, and he could hear the breath in her mouth. The whisky, or madness, or love was swinging in his head as he put his arms in agony around her, and her mouth came wet and moaning to his mouth.

"Hey, Fogarty——" shouted the chemist's son, and Kingdom looked back, whining, from the wheel.

"Say, I've been among the onlookers just about long——" he began, but he did not finish. What they took for a sudden downpouring of the rain hit the glass of the windshield like a wave, and the lights went out with it, without terror, and without sound. The movement of the car had ceased as if a hand had closed upon it in the dark.

It was not until the next afternoon that anyone thought of looking into the lake for the doctor's car, and there it was, sure enough, with the marks showing clearly where it had left the road. The four corpses were sitting in it, the four young people, just as death had found them, inside the curtains of isinglass.

▲▲▲▲▲▲▲▲▲▲▲▲▲▲▲▲▲▲▲▲▲▲▲▲▲▲▲▲▲▲

French Group
1939–1966

▼▼▼▼▼▼▼▼▼▼▼▼▼▼▼▼▼▼▼▼▼▼▼▼▼▼

Major Engagement in Paris

It was Mrs. Hodges' American dentist who introduced her to the toothpicks. They were called Hav-a-Picks, the name bearing an obvious double meaning, and they came in flat cardboard packets, like the matches they give you in hotels. Mrs. Hodges took a liking to them at once. The dentist gave her the first package around three o'clock one afternoon, and at five she took them out to tea with her, a grim-lipped, imperious old lady sitting upright in the elegant teashop with the packet of toothpicks laid out in preparation on the table with her gas mask in its case slung over her shoulder. She was wearing one of the new small hats, a black one with a crisp white flower on it, set firmly forward on her brow, and her hawk-thin, aquiline nose arched regally beneath it. She told the girl who came for her order that she was waiting for Mrs. Peterson, and that she would order her ice-cream soda when Mrs. Peterson came, the ringing accent which thirty years of Paris had not yet worn into French stating:

"*Mon am-ee*, Madame Pee-tair-song, *doit vanir.*" She had put her black bag on one chair and her umbrella on the other, and she told the girl rather tartly that last war no one had bothered to hang up curtains like that or gum strips of paper on the plate glass. "Last war Big Bertha's range moved right down our street," she said. "One day it got the house at one corner and the gentleman who had been dining with us got his bedroom shot away. He came back, very apologetically, of course, and spent the night on the divan in our sitting room." Because there were only three or four other ladies taking tea in this place where American girls in their sheer silk stockings and American matrons had swarmed before the war began, the girl had time to stand and listen to it. "The next day it got the house at the other corner," Mrs. Hodges was saying, loud and clear. "That's why I never like to sit near glass. Every geranium Mrs. Peterson had put out that year was cut to pieces. She lost her *bonne* too with it."

"*Affreux!*" the waitress murmured, but without much passion, for that was the other war, not the war outside and in the newspapers today.

"Her nerve broke and she went back to Brittany," Mrs. Hodges said. "Mrs. Peterson had a hard time getting another one who could cook so well."

And now Mrs. Peterson herself came through the revolving glass doors, dressed all in mauve, except for the dark fur cloak across her fragile shoulders. She came hesitantly into the tea-shop, garbed in a series of unbelted, silken, mauve garments which fell straight to her ankles as if they covered nothing but stark, white, unfleshed bones. A canopy of violet drifted from her hat and draped one side of the frail, ladylike face, and her gas-mask case hung rather rakishly on her shoulder. She came through the doors and stood there in bewilderment a moment, seeking Mrs. Hodges out of the endless repetition of mirrored tables and mirrored faces and mirrored mauve garments, so nearsighted was she that Mrs. Hodges must lift up her umbrella and wave it at her.

"Hi, there, Helen!" she called out, the strong, thin-lipped face, the head with the waved gray hair and the new hat on it raised commandingly. "Helen!" she called out to her former brides-maid, and Mrs. Peterson turned, faintly and vaguely smiling, in the direction of the voice, still undetermined toward which of the reflections she should float.

Once the chocolate ice-cream soda and the banana split were ordered, Mrs. Hodges could wait no longer. She seized the package of Hav-a-Picks and began.

"Hav-a-Pick!" she said in grim hilarity, and Mrs. Peterson looked up at her, startled for an instant, and then smiled bravely at her girlhood friend. "The newest rage in America, Dr. Havi-lock tells me," Mrs. Hodges went on. "They stimulate the teeth, disinfect 'em, get the tartar off. He says that the film stars always carry a package in their handbags."

"Why, I had no idea that Americans——" Mrs. Peterson's frail voice began, but Mrs. Hodges stopped it short by snapping the package open before her. There they were, rooted upright in one piece like a strip of fragile, golden matches.

"Take one," ordered Mrs. Hodges. "Just bend it off. You'll need one after your banana split."

Mrs. Peterson, visibly affected, lifted her hand in its pale gray glove, then let it fall helplessly into her lap again.

"Marion," she said gently, "I'm afraid you'll think me very silly, but I've never used—I mean, I really don't think I ever met anyone who used—— Of course, I've seen people in restaurants, I mean French people, foreigners, of course, but——"

"Rubbish," said Mrs. Hodges, removing a toothpick expertly from the group. She held it an instant in her fingers so that Mrs. Peterson might study its contour, and then she said: "It's not like an ordinary toothpick. You don't just stick it in. First," she said, proceeding to demonstrate, "you wet it with the tip of your tongue so as to limber it up and get the disinfectant working. Then," she said, continuing with the demonstration, "you work it —gently—in—between—each—tooth——"

She sat on the green velvet cushions, concentrating severely on it, her upper lip drawn up and her teeth revealed like a squirrel's. Mrs. Peterson looked at her in faint dismay a moment, then flung a shortsighted but despairing glance around at the neighboring tables and the beautifully appointed room.

"Don't you think," she murmured, drawing the folds of her mauve canopy about them, perhaps in the hopes that this or some intervention from heaven might succeed in veiling Mrs. Hodges temporarily from the public eye, "don't you think, Marion dear, that certain, well, certain intimate functions, that is, like washing the face or pick—I mean, going about these things where people——"

"Brings the gums to life," Mrs. Hodges snarled through her Hav-a-Pick. Once the chocolate ice-cream soda and the banana split had been set down on the table and the tray of variegated pastries was borne to them, Mrs. Hodges' glance lit on the piece of orange layer cake and the conversation altered. "Everyone eats in the Automat now in New York," she said, speaking as one

fresh from the metropolis because she, at least, had been there
six months before. "Much nicer places than they used to have
when we were young, all white and clean and the food tastes
good."

"I don't know if I could bring myself to go into an Automat,"
said Mrs. Peterson in her failing voice. "It's so dangerous, isn't
it? I always think of that dreadful, dreadful story about the old
beggar-woman who had her walls lined with thousand-dollar
bills they found out later." Mrs. Peterson dabbed her lip with her
handkerchief as her voice expired. "She went into the Automat,"
she said, scarcely audibly, "and bought a bun and filled it with,
you know, Marion, filled it with—with——" The words trailed into
silence and her gaze wandered helplessly around the room, and
Mrs. Hodges, loathing senility and the decay of the flesh and
memory, snapped out:

"Jam, butter, sausage, treacle—say it, Helen, say it."

"Oh, no," gasped Mrs. Peterson, "with something, you know,
fatal. I think it was strychnine or arsenic—anyway, something
deadly. And she ate half the bun and left the other half on the
counter," said Mrs. Peterson, holding on to her spoon, with the
piece of banana in it, for strength. "And she went off into the
rest room and died there in the most awful agony. That's the sort
of thing that happens in New York," she said. "And then somebody came along, quite a young man I think it was, a working-
man but still a perfectly healthy fine fellow with a wife and a little—I don't remember, but I think the newspaper said he had a
little baby—yes, a little boy or a little girl, I don't quite remember which—and he picked up the other half of the bun and
ate——"

"Now you try one," said Mrs. Hodges, flapping the packet
open in front of her again, and before another word could be
said she broke a toothpick off and handed it to Mrs. Peterson.

"Why, Marion dear, I don't think I will," said Mrs. Peterson,
and as completely as a snail retires into its shell she retreated
into her own dim, well-bred haziness, but Mrs. Hodges had already put the slender golden wand into her hand.

"Now, do as I tell you, Helen," she said, and she selected another toothpick for herself and moistened its tip in her mouth.

Mrs. Peterson, helplessly drawing the folds of her violet canopy about her, did the same. "Wet it," commanded Mrs. Hodges. "Do it like this, and then force it gently—but very—gently—in—between——"

It was during the preparatory maneuvers that Mrs. Peterson's toothpick broke suddenly in two.

"Good heavens," she murmured in relief, and she put the bits of it carefully out of sight beneath her plate. "I don't think I could ever become an expert at it," she said, laughing lightly, but there was no escape.

"Take another," said Mrs. Hodges brutally. "You've got to learn." Mrs. Peterson's frail hand was trembling slightly as she placed the point of the second medicated stick upon her tongue. "You must do it gently. Don't rush at it like a bull in a china closet," Mrs. Hodges said. "Just work carefully at it—carefully—carefully—the way—I'm—doing——"

"Isn't that Mr. Bullitt's daughter over there?" murmured Mrs. Peterson. "I really would feel quite distressed if—Marion, I would feel very badly for both our sakes if that nice Mr. Bullitt ever heard anything that would——"

The words were scarcely out of her mouth when her second Hav-a-Pick bent over double. Mrs. Hodges was so annoyed this time that, although she knew perfectly well that it was she who had invited Mrs. Peterson out, she could not bring herself to pick up the check and walk to the cash desk with it. She got to her feet and she said: "My treat next time, Helen," exactly as they had said it a hundred times as girls to each other. The packet of Hav-a-Picks was closed safely away in her bag and she thought bitterly, I'll never give her another one, never, never. She stood there by the table, the haughty, imperious, rather haggard face set against the other tables of pastry-eating women, waiting for Mrs. Peterson to gather up her things, settle her gas mask over her shoulder, and come.

Nothing further was said about the toothpicks until the first early morning they met in the spacious, well-lighted cellars of the apartment house across the street. It was just three o'clock, and the sirens had ceased wailing. There were only about twenty people gathered underground with them, all fully dressed, quiet, respectable people. Mrs. Peterson had brought her knitting with her, and Mrs. Hodges had the Hav-a-Picks in her bag.

"Last war," Mrs. Hodges was saying as her former bridesmaid came drifting down the cellar stairs, "the sirens made quite a different row. They screamed out loud as if you were stepping on their tails, and there seemed some sense to it. More life to it than the mooing and growling they go in for now."

"Yes, I *do* know what you mean, Marion," Mrs. Peterson said as she merged rather timidly into the group. "It seems such an understatement, doesn't it?"

But Mrs. Hodges had not quite forgiven her yet, and she turned her profile to her and looked steadily the other way. The mother with the three-week-old baby and its uniformed nurse were walking slowly up and down as if in the Bois on Sunday afternoon; the young married couple were strolling from gas meter to electric meter to water meter, reading the numbers showing on them, arm in arm; the distinguished old gentleman with the white Vandyke beard had unfolded his campstool, tested its firmness, and then sat down with his glasses pinched on his nose and opened out his copy of *Le Temps;* the five cooks and the four chambermaids and the six concierges had all brought their stools, or sacks, or newspapers with them.

"Where are the seats?" Mrs. Hodges demanded in a moment, the grim eye raking the cellar from ceiling to earthen floor. "No seats?" she said. "Last war we had 'em." Without a word, Mrs. Peterson followed her in contrition the length of the cellar to where the drainpipe traversed the end, and meekly sat down beside her on it. "Last war everybody came down cellar," said Mrs. Hodges in her loud, ringing imitation of the Gallic tongue. She sat on the drainpipe, looking in contempt at the small gathering seated on their sacks or their newspapers or their stools. "Nobody lolled around in bed. We had card tables and the gramophone going and some *esprit de corps.*"

Before Mrs. Peterson had managed to extricate her roll of violet knitting from the chain of her lorgnette and the strap of her gas mask and the keys of her apartment, Mrs. Hodges had brought the toothpicks out.

"Hav-a-Pick, Helen," she said almost jovially, but Mrs. Peterson heard the note of bitter and brief reprieve in it. She knew this was just one more chance being given. "We may be shut down here for a couple of hours," Mrs. Hodges said, and Mrs. Peterson set her paraphernalia down on the ground and did as she was bid. "Now, do just as I tell you," Mrs. Hodges went on. "First you must notice that the Hav-a-Pick has one flat side and one pointed side—no, Helen, I did not say 'end,' I said 'side.'" As Mrs. Peterson studied the little golden strip of wood, tears came suddenly and hopelessly into her eyes. "Now, you must remember to keep the broad side down—the—broad—side—down, the broad—not the pointed—side—down——" Mrs. Hodges made the demonstration several times over before Mrs. Peterson had summoned enough confidence to begin. "Now, just go at it carefully," Mrs. Hodges said, and Mrs. Peterson gave one last, despairing look at the carefree, unwitting others in the cellar.

"I had hoped to get a few rows done on my *liseuse*," she murmured out of her inadequacy and dismay, and just as she finished speaking the toothpick snapped in half.

"Good gracious, Helen!" cried Mrs. Hodges. "I've never seen anyone go at it the way you do! You simply won't listen to what I say." She scanned the open packet, as if calculating the number that remained, and then she made the decision and selected another one for Mrs. Peterson. "Now try it again," she said. "Just try, if you possibly can, to moisten it without biting it in two."

"I didn't bite it," said Mrs. Peterson, close to breaking down before them all.

"Stop talking," said Mrs. Hodges as she worked scientifically across her mouth. "You're bound to get into trouble if you keep on moving your jaw up and down. Remember I can't get these easily over here. Just try to keep your mind on what you're doing."

At exactly what instant Mrs. Peterson's second Hav-a-Pick broke, Mrs. Hodges never knew. The only thing she was sure of was that Mrs. Peterson kept up the bluff for some time after the best half of it was gone. After a good minute of observing her former bridesmaid fumbling awkwardly away at her teeth, she said sharply:

"Let me see your Hav-a-Pick, Helen," and Mrs. Peterson could do nothing but take the remains of it out. "Just as I thought," said Mrs. Hodges briefly. "I simply don't know how you do it. I simply don't understand."

She was so annoyed that she could not bring herself to address another word to Mrs. Peterson. Only when the sirens had begun sobbing the all-clear signal did Mrs. Hodges manage to articulate a sentence in her mother tongue. She said: "Next time I'll bring a deck chair along and get a snatch of sleep, instead of thinking of other people." They walked up the cellar stairs and out into the street in silence and crossed it, their gas masks hanging from their shoulders, in the iron-cold white dawn of day.

Effigy of War

The barman at the big hotel on the sea front had been an officer in the Italian army during the last war, and somehow or other the rumor began to get around. Whether it was that he said too much to people who spoke his own language with him, saying late at night that the vines in Italy were like no other vines and the voices more musical and the soldiers as good as any others, no matter what history had to say about them, or whether it got around in some other way, it was impossible to know. But the story came to the director of the hotel (Cannes, it was, and the people just as gaudily dressed as other years, and the shops on the Croisette as fancy), and because of the feeling that ran high against the foreigner and against the name of Italy, the director stepped into the lounge bar about eleven one morning to tell the barman what he'd better do. He was a dressy, expensive-looking little man, the director, who could speak four languages with ease, and he had been a Russian once, a White Russian, so that France was the only country left to him now. He came into the bar at a quiet hour, just before the idle would begin wandering in out of the eternally springtime sun, and he jerked his cuffs inside his morning coat and screwed the soft, sagging folds of his throat from his collar wings and started speaking quietly over the mahogany-colored bar.

"Maestro," he said to the barman who had been ten years with them, "with all this trouble going on the management would quite understand your wanting to go back to Italy."

"Italy?" the barman said, and it might have been Siberia he was pronouncing as a destination and the look in his eyes was as startled. He stopped whatever it was he had been doing, setting the glasses straight or putting the ash trays out or the olives, and he looked at the director. He was a slight, dark man and his face was as delicate-boned as a monkey's, and the hair was oiled down flat upon his monkey-fragile skull.

"A lot of Italians are going back," the director said, and he swung himself up onto the stool as elegantly and lightly as a dwarf dressed up for a public appearance, the flesh hairless and pink, and the hand on the wood of the bar as plump as a child's. "Give me a glass of milk," he said, and he went on saying in a lower voice: "In times like these everyone wants to avoid all the trouble they can. Everybody likes to feel he's in his own country." He said it with a slight Russian accent, and the barman waited while the director took the cigarette out of the silver case, and then the barman snapped the lighter open and held the flame to the end of the cigarette in his dark, monkey-nervous hand. "We're perfectly willing to discuss things with you," the director said, and as the first bluish breath of smoke drifted between them, their eyes met for a moment across it, and the director was the first to look away.

"Ah, if we should all go back to the places we belong to!" the barman said as he put the lighter into the pocket of his starched white coat. He turned aside to take the bottle of milk off the ice, and he went on saying in strangely poetic sorrow: "If we all returned to the waters of our own seas and the words of our own languages, France would be left a wilderness——"

"Of course, there are some national exceptions," the director added quickly. "There are some nationalities which cannot go back." He took a swallow of milk and looked rather severely at the barman. "In countries where there have been revolutions, economic upheavals," he went on, his hand with the cigarette in it making the vague, comprehensive gestures of unrest. "But with Italians," he said, and the barman suddenly leaned forward and laid his small bony hands down flat upon the bar.

"Well, me," he said, "I've been fifteen years in this country. I'm too old to go back now. For me, Mussolini was an economic upheaval," he said. He picked up the bottle of milk again and filled the director's glass, pouring it out a little too quickly. "I've never gone back, not since fifteen years," he said, the words spoken sharply and rapidly, almost breathlessly across the bar. "I'm like a refugee, like a political refugee," he said. "I haven't the right to go back."

"That can be taken care of," the director said, and he took out his folded handkerchief and dabbed at the drops of milk on his upper lip. "The management would advance you what you needed to get back, write you a good testimonial——"

"I haven't done military service for them," the barman said, and he was smiling in something like pain at the director, the grin pulled queer and ancient as a monkey's across his face. "I can't go back," he said. "This is my country by now. If I can't go on working here I can't work anywhere. I wouldn't leave this country no matter what anybody said to me or no matter what they did to me."

"You never did very much about getting any papers out," said the director. He was looking straight ahead at the small silk flags of all the nations and at his own immaculately preserved reflection in the glass. "You never did much about trying to change your nationality," he said, and he took another discreet swallow of milk. "You should have thought of that before."

"I might have been a Frenchman today if it hadn't been for my wife," the barman said, and his tongue ran eagerly out along his lip. "My wife——" he said, and he leaned closer, the starched sleeves, with the hairy, bony little wrists showing, laid on the bar. "I haven't seen her for fifteen years," he said, and the director looked at the glass of milk and shrugged his shoulders. "She's in Italy, and she wouldn't sign the papers. She wouldn't do that one thing," he said, the eyes dark and bright, and the face lit suddenly, like a poet's, with eagerness and pain. "Not that she wanted me," he said. "It wasn't that. But women like that, Ital-

ian women, they're as soft and beautiful as flowers and as stubborn as weeds." He said it in abrupt poetic violence, and the director stirred a little uneasily and finished the milk in his glass.

"Now, you take a run up to the Italian Consul this afternoon
and have a talk with him," he said, and he wiped his upper lip
with his folded handkerchief again. "Tell him you're thinking of
going back. Put Raymond on duty for the afternoon. And another thing, Maestro," he said as he got down off the bar stool,
"don't keep that *Corriere della Sera* out there where everybody
can see it. Put it in your pocket and read it when you get home,"
he said.

It might have passed off quietly enough like that if the Dane
hadn't come into it. He was a snub-nosed, sun-blacked, blond-
headed little man who gave swimming lessons in one of the
bathing establishments on the beach. He had been a long time
there, walking season after season tough and cocky up and down
the beach with his chest high and his thumbs hooked into the
white belt of his bathing trunks. He wore a bright clean linen
cap down to his yellow brows, and royal-blue swimming shorts,
and the muscles in his shoulders and arms were as thick and
smooth as taffy. But after the war came, he didn't parade up and
down the esplanade in the same way in the sun, but stayed hour
after hour in the water or else in a corner of the beach café. He
still gave lessons, but he let the pupils seek him out in the shade
of the café, as if the eyes of the mobilized and the uniformed
and the envious could see him less distinctly there.

The one who started it all was the Greek waiter in the big
hotel who had got his French naturalization papers eight months
before and was leaving for training camp in a week or two. He'd
lean over the diners—what was left of the English and the American colony, and the dukes and duchesses, and the Spanish who
had got their jewels and their pelts and their money out of Spain
—and he'd say:

"What nationality do you think I am, eh? What country would
you say I come from?" showing his teeth in pride and pleasure at
them as he slipped the dishes of *filets de soles bonne femme* or
champignons à la Reine d'Angleterre down before them, provided the maître d'hôtel was looking the other way. Sometimes

the guests would say he looked one thing, and sometimes another: Italian, Rumanian, or even Argentine, and he'd smile like a prima donna at them, leaning almost on their shoulders, with his eyes shining and the serviette flung rather wildly over his arm.

"No, no, oh, *mon dieu,* no!" he'd say. "I'm pure French. What do you think of that? In another two or three months you'll see me coming in here with gold stripes on my sleeve, ordering everything like everybody else has to eat." And then he'd take out his mobilization order and show it to them, balancing the *homard à l'américaine* on its platter in the other hand as he opened out the stamped, signed paper. "I'm French," he'd say, with the garlic hanging on his breath. "I'm going right into the French army to fight. I'm going to fight for everybody sitting here having dinner tonight," he'd say, and he'd give the people at the next table their salad, holding his mobilization order open in his hand.

The Greek waiter had never liked the look of the Dane, and now that he had his military orders he couldn't so much as stand the sight of the cold-eyed, golden little man. In the hours he had off in the afternoons, he took the habit of walking out on the esplanade and stopping just above the bathing place to call the names down to him. There he would be, the Dane, with his white cap on and his royal-blue bathing trunks, talking half naked to the half-naked girls or women on the beach, war or no war, and going on making money just the same.

"*Sale étranger!*" the Greek would call down, with a fine Greek accent to it, and "*Crapule!,*" with his voice ringing out like an opera singer's across the sand and the striped bathing houses and the sea. "France for the French!" he'd roar over the railing, and the little Dane in his bathing suit would go quietly on with his swimming lessons, or if he were alone he'd turn and go into the beach café and sit down out of sight in the shade. There was a week ahead still before the Greek waiter would go, and all those days in the afternoons he'd stand on the esplanade and call the names down. In the end he appealed to the French themselves, exhorting them to rise. "The French for the French!" he'd shout down through the funnel of his hands. "Don't employ foreigners! Give a Frenchman the job!"

The last night of the week the little Dane came into the lounge bar for a drink before he went to bed; coming late, in discretion, when no one else was there. The two of them were talking there together, the Dane sitting on the stool with the glass of beer before him, and the Italian on the other side with his starched jacket on and the wisps of his monkey hair slicked flat across his skull, and in a few minutes the barman would have taken the bottles down and locked the safes and turned the lights out, and then nothing would have occurred. But now the barman was leaning on the counter, speaking the French tongue in a low, rather grievous voice to the swimming teacher, his thin hand rocking from side to side like a little boat as he talked.

"Drinking has ceased," he was saying in faultless pentameter, "in the old way it has ceased. Even before September there was a difference, as if the thirst of man had been slaked at last. To any sensitive eye, the marks of death were to be seen for years on the façades of casinos, palace hotels, luxury restaurants, and on the terraces of country clubs and vast private estates. Even the life of the big bars has been dying," he said. "For years now that I can remember, the lounge bar has been passing through the agonies of death." He made a tragic and noble gesture toward the empty leather armchairs in the half-darkened room, and he said in a low, dreamy voice: "All this is finished. There is no more place in the hearts of men for this kind of thing. The race that insisted on this atmosphere of redundance for its pleasure, that demanded this futility, is vanishing, dying——"

"War levels the ranks," the Dane said quietly. His sun-blacked, sun-withered face under the bright light thatch of hair was as immobile as if carved from wood.

"Ah, before the war even," the barman said softly, and then he stopped, for the men had come into the bar. The Greek waiter walked a little ahead of the others, wearing a gray jersey and a cap pulled down, and they both of them knew him; it was the others behind him they had never seen before.

"Get that one, the one on the stool," the Greek waiter said, and one of the other men stepped past him and walked toward the bar. Just before he got there he lifted his right arm and hit the swimming teacher on the chin. The little, light-crowned head and the strong, small body rose clear of the stool an instant, like a piece of paper lifted and spun sidewise by the wind, and then it sailed into the corner and collapsed there, bent double, by the leather chair. "That's the kind of language he understands," the Greek said, and he crossed the length of thick, soft carpet, jerking his cap up on his forehead. He was smiling with delight when he kicked the swimming teacher's body into another shape. "Walking up and down out there on the beach," the Greek said, and he turned back to the others and the Italian barman behind the bar. "Giving lessons just like men weren't bleeding their guts out for him and people like him——"

"He volunteered. I tell you that man volunteered," the barman began saying, and his bones were shaking like a monkey's in his skin. "I've seen the paper he got. I know he volunteered to fight like anybody else would——" And when he jumped for the bell the Greek waiter reached over and took him by the collar of his starched white coat and dragged him out across the plates of potato chips and the empty beer bottle and the glass the Dane had been drinking and slung him across the elegant little glass-topped tables into the other corner of the room.

"Pick him up and take him along too," the Greek said. "I know all about him I need to know. He was an officer last war, officer in the Italian army, so you'll know what side he'll fight on this time. Take them both out," he said. "This country's not good enough for them, not good enough for either of them."

They did it by moonlight, taking the two men's clothes off on the sand and shingles by the Mediterranean water, and giving it to them in fiercely accelerating violence. They broke the swimming teacher's jaw, and they snapped the arms of the barman behind him like firewood, beating the breath and the life from them with whatever fell under their hands. The Greek carried over an armful of folding iron chairs from the bathing establishment's darkened, abandoned porch and, with these as weapons, they battered the two men's heads down and drove their mouths into the sand.

"So now repeat this after me, foreigners," the Greek began

saying in wild holy passion as he kneeled beside them. He had taken the flag out of his jersey and was shaking out its folds. "So now repeat what I'm going to tell you," he said in violent religious fervor against the pulsing and murmuring of the water, and his hands were trembling as he laid the flag out where their mouths could bleed upon the tricolor emblem, the cotton stuff transformed now to the exigencies of a nation and a universe.

Diplomat's Wife

I

He was a wonderful sight to see on any landscape, coming swiftly and effortlessly down the snow in winter with his strong slender legs held close, one knee locked fast but limber a little behind the other, using skis as portion of a natural and inevitable intention. But it was not only that: there was as well his hair, and the light pigment of his hands and face, so that whatever the weather was, the snow falling or the rain, it seemed a strong sun were shining on him. He was not French, he could never have been French no matter what they did to him. His name was Toni Gratz and he had left Austria in 1934 when times were hardest and the political tension was high coming to France to make a living at showing the French how to ski. In those days it was still strange enough, not yet having taken on the proportions of a national sport as common as tennis; it was still something to stand still and watch when you saw it: that miracle of one man coming down a precipitous winding mile of snow through pines and over gullies, the swift sloping figure lost for an instant in the clots of needle trees and then curving forth on the pure white again, streaming faster and faster with that quick oblique sweep and arch to the unseen and undivulged shape of the land.

That first autumn he rented a cabin from the peasants; it was high on the mountain, far above the village, and he began at once to do what had to be done. All through the dark sogging October and November he fixed up the two long barnlike rooms and the loft: inside he whitewashed the stone walls and broke two windows through them and set in the timber jambs and glass. He borrowed a horse and carted the secondhand cookstove and the half-dozen divan beds and mattresses, and the utensils and fuel he would need up the lumber track alone, alone putting his shoulder to the wheel when the cart bogged in the knee-deep muck or where the way grew steeper; alone laying the wood floor in the cabin where only cattle had been before, and manipulating the rocks into place to shape the terrace toward the sun. By December he had his supplies in and his firewood stacked along the south side of the cabin, and enough coal, sparingly used, to see him through till spring. Here he was starting out single on the adventure of his own existence, the muscles in his arms and thighs and naked back swelling to bursting in his skin as he worked, the teeth that any woman would have cried her heart out for set down deep in the flesh of his lower lip in strain. Here he was, twenty-five that year, a scrupulous, stern, blond young man taking this honeymoon with his own identity; a man without a fatherland any longer, hauling and hacking and skiing his own way to redemption through the shale and the mud and the high mountain timber and snow.

He knew the language well, but there were other things he never became used to. All that first winter his puritanical young heart set colder and colder, harder and harder in foreign, reserved outrage against the women who took the funicular car up and came to him for lessons, or those who came with their men as transitory boarders in the chalet and slept in the loft, the wives and husbands, cousins, lovers, friends, all sleeping on the divan beds side by side as carelessly as children might have slept together. From January on, on the good days, they bared themselves as if for sea bathing and lay, their flesh stained with oil, tanning themselves on the boards he had planed to fashion the terrace with. He had hired a cook, a chef-apprentice, who turned out the meals for the skiers who stopped in for lunch, and for the boarders, but he himself served at table and carried the coffee out to them where they lay smoking and talking, the shameless painted women stretched in half-naked depravity in the sun. Even after dark when they danced to the radio's music in the whitewashed, cattle lean-to, he could not unbend. He might have been a priest, a recluse vowed to something higher, dancing with them in the same way that he served them, in remote, servant-austere equity; and those he embraced, putting his blond hands on their shoulder bones and drawing them against him, he could not warm to. His bright head lowered over a girl's head briefly as he kissed her mouth in the darkness, like a light, intense but glacial, falling for just an instant across her face.

It was the fourth winter he was there, in February, that the diplomat's wife and her two children came skiing over the *corniche* one hot afternoon and stopped there on the height of snow and looked down at the chalet. He was standing in the doorway, drying dishes in the sun, alone after lunch so late in the season, except for the male cook chopping wood at the back of the house. She looked for a moment down the steep, overhanging slope and then she brought her skis together and took it straight through the unbroken snow toward him. She was tall and lean, with black hair worn longish and caught back in a filet. Her mouth was painted, like every other Frenchwoman's mouth, he saw when she made the swift, arrogant stop at the terrace and leaned over to undo her skis. She was wearing a skirt, not trousers but a short plaid kilt, and white hand-knitted stockings, and her knees were bare. But the thing he could not take his eyes from, and which moved him with an actual physical motion of the heart, was the pair of earrings, the big ivory flowers blooming like home and country and the forgotten outline of other mountains and vegetation, as angular-petaled as starfish and as unexpected in this Frenchwoman's ears. She turned her head to watch the two children brake cautiously down the beaten run, and she called out:

"*Halte,* Michel! We'll have something to drink here!"

She had a straight, weather-browned nose and a straight, dark fearless eye, and in spite of the livid rouge and the edelweiss earrings, there was at once that other thing, startling and swift as a slap across the face: that racy and reckless distinction of the intrepid young (bullfighters, ski jumpers, aviators, automobile racers) borne casually and sexlessly either to victory or defeat. She walked directly to the Austrian, as a soldier might have, and put out her platinum-ringed right hand.

"*Grüss Gott*, I imagine?" she said almost grimly to him. It was not until a long time after that he learned her grandfather had been Maréchal This or Maréchal Somethingorother (whether Foch or Joffre or which one of the others he never could remember), but this might have been explanation in a woman so young for the absolute and stubborn way of speech and the handshake and the steadfast eye. She said: "I heard there was an Austrian keeping the chalet up here," and the girl and her brother, the girl perhaps ten and the boy younger, came up and shook the blond man's hand. There he stood, having put the dish and the dishcloth down, in tapering black ski trousers and a yellow linen shirt with the sleeves short and the collar undone, so that above the elegant narrow hips and the black brass-studded belt he stood tall and radiant against the timber like a god of the pre-Christian world. She said: "I've spent a lot of time in your country, that is, when it was still your country," and they sat down at a table together in the sun. "My husband was attaché at the embassy—oh, I know Vienna wasn't Austria! But I went other places with the children," she said. "We learned to ski in St. Anton and listened to music in Salzburg." He sat with a small core of happiness suddenly lighted in him, listening to her speak, listening to her and bringing the little bottles of fruit juice when she asked for them, and harking to her as he poured it out. She went on talking quickly and without subterfuge to him, a woman about thirty, a diplomat's wife, with her two black-eyed and black-haired children sucking at the straws. "I did what I pleased in Vienna," she said. "Wherever I am I make a point of doing what I please. Positions are there to be made use of, not to use the people who fill them. Whenever I wanted, I went on the other side of the river and didn't wear a hat and bought bad jewelry. I went on the scenic railways at the Prater every Sunday afternoon, and on that one that runs upstairs, you know, in the black with coffins opening and skeletons rising, and claps you into the tomb and out——"

"Yes," said the Austrian, and suddenly he burst out laughing. "We used to stand outside to watch the faces come out, before they expected it, into daylight on the rails——"

"Still fixed for death," she said. "And the dragon. Did you ever mount the illuminated dragon and move on his tin seats through the beautifully tinted scenes—soft music, stars in their tulle skirts, and almost always twilight——"

But it was not only this, not only because she spoke of his own country to him that his heart was moved, but because of the abrupt, disciplined giving and taking of her eyes, austerely taking sight and austerely returning it under the bare high brow. Her browned hand with the rings on it jerked nervously over the glasses and cakes, and over the children's jackets and hair, and suddenly she touched the white edelweiss in her ears and for the first time she smiled.

"Innsbruck," she said, and for a moment his breath stifled in him.

"They used to sell them in the postcard shop," he said, not thinking of the words any longer or if they were foolish or how they came. "The one on the square where they sell religious cards and wooden chamois. I went to the university in Innsbruck," he said, and the little girl looked up at him, sucking the pineapple juice up through the straw.

"They had imitation matchboxes there, didn't they, Mimi?" she said, looking at her mother. She was speaking slowly, as if seeking her way up the right street in the dark, moving hesitantly with her hand out for the feel of the right show window, waiting a moment to be sure before touching the handle of the door. "And when you pushed the matchbox open there was a tiny room inside with tiny little furniture in it. That was Innsbruck, wasn't it?" she said, watching the side of her mother's face.

"Yes," said the diplomat's wife, and the little boy said:

"And you bought me the matchbox with Mozart's room in it. It had a stove and a piano and three chairs and Mozart's sister in it."

"Yes," said his mother, and she smiled quickly at him, her mouth painted, her teeth white as a dog's.

"Then you may remember the man who watched the cars on

the square when you parked there," said the Austrian, leaning forward on his slender, strong, bare arms and speaking eagerly out.

"Ah, yes!" she said, and she laughed rather grimly across the table. "Even if I was French, he liked me. He stopped the tram behind the monument whenever he saw me and gave me three salutes, the Nazi, the Heimwehr, and the Monarchist, just to be certain."

"I used to drive down from Igls every morning in my father's little car," he said, and even if she had shocked him he was smiling at her.

"Ah, your father," she said, looking straight but incuriously at him, as if everything that touched him, country and blood and kin, must have now its exact definition for her. "I should like to know about your father."

"He had a little *Gasthaus*," he said quietly, and without knowing that he had wished to say it aloud or that he was about to say it, he added: "He died. My father died. If he had not died, even with things difficult as they were—making a living, politics —I mean, if he had lived I would not have gone away."

"Yes," she said, looking down at the rings on her hand. "Yes. Mine died too. My father. I missed him—you understand how it is, I missed him. So I married; I married a friend of his." Her eyes looked over the sun-dazzled bottles and glasses and paused, clear and artless as a man's, upon his face. "We live in Paris— house, servants, functions." She shrugged her shoulders. "And yet one goes on," she said in the quick, blunt, nonchalant voice. "Habit of discipline, loyalty, diplomatic candor, tommyrot."

Now that they had spoken out they looked for a moment in what might have been comprehension at each other across the table, only it was too proud, too shy, too uncommitted a declaration to be given that name. But for one instant, before she got up to go, he felt his heart stop at the incalculable brink and quiver there in indecision. He sat looking at the side of her face, the nose, like the brow and throat, bronzed and straight, and the dark, delicate eyebrow lifting a little at the temple as if for flight. He saw her narrow wrists as she drew her gloves on, and now he believed it was for this, not for love but for this, that he had worked humbly and servilely here year after year; for this that he had come up the mountains alone and dragged the means of life and subsistence up them, alone hoisted the rock and nailed the timber into place, and passed the black autumn months and the spring months of roaring thaw in solitude, outwitting water, tempest, wind, night after unaltering night outwitting the implacable cold. It was for this manifestation of a sterner purpose, pride or valor or incorruptibility, that he had mounted rucksack after rucksack packed solid with weight that would have bowed another man's back double; not for any conception of love, not a woman to kiss or marry or make a life with, but this that had come for a brief time one afternoon and gone, leaving nothing behind it but the challenge, and a visiting card engraved Marie-Angèle de Castnelnau, and the marks of her skis and her children's descending through the snow. She had said, "I'll doubtless be back next winter," and he answered: "There's still two or three months of skiing ahead now, and the spring snow's the best," but he did not say out loud: "Don't go. I have something to say to you. Please don't go."

The books he had at the university in Austria stood on a little shelf above his bed, and with them a few of the poets and playwrights; but because of the skis to be greased and scraped and pressed, the skins to be dried, the lessons to be given, the food selected, the planks and dishes and clothes to be washed, he scarcely ever took them down. If she had not stopped there, speech and bearing and name a rebuke to what had become of the student and gentleman a long time back, he might never have carried the little volumes into the other room, carrying them, after so long as awkwardly and unfamiliar as the newborn in his arms, and put them down on the table under the light. But that evening or the next he began reading, and kept on reading every night during that week before she came back; at first reading whatever happened to fall open under the ski-broadened and labor-broadened hands, and then beginning to seek those passages in Goethe or Heine, or Schnitzler even, that might be transformed to apply, in the end paraphrasing sense and logic, time and space, for the small violent excitement of imagining he read of her or for her. "But of hell, Madame," he read, as if the mere salutation evoked her face, "you have not the slightest idea. . . . I heard one of the burning heathen cry out from his pot—'Spare me! I was once Socrates, the wisest of mortals! I taught Truth and Justice and sacrificed my life for Virtue!' "

Truth and Justice, he thought, springing up from his chair; Justice or Truth or Virtue! I have been, above everything else, just and truthful and virtuous, and he began walking up and down in the warm room, thinking of his own life, and of how he had been in his student days, not twenty yet, walking in young righteous vanity the cobbled streets of Innsbruck, his overcoat hanging from his shoulders as Viennese artists and literary men wore theirs with the casual, daring grace of musicians or actors to inaudible but undying feminine applause. Never, he thought, never in those days would he have walked into a public room or a wine house with his arms thrust into the sleeves of a coat, but entered wearing it across his shoulders and stood for a moment just inside the doorway with his head bare so that the girls serving and the seated girls and the women might see the icy blue of his eye, and the golden sideburns cut short and fluffy on his cheeks. If he had died for the gesture, it was like this he must enter any place, the head lifted, the shoulders spread, the hips narrow beneath the theatrically mantled coat; entering in truth, justice, virtue, and conceit into Herr Niederkirchner's inn, where the portraits of Andreas Hofer and Napoleon Bonaparte and Louis of Bavaria hung side by side. So it was once, he thought, and is so no longer, and he walked in sudden grief for what he had been up and down the empty room. All of it came to nothing, he thought in bitterness: gusto and learning and the stamping, shouting, swash-buckling gesture of youth come to exile on a mountaintop and perhaps to conflict, perhaps to a war in which he would be trained on this side like a Frenchman to fire on those same young, arrogant, insouciant students with their coats worn over their shoulders, aping, as he had aped, the Viennese artists and literary men. And as if to escape the sight of this, he sat down quickly again and began reading Heine's words in his own tongue: "Madame, that old play is a tragedy. . . ."

The day she came back she had a woman friend with her, perhaps a young woman, but half blinded now by the sun and the

snow and by what the diplomat's wife had become for him in
solitude, he did not know. She had shaken hands with him when
she came, and then she and the other woman sat down at a table
at the end, away from the others eating on the terrace. He
brought the neatly turned little omelet with the green herbs
sprinkled on it to them, and the cold mutton and salad, setting it
down before them, and she did not lift her head. She was saying
across the table that she was going back to Paris, the direct,
clipped speech giving with military precision the school, the
mother-in-law's tea and cocktail reception, the time of year, as
steps or movements in the established but unreconcilable and
endless dance. Back to it, she was thinking, back to it: the house
in Paris, the functions, the demands, but instead of seeing the
gray Passy Avenue, and the city woods turning already toward
spring, she saw him as she had seen him the afternoon before in
the village just at dark. The snow was falling a little in the early
bluish dusk and the lights from the teashop and the butcher
shop and the sports-clothes shop fell in great squares of light
across the shallow darkness of the road. There was snow underfoot and sleighs were driving past, and the street at that hour
was filled with people in ski dress and furs walking arm in arm
together under the airy little sprinklings of snow. Even then
when she had seen him she had thought it of him, even while the
blood moved suddenly and inexplicably in her heart she had
thought: *There he is again, one of the incredibly cinematic
sights, one of the outstanding picturesque attractions of the resort,* and she walked on through the babble of the sleigh bells
and people's voices, seeking not to see him because seeking to
pretend now while there was time that nothing had begun. She
was dressed for some other place, with an elegant black corduroy skirt and jacket on, and silk stockings on her ankles, crossing the arch of the village bridge under which the stream
scarcely murmured in the drifts of its bed. In hard bright willful
solitude she passed through the carnival-like scene of costume
and flung white confetti, thinking: *I might be a single, unwanted
woman walking alone like this, having always refused to believe
in, conceive of, admit that it could ever touch me, so that now I
can perhaps no longer recognize the clear unperjured look of*

love. And she remembered now, sitting in the sun at lunch, as if
remembering someone who had died young a long time ago,
how he had paused to talk in the evening with three light-haired
girls, three pretty, bareheaded young girls who glanced sideways
up at him and laughed and clung to each other in their fur coats
in the dark, like folly-struck girls fainting at last before the mi-
raculous flesh of a beloved stage or cinema star. He had stood
there, stooping a little from the weight of the sack on his shoulders, talking and even smiling at the three senselessly laughing
young women while the dry descending snow fell lightly across
his hair.

Only when he brought the filters of coffee out and set them on
the table did she raise her head and look into his face.

"I see you have a book," she said, looking rather mockingly up
at him, and now the friend was watching him too from behind
her dark glasses, and he felt the color burn up across his cheeks
and brow. She had picked up the little red volume of Heine's
travels from where he had forgotten it on the bench and she was
turning the pages idly over. She said, looking up at him still and
her mouth smiling: "My friend has just come from Paris, and of
course the hotel proprietor told me I should bring her up at once
to see you. He said you were one of the natural——" She did not
say "beauties" or "sights," but paused, seeming to seek the word
as her fingers turned the pages of fine gothic print. "I mean,
something like a waterfall or a gorge—that is, something one
mustn't on any consideration go away without seeing," she went
on saying through her straight red lips. Her eyes were squinted
up to see him as he stood there against the sun. "They said I
mustn't think of leaving without taking my friends, that is, my
young lady friends, of course, up to see the handsome blond
Austrian in the chalet just below the *corniche.*" The face was the
same, and the paint on the mouth, and the edelweiss flowers in
her ears, but now he had begun to believe that it was not this
woman, not this woman at all but some mistaken sight or memory of her who had opened the little volumes of the poets with
him at night and walked the streets of Austrian towns with him
again as his young loves had walked it. She was saying: "So obviously I had to come back, probably so that I could boast of

having come up twice and gone down—how shall I put it?—unscathed, I suppose——" She was looking at the pages of the book now, and suddenly she began laughing, the boylike body in the striped flannel shirtwaist bending forward over the table, the slender brown throat jerking with laughter above the cameo brooch that held the collar fast. The teeth showed sharp and stainless as she laughed. "Just listen to this," she cried out in a stifled voice to her friend. "Just listen to this," and with one long unvarnished fingernail following the words across the page, she began translating swiftly and easily aloud: "The Tirolese are handsome, cheerful, honorable, brave, and of an inscrutable narrowness of mind. They are a healthy race, perhaps because they are too stupid to be sick." She looked over the table at her friend, laughing, and then up at him for an instant, the dark eyes incredibly young and gay. "The girls," she went on reading, holding the laughter in, "greet you so amiably and the men press your hand so severely and behave themselves with such—such ornamental earnestness that you can almost believe that they treat you like a near relation, or at least like one of themselves, but this is far from true. They never forget," she read out, and now she bent again over the table edge, laughing, the thin arched back and the curled line of the lip and the white teeth wolflike as she laughed. "They never forget that they are but common people and that you are the gentleman who likes to see common people speak to him without shyness. These dealers in variegated table covers——" He saw her brown hand with the silvery rings on it holding the delicate little volume fast, and heard her voice continuing to read: "They set a price on their personality and their nationality," and then he walked off across the terrace in the sunlight and stopped at other people's tables and leaned his bare arms down and talked a moment before he went out of the sun and in through the chalet door.

They finished their coffee, then, like the others, and like the others paid the chef-apprentice for their meal and stepped off the terrace to strap on their skis. They were the last, and in a moment the place would have been free of them all, but suddenly the diplomat's wife turned her head and then savagely kicked her feet loose. She called back "wait a minute," or "just a minute," to the woman who was with her, and then she ran across the terrace boards and in through the doorway, running quickly, like a tall, beautiful young girl running eagerly toward love. She stood there blinded a moment, coming in from the bright white glare to the room where the timber tables and benches stretched the length of the walls, facing nothing now but the equivocal dark. Waiting just inside the door, she watched it perish slowly, ebbing inch by reluctant inch from chair and bench and table, until she could see the split ski tips mounted and crossed on the rafters like trophies, and saw the fox brushes and the martenhides and the snow rackets hanging from the whitewashed stone. Only at the last she saw him, the Austrian, with his back turned to her, leaning over the farthest table, working at the radio. She walked straight across the room to where he was, and looking at his shoulders, and the brass-studded belt at the narrow waist, and the back of his neck, like a child's neck with the hair growing yellow in it, she began speaking to him, saying the words quickly and without sentiment.

"You could give me lessons," she said. "I mean, in what I've always prided myself on respecting—high-sounding things like veracity and honor, or perhaps a military born-and-bred vindication for having turned out a woman after all. If you could see it exactly like that and take my apology," she said. And he straightened up from the radio and turned around to face her, and now that he saw her again standing before him and asking in boylike humorlessness and chivalry for a pardon she couldn't want and wouldn't know what to do with, his chilled heart smote him, striking a blow of indescribable tenderness and longing in his breast. "I like being the star of the piece," she was saying in quick stubborn honesty. "I like to play the lead without any competition. I suppose I minded because you play your part so much better than I've ever played mine." He stood watching the straight, painted lips shaping the words, and the unflinching eyes, and the head lifted, refusing beauty as if refusing the obligations beauty might incur, and he thought, *When she goes I'm lost again, I'll be lost again among them, a foreigner again, a foreign ski teacher shouting "Hands on the knees, chin forward, hands on the knees, hands on the knees"* to them, after having

been a man again for a little while; while her voice went on saying: "Last evening I saw you in the village. I just happened to see
you, and you were talking to three girls. And that's what it was,
you see, that's the kind of small, destructive pride I have, a thing
that can't bear to see you talking to three younger, prettier—
But even that," she said, and her eyes did not falter, "even the
nonsense of silly, foolish women you keep clear of. Everything
you have you could ruin overnight, I mean from the point of
view of all the high-sounding things I've respected, you could
ruin it. Everything that makes people stop and look at you and
sit down looking at you could be worth nothing, not even a snap
of the fingers, if it wasn't that—" He had stood there a long
time listening to this direct, unwooing statement of her speech,
and now he put his hands out and took her shoulders hard in
them and drew her against him. Before he kissed her, she said:
"If we have any sense we'll put it out of our heads at once," but
her voice was swooning in her throat.

"I've never wanted anything else," he said before or after or as
he kissed her mouth, his blood, or his heart, or his lips repeating
it to her. "I've never wanted any substitute for you here or
anywhere—"

That was two days before the blizzard. In the early morning
the high mountains began smoking like volcanoes along the hori-
zon, and by two o'clock in the afternoon it was snowing and
drifting so fast that the busses could not attempt the road down
to the railway station in the valley. So the diplomat's wife and
her children and the neat blond Swiss nurse were snowbound
with all the other guests in the extravagantly rustic sports hotel.
The time was long all afternoon and some of them played ping-
pong, and some of them danced to the music of the band in the
tearoom, and some swam in the heated indoor pool, their voices
echoing single and prolonged and summerlike across the stretch
of water and against the tiles, while outside the wind tore wildly
up the pass. The flexible blinds were lowered and hooked fast so
that none of the guests need witness that monstrous spectacle
without, shutter and glass and wall protecting them from the implacable primal hand that struck the trees and house and mountains not once or twice but in tireless violence hour after hour,

flaying, like wild horses up the valley and through the forests, the horizontally racing flanks of snow.

There were books left out on the table, but she was not reading; she was not knitting the coarse colorless wool into the endless smart and manlike sweaters, or doing her nails over, or cutting out cardboard boats or paper dolls. She was standing at the window of the hotel bedroom with the blinds up, watching the wind drive the snow in icy fury against the glass that might at any moment abjure its purpose and splinter, thinking that at least by tomorrow they would be able to go. Back to it, she thought in stern, chaste resignation: back to the house in Paris, to the man who came occasionally to table, and the twenty, thirty, forty others, the political experts, the accepted portrait painters, the diplomatic circle, the wives, the teas, the proper rationale to folly. In stern, chaste relinquishment of nothing, she thought, of absolutely nothing except five minutes of a blond young man on a mountaintop taking me in his arms and saying these things, saying: You are that river, and that place, and every separate day of my youth and every note of music I remember, and saying: Without you I have never been anything and what will I be now except that shade, that ghost, that spirit without flesh or meaning wandering blindly and fatally through hell, hearing the voice of Socrates cry out, "Spare me! I taught Truth and Justice and sacrificed my life for Virtue!" And suddenly she sat down by the cold white window and put her hands over her face and began to laugh. She sat there laughing in a sort of sad strange wisdom, seeking to see Paris now, and the water birds coming out and moving across the lake in the Bois on Sunday afternoons.

In a little while she turned away from the darkening window and the sight of the storm, thinking in sudden impatience that she had no use for idleness and for this superheated, superequipped place. She went quickly across the room and touched the electric button by the door, but no light sprang up in the milky basin in the ceiling or under the pink lamp shade on the table by the bed. But they brought her a lighted candle, saying that the electric pylons had gone down an hour back with the weight of the snow and the ferocity of the storm. Downstairs the

wide entrance hall was illuminated by the separate cones of the
oil lamps' light and the wood burning high in the granite fireplace; and the guests were gathered there now, playing cards or
seated talking or drinking, their lumberjack shirts open at the
neck and their feet in fur-lined and fleece-lined slippers as they
took these attitudes of safe, incurious leisure in the heat. But
passing the window in the stairs, she could hear the wind coming wilder and wilder up the valley, the thin, deathly wail and
whistle of it as it passed over what had been grass, tree, stream,
or man or animal quick with life once and was now lashed brittle and bloodless to one indistinguishable species by the wanton
transports of the storm. The house itself seemed to advance with
the racing torrent of ice, tipping, stem-up, rudderless and route-
less as a boat might on the strong, perpendicular crests, not of
water, but of snow that froze in the wind's velocity as it fell. She
stood a moment, waiting, as if for the crack and splinter of disaster, and now she saw him with an almost unbearable clarity, the
light bright hair, the lowered eyelid with the stubborn golden
lash along it, the stern, young, tender, violent mouth, the clefted
chin. He was sitting by the stove in the chalet's big room, reading Heine or Goethe or Immermann perhaps, sitting alone there
in the candlelight with his heart harking to the storm that swept
around him on the mountain as she stood alone here in the
candlelight on the stairs, harking to the storm in like unrelenting
and solitary fealty.

Two men in different parts of the hall saw her coming down:
the English army captain stood up and put his cigarette out, and
the young man she had danced with the evening before looked
across the card table and smiled. But she was looking at the
third one whom no one else had seen yet. He had come in from
the darkened dining room and was perhaps on his way to the
kitchen, a thin, rather ill-seeming young man with the look of a
waiter off duty about him, or the unfamiliar look of a taxicab
driver seen for the first time without his cab. He had meant to
hurry through the hall, drawing himself into his overcoat and
keeping his head down, perhaps delivering a message or a package; even as she went toward him she was not quite sure where
it was he had been or what function he had fulfilled. She

thought she had seen him chopping wood, perhaps, the end of a cigarette hanging on his dark, wet lip, and a cap on; connected in some way, close but inexplicable yet, with a thing as preposterous as hope. She had turned her back on the others in the hall and walked over the deep-napped, beaver-colored carpet to him and stopped him near the door. And suddenly, as he took his ski cap off, she knew.

"You come from the Austrian's chalet, don't you?" she said.

He said *bon jour* to her, and he told her he was the cook up in Mr. Gratz's refuge, and he went on saying, looking a little uneasily at what was lady and wealth and command, as if she might use this prerogative to ask him for explanation:

"He sent me down before the wind started. He said it was all right leaving him," with the He's and Him's capitalized as if referring to divinity. "I started in good time, but inside an hour you couldn't see your hand before your face. So the chef at the hotel here's letting me help him out tonight and share sleeping quarters with him. I'll get up there tomorrow if the wind stops."

She stood watching his face in patient urgency, watching the eyes as if they might divulge some portion of that sight they had of him day in and out, and the lips that might say without warning: This is the way he looks when he comes in from skiing and takes his gloves off, and this is the way he holds his fork and the way he drinks, and this is how he straps his boots around the ankle. The cook was gazing away in ailing, hollow-cheeked longing across the heated and peopled luxurious room.

"Why didn't he—why didn't Mr. Gratz come down?" she said, the voice quiet but the eyes moving eagerly on him.

"That's what he sent me down for," the cook said, shifting again uneasily. "He sent me down for compresses and liniment, but by the time I was through at the chemist's it was already blowing too hard. A native might get up there tonight, but I couldn't. I don't want to leave him up there alone on a night like this, but I haven't got the strength for it. I might make a start, but I'd never get there," he said.

"I don't think I understand," she said, and now she felt herself stirring, waking from the dream of acceptance and torpor and relinquishment. "Tell me exactly what it is."

"Well, it's his leg," the cook said, not looking at her but off across the room. "He's got a bad place in his knee from breaking it six times ski jumping when he was a boy going to school. He turned it again last winter and was three weeks getting around again."

"His leg?" she said. In a moment she said: "He has food and coal, hasn't he? It's just that he's turned his knee, isn't that it? He can't starve, he can't freeze, can he? It'll just be one night and then you'll be up there tomorrow. Anybody can stand a little pain."

The cook moved his feet again and looked down at his boots and the nap of beaver-colored rug flattened beneath his soles. And seeking his face deeply and relentlessly for truth, she saw in the empty temples and the hollow throat and in the cheeks' caverns the inescapability of his doom. Next spring, she thought, or perhaps next autumn, anyway at one change of the seasons, he'll be gone, and for an instant she perceived it clearly, this inevitable and almost impersonal death before the fact of it faded and she heard him say:

"There isn't a lot of food, but there's enough if he can manage to get to it. The wood and the coal—the coal's outside. It's not far outside, but it would mean him having to get over to the door and open it against this wind, and getting a drift of snow off it, and then carrying it in. I'd have got more in this morning before I came down, only nobody——" He dropped his eyes from hers again. "It ought to be soon enough if it quiets down tomorrow, but they're saying in the village it may go on three days like this. If it does, I can get a party to go up——"

"And the coal?" she said. "You don't think he has enough inside to see him through tonight?"

"Well," said the cook, shifting again. "That's what I wasn't sure about." He looked across the big warm hall, asking nothing more, nothing ever better and safer than this. "Only I can't get up there. I can't do it. I wouldn't get there," he said.

The Austrian sat wrapped in a blanket, moved close over the fire in the stove, with his leg on a chair before him. She saw him there and the clock on the wall saying one o'clock, when she got the door open and stamped in on her skis. She walked in stiff and erect as a mechanical toy, as a soldier wound up to go might walk directly and impregnably through barrier and impediment until the mechanism within his breast jerked more and more slowly and then ceased. She was masked white with sleet, so that he did not know her at once; because of the great rucksack on her back and the manly shoulders and the canvas, sleet-stiffened hood on the head, he only knew her when the lips began to move.

"I asked two men," she said, still standing straight. "But they refused, so I came up," and then the mechanism ceased and she sat down on the floor.

II

That was in February, 1938, a long time back, and if this had been another continent it would have ended like this. They would have lived on there, two people bearing the rucksacks up the long steep way through the pines and the high fields summer and winter, once the skiers and vacationists were gone saluting and saluted by only the peasants they passed, not man or woman any longer but legendary figures set apart from others by the mere enactment of other men's hopeless dreams of passion and love. But in this country there was something else: there was another presence as impelling as that of a third person sharing the night and the day with them, in intimacy or in public places, walking up the hill with them and sitting down at table with them and standing there in the chalet room, listening and giving their talk and their laughter another sound. No matter how high they went, up past the chalet to the higher mountains, and up glaciers and over passes where there was no human sign, no matter how recklessly they went or into what danger, they were not alone. For over a year the presence lived there with them, laying its hands on their hearts as it did on the hearts of other men and women who lay down at night and rose in the morning silent before the unwritten and unarticulable vocabulary of individual and national and racial doom. On the third of September of the next year, the presence was visible even to the most incredulous eyes at last.

On the morning of the fourth, about eight o'clock, a small closed car coming down the rocky alpine road through the already wintry-seeming gorges made another of the violently blind turns between the wall of dripping mosses and the precipitately rooted pines, its klaxon echoing in the wilderness, and then halted abruptly beside the two people standing in the roadside. It was the woman who had lifted her hand and made the sign. She had no hat on, only a dark silk filet holding back the smooth black wavy hair; she was wearing a camel's-hair coat and her mouth was painted. The blond-headed young man stood taller and broader but a little behind her against the dripping rock, wearing a city suit and carrying a city hat, like a swain dressed up for a country fair, as people used to living out of towns look when dressed up for an occasion. There was mud thick on their mountain shoes, and her eyes were hollow; the blond face behind her, perhaps younger than hers, seemed incongruously drawn and white above the strong, lean, country-bred bones of the frame. To the man sitting in the abruptly stopped car with his foot on the brake still they looked as if they had come a long way both in distance and in desperation.

He was a Frenchman from the north, a commercial traveler for a manufacturer of leather goods: straps, belts, fancy buttons, dog leashes, muzzles, canine and equine trappings and whips. Pasted on the rear window glass was a police dog's head, depicted in life size and color, the eyes bright, the sand-colored ears erect, and there was a stack of glazed-paper catalogues tied neatly together on the back seat of the car. The commercial traveler was in a hurry, having a wife and three children waiting for him in the *banlieue* of Paris and a third-day mobilization order in his mind. But when he looked through the glass of the finickily kept car at the woman standing in the roadside, he stopped thinking of these things and of the six hundred kilometers still to go. He leaned forward across the wheel to open the door for them, a man over forty going gray and his paunch going to fat, thinking either the cut of her face, or the way she wore the white earrings and the camel's-hair coat, or the urgently but

quietly spoken words gave her a quality as glamorous and exciting as if she moved toward him across the boards of a stage, and
at the same moment he thought: *Something terrible is happening to them, something as hopeless and final and inescapable as
the war.*

She said that they wanted to go to Voirancy and that they
had to get there before ten, and the commercial traveler pulled
the hinged seat beside him forward so that they could pass behind it and sit down. First she got in, in her coat and her white
hand-knitted Tirolian stockings and the soiled mountain shoes,
bending her head to enter so that her face came close to his as
she passed. Her eyes, undaunted and incurious, looked for an instant straight into his before she took the place by the stack of
catalogues behind him. And then the young man followed her
in: not a Frenchman, he thought, because of the heavy blond
head and the light-blue, light-lashed eyes, and the sound of the
pardon he spoke as he came, slender but strong, and so light that
it might have been the sun that had come now, through the
depth and shade of the gorges, into the small, low-roofed car.
Scandinavian, or Dutch, the commercial traveler may have
thought of him, if he thought anything at all; but it was not until
some time the next day, still driving toward Paris, when he
began seeing and reading the printed notices posted on the bill-
boards of police stations and city halls and post offices next to
the notices of the general mobilization whenever he got out to
have a drink or eat a meal, that he began to recognize him as a
German or an Austrian. Then he read that all past or present or
exiled citizens of the Greater Reich were to report without
delay; but on that drive down through the gorges he scarcely
considered the man at all because of the woman sitting there
behind him with the picture of the police dog's head just over
her shoulder. In the glass above the windshield he could see the
dark brush of hair and one edelweiss earring and the slash of
red, that partial portrait of a woman quivering with the car's motion as if reflected on water, and he drove, making conversation
almost shyly with her, this being the nearest he had ever come to
speech with the glamour and mystery of a woman of the stage.
She was saying that the young man had to be in Voirancy before

ten because he had been called there, a telephone call the night before to the chalet where they lived requesting him to report for service, and the commercial traveler saw the reflection quivering under water as she took the dark silk scarf off her own neck and put it around the young man's throat.

"No, no," said the quick, low, foreign voice in protest, and she said:

"Yes. You haven't taken a stitch with you. You'll need it."

And seeking to find her eyes in the traffic mirror and not caring what the answer would be, the commercial traveler said:

"What class is he?"

"He isn't any class," she said. "He volunteered. He volunteered the first day and now they're calling him for examination. That is, it must be for examination. It's probably just for that, and then they'll dismiss him and let him come home until they need him."

Because her voice was saying it, even that did not sound irregular to him then; it was only afterwards when he was driving alone toward Paris that he began to get one angle of the truth, and then he said out loud: "She believed it, I'm sure she believed it. I'm sure she thought up to the last minute, up to the minute when she had to take the cognac, she thought it was all right and that he was going to be sent to a training camp with Frenchmen." He said to her:

"I'm driving back to Paris in a hurry. I'm mobilized the third day."

But still he didn't just put them down in the main square at Voirancy, as they asked; instead he drew up by the curb and got the directions from a boy delivering bread. The boy said they had passed the prefecture back on the avenue, behind the trees, and the commercial traveler turned the car and drove them back to it and halted by the drive. The young man got out first, and when the woman got out the commercial traveler leaned forward and said in a lowered voice and almost sternly to her:

"You can't go in with him, of course." The French husband and father, the defender of family and convention speaking, Frenchman to Frenchwoman, as if recalling her to her own rigid and fearless conception of her role. "You'll have to wait out here while he goes in."

"Yes," she said, "I know," and she made no move but stood there on the sidewalk, watching him go in through the carriage gate and walk up the gravel drive under the trees toward the double flight of steps. He did not turn around, the tall, straight-backed, blond, young man, but walked quietly toward the stone stairs of the official buildings, his head raised to the barred windows and the printed signs. "I know," she said standing there with her hands in the pockets of the camel's-hair coat. Even at the door he did not turn, but, carrying his hat still, stopped to scrape the mud from the mountain boots on the wire mat and entered.

"Look," said the commercial traveler quickly. "You come across the street here with me and we'll have a drink while you're waiting for him to come out."

She turned around and looked blindly at him a moment and then she said:

"I don't drink."

"All right," said the commercial traveler, "but you'll have to sit down somewhere. You may have a little while to wait," and all the next day alone he kept saying to himself, "Me, a father, a husband, a cynic, sitting two hours and a half there for the pleasure of watching her take *café crème* and listening to her, who-ever she was, telling me about the children she hasn't the right to see any more—me, after three drinks getting teary-eyed just because she didn't, me playing the bereaved mother's and the bereaved lover's part because she refused to play it—sitting two hours and a half there when I ought to have been in a hurry, and she never mentioned the word 'love' once or the word 'foreigner,' leaving it all to me to put together——"

Sitting there, he had said: "You might be my daughter. Any-way, you look young enough to be my daughter," but in sudden helplessness and weakness he had thought: *This could be the end of a man, this could be the finish of him as far as anybody else or anything else was concerned.* "That last half-hour I know I said it over and over to her," was the way he told it after. "I said to her what I've never said to wife or mother or brother or child,

I said, 'I don't care what I am, Frenchman or German or Pole, so long as I can do my work in peace and have my drink before dinner and go to my cinema twice a week and then go home to bed to my wife at night.' I said, 'I don't want to fight any more than any man living whoever he is and whatever he is wants to go and fight,' and for two hours and a half she listened to me and I listened to her, that being probably the only conversation I've ever had where the weather or people's names weren't mentioned, because that sort of thing didn't even exist any more. It was the way you might have talked and might have listened twenty years ago when the first war was just over and there was nothing ahead but a lifetime of peace and youth, and in the end the messenger came across the gravel drive from the prefecture. We could see him coming through the gate and across the street among the requisitioned cars, and he looked around a bit and then came up to us on the café terrace, and she stood up to read the letter, standing as if to face a firing squad instead of words on paper, and afterwards she gave him two francs and said there was no answer. And even then she didn't give in to it," the commercial traveler would tell it. "She never said what it was, she just said: 'He hasn't any clothes with him and it's going to begin getting cold now,' and then she put her hand out over the table and took my hand hard, not foolishly but the way a man might have taken it, and she said: 'Please order me a cognac. Just order it for me quickly, please.'"

Men

The Baron had been set to work with the others on a road that lay in the Isère valley, running side by side with the river with only a row of trees standing tall and almost lifeless-seeming in between. He was a strong man and he liked the air he breathed and the unaccustomed action of the work after the months of being closed away. It was in the early spring, and the war not over yet, so there was still the movement of troops to be seen as there had been all winter and the passage of camouflaged liaison cars and lorries on the roads. It was then, in March, that the French had got the idea that there should be no more railway crossings to hold up the military traffic, and that bridges should be built instead to carry the thoroughfares up over the rails. So they took the men that they couldn't do anything else with and put them to work on the roads in the south and in the north and in all parts of the country, as if this sudden hastening of animate and inanimate material from place to place could alter the look of history in the end.

The railway line came across the Isère from the direction of Italy, from Modane, and cut across the highroad, but it was such a little line that the Baron could not see the sense in what they had to do. Only an occasional freight train moved idly along it, so it seemed it could not offer much interference. But still the powers that were had decided to hoist the highroad up over the rails, and the group of foreigners had been sent out into the bleak retarded springtime of the valley, perhaps fifty or more of them, to hack at the black surface of the road and the still hard soil around the condemned trees. The sky was heavy, as if there were snow yet to fall from it, and the flat shallow river that passed so close to them as they worked was cold, metallic, deathly, like a needle of ice that pierced their hearts. A little ahead of them, perhaps half a kilometer or less, there was a house to be seen on the field and swamp side of the road: a humble, rather dilapidated little house with a low-pitched roof fading between the tree trunks into a piece with the road's and the valley's flawless imitation of November. It was only when the Baron turned his head and looked the other way, up toward the mountains and saw the snow lying miraculously fair and high on their crests, that he believed again in the actual living world of natural ritual: of moon and sun, men and women, and the changes of the seasons instead of in this phantom and twilit rendering of fixed despair.

The Baron was twenty-eight that year, and from the look of him he came from a cold-stoned, dour-climated, castle country which might have been Scotland just as readily as Austria. He was tall and big-boned, with a longish, weather-flushed face, and shy, strained, rather prominent green eyes. If you were seeking for other things to place him than what women would call handsome you might not have seen that he was at first, and yet that too was there. Anyone knowing the German statuary of the Renaissance would have recognized him at once: Theodoric, King of the Ostrogoths, or Emperor Rudolph of Habsburg, or even Arthur of England somehow taken out of his century and his armor and put to work digging a roadbed in sight of the Alps. His hair might have been light except for the amount of water it needed to slap it, like a schoolboy's, into place; and his nose was fine enough for any member of royalty to have worn with pride. But it was his laugh, just after you had decided he was too reserved or grave for that, which it did you good to hear. Dostoevsky has written that one can know a man from his laugh, and that if you like a man's laugh before you know anything of him, you may say he is a good man. It was perhaps this laugh, so pure and hearty, so entirely without venom, which made the others come close to him and allow their hearts to open just a little, like men spreading their cold fingers before a flame.

But if the Baron looked now and again at the mountains, the other men had had enough of scenery: it was the house they liked to look toward down the road. The seven months they had spent in internment had altered their eyesight for them so that the little house appeared singularly sweet and touching to them; it had a homely, nearly familiar look to them all as if they had seen it somewhere before in another country. There was one man among them who was a Spaniard who couldn't take his eyes from it, and he would stand there putting his black hair back off his forehead with his fingers, letting the shovel fall idle between his narrow legs. He had something like a red stocking knotted around his neck because his throat was sore, and the ends of it hung down in front inside his raveling jersey. To him the house half a kilometer away seemed like his own house, the size of it and the shape, if only the sun had been out to give it the color of plaster, and if the doorway had had a beaded curtain hanging in it to keep the flies of another climate from getting in, and if the roof had been flat, and if there had been melons and gourds ripening on the step. Otherwise, it was exactly like his house in Pastrana, seen through the Spanish tree stems, at the end of town. Even the Baron made a rather foolish remark about it that first day. He said that the side of it which was turned toward them, with the two windows and the shape of a door and the dark headdress of the sloping roof, looked to him like a woman's head; and then he burst out laughing.

"*Regardez*, my house," the Spaniard said, and he showed his bad young teeth as he smiled. He spoke the words in French, but with a strange, untamed accent which gave them another sound. "Chicken cooking in tomatoes, and the woman waiting," he said. "That's where I go to sleep tonight, in a bed too. Nobody's going to get any of it but me."

He stood there, slouched thin and dark on the road, drawing his dark-skinned narrow hand under his nose to wipe the bead of cold off while the others went on hacking at this doomed portion of the highway, their backs bent, their heads down, digging the public and unhallowed grave. He might have been saying these words to any of the men working there around him, to the Hungarian doctor who had glanced once or twice down the road and believed there was a certain portion of the wall of the house, the tilt of the right side of the roof or the placing of the windows, which made it peculiarly his, better and closer than memory to him; or spoken them to the Czech tailor who had a wife and two children waiting in Avignon for nothing better than the cards he could send them twice in the month saying his leg was better or wasn't better or that he limped still (he, too, who had looked down the road and thought for an instant that he saw their faces at the windows of home, and the color of flowers on this side of the glass). But they all knew well enough that the Spaniard had spoken to the Baron and that he was tittering his rather vulgar girlish laughter for the Baron to hear; for it was the Baron, the strongest and the hardest worker among them, who seemed to keep night and day the patience to give ear and interest to what anybody had to say.

"*Regardez*, my house," the Spaniard said, croaking because of the soreness in his throat, and the Baron did not stop working while he said:

"It's a very good reproduction of a *Schloss*. Allow me to compliment you on your taste. It's exactly what I myself would have chosen." He straightened up for a moment and looked down the speechless, colorless road to the humble little house in the trees. "I like the turrets," he said. "Strikingly medieval," and he made a rather awkward gesture toward the slanting-roofed cottage, covered with tiles or corrugated tin or whatever material they could not tell from here. "And the way you've repeated the armorial bearings in red on the shutters, quite in keeping with the earliest German baroque. If I might make one or two suggestions," he said, saying it earnestly as he leaned again and struck the pick into the stone-clogged soil, "I'd have the iron deer moved back from the bridle path and placed a little more centrally on the lawns where they'd show to better advantage and at the same time do away with any possibility of the hunt taking fright." He spoke French a little heavily and carefully, but with the vocabulary of one who has read the words a long time and knows them well, although he has not had the habit of speaking them aloud. "I take it the banqueting hall overlooks the river," he said, hacking at the hard, alien earth and stone. "If so, I should have the statues placed nearer to that magnificent fountain which plays in the vicinity of the grottoes, and thus disengage the view of the façade."

The sentry was coming down the line toward them, a young man in uniform with a gun on his shoulder, callow and harmless enough looking, but at the sight of him coming the Spaniard picked up his shovel and seemed to set to work again.

"So if I didn't go back the same direction as you tonight," he went on saying in a low, almost wistful voice to the Austrian's strong bowed back, "you'd know where I'd gone. You'd know this time I decided to go to my house. I decided to go home."

The Baron could hear the scrape of the other man's spade as it struck on rock, and then the patter of the loose soil on soil as he flung the shovelful out on the road. In another moment the sentry's shoes had passed them, and without turning his head the Baron said:

"What is the name of the place you come from?" as a teacher might ask it of a child, or a doctor ask exactly where the pain might be.

"Pastrana," said the Spaniard. "Between Teruel and Madrid," and the sound of it laid such a languor on his blood that he must put the spade aside again and look down the road. "Pastrana," he repeated, and he leaned on the shovel and wiped his nose slowly and absently with the ends of the stocking or scarf that was knotted around his neck. "Pas-tra-na," he said again, pronouncing it lingeringly.

"That would be a long way," said the Baron, and as he worked he saw the geographical picture of it, the line of the coast from Marseille to Castellon and the journey inland in the heat. And now the Spaniard spoke to him in winning, playful slyness.

"Maybe just half a kilometer. Just over there," he said, tittering like a vulgar girl as he looked down the road. "I can smell something. I can smell the olive oil heating on the coals."

Still the Baron did not look around, but he knew well enough that the Spaniard was looking toward the house clamped fast between the tree trunks in the cold.

"That isn't Pastrana," he said. "You've made a mistake. That's Schloss Weidlingau. They're having venison and kraut for supper."

"No," said the Spaniard, the young but already corrupted teeth showing between his lips again as he spoke. "I can even say how the woman looks——"

"Ah, the woman," said the Austrian. For a moment he felt the thing stifling his heart, and then they both began laughing without warning, the Spaniard behind him laughing in quick high foolish gasps as he leaned on his shovel, and the Austrian in pure loud guffaws of blank and terrible despair.

Every day that they came out from the camp to work on the road brought them a little closer to the house, and day by day now it seemed to have become some sort of goal, almost an actual destination to them. They never saw smoke coming from its chimney, nor light in its windows, and toward evening they waited almost in grief for that cold quick rush of valley darkness which would engulf it with gloom beneath the trees. In the

mornings, while their hearts were fresh still, they had the inexplicable feeling that once they had come abreast the house, work
must somehow cease of itself, that merely reaching it must be
the end, the signal for them to fling down their shovels and
picks, as absurd as if the actual announcement of an armistice
had been made. It might have been that the war itself and its
issue had been waiting all winter for this little group of foreigners
to come up the road by the river to where the house stood before
the word of respite could be given.

During the final days, as they approached it, the Spaniard
would be seized with sudden insane transports of joy and would
fling his hair back and sing wildly to the trees; and as he worked
the Hungarian doctor's eyes would fill incomprehensibly with
tears. The others were nervous, ill at ease among themselves, like
animals when the wind is changing: their heads lifting quickly
from their work at the sound of a car or a lorry coming out of
the distance, as if it might be the purveyor of the message to
them, and their speech would be suddenly heated against one
another when, keeping to the still unbroken side of the road, it
would pass them by. The strings of army mules and soldiers who
trailed past once or twice in the day, picking their way across
the destroyed ground, seemed at one moment objects of humor
to them, the mules' ears and lips and even the sketchily clad soldiers ludicrous to the Baron and the Spaniard, and the next moment they recognized them in hopelessness as the delegates of
some final and inexpressible tragedy. Perhaps they had really
come to believe that once they reached the place where the house
stood the fighting would have to cease, the conflict stop forever,
although what they felt or what they thought they could not find
the words to say.

The Baron listened to the Czech speaking of home as he
worked near him, for some reason speaking of the iron fencing
which had stood around the garden of the tailoring shop as if it
were an emblem of freedom rather than injunction, and as he
broke the ground with his pick and listened to the other man
speaking, the same pure vision of justice and freedom and peace
was in the Baron's thoughts: that of freed men returning miraculously to their salvaged countries and their peoples, but in some

way it seemed to have grown clearer, sharper, even more painful to him, as if the realization of it now that they approached the house could not be far.

One day at noon they came so close to it that they saw the scrawny, tough-footed chickens in the enclosure that stood, fowl-picked-clean, behind the house. It was at two, just after the mid-day rest, that the sergeant took it into his head to send two men on before the others to start getting the branded willow out. He picked the Baron for his size and his reliability, and the Spaniard because he seemed to be doing nothing but lounging there with the shovel in his hands.

"You two go on ahead and get to work on the tree," the sergeant said, and he looked at the width of the Baron's shoulders, and in something nearer to contempt at the Baron's absurdly noble and vulnerable face. "You'll have a day's gain on the others, so by the time they're up with you you'll have it out," he said.

So it was in this way that the Austrian and the Spaniard happened to be the first to walk up the still untouched road and pass the house. The others paused a moment in their work and watched them go: the big, strong, blondish young man in the corduroy breeches and the French-cut shabby jacket with his wrists hanging naked from the sleeves, and the delicate-boned, gypsy-dark one with a red string knotted around his throat, carrying their pick and shovel straight past the house to the tree that stood on the other side. But even now that they had passed it, nothing happened, nothing altered in the air, and the other foreigners of the road gang stood there as if stricken with disappointment an instant, and then the sentry moved down the line and they lifted their implements and savagely attacked the soil. It was only when the Austrian and the Spaniard had reached the other side of the house that they saw what none of the others could: they saw the girl standing in the doorway looking out over the marshy fields that lay on this side of the road. She was simply standing quietly and innocently there, and at first she did not seem to see them. But when the Spaniard said: "Blood of God, there's a woman," she turned her head and looked at them where they had halted by the tree.

"Get on with the work," said the Austrian, but however immune his voice was when he said it, he had to turn his shaking heart away.

What she looked like it was never possible to say after. She was merely a young girl, perhaps seventeen, perhaps a little older, wearing some kind of fresh, clean dress, a blue one, or maybe a white one, who came down the one step from the doorway of the house and walked partway across the clean-picked, barren yard toward where the Baron had already thrust his shovel into the soil.

"What are you going to do?" she said. "Are you going to take the tree down?" Or, "You're not going to take that tree down, are you?"

The Spaniard gave a sly little sideways glance at the Baron, who had not moved from his place by the tree, and then his quick dark furtive hand went up to the string of red around his neck and his fingers undid it and slid it down, out of sight, inside the jersey's raveling wool.

"You're not going to take the tree down, are you?" the girl said, and all the time she walked toward them saying this the Baron was repeating to himself: *This isn't it, of course, this isn't the thing we were waiting for.* She was almost at the edge of the road, almost visible now to the others working beyond, and suddenly the Baron knew that for the sake of every woman they had not seen in months he must stop her from coming further. He threw his head back on his neck and he turned around, and again he thought: *This isn't it, of course;* so afraid he was that she would be different from what he wanted her to be.

"Yes, Mademoiselle," he said in his heavy, rather awkward French. "That is what we have to do, Mademoiselle. We have to take it down." He was facing her, drawing his hand back over his hair as a boy might do, but he could not bring himself really to look at her, only at the light, perhaps cotton, perhaps something else, but wondrously clean stuff of her dress. "Please, if you would go back there, back by the house," he said, and as he walked toward her she took first one step and then three or four backwards in obedience before him. "If you would not go out on the road, please, but let me tell you there by the house, then I could explain to you, Mademoiselle," he said.

He had put himself between her and the sight of the Spaniard who had not moved from his place by the tree, shielding her it might be from the Spaniard's dreams of love as from what the Hungarian or the Czech or any man might remember of her night after continent night in sleepless, frustrated memory. She was standing near to him, her hands and her bare arms hanging in her dress, her look moving curiously but without any quality of fear in it across his face. Even now that he looked at her, the Baron could find no human judgment of light or dark, pretty or not, to bring to her; he could not say what the color of her hair or mouth or skin was, or what the sound of her voice was like, although he had listened to her speak. He knew from the fact that her face must be lifted to his that she was shorter than he, but apart from this there was nothing, no physical sign or mark, to distinguish her from a thousand women—only the endowment of womanly purity which lay like a lovely garment on her flesh.

"Let me tell you, Mademoiselle," he said a little wildly. "Let me explain to you that we are altering the road here. There are certain changes which have to be made in preparation for the bridge which will go up over the railway line."

She did not move, she did not seem to hear him even, but her glance moved clearly and innocently, transparent in its curiosity as a child's eyes, over his cheeks and mouth and hair.

"I'm not from this part of the country either," she said, and she stood looking at him. "I've been evacuated from the north with my little brother. What language do they speak where you come from?" she said.

The breath caught in the Baron's throat, and he waited a moment. As he looked at her even his heart seemed stilled in his breast. At first he believed he would lie, and then he knew he could not, for it was no longer merely this, merely a girl in a clean dress putting a question to a stranger working in sweat and filth and hardness on the road. It may have been music like this, he thought, which the middle-aged, the older men heard playing when they had drunk too much in camp on Saturday nights in the winter and begun to weep among themselves, and to babble their wives' names, or their mothers', or their children's, though if they had families any longer no one ever knew. The Baron's ears had been deaf so long to everything except the cries of men calling out at night that he could scarcely hear it and scarcely credit it now that he heard: the voice of ineffable and nearly forgotten tenderness finding the questions to put to him at last.

"I speak German," he said to her, his hands thrust down in his breeches' pockets as he spoke. "They speak German in my country."

"German," the girl repeated. She said it gently, trying it out, almost as if it were a word she did not know the actual meaning of. "But you don't look like a German," she said, and the Baron said quickly, eagerly to her:

"No, Mademoiselle, the truth is that I am not a German. It is only that my country and Germany have that language in common." He took one hand out of his pocket and made a gesture toward the road. "You see, I am working now for the French," he said.

She looked at him another moment in silence, standing before him pure-skinned and guileless and young. And then she went on with a child's exact, curious persistence:

"But why do you do this work? It's funny work for you to be doing. Why don't you do some other kind of work?"

"Because we are not allowed to choose," said the Baron, and as he said it he felt the color come into his face. He might have stood there a little longer in uneasy silence, half ashamed, half shy, seeking to look beyond her and even beyond himself upon the spectacle of his own disastrous fate, had not his pride and his humor suddenly delivered him and he looked as if he were about to start laughing out loud. "That is, this isn't our war, at least to fight in, the one you read about in the papers," he said. "We're rather special people, all of us, very much enlightened, educated, scholars even, so obviously they couldn't put us into the trenches with ordinary men. Therefore they gave us our own battlefield," he said. He jerked his head in the direction of the road, and his mouth was smiling. "A very pleasant, peaceful one with a nice view of the river, only they can't decide what sort of uniforms to put on us yet or what grades to give us——"

All this, from the very beginning, may have taken no more than a minute or two, but when the Baron looked back on it the conversation seemed to him to have been marvelously complete and varied, as if they had talked profoundly and for an incalculable length of time. He had scarcely finished speaking when he saw that there were tears in her eyes, but her voice did not alter and her chin did not tremble as she said:

"Because you are prisoners. I thought you were prisoners when I saw the sentry walking up and down there all week with a gun."

"Yes, Mademoiselle," said the Baron quietly. "That is true. But our sentences are all for the same crime and for the same period of years, which somehow divides the burden among us."

"I am sorry for you, I am so sorry for you," the girl said, and she stood looking at him and slowly moving her head. It seemed she might put out her hand and touch his arm but she did not; instead she said: "It is not warm out here. Come into the house before the sentry passes again and I will give you a little glass of cognac. It will do you good," and because it was her voice that said it even the liquor's fiery, bitter little word sounded cooler and purer to him than any water she might have drawn from the faucet and offered him to drink.

"Yes," he said helplessly. "Thank you, Mademoiselle, I will," and as he followed her in over the step he heard the Spaniard's whistle, long, low, derisive, coming after him from underneath the tree.

She said two or three things more: she said she could make real lace and she showed him the hook and the spool of linen thread while he drank the cognac down in one quick jerk; and she asked him how long he had been away from home and how long since he had seen his people, and he answered that it was two years now, and, standing hooking the nickel needle through the thread, she said to him:

"But afterwards it will be all right and you can go back to them. After France has won the war it will be all right," and the Baron said quickly:

"Of course it will be all right then. It will be all right after France has won the war."

He stood tall and young, outsized and weather-hardened, in the little room near the stove, his hands in his pockets, the blondish pieces of his hair beginning to stand up of themselves. There he hesitated in the low-roofed kitchen that seemed too small for him, looking strangely and intently at her and trying to speak. He was trying to say that for a long time now he had come to believe it was not the loss of home, not the loss of country or freedom even, not even the loss of identity that was defeating them, but that it was something else, it was something else, but he could not find the name to give it. He wished to say that it was something as good and as necessary as the air they breathed that had been taken from them and not replaced: not the emotion of love or pity, but perhaps the flesh of these things, and he stood there silent, watching her hook the needle into the thread and draw the new loop through. He wanted to say: "Sometimes lying awake at night in camp among the others I scarcely believe in country or home or freedom or even in humanity any more, that all this is a fool's dream, all less than nothing to us. It is something else that has perished for us, that thing you gave us by walking out of the door and coming across the yard to us," but he could not say it out.

In another minute or two he was back on the roadside again with the taste of the cognac still in his mouth, and the fluid of tenderness pouring softly in him. Even with the shovel in his hands and his back bent, he moved still in the strangely perfect substance of the dream. It was only when the Spaniard, smiting the earth beside him with the pick's beak, said: "What about us? What about the rest of us? What do we get out of it?" that he started awake and stared about him in bewilderment.

"Out of what?" he said, and even as the Spaniard said the words he saw the sentry coming. It was not the exact meaning he heard, for hearing and sight and action had merged singularly into one. The shovel had fallen and his hand had lifted and struck hard across the Spaniard's mouth at the same instant that the sentry came toward them, his gun lowered, up the broken road.

They Weren't Going to Die

They were most of them rather tall men, tall, lanky black men with their heads carried high and with dignity on their smooth straight necks. If you walked behind a group of them wandering idly and with almost girl-like flippancy of gesture down the road, you could hear their shy, giddy laughter and speech, and you saw at once that the uniform they wore had nothing to do with their bones or their gait. The tunics and trousers and boots had all been made for somebody else, for some other race of men who knew when they came to a town what they wanted: *bistrot*, or a *tabac*, or paper and ink to write to somebody at home. They were never made for the softly hee-heeing, melodiously murmuring Senegalese, who went plucking the heads off daisies and nudging each other like school girls as they ambled through the springtime evening toward the river and fields, out of the direction of and the setting for war. Their necks rose rounded and smooth from the khaki cloth, with a little spring in the arch of them just before the hair began growing high on their pates, and from the back like this you could see the ears lying close to the small, elegantly fashioned skulls.

There was a general term for them, for the Senegalese: one that covered the whole foolish, aimless-seeming catastrophe of them, the long, loose-hanging hands and the narrow hips and the quickly lipped and unlipped smiles. In cinema theaters they were recognized as this, where they might be seen in the actualities of the week marching half indolently in military formation across the screen toward what nobody had taken the trouble to show them a picture of or told them how loud the noise was going to be. And Frenchmen, marking with colored pins on the wall map the drastic sweeping line of the German descent through France, would put their fingers down south of Lyon and speak the name for them again and again. They would say: "Here's where we're pushing the *chair de canon* up," and if the

black men had heard it they would not have known what it
meant or, anyway, that it was meant for them. But they wouldn't
have heard it because they would have been wandering off toward the river, the incongruous army boots heavy and dusty on
their feet, and daisies or the flowers of other weeds broken off
and brushing switchlike in their hands. They knew they were
going to kill people, maybe a lot of people, smiling big soft-
lipped smiles and looking sideways in the evening at each other,
but they hadn't come all the way out here just to die. They
hadn't walked down the hills of home, descending the paths
with their hands in their fathers' or their uncles' or their male
cousins' or their older brothers' hands toward the colonial towns
and military service, for absolutely nothing. They had taken a
long time learning which was the right and which was the left,
and how to count up to forty-six or -seven, and what the foreign
orders meant. In a little while they knew they were going to start
singing again, and do the belly dance to the tom-toms that summer, but one thing they weren't going to do: they certainly
weren't going to die.

Twenty or more of them had been billeted in the Count's stable on his property south of the city, and the first evening the
Count left them alone. But in the morning he put on his gray
tweed jacket and smoothed his oiled, thinning hair back in his
hands and stepped down the driveway to look them over in the
sun: a big, well-manicured gentleman of fifty maybe, with heavy
shoulders and a sveltely corseted *tour de taille*, and his pince-nez
hanging on a ribbon. He had been an Anglophile so long that it
showed by this time in the way his eyelids fell halfway over his
sight and hung there, and the way his chin returned to his throat
and vanished whenever he opened his mouth to speak. He stood
in the stable door with the light behind him, the height and the
weight exaggerated so, and the baby lieutenant whose family
kept a good hotel on the water front at Cannes stood before him
in the darkness of the stable, not quite certain how to address
him or exactly what to say. But the Count said at once:

"I gathered there was someone too young for it in command,"
and he snapped the pince-nez on the high hard arch of the nose
his ancestors had handed down from one generation to the next.

There it hung between the hard, well-shaven jowls, as outmoded
as the battle-ax tacked up among the relics of another time and
the armorial bearings in the dining hall. "There's one of them
got into the house," the Count said. "I saw the back of him making down the corridor as I came out," and the little lieutenant
straightened up like a flash and settled his leather belt in a military way.

"I'll have it taken care of at once, Monsieur," he said, but the
Count wasn't finished with him yet. He took off his pince-nez
and with the rim of one glass he tapped the lieutenant sharply
on the khaki breast where the decorations hadn't yet been
pinned.

"I don't know what the army's composed of this time or what
kind of war you're running, young man," he said, and the lieutenant's color ran up under his delicate skin to his black silk
brows, and he bit his lip. "As far as I can see there's no discipline, no order, not an ounce of stamina in the superiors." He
drew up his heavy, stooping shoulders in the London-cut tweed
and sucked his waist in, as if for military bearing, and looked
down on the young officer with his bleak, withering eye.

"I feel certain it won't happen again, Monsieur," the little
officer said, but for all of that it happened three times again that
day.

It seemed there was nothing to be done with the tall, black,
grinning fool who went sidling out of the loft no matter whom
the lieutenant set to guard him, and went ambling back through
the château's ancient, imported trees and in through the window
or the door and down the ground-floor corridor to the place he
liked so well. There they found him the first time when they
searched the house, and there he was the second, and the third,
not even taking the trouble to lock the door as other people did
when they entered this particular place. He was sitting on the
window sill above the porcelain receptacle, his puttees unwound
and his breeches drawn up high, and his bare black feet hung
down in the water that was there for another use entirely. The
servants said they could hear him laughing out loud all the way
in the kitchen whenever he pulled the chain and the water
flushed up across his shins. Even the third time the lieutenant

opened the door, the black man was sitting there, smiling right across his face, and reaching up to pull the chain again.

"What in the name of God do you think you're in France for?" the Count exploded before the lieutenant could clear his own throat of the youthful hesitation in it and snap the orders out.

"Kill Boche," said the Senegalese, with his feet dabbling in the water still. "Come kill Boche," he said, and he was reaching up to pull the porcelain handle when the lieutenant took him by the neck of his tunic and jerked him off the sill.

The weather held six weeks for war that time as it never did for pleasure, and the Count told the lieutenant that afternoon to get the blacks busy on the soil. His gardeners had been mobilized and he had been making out with a boy as best as he could, but now he had had quite enough of this military horseplay. The potato plants were waiting for the earth to be hoed up compactly around them, so a half dozen of the Senegalese were set to that, stripped to the waist and bent like oarsmen under the sun. Others were put to work the length of the strawberry beds, weeding and raking out between the clumps of low glossy leaves and the just-shedding strawberry flowers beneath the southern wall. The pear trees had been trained to spread out like vines across the hot stones of the wall, and on the other side the main road from Lyon led on around the curve and dropped down the hill to the village. Whenever the Senegalese turned their heads that way they could see over the top of the wall, through the pear leaves, whatever happened to be passing by.

They could see the trees and the fields and the waters of the river moving off beyond, and they leaned on the rake handles and the spade handles, talking among themselves. They would strike at the ground a little, and then the Senegalese melody rose sweetly on their tongues and they would pause again, giggling like women at each other. It was not from indolence that they ceased to turn the earth or pluck the weeds out of the Count's rich soil, nor out of what might have been native languor that they leaned on their implements and looked off through the leaves. They might have been merely waiting there, waiting for the name and the look of the thing that was to come, and work was not in them, for this was not the promise that had been made. The Count came out after tea and he saw them leaning in these long, loose attitudes of ease, their big hands hanging from their idle wrists, or clasped at rest on the rake handles and the spade handles and the hoes. There they had paused, like children halted on the edge of Christmas Eve, the blood humming with it, the babble of credulity tittering from lip to ear to eye.

"What are you canaille waiting for?" the little lieutenant called out as he hurried across the drive. He was beginning to play his part quite well, although in a panicky, puerile way. The Senegalese shifted the instruments in their hands, and moved their feet, and looked out toward the river. "What are you waiting for to get on with the job?" he shouted out, and one of the black men lifted his hand like a black lily drooping from the wrist and moved it toward the sky.

"Kill Boche," he said. "Waiting for the sun to go."

The Count seemed to have set the worldly manner aside for the moment, and he opened his arms in his gray tweed jacket and looked around in mock bewilderment.

"But where is the Boche? There's no Boche here as far as I can see," he said. It was he, by his own cunning, who was to establish himself the unmistakable master of the situation as he was the master of the château and the lawn. "Everything's very peaceful and quiet here," he went on saying, and as he spoke to the blacks he put an innocent look on his long outmoded face. He was going to get the better of them in their own way now, steal their blue-black thunder from them by his utter guilelessness and charm. "No Boche, no kill," he said, and his chin collapsed into his neck as he smiled around the vegetable garden at them. "Work," he said, and he made the gestures of spading, hoeing, raking before them on the air.

"Boche tomorrow, maybe Boche tonight," said the black man, and he lifted his hand again and moved it in casual indication from place to place. "Kill Boche there—there—there—there," he said, letting it fall from the wrist once toward the trees and once toward the wall and twice beyond it, and the Senegalese music of talk rose on their tongues again, then waned and died.

It was just before six that evening that the first motorcycle was heard coming down the road. The three Senegalese near the pear trees straightened up from the strawberry beds and their vision came level with the top of the wall and sought beyond it. They saw first the trees on the other side and then the surface of the road and at last the color of the solitary rider's jacket as he came leaning to the handle bars. They spoke the word or gave the sign in silence, and then their feet raced naked and wild back across the garden and the drive to where the guns were stacked in the stable yard, their legs reaching, their mouths splitting wide. They went so fast they were back in time for the second one: he dropped from his machine just where the brass studs began marking the curve of the turn and the motorcycle ran of itself a little way down the hill before it hit the tree. The third had a sidecar with a machine gunner riding in it, but neither the driver on the leather saddle nor the gunner behind his curved glass shield had time to see the khaki drape of the turbans or the guns along the wall. It did not make the turn this time but ran with the two dead men on its seats into the ditch and sputtered out there, and the others coming along behind were thirty seconds too late to see. There they came hastening down the road from Lyon, sidecar after sidecar of them driving fast, and as they came the black men picked them off over the garden wall and jumped up and down on the strawberry plants on their naked feet in glee.

The seventh or eighth was a single rider again, and this time the warning was there, splattered out on the road before him. He lifted his head to the pear leaves on top of the wall and braked so that the tires cried aloud, and swung the machine on its haunches, rearing and pawing the air. When he poured into speed and streamed back up the road, crouched flat to the bars, the black men's hearts stood still in pain. They waited there for a moment, and then they looked at each other and they could no longer find the sounds of laughter or speech. It might have been just after six on Christmas Day, and the stockings emptied, the presents all opened, the candles on the tree put out. They hadn't quite got over it when the nimble little tank came down the road, its eyes, like those of a snail, fingering them out, nor when the second tank came down behind it and the piece of the garden wall suddenly blew in.

The look of disappointment was on their faces still when the Count came out to have a look at them lying there. The machine gunners who had finished them off were removing their smoked goggles just inside the gate, and the German officer was chatting amiably with the Count as he walked with him out through the rose garden which shielded the vegetable beds from the drive. There were the black men, foolish-looking and rather giddy even in death, lying among the strawberry flowers and the potato plants.

"The staff will be along almost at once," the German officer was saying in a rather heavy but easy French. "I'd like to get this cleaned up without delay. It's a charming place, really charming. Regrettable that it was necessary to touch the wall."

The Count put his pince-nez on with a hand that did not tremble, and as the thought struck him with singular force, *Gentlemen, actually well-bred men this time,* he said aloud:

"The bodies removed?" and he felt himself sickening and turned the other way.

"Buried," said the German officer pleasantly. He had a kid glove, as scrupulously clean as if just lifted from the haberdasher's counter, on the hand with which he touched the Count's tweed. "I'm sorry to give you all this trouble," he said. "The staff will require most of the bedrooms for the moment at least." Then he turned toward the black men again and gave his orders. "Right where they are," he said shortly. "Snipers' burial."

"Right there—there, you mean?" said the Count. He was thinking confusedly of the potato plants and the strawberry flowers, but he could not bring himself to turn and look at them again.

Defeat

Toward the end of June that year and through July there was a sort of uncertain pause, an undetermined suspension that might properly be called neither an armistice nor a peace, and it lasted until the men began coming back from where they were. They came at intervals, trickling in twos or threes down from the north, or even one by one; some of them having been made prisoner and escaped and others merely a part of that individual retreat in which the sole destination was home. They had exchanged their uniforms for something else as they came along, corduroys or workmen's blue or whatever people might have given them in secret to get away: bearded, singularly and shabbily outfitted men getting down from a bus or off a train without so much as a knapsack in their hands, and the same bewildered, scarcely discrepant story to tell. Once they had reached the precincts of familiarity, they stood there where the vehicle had left them a moment, maybe trying to button over the jacket that didn't fit them or set the neck or shoulders right, like men who have been waiting in a courtroom and have finally heard their names called and stand up to take the oath and mount the witness stand. You could see them getting the words ready, revising the very quality of truth and the look in their eyes, and then someone coming out of the local post office or crossing the station square in the heat would recognize them and go toward them with a hand out, and the testimony would begin.

They had found their way back from different places, by different means, some on bicycle, some by bus, some over the mountains on foot, coming back to the Alps from Rennes, or from Clermont-Ferrand, or from Lyon, or from any part of France (as colloquial and incongruous to modern defeat as survivors of the Confederate army might have looked transplanted to this year and place with their spurs on still and their soft-brimmed, dust-whitened hats, limping wanly back half dazed and not yet having managed to get straight the story of what had happened). Only this time they were the men of that tragically unarmed and undirected force which had been the French army once but was no longer, returning to what orators might call reconstruction but which they knew could never be the same.

Wherever they came from, they had identical evidence to give: that the German ranks had advanced bareheaded, in short-sleeved, summer shirts—young, blond-haired men with their arms linked, row on row, and their trousers immaculately creased; having slept all night in hotel beds and their stomachs full, advancing singing, and falling singing before the puny coughing of the French machine guns. That is, the first line of them might fall, and part of the second possibly, but never more, for just then the French ammunition would suddenly expire and the bright-haired, blond demigods would march on singing across their dead, and then would follow all the glittering display: the rustproof tanks and guns, the chromiumed electric kitchens, the crematoriums. Legends or truth, the stories became indistinguishable in the mouths of the Frenchmen who returned: that the Germans were dressed as if for tennis that summer, with nothing but a tune to carry in their heads, while the French crawled out from under lorries where they'd slept that night and maybe every night for a week, coming to meet them like crippled, encumbered miners emerging from the pit of a warfare fifty years interred, with thirty-five kilos of kit and a change of shoes and a tin helmet left over from 1914 breaking them in two as they met the brilliantly nickeled Nazi dawn. They said their superiors were the first to run; they said their ammunition had been sabotaged; they said the ambulances had been transformed into accommodations for the officers' lady friends; they said: "*Nous avons été vendus,*" or, "*On nous a vendu,*" over and over until you could have made a popular song of these words and music of defeat. After their testimony was given, some of them added (not the young, but those who had fought before) in sober, part-embittered, part-vainglorious voices: "I'm ashamed to be a Frenchman," or "I'm ashamed of being French today," and then gravely took their places with the others.

There was one man at least who didn't say any of these things, probably because he had something else on his mind. He was a dark, short, rather gracefully made man, not thirty yet, with hot handsome eyes and a clefted chin. Even when he came back without his uniform and without the victory, a certain sense of responsibility, of authority, remained because he had been the chauffeur of the mail bus before the war. He didn't sit talking in the *bistrot* about what he had seen and where he had been, but he got the black beard off his face as quickly as he could, and bought a pair of new shoes, and went back to work in stubborn-lipped, youthful, almost violent pride. Except one night he did tell the story: he told it only once, about two months after he got back, and not to his own people or the people of the village but as if by chance to two commercial travelers for rival fruit-juice firms who were just beginning to circulate again from town to town in the unoccupied zone. They sat at the Café Central together, the three of them, drinking wine; the men perhaps talking about the anachronism of horse-and-mule-drawn cannon in Flanders and the beasts running amok under the enemy planes, or saying still what they had all believed: that the French line was going to hold somewhere, that it wasn't going to break in the end.

"At first we thought it would hold at the Oise," one of the traveling men was saying. "We kept on retreating, saying the new front must be at the Oise, and believing it too, and then when we dropped below the Oise, we kept saying it would hold at the Seine, and believing it; and even when we were south of Paris we kept on believing about some kind of line holding on the Loire——"

"I still don't know why we stopped retreating," said the other commercial traveler. He sat looking soberly at his glass. "We can't talk about the Italians any more. I still don't see why we didn't retreat right down to Senegal. I don't see what stopped us," he said. And the quiet-mouthed little bus driver began telling them about what happened on the Fourteenth of July.

It seems that in some of the cities the enemy hadn't taken or had withdrawn from, processions formed on the Fourteenth and passed through the streets in silence, the flagstaffs they carried draped with black, and their heads bowed. In some of the villages the mayor, dressed for mourning, laid a wreath on the monument to the last war's dead while the peasants kneeled about him in the square.

"I was in Pontcharra on the Fourteenth," said one of the traveling salesmen, "and when the mayor put the wreath down and the bugle called out like that for the dead, all the peasants uncovered themselves, but the military didn't even stand at attention."

"By that time none of the privates were saluting their officers in the street anywhere you went," said the other salesman, but the bus driver didn't pay any attention to what they said. He went on telling them that he'd been taken prisoner near Rennes on the seventeenth of June, and there he saw the air tracts the Boche planes had showered down the week before. The tracts said: "Frenchmen, prepare your coffins! Frenchwomen, get out your ball dresses! We're going to dance the soles off your shoes on the Fourteenth of July!" He told the commercial travelers exactly what use they made of the tracts in the public places there. He was more than three weeks in the prison camp, and on the night of the twelfth of July he and a *copain* made their escape. They went in uniform, on borrowed bicycles. They kept to the main road all night, wheeling along as free and unmolested in the dark as two young men cycling home from a dance, with their hearts light, and the stars out over them, and the night air mild. At dawn they took to the side roads, and toward eight o'clock of the new day they saw a house standing a little in advance of the village that lay ahead.

"We'll ask there," the bus driver said, and they pushed their cycles in off the road and laid them down behind a tree. The house, they could see then, was the schoolhouse, with a sign for *filles* over one door and for *garçons* over the other. The *copain* said there would be nobody there, but the bus driver had seen the woman come to the window and look at them, and he walked up to the door.

The desks were empty because of what had happened and the time of year, but it must have been the schoolmistress who was standing in the middle of the room between the benches: a young woman with fair, wavy hair, eying them fearlessly and even sharply as they came. The bus driver and his *copain* said good morning, and they saw at once the lengths of three-colored stuff in her hands and the work she had been doing. They looked around them and saw the four French flags clustered in each corner of the classroom and the great loops of bunting that were draped along the walls. The first thing the bus driver thought was that she ought to be warned, she ought to be told, and then when he looked at her face again he knew she knew as much or more than they.

"You ought to keep the door locked," he said, and the schoolmistress looked at him almost in contempt.

"I don't care who comes in," she said, and she went on folding the bunting over in the lengths she wanted to cut it to drape across the farthest wall.

"So the village is occupied?" the bus driver said, and he jerked his head toward the window.

"Yes," she said, but she went on cutting the tricolor bunting.

"There's one thing," said the *copain*, looking a little bleakly at them. "If you give yourself up at least you don't get shot," he said.

But the schoolmistress had put her scissors down and she said to the bus driver:

"You'll have to get rid of your uniforms before there's any chance of your getting through." She glanced around the classroom as though the demands of action had suddenly made it strange to her. "Take them off and put them in the cupboard there," she said, "and cover yourselves over in this stuff while you wait," and she heaped the blue and white and red lengths up on the desks. "In case they might come in," she said. She took her hat and filet off the hook as she said: "I'll come back with other clothes for you."

"If there would be any way of getting something to eat," the bus driver said, and because he asked this the tide of courage seemed to rise even higher in her.

"Yes," she said. "I'll bring back food for you."

"And a bottle of *pinard*," said the *copain*, but he didn't say it very loud.

When she was gone they took their uniforms off and they wrapped the bunting around them, doing it for her and modesty's sake, and then they sat down at the first form's desks, swathed to their beards in red, white, and blue. Even if the Boche had walked into the schoolhouse then, there probably wasn't any military regulation made to deal with what they would have found, the bus driver said: just two Frenchmen in their underwear sitting quietly inside the color of their country's flag. But whether he said the other thing to her as soon as she brought the bread and sausage and wine and the scraps of other men's clothing back, he didn't know. Sometimes when he thought of it afterwards he wasn't quite sure he had ever got the actual words out, but then he remembered the look on her face as she stood by the tree where the bicycles had lain and watched them pedaling toward the village just ahead, and he knew he must have said it. He knew he must have wiped the sausage grease and the wine off his mouth with the back of his hand and said: "A country isn't defeated as long as its women aren't," or "until its women are," or "as long as the women of a country aren't defeated, it doesn't matter if its army is," perhaps saying it just before they shook hands with her and cycled away.

That was the morning of the thirteenth, and they rode all day in the heat, two what-might-have-been peasants cycling slowly hour after hour across the hushed, summery, sunny land. The war was over for them; for this country the war was over. There was no sound or look of it in the meadows or the trees or grain. The war was finished, but the farmhouse they stopped at that evening would not take them in.

"Have you got your bread tickets with you?" the peasant said, and even the white-haired sows behind his legs eyed them narrowly with greed.

"We're prisoners escaped, we've got a bit of money," the bus driver said. "We'll pay for our soup, and maybe you'll let us sleep in the loft."

"And when the Boches come in for the milk they'll shoot me and the family for having taken you in!" he said, and the bus driver stood looking at him bitterly a moment before he began to swear. When he had called him the names he wanted to, he said:

"Look here, we were soldiers—perhaps you haven't got that yet? We haven't been demobilized, we were taken prisoner, we escaped. We were fighting a little war up there."

"If you'd fought it better the Boches wouldn't have got this far," the peasant said. He said it in cunning and triumph, and then he closed the door.

They slept the night at the next farm, eating soup and bread and drinking red wine in the kitchen, and when they had paid for it they were shown up to the loft. But they were not offered the side on which the hay lay; the farmer was thinking of next winter and he told them they could lie down just as well on the boards. They slept heavily and well, and it was very light when they woke in the morning, and so that day, the day of the Fourteenth, they did not get far. By six that night they were only another hundred and thirty kilometers on, and then the *copain's* tire went flat. But a little town stood just ahead, and they pushed their bicycles toward it through the summer evening, and down the wide-laid, treeless street that had been road a moment before and would be road again in a moment once it had passed the houses. They hadn't seen the uniform yet, but they knew the Germans must be there; even on the square in the heart of town they saw no sign. But still there was that unnatural quiet, that familiar uneasiness on the air, so they pushed their wheels through the open doors of the big garage, past the dry and padlocked gas pumps, and stood them up against the inside wall. There, in the half-security and semidark of the garage, they looked around them: twenty or more cars stood one beside the other, halted as if forever because of the lack of fluid to flow through their veins, and the little Bibendum man astride the air hose on wheels was smoking his cigar the way he would never smoke it again. Over their heads the glass panes of the roof were still painted blue; the military and staff cars parked in the shadowy silence still bore their green and khaki camouflage. The war was over, everything had stopped, and out beyond the wide-open automobile doorway they saw the dance platform that had been erected in the square, dark, heavy, leafy branches twined through the upright beams and the balustrade, and the idle people standing looking. There were no flags up, only this rather dismal atmosphere of preparation, and the bus driver and his *copain* remembered it was today.

"It's a national holiday and we haven't had a drink yet," the *copain* said. He stood there in the garage with his hands in the pockets of the trousers that didn't belong to him, staring bleakly out across the square. Even when the two German soldiers who were putting the electric wiring up in the temporary construction came into view, his face did not alter. He simply went on saying: "We haven't had the *apéritif* all day."

The bus driver took a packet of cigarettes out of his jacket pocket and put one savagely on his lip. As he lit it, he looked in hot, bitter virulence out to where the Germans were hanging the strings of bulbs among the fresh dark leaves.

"'Frenchmen, prepare your coffins!'" he said, and then he gave a laugh. "They've only made one mistake so far, just one," he said, and as he talked the cigarette jerked up and down in fury on his lip. "They've got the dance floor and the decorations all right, and they've probably got the music and maybe the refreshments too. So far so good," he said. "But they haven't got the partners. That's what's going to be funny. That's what's going to be really funny," he said.

He sat there in the Café Central some time in September telling it to the two commercial travelers, perhaps because he had had more to drink than usual telling them the story, or perhaps because it had been weighing heavy on his heart long enough. He told them about the dinner the garage owner gave him and his *copain:* civet and fried potatoes and salad and four kinds of cheese, and Armagnac with the coffee. He said they could scarcely get it all down, and then he opened a bottle of champagne for them. That's the kind of man the garage owner was. And during the dinner or afterwards, with the wine inside him, it seems the bus driver had said it again. He said something about as long as the women of a nation weren't defeated the rest of it didn't matter, and just as he said it the music struck up in the dance pavilion outside.

The place the garage owner offered them for the night was just above the garage itself, a species of storeroom with three windows overlooking the square. First he repaired the *copain*'s tire for him, and behind him on the wall as he worked they could read the newspaper cutting he had pinned up, perhaps in some spirit of derision. It exhorted all Frenchmen to accept quietly and without protest the new regulations concerning the circulation of private and public vehicles.

"Without protest!" said the garage owner, taking the dripping red tube out of the basin of water and pinching the leak between his finger and thumb. "I'll have to close the place up, and they ask me to do it without protest!" He stood rubbing the sandpaper gently around where the imperceptible hole in the rubber was. "We weren't ready for war and yet we declared it just the same," he said, "and now we've asked for peace and we aren't ready for that either," and when he had finished with the tire he showed them up the stairs.

"I'll keep the light off," he said, "in case it might give them the idea of coming up and having a look," but they didn't need any light, for the illumination from the dance pavilion in the square shone in through the windows and lit the rows of storage batteries and the cases of spare parts and spark plugs with an uncanny and partial brilliancy. From outside they heard the music playing: the exact waltz time and the quick, entirely martial version of swing.

"Somebody ought to tell them they're wasting their time," the bus driver said, jerking one shoulder toward the windows. He could have burst out laughing at the sight of them, some with white gloves on even, waiting out there to the strains of music for what wasn't going to come.

The garage owner shook out the potato sacks of waste on the floor and gave them the covers to lie down on, and then he took one look out the window at the square and grinned and said good night and went downstairs. The *copain* was tired and he lay down at once on the soft rags on the floor and drew a blanket up over him, but the bus driver stood awhile to the side of the window, watching the thing below. A little group of townspeople was standing around the platform where the variously colored lights hung, and the band was playing in one corner of the pavilion underneath the leaves. No one was dancing, but the German soldiers were hanging around in expectation, some standing on the steps of the platform, and some leaning on the garnished rails.

"For a little while there wasn't a woman anywhere," the bus driver told the commercial travelers. "There was this crowd of people from the town, perhaps thirty or forty of them, looking on, and maybe some others further back in the dark where you couldn't see them, but that was all," he said, and then he stopped talking.

"And then what happened?" said one of the traveling men after a moment, and the bus driver sat looking in silence at his glass.

"They had a big long table spread out with things to eat on it," he went on saying in a minute, and he didn't look up. "They had fruit tarts, it looked like, and sweet chocolate, and bottles of lemonade and beer. They had as much as you wanted of everything," he said, "and perhaps once you got near enough to start eating and drinking, then the other thing just followed naturally afterward, or that's the way I worked it out," he said. "Or maybe if you've had a dress a long time that you wanted to wear and you hadn't had the chance of putting it on and showing it off because all the men were away; I mean if you were a woman. I worked it out that maybe the time comes when you want to put it on so badly that you put it on just the same whatever's happened, or maybe if you're one kind of woman any kind of uniform looks all right to you after a certain time. The music was good, it was first class," he said, but he didn't look up. "And here was all this food spread out, and the corks popping off the bottles, and the lads in uniform great big fellows handing out chocolates to all the girls——"

The three of them sat at the table without talking for a while after the bus driver's voice had ceased, and then one of the traveling men said:

"Well, that was just one town."

"Yes, that was just one town," said the bus driver, and when he picked up his glass to drink, something as crazy as tears was standing in his eyes.

Let There Be Honour

I

It was one night in March that the first group of Foreign Legionaries came into the military canteen: there were five or six of them in khaki, with their heads under their beaked caps still shaved. They strolled in from the station platform casually enough, but as soon as they set foot inside the door their eyes began seeking for what they'd been told she would be like. They'd heard it first in Damascus, and the second time on the cattle train going to Beirut, and the last time they'd heard it was on the ship coming back to what had once been France. It was just as explicit as if the details of the story had been typed indelibly out. Only it was never written out; it merely went like this from ear to ear, and the men who heard it believed it because they wanted to believe in something; by this time they had to believe in something or else there wasn't any sense in giving the salute or wearing the uniform any more.

They believed every word of it: they believed that once you got to this city, either by boat, or by train, or on bicycle, or on foot, all you did was to walk to its terminus and get past the gendarmes at the gates (and some of them even believed that the gendarmes closed their eyes, for what were they but Frenchmen with their contraband hope in it too). And there you crossed the station to the left-hand platform and you walked into the canteen, and when you got near enough to her, to that one girl behind the counter (not to the lady at the cash desk or any of the boys helping, but to that particular one), you said the first word of the ritual to her; you said "Honour" to her, and she would answer: "Honour Higgins." The story had it that she was a Lady, that her name was actually Lady Honour Higgins, and then she would say: "Did you want coffee?" and you would answer: "I've come a long way for it, and I'm willing to go further."

They believed all this: all those weeks or months or merely days it took them to get there, they believed in this, but when they had got inside the door the terrible moment of misgiving came. Perhaps after all it was hoax or lie or legend, and perhaps this had nothing to do with the way to do it in the end. So the Foreign Legionaries paused that night in March as other men had paused after stepping just inside the canteen room, and then the big blond man who had taken the lead began making his way through the crowded tables to her. He was taller and stronger than any other man in the room, and he elbowed his way past the others, kicking aside the knapsacks in the aisles when they stood in his way. Men were collected two deep at the zinc, drinking their coffee and looking at her, and he made his way past them as well with the other Legionaries following behind. Once there before her, he stopped short and took off his cap: before the girl with light, longish hair with a blue veil over it (perhaps the same color as her eyes if he could have seen them by day), and the red cross on the white band on her forehead the same red as her lipstick (or as nearly as he could tell in the railway station's equivocal light).

She was pouring coffee for two recruits, but the Legionary had waited too many weeks already, and his patience was at an end. He wet his lips, and he leaned forward and said the one word to her. He said: "Honour," pronouncing the single word as well as any Englishman might have, and then he waited, his eyes on her. The girl had glanced at him once, but now that he spoke she gave no sign of having heard. She had asked the recruit how old he was, or where his father had fought the last war, and she waited for the answer while the blond Legionary's eyes and the eyes of the others with him did not leave her face. Once the recruit had answered she looked at the Legionary again, at the decorations on his left breast pocket, and at the width of his shoulders, and she said:

"Honour Higgins," but nothing had altered in her. It was in the men's faces that the change had come. "Did you want coffee?" she said as she wiped the zinc dry.

"We've come a long way for it," the blond man said, still speaking the flawless English to her. "We're willing to go further."

"All of you?" said Lady Higgins.

"Yes, all of us," said the Legionary, and Lady Higgins turned and took six cups from the stack drying on the wood and set them on the counter one by one.

So that was, after all, the way the thing began. Madame Pichot working there with her at the cash desk knew that much of the machinations of it, but what happened afterwards was never spoken of. Lady Higgins made her own dates and kept them, and the next afternoon the blond Legionary went alone out to her little house on the sea. She didn't have a veil on her hair. She was wearing slacks, light gray like the shirt, and she was smoking by the fire. When he was shown in by the Frenchwoman in espadrilles, she stood up for a moment and gave him her hand.

"You're a very good imitation of an Englishman," she said.

He said he was Viennese, smiling the bright white smile a little too much on his sunburned face. He looked even bigger here in his khaki in the fisherman's low-ceilinged plaster room.

"I was educated in England," he said.

"What are they doing with the Legion?" she asked. She offered him a cigarette from where she sat by the fire.

"They're sending a lot of us back to Austria," He said.

She sat looking at him a moment as he ate and drank the tea; the hair on his head was just beginning to grow in, and the skull that bent to the cup had a heavy, naked, almost Prussian look.

"And you don't want to go back to Austria?" she said.

He said he had been a Heimwehr, and then he cleared his throat.

"I don't fancy the idea of facing a firing squad one early morning over there," he said. He took another sandwich of synthetic anchovy paste spread thin on zwieback and gulped it down with tea. "They say Vichy's handing us over in exchange for potatoes," he said. "We're a commodity, we're not men any more," and he went on saying: "But those of us who went to see you last night, we want to make the break——"

Lady Higgins sat by the fire, smoking, with her ankles out of the gray slacks stretched and crossed. They were almost as slender as her wrists, and she saw his eyes were on them. The firelight moved on his face, laying quick, uneasy shadows there, and the thoughts came, not for the first time or even the second, but this time almost with conviction to her. She could hear the sound of it as clearly as if a voice were saying it aloud: "Some time you may make the mistake, Honour Higgins. Some time you may fatally mislay judgment's quality."

It was about half an hour later when they walked out through the sea-burned cactus and palms to the sandy road that he himself said it aloud. He had to be in barracks by seven, and she came this far with him and repeated the last things to him in the sea-washed dark. She had said: "So I wish you good luck," and then he said the thing she had been thinking.

"I should think you'd be afraid of one thing," he said in a low voice, and because he stood so near to her she said:

"Not of men, anyway, my friend. Only that they may not be heroes in the end."

There were a few stars out, very big and bright through the palm's papery leaves, and she took a step away from him and waited there.

"I mean, someday you may make a mistake," he said. "Someday someone who isn't an Austrian or who isn't whatever he says he is may walk in and say 'Honour' to you, and then it will be all over. Someday it's going to be somebody else, and then the gentlemen in gray will get you up one morning before sunrise too."

"That's just a chance I happen to be taking," said Lady Higgins, and without warning the Legionary took her in his arms and kissed her mouth.

When she could say it, Lady Higgins said:

"That isn't such a good imitation of an Englishman." She took out her handkerchief and smeared it hard across her lips, rubbing the feel of it and the violence and even the memory out. "Now, just get out," she said quietly, and the Legionary or whatever he was turned and went down the road.

II

It was done like that, only some of them were better men than others. Two Belgians came through the canteen the next night, and three Czechs the night after that. The Czechs stood up at the zinc counter and they said they wanted to fight the Slovaks; that was all they wanted to do. They would wear any uniform and use any weapon you put in their hands as long as they could fight the Slovaks. Next to them stood a Spaniard in a ragged shirt, with little gold earrings pierced in his ears, and beyond him stood the gendarme. The Spaniard said in a quick, gentle voice that he wanted to fight the Spaniards, and his French was so simple and strange to the others that they burst out laughing when he spoke. It was only after a little while, when the Spaniard tried to lift his cup of coffee up, that you saw his wrist was handcuffed to the gendarme's wrist.

"Got loose from the concentration camp near Perpignan," the gendarme said to Lady Higgins when she poured his coffee out, and the Spaniard stood there with his eyes gone soft, looking at her hair. "He's a nice, quiet fellow," the gendarme said. "Just wanted to see his brother on the other side."

The three youngish-looking Czechs were there, talking among themselves and drinking coffee and watching a little warily for the gendarme to go. They knew by heart the words they wanted to say, but they weren't going to say them before him. One had been a medical student, and one a chemist's son, and one had been studying law in a world that now had ceased to be. They had been afraid so long that they were afraid to speak out loud in any tongue before a uniform, they were afraid of their shadows at their heels, afraid when a door opened and closed, afraid to look anywhere except into one another's face, as if finding only there the landmarks of security. But the Spaniard was not afraid; the bangle on his wrist was nothing. After he had swallowed the sandwich and the coffee, he started looking at Lady Higgins again.

"Give him another chopped dog," the gendarme said. "He's

hungry. We picked him up after forty-eight hours in the maquis." When she handed the sandwich out over the zinc, the Spaniard ceased thinking of love or beauty or anything else except the bread and the meat she held in her hand, and they watched him eat it. "Give him another," the gendarme said. "That's better than what he'll get where he's going back to tonight."

The gendarme began telling her then about the gasoline the Germans made out of capsules you just dropped into ordinary water. You dropped the capsules in and stirred it around with a stick, and there it was, he said. This was perhaps the three hundred and fiftieth time she had heard the story, but Lady Higgins gave no sign: sometimes the capsules were as big as pie dishes and sometimes they were no larger than an aspirin tablet, and sometimes they became a shower of crystals tossed out in the hand. But however the miracle was performed, the *mise en scène* didn't alter: the Boches always drove up to a village pump and stopped their car there, and the chauffeur got down and asked for a bucket in French even more correct than a French peasant's would be. And when he got the bucket, he filled it with water at the pump and, with the whole village looking on, he dropped the pie dish or the aspirin tablet in. But the Spaniard didn't listen to what the gendarme was saying; the gendarme might not have been talking at all, as far as the Spaniard was concerned. He was merely handcuffed to him, and there their relation ended. He was thinking of something else entirely, and after a minute he spoke about it.

"I want to go to England," he said in his strange and simple French to her, with his eyes fixed on her face. "No Fascist," he said, and he pointed to the scarcely covered bones and the dark skin where the shirt lay open on his neck. When he lifted his hand, the movement was jerked short by the chain on his wrist. "You tell me, please, how to get to England," he said.

That sort of thing might happen right out like that any night and it didn't matter. Said like that, there could be no implication to it, and the eyes or the voice confessed to nothing at all. It wasn't even good enough to be a joke; the gendarme didn't see anything funny in it, although the three Czechs had begun to laugh uneasily among themselves. The gendarme said:

"There's a lot of them still locked up down there. There're twenty thousand or more like him. Nobody wants them, in the country or out of it. There's nothing to do with them," he said.

Lady Higgins stood on the other side of the zinc, looking at the Spaniard's face and seeing not one but the other twenty or thirty thousand of them, the tattered, exiled army of despair still undespairing as it gathered, dark-eyed and hungry, behind him in the canteen room. There weren't enough cups to set out for them, or enough imitation sandwiches to cram into their mouths. There weren't enough benches to ask them to sit down and make themselves at home on, so they stood there in silence with their eyes on her, asking in silence for nothing that anyone could give, not men any more but the shadows and shapes of men with chains on their wrists to link them with reality.

That was in March, and in April the thing that really mattered happened: about two o'clock one morning the Englishman walked in. He was not too tall and not too young, and his hair was a little blond at the temples as if the sun had done it, and he came right over to the counter and leaned his arms on the zinc. He was wearing a darkish jacket that must have belonged to someone else before him, and blue workmen's trousers, still quite new. His nose was short, and his upper lip was longish, and his eyes were casual but steady.

"Hello, Honour," he said, saying it wrong from the beginning. He didn't look at anyone or anything else in the room, but leaned there on the counter.

"Honour Higgins," she said, without a trace of anything in her voice. He pushed the beret on the back of his head, and as he did it she saw with something like tenderness the small-knuckled, boyish hand. It might have been hand of brother or cousin out of its glove for a moment and on the snaffle rein at home, or lifted to slap a horse's shoulder, or just lying will-less on English paddock grass. "Did you want coffee?" she asked. Either he was English, or else marvelously cast in the role, and then she heard him miss his cue.

"I don't know. It's pretty foul stuff these days," he said. He leaned there, his fingers cupping his elbows where the sleeve lining showed, looking not intently, perhaps even without so much as expectation, at her.

"If you'll show your military papers at the cash desk and get your ticket, I can serve you," Lady Higgins said. The others had always been simple enough: lost foreigners asking a direction, and their faces lighting like children's when you spoke the words they knew. But this one had put the rigmarole aside, and even when she pointed out Madame Pichot at the cash desk to him, he made no move to go. "You're the first we've seen come through," she said, countryman saying it to countryman, and she wiped the zinc off. "Did they give you a bad time getting down?"

"I forget," said the Englishman. "Ran into a few prisons sort of thing," he said, and without any drama in it, he added: "I've been six months on the way."

Lady Higgins had set the clean thick cup down in readiness before him, and now she spooned the sugar out, but whether or not he got anything to eat or drink seemed of no interest to him at all. He simply wanted to lean there, telling her in bits and pieces this thing which might sum up one man's history in the end. There were lines at the corners of his eyes, and lines on each side of his mouth, and his cheeks were a little hollow, but he hadn't a word to say about hunger or cold or any kind of pain.

"Good old organization," he was saying, and he said that in German prison camp at least you knew where you were. "I take off my hat to organization," he said, and Lady Higgins said:

"You've still got it on."

He reached up when she said this and took his beret off and put it in his jacket pocket, and Lady Higgins liked the way he moved his head and hands.

"That's for the French look of the thing," he said about the beret. "The French lock you up," he went on with the story, "and then they forget you're in prison and they give you a bottle of wine by mistake or shoot a game of billiards with you. All that leads to confusion."

"They're not such an easy lot outside," said Lady Higgins about the French. "You'll have trouble getting past them."

"I've had trouble before," said the Englishman. "When I skipped the Jerry camp, the French locked me up for six weeks for swimming without a bathing suit. I didn't do it out of choice, because it was nearly Christmas. It was just one way of getting across the line."

"If you'll get your ticket at the cash desk," Lady Higgins began again, and she added: "I'm sorry. It's regulations."

"Good old regulations," said the Englishman, and he turned and looked for Madame Pichot. When he saw her, he turned and walked the length of the counter to where she sat.

Lady Higgins stood there, her eyes on him, watching him go, watching the part-casual, part-arrogant English-gentleman walk as he crossed the boards, watching him pause there at the cash desk and fish rather vaguely in his pockets for his military papers, as if it were of no importance where they were or if they were actually on him, and finding them where he didn't expect them to be. She didn't hear the wash boys talking behind her, or the train whistles crying outside in the dark, but stood there simply watching him as if, after the months of exile, she could never see enough of her country's blood and bone. It was only when he turned around again that she saw his face was harder and more bitter than any man's under thirty had the right to be.

"The second time, it was because I didn't have a license plate on my bicycle," he said, leaning on the counter again. He took a swallow of what nobody called coffee any more. "I should have traveled by night, but mad dogs and Englishmen go out in the midday sun," he said. "I'd been locked up so long I thought once I got over the line all I had to say was 'Look here, I'm English. Bad luck Dunkirk and all that, what?' and then we'd sit down and have a drink together. But it didn't work out like that. 'So you're English sort of thing, are you, my lad?' they'd say, and then the fun'd begin."

"How funny was it?" asked Lady Higgins, and the Englishman looked at her.

"Not very funny," he said.

It was just beginning to be dawn now, and the little coast omnibus was rattling into shape outside. The repatriated wounded had begun packing up the remains of their food, and folding their bits of paper carefully away. The Englishman heard the movement behind him and he stopped what he was saying.

"I'd better clear out with them," he said, but Lady Higgins shook her head.

"They aren't going out," she said. "They're taking another train. They're going home," and the Englishman said, with no perceptible interest in it:

"That's where I want to go."

He had seen the scrap of bread somehow left forgotten on the table when he turned his head, and now that they had gone he took the two steps to retrieve it and laid it on the zinc.

"Jerry bread," he said, "you can tell by the color of it." There it lay between them, whiter than any bread she'd seen in months. She told him the wounded were back from Germany, and brought provisions with them. "It's nearly the same as we used to have in Munich on a summer night between the acts of *Lohengrin*," the Englishman said. He stood looking at the bit of bread as though it were a dove of peace come quietly to rest there. "Lady Higgins, my dear, there's something rather odd about the whole show," he said, and then, as if continuing the same sentence and without looking up, he said: "How do I get across?"

It was Madame Pichot who brought the matter of his papers up: she said they looked too authentic to be true. She said this to Lady Higgins at half-past four in the morning when she came past the cash desk to get more sugar from the reserve. Madame Pichot leaned forward from her chair and touched Lady Higgins' arm and whispered it through her teeth so that no one standing near might overhear. She said she liked the look of the young man, and the way he spoke, but she didn't like his papers.

"I've never seen anything so complete on a military fugitive," she whispered, and the light glinted on her glasses as she brought her face closer to Lady Higgins' face.

"He comes from Mousehole," said Lady Higgins. She stood

there, wondering, with the empty sugar tin hanging from her hand. "He's absolutely all right."

"How do you know?" asked Madame Pichot.

"I was born and bred with them," said Lady Higgins. "I've hunted with them, was brought up with them, married one even," she said a little grimly.

"What about Lord Haw-Haw?" whispered Madame Pichot through the steel-white light of dawn.

"But his people——" Lady Higgins began, and then without warning the Foreign Legionary interrupted her. He might just as well have been there, big and blond and smiling in the flesh, aping to perfection the English tongue. "Someday you may make a mistake, a bad mistake," said the phantom Legionary to her, and Lady Higgins felt the blood run suddenly cold through her heart. "Someday somebody may walk in and say 'Honour' to you who has no sense of honor," the Austrian said, and because of all that hung on the doubt she let him go on. "You can't get away with it forever, you know," he said, and then Lady Higgins brushed the two of them, the Frenchwoman at the cash desk and the memory of the Austrian, impatiently aside.

"I ought to know my job by this time," she said, and she went to the door of the reserve and savagely pulled it open, and savagely jerked on the light. "Mousehole and Noel Coward," she said, but the thing was spreading like poison in her as she filled up the empty tin. When she came out, her gaze fled down the room at once, and he was there still: his feet in the ancient tennis shoes crossed, and his shoulders hunched, and his arms in the worn sleeves folded on the zinc.

At six there were three trains in, and Lady Higgins served the recruits who walked into the canteen and slung their knapsacks down. At quarter-past six the Englishman said:

"I ought to be clearing out now." He dropped the end of his cigarette on the floor and put his heel on it. "I wish there were someplace where we could sit down for five minutes together," he said, but his eyes were asking her nothing at all.

The gendarmes were busy at the gates, checking the papers of those going out, so she took the Englishman across the tracks and up on the other platform and into the Buffet de la Gare. The place was big, and perhaps not more than a dozen people were seated at the marble-topped tables, with their bags beside them and their faces weary from the distance they had come. At the farthest end, in the shadows still, was a swinging door, the top half of it mottled glass and lettered across it *Hôtel de la Gare et de l'Univers,* elegantly, in gold. The Englishman ordered white wine because she said she wanted that, and then he looked around him. When he saw the swinging door, half lost in the dark, his eyes stopped moving.

"So that's the way I might go out?" he said.

"You might," said Lady Higgins. She took out her cigarette case and took one from it. "I should think it might save you from showing your papers to the lads outside," she said. She didn't add that over a hundred men had come into the Buffet with her and gone out that way, some by night and some by day, and none with papers on them. The Englishman struck a match and they both waited in silence until the sulphur perished from the air. "You picked it very quickly," she said. She sat there looking steadily at him.

"I had to find it," he said. "I didn't see any other way."

The waiter had put the bottle and glasses down, and the Englishman poured the wine out, a little in his own glass first, and then hers full before he filled his own.

"So if it's poisoned, you'll die too," said Lady Higgins. "I think that's how the whole thing began."

"It's better than the version about the cork," he said. He lifted his glass and took a swallow of wine. "So I just walk out there," he said. "And then what do I do?"

Even though she didn't say anything then, he still seemed to believe she was eventually going to say it. But she talked instead about the way they had of growing the wine here, with the vineyards tilted up among the sea coast's stones, and about the legends. She said:

"Maybe you could add to the German legends," watching him a little narrowly. "There's the one about changing water into petrol," she said, sitting there drinking her wine and smoking. "It's like the Indian rope trick. I mean, you never meet the person who's actually seen it. But still you hear it everywhere, over and over. And the one about the man-eating crematoriums——"

"There's one about every lift boy in every newspaper building in Paris wearing a *Feldgrau* uniform under his mufti," the Englishman said. He offered her his packet of Bleues across the table.

"And the tiresome one about the correct German officer," said Lady Higgins, taking a cigarette from the paper in his hand, "who gives his table to two Frenchwomen in a restaurant, and then turns and announces to all the Frenchmen still seated in the room that he is giving them a lesson in French gallantry——"

"And the one about Lady Honour Higgins," the Englishman said in a quiet voice. "I believed in that one," he said, and he held the flame to her cigarette and watched her suck the smoke in. "I still believe in it." He didn't touch his wine now, and he hadn't taken a cigarette. "Look," he said, in the same quiet voice. "Is there a Lord Higgins somewhere?"

Lady Higgins sat still for a moment, saying nothing, her eyes not looking at his face any more but at the familiar, narrow-wristed, cousinly or brotherly hand.

"There was," she said in a little while. "He brought down fifteen of them before they got him. He was one of those 'pilots lost.'" She sat looking into the clear light color of the wine. "He was pretty good while he lasted," she said, and as if to stop the sound of it she looked straight up into his face. "How do you expect to get over?" she said.

"I know how the country lies pretty well," said the Englishman. He was asking absolutely nothing of her; it might have been that he had never expected anything at all. "It'll go off all right," he said, and she sat on the other side, watching him. "Maybe we could drink one drink to Lord Higgins before I go," he said, and nothing happened to her face.

They touched glasses without looking at each other, and he didn't say much more. After a moment he stood up and laid the pieces of money down, and he took the beret out of his jacket pocket and put it on for the French look of the thing, and he said:

"My name's Dorset, Chris Dorset. I'll send you a postcard if I get through."

After that he crossed the Buffet with his rather casual, rather arrogant walk and went out by the elegantly lettered door, and the mottled glass swung into place behind him. Now that he was gone, Lady Higgins sat there at the table for what must have been a certain length of time, not knowing why she sat there like any traveler in any station, waiting in blank, speechless listlessness for time to pass, or for a train to come, or for the name of a destination to be called aloud through the amplifiers in the four corners of the hall. She didn't know what sense there could be in sitting there facing his empty glass and his empty chair, and yet she could not bring herself to get up and go. It must have been the wine, she thought; the wine, or else the very face and features of home denied, which had left her sitting hopelessly and helplessly there. She watched the black iron arm of the big clock above the entrance to the platforms jerk slowly from one minute to another, and she thought: *He didn't have anyone to tell him how to do it before, and he made it. He got on all right alone before,* but it was her own tears that stopped her. She felt them running hot and senseless down her face.

"Oh, damn you," she said. "Whoever you are, damn you for coming," and she could hear the sound of his voice in her ears still. She dried her cheeks savagely, and blew her nose, and painted on her lipstick. It was just past seven when she got back into the canteen. There were four recruits drinking coffee and eating sandwiches at the counter, and a dozen or more asleep on the benches. Beyond them, the wash boys were making fresh coffee and stacking the clean cups. There was an hour still to go.

III

The secret police had nothing in common with the gendarmes. They wore plain clothes and the look in their eyes was different, and usually they weren't meridional men. They'd come into the canteen in shifts, two at a time, at any time of night, for coffee, and when they came to the counter the French would shut their mouths. Madame Pichot would give them a grim-lipped smile from behind the cash desk, and Lady Higgins would put clean cups and saucers out and set the sugar extravagantly before them. They liked standing there talking to her, talking about anything to her: the weather, or the food situation, or the last small country to have folded, or talking about England. But whatever they talked about may have been the excuse to stand there looking at the unfading color of her eyes and mouth and hair.

"When are you going to write that letter home and tell them to let a few boats through?" one or the other might say to her, holding in his hand the synthetic bread and the meat they called chopped dog. "Down in Brazil they're dumping coffee into the sea because they don't like it any more. I saw the pictures of it."

"There'd be bloody revolution if they showed them here," the other one might say, and then he'd offer a cigarette to Lady Higgins.

"This is the last night of sugar," she said to them one night. "You'd better help yourselves while you can. You'll have to bring your own with you the way you do everywhere else. It's a bit thick for the soldiers coming through."

"You drop a line to Churchill and tell him that," said the secret police. "You tell him we don't like the way he's running this blockade." He'd hold the flame with a certain careful gallantry for her, his shirtcuff and his hand and his nails soiled from the grime of the station and from the lack of soap, and he'd say: "He'd listen to you. Even an Englishman might turn almost human if you talked to him."

Because they said almost everything in front of her there, one night toward the end of April they said something else.

"Did you see that Englishman they brought in last week?" one of them said, and the other one shook his head and picked up his cup from the zinc and drank.

"Have you got your bread tickets, gentlemen?" Lady Higgins asked, and she knew her voice was as steady as her hand. "Fifty grams each," she said, and she brought the stork-billed scissors out.

"They picked him up near Fontac," the first one went on. "Military age, trying to cross the frontier. When they brought

him in, I asked him why he hadn't saved his skin with the rest of
them at Dunkirk. 'Took you some time to make up your mind to
skip,' I said to him," and the two secret police laughed.

"So what will they do with him?" asked Lady Higgins. She cut
the green bread coupons steadily off. The first one shrugged and
felt for his sugar in the pocket of his coat, and when he had it he
undid the bit of paper there was around it and dropped the one
lump in his cup.

"Someday the prefectures of this country are going to be reor-
ganized, and like everything else they need it," he said. *Good old
organization*, said Chris Dorset's voice from somewhere out of
the long, lonely corridors of memory, and the secret police
stirred the liquid with his spoon. "Absolutely fresh-roasted
coffee being dumped in the sea," he murmured, and then he
thought of the Englishman again. "Unfortunately, being English
isn't a crime yet in the unoccupied zone, so they don't know
what to do with him." He had his mouth open to say more, but
suddenly he put his cup down and he didn't say it. The siren in
the station had begun to blow.

The call began in the station yard, it seemed. It jumped the
rails and fled to every corner of the canteen room. "Lights out,
lights out!" the voices bawled, and above the sound of them the
siren cried out in anguish to the night. Madame Pichot had gone
at once to the switches and brought them smartly down, and instantly the benches, tables, the sleeping recruits, the police with
their hats on, were jerked into obscurity.

"They'll never learn to stay home, the English won't," was the
last thing Lady Higgins heard the police say as they started
across the blotted-out room. She could hear them colliding with
the tables and the benches and the still sleeping men, but cursing only the English and the roar of their bombers passing overhead.

They came in waves, and at intervals, and the siren's wail
soared higher, almost beyond human hearing, in wild inhuman
pursuit. It assumed an uncanny presence in the nothingness, no
longer a signal of warning but a tall, bereaved woman standing
wringing her hands in grief and crying for the dead. Lady Higgins felt the cold of it on her flesh and she shivered a little. Then

she felt her way down the counter to the cash desk and asked Madame Pichot where the candles were.

"That's just it," said Madame Pichot through the dark. "We melted them down for soap last month."

Lady Higgins leaned on the counter near Madame Pichot, unseeing and unseen, and listened to the English passing. As soon as one throbbing wave of sound had almost ceased, another rose behind it, swelling and boiling hard over them a moment, and then rippling evenly away.

"There're a lot of them tonight," Lady Higgins said, and waiting there it seemed that the dark was alive with their faces, tough little grim-lipped English pilots' faces, flying high and fast. In another half-hour they'll be crossing the big mountains, she thought; they'll pass over Mont Blanc and the glaciers in starlight and cross Geneva's quiet, neutral lake and leave Switzerland behind. And then she said something aloud to Madame Pichot about Chris Dorset.

"The *flics* picked up an Englishman at Fontac last week," she said. "I suppose that clears him."

"Except that he didn't get the information they want," Madame Pichot whispered. "They'll have to get him back here to try again."

"So you think he'll come back," said Lady Higgins, and the thought of it stirred her a little. "It's been just about three weeks," she said, and she closed her eyes. They might have been falling asleep there in the darkness, their voices murmuring while the bombers droned with the siren's wail toward the extinction of sleep or silence. "Whatever he was, he was very convincing," said Lady Higgins softly. "He played the part very well. He was much better than the old English colonel they sat on the park bench with the tropical bronzed skin and the clipped military mustache."

"But still you went up and spoke to him," murmured Madame Pichot severely. The sound of planes was growing fainter in the night.

"I said 'My goodness, my Guinness' to him," said Lady Higgins, and Madame Pichot yawned beside her and asked her what that meant.

"*Mon Dieu, mon demi,*" said the man's voice without warning from the other side, and Lady Higgins jerked her head and held tightly to the counter in the swinging dark. He must have been there just within hand's reach, and perhaps been standing a long time there with the beret on the back of his head and his jacket out at the elbows and the blue workman's trousers still looking new. "Or even Sainte Thérèse, *ma bière anglaise,*" he said. "This could go on forever. You might have told me about it before."

"Hello," said Lady Higgins, as if he were anyone at all.

"I came back to tell you I muffed it," the Englishman said. He said it casually and not very loud, and Madame Pichot laid her hand on Lady Higgins' arm. "I'm out on parole," he said. "I'm a free man since an hour ago. That makes my thirteenth jail," he said. "Maybe it'll change my luck," and Madame Pichot's fingers still pressed in warning. There he stood on the other side in the darkness, and Lady Higgins knew there was no possible small talk to exchange with him. There was only the one thing to say.

"Madame Pichot doesn't like the look of your papers," she said. "They haven't been through as much as you have."

"They're new," said the Englishman. "I bought them from a Jerry about six weeks ago. You can buy everything from a Jerry except his uniform," he said, and he added that he was in a good position now, better than he had ever been before. "They're getting me a *carte d'identité* and a *permis de séjour* at the prefecture," he said. "They've done it for so long for the English—ever since Warwick probably—that they don't know what else to do."

"So you're staying here then?" said Lady Higgins, and she said it rather savagely. "So why have you come back to the canteen?" she said, and her voice was as cold as stone.

"I wanted to ask you about the address," the Englishman said. "I thought if I sent you the postcard here, it might look a bit on the queer side to them."

Lady Higgins wanted to put out her hand and touch him and start laughing aloud over nothing as you could with brother or cousin or any one like him at home. She said: "I live out on the sea," and she told him the name of the town and of the house, with the sense of pride and triumph rising in her. "That's where my people write to me," she said, and even now Madame Pichot tried to keep her from going on. "Just send it to me there," she said.

It was then that Madame Pichot said she was going to switch the lights on now that the "all-clear" signal had begun to blow.

"Not before he gets out," said Lady Higgins, and she linked her arm through the Frenchwoman's arm and held her where she was. "Good luck, Dorset," said Lady Higgins. "You'd better go."

He said: "Good night, Lady Higgins," and then he said: "Look, you'll be coming back to England, won't you? I mean, if I get through this show, you might like coming down to Mousehole. It's quite a country," he said, and then he didn't say any more.

The voice seemed simply to be wiped away, and then Madame Pichot crossed to the switches, and with the return of the illumination a little breath of "ah" went around the room. The recruits were on the benches still, and the boys had begun clearing the cups and saucers off the zinc, but the Englishman and the sound of him were no longer there.

IV

The next interval was a shorter one; it was only three nights later that the secret police walked in and went straight to where Lady Higgins was. The weather was getting warm, and their hats looked too tight on their heads, and their waistcoats and jackets more soiled than ever, and heavy in the heat. But they didn't want to talk about the weather; they didn't even want to talk about the two Italian women who had been killed that morning outside the butcher shop. Everyone knew about the two Italian women who had been waiting in line for meat with twenty or thirty Frenchwomen in one of the back streets of the town. The Italian women had told the others that they were the conquerors, and because of this they had the right to pass before them (whether it was true or wasn't true, this was how the story went). And out of the Frenchwomen's marketing bags had come their bottles empty for wine, and their other bottles empty for what oil they could get, and they'd laid hold of the campstools the French carry with them now to sit down on and wait, and they had killed the two Italian women. There in the street, where anyone who had turned his head might easily have seen it happening, they had killed them silently. But it wasn't this, it was something else the secret police had on their minds: it was that the Englishman they'd caught trying to get over the frontier at Fontac had been let out on parole.

"He promised to be good, so they let him out, that's what the prefecture did," the first secret police started telling it. "Here we are, sweating ourselves to the bone to keep anything queer-looking from passing the gates out there, and what do they do but let an Englishman of military age out on parole. Someday," he said, "they're going to see things as they are and they're going to put every gendarme in this country under arrest."

"And then?" said Lady Higgins.

"So then he walks out on them," the first one said, and Lady Higgins remarked that it didn't sound much like an Englishman.

"Not like an Englishman?" said the secret police in a high, baffled voice. He pushed his hat up on his forehead and seized a chopped-dog sandwich off the wire tray. "Not like a—what? Not like a——"

"Don't say it," said the second one. "Don't waste your breath on it. The dice are cast."

"Wait," said the first one, his cheek big with bread or whatever went by that name now. Lady Higgins asked for his tickets, and he took out his ration card and slapped it down on the zinc. "Just wait," he said. He didn't even watch how many coupons she cut away. "That Englishman simply walked in past that row of gendarmes out there and took a train," he said bitterly. "Nobody knows when he did it, but that's what he did. It was only when he didn't report next morning that the prefecture woke up and telephoned Fontac and Pertinau to keep an eye out for him. So when he got off at Pertinau, they were there to meet him with their guns loaded and even a pair of bracelets for him. They telephoned up here to the prefecture to ask what they should do with him, and the prefecture said to bring him back," said the secret police, his voice soaring again with the absolute fabulousness of it. "They couldn't trust Pertinau with him. They were better equipped for the really big criminal types up here!" Lady Higgins watched him bring his open hand down hard on the zinc. "And every word of this is true," the secret police was saying in actual pain. "I talked to the gendarmes who brought him back from Pertinau. They were five hours in the train with him, and they spent it playing cards and drinking *pinard*. I asked them if they knew their prisoner was an Englishman, and if so what in the name of God they were doing playing——"

"Don't waste your breath on it," said the second one.

"So they brought this Englishman back from Pertinau," said the first one. "That was this afternoon." And suddenly it all got beyond him again, and he stood there, a big fat man in a brown suit, looking as if he were going to cry. "They took him up the three flights of stairs to the captain's office, and the captain got up and shook hands with the prisoner when they brought him in."

"The captain told him the place had been lonely without him," the second one said, and the first secret police leaned his head on his hand and groaned aloud.

"The gendarmes had a train back to Pertinau that evening— that's this evening," the first one went on, "and there didn't seem to be any reason to hang around. A fellow'd broken his parole, and they'd brought him back, and so they thought they might as well go home. They'd seen a lot of handshaking going on, and anyway they had five hours of drinking behind them, so there was nothing for it but they must shake hands with the Englishman too. Oh, it must have been wonderful!" said the secret police in agony. "And now, just listen to this! The prisoner said: 'Wait a minute and I'll go down the first flight with you. It's no trouble at all. It's right on the way to my cell.' And after five hours of *pinard* and all the handshaking, this sounded all right to everybody there. How the captain was filling in his time just at that moment, nobody knows. He was probably putting the champagne on ice in preparation for the evening game of cards. So the gendarmes' story is that they said good-by to the prisoner on the second-floor landing and told him how much they'd enjoyed the day with him and hoped they'd get together soon again, and the Englishman said he'd accompany them down the next flight." He stopped talking for a moment, and with one hand he shoved the cup impatiently aside. "So the man they've just brought back under heavy guard walks down the three flights of stairs with them and straight out the door. That's how he did it," he said. "That's how he walked out on them a second time."

"That's one up for the English," said Lady Higgins, smoking.

"Not yet," said the secret police, "because we're out to get him. We're going to reorganize this city's police system if it means crossing the Channel to do it."

"Good old organization," said Chris Dorset's voice from a long way away.

It went on all that night for Lady Higgins in blame and bitterness and fury, and when she went home to fall asleep in her own bed in the morning, the dream of failure, outraged, violent, implacable, was there. So you let them down, the voice of conscience repeated in the room, you let down brothers, cousins, the dead and the living, the pilots' faces, and whatever country is. You let him go off through the uncertainty of that again, the first time and the second, and now the third, out of suspicion or doubt or fear.

It went on all day as she slept, and toward evening as she dressed she kept saying: "Perhaps it isn't too late, perhaps he'll remember the name of the town and the name of the house and come." Out of all the possible ways to his destination, perhaps he might still come by this one, but she couldn't see it happening that way. She tried picturing him on the port, or walking into the hotel bar, or climbing the rocks by moonlight, but she could not see the Englishman anywhere in it. So that when she actually did see him, she didn't believe it any more. She had just begun walking up the sloping lane toward home, and frogs were calling out deeply and sorrowfully in the orchard reservoirs. It was past dusk, and the light was going fast now, when the Englishman came walking down between the cypress and the olive trees.

He said: "Hello," and he looked at her for a moment. "It's the first time I've seen you without a veil," he said.

"It's madness for you to go about like this," she said, not listening to him.

"I was looking for you," he said, and they started together up the road.

"You'll have to get out tonight," she said. Ahead of them was the line of the cliff, sharply defined against the fading sky. And as they walked she began telling it to him, speaking in a low unhurried voice as they climbed up the road between the lizard-infested walls. "You see, it can't be the question of a frontier any more," she said. "There's been too much of that and they're watching for it. You follow down the coast," she said, pronouncing the names and the possibilities with dogged exactitude for him, repeating parts of it for clarity, keeping nothing back. "You cross that cliff," she said, just as she had told all the others who had done it before him. "You do it by night. There's a good path and the stars are out and you won't have any trouble. It's the fourth town after you've passed the cliff that is your town, and there you walk up the rue Principale to the Bar de la Marine." She told him the name of the man who sat behind the counter all day and slept above the *bistrot* at night, and she said: "He'll have the papers for you, and he'll give you the sailing date, and he'll see you through. You'll wait where he tells you to, and until Casablanca you won't be Chris Dorset any more: you'll be Louis Blanc or Jean Dupont or whatever the papers will say you are, and on the boat you'll work as one of the crew. The French identification is the only one you'll have with you. Don't try to take your other papers, because that sort of thing has been the end of other men. You're Louis Blanc or Jean Dupont and you've never heard of the English until you get to the rue de la Sphynx in Casablanca," she said, and she repeated the number to him, and told him whom to ask for there. "You can talk to him as you've talked to me, and he'll get you through to Lisbon." It was only when she had finished talking that she knew he had scarcely heard it, that she would have to say it all over again in a little while to him because he had probably not even been trying to listen to what she said. "I should have told you all this a month ago," she went on saying, and her voice had altered as she walked up the land beside him in the growing dark. "I don't know why I had to have so many proofs from you. Perhaps because I couldn't believe I'd ever meet anyone again who was everything I wanted him to be."

"But, look," he said quietly, "I always thought all this was what you call the legend. I mean, after I saw you I believed that the first part was true, that you were English and that you were there and that you were so beautiful that men never stopped trying to get there just to look at your face. But as for the rest of it, I thought I only embarrassed you when I asked the ways and means. I thought it was pretty rotten of me to go on insisting you tell me something that you yourself didn't know." They were far from any house now, mounting through the dark maquis; the stars were out, and the sea moved hollowly and distantly on the shore. "So it wasn't for that I wanted to go on seeing you," he said, and Lady Higgins knew this must come to an end.

"Now it's the war," she said, "but next year when I go down to Mousehole, I'll remind you where the conversation was when we left off."

But whatever Lady Higgins said, however she explained it time after time in the slack hours of the night, Madame Pichot would have none of it. She knew what he was: she had known it from the game of come-and-go he played, and the state of the papers on him, and even when the postcard came from England it did not change her mind. It was sent from London, and Lady Higgins brought it into the canteen to show it to Madame Pichot behind the cash desk. It had taken more than a month to come, and it said:

"Let there be Honour," without making any attempt to take the grandiloquence away.

This They Took with Them

Everyone who came streaming down the highways of France that month of June, coming on foot or by bicycle or cart or car out of Paris and from the north, carried his separate past, like his suitcases, with him. There were those who came by car, and when the road was blown up or when the gas gave out, they abandoned their cars as others had done before them. There were those who came on foot and one after another left their suitcases in the roadside because they could carry them no further. Day by day as they went they cast aside what no longer had application to fear or grief or pain, doing it ruthlessly and without stopping so as not to lose their places in the inexorably ebbing tide. There was only one thing they could not rid themselves of as they went, and that was the accumulation of unalterable experience which made each of them what he was. This they carried with them, and no matter how irrelevant it might seem now, they could not put it down.

They did not go fast; they moved at the pace of bewildered children wandering among the handcarts and the horse-drawn wagons down the hopelessly encumbered highways of France. Even the elegant cars that had fled from Holland and Belgium had mattresses roped on them as the poorest cars and the handcarts had, with only the quality of the ticking differing. To the army of walkers who moved sightless and will-less as if in sleep through the incurable dream, the cars were in some inexplicable way the given proof that food and drink and shelter must be waiting, not here but a little further, not at this town or in this valley, but somewhere just beyond.

Baldomero walked with them, a tall, rather heavy man with the good head and the high chest of an opera singer, moving along as casually as if he were drifting with the departing audience through a theater lobby after the final curtain has come down. He carried his soft-brimmed, dark plush hat hanging in one hand, and in his face was the same look of weariness that is seen in the faces of spectators for whom the show has lasted an act too long. He did not look like a Frenchman; the complexion was darker, and the step gentler and more indolent—scarcely the gait of a white man even—and the eyes were dark and richly lashed. He was a man of forty-two or -three, with straight, Indian-lank, Indian-black hair combed back from the widow's delicate peak upon his square, sallow brow.

Just after dawn he spoke to the first woman whose features he

could make out in the anonymity of this particular instant of retreat. He had seen the thin little jaw set, and the shoulder bones
held sharp and austere in her jacket, and he had said:

"Could I carry your brief case for you?" and the little woman,
her eyes fixed on some vision of irremediable disaster which no
foreigner could see, mutely shook her head. But he went on talking: he was on his way to Bordeaux, he said, and he walked
quite close to her for a moment, looking down on the dark, nar-
row-brimmed straw hat that was pinned to her graying hair. It
might have been that the alienness of his accent was just one
more blow struck at her heart, for when he said, as guilelessly as
a child would, "Could I take your umbrella for you?" she
marched on in tight-lipped, grim-eyed silence, refusing, as if it
were as distasteful as love to her, anything he had to give.

He may have been many things to many women, but to her he
was nothing. He was merely a foreigner in patent-leather shoes
and a black, pin-striped suit who walked sometimes beside her
in the slowly advancing ranks, or else ahead of her on that second day on the road. He was just one of the figures following
behind the American ambulance which shifted gears and jerked
into motion or halted as the crowd progressed or halted, and
whose radiator kept boiling over as it crawled forward in the
heat. He began talking now to the Frenchman who walked on the
other side, and he said he was a Mexican, and that he'd been five
years in the Mexican Legation in Paris, and that they'd closed
down a week ago and transferred with all the other diplomatic
services to Bordeaux.

"Two days' leave I asked them to let me have," he said, and he
smiled with his handsome teeth at the Frenchman. "I wanted to
say good-by to a few places, a few cafés in Montmartre, a few
friends," he said, and even if he did not specify "women," Mademoiselle Biche who walked beside him visualized the friends'
faces as he spoke. She saw the faded flesh and the bleached hair
and the rimmel on their lashes, and her heart went small and
hard with contempt in her breast. The Legation had gone on to
Bordeaux, the Mexican was saying, while he got caught in Paris;
and as he talked, the paraphernalia of his own youth appeared
piece by piece with the colored stickers of where he had been

and what he had seen still not peeled away. He said he had cleared out from Mexico young, and his plush hat hung between him and Mademoiselle Biche in his delicate, Indian-hairless hand. Whether he knew it or not, the crown of his hat touched her skirt now and then as they walked, and when it did she drew herself slightly away.

The country was sweet with early summer all around them, and the sky was clearing, but Mademoiselle Biche did not take off her gloves. They were buttoned at the wrist, navy blue with three white ribs stitched down the backs of them, and she carried a blue-and-white silk umbrella furled like some final charter of amendment or repeal beneath her arm. Whatever else she had was in the attaché case: a towel, a cake of soap, her dead mother's bracelets, and, out of some still uninterrupted recollection of duty, the neatly folded *rédaction* examination papers of the fourth class of the *lycée* of the sixteenth *arrondissement,* still uncorrected, and a small, yellow-backed copy of George Sand's *Elle et Lui.* Her own name, Madeleine Biche, was written on the book's title page, thus compromised forever with illicit passion, and carried hot, fierce, and unspoken in her flesh was her own committance to love's vocabulary.

"Three years I was telegraphist for Pancho Villa," the Mexican was saying to the Frenchman. "I ran away from home at fifteen. I grew up fighting for him."

"He was a bandit, Villa," said the Frenchman, and Baldomero said:

"Yes, he was a bandit. If you took his pistols away from him, he cried like a child," and he sighed after he spoke, as if in sorrow for the paraphernalia of youth that was clearer and more alive in his heart than anything happening now. "One Sunday afternoon," he said, "they kept telephoning up the mountain to us to send men down the valley. There was going to be trouble: the crowd was going to crucify a man. Villa was asleep in the bunk, and I had to wake him up to give him the messages. He never undressed," Baldomero said. "In six years I never saw Villa undress, and when you woke him his hand always went under his head, quick as a serpent, and found his gun. He asked me what village it was, and when I told him the name of it he said: 'Let them do it. They've got to do something. It's Sunday afternoon and there isn't a movie house within twenty miles of them.' And he put his pistols back and went to sleep again."

"What a country!" said the Frenchman in weariness as they walked. "What a civilization!"

The Mexican looked from one to the other of them as if a little injured, and when the plush hat stroked Mademoiselle Biche's skirt she drew herself away.

"So after a while I got on my horse and I went down to see it," Baldomero said. "I was fifteen. I'd been wounded eight times for Villa. I have the scars," he said, as if this might exonerate him in the end. "I rode down the valley Sunday afternoon, and the people were thick as bees around the town. I tied my horse up and I walked into it. The man they were going to crucify was standing there with the crown of thorns already on his head and a little blood running down. And then they drove the mules out, dragging the big cross behind them on a chain. They drove the mules ahead of him up the pathway to the mount," the Mexican said, "and the crowd started following after him, with the village kids jumping around like crazy——"

"What a civilization!" said the Frenchman, wearily, and he wiped his brow as they walked.

The American ambulance ahead had come to a stop again, and now the driver got down. He wore the Field Service uniform, and he looked incredibly tired and incredibly naïve as he made his way among the others to where the rust was boiling thick as ectoplasm from the radiator of the car. He stood there, with his cap pushed to the back of his head, staring in bitterness and helplessness at it.

"It isn't just needing water," he said, speaking American as if not caring any longer if anyone knew what he said. "It's no oil, it's everything. It's the whole damned works." But the Mexican had somehow got to the side of the road and was scooping water up in his dark, plush hat, and carrying it carefully back through the people to the ambulance's steaming mouth. "It isn't just water," the American kept saying, but when the Mexican had poured the fourth hatful in, he went to the driver's seat again and slid in over the two women with the two sleeping children on their knees, and started the motor up.

"He did the fourteen stations of the cross," Baldomero said, when he was in step with the Frenchman and Mademoiselle Biche again, "and the whole crowd, the people of six villages, followed after him, step by step. And up on the mount, the men with the mules set the cross up. They had it all ready when he arrived. He took his robe off there, and they lifted him up and drove the nails through his palms and crossed his feet over and drove the big nail through them," Baldomero said, "but they did not pierce his side."

"What a country!" said the Frenchman again, and the Mexican looked in slow, shy disappointment at him.

"His wife passed the plate around in the crowd when he was crucified," he said. "If you wanted to touch his wounds afterwards, you gave something more. I touched them. They were not raw," he said, as if this would save the story for the Frenchman. "There were calluses all around them. When he got down, we had a drink of beer together. He'd been doing it for twenty years, he told me. He was a trouper. That was his show," Baldomero said, and he smiled first at one and then at the other of them, but the Frenchman only shook his head.

He was nothing, he was a clerk from the Mexican Legation, he was nothing at all to Mademoiselle Biche until toward evening when the American ambulance began burning quietly and without sensation in the midst of all these people whom, it seemed, nothing could touch or startle any more. The retreat came to a halt, stopping as a herd will, not in fear but blankly, when there is impediment before it. The ambulance driver got the two women and their children down from the seat, while Baldomero ran back and forth with water in the crown of his hat and cast it in little, spitting hatfuls on the flame. Then the driver came, young and white-faced, to the back door and opened it, and for the first time they saw the three wounded men lying inside. Mademoiselle Biche stood back with the others from the heat of the fire and watched the Mexican help lift the wounded on their stretchers out, watched him bear to the slope of the embankment the broken, symbolic figures of what now was France and lay them gently on the grass.

"What will happen to us now? What will become of us now?" one of the soldiers cried out from the stretcher in such terror not only to the men who bore him but to life itself that the herd, halted there in the road, shivered and shifted closer in itself. "Are you going to leave us here? Will you leave us here?" the voice screamed out, and the Mexican answered:

"I will stay with you. The driver will get help while we wait here," and his voice was so calm and filled with promise that, however strange his accent was, they no longer cared.

Ahead in the road, the ambulance was burning, the roar of its conflagration in the stillness of the country like a furnace's wide open mouth. When the gasoline tank went, in flames pouring soft and fresh as the sound of rushing water, the herd broke in two directions and began climbing off through the fields. The handcarts went with them, with the saucepans, the baby cribs, the washing machines, the mattresses they carried tipped sideways on them as they lurched through the ditches and up the embankments. The horse-drawn wagons rocked off the highway, the horses' feet scrambling in effort, and their ears cocked to the thick, pouring cubiform of flame. The ambulance driver with his hat on the back of his head ran first to one side and then to the other after the wagons, laying his hands on the dashboards and the sides of them, asking them to take the wounded in.

"Stop, stop!" he cried, and he even ran up the embankments and into the fields a little way after them, running beside the wheels. "Stop and take them!" he cried. "Take them with you!" But the men with the reins in their hands only lashed the horses harder.

"Where have we room? Where could we put them? We'd jolt them to death before we got them there!" they said to him, and the weary, white-faced little driver cried out:

"Throw out the other things, the washing machines, and take the wounded on your mattresses! Take them as far as Orléans! There must be doctors left in the hospital there!"

But these were the things of the living: the mattresses, the baby cribs, the saucepans for the living; it was not for the dying that they could be cast aside. Women and children rode huddled on these monstrous monuments to daily life, and as the ambulance driver ran beside them their faces did not alter. They watched him as if he were merely some curious animal running like this abreast the wagon wheels.

"Stop and take the wounded in!" he would cry in his strange, high-pitched American-French, in his almost incomprehensible lingo. "One of them, gangrene," he said, "maybe gangrene," and he touched his leg at the knee in indication as he ran.

Mademoiselle Biche stood in the road and watched him turn from one fleeing wagon to another, the look of hope in his face still unextinguished until the last of them had gone. On the highway behind them stood the accumulating, halted cars, the growing line of them stretching northward into the far, dark, focal point of dusk; and as fresh ranks of marchers caught up with the fire, these ranks too divided and scattered slowly off through the fields. Cyclists forced their wheels into the ditches and up over the embankments, and handcarts followed them, and ahead on the road, toward Orléans, the dispersed lines of marchers and carts converged again and flowed on in that lame and almost ludicrous grotesque of direction and intent.

It was only the cars that had not the place to pass and must wait there, halted, as if in reverence, before the tough, tearing banners of flame. When the fire would be done, and the car frame cooling, the other men would get down, as they had before on their journey, and, as they had before, push the twisted skeleton to the side of the road to let it rust there, and then they would drive on, impervious as tanks, forgetful of the shape it had had or of what it had borne.

The Mexican had shaken the wet from his hat and laid it on the grass beside him, and he sat there by the stretchers with his legs spread and his hands hanging loosely on them, seemingly in some sort of conversation with the nearly dead. The people left the road and passed on one side and the other of him, and after a while Mademoiselle Biche climbed the embankment to where he sat by the wounded, climbing sideways and slipping in the trampled earth of the incline, the attaché case in one hand still, and the umbrella under her arm.

"So you intend to stay here?" she said, speaking as sharply to him as if he were sitting at a pupil's desk before her with his copybook open and ink on his hands.

"The American's gone on for help," he said. "He will find a cart and come back for us. Or when the cars start moving again, they'll take us in. We won't be long here," he said, saying it calm and loud so that the wounded might hear. Don't tell them, he did not say, that the cars are for the living; don't tell them that no vehicle could ever fight its way back against that imperviously ebbing tide. And as she listened to him speak, her thoughts took shape about the wounded: perhaps that they who were Frenchmen, or who had been French soldiers once, had come to this, and that now there was no priest or nurse left to sit with them as they died, but only a Mexican in patent-leather shoes and a pin-striped suit to brush the flies away. "While we're waiting, we can talk," he said, and she relinquished neither brief case nor umbrella, but sat down a little apart from him on the grass. "My mother was pure Indian," he said. "I never saw her smile. She has never kissed me. It may seem strange, but Mexicans do not kiss. We see it in the movies, but among ourselves we cannot bring ourselves to do it," he said, and he lit a cigarette for the one man on the stretcher who still could smoke, and Mademoiselle Biche saw the white mouth part and smile.

Now that the light was going, the glow of the burning ambulance seemed stronger and richer than before, and the iron frame writhed slowly in it. One of the wounded sought to utter the syllables of a woman's name, and another would whisper the one thing at intervals to the falling night. "Please," he would whisper carefully, "give me something to stop it, please give me something to stop it," and then he would save his breath, hoard it and hold it, to pay it out carefully to them, word by word, again.

"He'll be back," said the Mexican to the night. "He'll bring it with him. It's a big place, Orléans. They'll have it there."

In a while there was nothing left in the dark but the hot refulgence of what had been the ambulance. The people had ceased to move on the highway, halted in the same stooping postures of fatigue in which they had walked and the cars, with mattresses roped to their roofs, waited in silence for the iron to cool.

Crickets had begun to sing in the ditch below, and the Mexican did not cease talking; he told them of the women in Mexico plowing the fields who stopped to give birth and then went on with their plowing; and in the darkness the wounded listened to him and spoke their terrible vocabulary of pain.

Mademoiselle Biche had laid neither the umbrella nor the brief case down, and she sat erect on the embankment, thinking: *There are men with the breath of life in them who can teach the rest of us to breathe; there are men with the breath of life in them, we can learn strength from them.* Her blood was faint with hunger in her, and even when she felt the fingers moving on her hat, drawing the pins from it, and laying it aside, she could not move.

"There," said the Mexican's voice softly in the darkness, "there," he said, and his hand smoothed back her hair.

"Don't, ah, don't," she said, "don't," but her mouth was so dry that the sound that came from it was strange in her ears, and she could not turn from him.

"Listen," he said, "the dew is falling. It is drenching everything around us," and she could feel his breath on her face as he put his coat around her. "Lie down like this, like this," he said, and he took the brief case and the umbrella gently, as if these were the last defenses taken away. "Lie down as the wounded lie," he said, and she lay down in sudden and terrible relief upon the grass. "It is wetting your hair," he said, "and wetting the faces of the wounded," and she lay like a wanton woman with his arm beneath her head. "It is unparching their lips for them," he said, "so that they can say their women's names aloud."

"Will they die?" she whispered fiercely against his shoulder. "Will they die?"

"No, they will not," he said. "Go to sleep. They have already gone to sleep. They will not die."

He thought of the ambulance driver's small white face, and it might be, he thought, that the American had found a plate of soup somewhere and a place to lie down in and that the flesh at least had forgotten. It might be that he would never find his way back here again, or would not come until it was too late. He remembered other nights, the night near Jalisco when Villa's

mother was dying, and the look of the country in the moonlight,
bathed in the pure, clear, lambent flood. They had gone out from
her room near three in the morning, the little group of men, and
sat beneath the great plane in the patio. In the bright quiet illumination of the moon, they had gone on shelling the white
pearls of corn into the baskets under the tree. The boughs of the
single plane had stood over them, smooth and strong and the
bark radiant with light, and the roosting chickens, with their
wings folded, slept in the darkness of the leaves.

Outside the chalk-white wall of the patio the country had lain
with the limpid, wondrous silence on it; and then, without warning, the grass had begun to stir, the crests to feather and rise as
if upon wind, but there was no breath of wind about them.
Whatever it was, it passed swiftly through the open gates and
into the patio, and struck cold as a glacial blast upon their flesh.
It made no sound and carried no dust with it, but as it came the
chickens asleep in the plane tree were stricken by it too, and
they had suddenly risen, the hundred or more of them, and
flown screaming from the branches. Villa stood up with a pistol ·
in each hand as they fell through the night to the milk-white
earth and fluttered as if beheaded there, and the other men
stood with him, their blood motionless, underneath the tree.

It had not been a wind, for the leaves had not stirred and the
doors were silent. It was merely death that had moved in
through the gates and up the stairs. When they ran into the
house and into the mother's room, they had known it; and Villa
stood by the bed, for the first time confused by the sight of it,
and made the sign of the cross with the pistol in his hand. It was
merely death, Baldomero lay thinking as he watched the light of
what had been the ambulance dying beyond on the road. Merely
death, he thought, and through his shirt he felt the cold of the
ground on which he lay. The schoolteacher was asleep on his
arm, and so as not to wake her he spoke in a low voice, asking
the wounded man on the stretcher near him if he wanted another cigarette. There was no answer, and he asked it again, in a
louder voice, but still no answer came. He drew his hand back
over the schoolteacher's hair and yawned, and in her sleep she
murmured the words to him that may have been George Sand's

or else some other woman's, but he was thinking of Villa again, he was thinking of the last ride up through the lemon groves, and he did not hear.

Their Name Is Macaroni

The Italians had been a long time in this part of the country, some of them since two or three generations, come over in search of work or in political protest, but the quality of their speech had not altered much, and their eyes remained more credulous than Frenchmen's eyes. They were strong men, used to the sun, and they worked in the quarries of the new road that would cut across the clifftops through the unbroken stretches of dry, meridional maquis; or else they worked in the shipyards. The town they went home to at night was small, and either by land or water it was a short way from it into Italy. But none of the Italians who had left there had been back or ever seemed to want to go back, except a wife or two who had gone over once or twice or three times for a funeral or a wedding or to settle a piece of business, wearing no hat in the third-class carriage of the train and carrying her salami and bread wrapped in paper in a basket, and staying only the necessary number of days. But even these women returned as shyly and hesitantly as deer to their own country, for in all their hearts was the same baffled, speechless tremor for what had happened or what was happening on the other side.

The Italian women had always found work in the villas and hotels of the town: they worked for the English and for the Americans and for the other foreigners who stayed a winter or a summer, as well as for the French whose soil it was, until in 1939 and 1940 the visitors went home and the look of everything changed. Everything changed, that is, except one thing: what the French think of the Germans has never ceased to alter, but what they think of the Italians will always be the same. Their

name is macaroni and their blood is water, and in any kind of
area or weather, and armed or unarmed, they can outstrip Nurmi
when in retreat. But suddenly in June, the Italian nation was
given a new role to play and it dressed up elegantly for it, even
though it was nothing better than the buffoon's part in this uproarious burlesque of victory.

Every week after the armistice was signed, the Italian officers
of the commission drove up the coast and into the towns in their
steel-gray cars, and there were the signs of the times chalked up
on the walls and the sides of the houses to greet them. Not *Duce
Duce Duce* as it was at home, but *Les Macaronis sont tous
foutus*, or perhaps something about where the Italian armies
might then be taking their defeat. At times the things would be
written out, in letters as tall as a man, on the boulders which the
earth's primordial boiling or cooling had cast out upon the
coast's maquis. There where these other self-exiled Italians broke
stone for the new road, the commission in its triumphal cars
would rock slowly past, reading and pretending not to read the
single words *Tobruk,* or *Mogadishu,* or *Taranto,* chalked up in
silent derision in the wilderness.

No one in the town could say who wrote the words out.
Angostini was foreman at the shipyards, and when the words
began appearing there, painted pure white across the ribs of a
ship's scaffolding, and the mayor called him in and questioned
him, he spread his hands and could not say. He was a small
slight man, thirty or thirty-five, and quick-eyed as a monkey,
with a monkey's shrewd wrinkles arched on his brow. He had
been all his life there, and perhaps because he believed—as perhaps all of them believed—that the miracle of revolt would one
day come in Italy and he would be Italian still to share in its
glory when it came; or perhaps because he thought of himself as
a part forever of this other nation, he had never done the things
there were to do about French citizenship papers. He was
merely an Italian in a Frenchman's country, but he didn't know
it any more. When he left the yard at night, he'd stop to pass the
time of day with the others sitting on the port: with the doctor,
or the hotelkeeper, or the fishermen drinking *pinard,* and their
feet still wet with brine. He'd speak of the French, and he'd call

them "we"; he'd say "we Frenchmen," and no one ever saw anything peculiar in it, not even Colonel Pinhay, who would sit on the port with him in the setting sun and have a glass of wine.

"There was something written up on the front of the *mairie* this morning," Colonel Pinhay might say, with his voice unshaken yet by age. "I could see it at half a kilometer's distance as I came down the road." He had stood there with the others on the Place des Sardines, his hair under the pith helmet and his mustaches white and clipped short as if for military precision still, and his market bag hanging in his hand; and he had watched the mayor himself, because nobody else would do it, come out with a bowl of water and a little rag on the balcony where the flag didn't hang any more, and wash the words away. "It was printed up right underneath the *liberté, égalité,* and *fraternité,*" the Colonel said. The bloodhound folds of his throat hung slackly in the breach of his collar, and the bloodshot eyes held in them the singularly undimmed vision of twenty years of Karachi. "It said 'Sidi Barrani,'" the Colonel said, and Angostini swore aloud with pleasure, and the two of them went through the ceremony of touching glasses and drinking to victory's still untarnished name.

This was the sort of underground literature that was printed in public all that winter and spring, and everybody read it. Everybody needed fuel for their fires, and food to keep their children alive, and bigger and finer, month after month, the Italian commissions kept coming through. They requisitioned this, and they requisitioned that, and they sent everything they liked the look of back across the frontier to where they'd come from. Because of them, strawberries were eighty francs the kilo on the coast that spring, and asparagus had acquired the fabulous quality of orchids with their stems wrapped elegantly in silver foil. And still the Italian commissions came: they were there when the American food ship came in to port and docked in the harbor city that lay thirty kilometers away. It was perhaps the second or third ship to arrive, and the French flag and the American flag were hanging together like lovely sisters from every window on the water front when the officers of the commission walked up the gangplank and told the Americans what percentage of the milk and vitamins and flour they would like to have.

Colonel Pinhay was there on deck when the Italian officers began playing this part they'd been understudying all their lives for. He was the last of the English left, and he had been called to serve on the American committee of distribution. All of the other English had left the place, but he had never talked of leaving. He said there was a name for the people who left France now, and it was the same one you used for a man who left a woman once her money was gone, and the folds of his throat trembled in outrage as he said it.

"When they came on board, we were all being photographed for the newspapers," the Colonel said. He told the story to the mayor, and to the doctor, and to the hotelkeeper; and that night, sitting in the Marine Bar with the semaphore's ray flashing twice, and then once, and then twice again across the sea outside, he told it to Angostini. "They came on behind us, so we didn't see them at once," he said.

"*Sacré merda*, I hate them," said Angostini rapidly and bitterly.

The Colonel said their faces were the wrong color, they were slightly green as they stood on deck in their uniforms and told the Americans how much of the cargo they considered their due.

"I thought perhaps one of the cameras might have got an Italian kepi or an epaulet in a picture by mistake, so I smashed the lot of plates," said the Colonel. "If anything like that got into the public prints, there wouldn't have been any explaining it away. So I did for the lot of them, while the ship captain ordered the officers off—and they went," he said. "The captain told them he'd pull up anchor and go straight back where he'd come from if they laid a finger on anything on board, and they went," said the Colonel. "I can't say I liked the color of their faces, but they didn't hang around."

"I wish to God I'd seen them," said Angostini. "I wish I'd seen them run."

Colonel Pinhay told the story a good many times about the Italian officers coming on board the American boat, and what the ship captain had said to them. Sometimes the captain had said that if they didn't get off at once he'd throw them off, and sometimes he'd said that he'd turn the machine guns on them, but however it was, the Colonel had given them a piece of his mind as they went down the gangplank to the shore. Either he told them that every tin of milk and every bag of flour was going to feed French babies under two, or else he had said that gentlemen had let this boat through the blockade and as long as there was anything like honor left only gentlemen would see to the distribution of what they had on board. So when the other things came up, some of the people in the town couldn't make the second part fit the first. It happened the day the American food was to be handed out at the *mairie*, and they couldn't understand why he did it. Colonel Pinhay handed in his resignation; he said he wouldn't serve on the committee of distribution any more.

He sat having a glass of wine with Angostini just after the twelve-o'clock whistle had blown, and Angostini was telling him the one about the Duce telephoning to Hitler or Hitler telephoning to the Duce, or the one about the two Italian officers insisting on being served first in a restaurant in Nice because they were the conquerors, and the maître d'hôtel saying: "Oh, excuse me, *messieurs!* I didn't recognize the Greek uniform," when the mayor stopped at the table and leaned down and fumbled the red ribbon in his buttonhole and didn't look once at Angostini. He said to Colonel Pinhay:

"So you don't want to be on the committee this afternoon?" and the Colonel said he didn't. His two old hands were folded on his cane and he looked straight out across the sea. "Because of the regulations?" the mayor said in a low, conciliatory voice, and the Colonel answered sharply:

"Yes, because of the regulations."

"Because there's to be no food from the American ship given to the children of the Italian population?" the mayor said, and the Colonel's grieving, bloodshot eyes came back from sea.

"Because that means three quarters of the children in this town!" he said, and the cane danced savagely under his hands.

"They're Italians," said the mayor, and he looked uneasily around. "The regulations specify only the French, and legally they're Italians——"

"Only on paper!" shouted the Colonel. "Not on stone!"

He flung his cane aside, and with one hand he pointed to the port before them, and the mayor straightened up and turned around to see. There on the semaphore wall where the shipyard men had just walked past were the words freshly written up in chalk. They said: *A bas les macaronis!* and they were large enough for even an airplane to read them as it passed.

After the mayor had put his hat on and gone off along the port and crossed the Place des Sardines, the Colonel did not speak. It was Angostini who spoke first, and who reached across the table with his dark, monkey-nervous hand. He said *"Merci"* to the Colonel, saying it not very loud, and saying it as if this one word in just this language were the only word that was there to be said. As he said it, he laid his hand over the Colonel's hand as gently and as romantically as if it had been a young girl's long-fingered, milky-skinned hand that lay there on the marble in the sun. After a little while he began telling the story about how he'd given the macaronis a run for their money that morning, and the Colonel ordered them both another glass of wine.

"The commission came out to go over the shipyards," Angostini said. "They were all of them young this time, and this was their first trip over on our side. They had gold braid on, and their boots were shining like glass, and they were scared to death of stepping out of the role that fate had cast them in," and he made a grimace at the Colonel. "It was raining hard then, and when I'd shown them over the first ships, I told them that to see the rest of what we were doing for them they'd have to walk up the hill and come down on the bigger yards on the other side. They asked me if they couldn't drive there, and I looked at them in great surprise, and I told them of course there wasn't any road. I spoke Italian to them, but I didn't give the salute," said Angostini. "I said the other officers were familiar with the way the whole thing was laid out, but of course this being their first time over," and he shrugged his shoulders. "So I led them right up the Crête de Poisson," he went on saying, and Colonel Pinhay opened his mouth and roared aloud. "The mud was up to their knees," said Angostini, "and their breeches had never seen anything like it before. The way their boots looked must have made them sick at heart, but I didn't stop for a second. I took them down the Escalier de Boue, and one of them slipped on his spurs at the top of it and slid three steps on the seat of his pants——"

"Ha, ha, ha!" roared the Colonel, and he slapped the café table with his hand.

"In half an hour I brought them down just twenty yards from where we'd started off," said Angostini, "and one of these little officers, he looked around and he said: 'It seems to me this is just where we came from.' 'That's what everyone thinks the first time they go over the yards,' I said. He was trying to get the rain wiped off his sword and his gilt before it started to tarnish, and I said: 'You've come a long way, but it wouldn't have done to have missed it. Here are the three biggest boats we're turning out for you.' I didn't tell him there wasn't a man in the yards who wouldn't have set them on fire before they'd have seen them put into Italian hands."

It wasn't until the next morning that the Colonel knew the committee had reconsidered at the mayor's suggestion, and that they had given the tinned milk and the flour to every mother who came up with her baby in her arms. They gave it to the French, and they gave it to the babies called Ferrari, and Perelli, and Palavacini, and Angostini, but whether or not it was because the Colonel had resigned, neither the mayor nor the committee ever told him. He only knew it by what he found outside his door. He had opened it in the morning, and there was the driftwood, the endless, pointed, dry, bleached arms of it in a time when driftwood couldn't be had for money, and there were the packets of charcoal, enough for six months' cooking, it seemed, piled neatly along the wall. The Colonel had carried it into the house all that morning and stacked it, log after sea-bleached log, and bundle after bundle, by the cooking stove, and no one in the town ever spoke of how it happened to be there.

But before this, quite a long time before this, something else happened; just before the French asked for the armistice something happened in this town which ought to be set down. Perhaps the whole thing should begin with the two Italian bombers coming up the coast that lovely morning in June, and the air-raid warning sounding in the city thirty kilometers away, and in the town, and crying out across the water, and the French antiaircraft guns coming to life and spattering ammunition into the air. It was no more effective than that, just coughing and spitting at death itself, and Colonel Pinhay stood on the port in the sunlight and watched the Italian bombers make two strikes: one on the old fort that had stood at the head of the cliff, and one on the lighthouse, all but missing it and merely cracking a handful of white plaster away.

After that, the bombers might have continued up the coast, and the little antiaircraft guns sputtered into silence again, except that, according to any Frenchman, the Italians could always be counted on to do exactly what they did. The first bomber circled too near the cliff's nose beyond the port, and in righting himself he hooked the second bomber, and the two of them locked and crashed together, and Colonel Pinhay struck the pith helmet on his head a smashing blow and roared aloud with joy. It was the same sort of thing, he said later, that they did when they fired torpedo after torpedo at Taranto from one Italian destroyer into another, sinking their own navy with wild precision and ignominiously.

So the two Italian planes went down, and the bodies of the men were brought ashore, and in a day or two they made a funeral for the pilots. The coffins stood open in the church, with candles lit at the head and feet, and all the people of the town filed in and looked at the two youths lying there. Their shirts had been washed clean of the oil and the blood, summer shirts made of silk with elbow sleeves, and they had dressed them up in them again and crossed their bare arms on their shattered breasts. Each man wore his identity bracelet still, and his wrist watch on the other arm, with the time on it halted forever at the hour he fell. Angostini said there was three minutes' difference in the time the needles marked, either because one watch had been running faster than the other or because one of them had hit harder and died quicker than the other had.

He stood there a long time looking in bitterness at the two dead pilots in their coffins: at their faces with the one or two marks of violence on them, and at the long slender legs in the green military trousers, and at the cotton socks the French had put on their feet. One was nineteen and the other one was twenty-one; that is what their identity papers said about them, and they said as well that the youngest one came from Naples, and that he was a count. The French had combed their hair for them, as well as it could be done, and cleaned their nails for them, and there they lay, the conquerors, in the church's gloom. Their faces looked a little tired, but quite pure, as if nothing had touched them yet, not even death, not even a faith in the thing in which they had taken part.

Colonel Pinhay came in with the other people from the town, and he stood there, seemingly searching the faces of the two young men he had seen die. There was a vain, rather petulant look around the Count's mouth that he did not like, but still he stood there, stubbornly searching the features for something he could not seem to find. The lashes lay long and dark on the dead boy's cheeks, and his chin was clefted. His nostrils were white and arched in distaste, it might have been, for the air they had given him to breathe. After a little, the Colonel went past him to where the other lay, and Angostini came just behind him, stepping without reverence over the great bare slabs of stone. Angostini was standing by the coffin, thinking his own savage thoughts, at the moment the Colonel seemed to find at least some shadow of that thing he sought, or else some way to endow with figurehead the body of fallen youth, or of perjured youth, or the single word of helpless youth spoken so briefly and sharply to eternity. Angostini stood there while the Colonel took the small silk flag out of the breast pocket of his English tweed and leaned over and laid it in the fingers of the pilot's hand. It was the Italian flag, and *Souvenir of Venice 1920* was printed on the side of its little stick, and the edges of it were fraying out.

"Military honors, and one thing and another," the Colonel said, and he closed his mouth, but he was not apologizing for it. Angostini stood a moment longer looking bitterly down at the flag and at the dead Italian's face before he spoke, and then he said:

"Fascist." He said it three times over, spitting the words through his teeth. "Fascist. Alive or dead, that's what he is. Alive or dead, I hate him. Fascist," he said, and whether or not he actually spat into the dead man's face, Colonel Pinhay did not know. He had left him standing there, and moved on up the aisle between the benches, and the others approached and looked into and then passed by the open coffin where the dead man lay unaltered except for this relic of an Italy that Mussolini had not yet come to touch held in humble exoneration in his hand.

French Harvest

A country, like a person, is not an easy thing to return to once you have left it; for if you demand pride of yourself as well as of others, you have no patience with the duplicity of sentiment. I did not come back to France to walk the streets of Le Havre, or Lyon, or Paris with my heart gone fluid with recognition; not this year or any year would I do it, for I had come back to find the living, not the dead. If you believed some of the living who talked to you, the Resistance had been forgotten, and the men who had survived it forgotten, as well as those who had not survived. Some of them who had survived needed arms and legs, having lost their own, and some of them needed pensions, but no one had got around to that yet. Everything belonged to the new race of people, the black marketeers, with their full, pink cheeks and their bloated limbs and the diamonds on the fingers of their plump, clean hands. There were only a few among the living who remembered still. There were the families who kept the flowers eternally fresh in the vases that hung at the Place de la Concorde by the *métro* stairs—there where the names of their sons were inscribed and the dates when they had met their death. And there were others. There was the wife, it may have been, who kept the ivy green in the little jar fixed at the height of a man's heart on the apartment house wall, with the legend engraved on the slab of stone above it saying that here Louis Vaillant, a *gardien de la paix*, had lost his life on August 19, 1944, after having attacked a German tank and destroyed it with a hand grenade.

The rest of the people talked of wheat—of the wheat that

America had sent, or the wheat that Russia had sent—and whether it was white wheat or red wheat was of no importance, they said. What mattered was that it be made into bread to fill their children's bellies, and no questions would be asked as to the soil in which it grew. There was a little woman who used to sit behind the wicket in a post office in Montmartre, and she was sitting there still, with the colored pages of stamps laid out like the map of a foreign country before her. When she recognized my face she said:

"Where is the American wheat? What did our government do with the wheat you sent?"

And the man who stood in the line behind me, leaned over my shoulder to speak. "Is it true that the official our government sent to Washington to negotiate for wheat looked up the wrong word in the dictionary and asked for corn instead?" he said. "Is that why our bread turned yellow overnight?"

Or, in the bake shop, a man might take up a length of bread from the shelf, and the feel of it in his hands would cause the rage to rise in his throat and throttle him anew.

"You bakers! You're bandits, the lot of you!" he would cry out. "You give us this stuff like an iron bar and call it bread! And you bake white bread to eat at your own tables, and to sell to those who can pay the price for it! That's where our flour's gone!" he would shout.

And the baker would smile a little as he took the frail green tickets and the money, and no matter how many people waiting in line for bread had heard the accusation flung at him, there would be no sign of anger in his face. It may have been that he had heard it said so many times a day or during the week or month that the bread ration had been cut that the accusation no longer mattered to him. Or it may have been that he—like those who waited in line in bleak and still, unexhausted patience—knew that the words the man had shouted out were true.

If you believed others who talked to you, times had been better under the Occupation, and there had never been any conquerors to speak of except the Americans who had come raping and pillaging and desecrating across France's soil. The gas chambers had been forgotten, and the deportation trains, with the travelers who had ridden upright in the boxcars, all forgotten. There were many among the living who remembered nothing of the armies that had lingered on their territory except the GIs who had climbed one night onto the Jeanne d'Arc statue which stands at the Place des Pyramides and straddled in drunken triumph her gilded horse, riding like liberators behind her armored figure, aping even the gesture of the lifted sword; or remembered those other GIs who had removed the swinging doors of the ladies' rooms in restaurants, because of the *"dames"* stenciled on them, and had borne them through the streets of Paris on summer evenings, roaring their shameless songs aloud.

"It might have been better if the Germans had won in the end," the shopkeepers and hairdressers and hotelkeepers could find it in their hearts to say to you now. "When they were here, at least we had discipline, order."

"Look," I said quickly to the hotelkeeper, "I'm going out into the country and talk to other people. I'm not going to sit here and listen to it being said to me any more."

"*Quand même*," said the hotelkeeper, making out the bill, "there was one thing about the Germans: whatever they did in other countries, there was nothing to complain about what they did to our hotel rooms—never a broken window, never a scratch on the furniture . . ."

As soon as you saw the fields and the forests, however, you believed in France again. As the bus moved past the rippling meadows and the leafy groves, it was clear why this vision of beauty, of profligate foliage and rich earth, had turned the blood of the conquerors hot with love. How the pulse of the Germans must have quickened to swooning as they took possession of this country, they with their scrupulously counted and labeled timber, and their highways lined by milestones as cold as those that mark men's graves instead of by the tall lovely bodies of living trees. If you accepted as testimony the full green and golden fields, you would have believed that France was a flourishing country still, and the potato crop and the rye and wheat crop abundant. In spite of the talk of want, and in spite of the drought, when you looked from the bus windows, you believed

in the fabulous richness of the earth that stretches forever between the châteaux and the rivers of France, growing food
enough and to spare to satisfy the hunger of its people, growing
such grapes for wine as does the earth of no other country, perhaps because of the blood of Frenchmen that has been shed
there generation after generation.

The house to which I went stood outside the village, a small
unturreted château approached by tree-lined lanes leading from
the highroad and the broad, deep stream. I had not seen it since
before the war, but, however you approached it, it was still a
place of freshness and of ineffable charm, with its stone painted
white, its shutters gray, pleasing and flattering you whichever
way you turned your head. Pastures unfolded toward it from the
stream where the poplars trembled delicately in every leaf, and
as I came up the short-cropped meadow in the afternoon, there
was no sound except that of the skylarks' singing and of the cattle's lips pulling at what remained of the grass. I carried a rucksack on my shoulders, and in the pocket of my skirt was the key
to the front door and a letter from French friends saying they
were going to stay in the south a little longer, and that I could
live in peace there until they came back. I crossed the lane that
ran along the garden wall and opened the white door by the carriage gate. Nothing had changed in the courtyard, and the liz-
ards flicked quickly before me between the stones; and nothing
had changed in the gardens, except that the grass had not been
cut, and moss had grown across the faces of the statues that
stood beside the fountain in which water no longer played. Inside the house, too, nothing had changed, except that the signs
of any personal life were gone, and, visible still but a little faded,
the word *Kommandantur* remained on one of the bedroom
doors.

When I awoke the first morning, I lay in quiet a moment, looking around the room that was filled with light. There were yellow rag rugs on the waxed floor, and a single white shelf, with
paper backed, variously colored French novels standing the
length of it, ran along one palely tinted wall and halted at the
clean, white wooden chimney piece. At the two long windows
hung yellow curtains, as transparent as glass, which must have

lent a look of sunlight to the room even had there been none. On the table by the bed the candlestick stood where I had put it the night before, the candle burned low in it and icicles of wax dripping static from its fluted brass.

"Today I must call the village electrician," I said, but I did not move. Beyond the windows was the music of cowbells, and the voices of rooks as they congregated as thick as thieves in the tall trees of the forest behind the house. I shall stay here a long time, I thought, and in the fields and along the roads and in the cafés I shall hear another kind of talk. I shall forget the strikes, I thought, and the look in the women's faces when they say to you: *What do you do when your husband brings you home eight thousand francs at the end of the month? What do you do with eight thousand francs when butter's a thousand francs the kilo? I'd light the fire with what he brings home if I had any coal to shovel on after* . . . "I shall forget the sound of the hotelkeeper's words and the hairdresser's words," I said to myself, "for there will be men here among the living whose memories will be all of a piece, not broken and scattered through the years."

But as I lay watching the curtains stir at the windows like softly drifting veils of sun, I did not know the names or the faces of these other men, and I did not know the electrician would be one. I telephoned the electrician before noon, and when he heard it was for the little château outside the village, his voice went wary across the wire.

"So you are the friend who was there before? So you have come back again?" he said.

"Yes, I've come back," I said. "But it's been a long time."

"Not a very long time," said the electrician's voice, speaking carefully, warily.

He said he would not send a workman but would come himself, and, within the hour, he pushed his bicycle through the door that stood open in the wall. He was a youngish man, and he carried his tool bag slung over his shoulder on a leather strap. As he stood his bicycle up near the courtyard gate, his eyes looked darkly, sharply at me. He had a gray cap pulled down on his head, and the roses left on the vine above the kitchen window touched the stuff of it as he turned toward where I stood. His jacket had once been navy blue, perhaps, but now it was faded, and there were patches of other cloth at the elbows; his trousers were GI khaki, which someone had turned up at the ankles for him—a Frenchman's legs are sometimes shorter than an American's—and he wore rope-soled shoes. He came across the garden, and shifting his tool bag on his shoulder, touched his soiled gray cap in greeting as he stopped before me in the sunlight.

"The lights," I said at once. "I didn't know they'd be off. I found the meter last night, but I couldn't do anything with it."

But he did not seem to be thinking of the lights at all; it may even have been that he had not heard what I said. He had thrown back his head, and I could see that his cheekbones were high in his long, narrow face. His nostrils were pinched and colorless, as if from hunger or suffering, but it did not seem possible that he could be a hungry man. He stood looking up at the delicately turned stone of the cornice above the château doorway, and under the visor of his cap his thick, black eyebrows met across his nose.

"There used to be a bat's nest there," he said, and he jerked the line of his bony jaw toward the cornice. "A handful of baby bats up there one spring. That was when the Boche was here." And then he looked back at my face again. "You're not the woman I expected to see," he said, and except for the cold, quiet condemnation in his voice of the other woman who had been here, it might have been said in apology.

The electric meter was in the vaulted cellar where the wine had once been kept, but now the wine was gone, and the stone shelves and the iron racks stood empty. We could see them as I carried the lighted candle down into the well-like quiet of dark and damp. When we stood on the earth floor at last, the electrician took the candle from me.

"I turned the switches and looked at the fuses last night," I said, but I was thinking of the other woman now, and trying to see her as he must see her as I watched the side of his face. He had lifted the candle so that its light reached higher, and, for a moment, he did not speak. He stood in his old faded jacket, studying the meter, and then he slung his tool bag off his shoulder.

"She was a foreigner, too," he said, "so that's why your voice was like hers when you called. I thought she'd decided enough time had passed, that enough people like her had slipped out of the jails and nothing said. That's why I didn't send a workman. I wanted to deal with her myself," he said.

He stooped to take the tools from his bag, and as he worked, I held the candle for him, and his shadow stood taller than a man's upon the wine cellar wall.

"And if I had been that woman, then what had I done?" I said, and I held the candle higher in the darkness as I waited for his answer.

"Slept with them here, eaten at table with them here," said the electrician grimly. "The day of the liberation, the mayor and I and two Americans came in to get her," the electrician said as he worked, "but she had neutral papers on her, so we couldn't lock her up. She was a neutral—she slept with them and ate with them and drank French wine with them, that's all." And then he said another thing to me, saying it so clearly and simply that the voices of the hairdressers and the shopkeepers could not be heard speaking any longer, would perhaps never be heard to speak again. "The Boche gave his soul to the French a long time ago," he said, and he worked with the twisted bits of wire, "and now every generation of them tries to buy it back in blood. I said to the Boche when he was here: 'They can't be brought back, the things you want, the things you keep groping for in the dark.' 'What things are you talking about?' the Boche used to say in fury to me, and I'd answer: 'Your soul, and your honor, and your courage. Whenever you won, you lost all three.'"

Suddenly the light sprang up in the bulb that hung in the wine cellar, for the electrician had fixed the fuses at last. And now the talk of the Germans ceased for a little while, and the talk of wheat began again; it was to be heard that morning by the bread wagon that stopped before the village church, there in the mouths of the women as they counted their bread tickets and their money out across the wagon shafts. "If the harvest is good, the ration may be better next month," they said, and they looked at the face of the bread woman for some sign of hope, as if she, who dealt in a measure with officials, would know far better than they themselves, who merely worked the soil, how good the crop might be.

I went into the roadside café with the flute-shaped bread under my arm, and the café owner told me that the wage the harvest workers were paid was six hundred francs a day now, and from behind the counter where he stood he sold me a bottle of red wine. In back of him, over the mirror, hung the fly-specked yellowing likenesses, with their countries' flags crossed above them, of Roosevelt and Churchill and Stalin and De Gaulle. Men had left their jobs in the factories or had closed the doors of their little shops for the month or the six weeks that the harvesting would last, the café owner said to me; and when the grain was in, he said, the same men would move down to the wine-growing parts of the country, even taking their families with them, for women and children were paid well, too, to do the *vendange* there.

"Besides the pay, they give them a meal a day and a place to sleep," the café owner said across the two glasses of wine we drank. He had a sharp little face, as quick as a fox's, but when his mouth closed on his words, the shrewdness went from it, and it was set, like the electrician's, in a look of actual pain. Owing to the drought, 1947 would be a year famed for its wine, he said, and a good wine year was an omen. "It has always come as a warning to Frenchmen not to forget their soil. The warning was given in 1929, before the beginning of our corruption," he said, "and none of us heeded it. Everywhere you went in the ten years following that, you saw how the country had been abandoned. In the south, you'd travel for kilometers through hills of plagued and abandoned vine. Even before the war, we had forgotten how to grow wheat," he said, and in the shuttered darkness of the empty café, he took another swallow of red wine, and he drew the back of his hand along under his mustaches. "Now that we're bankrupt, we'll learn to be humbler, and we'll learn to grow wheat again," he said. As he talked, the prosperity of France seemed to lie just ahead, no further away than next year or the year after that, and, for a moment, there seemed no further cause for fear.

The second night as I lay in bed in the darkened house, I felt the moonlight like a presence in the garden, and because of it I could not sleep. I lay watching the panel of the open window at which the curtains had ceased to stir, and in which the light stood milky as dawn, and I thought of the armies that had passed along the highroad beyond the pasture and the stream, and the men who had turned off the highway to come here and sleep—first the Germans advancing, and then the Germans in retreat, and then the Americans coming. I thought of how the sound of their feet must have been on the stones of the courtyard and across the waxed floors of these rooms; and it was then, in the bright, calm silence, that I heard the voices speaking in the lane beyond the garden wall.

"*Heil Hitler! Geht's gut?*" the first voice said, and the other answered:

"*Heil Hitler! Wie die Erde dürstet!*"

For a moment, I did not believe in the voices. I got quietly from bed, and crossed barefooted to the window. I stood a little to one side of the brilliance, looking down across the garden and the lane. The moon could not be seen, and the clear, cold light of it seemed to rise as evenly as water from the garden paths and from the soft deep grasses of the orchard; it mounted the whitened stones of the wall and poured out across the lane and the short-cropped pastureland. The alleys of trees that led away to the stream were no longer conduits of darkness, for the leaves were lacquered with light, and the trunks themselves and the boughs were lambent and as smooth as sculptured stone. And then I saw the two men standing just beyond the garden wall in the moonlit lane. Their heads were bare, and, in the warmth of the night, their shirt sleeves were rolled up from their forearms. They must have called out at first at a little distance from each other, for now that they stood close I could hear the murmur of their talk, but I could not hear the words they said. But even with the sight of them below me in the countryside washed marvelously clear with light, I still did not believe in the language they had spoken, or in the greeting they had given. I did not believe that a voice had said in German in the hot European night: *The earth is thirsting,* or *How parched the earth is,* or *The earth is parched for rain.* It was because of the memory of the armies that had passed by these walls that I had seemed to hear men's voices greet the dead, I thought; or it was an echo of other years that the stones returned now, and I waited by the window. In a little while, the two men moved off through the moonlight together, and I could hear the sound of their boots like the steps of living men upon the thirsting soil.

And *ne l'oubliez pas*—don't you forget it—they were living men, the café owner said when I told him of it; and that was their native tongue they spoke, and those certainly the words they said. I met him the next afternoon by the pump as he set out to look for fodder for the rabbits he kept behind his house, and when he saw me, he set down the wheelbarrow handles and shook my hand. Here in the open, he seemed a tougher, more muscular man than he had before, and his eyes were quick and brown. He wore a beret low on his brow, and his eyebrows and the hair in his ears and the mustaches on his lip were as bright and dry as fire springing across his face. In the seams of his strong, short neck, nailheads of dirt had been driven, and they studded as well the nostrils of his pointed nose.

"If you go as far as the farmer's market place, you'll see them —the German prisoners," he said, and you knew from the sound of his words that his memory had not split in two. His jacket was black alpaca, polished high, with the faded ribbon of the *Croix de guerre* fixed in the left lapel. As we walked out of the little cobbled square where the single, ancient dark-leafed tree and the pump beside it made an oasis of shade and damp in the desert of the stones and streets, you could see that his gray and black-striped trousers—like those that a diplomat of another era might have worn—were patched across the seat. Along the walls of the country lanes were posters, some showing a fat bag of grain and some a richly burdened spray of wheat, with legends saying: *Deliver your wheat—ALL of your wheat! Deliver it NOW to give your country bread!* "We lost too many in both wars, and so now we need help in the fields," the café owner said. "Dead men can't work the soil. They only fertilize it," he said, and the wheel of the barrow he pushed before him cried aloud as it turned in the ruts of the road.

Now the wheat had been cut; it lay in field after field on either side as we followed the wagon roads, with the wagon tracks carved deep in the hard-baked soil. And now the men worked at binding it into sheafs, scattered groups of them to be seen as far as the eye could reach, their backs bent under the solid weight of sunshine. Above them, flapping black above the burning golden world, the crows flew, cawing singly, hovering like vultures above a plagued and dying continent. For the first time in the memory of the country people, said the café owner as we walked, horses had dropped dead in the fields before the plow this summer. He said that last week a man who had come from the mountains had told him that even the glaciers were shrinking slowly in their beds, their substance pouring from them like a man's blood running dry. This year the rivers of France had become too shallow to move the shipping from one port to another so that now throughout the country you saw the canal boats lying idle between the locks. Coal could not be moved from one place to another, he said, and potatoes lay rotting where they were. And he spoke of another thing: of the sugar that went by truck, at night, clandestinely into Germany, and, as he talked, the iron wheel of the barrow he pushed cried out as if in pain.

We had come in sight of the farmer's market place when the first German prisoner, his strong, tanned torso bare, came down the wagon road toward us, walking slowly along the wheel ruts. He carried a spraying machine strapped to his naked back, and, as he approached, it could be seen that he was a handsome dark-eyed boy not twenty yet, with thick black curls and a rosy face. Over his torso and his cheeks and hair, and over the canvas trousers and the broken shoes on his feet, a delicate film of white had been cast by the spray, but, for a moment, it seemed that he had in some profligate gesture of irony been powdered with the flour that no Frenchman could buy. When we passed near to one another on the road, the German boy smiled a little hesitantly at us, and then he shyly turned his finely powdered, ignorant face away. The café owner, still pushing the wheelbarrow, jerked his chin in his direction, but his eyes did not falter; no word was uttered in greeting, and in silence we passed by.

"There're twenty of them working at the farmer's wholesale

market place," the café owner said as we followed the wagon trail where it led beneath the apple trees. Now and again, we stopped for a little to pull at the vines that clung to the roadside rocks, and we piled onto the barrow these winding garlands of dusty green. The rabbits' hearts would shrivel in their breasts at the sight of it, I thought, for the leaves of the vine were dry to the touch, and the sap had hardened in its veins. "They must have taken that one out of the classroom to put the uniform on him," the café owner said, and for the first time the sound of bitterness was in his voice. "He's a child, but child or not, there's no reason for any of us to pass the time of day with him. *Bon jours* didn't come so easy in 1944. You couldn't hear them very well above the gunfire executing hostages," he said, and his hands pulled fiercely at the vine.

Now we could see the rest of the prisoners, the far line of them working like men on a chain gang, with their naked backs bowed over the fallen wheat. There, against a backdrop of yellowing birches, the far line of bowed enemy figures harvested the grain for France this year as they had foraged the same grain in the years of the Occupation that were scarcely past. There they bowed in labor above this coveted soil, as if giving aid to the stricken or the dead, their toil mingling now with the toil of Frenchmen in singular, silent union, as their blood had, through generations, never ceased to mingle in violence with French blood. And *wie die Erde dürstet!* said the memory of the prisoner's voice, speaking softly across the land.

"They've lived here three years or more as Frenchmen live," I said. I was looking for pimpernel flowers among the tall weeds we had broken, for, even though faded, they might bring death to the rabbits who waited in their cages, their fleetness and nimbleness subdued behind the wire to a crouched, trembling expectancy.

"Next month the prisoners will be repatriated," the café owner said. He stood looking away at the far, bowed line of them, his mustaches burning across the side of his foxlike face and a tuft of fiery down springing from his ear. "They will go back having learned one thing. They will have learned that the story they were always told of France's soil being richer than that of their own country is true, and they will remember it, and they will not sleep easy until they can return—but not to return as prisoners," he said, and as he stooped to pick up the handles of the wheelbarrow again, the look of shrewdness had gone from his face, and only the look of grief was there.

From here it was not far to the farmer's market place. It lay just ahead, basking in peace in the embrace of a winding, low stone wall. The road that we followed led to the gates of the farm and through them, and there five black Great Danes, as large as deer, perceived our coming and leaped upright before their thatch-roofed kennels, their shining flanks quivering. They bayed and slobbered in outrage, and strained at the ends of their chains as we passed them by. The main buildings of the farm formed a fortress in themselves within the outer wall, and the bridge we crossed to the three-sided courtyard may have been a drawbridge once, but now ducks lay in the shade that it cast into the dust-filled moat below. The courtyard that opened before us was as clean as a freshly swept room, and the wall of strong, gabled buildings held it fast. On either side, as one entered, stood the watering troughs for the livestock, with the miracle of water lying untroubled in their mossy depths and pink-tiled roofs standing over them to keep them from the sun. Here, by the shaded pump, the café owner set down the legs of the wheelbarrow; he turned and looked with satisfaction around the orderly place.

The first building to the left was that which housed the sheep, and the upper halves of the handsome oak doors stood open so that as we approached we saw the multitudinous faces of the flock within. They lifted their heads and looked at us, as silent as spectators in a motion-picture theatre, their small chins shifting as they chewed, their weak, pale eyes fixed on the screen of sunlight on which we had appeared. Next to the sheep, in the same unbroken block, came the dairy, with the tall, clean milk cans visible, standing in shining pillars in the partial dark. Beyond that, the barn, with no pile of manure before its doors, made the angle of the corner; and next to the barn was the farmhouse itself, adjoining it, so that in winter the warmth from the cattle might lean against it in a strong, fragrant wall. The farmhouse ran the full width of the courtyard, flanked on both sides by its auxiliary buildings. Only the lace curtains and the pots of geraniums at the barred windows of the lower floor distinguished it from the other buildings, for it was like them in height, and the pink tiles of its gabled roof were the same, and its substance the same grayish stone. And there was another difference: the lofts beneath the eaves of the other buildings could be seen to be packed with fodder of alfalfa and dark clover heads, for the loft doors stood open, while under the eaves of the farmhouse was the honeycomb of the pigeon-cote, and the high façade of its circular openings murmured with their voices, and the lime-hung ledges were aflutter with quick-winged pigeon life.

On the other flank of the farmhouse lay the stables, and in the shaft of sunlight that fell across the open doorway, the great tasseled fetlocks and the hoofs of the work horses could be seen as they stamped at flies in the stable's shade. Then came the poultry houses and runs, as finely equipped as aviaries; and next to them the well-stocked wood house, and the lofty wagon shed, in which the farm implements and the vehicles were arranged. Everything was in order in the shed as well: the plowshares scraped clean of the earth through which they had traveled, and the planks of the ancient farm carts scrubbed white as fresh, sawed timber; but in this country where, in eight years, little had been produced for the use of its own people and little replaced, the iron-bound wheels of the wagons were warped to another shape from use.

The farmer's wife came out the door to greet us, a blondish-haired woman, still under forty, who wore a dark-flowered, long-sleeved apron, and black cotton stockings on her well-turned legs, and black felt bedroom slippers on her feet. She said *bon jour,* but there was no look of pleasure in her flushed, amber-eyed face, and she gave us each in turn a damp, limp hand.

"So things are not going well?" asked the café owner, and she shook her head. "A little water wouldn't hurt any, would it?" said the café owner, with what might have been taken for humor.

"If it came now, it would come too late," said the farmer's wife.

"Not too late for the autumn sowing," the café owner said. A piece of blond hair had come down across the woman's perspiring brow and cheek, and she set it back with the fingers of one hand. Her husband was out in the fields with the workers, she told us, and the café owner said we had not come to call, but that we were out after rabbit fodder and had just happened to pass by. "Next month you'll be twenty workers short," he added.

"We're going to have trouble getting the planting done without them," the farmer's wife said. "First they stop the rain with their atomic bomb, and then they tell us we have to send the German prisoners away." A black and white puppy, bowlegged and as soft as suet, came out the door from under her skirts. The agitation of his outsized tail unbalanced him, and he fell down the one step and onto the cobbles of the courtyard, still wagging his tail as he fell. "They keep everything clean. They've been disciplined. We'll never find anything like that here," she said, and she stooped to pick up the soft, fat puppy, turned him over, and set him upright on his paws.

"What kind of men are they?" I asked her. She looked at me slowly for a moment, her fingers setting the pins straight in her hair.

"There're two kinds that I know of," she said. "There're the old ones and the young."

"And what do they talk about?" I said, and the farmer's wife looked at me slowly for another moment.

"The old ones talk of going home," she said, considering it. "The young ones talk of Hitler. They say if we had a dictator, we'd be better off in France." She turned her amber, heavily lidded eyes toward the café owner. "Maybe they're right. You hear so many people saying it that maybe there's some truth in it. Maybe we need a dictator to straighten the country out," she said.

The café owner looked out over the courtyard, and over the bridge, and over the dusty wagon road that led away beyond it, his eyes seeking beyond the apple trees to the parched fields, seeking far across the thirsting earth of France.

"No," he said. "Our needs are simpler than that. Do not let

them confuse you. We need wheat, we need grain, we need rain."

Perhaps it was not until the very last days of the harvest that the women of the village believed in the failure of the wheat. They knew of the frost that had blighted it when the crop was young, and they saw the cabbage plants moulting like palm trees, row after row of them in the fields; they saw the leaves of the potato plants turned to scorched paper by the sun; but in spite of the signs their faith in the wheat had not yet left them. It was with them still on the Saturday night when the village fete began. The carousel and the shooting gallery and the nougat booths had come in their motorized caravans the day before, the train of them as shabby as a convoy of gypsies coming up the road. Even the dance pavilion was brought on a caravan, one that had been a Paris bus, they said, perhaps twenty years before; and owing to the length of the boards and the poles lashed to its trailer, it took the curves slowly, and its motor died twice as it came up the hill. On Friday evening, the caravans drew up beside the commons that lay between the mayor's house and the church, and, as darkness moved across the country, the thin blue threads of smoke from the caravan kitchens faded, and the separate glow of their fires could be seen in the still night air. The troupers dined late, and they did not begin to drive their stakes into the ground until the moon rose, and then the planks and the beams and the grim paraphernalia of festivity were unloaded from the vans. The frame of the shooting-gallery scene, and the fortune-telling wheel, and the tiers of the prize-winning booths were lifted out, and from the road you could see the horses of the merry-go-round with their forelegs arched and the curved-neck swans as they lay, sculptured to singular fantasy and beauty by the moonlight, in static flight upon the dew-wet grass.

And then, on Saturday night, the dancing began to the sound of the accordions, and the young men of the countryside came into the dim yellow light of the tent, wearing suits and shoes so new that it seemed they had never been worn before. There were those who had brought their wives in pale silk short dresses with them, and they paid for their strips of tickets at the entrance and guided their wives carefully in their arms as they moved across the boards. The others chose partners from the row of girls seated in chairs along the canvas wall. Above the collars of their shirts, the backs of the young men's necks were red from the seasons of sun, and the black of the soil was in their nails still as they held the women close to them. The sweat shone on their faces, and the pavilion shook with the weight of their steps as they danced in the heat and tumult on the crowded floor. And "a little water wouldn't hurt any," the men might say to each other in greeting, thinking of the fields still. It was only later when they had drunk well at the café that the dancing grew wilder, and they began to think of love.

"You have to dance until five o'clock in the morning," said the electrician, and we danced together. He was dressed elegantly now, in a dark green suit, with his thick hair back in a cowlick from his brow. "On the two nights of the fete, you have to dance until five in the morning," he said, and he danced quickly and well in his narrow, pointed brown shoes, with his shoulders hunched a little. "During four years there were no fetes, and we didn't dance," he said, "so now there are four years out of our lives that we have to make up for."

In between dances the measure of the accordions ceased in the tent, and then the music of the carousel could be heard as it turned outside in the breathless night. The men would go under the canvas flap and cross to the café to drink again, and the girls would sit down on the chairs and wipe their faces, and talk and laugh among themselves as they waited for the melodious breathing of the accordions to begin again, and for the men to return and take them in their arms.

"Let's go to the café and have a glass," said the electrician.

Outside, the merry-go-round was turning, its jeweled canopy overhead and its glass panels glittering with light. Above the sound of its pianola playing, one could hear the clear high "ping" from the shooting gallery as a clay pipe or a bird went down. And on the revolving white horses and the swans of the carousel, young lovers rode with their arms about each other, and others, on the plush-covered seats of the ornamented sleighs, kissed gently, mouth to mouth. As we passed the illuminated booths, the women in their white aprons cried out:

"Nougat! Nougat! Nougat from Montélimar!"

We had come beyond the ambit of light when the electrician said: "The population of France is on the increase now. Perhaps that's because of the village fetes—" and in the darkness I could not see him smiling, and I knew, for the first time, that the moonlight was not there.

What was to happen did not come at once. The door of the café stood open; men stood drinking and men sat drinking at the tables, some with their Sunday hats on still, but in their vests and shirt sleeves, having taken off their jackets in the heat. The air was filled with the smoke of their tobacco, with the tumult of their arguments, and we edged our way between them to where the café owner stood. He was at his place behind the counter, serving drinks, watching the packed tables, and rinsing the glasses in the tub of water set beneath the *zinc*. He turned his head quickly, sharply, as he worked, alert to the speech of the living in the café, and harking as well, it might be, to the dead. He wiped his palms dry quickly on his apron, and shook our hands. He spoke in a low voice.

"The radio says rain," he said, as he lifted bottles and poured drinks. He said he would take a cognac with us, and we drank together. The talk of the men grew louder at the tables, but the café owner stood like a deaf man before us, no longer listening to them speak. For outside lay the dark, exhausted earth, stricken by drought and spent by the contests in which it had been the promised trophy, and the café owner turned his head toward the doorway now where the earth lay burdened with its uneasy dead. "The radio says rain," he said again, and then suddenly he jerked his head up, and the lights in the café faltered an instant as the sound of thunder split the dark. "Hush!" he said, and the room went quiet. *Wie die Erde dürstet, wie die Erde dürstet,* whispered the memory of the prisoner's voice across the silence, and then, above the music of the merry-go-round and the accordions in the dance pavilion, we could hear it coming like a great sea roaring in across the trees.

Fire in the Vineyards

The house to which the mother and the children had come to live in for a little while was ornamental enough to bear the name of château, and it stood on sloping ground among the vineyards of southern France, two miles or more out of the fishing town. It was an Englishman's property, a place on which wine was grown, and bottled, and sold to restaurants, or else for export, or to individuals who came in their own cars for it, knowing the value of its name. But now the Englishman was dead, and his wife had gone to Cornwall to visit her people for the summer, leaving the house to the mother and children until the vintage time would come. So it was theirs, but it was no more than a fragment of possession, the mother knew, this temporary title they had been given. They were allowed access to the château's material residue, to the garden hedged by tapering cypress trees, to the stagnant lily ponds, and the crumbling walls on which scaled salamanders moved quicker than light.

But the essence that kept the place from dereliction was not theirs. Father and son, down to the third generation now of men and their women, it was the beat of the peasants' hearts that could be heard in the somnolent quiet, and the movement of their life in the cellar chambers, and the murmur of their voices through the heat as they worked among the vines. Men and their wives and their children labored together, tending the vineyards and the orchards, picking the grapes and pressing them when the right season came. They filled the vast, ancient kegs, and bottled, and corked, and labeled the wine, and pruned the vine in late December. In August, they gathered green almonds and dried them for winter eating, and they plucked the olives from among the trembling silvery leaves, and crushed them under the horse-drawn, granite cylinder to oil that ran, slower than honey, into the great stone jars.

All summer the peasants would be at their work of washing

the wine bottles clean, and filling them from the giant casks that
stood in the dark cellars at the back of the château, transforming
the ritual of the seasons into commerce as the retired English
army officer had disciplined them to do. Whenever the mother
and the children passed the open door, the peasants would look
up and say *bon jour,* and roar the words out about the weather,
their voices continuously amazed, although, now that it was summer, the weather scarcely altered. The sun was as unremitting as
the grinding whispers of the cicadas in the trees, and when it set,
the cicada voices died with its light, and an uneasy silence fell
upon the evening air. But the peasants spoke neither of sunshine
nor rain, but of the wind, like fishermen. One day the *mistral*
might be blowing, and that was good wine-bottling weather, for
it wiped the foreground and the rocky skyline clean. It blew in
from the northwest, across the Gulf of Lion, cold and arrogant
and alien as it strode across the beaches and the flowering cliffs.
But it was not alien, for it was there, hammering the coastline,
for two hundred days of every year. After it had gone on its way,
a fitful, pleasant breeze, with the taste of salt in it, might cavort
in off the Mediterranean waters, and then the heat would close
down again in suffocation on the prostrate land.

"It's good for the vine, the drought!" the peasants would say,
their voices as loud as if they called across a long distance to the
mother, for theirs was the vocabulary of the vine, and, because
she was American, it must seem to them that hers would be of
war and the atom bomb, and they were not sure that they could
make her hear. Let the springs go dry in the rock, and the goats
tethered in the fields cry out with thirst; let artichokes hang like
blackened skulls on their ashen stalks, and it did not matter,
their dedication protested, for such things meant that the vine
would flourish as in no common year. "It will be a good crop!"
they would roar out of the damp, cool caverns where they
worked, knowing that drought is the climate in which the vine
draws body and power from the diathermic soil.

On another day, the peasants might try to speak to her of the
thing that stood between them.

"You're American, but you've been to England?" they would
say. "If you talk to the English, they'll tell you they've had

enough, the way we French have had enough." They would stand in the shadows of the cellar rooms, their faces masked by the obscurity, saying: "You are American. You live so far away that you are not afraid of war the way we French and the English are afraid."

At that time of the year there were the customary number of English travelers, red-kneed, big-wristed, young men in khaki shorts and dusty boots, with the Union Jack spread like a declaration of their neutrality across the knapsacks on their backs. In hobnailed boots, they tramped the southern roads between the vineyards and the olive groves, their backs bent under the weight of their portable stoves and their utensils, under their books and their shabby clothes, because of their poverty and their determination, already aged, dogged men. Or there were the other English who rode, two by two, erect on motorcycles, with their tin pots and pans strapped to the canvas rolls behind them; or the English families who traveled in cars of such dilapidated distinction that there was no need for the "G B" above the numbers of the license plates to indicate from where they came.

They had a look of earnest shabbiness about them, these English, thought the mother as she walked with her three children along the port of the fishing village, with the Mediterranean lapping at the stones. They had none of the assurance of the German tourists, for the Germans, with so much to answer for in every European country, now carried their heads higher than any other visitors, in order not to hang them low in shame. The English looked as poor as beggars as they passed the Germans sitting in the cafés, and their motorcycles were enough to make you split your sides with laughter as they stood parked along the waterfront beside the shining American cars.

"You are American," the fishermen would say to her as she and the children bought the fresh sardines from the baskets lined with seaweed laid on the harbor stones. On the delicately tinted wall of the wharfside café would be written in strong black lettering, as it was written on the gas-station roof at the entrance to the town: "Amis, Go Home," or "*Les Américains en Amérique!*" "You are American," they would say, the rejection so impersonal that there was no venom left in it. And their silence added: *You are not afraid of what may happen the way we are afraid.*

"I can tell the difference between the English and the French," said Fife, who was eight that summer. The mother and the children walked up through the parched fields, carrying the fish, and the lengths of bread, and the fresh fruit in their rucksacks, and the children would look at the words lettered faintly on the garden walls, "U. S. Go Home," and then they would look away. "The English get the reddest on beach," Fife said. He wore blue jeans, and American sneakers, and his voice sounded high and clear above the rasping of the cicadas in the almond and the olive trees.

"I can tell Frenchwomen because their hair is rusty," said Candy, who was ten. "I can't tell the difference between any of the men yet. Wherever they come from, they all turn around and stare," she said.

"Frenchmen's hips are higher up, nearer their armpits," said the girl named Claude. "Englishmen have theirs nearer their knees." She was slender, and tanned, with the small, grave face that had been hers at three years old no different now that she was twelve, except it was borne higher on her lengthening bones. "There are several other differences," she said, with dignity.

"Frenchwomen kiss louder than other women do," Candy went on with it, and her wheat-colored braids swung forward in the sunlight as she made the explosive sound of their embrace on the back of her own brown hand.

"Americans kiss very, very silently," said Fife. "In the movies I've seen of Americans kissing, they never make a sound."

"Oh, it's hot, it's much too hot!" Candy cried out in sudden impatience. "I'm too tired to go any further, and there's a cicada caught in my hair!"

And then one day, as the *mistral* blew, the forest fire began to burn. It was just past noon, at the hour when all life and all activity attenuated toward food and sleep, that the siren wailed its prolonged warning from the fishing town below. The peasants stood in their doorways, shading their eyes against the midday light, and the American children stood up by the château's lily ponds, where they had set their boats afloat in the high wind, their hearts chilled by the sustained, unearthly cry.

"It could be a drowning or it could be a fire," one of the younger peasants said, and an older one who stood near him, his grim face shaded by his copper-skinned hand, said:

"It could be for twelve o'clock. Sometimes they blow their whistle a half hour off."

It may have been that they were all blinded by the mere presence of the meridional noon, for it was a minute, perhaps longer, before they saw the smoke through the blowing tracery of the olive trees. The mother and children followed the peasants out onto the wagon road to watch the smoke now billowing in creamy fury across the wooded hill. It took them another long moment to see that a wheat field had gone first, and then an orchard, and that the fire had charred fig, and olive, and cypress trees across the shallow valley, and was climbing fast to higher land. As they watched, the *mistral* unfurled the flames in sudden, flapping banners above the scrub and the writhing treetops, waving them ever higher in its strong relentless hand.

"This isn't the time of day for a forest fire," said the older peasant as the vertical note of the siren began its wailing fall. "The *pompiers* are fathers of families like anybody else. They've got the right to eat their lunch in peace," he said.

"Even if Monsieur Mistral laid down now," said the younger peasant, speaking of the wind as if it were a man, "you'd still have the birds and the rabbits carrying the fire on them. A wild pig will carry fire twenty–thirty kilometers a day, from the sparks caught in his fur as he runs before it. If there's no more than just one cicada flying with his wings lit, you can't say the forest fire's out."

Again the cry of the siren rose, and in the blinding dazzlement of afternoon, the deeper, hotter texture of the flames sprang in dark-plumed triumph above the land. And now a rust-colored jeep, it's warning signal gasping in puny alarm, could be seen moving up the valley road, with a fire engine following behind.

"That's the fire chief," said the older peasant, not saying it to the mother or the children, but to the implacable wind.

"He's known Monsieur Mistral thirty years," the younger peasant said.

From where they stood, neither jeep nor fire engine seemed larger or better equipped for action than a child's mechanical toy. The two minutely laboring vehicles proceeded up the bleached, walled road, passed the charred area the fire had left behind it, bypassed the fire itself, as if their destination lay still farther, and, at a break in the slumbering wall, turned off the road and into the tilted fields. There they rocked ludicrously upward, not toward the fire, but still higher, and when they halted, the firemen in their light-blue shirts scattered like confetti across the faded pigment of the grass. But they were men, with the ruse of men in their heads and in the white rope of the hose they carried, and so they could outwit the mindless torrent of liquid flame that poured across the thirsting hill.

It was more than an hour before the strong, flapping flames fell, tattered, from the black masts of the trees, and the smoke thinned out to mist which the *mistral* swept away. By evening, there was only the smell of fire left in the nostrils, and the eye saw the dark scar left on the wooded land, like the shadow of a cloud cast on sunny water, or on a field of yellow grain.

But that was not the end of it, for the story of how the fire had begun was still to be recounted, and whether it was truth or rumor, or who had told it first, nobody knew. But it was told in every shop and café of the fishing village, and repeated even by the fishermen as they mended their nets along the harbor, and by the peasants as they washed the bottles in the cellars on the north side of the house. It was this: that an American soldier, on furlough from Paris or Orléans, had driven that morning into the village in his fine, big car and parked it under the sign that said no parking was allowed. The soldier had drunk three *pastis* on a café terrace in the sun, the story went, or drunk half a bottle of cognac, and then refused to pay. When the café proprietor said he would call the police, the soldier had said: "France never did nothing but sit on a corner holding a tin cup out, and we're sick of dropping the dollars in"; or said: "France died a couple of centuries ago"; or said: "There's eighteen cafés in this town, and there's one church. That's all any Christian needs to know." Then the soldier had walked unsteadily across the cobbles of the port, and raced his car through the narrow streets of the fishing village, and out the pastoral valley road, mistaking it for the coastal road, because by that time he couldn't read the signposts any more. And, driving crazily between the long, low, orchard walls, he must have flung his cigarette away, and the paper-dry field of wheat went first, and then the orchard, and it was even said that two milk-giving goats had perished. A farmer coming home had heard them bleating in the flames.

It was no longer said that there had been a forest fire near the fishing town, and that the *pompiers* had extinguished it, for now another element had come alive in it. Whether or not there was an American soldier who had drunk too many *pastis* in the sun no longer mattered, and the name of the café where he had sat was of no consequence, nor the words he might have said. Whoever he was, he had been endowed now with political distinction, and as he reeled across the stones he became the figurehead for whom the slogans were written out in letters taller than the orchard trees. Fife stood in his black rodeo shirt, and his black rodeo trousers, on the quayside, his hands thrust in his jewel-studded pockets, his eyes fixed on nothing, perhaps seeking to see the soldier, with the cigarette on his lip, making his way like a blind man to his car.

"I don't believe it was an American that did it," Fife said.

Claude had carried the fishnet that afternoon, and there was a hermit crab caught in the meshes of it, and she watched with gravity his small, evil, almost human face, his outsized thumbs, his irritation. Her feet were bare, and there were viscous ribbons of seaweed between her toes. The muscles tightened in her long, brown, slender legs as she crouched down.

"Sometimes soldiers in foreign countries get lonely," she said, watching the crab, "and then they take too much to drink."

"But even if a soldier was lonely," Fife said, and he looked out over the moored boats riding quietly, "and even in a foreign country, I bet he wouldn't forget the things he learned about fires when he was a Scout."

"Oh, Fife," said Claude, "then you grow up, you smoke, and you drink, and your memory fails you!"

She held the hermit crab on the palm of her open hand now, and Candy squatted beside her, her braids bleached white as cotton by the sun.

"Does every hermit crab live with an anemone?" Candy asked the mother, but it was Claude who answered.

"They live in discarded mollusc shells," she said almost in rebuke, "in association with annelid worms or sea anemones. But whether they're parasites or just flowers the hermit crab wears as ornament, nobody really knows."

But Candy was lost to them now in other conjecturings, her head turned from them. There were two lovers sitting on the moss-grown landing steps beyond, the water rising and falling in slow, unceasing motion just below their naked entwined feet. Their clothes were poor, their flesh was smooth and dark, and bronzed still darker on their throats and forearms, and they shared one cigarette between them, the girl taking it in her narrow fingers from her own mouth once she had drawn a deep breath in, and then placing it in the boy's pale, handsome mouth. When the cigarette was done, she put her hand on the back of his sun-blackened neck, and drew his face to her face, and kissed him long and sweetly in the golden light. These were the two that Candy watched, her thin, brown arms around her drawn-up knees, her nose a little wrinkled; and when she had watched them from this side for a space of time, she moved in her faded shorts to the other side, and squatted down again, her eyes quizzical, her toes spread on the stones, and she watched the sight of love for a little while from there.

"You Americans, you've got a country all to yourselves as big as Europe," one of the fishermen had begun saying to the mother, his blue eyes as cold as metal on her. He stood barefoot, broad-shouldered, in his singlet, a man of fifty maybe, with his blue cotton trousers rolled below his knees. In one hand he held the soft lifeless body of an octopus, its long, rose-colored legs, which could no longer reach and writhe, like the delicate roots of some exotic plant he had taken from the sea. "You've got so much territory, you Americans," he said, "that one side of a hill burning, it isn't the same as it is to a Frenchman or an Englishman. In America, you've got so much of everything, you can afford to blow some of it up in those atom bomb experiments, so what's it to you, a hill burning, or an acre of forest trees wiped out?"

"I don't believe the story about the American," Fife said, and he looked out past the semaphore at the harbor entrance to the cliffs that built up from the sea.

A few days after that, the summer was suddenly done, and the stony hills, the long-eroded cliffs, the sapless vegetation, took on another, more heterogeneous look. There were shadows cast, and the wine cellars, with their ancient barrels taller than a man, loomed strangely in the evening. The château tower, its windows thickly webbed by spiders and sibilant with the stirring of many dying insects' wings, was a place to turn from when the night had come. Once the peasants had closed the heavy cellar doors, and left for their houses down the cart road where the vineyards sloped away, the mother would make the shutters of the windows fast, moving from one hushed room to another while the children slept. Downstairs, there were branched candelabra on the walls the length of the quiet salon, with crystal lozenges, blackened by time, hanging like trembling tears beneath the pear-shaped bulbs. By their uncertain light, she could see her own figure, slender and tall in the long, blue dress, cross quickly toward the mirror in its massive, gilded frame, and she halted there, and looked behind her, as if in fear, before she faced her own eyes in the glass. It seemed to her then that the shadows in the long room had come alive with the movement of many people, people from different countries, and all of them empty-handed, shabbily dressed, and some of them gaunt with hunger, and the words that they whispered like the final dying of insects' wings were: *Peace, peace, peace, for God's sake, peace. We have had enough of war.*

"Yes, peace," the mother said aloud to her own reflection, not allowing her eyes to look away. "What are we doing in uniform in every European country? What are we doing here?"

Outside in the water-lily ponds she could hear the throbbing of the frogs, as rhythmic as breathing, and she turned from the mirror and walked to the handsome, spindle-legged desk, with its brass-encrusted drawer handles, and she sat down to write.

Whenever the frog voices abruptly ceased, as if at a signal, she knew it was because a white owl had swooped down through the moonlight to a plane-tree branch above the stagnant water, and that the frogs would be silent in caution until he flew away. It happened every night, and every night she thought that this time it might not be the white owl drifting down on his spread wings, but the movement of a great many people gathering outside that had brought the deep, clonking music to a pause.

"Dearest man," she began to write in almost overwhelming tenderness, "I think the children and I should meet you somewhere else. There doesn't seem much point in you coming so **far** to join us here." She did not add: *Perhaps somewhere more neutral; but where in Europe can we turn?* "The *mistral* is blowing colder and colder two days out of three," she wrote, "so I think we should plan on another place for your time off. I'm going to start packing tomorrow morning. Send us a telegram, and we'll meet you wherever you say. Perhaps Switzerland?" she suggested. She would wait until his arms were around her before saying: *I too, I too, am afraid of what may happen this year, or next, without us knowing that it is taking place. The wrong voices are speaking out for us in our country, and we cannot be heard—we, you and I, and Claude and Candy and Fife, we have been silenced. You could not possibly come here.* "We could meet you in Davos," she put at the end of the letter, and the frog chorus ceased outside as the owl swept down, or the people of other countries gathered outside the windows, and she addressed the envelope quickly to the U. S. Army colonel's name and his outfit in Frankfurt, Germany.

▲▲▲▲▲▲▲▲▲▲▲▲▲▲▲▲▲▲▲▲▲▲▲▲▲▲▲▲

Military
Occupation Group
1945–1950

▼▼▼▼▼▼▼▼▼▼▼▼▼▼▼▼▼▼▼▼▼▼▼▼▼▼

Hotel Behind the Lines

I stood at the window of the hotel room and looked out across the stone balcony's balustrade, and beyond it across the square to where the river flowed, as clear and unbroken as peace itself, and marvelously impervious to demolition. A long way below, a dozen or more people stood waiting on the stones of the Arno's beach, faceless and sexless and scarcely human from the window's height, but more like the black, explicit letters of a caption saying: "Italian workers in blasted Florence waiting on the bank of the Arno to be ferried home at night." The rowboat for which they waited had no oars, but a cable had been strung across from the beach of shingle to the other bank, above which the cypresses stood, and the boatman's hands on the cable wove back and forth, back and forth, delivering the people who crossed with him into the brilliance of the sunset, and then weaving back across the shining surface of the water to the shingled beach again.

The front must be up there ahead, lost in the misty, bluish folds of the Apennines, but I did not believe in it yet. The roar of the airplane's motors had ceased in my ears just a little while before, and I believed now only in this pool of evening quiet that lay, unquivering, in the violent landscape of war. The front must be up there, with men I knew fighting on it; but here there was no echo, no whisper on the water. Outside there was the cable, strung, a delicate vein, through the stillness, and the boatman's hands on it drawing the people home. In the room, on the table behind me, were the daffodils Mario had sent, with a card saying to telephone him as soon as I got in. *In a moment I will call him*, I thought; *in just a moment, when I've stopped looking at Italy. I will call him, and see him tonight, and get the shape and the taste of things from him. He'll have grown up since 1937—he'll be twenty-three-or-four, and as free man and a poet he has somehow managed to survive.*

And then the telephone rang quickly on the little table by the bed and I went to it, and lifted the mouthpiece and receiver up.

"This is Colonel Sarett," said the Englishman's voice from the other end of the wire. "Stranger to you, I'm afraid. I just bumped into your name on the hotel list downstairs—"

"Oh, yes," I said, and there was silence for a moment.

"Once had a cousin from Dublin by the same name," said the Englishman's voice. "Occurred to me perhaps some member of the family. I thought I'd simply ask."

The family, my part of it, I said, left Ireland three generations back. I added that there wasn't much to say for it as a name, and the Englishman laughed.

"There was always Robert," he said. "Wintered here, you'll remember, studying the works of Galileo. I think it was 1642."

"They had a weakness for Italy," I said. "There was John, the Earl of Cork and Orrery. But probably we're none of us related."

"Oh, doubtless not," said Colonel Sarett. "Right you are. You'll forgive me for calling, won't you? I'm just down from the front for fifteen hours, covered with muck and grime." It might have been that he brushed at his blouse a little as he said it. "Awfully decent of you to have talked to me at all," he said.

After I had put the telephone down, I felt the singularly rebuking silence in the room. *You could have gone downstairs, sat five minutes at the bar with him, asked him what part of England he came from, not mentioned Greece, but spoken of the look of London ten days ago, and of England's inarticulated courage. You could have done it for five minutes between the time of arriving here and having dinner with Mario. You could have done it for the sake of the muck and the grime and the fifteen hours he has of absolution.* I stood looking out again over the roofs, and I thought of Eden in the House of Commons crying out like a petulant woman to the questions the Labor members put to him, but I laid the thought of that aside. There had been other Englishmen; there had been the quick, good words of the air marshal saying to me two weeks ago at lunch,

"If the time has come when the common people of the world have found a party that can speak effectively for them, then, for God's sake, let the rest of us rid ourselves of our outdated prejudices—" and then the telephone rang sharply again.

"Damned cheek, I'm quite aware," said Colonel Sarett's voice, "but I've waited a decent interval, and I still want to say it. I want to ask you if you'd indulge in a spot of pity and come down and have a drink with me?"

I said I would. I told him I was in uniform; and in the lobby downstairs there was nothing but the military—the young, the middle-aged, the Americans, the British, the Scotch, the military without relief.

"It won't be easy to find you," I said.

"You'll know me at once," said Colonel Sarett from five flights below. "My hair is going thin—you know, receding from the temples. I'm definitely battle-worn, and there are bags under my eyes."

I said I would put a daffodil in the front of my blouse.

"You mean there are actually flowers blooming?" asked Colonel Sarett. I said there were lots of daffodils—cartloads of them in the streets. "Good God, flowers—flowers blooming in all this mud!" said Colonel Sarett. "I got in half an hour ago. I haven't had time to look around . . ."

The lobby of the hotel was marble-paved and built tall and dark for Italian summers. It was not made for the military at all. Yet here was the sharp, nervous weariness of men on pass drawn taut as a wire from pillar to pillar, and the nameless hunger, the nameless thirst of tired men and lonely men sunk in the split leather of the armchairs, or pacing back and forth on the marble flags, or grouped in nothing as absolute as hope by the revolving doors. But the man who stood quite alone, and a little nervous, by the central pillar, was watching over the heads of the others who passed him. He was watching the stairway that opened, fanwise, into the crowded place.

He was tall and rather slender, with a high, solid, broad chest—a man of forty-five it might be, standing there with the light, smooth hair receding from the peak of it on his forehead, and a clipped mustache on his lip. In spite of the wash of weariness across his face, his eyes were quick and sharp, and when he saw the daffodil, he came forward, pulling a little uneasily at his cuffs. He had not spoken of the campaign ribbons, the decorations, but they all were there.

"I say, this is sporting of you," he said at once. He must have washed his hands while he waited, for when he shook mine, the palm of it was fresh still. "We can have incredibly bad liquor in there, if you don't mind," he said, and he jerked his chin toward the door of the bar. We went in through the archway, past the uniforms standing, the uniforms seated, the great, featureless, khaki-clad army gathered in simulated ease, which turned its eyes to the sight of a woman coming, even though the look of the women loved and the women wanted had ebbed from the realm of possibility a long time back. We sat down on the only two seats that were left on the cracked, dark leather against the wainscoting. "You don't quite believe it at first—I mean, for the first few hours down from the front, you never quite believe you've got here," he said, and as he ordered the drinks of synthetic fruit juice and Italian gin, his eyes were on me carefully. "You're just beginning to get the feel of it when you have to turn around and go back again. This isn't a complaint," he added quickly, and there was the relentless military eye turned inward in self-interpellation as unflinchingly as it would have censored anyone else.

"Fifteen hours isn't much time," I said, and the drinks came then, and we lifted the short, thick-bottomed glasses, and Colonel Sarett said:

"Cheers." The taste of the drink was bad, and he ran his tongue in quick repugnance along his lip. His face was short-nosed and neat, with none of the soft betrayals of indulgence in it; the mouth was stubborn, exact, tenacious, above the cleft chin. "I could, of course, stay down longer," he said, and his eyes moved quickly to me again. "Twenty-four, thirty-six hours, you know. But I can't bring myself to it. Vanity, possibly. Probably nothing more admirable than that. But I have to get back," he said.

"You mean, the war is being won, and you're here—you're out

of it for fifteen hours?" I asked, and he turned his glass in his fingers a moment.

"Lost causes," he said. "Damn it, they get under your skin." He looked up; his eyes, with the drink beginning to fuse in them, were brighter and less weary under his lightish brows. "I remember watching the planes go out over Maidenhead in the evenings—1940 that was," he said. "Old crates scarcely able to make the hop and drop their load. And even if they did get over —Norway and stuff—God knows how many managed to make it back. Isn't the smoke awfully thick in here?" he said.

"After the mountains, it's like that. It always is," I said. "You come down, and rooms seem smaller, and ceilings lower, and you can't breathe the air."

"It's true," said Colonel Sarett, and he ordered the second drinks. "That summer I'd watch them going out at night," he went on saying, "and I'd listen for them to come back at dawn. I was convalescing from a wound I got in the Dunkirk show, and I'd lie there listening for them. When they'd begin to straggle back, I'd start counting the sound of their motors, and they'd be coughing their hearts out as they came. No recent models, no modern gear, just crates that spring and summer, but they kept on going over, and coming back when they could come back— coming back with their rudders out, and their landing gear gone, just to say that they hadn't cracked up in a foreign field—for God's sake, how did I get on to this?" said Colonel Sarett. "This isn't small talk, but I swear I've forgotten how it goes. I ought to be talking about your eyes, or the way you smile, but I've forgotten how to begin. I could tell you that the reason I telephoned the second time to your room was because of the sound of your voice, and that would be true. Or I could tell you that the sound of any woman's voice heard here is like a pain in the heart—not a sharp pain, but a really beastly, nagging pain, provided you have time for that kind of pain," he said. "Perhaps better to tell you about the mountain goats up there in the hills, just born you know, right in the middle of war, sticky as lilac buds. Rupert Brooke was awkward as hell with images—foreign fields and lilacs and all the rot. But still in 1940 those planes kept going out," he said, his stubborn voice jerking back to it again. "Theirs was the lost cause then, absolutely lost, there wasn't a chance. But we had faith in them. We had to, because there wasn't anything else, and, by God, they won—"

It was when the second drinks came that he began to say other things, looking straight down into the evil-tasting and evil-smelling liquor as if the revelation of all that he believed lay there. He said, speaking quickly, that he had his own army, the men of it his own men, his people, who bore their arms in personal loyalty. He had trained these men, he said, and he had armed them, and up there in the Apennines they were fighting their own individual and dogged war.

"Eighteen thousand of them," he said, and as he spoke the fire kindled slowly in his face, and the actual flesh of Lawrence of Arabia's legend seemed to come in its pride and passion to the table and take its place with us there. "They've fought their way up from southern Italy, because they want to be up there, they want to be in the show. They've kept the supply road through the snows open all winter, done it against all the odds the elements had to offer," he said, and his eyes were on me in unflinching estimate. "Two hundred and fifty more came up the pass yesterday, the survivors of a brigade of seven hundred operating in the northern Apennines," he said, "asking to sign up with me —tough, hard men who know there's a job of work to do, and who'll do it." He had been a soldier a long time, and there was nothing of forbearance in him, and the appraisals he made were perhaps nothing more than the soldier's assessment of what functioned adequately and what did not. I'm talking about the Italians," he said. "Italian partisans."

He said he had begged, borrowed, lied, and stolen to get their paraphernalia for them. He had got them dark blue ski suits from American stock; he had got them shoes, signing chits for them that he had no authority to sign. He had kept them covered, and fed, and armed, and fighting up there all winter. As he talked, he took his drink quickly down. In a minute, he said, in a minute he'd have a hot bath and a change of clothes, but it was not this that mattered. What mattered was that the others, the eighteen thousand of them, were up there in the dark of the mountains without him, wearing the uniform and the shoes of no regulation army, keeping the road clear of landslides, and enemy destruction, and high mountain snow.

He was saying these things at the little table in the smoke-filled crowded bar when the American major walked in and paused beneath the arch for a moment. There he stood, looking, in something not nearly young enough or lost enough for loneliness, for the sight of anyone he knew. When he saw Colonel Sarett's face, the relief came swiftly across the broad, square expanse of his own and lingered, the lines grew easy about his mouth, and he made his way through the uniforms toward us. Then he halted beside the colonel, and he nodded to me, and he leaned over and stretched his arm across the colonel's chair.

"I was thinking about you today, Colonel. A matter come up that put me in mind of you," he said. The voice was middle western, the features rugged, with wrinkles drawn deep across his heavy brow.

"I say, sit down with us," said the colonel, coming abruptly back from the front. "This is Miller, Major Miller," he said to me. "A countryman of yours. An agricultural chap from the AMG."

"Call it plain farming. That's what it is," said the major, and he said, "Pleased t' meet-ya, ma'am," and he sat down. He had narrow, bright, black eyes, and his ears were big, and the hair sprang black and curly and lively on his head. "Ran a farm journal back in Oklahoma. Doing something like it here," he said.

"The major's draining the marshes out, getting flood walls rebuilt from Marina di Pisa down," said Colonel Sarett, and he raised his hand and snapped his fingers for the drinks.

"The colonel here's mustering an army of his own," said the major. His mouth was wide, and when he smiled the wrinkles scarred deep and crescent-shaped in the flesh of his cheeks. "He speaks the lingo, and they listen to him as if they liked it, the Italians do," said the major, and he sat there, the jagged crescents of the smile in his face. "I've run into a couple of Englishmen who don't like it quite so well," he said.

"All Lombard Street to a China orange," said the colonel, "but they'll take it. You can't dispense with a country's population, somehow, not even a liberated country's."

"Floods raising Cain all over the place," Major Miller said, and when he thought of the floods he stopped smiling. "You get floods, and no sewer systems, and then the epidemics get going. Our medics are up there shooting the people full of inoculations." The Italian barman brought the drinks and set them on the table, and the major raised his glass in his broad, clean hand and said, "Here's looking at you, ma'am," and he took a drink of it. "Jiminy crickets, that's lousy booze! I'm sure you're of the same opinion about it, ma'am," he said politely over his glass.

"There's a lot of future in it, my man," said Colonel Sarett. "It's keeping us here talking together. I think we might have another," he said.

"We'll drink it to Colonel Sarett's army," I said, and the major stopped smiling abruptly again, and the crescents were blanked out of his cheeks.

"I was coming to Colonel Sarett's army," he said, and he looked at the colonel. "I heard about thirty thousand Italian soldiers we're holding as prisoners of war. I just heard about them today," he said. "Question come up about disposing of them—thirty thousand of them that we took prisoner when we come in, and by the law of Acquisition, Retention, and Confusion, they're POWs still. Now maybe we'll conscript them into battle, and again maybe we won't," the flat middle western voice went on, and the bright black eyes watched Colonel Sarett in sanguine belief. "But if you put in a claim for them, I'll bet they're as good as yours," he said.

The colonel hesitated a moment, took a swallow of the synthetic juice and gin, and put his glass down. "There's no way of knowing what their politics might be," he said.

"There's nothing to keep you from making Englishmen, or Americans, or even Russians out of them. Nothing on earth," said the major.

"Thirty thousand," the colonel said, musing on it. "I wouldn't know where to begin. I wouldn't know what to do with a lot of blokes who don't know by this time which way the wind is blowing. They wouldn't fit in with my blokes up there."

"Colonel, it could very well be that you're just not giving them a break," said the major, and he shook his head. "They've had twenty-five years of not acting like themselves, the Italians have, ma'am," he said in explanation, "and now they got to start learning how. You got to help them to get everything new, right from the inside out. It's like draining the marshes first and getting the crops in afterward. You can't do it quick, so you do it slow. And in the end you get it right," he said.

He lifted his glass to drink, but Colonel Sarett spoke almost sharply across the table, and the major put his glass down again.

"You've forgotten one thing," said Colonel Sarett. "The whole blooming lot of them in this country weren't in it, not by a long shot, Major." He chewed quickly, savagely, at his upper lip a moment, and then the vehemence died from his face. "Thirty thousand POWs," he said, musing on it again. Thirty thousand Italians out of prison, his men to clothe, to feed, to arm, to cherish. "Thirty thousand of them," he said, and the thought of them was alive now, moving up the mountain with him. "By Gad, who should I talk to about it?" he said, and the light of it was shining in his eye.

I remembered Mario then, and I got up from the table, and I gave my hand to Colonel Sarett.

"I have to telephone," I said. "I am having dinner with a man called Mario."

"Blast Mario," said Colonel Sarett, and he got up quickly from his chair. He stood there, tall and straight, his thumbs hooked in his leather belt, his mouth twitching under his clipped mustache. "If I had a bath and a shave and that sort of thing—made a decent job of myself—would you dine with me instead of him?" he said.

We had dinner in the mess hall, meat and carrots and white American bread, and red Italian wine—the colonel, the major, and I. It was the major who had the jeep waiting at nine in the hotel's moonlit square, and he said good-by to us there. Colonel Sarett, with his cheeks shaven clean and his fresh clothes on, followed me in over the jeep's side and sat down beside me on the boards of the back seat. The doors and the sideflaps were buttoned on, for the night was cool, and our coats were belted around us. The address I gave the corporal at the wheel was not

Mario's address; it was the name of the street and the villa where Mario would be.

"He said he would be there with his friend, the newspaperman, tonight," I said to Colonel Sarett, and the jeep took the corner of the square and jerked into the narrow street. "A man called Valdarno," I said. "They can tell me exactly how things are in Italy."

"Who the devil would Mario be?" said the colonel.

Mario's mother was English, and his father had been Italian; I had known them in Florence eight years ago, I said. There had been an older brother then, a boy called Michele, who had played the mandolin and sung. He was nineteen when I knew him, and very beautiful—a good swimmer, a good runner—and he had gone to boarding school in England and liked it there.

"What school did he go to?" asked the colonel in spite of himself.

"That has nothing to do with it," I said in impatience.

"Very well," said the colonel as we rode, and he drew the skirts of his overcoat around him. "I merely wanted to know."

"They live up on the hill, in the same house still, Mario told me when I telephoned tonight," I said, and I could see it clearly. There were almond and mimosa and olive trees growing fresh on the slope below it, and two little stone-walled terraces baked hard by the sun, with the shade of the cypresses marked sharp and conical, as dark as if drawn in ink, upon the terraces' pure white. "It was in the autumn, early October, of 1937, and the English mother set off for a day or two in Rome. And Michele came to the door, and he was angry, he was in a rage. His mother wrote me all this afterward," I said. "He called out after his mother as she left not to forget to bring him back some tennis shoes from Rome. 'For the damned Fascist relay races—I have to have them for the relay races,' was what he said."

"The night of the day she left, Mario came down into Florence for a concert," I said, "and he left Michele alone in the house. And then he did it."

"He did what?" asked Colonel Sarett, and his voice was a little shocked, as though he knew exactly what was to come.

"He shot himself. He killed himself," I said. "Mario came

home from the concert, and there was a letter on the table, with Michele's cameo ring lying on it. The letter just said that he had had trouble finding the gun, and after he'd found it, it was so rusty that he didn't know if it would work. But it did work."

We were out of the city now, and the jeep was moving tentatively along what was no longer street but road, as if feeling its way across the temporary planks of the bridges, and between the moon-blanched walls. Then it came to a stop before a gate.

The house lay close to the road beyond the garden wall, bright white and palace-like under the moon, the substance of it seemingly too lambent for stone. Colonel Sarett rang the bell, and as we waited the trees stood close around us, motionless, fragrant, and mysteriously leafed.

"In another month the nightingales will be singing," Colonel Sarett said. He had taken his cap off, and the moonlight lay in a sharp, metallic blade across his lightish hair. "The presence of a thought," he said in a low voice, "is like the presence of a woman we love. Schopenhauer and the moonlight making me eloquent again," he added in quick apology. Then the door opened, and I saw it was Mario, eight years older, standing hesitant in the dimly lit hall.

"I hope it wasn't too difficult to find the villa," Mario said, and he closed the door behind us. Inside it was colder than it had been outside in the evening air. Mario said that Valdarno was upstairs waiting; he said that if it had not been for the state of Valdarno's health, and the lack of transportation, they would have saved me the trip out and come in to the hotel themselves. "But there are no buses, and no way of getting from one place to another," he said, "and Valdarno is not well."

Mario seemed a shy man, and at first you believed that he was shy, this delicate, slightly stooping figure with the wealth of black hair on his Latin head. You believed it until he began to speak, with his large, dark, fearless eyes on you, and then you knew that it was something more admirable than timidity which marked his bearing and the features of his face.

"Valdarno was imprisoned, you know, because of the articles he wrote," he said, and he lowered his voice a little as we started up the stairs. "A friend has lent this place to Valdarno and his wife," he said. "When Florence was liberated, Valdarno was set free, but he was penniless and he had no house in which to live." At the top of the first cold, echoing flight, he turned to the door on the right of the hall, and laid his hand on the iron latch. "He is extremely eager to meet you," he said before he opened it, and his voice was low. "We want to know what is happening in other countries—in France, America," Mario said, and he turned his head and smiled at us, a quick, gentle, half-apologetic smile.

Valdarno sat alone in the room, seated by a table on which the lamp was lighted and shone dimly, and his wild black eyes were fixed upon the door. When we entered, he stood up, trembling a little, his chest concave behind the façade of the gray tweed jacket, and he shook our hands and spoke our names.

"Sit down, sit down, please," he said. He spoke in English to us, turning in agitation and uncertainty from empty chair to chair. "My wife, unfortunately, is not here. She works at the telephone company at night. Here is a chair, Signora," he said, and he leaned to it, and drew it forward in his trembling hands. "And for the officer—for the Colonel," he murmured, and he was turning like a swift, dark animal from side to side. There was a fine, black, silky mustache under his long, narrow nose, and his lips were thin-skinned and of a red so precarious that it seemed the blood might spring from them if he spoke his words too loud. "For the officer, the large chair here—"

"Please be seated, Signor Valdarno," Colonel Sarett said, and suddenly, at these words, the flurry of movement ceased in the room. Valdarno, his eyes fixed as if in fright on the colonel, sat slowly down in his chair. Colonel Sarett undid the belt of his trench coat, unbuttoned it without haste, and drew his arms from the sleeves. "I ask you please to forgive my coming here, Signor Valdarno," he said, and he spoke Italian to him, speaking it softly, and quickly, and well. He was leaning forward as he talked, his elbows on his knees, his fingers interlaced, as if in this bowed position he somehow discounted the breadth and the depth of his own chest as he faced Valdarno, and the display of ribbon on it. "I'm down for a few hours from the front," he said, "and I wish you would go on talking exactly as if I were not here. I came because I wished to be with the Signora, and because it is good to be with men who are not in uniform for a little while."

He had made his explanation, he had offered his apology, and I wondered a moment; and then, as Mario began speaking again, the thing became clear. Not to Valdarno, and not to Mario, and not to himself was Colonel Sarett merely a man come in from the moonlight to sit and hear them talk of their country, or their country's shame, or to speak of their country's future. He was not a man come casually, briefly in of an evening as any visitor might have come. He was something else, and he did not like the role he had been given. He was the Army, he was the British Army; he wore its uniform, he wore its honors pinned on his breast, and nothing could take the look of it away. To them, and even to himself sitting there in the badly lighted, the unheated room, he was the Army with its ear to the ground for the subterranean whispers; the Army with its machine guns leveled; the Army prepared to wipe out the weak and the hungry and the desperate as they came.

"We can talk of nothing but Roatta's escape," Mario was saying, quietly, evenly, as if with intention. "We can think of nothing else just now—I suppose because of the symbol it offers, the play within the play. The proceedings of Roatta's trial would have stripped the story of all but its essential drama and made it simple enough for everyone to have understood. The story, I mean," he said quietly, "of the criminal policies which ravaged this country for more than twenty years and brought her to disaster. We could have enacted in that trial—the courtroom as stage, the people of the world as spectators, and all the players perfectly cast—the history of our shame and our atonement."

"It's been a match set to tinder, that rotter getting out," said Colonel Sarett. "Demonstrations in Rome, students marching in protest—" *The kind of conflagration,* said the silence when he had ceased to speak, *that we British have extinguished with such generous mercy;* and as his voice broke off, the colonel chewed nervously at his mustache an instant.

"Our government," Mario went on saying, "has created the climate for evasion. The accomplices in Roatta's flight are men who are still in high places, and who feared the revelations he would make—"

And *Hush,* said the furtive silence in Valdarno's face, *hush, hush now, Mario. These things are true, they are all true, but before the British uniform they cannot be said.* And Colonel Sarett sat, leaning forward, his fingers interlaced, his eyes on Mario.

"The farce we are enacting here in Italy—the farce, instead of serious, responsible theatre," Mario was saying, "the monstrous farce of purging ourselves clean! Do you know how many public figures southern Italy has executed?" he said, and he looked at us, half-smiling. "One, precisely one," he said, and he lifted the forefinger of his right hand. "Free Italy has executed one man of all those accused of specific crimes committed at a specific time. At his trial Roatta, former Italian Chief of Staff, head of the Military Intelligence Office, one of the most iniquitous and murderous organizations in the world, Lieutenant General Roatta testified that he had organized two Fascist brigades called the Black Arrows and the Blue Arrows to support Franco, but declared that he himself was neither Fascist nor anti-Fascist but an Italian general who obeyed his government whatever its color might be. He said that he had once helped many Polish soldiers and more than five thousand Jews who were wanted by the Nazis. Do you see how they are going to try to save their skins?" said Mario. "Now if our slate is to be sponged clean," he said, and his clear, dark, sober eyes were on me, "then one must begin at the top and wash down the slate, as we did when we were school children. Thus, we should begin with the King—only, of course, that is absolutely unheard of. Too many Englishmen like our King—they are really devoted to our King. So, obviously, we cannot begin at all."

Hush, said the unspoken anguish in Valdarno's face. *Do not bare yourself like this before him. Do not betray us all into his hands.* "And the King," Mario went on, "recognizing himself in private as the perfect representation of our public treason and shame, hastily retired, hoping that if he got out of sight quickly enough the Italian people would not have the time to get a really good look at what he was. He decided, our little King, he decided very quaintly and humanly that it would be very silly indeed to execute himself, and probably quite unnecessary," Mario said, and then, abruptly, he ceased speaking, and the humor was gone, and only the bitterness was left to pull at the corners of his young mouth. *To execute himself,* said the silence; *to execute himself,* and Mario sat motionless, and he stared straight at the floor. And it might have been that the figure of Michele lay there on the boards, in the little lake of blood as he had found him eight years before—lay there, eternally nineteen, eternally silent, the voice no longer impatiently asking for tennis shoes for the Fascist relay races, and the pistol lying near his hand.

"You know, here in Italy a great many good and brave people have died," Mario said. "They died," he said, "and their lives and their deaths have become the words of a kind of vocabulary of violence for us, and now there is no other vocabulary that men of honor can use—"

And *Hush, do not say it so loudly,* said Valdarno's eyes as they moved in trepidation from Mario's to the colonel's face. *We have come through prison, starvation, through torture for it. Do not give it all away to him now, do not lay your heart in his hand.*

"We speak the same language," Colonel Sarett said, and because of the modest sound of petition in what he said, it might have been he who wore the thin-soled, ancient shoes and the shabby coat. *Allow me,* he did not add, *to address you not as a unit, but as a man. Overlook the khaki and tin and the record,* his humility asked of them, but he did not say the words aloud.

"And yet one would scarcely say that it was English," said Mario bitterly. "Roatta's escape was a match set to tinder, as you said—Fascist riots in prison, buses turned over and burned. The police have been denying ever since the alleged mass escapes from the Soriano nel Cimino and the Vierbo prisons, and when a situation comes to the point of denials, it means that something is about to happen. It will have to happen—it will have to happen in spite of the English and because of the English, in order to save Italy from the fate of Greece—"

Hush, for God's sake, keep quiet, said Valdarno's agitated silence, and he turned one more look of desperation on Mario. Then he leaned toward me and spoke a few low, hurried words across the light. "And France?" he said. "In France how is the *épuration* going?"

I said there were trials, sentences passed, executions every week: prefects, mayors, journalists—the little men. The big men in France had not yet been touched—the industrialists were still to be taken into custody. And as I spoke, Valdarno watched the shape of the words on my lips and shaped them in silence with his own; watching eagerly, harking, waiting for the small, faint sound of promise or hope that might be in them, as a famished man might wait at a table for what crumbs of sustenance might fall.

"Puységur has been condemned to death," I said. "Stéphane Lauzanne has been given twenty years' hard labor. General Pinsard escaped capital punishment. No one quite knows why. Two of Mandel's murderers are to be executed—"

It was like a bar of music begun, the notes struck separately, precisely, but not completed, and as I ceased speaking, the rest of the tune hung curiously unplayed between us on the air. They ask for purity, the young men of Europe, I thought; they ask for the *épuration* of their countries and their souls.

Valdarno leaned one emaciated arm in the gray tweed jacket on the table beneath the light, and his long, fleshless fingers tapped quickly, nervously on the wood.

"Signora, we are not like the French," he said in a low voice, looking as if in entreaty at me. "We are less spirited, humbler, and we have been cripples for a quarter of a century now. We have been very ill," he said, and his bright red lips were trembling with intensity. "We still are not quite able to get up from bed and make our way across the room to the window where we know the light and air must be. Signora," he said, "we are just beginning to get well again, we are just learning now to get our pride back, but we are still unsteady when we try to stand alone. We need you, you Americans. Do not leave us yet. We need you until we can learn to do the mere physical things, like eating and drinking, for ourselves again. Signora," he said, and the wounds were there, unhealed still, the avowal of their pain marked in his eyes. "Do not leave us, you Americans. Do not leave us for a little while—"

"Blast it, there's no need to ask favors of any of us," Colonel Sarett cried out, and he jumped up from his chair. "The number of patriots fighting the Germans in northern Italy is twice that of the Italian regular army troops." He paced back and forth, impatient now with inaction, back and forth across the floor. "I tell you I've got an army up there on the front, an army that is fighting, damn it, bearing arms and fighting. We have camps set up where we're reclothing, re-equipping them as fast as they come. I'm talking of Italians, Italian partisans," he cried out. "They've established their own airfields at Cuneo and Pinerolo— behind the enemy lines. That's a resistance movement for you. More than two hundred and fifty thousand of them dead, resisting—"

"My sister and brother died with them," Valdarno said, and his pale hand on the table trembled, and the lamp's light shone dimly on his bloodless nails.

"Look here, Signor," said Colonel Sarett, and his voice was quieter now. He sat down on the chair again before Valdarno, leaning forward, the singular fire and vision in his eye. "There's a question on the boards now about a batch of Italian POWs interned down south. I want to get them, give them a battlefront, make men out of them," he said.

"What kind of men?" asked Valdarno, and his black, desperate eyes were halted as if in fear on the colonel.

"Men," said the colonel impatiently. "Men taking their part in this bloody show. Thirty thousand of them," he said, and he leaned forward, watching Valdarno eagerly. "I'm going to try through channels to get hold of them, fit them out, march them up here into the mountains with me—"

"And when the war is finished," said Mario's bitter voice; "when the north of Italy is liberated and they and the other free men come marching down on Rome to protest our decadent government, will British machine guns be turned on them as they were turned on the people of Greece?"

"If they turn their blasted machine guns on the partisans," said Colonel Sarett, and he had got to his feet again, "then they'll turn them on me as well, for I'll be marching with them. Out of thirty thousand," he went back to it as he paced in the room, "we can count on a third of them at least being rebels, and that leaves two-thirds of them fools, but rebels are far more eloquent than fools, and they'll do the job, a smashing job," he said.

"What job?" asked Valdarno, and his voice was cautious, and his eye was on the colonel warily.

"The job of saving a country, blast it. This country, Italy," the colonel cried out, and when I looked at Valdarno, I saw that the thing had happened to him: he had dropped his head forward on his hand, and the tears were running down his face.

Summer Evening

Toward seven o'clock of a dreamy, bluish summer evening, the cocktail party, which was taking place at a terraced villa overlooking the eleventh-century Hessian town across the valley, was well under way. The first guests had come scarcely an hour before, driving up the hill in their shining American cars, and now, some in uniform, others in civilian clothes, they strolled out through the long open windows onto the gravel of the upper terrace, bearing their frosted glasses with them and talking and laughing as they came. On the opposite hill, the ancient *Schloss* rose, sombre and monumental, above the treetops, its façade and turrets turned toward the widening river valley, appearing to watch, as it had watched century after century, for armored knights on horseback to take shape in the twilight of the distance, or for armored vehicles and low-flying planes to advance, as they had come in April, four years before, out of the area of perpetual dusk that lay fifteen or twenty miles away.

Except for the German musicians, who bent their heads to violin and zither and accordion, and for the *Hausmeister*, in his starched white jacket, who moved among the guests, there were only Americans present, and it was their voices, both men's and women's, and their laughter that rang out above the tender striving of the instruments as the music cast its spell of longing on the summery air. For the uniformed men who leaned on the balustrade or who strolled on the terrace were officers of the American Army of Occupation, and the civilians were men attached to the Military Government offices—men, some with wives and some without, whom the call of duty had brought to this defeated land. But to anyone passing on the road below the garden wall it might have seemed that it was the Americans who were at ease on a familiar soil and the musicians, playing their nostalgic music, who were exiled from a homeland that lay far across the sea.

"You have to be as careful about who you take for a *Hausmeister* as who you marry," Major Hatches was saying to the view of the peaceful valley and the town and the domineering *Schloss* above it. He was a handsome figure of an officer, probably forty-five but appearing younger, standing, spruce and lean in his green blouse and his pinks, against the deepening tide of twilight, with his glass held in his boyish hand. "You have him underfoot twenty-four hours every day of the week," he was saying to the pretty women— Occupation wives with brightly painted mouths and glossy hair—and to the younger officers in the group around him by the balustrade. "He knows how many cigarette stubs you can be counted on leaving in which ashtrays between the morning shower and the time you leave the house," the Major said, and he took a chopped-egg-and-anchovy canapé from the platter before it passed from reach.

"Fellow I knew down in Nuremberg used to fox his *Hausmeister* every time," said Lieutenant Pearson, already beginning, or perhaps never, even in sleep, having quite ceased, to laugh. He stood six feet tall, and despite his youth three rolls of flesh lay on his jacket collar, for his good nature had larded him since childhood with excessive fat. "Used to drop his stubs out of the window, so the guy'd have to crawl through the shrubbery for them," he said, shaking with laughter, and he drew one plump hand across the bristles of his close-cropped hair.

"That's not according to Hoyle," said the Major, whatever there was of reprimand in it tempered by his smile. "It's one of the articles of the Occupation Statute that you leave your cigarette stubs in plain sight," he said, and the group around joined in Lieutenant Pearson's laughter. He stood there shaking, with his cheeks squeezed up as if in actual pain. "A *Hausmeister*'ll make enough out of what's left in the ashtrays after one of these shindigs to keep him in luxury six months," the Major went on. He jerked his chin after the stooped man in the clean white jacket who bore the platter of canapés from guest to animated guest—an aging man, with his legs warped in his shrunk cotton trousers, and his thin gray hair combed neatly on his skull. "Ours has to be watched. He has a weakness for the bottle," he said, and he drank from the depths of the ice-and-fruit-encumbered glass he held.

Beyond them, in the thick of the fray, Mrs. Hatches flew at her guests with cries of pleasure, her bosom swollen like a pigeon's in her flowered dress. She was older than the Major, and she bore the knowledge of this with some hysteria, painting her soft-jowled face high in denial of it and tinting her iron-gray hair blue.

"That's twice you-all gave you' wud you'd come on ovah and play bridge with the Majah and me!" she might cry aloud as she fled among them, but it was not their faces that had meaning for her. While the Major was a lieutenant still, her blank, dazzled eyes had been blinded to recognition of any man's or woman's features, placing them only by company and field grade, so civilians always troubled her. "You promised me that lemon-meringue recipe two weeks ago," she might cry out in her uncertainty, "an' you nevah kep' you' wud!"

But because of the longing of the music and the gentleness of the evening the attention of the guests was not held by these subjects but wandered to far sweeter and stranger things. The men's thoughts were concerned with the charm of the women in their fresh light dresses, and their unexpected beauty in the fading light, and the women, drinking quickly, viewed with excitement the homage offered in the men's attentive faces, knowing that in this interval all dreams and all desire were contained in the rising and falling of their laughter, and in the stirring of their limbs within their clothes. There was, for instance, Marcia Cruickshank, lying back in the wicker chair, drinking her drink, and looking in lazy shamelessness at the young man seated on the terrace balustrade.

"You're new," she said, liking the bronze of sunburn on his hands and neck and brow.

"Berlin," he said. He was wearing a well-cut navy-blue suit and a conservative tie, with the white of his silk shirt pleasing to see against the clear brown of his skin. He had lit a cigarette now, and he sat looking down at Marcia Cruickshank, whose eyes were wide-set in her blond, Nordic face, eyes aquamarine in color and transparent. Beneath them, her high cheekbones were flushed with the fever of either drink or love.

"I've been here a year. I'm going crazy," she said, her voice husky and low. Her arms were naked to the shoulder and as white as milk, and her hair was brushed up, light and silky, on her head. Her legs were stretched from under the gray stuff of her dress, long and smooth-skinned, and the young man followed the line of them with his cool, dark, diabolical eyes. "So tan, aren't you? So really athletic?" said Marcia Cruickshank, her voice too languorous for mockery.

"Tennis," the young man said, not looking at her face.

"Oh, God! When you're not married, there's time for everything," she said, saying it softly, lazily, still, but speaking bitterly.

"Not quite for everything," the young man said. He might have been asking her now for what he wanted of her, except for the casualness of his hand as he tapped the ashes from his cigarette. "I'm with Intelligence," he said quietly. "That means eighteen hours a day. I've never had time, for example, to play house with anyone like you."

But the *Hausmeister* had come between them now, and the young man took a canapé from his platter, and Marcia Cruickshank stirred in the deep-seated wicker chair and offered the *Hausmeister* a Camel from her pack. He had a queer sort of twist to his body, which gave him a dwarfed, gnomelike look, it being doubtless lumbago that had closed on the small of his back a long time since and caused his spine to slip a vertebra or two. His false teeth were bared in his leathery face, in a grimace intended to express his deference, and he quivered with pleasure when Marcia Cruickshank reached out her hand, with the finger-nails varnished scarlet on it, and laid it on his arm.

"For God's sake, go and have yourself an Old-Fashioned, Pop," she said. "Just get behind the pantry door and have a quick one. It's the only way to beat the rap," she said.

"Old Pop's O.K.," said the *Hausmeister*, but a bead of self-commiseration stood bright in the corner of each eye. "Good German music. Makes Pop remember other times," he said. He shifted the platter of canapés from one hand to the other to take the cigarette from her pack. "Everything bombed out. Everything lost. Nothing left to Pop," he said. When he had put the cigarette into his jacket pocket, he pulled himself nearly erect, brought his heels together, and saluted Marcia Cruickshank with his stiffly cupped right hand brought smartly from temple to brow.

"Now give it a rest, dear," said Marcia Cruickshank wearily, and the young man sitting on the balustrade turned his head to watch the *Hausmeister* sidle humbly, grievously, away.

"Pretty tough on some of these old boys," the young man said, and Marcia Cruickshank looked lazily up at him, at the line of his throat and jaw, and the cool, dark, diabolical eyes.

"Probably had great, big, luxurious concentration camps of their own once," she said, putting a catch of emotion in her voice. "And now what have they got? Nothing but Scotch and rye."

"Your glass is empty, Mrs. Cruickshank. It is *Mrs.* Cruickshank, isn't it?" he said.

"I wish to God it wasn't," said Marcia Cruickshank, in sudden bitterness. "I like to look at you. I like to listen to you."

"I'm going to get us another drink. We can talk better after another drink," he said, and he slid down from the balustrade.

"Don't go," whispered Marcia Cruickshank, scarcely aloud. "For God's sake, don't go."

Captain Pete Forsythe stood a little apart from the central groups of animation, his back leaning in comfort against the grapevine whose pallid, flexile leaves spread across this side of the house. He was nursing a glass of Scotch-and-soda in one hand, his mouth smiling gently, his half-closed eyes reflecting on the beauty of the valley, as the young man in the dark-blue suit came past in search of drink.

"I'm against it. I'm against organized, uniformed annihilation," Captain Forsythe said, in a quiet voice. He was slight, sandy-haired, and barely thirty, and he had stopped the young man who was passing merely by looking straight into his eyes.

"That depends on who gets annihilated," said the young man, making it light, but his glance was tense as it moved across the people, seeking the *Hausmeister* out.

"Over there," said Captain Forsythe, his voice gentle as he looked across the valley to where the *Schloss* stood, drawn in sharp relief now against the yellowish sky, "over there—the other side of the hill—there's a tank, a big Sherman tank, rusted and gutted and turned on its back, with field flowers growing through the carcass of it. I saw it when I rode through the country one day last week. It made me think of the wreckage of fighter planes that we used to see in the fields near Carthage— engines and fuselage more archaic than the two-thousand-year-old stone plows the oxen were dragging through the soil perhaps five yards away. The meaningless paraphernalia of war," said Captain Forsythe, as if speaking from a dream, and the young man's cool, dark eyes surveyed him carefully, with a certain shrewdness even, as the Captain lifted his glass to drink. Had it not been for Mrs. Hatches, he might have encouraged the Captain to go on with it, but Mrs. Hatches had run toward them, crying aloud, the gravel and her heels conniving to produce her wild, unbalanced gait.

"Why, that's agains' all the rewls!" she cried out. "The tew of you standin' up theyah talkin' togetheh, sobah as jedges, and one without a glass to cheah him! Now, we cain't have anythin' like that!" she cried, and her eye, too, was sharp for where the *Hausmeister* might be. Because she was drawn to no man's flesh in lust or love, and no man's flesh was drawn to hers, nothing remained to her but to flee like one possessed among the drinking, laughing people, as if in flight before the lonely spectre of old age. She would seize up empty glasses to fill them anew, crying the *Hausmeister's* name aloud in panic when she could not find the stooped white shoulders of his jacket sidling through the dusk; calling him to bear more sausages stabbed with toothpicks out, more brimming glasses, and to pass them with greater speed among the guests, urging him to race, neck and neck, with her on the homestretch of social vigilance before the field grades would begin to go. If ever she let him from her sight, she knew he would sidle to the whining of the music, to the rear, and get one or two drinks down behind the kitchen door. "Now let's the three of us—Pete Fo'sythe and you and me—" Mrs. Hatches began, but was interrupted by the personable young man whose civilian rating she did not know.

"Please allow me to go for the drinks," the young man said, and he escaped them, making note of the name Forsythe and thinking in controlled hot passion of Marcia Cruickshank's milk-white legs and her naked arms as he stepped in absolute composure through the long window, which stood open like a door.

Captain Pete Forsythe, still leaning against the vine leaves, lifted his glass and drank before he spoke. "You're standing on my wife," he said in his quiet voice, and Mrs. Hatches looked behind her hastily and gave a loud, apologetic cry. There, on a garden footstool, obscured by the vines and by the gathering darkness, sat a slender, fawn-eyed girl in a low-cut scarlet dress, with the lengths of it spread around her on the pebbled ground. "My wife has been crying," said Captain Forsythe, with the contemplative smile on his tilted mouth. "We read Proust until late last night, and the world was recreated. Then you come awake."

"Oh, Pete, Pete, my love," said Mrs. Forsythe from where she sat, below them, "I'm not crying for a dream. The dreams are finished. They've all curdled in my heart," she said. She was perhaps twenty, with a teenlike thinness in her bones still, and her face was as delicate as a flower, with the fawn eyes and the soft mouth too big, too vulnerable, in it, and filled now with a passionate gravity. Behind each ear was thrust a fragrant live rose of the same rich color as her dress, and these held back her feathery dark hair. "I'm weak as water. I hate it, but I'm weak," she said, and she looked up in supplication at the faces that were there above. "I'm crying for a reality, Mrs. Hatches, not for a dream that Proust lived once. I'm crying for the whooping cranes, who stand as tall as the Indians who hunted them, and who are going to die."

"Wendy, I don't think you' feelin' quite yo'self," the Major's wife said. "Let's you and I go inside the house togetheh and have a cup of coffee, jus' us tew," she said, but Mrs. Forsythe might not have heard her speak.

"I don't want a world like this," she said. "I don't want a world in which birds who stand as tall as men are wiped away."

"Pete Fo'sythe, you git along and git yo'self anotheh drink while I have a little talk with Wendy," Mrs. Hatches said, but Captain Forsythe did not go. He set his empty glass down on the window sill beside him, instead, and he folded his arms across the breast of his battle jacket, and his head moved to the pain and beauty of the music that the violin and zither and accordion played.

"Like the Labrador duck, the passenger pigeon, and the heath hen," he said, saying it slowly, like the words of a line of poetry he was trying to recall, "like the great auk, and the ivory-billed woodpecker, like man himself, the whooping crane is doomed to go." He leaned back at his ease against the wall, his half-closed eyes looking past the talking, drinking people on the terrace, which was partially lit now from the lamps that had been lighted, one by one, within the house as the twilight died. The outline of the hills that enclosed the valley was gone, and the *Schloss* was lost in darkness, and the musicians' instruments cried sweetly, piercingly, in the night for the look of one city, for the streets and the parks, for the stones and the trees, the wine cellars, the palaces, the wit, and the women of Vienna, as the stars came, far and isolate, into the Hessian sky. But Captain Forsythe's thoughts had nothing to do with these things, this place; it was the vast expanse of another country that he saw stretching away. "The wheat growers came down across the plains and the marshes and the open prairies," he was saying softly, "and the whooping crane lost its breeding ground. Like the Indian, the bison, the poets, their time is finished. There is no role left for them to play."

"So they are asked to take their wingspread somewhere else," said Mrs. Forsythe. She sat on the footstool below them still, pressing her two hands tight between her knees. "It's pure white and greater than an archangel's, but there is no place but extinction left for it to go. I read about one, Mrs. Hatches, who had lost an eye and broken a wing, and they put him in a refuge," she said, speaking quickly. "They offered him the Mackenzie Delta, and Iowa, and a part of western Illinois, and the region stretching from southwestern Louisiana to Mexico. Because that's what they'll do for you when you can't fly any more and are nearly extinct," she said, her voice almost breaking with its grief. "But it wasn't that that he wanted, Mrs. Hatches. He wanted a mate, he wanted a wife, so the kind of thing they had been for centuries wouldn't have to be extinct," and her tears began to fall.

"He wanted a thin, sweet wife," said Captain Forsythe softly, "with red roses stuck behind her ears."

A feeling of space, of peace, seemed to spread across the terrace now; it might have been that a burden had been lifted, that they were given air to breathe, for the guests were thinning out at last. Mrs. Hatches' glance fled here and there in inquiry, noted that Colonel and Mrs. Smith and the senior Military Government officer and his wife no longer stood chatting by the balustrade, and that the Major stood on the stone steps that led down to the drive, which curved below the lower terrace, calling goodbye to the headlights of the departing cars. The *Hausmeister,* thought Mrs. Hatches, in sudden panic, and she began to run from uniform to uniform, insignia to insignia again, among the scattered people who remained. The *Hausmeister,* she thought, with determination, her eyes outraged by the overturned glasses, the cluttered ashtrays, the canapé platters littered with olive stones and soiled by mayonnaise. The music came abruptly to an end, for Lieutenant Pearson had taken the violin from the musician's hands and now sought to accompany on the delicate catgut strings his own loud, jovial rendering of "Clementine."

"How'm I doin'?" he called out to Mrs. Hatches as she passed, his flesh convulsed with laughter.

"Why, fine, jes' fine!" said Mrs. Hatches, crossing the gravel on her high, unsteady heels. As she reached the long open window that served as door, Captain Cruickshank came through it, his young eyes bloodshot, holding his wife upright against him, urging her limp legs to bear her on at least as far as the driveway and the car. Marcia Cruickshank's mouth was clean of lipstick, her eyes were sightless, and her face was bleached colorless from drink.

"It happens every damned time. Every damned time we go out, it happens," said Captain Cruickshank, swaying forward. In the brief moment that they faltered there, Captain Cruickshank's face was not that of an officer any longer but of a tired, disappointed boy, perhaps having learned just then, at that instant, that the ball game had been called off forever, the swimming hole been permanently drained dry. "She ought to stick to lemonade," said Captain Cruickshank, and Mrs. Hatches smiled politely and hurried past them, her voice quite musical as she called out the *Hausmeister's* name.

But even after the other guests and the musicians were gone, Lieutenant Pearson and the young man in the dark-blue suit lingered by the balustrade. The Major had offered them a final drink, and as they talked together on the half-lit terrace the young man rubbed discreetly with his Scotch-plaid handkerchief in quiet colors at the stain of lip salve that lingered on his mouth. The Major was speaking in satisfaction of antiques to them, his tongue only slightly thick as he said the collecting of antique silver and handmade linens and porcelain was one of the artistic pursuits that he and Mrs. Hatches shared.

"We picked up some very fine pieces over here while times were hard still," the Major said, standing tall and elegant and almost steady against the stars. "Museum pieces, in their way. I'd like to show them to you sometime. We've got a Biedermeier silver coffee set that had been handed down from one generation to the next, without a scratch on it. And my wife got hold of a seventy-four-piece Dresden dinner service with gold inlay. I know they're going to mean a lot to us when we get home," he said.

"I see you're a connoisseur," said the young man in the navy-blue suit, and he folded his handkerchief carefully and put it away. "Let me tell you that Berlin's the territory for the man who's got a flair. They're still pretty hungry over there, so they come to terms without too much of an argument." His tanned face was illuminated for an instant as he took a light from the match Lieutenant Pearson held. "I picked up a tablecloth from a professor's wife last week who'd spent twenty years making it. Every inch of it lace. You'd appreciate it, Major. Experts tell me it's a thing that would bring five to six hundred dollars at home." The Major gave a long, slow whistle as he poured them each another drink. "I got it for a song," the young man said.

"Which one?" asked Lieutenant Pearson, his eyes squeezed small by his firm, shining cheeks, his mouth distorted by his silent mirth. " 'Lili Marlene' or 'Dinah, Won't You Blow'?"

"They'll part with their back teeth if you have coffee or lard," the young man said, in answer.

"Just for future reference, in tins or in the bean?" the Major said.

"They don't make conditions over there. The market's good still," said the young man sitting smoking on the balustrade.

It was then that the *Hausmeister* appeared before them, having arisen, it seemed, from the shrubbery of the terrace below. He came, weary and stooped, his starched white jacket shining like moonlight in the dark, his warped legs rocking under him, emerging from the deep, cool well of night and coming up the stone steps from the drive.

"Pop, I bet you've been snaring cigarette stubs again!" said Lieutenant Pearson, beginning to laugh.

"Pop, come and have a drink," Major Hatches said, in kindness, at the sight of him standing there, leather-skinned, gnome-wizened, small.

"Major, I want to speak to you," the *Hausmeister* said, his bright, grieving eyes, which belied the deferential eternal grimace of the china teeth, turned sharp now as he watched the Major pour the whiskey unsteadily out. "I'm American man. I want to go home to U.S.A."

"American?" said the Major. He handed the glass to the *Hausmeister*, and then he turned to the balustrade and set the bottle down.

"Sure, and I'm Rooshun," said Lieutenant Pearson, and he

rubbed his big, dimpled hands together in delight. "Paderewski, *nyet, stoi,* Henry Wallace!"

"My mother, she American woman," said the *Hausmeister,* the glass of whiskey swinging in his aged, gnarled hand. "She *geboren* New Joisey. She no Joiman. She married wid a Joiman."

"Now, let's get this straight," said the Major. He could hear his wife calling the *Hausmeister's* name as she stood in the long open window for a moment, and then she must have perceived him standing there drinking with the others, for she turned back in to the lighted living room again. "You say your mother was born in New Jersey, Pop," the Major said, but he felt too weary, too confused, to bother with any of it any more.

"I *geboren* in New Joisey by my mother," the *Hausmeister* said, with a certain ferocity. "Den my father, he take us to Joimany." After he had said this, he looked in sudden, bleak appeal at the three men there before him. "I want American passport. I go home to U.S.A.," he said.

"Sure," said Lieutenant Pearson, and he gave the Major a wink. "Sure you do, Pop," he said. He lifted one soft, heavy arm in his battle jacket, and laid it around the shoulders of the young man in the dark-blue suit, by this gesture abruptly dwarfing him, making a frail and irresolute figure of him merely by the proximity of his own outlandish weight and size. "Here's who you want to talk to," said Lieutenant Pearson. "Here's the American Consul General, just in from Berlin. Here's the only man in the E.C. who can get a passport for you overnight," he said, for once not laughing, for once the hard-packed rolls and creases of his swollen face immobilized by gravity.

"No kiddin'?" the *Hausmeister* said. For an instant, the warped legs ceased to rock.

"Cross my heart, hope to die," said Lieutenant Pearson, saying it as a boy might have, not as a drunk man seeking to maintain with dignity a fat boy's innocent, unsmiling mien. He looked down at the young man, his arm half crippled, half embraced. "How about it, Consul General?" he said.

They did not know it was going to be like this; they did not expect the *Hausmeister* to cry any more than they expected him to say his age was seventy-three. But once the young man had accepted the role of Consul General, the thing had already gone beyond them; it had become, of its own momentum, something that two other men were acting out on another terrace, with no sense and no humor in it, and no way to bring it to an end. The young man in civilian dress had found a bridge score card in his pocket, and as the *Hausmeister* gave them to him, he set the names, the dates, the two words of a place, "New Joisey," spelling it like that, on the lines of the score card, with the greatest care.

"You get me passport? You get me passport to U.S.A.?" the *Hausmeister* asked, watching the hieroglyphics being written down.

"Sure, he's going to give you a passport. He's going to give you a passport, Pop. Now all you need is an airline ticket," Lieutenant Pearson said. The waves of nausea were rising in him, the taste bad in his mouth. And then the sobs began to rip from the *Hausmeister's* breast, the sound of them akin to foolish laughter, and the tears of helpless gratitude streamed from his eyes. "You just get four photographs taken," Lieutenant Pearson said, and whatever it was that had sustained him until now collapsed within him, and he slid down between the young man and the Major and came to rest on the gravel of the terrace, his head and shoulders at ease against the pillars of the balustrade.

"Stop crying!" the Major roared suddenly, and the *Hausmeister* drew himself nearly erect, put his empty glass in his left hand as he brought his heels together, lifted his chin, raised his right arm in the starched white sleeve, and cupped his hand stiffly at his temple, in salute. "Seventy-three, and crying like a child!" the Major said. He reached out and took the score card from the young man's hand. "We'll have another drink around, and then we'll put Pearson and ourselves to bed," he said, and he tore the score card in two. Then he stood motionless, silent, a moment, not only surveying the men before him but looking in wonder and question· upon himself as well. *What are we doing here, any of us?* he asked himself, in sudden bewilderment, almost in fright. *What has become of the lot of us here?* "Go get some soda and ice in the kitchen, Pop," he said.

"Forsythe, Captain Pete Forsythe," said the young man in the dark-blue suit, and it might have been this, or something like it, that he had been saying all the time. He took his cigarette case out of his pocket and offered it to the Major before he selected one himself, watching the *Hausmeister* weave his way over the terrace toward the lighted windows of the house. "Seems a bit on the appeasing side—Captain Forsythe—doesn't he, Major?" he said.

The Criminal

The family had lived since May in the pleasant, sun-filled house on the German hillside—a house that might have fitted into the setting of a shabby, obsolescent Hollywood—with long, wide windows on the south side, facing the softness of the river valley, standing a little lower than the eleventh-century castle that rose in dignity on the opposite hill, above the gray roofs of the town. Although the house had a forest behind it and a road instead of a street before it, it could not rightly be called isolated, and if the mother and father felt that it was so, it was more because every American who took part in the Occupation of this country felt within himself this sense of isolation from everything that he had known before. In the mornings, the father of the family would rub an American-brand shaving cream onto his jaw and chin and shave with blue blades, as he would have done at home, and then he would put on the same clothes and eat the same breakfast as he would have had he been catching the eight-fifteen from Scarsdale. But it was not home, and the destination was not Grand Central. The look of the world outside the windows was different, and the taste of the air when he stepped out onto the balcony was not the same. It was a former Nazi *Block-wart's* house in which the family lived, and the place to which the father drove at eight-thirty every weekday morning was Military Government buildings, with the American flag on the tall white flagstaff—where the swastika had hung once—fixed in the plot of grass before the guarded door.

The first-floor windows of the hillside house were barred, like the windows of a prison, as if the Nazi from whom the place had been requisitioned had himself feared what lay outside. But the second-floor windows, where the balconies were, were quite without protection, and because of the record of what had taken place in other houses where American families lived, the father of the family had hung the Walther pistol that he had liberated in 1945 in its leather holster by his bed, and the ammunition lay ready in the table drawer.

"There was Pritchard," the father said, telling the story to the mother soon after they came. "He'd come back from skiing in Switzerland, after Easter, and he had his right arm in plaster, having fractured it out there. It was still in plaster the night he woke up and heard someone walking around downstairs. He told his wife to stay with the baby, and he took his pistol in his left hand, and when he got halfway down the stairs, the first shot passed him." The man who had broken in had shot it out for twenty minutes with Pritchard before taking off, the father said, and neither had hit the other, but there were two holes left in one windowpane, and the mirror over the hall mantel had lost a corner where a bullet struck it. "He got away," the father said, and the children listened to the story, but without much interest. It had not happened in their time or in this house; it was somebody else's history. "He ran off through the fields, whoever he was," said the father. "In the morning, they could see his footsteps marked clearly in the dew."

There were other stories—stories the children heard or overheard as they went about their own affairs. There was the one about another man the father had known before they came—an American called Johnson, who had a turquoise-blue Ford car. One night in April, as he drove from one town to another on the Autobahn, the headlights of his car must have picked out the figure of a man standing there with his hand raised—so the police had reconstructed it—a disreputable figure, they knew for certain, asking for a ride.

"And Johnson must have stopped, poor guy," the father said, telling the story to two Army men who were dining with them on the terrace in the dusk, "and he must have taken the German in on the seat beside him, because that's where the dead German was sitting, in his rags, when they found the wreck next day. The car had jumped the ditch and smashed head on into the iron pole of a deer-crossing sign, and Johnson himself was dead behind the wheel." The father poured fresh drinks into the officers' glasses and into the mother's glass and into his own. "But it wasn't the accident that had killed him. He'd been stabbed three times, in the ribs, as he drove, and the knife was in the German's hand still, and Johnson's wallet and papers in the inside pocket of the German's coat."

"He couldn't have had much use for them where he was going," one of the Army officers said, and the other one in uniform laughed, but there had been no sound of amusement in it in the twilight.

"Perhaps Heaven and Hell stopped coming into their calculations a long time back," the father said in bitterness, for Johnson had been his friend, and he didn't like the way he had died.

It was only the children of the family who did not feel the sense of isolation, for they were too young to miss the soda-water fountains or the baseball games of home. Behind the house, the woods rose, tree by tree and path by tortuous path—leafy and murmurous, half shade, half light, all summer. It did not matter to the children that the great stones that stood at the entrance to the caves that had served as air-raid shelters once were engraved with savagely hooked crosses, or that they lived in an alien country, among alien men. For the children shared the life of their mother and their father in this house, as if it were a place they had chosen themselves, not knowing—or caring, had they known —that it had been confiscated from its owner, a man who had, in the war years, eavesdropped at the doors of neighbors for the sound of Allied broadcasts and turned in the names of the offenders to the local authorities.

The owner's name was there still, in brass plates on both the front and kitchen doors, and the owner himself was not an unknown figure to the family. He could be seen from time to time in the garden or the orchard, a heavy man wearing the traditional Hessian gray-and-green forester's jacket, with his white hair clipped so close on his long, tapering skull that bony protuberances were bared below the brim of the small green felt hat, in the space above the rosy, white-bristled rolls of flesh that trimmed the collar of his coat. To his hatband was affixed a *Saubart*, which, even when he stooped to his work, stood upright in still glossy, still untempered arrogance. They had seen him first in May, with his heavy-limbed daughters, breaking sprays of lilac from the bushes by the front-garden gate, for, provided the current tenants did not object, it was permitted the owners of these properties to plant and tend and take the produce of the gardens that were, for the moment, no longer theirs. And the father could find no reason to object, for the *Blockwart* had had his trial and paid his fine, and when the Occupation was done, the house would again be his. So in June they saw him come for the vegetables—the radishes and lettuce and young carrots—and for the giant, drooping mauve poppies and the jasmine and peonies, and in July, with his forester's coat folded over his arm and his long, naked skull flushed red with heat, he came for the roses and red currants, and in August for the firm purple plums and the string beans, and in September, with a hand-drawn wagon, for the apples and the pears and the potatoes, while his daughters, with baskets over their arms, plucked the bunches of white grapes from the vines that hung heavy across the kitchen windows and shaded the balconies with green. Whatever the month, they left nothing of its bounty behind them—not a plum or a grape or a currant for the conquerors—bearing even the goldenrod, in great armfuls, down the dusty road.

But now the summer was through, and the children believed in another world entirely—in a world of acorns and horse chestnuts and of white-breasted squirrels flashing, red as fire, through the forest trees. In the house that belonged to them now, there were sheepnose apples from the American commissary, and peanut butter, as thick as clay, in glass jars on the pantry shelf. Not until the tall, thin man came to the basement kitchen door one morning did they think of hunger or of anyone's wanting the things they had. The man wore a torn khaki shirt and Wehrmacht trousers and a battered felt hat, of the quality of a soiled and ancient hound's ear, with the limp brim hanging low across the caverns of his eyes. He came to the kitchen door, and he asked the mother, saying some of the words in German and some in English, for the spade the owner of the house had told him was in the cellar, and as he spoke, he hitched up, with the inside of one big, bony wrist, the stained and faded trousers that wouldn't stay where they were intended to, because of the substance of his body, which hunger had hacked away. He said the owner of the house—and one soiled, thin finger pointed to the brass plaque on the door—had sent him to dig out what remained of the potatoes. The plants had already been uprooted and the best of the potatoes carried away, but he was to pick up the ones that had shaken loose in the soil, and the owner would pay him five marks for the work he did.

"Maybe he'll give me something to eat, too," he said, and there in the dark caverns of his eyes they saw the lurking thing come furtively to life and wait in trembling, bleak pain.

In the kitchen, there was the smell of eggs and bacon frying, and of cocoa warming, for the mother was making breakfast, and whether or not the children understood the words he spoke of food, they could not mistake the meaning that was in his face. To them, it seemed that if he could not have a little of what they were about to eat, then the sharp bones of his big hands and wrists would break through the useless, fleshless skin to get at what they wanted. The mother thought of the stories that had been told, and because the father was not there, she did not ask the thin man to come in. Instead, she went through the kitchen to the cellar, and she carried the spade back to him. The thin man looked at them for a moment out of the deep pits of his eyes —looking strangely, almost timidly at them—and then his long, bloodless fingers closed on the handle of the spade, and they saw him turn away.

He worked all day in the plot behind the house, turning the earth slowly, laboriously, and stooping to pick the earth-clotted potatoes out. And once, when the children passed near him, following the flight of the squirrels in the first of the forest trees, he leaned on the handle of the spade and tried to ask questions of them. Perhaps he was asking from what city they had come and by what means they had travelled, and then he seemed to speak to them of the city or country he himself had come from, for he

flung his arm out toward the distance, toward places that lay beyond the river valley and beyond the yellow, wooded hills.
When he saw that they did not understand his words, he made
the motions of walking, bending his long, spare legs in the
threadbare trousers, the boots, laced with knotted string, coming
down in the same places in the earth of the potato patch, coming
down over and over in dogged resolution, over and over without
pause, until the children who watched him felt the weariness
and the hopelessness, perhaps even recognizing for an instant
the stretch of distance he had come. He worked all day, but
once, in the afternoon, he took an end of black bread as small as
a child's fist from his pocket and ate it, sitting with his back
against a tree.

When the father drove home from work, at half past five, the
man was stooping over, buckling the full bag of potatoes closed,
preparing to go. The father made the circular turn of the drive
and drove the car into the garage, and locked the door behind
him when he came out. As he walked toward the house, he saw
that the man had cleared about three-quarters of the plot. And
then, when the man stood upright, the father saw him clearly,
and his heart went sick within him—a figure so eloquent in its
suffering, so dramatically conceived, that it might have been a
portrait done in sombre oils, the dark, despairing eyes, not of a
living man but of an El Greco head, following him now from
where the canvas was placed upon a museum's shadowy wall. It
was not that he had never before seen a man so thin and so
degraded by privation that any estimates as to age, background,
character, history were rendered futile; it was precisely because
he had seen men like this before that his heart went sick with an
old horror, an old fear. He had seen them in 1945, in Dachau,
when he and the other Americans had come in—skeletons that
had seemed to rise from the heaps of them in the courtyard but
that were somehow still-living men, ageless, pastless, coiling the
rope in the claws of their hands to hang the S.S. guards who had
not been able to get away. And none of the Americans had
moved to stop them; even the father had stood, bearing witness
to murder, with his head bowed in contrition and humility. As
the man passed beyond him along the strip of frost-yellowed,

withered grass, the father opened his mouth as if to speak to him, but he did not speak. Instead, he stood silently there, filled with a nameless emotion, watching the man go.

At seven in the morning, when the mother went downstairs to put the coffee on, she saw what had taken place. A wild wind had seemingly blown through the dining room and the sitting room, carrying all things before it, blasting the drawers and doors of the sideboards and tables and cupboards open and sweeping them bare. All that had lain in order within them—silver and linen, checker and chess and domino sets, bills, papers, maps, telephone books, and sewing materials—was there in chaos upon the floor. For an instant, the mother stood motionless, trying to make some sense of it all.

Do you mean this happened, do you mean the children did this when they went to look for the package of pretzels before going to bed, she asked herself in bewilderment, and then she saw that the pane in one of the sitting-room windows had been cut away.

The father came down in his pajamas when she called, and the children awoke and came, too, standing there without slippers and shivering with pleasure at the sight of this anonymous disorder, this chaos and disruption in which they had played no part.

"He didn't take my cigarette case," was the first thing the father said. It was lying with the scattered letters, the newspapers, the carbon and typewriting paper on the floor, lying open, with the cigarettes gone from it, and the father stooped and picked it up. "Sterling silver," he said, a little ruefully, "but he didn't want it," and he snapped it closed.

"He wanted the cigarettes, but he wanted something else," the mother said, and she picked her way through the hopeless clutter of objects that, it seemed, might never find their proper place.

"My stamp collection," the father said, in true concern.

"Perhaps your passport. It was in the desk," the mother said quietly, and they both sought among the confusion of books and papers and photographs a moment. The albums of the stamp collection lay under the litter, unharmed, and the passport, in its cellophane cover, was there. All through the rooms was a trail of burned-out matches, testifying that the man had carried no flashlight with him, and here and there was the darkening print of blood. The mark of blood was on the dining-room silver, which he had emptied out onto the table, not daring to take it, perhaps, because of the monogram on it, or else not wanting that at all. And the blood was there on the salmon-colored brocaded tablecloth, which they kept for dinner parties, and on the napkins, still folded corner-wise but marked with red, and there was blood on the wicker of the sewing basket, for he had overturned it in his haste and then made some effort to stuff the contents back in it again. But he had not wanted the scissors or the silver thimble or the skeins of wool it held. "It was something else," said the mother—not the crystal liqueur glasses, which he had touched, leaving the four or five charred, twisted matches beside them once he had viewed them in their beauty, and not the silver ashtrays or the napkin rings, which his fingertips had clouded when he picked them up. "It was something else he wanted," the mother said.

The instrument with which he had cut the pane out lay, as idle as a paperweight now, on the pile of disorder on the sitting-room table—an iron tool, staple-shaped and evil, with one dull, broken end and the other end filed as fine as a strong needle, with the tip worn white from the work of cutting it had done. The father picked it up and studied it a moment.

"This is the kind of thing that is used to grapple logs together when they float them down a river. Perhaps he came down the valley with logs. Perhaps he came from a long way off," the father said.

In the hall, he had not touched the hunting rifles, which hung on the coat hooks, or the binoculars or the optical sights. He had been looking for something else, something that was not to be found in the ground-floor bathroom, either, for the new cakes of soap and the razor, in its imitation-leather box, had not been taken, although he had touched the razor for an instant, for the trace of blood was there. It was only when they went down the cement stairs to the kitchen, where he had passed the two pairs of the father's shoes on the shoe rack, and not taken them for his own, that they understood what he had been after. The refrigerator door stood open, and the mother went at once to it, but the shelves looked as burdened as they had before. The uncooked chicken and the uncooked joint of beef were there, and the eggs and the bottles of beer, and the bottles of good Danish milk. He had taken nothing but a half pound of butter from the icebox shelf. They followed the way he had gone by the trail of burned-out matches left behind him, and in the storeroom, having struck match after match and studied the labels by their light, he had found the things that he wanted to take away.

"Just what he could eat on the side of the road somewhere," the mother said. But he hadn't been able to wait that long; they found the paper of a half-pound bar of unsweetened baking chocolate on the floor, where he had dropped it, empty.

"Oh, God, he must have been hungry to eat that!" the father said.

He had taken two cans of sardines—and left them two—and the smallest can of frankfurters, and a half-size can of salmon and one of shrimp. From the kitchen-table drawer, he had taken one knife and a can opener, and from the breadbox a loaf of raisin bread.

"He took only what he needed for the road," the mother said, and the "he" indicated a man who had walked for a long time, and who would go on walking, as explicitly as if her suspicion had spoken a proper name.

Whoever he was, he had gone out through the cellar door, leaving it open behind him, and as the mother and father stood there looking out across the orchard, they could see the marks of footsteps in the deep, cold dew. They believed then that they could see him going, accepting without question, and with a certain sense of guilt and sorrow, that it should be he. They could see the great, bony shoulders stooped, the wilted felt hat drooping low about his ears, the string-tied boots scarring their way across the orchard grass.

"It would have been less trouble for him to have rung the bell last night and asked for food," said the father, his voice irritable with his own shame.

"He must be a long way off by this time," the mother said.

But, just after eight, there he was in the potato patch again, taking up the work where he had left off, slowly and wearily spading the earth away. The maid had come, and she and the mother were in the kitchen, busying themselves with the setting of the place in order, and the father had gone out the door to take the car from the garage when he saw the skeleton, in a long coat this time, at work in the misty morning air. So the father dropped his bunch of keys into his pocket, and he crossed the drive and went up the stretch of sloping ground. The coat that the thin man wore came almost to his ankles, a coat that a German officer had worn once—rusty and greenish, with a braid-edged velvet collar and high, smart, flaring lapels.

"*Guten Tag,*" the father said, and the man looked up from under the hanging brim of his hat. Oh, God! thought the father, the sharpness of the pain returning. That look that men have the power to put into one another's eyes!

"*Guten Tag,*" the thin man answered, and his voice was gentle, but it was clear that he was not convinced of the truth of the words he had just said.

"You're a stranger to this part of the country, aren't you?" the father said, speaking German still. The Army coat that the thin man wore had certainly never been his, for the sleeves rode half-way up his bony arms, and although there could be no question of buttoning it across, still, even as it hung open, the breadth of his carcass had split its seams.

"Yes," said the man. He had thrust the spade upright into the soil, and his big-wristed forearms hung motionless now from the too short, too tight frayed velvet cuffs of the sleeves. "I've been walking three weeks. I'm working my way to Fulda," he said.

"You've been doing some work with lumber, bringing trees downstream?" asked the father in his quiet presentable German.

"Yes," the man said again, and the lurking, ailing thing that the children had seen in the deep pits of his eyes looked warily at the man who stood, in his good clothes, before him. "I've been doing anything I could get," he said, and he lowered his head and shifted on his feet, dragging the cadaver of his destitution a little nearer to the father in the cold.

"Look," said the father, speaking firmly, "you come over to the house with me." The man followed him down the slope of

frost-burned grass and across the drive and onto the pavings of
the terrace, following in the half-helpless, half-eager acquiescence with which a well-disciplined dog comes to heel. The father opened the front door of the house with his latchkey, and
the thin man in the comic-opera overcoat followed him in and
wiped his feet, as the father had, on the mat inside the door. As
they crossed the hall, the father could hear the mingled voices of
the mother and children and the maid, below them, in the
kitchen, speaking quickly, with excitement, among themselves.
The father led the man through the sitting room, past the chaos
of papers on the table and the floor, through the disorder of the
dining room, and out onto the balcony, and he asked him to
stand there. The man had taken his hat off, in respect, as he
came into the house, and when the father went back through the
dining room alone and into the sitting room, he could see the
macabre figure framed by the broken windowpane standing abjectly, obediently, on the balcony, under the dry ropes of the
grapevine, with his head bare in the wash of the morning sun.
The man's hair was sparse, and high on his big, domed forehead
there was a violent scar that slashed into his scalp, marking a
crescent of white, waxlike flesh, hairless and nearly opalescent,
above one bloodless ear. The father looked at him for a moment,
and then he picked up the iron grapple from the table where it
lay, and as he walked toward the window, he did not take his
eyes from the man who stood on the balcony, beyond the broken
glass. "Here," the father said quietly, and he put his hand, with
the iron grapple in it, through the opening in the pane. "Take
this," he said. "Show me how it was done."

The man's eyes shifted toward the sound of his voice, and
when he saw the father extending the grapple to him, he crossed
the stone of the balcony with a humble, eager step. He took the
instrument from the father's hand and he looked at it curiously a
moment, not as if it were a strange thing to him but as if seeking
to determine how it happened to be here. Then his eyes focussed
slowly on the father, standing on the other side of the glass.

"Like this. It was done like this," he said. He had sought for
and found the sharp end of the grapple, and now the point of it
was raised, and he looked at the father eagerly. He seemed to

feel that by showing a wholly cooperative spirit he could establish his right of belonging to the father's side. "The point was
put in here," he said, his face gone sober with interest as he
fitted it to the broken edge. "And then, with the weight put
against it, and turning it all the time, the glass would be cut
out," he said, and the point of the grapple followed the arc
down. "You have to do it over and over, with great care," he
said, "and then the glass will give."

"And then, when the piece of glass is gone, you just pass your
hand in through the opening and turn the handle and open the
window," the father said, speaking quietly to the thin man. "But
in the dark you might cut your hand doing it," he said.

"Yes," said the man. "You'd put your hand in like this," he
said, and he laid the grapple down on the stone of the window
sill and passed his right hand inside and felt for the handle.
When he did this, the father saw the cut on the yellowish flesh of
his palm.

"So. Now tell me," the father said, speaking just as quietly as
before, "how long did it take you to cut the glass out?" And his
fingers closed strongly around the big, flat bones of the thin
man's wrist.

"How long?" asked the man. With his wrist caught there, as if
in a trap, in the father's fingers, he seemed to reflect on it a moment. "Perhaps an hour, perhaps two hours. You have to go very
carefully," he said, and then the look that had been wiped from
his eyes came back, and the tracked and circumvented beast lay
waiting in the sunken pits. "Who, me? Not me!" he said, and he
ran his tongue along his lip. "I didn't do it. I didn't have anything to do with it. I wasn't here last night," he said.

"Come in," the father said. His fingers let the man's wrist go,
and he motioned to the balcony door. The man turned slowly
and crossed the balcony, and he came through the dining room,
walking slowly, abjectly, in the German Army officer's coat,
through the disorder and into the sitting room, where the father
stopped. "Sit down," the father said, and when he was seated,
the father sat down on the other side of the table and he held a
packet of cigarettes out to him. "What's your trade?" the father
said.

"I'm a salesman, a shoe salesman," the man said. His fingers were shaking as he took the cigarette, and even in his mouth it shook as the father held a light to it. "I'll be all right if I can get to Fulda," he said. "I have an uncle and some cousins there."

"Where did you sleep last night?" said the father, lighting his own cigarette.

"I slept in a tool shed in one of the vegetable gardens down the road," the thin man said, and as the father studied him across the faint blue vapor of smoke, his eyes fled bleakly through the room.

"And the hunger got bad. It got a little worse than it was before," said the father, drawing slowly, deeply, on his cigarette, "and so you came up here."

"No," said the man. "It was the first night in three weeks I had a roof over me. I went to sleep."

"Oh, Christ!" said the father, leaning forward. "Don't you think I'd understand it? Do you think I'd judge you for it?" he said impatiently. "How low do you think the human being can sink, to what depths of censure and condemnation do you think the human being can go? Tell me any story you like about the cut on your hand," he said in a kind of fury. "It doesn't matter! It's past a matter of telling the truth or telling a lie, or recognizing the truth if you heard it. You're dying on your feet, starved, famished, discussing ethics with a man who's eaten. . . ."

The skeleton sat looking strangely, uneasily, at him, not certain whether this was anger or not, not comprehending what the father was seeking to say. And then the doorbell rang sharply out, and the father jumped to his feet, as nervously as if his name had been called aloud. He went out of the sitting room and downstairs quickly and opened the front door. There, in his Hessian forester's jacket, stood the owner of the house, holding the hat with the *Saubart* in it in his handsomely gloved hands. He stood there somewhat obsequiously, somewhat like a trespasser, at the threshold of his own front door, his shoulders back but the white-bristled skull tilted as if in apology. Beneath the forester's jacket, the father saw that the *Blockwart* wore a shirt of soft-gray flannel and that his shoes—beneath the knife pleats of the gray Loden trousers—were obviously American-made, black-market, new.

"*Guten Tag,*" the *Blockwart* said, and as the father looked at the officious, the fiercely bigoted face, he was filled with a wild, unreasoning anger, an almost unbearable fury, at the sight of the corpulent, rosy flesh before him, and the handsome, traditional clothes.

"What is it you want here?" he shouted, and it came to him that this was the first time they had ever come so close or looked into each other's eyes.

"I beg your pardon for the intrusion," the *Blockwart* said, tilting his naked head, "but I came up to pay the man who was getting my potatoes out, and your servant tells me it is possible he broke into the house last night. It is a mistake to deal with anyone who hasn't a roof over his head, and I should not have done so," he said, but it was almost as if he were catching the father up on some negligence. "I feel a certain responsibility for his being here. A certain responsibility," he repeated. "I see the spade and bag out there, and I believe you are questioning him. I would be quite willing to relieve you of the matter and turn him over to the police myself," he said.

"No," said the father, speaking carefully. "You can't do that. He isn't the man."

"Not the man?" said the *Blockwart* sharply, and it might have been an order that he gave. "But it must be the man!" he said, and it behooved them now to jerk their chins up as they faced each other, bring their heels together, clap their arms, rigid, by their sides.

"There is no indication that he is the man." The father confirmed it. "His hand is not cut, while the man who broke in left blood on everything." And then he closed the door.

The *Blockwart's* clock in the hall was just striking nine when the father walked back into the sitting room, and the thin man was sitting on the edge of the armchair still, smoking nervously at his cigarette. "Come on downstairs and have some breakfast," said the father, and the skeleton did not look at him but drew his bones together and got up painfully. As he and the father went down the stairs, to the sound of the women's and children's voices, the father said, "I'll drive you to the station afterward and put you on a train. You'll get to Fulda quicker that way."

Fife's House

Now summer was over, and the children would not be coming into the house any more; school had begun again. But in whatever community classrooms of the Zone the American children sat now, the sound of their voices lingered in this house, which had been built for people of another nationality. All summer, the children had come in from the other back yards, come down the hedge-lined pathway, where garbage cans marked "U. S. Property" stood at each gate, and in through the door that opened into the living room, where some petty official of the I. G. Farben works had sat in righteousness with his family once. Or if this door was closed, the children had climbed in across the window sills, some in child-size M.P. outfits bought at the Post Exchange, with handcuffs jangling at their belts, and others with strings or ribbons tied across their brows and a feather or two stuck upright at the back, warbling their Indian war cries as they came. They would mount the stairs looking for Fife, who was six that summer, sometimes half a dozen of them at a time and sometimes more—little girls in sun suits bought at Macy's or Bloomingdale's (or the Midwestern or Southern equivalent of these), or else picked from a Sears, Roebuck catalogue page, and little boys in faded corduroys and striped T shirts, coming barefoot or with soiled canvas sneakers on their feet, invading every corner of the Army-requisitioned house in their incurable sociability.

None of them had any last names, these children who crowded into the small, square rooms all summer. They were merely Linda, and Peggy, and Rosemary, and Joan, or else Douglas, and Michael, and Edwin, and Bill. And there were those who did not stay long enough in the block to be identified by any name—strangers in blue jeans or seersucker who came once or twice, in curiosity, to see Fife's crane work or to listen to his phonograph records before they moved away. But whoever they were or however long they stayed, they would come into the room where Fife's mother sat typing on her bed, and they would talk of the Stateside places that had been their homes once, and of the bikes and roller skates and the Flexible Flyers that had been theirs before they had had to come and live in Germany.

"Bluebells, cockleshells, evie, ivy, over," the children's voices would begin in the morning on the path, which ran the length of the block in back. These were the skipping-rope jumpers, and "Your mother, my mother, live across the way!" they would sing, skipping out the rhythm of it as they came. They and the M.P.s and the Indians would pass through the I. G. Farben official's living room and mount the stairs to where Fife's mother sat, and they would lean their tanned arms and place their skipping ropes and their handcuffs on the papers scattered on the table by the bed, and her fingers would come to a halt on the typewriter keys. "Why is half of the ribbon black and the other half red?" Rosemary, or Linda, or Joan, might ask, and Fife would know the answer.

"The red is to write the exciting things with," he would say, "and the black is to write the ordinary things, like—you know, 'Once upon a time' or 'So the next day.'"

"Go to the end of the line, so we can hear the bell ring," the M.P.s or the Indians might plead, or they might ask for the carbon paper that was too worn to use any more.

The back yard of Fife's house was the same as every other back yard in the double block of identical two-story, attached houses, except that the lilac bushes by the cement steps, and the sour-cherry tree in the middle of it, had grown taller than those in the other yards. It was perhaps that the official who had lived there once had been allocated a greater share of sunshine than the others, because of particular services he had rendered the chemical industry. But, however it was, only the sour-cherry tree in Fife's yard was strong enough to hold a rope swing on one of its branches, and right after breakfast the children would come to it, as noisy as starlings in the spring. They would fight for a turn on its plank seat and twist its rope into a spiral as they sat on it, for the pleasure of unwinding again in furious rapidity. These were the rope-swing swingers, and there were other groups that came. There were the doll-coach pushers, and the tricyclists, and those who drove their soapbox cars as far as the steps and parked them there before entering the house, calling out Fife's name as they came.

"Can Fife come out?" the voices would ask, and, loud and shrill in half a dozen voices, the "ack-ack-ack-ack" of anti-aircraft fire would begin as Fife slid down the banisters, or down the rain pipe to the yard below.

Fife was small and slender and quick, and the back of his neck was burned dark by the sun. His eyes were blue, and in spite of the visions of Superman and Captain Marvel Jr. and the Man with the Automatic Brain that dwelled within them, they were as gentle and long-lashed as a poet's eyes. There were a few things that Fife owned with pride: a toy garage filled with partially or totally disabled trucks, trailers, and cars, and a Flit spray gun and an egg beater, both of which functioned imperfectly. But in a different class from these was a wristwatch his father had bought him in Switzerland, which was kept in a silk-lined box in his mother's bureau drawer. It had a delicate, copper-colored face, and a stop-watch gadget on its bevelled rim, and, besides hours and minutes and seconds, the days of the month unfolded on it, and the mutations of the moon were marked on its disc, in accordance with the rising and waxing and waning and setting of the true moon in the sky. On the occasions when Fife had worn it for a little while—on Sundays, and on his birthday once—it had hung cumbersome as a clock on his wrist, for it was made for a man, and only when he became twelve would it be his to keep and wear.

Fife could wail like a fire engine for unbroken periods of time, and he could imitate with distressing accuracy the whirring of the motor of a car that will not start. He could reproduce the whine of a dive-bomber as it dived, and the sound of airplane wings ripping, in full flight, from a fuselage. And he would reproduce these sounds, and others like them, over and over, as if

they were music in his ears. So when the fish game was inaugu-
rated, sometime in August, it brought a curious quiet to the yard
and house. It began when Rosemary's father was transferred to
Heidelberg, and Rosemary gave her goldfish to Fife before she
moved away. This respite came in the hottest part of summer,
and Fife and the other children drifted in nearly perfect silence
through the living room and up the stairs toward the steady ticking of the mother's typing, their tanned arms in their T shirts
weaving through the currents of this mutual vision while their
mouths opened and closed, opened and closed, emitting no
sound.

How many hours, or days, or weeks, the children might have
continued to swim cannot be said, for hardly had this begun
when, one afternoon, Fife found the German boy called Horst,
and then everything was altered, and nobody came into the garden, and no one played the fish game any more.

It happened because the pathway that ran the length of the
block behind the houses stopped short at the broken asphalt of a
pavement, in a little clearing of parched, worn grass. And twice
in the week the housemen rolled the garbage cans down the
path to this clearing for collection, and twice in the week German children came in from the outer avenues and lifted the lids
marked "U. S. Property," and went through the refuse that lay inside. Whenever this took place, Fife and the others gathered to
watch the German children in envy as they sorted and selected,
and carried away the things they wanted. And one afternoon a
tall, strong boy in leather shorts was there for the first time
among the others, salvaging the best from the stack of garbage
cans. His name was Horst, and he was ten, Fife told his mother,
having brought him in pride and awe, with a rucksack hanging
on his shoulders, into her room, where she sat on the bed with
the typewriter on her knees.

"He's got real deerhorn buttons on his pants," Fife said. There
he stood before her, small, almost puny, beside the German boy,
with his thin chest rising and falling fast. Horst's hair was flaxen,
and it grew gracefully on his head. His cheeks were downy as
peach skin in the summer light, and his long, bare arms and
thighs were muscular and brown. "He says he'll be my friend,"

Fife said, and with these words the lineaments of the others—their blue jeans, their sun suits, and their familiar faces—were erased as drawings on a blackboard are erased. The voices of the skipping-rope jumpers droning "Evie, ivy, over" and the war cries of the Indians were heard only faintly and far away, through the window that stood open on the yard below. "His father shot the deer himself, and Horst helped him cut the horns off," Fife said, and the German boy's light eyes were fixed without emotion on him. "His father's a hunter," Fife said.

"What your father do?" Horst asked, saying it in a stubborn, untroubled English to him, and the mother, with her typewriter, might not have been in the room with them, for he did not look her way.

"Oh, he works in Military Government," Fife said, but this was of no importance and he went on quickly, "I'd like to go hunting," and he looked in shy, bleak hope now at the other boy.

"You get bullets, my father take you hunting," Horst said. He ran his thumbs inside the rucksack straps and jerked the full bag higher on his back. "My father need bullets. You get him bullets," he said, and Fife stood nodding his head in acquiescence before this figure of strength and comeliness that had taken shape before his eyes.

"Maybe Fife's a little too young to go hunting yet," Fife's mother said, but the words sounded frail and feminine in her own ears as she said them, the protest irrational and impotent.

Horst turned his head on his strong, sunburned neck, and he looked for the first time, and without any sign of interest, at her. "First time I go hunting, I'm four," he said.

This was the way it began, and in the days that followed the swingers no longer gathered at the swing behind the house, and the doll-coach pushers moved, two by two or in single file, in other directions. The Indian war cries sounded in the distance now, and the skipping-rope jumpers' voices said faintly, as if in sorrow, "Daisy, Daisy, touch the ground. Daisy, Daisy, turn around," but they did not come near. Fife's room was at the end of the hall, and Fife and Horst stayed there together, not playing on the floor with cars that wound up with a key, and not listening to the phonograph records, but talking in lowered voices, with circumspect pauses between their sentences, as older people talk. And on the second or third morning Fife came down the hall to his mother's room, coming quietly through the half-open door, and halted beside the bed.

"Look," he said, and he drew one finger along the painted metal of her typewriter. "That wristwatch you're keeping for me —it's my wristwatch, isn't it?"

"It's going to be yours," said his mother, and she went on typing, so that she need not see the tight white mark of pain around his mouth.

"Well, if it's mine, I can do what I want with it, can't I?" Fife said, but he still did not look into her face. "I told Horst about my wristwatch, and that's the kind of wristwatch he wants. If I give it to him, his father's going to take me hunting," he said.

"But you can't give something away that isn't yours yet," his mother said, and her fingers halted now on the typewriter keys. "You can't just skip five or six years like that. It's like trying to make Christmas come in the middle of summer."

"You told me Christmas comes in the middle of summer in Australia," Fife said.

That wasn't the end of it; it was nowhere near the end of it. In the afternoon, it was Horst himself who stood, bronzed and tall and handsome on the threshold of the room, looking Fife's mother in the eye. This time he wore black leather shorts, with edelweiss embroidered on the suède-like braces of them, and his blond hair gleamed as clear as light on the edge of the dim, shuttered room.

"I come for the vatch," Horst said. Behind him, small as one of the gnomes on his bibbed blue jeans, Fife lingered in the shadows of the hall.

"It doesn't belong to Fife yet," said the mother, and she slowly "X"ed out the last words she had written, for they were not the words she had wanted to set down. "He has to wait until he's older, and then he can do what he wants with it."

"O.K. I vait *bis* five o'clock," Horst said.

During this week in the summer when the children came no longer to the house, there was no language to speak to Fife in, for the substance of his being had seemed to change. He had entered an errant male world from which neither mother nor fellow countrymen could recall him, and in the early morning there was the sound of only one boy's footsteps coming up the stairs. Day after day, the two boys' voices murmured in Fife's room at the end of the hall, but it was only when the mother paused in her typing that she could hear the words they said. The argument may always have been the same one, for the bits and pieces of it were concerned with interchange and barter, and the mother heard Fife offer his Flit gun to Horst, and heard the gasp and wheeze of it as the German boy tried it, before the air pump jammed.

"It only jams every other time, not every time," Fife said in a low voice.

"I take the vatch instead," Horst said, and she heard him put the sprayer down.

Horst did not want the toy garage, or the cars that were in it, but it may have been that he considered for a moment the egg beater, which Fife kept under his pillow when he went to sleep, for the mother could hear the whirring of its flections. And then the sound of rotating ceased abruptly and there was silence in Fife's room and in the hall.

"When it sticks like that, all you have to do is turn the handle a little bit the other way. Like this," Fife said, and he seemed to be working with it. "It's a pretty good egg beater except for that one thing," he said.

"I don't vant it," said Horst, and the mother did not hear what he went on saying, for she had begun her typewriting again.

And then, at the end of the week, they made a final bid for the watch. They came to the mother's room, one bronze-limbed and flaxen-haired and tall, and the other almost dwarfed beside him in his shabby overalls.

"I wanted to show him my wristwatch," Fife said. "Just to show it to him."

"All right," said his mother, and she kept her eyes on the last line she had written. "Look at it quickly and then go away."

She did not have to turn her head to know how Fife would lift it from the silk-lined box. She could feel the delicacy and caution in his fingers as palpably as if he touched, not a cold gold shell in which the instants of life ticked brightly, mechanically, away, but the swift, impatient pulsing of her heart. She did not look up from the page before her until they had started toward the door.

"I vear it home tonight. I show my father," Horst said, and she saw that he had strapped it on his own brown wrist. "I bring it back O.K. tomorrow," he said.

"Look, Horst," said the mother, and now she set the typewriter aside, and she swung her legs in the blue silk housecoat down from the I. G. Farben official's varnished bed.

"He'll bring it back tomorrow. He just said he would," Fife said, but his dusty sandals wavered in pain and indecision on the shade-and-sun striped floor.

"Horst, I'm sorry. His father wouldn't like it," Fife's mother said.

"My father—" Horst began, but he did not go on with it. Instead, a look of fury came into his cold, light eyes. "That vatch not gold. I don't take it. I don't vant something phony," he said. He jerked the strap of it free of the buckle, and he tossed the wristwatch from him, toward where the mother sat upon the bed. It struck hard against the metal of the typewriter and fell upon the flowered cover with its coppery-colored gold face down. Once this was done, nobody moved, nobody seemed to draw breath in the room, and then Fife whirled on his dusty sandals, and he drove his fierce, small, unaccustomed fists into Horst's impervious flesh and bone.

That was the last time they saw Horst. He may have come back sometime in the evening of that same day, but that they never knew. It was known only that after dusk spirals of smoke began to rise in the hot, still air, each helix of it rising from each gate cut in the double hedgerow, and, standing at the open window, Fife's mother saw that the lids had been lifted and that flames were fanning, indolent and loose and golden, in the open garbage cans. There had been no outcry, no sound of footsteps rushing down the pathway, and yet these fires of rubbish burning had served as signals for assemblage. For now the children came out of their houses into the summer evening, came with watering cans and saucepans filled and splashing over as they ran across the grass. The skipping-rope jumpers and the rope-swing swingers and the soapbox drivers and the Indians crowded in ecstasy and disorder onto the common pathway, and, shouting and screaming, they fled from garbage can to garbage can, flinging the water they carried in upon the flames. The child-size M.P.s had fixed a garden hose to the faucet of one kitchen sink, and they played the jet that sprang from it onto the fires, while the others ran back through the yards, their voices piercing the evening air, to fill their receptacles again.

No bell had sounded out in summons, but after a moment Fife opened the door of his own silent room, and he came down the hall and crossed the threshold to where his mother stood.

"I can smell smoke, can't you?" he said, and he and his mother did not look into each other's faces yet but out across the lilac trees.

"Someone set fire to the garbage cans," his mother said, and Fife swung himself by his thin, braced arms onto the window sill.

"Golly, the whole row's burning!" he said, kneeling in wonder on the broad stone ledge.

Now the doll-coach pushers came hastening out, one behind another, the doll coaches careening crazily before them as they ran. The cushions, the covers, the dolls themselves—all the paraphernalia of motherhood—were gone, and the coaches carried tins of water. And with each slap of it cast on the flames it seemed to the mother that the hot, sore memory of Horst, and the features of his face, and the words he had said were extinguished. He was nowhere among the wildly leaping others as Fife stood up, holding with his hands to the iron ribs of the lifted blind, and moved on his rubber-soled sandals to the edge, and slid, calling their names out hoarsely as he went, down the rain pipe to the yard below.

The Lovers of Gain

The days in Germany were like the days in no other country, there to be breathed into being as one might breathe into the lips and nostrils of the dead. The hours of them seemed suspended, perhaps brought to a halt by the monumental rubble, but halted so long ago that it could no longer be recalled in what month, or year, or even in what lifetime, their sequence had reached this pause. Perhaps the bleak Teutonic twilight had set in as the reverberations of the final bomb faded to silence in the ruins, thought Mrs. Furley as she walked through the American Commissary door. Perhaps the meaning of night and day, of summer and winter, of peace and war, had been lost to this country in the instant when the last hope of German victory had died.

But once you stepped from the German city street, and into the Commissary, here, for better or worse, was the look of home. Metal push-wagons waited in a double row in the overheated entranceway, as they waited in the chain stores of any Stateside city you might name. Mrs. Furley showed her identification to the German girl seated at the desk, and picked up a meat number, and then she moved on with the others, as she had day after day of the year that had just elapsed—moved on with the young women in their saddleback shoes and bobby socks, pushing her wagon as they pushed theirs before them, moved into the thick of it with the matrons, the teen-age girls, the displaced grandmothers, some of them newly come from the States, who clung to the handles of their vehicles as if to the last remaining vestiges of a civilization they had always known. Scattered among them moved the men in uniform, the corporals, the staff sergeants, the lieutenants, the captains, the majors and colonels even, pushing their wagons as carefully as if babies rode in them, while they studied the lists their wives had written out.

On the shelves which lined and bisected the vast low hall were stacked the familiar cans and bottles—the names of Campbell, and Heinz, and Van Camp, and Fould, and Kellogg, to reassure the exiled, and beans and pancakes illustrated in color so that the fears of the lost and the bewildered might be allayed. But here the likeness to home came to an end, for nothing else was quite the same. Behind the vegetable counter, as behind the illuminated cases of meat, there were Germans, some lean and bespectacled and professorial, their natural habitat a laboratory or a lecture hall; and others solid and blond and canny-eyed, and still others as delicate-featured and long-haired as poets, all wearing the long, white chain-store dress. And the voice was German which pronounced the meat numbers slowly, painfully, through the microphone, saying: "Dirty, dirty, blease." Having drawn number sixty-one, Mrs. Furley pushed her wagon toward the corner where oranges and apples, and potatoes and cabbages, lay in refrigerated bins, their paucity enhanced by mirrors set above them along the walls. And here, one slender German poet came to life at Mrs. Furley's approach. She saw him slipping quickly through the other white-robed salesmen, maneuvering himself into position until only the bare wood of the counter lay between him and the American woman who had lived in Paris too.

"Bon jour, madame," he would say in a low voice to her, as he stood putting his dark hair back with his black-rimmed fingers, a shy and tender look of yearning come into his eyes. *"Je suis* contented," he would say. He was no older than twenty-three or twenty-four, but, dressed up as a soldier in the Wehrmacht, he had occupied Paris with the others, and he liked to speak of the parks, and the avenues, and the monuments of a city that was never his, his voice lingering on the music of their names. *"Champs-Elysées, Champ-de-Mars, l'Arc de Triomphe,"* was one of the lines of poetry he recited to Mrs. Furley through the summer as he weighed the melons and tomatoes from Italy; or *"Place du Panthéon, Place de la Concorde, Boulevard Saint-Michel,"* he would say as he weighed the celery from New Jersey or the endives from Holland in the winter. But this time he said: "You did not come for one week. *Vous n'êtes pas venoo pour une semaine."*

"Dirty-von, dirty-doo, dirty-tree, blease," said the voice from the meat counter, speaking through the microphone.

"Because I went to Paris for a week," said Mrs. Furley, and his eyes went dark with wonder in his eager face. (Once he had said to her that there were things which had disappointed him in Paris. The *Métros* were not kept clean, for instance, not as clean as the *S-bahn* in Berlin had been, he said. And he had spoken of the Paris pigeons, whose droppings defaced the statues in the public gardens, and the elegant façades. "Perhaps the Americans could tell the French to keep things cleaner," he had tried saying to her, smiling shyly.) "I brought you some cigarettes from Paris," she said to him now, and, as he passed the five-pound paper sack of Idaho potatoes across the counter to her, she put the packet of *Bleues* into his hand.

Or there was the one she had come to call Philip Morris, because that was the brand of cigarette he preferred. He had been three years a P.W. in England, and now his work was to roll the three-tiered carriers of bottled Danish milk in, rattling and clanking from the stockroom, and, as fast as the refrigerating-unit shelves were emptied, he would stack them full again. He was a man of fifty, or more, Philip Morris, with a wearily lidded eye, and hair turning gray, and he had a distinguished, high-bridged nose. His jowls were always cleanly shaven, the English he spoke was public school, and it would have seemed more fitting had he stood at the head of an operating table instead of trundling the milk carriers in in his long white surgeon's gown. He had spoken first of his insurance policy to Mrs. Furley, citing clauses which had been inserted, he said, in flagrant defiance of Occupation directives. He had even suggested that the matter be brought to the attention of Decartelization Branch, for the Germans, certain Germans, would be up to anything, he inferred, once the backs of the democratic and the just were turned. And another time he had spoken of Nietzsche to her, and once in a while of Schopenhauer; and on this occasion he opened the door of the refrigerating unit, as if drawing back a chair at a dinner table so that she might take her place among the enlightened who were already seated, and he spoke Plato's name.

"You will recall Plato's assertion that there are three classes of men," he said, and he selected the milk bottles for her from among those standing, long-necked and iced, upon the slatted shelves. "He defined them as the lovers of wisdom, the lovers of honor, and the lovers of gain," he said, as he set the bottles carefully in her wagon, side by side with the Super Suds, and the Crisco, and the Rowntree cocoa cans. "The lovers of wisdom," he said, his weary but masterful eyes on Mrs. Furley, "have been forgotten. They have not been called to the council tables, but are serving in menial positions in every fallen state. I study the faces of the men and the women who come through these doors, and it is not difficult to classify them. The lovers of wisdom are rarely observed among them," he said, and he closed the refrigerator door.

"And what of the lovers of honor?" said Mrs. Furley, and the voice at the microphone said, "Fourteen-sex, fourteen-seben, fourteen-ocht," while the bobby-socks wives, and the soldiers, and the grandmothers, moved forward in formation, pushing their burdened wagons as they came. "There are lovers of honor among them," Mrs. Furley said.

"Plato referred to the warriors when he spoke of the lovers of honor," explained the man called Philip Morris. "But the warriors are no longer the lovers of honor," he said, and he fixed the soldiers now with his cynic's gray eye. "The warriors are dead. They died in two world wars. Those who remain are the barterers. They know the price of coffee and cocoa and sugar and flour in a defeated country"; and, beyond him, the corporals and sergeants, the captains and majors, oblivious to the classification they had been given, moved, one behind the other toward the frozen meat, the lists their wives had written out for them held submissively in their hands.

"Won't you have a Philip Morris?" said Mrs. Furley, as she had said it week in and week out to him in the twelve months that had passed. And, although he seemed to have no great interest in it, he selected first one cigarette, and then a second, from the pack she held out to him; and he placed them with care in the monogrammed, silver case which he carried, with his pince-nez, in the pocket of his long, white, surgeon's gown.

The numbers fifty-two-and-three-and-four were called aloud

now, and Mrs. Furley wheeled her wagon toward the shelves of
Jack Frost sugars, and Crosse and Blackwell jams. And there a
little woman with loose, white, flying hair, and a ravaged face,
swept quickly, belligerently, with a broom made in Missouri, at
the Commissary boards. The first thing she said was that she
needed help, saying it in German under her breath to Mrs. Furley, but the plea already soured in her mouth, knowing there
was no way for help to come.

"It's my husband. They put him in jail last night," she said, the
tongue wagging, the broom sweeping, and the wild eye after it
in pursuit while the tatters and remnants of the story fluttered on
the air. "They oughtn't to lay their hands on him, the German
police, as long as he's working for the *Amis,* but they picked him
right up off the street and put him in jail!" She had been a beer-
hall singer, a cabaret artist, she had once told Mrs. Furley; in
the early twenties, she had danced the can-can for beer-hall
drinkers in Berlin. "Maybe if an *Ami* went and spoke to the German police, they'd let him out," she said, not looking at Mrs.
Furley, while the broom swept savagely across the boards. "He
was walking along the street last night, and there, *Herr Gott,*
was a man he hadn't seen in six long years, a man he wouldn't
forget in all his life, and my husband went right up to him, and
he got hold of him by the throat, and he started squeezing the
life right out of him, the way he'd wanted to do for six long
years, started shaking and squeezing him, and calling him the
only names he deserved!" Her own throat seemed to choke now,
for she could no longer find the breath to speak, and her fingers
closed so tightly on the handle of the broom that the bones
showed sharp enough to split the skin. "So the crowd that collected around them got hold of the police," she said when she
could speak again, and the broom from Missouri swept wildly,
crazily away. "And instead of letting my husband finish the
man off, the police began beating my husband up, and then they
dragged him off to jail! So he'll get the prison term, not the other
one he's been seeing for six long years in his nightmares every
night!" she said.

"But the man—the man he got by the throat—what had he
done?" Mrs. Furley asked, and it did not matter if the numbers

that were called through the microphone were nearing sixty now.

"So what had he done?" the little woman cried harshly out, and, as she whirled in her fury, the broom swept heedlessly across the feet of the lovers of honor or the lovers of gain who were passing, pushing their burdened carts. "So what had he done?" she cried out, her ire rising at the sight of them, for here was a torment, more profound than hunger, which no illicit coffee or cocoa or sugar, and no brand of foreign tobacco could assuage. "My husband's mother and sister, it was going to be all right for them," she said, her lips drawn back in a grimace from the bad taste in her mouth. "It was fixed up for them to get away. They were going to get to Geneva. That was in 1943. But they were denounced, denounced, denounced!" she cried out in a loud voice, not speaking to anyone at all. "That's what that man did, he denounced them. That's all he did, denounced them," she said, and, beneath the hem of the chain-store dress, her legs had the liveliness and spring still of a dancer's legs who had danced the can-can for beer-hall drinkers in Berlin. "Perhaps if an *Ami* spoke to the police," she said, and then she seemed suddenly to recognize the folly of calling as witness the humble dead. "You're always looking for Hellman's mayonnaise," she said, sweeping on past the angelfood and gingerbread mixes, past Aunt Jemima's smiling face. "They got some in this morning, over there with the bottled sauces," she said.

Mrs. Furley reached the meat counter as the man at the microphone said, "Zickstee." He was seated hunched on a high, leather-cushioned stool, with his legs drawn up beneath the white skirt of his dress. He was a small man, and his lips were full and ruby red, and his nose was flamboyantly nostriled, and a nest of tight, black, oily curls clung to the back of his skull. There were curls as well in his outsized ears, and his eyeballs were swollen, as if from a lifetime of falling, burning tears, and the whites of them were bound by scarlet veins. He was singular in that the names of Chesterfield, or Pall Mall, or Camel, could not be given him, as they could be given the others, for he had no interest in any brand of cigarette, as if by this one gesture of repudiation he cleared himself, and every member of his race, of the charge of barter and venality.

"Zo, hallo," he greeted Mrs. Furley when she paused by the microphone to surrender her number to him, and then he went on talking of the theatre to her, for the moment not calling the meat numbers aloud. Before the war, before Hitler's time, he had always worked in the theatre, he had told her from the beginning, but it was never made clear in what capacity he served. "I like the vork in the theatre better as vorking here," he would say, with a curved and painful grin stretching his mouth. "I begin vorking in the theatre in London. I learn to zpick the langvich there. That vas ober tventy years ago," he would say. And once he had said: "I vork for an American in London, a director-producer, a Jew from New York, but a nize Jew," sitting there hunched in his white dress on the stool, smiling his anguished smile at Mrs. Furley.

"Why do you say 'a nice Jew'?" asked Mrs. Furley. "What happened to you that you have to speak like this?"

But the answer had already been given in the history of the country, and nothing that had been said since had been said with power or passion enough to take that answer away. In concentration camp, and out of it, he had heard the radio voices and the other voices naming the outcast, heard them year after year, and over and over, describing the anatomy of evil until he had come to recognize in shame the stigma of his own reflection in the glass.

"Vell, zome Jews nize, zome not zo nize, that's vat they tell me," he had said, still smiling at her, and he had shrugged aside the responsibility for any of it. "Zo, hallo," he said to her now. "You vent to the theatre in Paris?"

"I saw a play called 'La Soif,'" said Mrs. Furley. "A play by Bernstein called 'Thirst.'"

"Oh, 'Zirst,'" said the little man on the stool. "'Zirst,'" he repeated in sudden bewilderment, and the sound of the word was whispered strangely through the microphone, as the voice of an entire people might have whispered it from a vast, still-open grave, before those lying in it had expired.

Mrs. Furley walked in past the illuminated cases where slices of beef liver, gray with frost, and suitable as tiling with which to roof a house, were spread on platters on display. The hamburger must be chiselled away in icy formations, she knew, and the brook trout pried from the granite block into which their once supple bodies had been frozen fast.

"I think I'll have a leg of mutton today," said Mrs. Furley, and the butcher she had named Lucky Strike peered through his thick-lensed glasses at her, as if studying the angles of a parallelogram.

"How many?" he asked, as he had asked it week after week across the shining counter, with a cook's white cap set gravely on his head.

"Well, I think one will be enough this time," said Mrs. Furley, as she had said it, with patience, all year to him, for it was perhaps the purest logic to believe that, dead or living, a mutton had four legs. "Won't you have a Lucky?" she added, and the German called Lucky Strike brought the pack of them slowly into focus behind his lenses, and then reached out his hand.

Army of Occupation

There was a train which left the Gare de l'Est at twenty-five minutes past nine every night, but it was not a French train. The guards at the platform gates were American MPs, and the ticketmen were GIs. They looked at the French girls who had come this far to kiss goodbye the men who were going back, and they passed their judgments and their comments on them. They watched the women and men who stood clasped together in a final embrace—Frenchwomen, and men of the American Army of Occupation going back for another stretch in Germany after a furlough spent in Paris in pursuit of love. The train known as the Duty Train, the "Main Seiner," made its thirteen-and-a-quarter-hour run between the two rivers of two countries. The German sleeping cars and the third-class carriages renounced their former nationality in defeat and became links coupling together the disparate states of America, and the sad, wild, longing outcry—no longer recognizable as singing—of the men of these states could be heard in the crowded corridors and the compartments even before the train pulled away. Even while the gates were sliding closed between the Frenchwomen and the last, racing uniformed men with the weight of their duffel bags balanced on their shoulders as they ran, the drunken speeches to Michigan or California or Maine were roared out through the open windows, and then the trainman's sharp, lingering whistle blew, and the lanterns swung, and the Duty Train pulled out into the dark.

It was a man's train, and yet a few scattered women used to ride on it—American women: Wacs, or Army nurses going back to duty, or War Department employees going where they had to go. Among these few women who went through the gates one cold February night, there was a slender, pretty girl in uniform, with the patch of a war correspondent on the right sleeve of her overcoat, and the letters "US" stitched on the left. She carried her Val-Pak easily in one gloved hand, and her hair was brushed out from under her army cap, glossy and soft and nearly black. As she passed beneath the platform lights, the men at the windows called out to her and whistled, but in spite of the rouge on her mouth and the shortness of her skirt, there was a look of modesty, of shyness and vulnerability about her, so that she seemed at once different from the other women hurrying by. Perhaps it was merely that she was alone, while the others hastened in twos or threes up the crowded, tenebrous platform, half running on their high, bold heels, with their breath showing white on the air before them as they talked or laughed aloud. Or perhaps merely that she walked with her head a little lowered, while the others did not, or else that the things that passed through her mind were different. She did not look toward the men, and she did not seem to hear them calling out.

When she came to the third-class carriage on which the letter "B" hung black on a square, white sign, she swung her Val-Pak up the high steps through the door. Although there were still six minutes before the train would go, the outcry had already begun in the packed, cold cars, and the girl made her way, a little hesitant, a little shy, past the soldiers blocking the corridor. "Roll me over / In the clover," wailed the voices in grief from behind the closed compartment doors, and far ahead, in almost unbearable sorrow, other voices cried out "Reminds me of / The one I love" in drunken, unmelodious complaint.

"Compartment 5, Seat 29," the girl said half aloud, holding her ticket in her hand. And then she had found the number, and she put her hand on the sliding door of Compartment 5 and pulled it back.

There were three soldiers sitting inside on the long, wooden seats, and one of them, a sergeant, who was in the corner at the right of the door, must have just ceased singing, for his mouth hung open still. He held an uncorked bottle of cognac in one hand, and he looked up at the girl standing in the doorway, and then he threw back his head and bayed the wolf call long and wild and loud.

The soldier who sat across from him got slowly, carefully to his feet. "Take a glance, gentlemen, at what they're passing around with the coffee and leecures tonight," he said, and he reached out and took the Val-Pak from the girl's hand. He was a big, pink-skinned young man with heavy, sloping shoulders, and his reddish hair was cropped close upon his broad, round skull. "They take away Montmartre, but they give us a war correspondent," he said, and as he raised her bag to jam it onto the rack, he lost his balance and caught at the handle of the door. "What paper you representing?" he said.

The girl stood in the doorway still, troubled and young, with her dark hair soft around her face. She looked at the sergeant, who sat holding the bottle of cognac between his spread knees, and at the soldier standing beside her, whose eyes had begun at the patch on her shoulder and moved slowly, unsteadily down to her sheer stockings and her brown tie-shoes. Beyond them, there was a third soldier. He was sitting by the window and had not turned his head, and now, as the Duty Train slipped into motion, she saw the platform lights flash in accelerating rhythm past his ear and the cap he wore pushed low upon his forehead.

"I'm free-lancing," she said. She did not say, *I'm going to Ger-*

*many to see him. He's showing them how to publish papers over
there.*

"Have a seat," said the big soldier, swaying toward her.
"You've never had it as good as this before. Everywhere else in
the train they're packed in eight or ten to a compartment. You
never had it so good anywhere you've ever been," he said.

"She's afraid. The poor little thing's afraid," said the sergeant.
He sat looking up at her, his pale, soiled hands closed on the cognac bottle that hung between his knees. "She's afraid of you
and me and this here bottle."

"No," said the girl quickly, "I'm not afraid." She stepped inside, and because of the cold in the corridor she pulled the door
shut behind her, and at once the sound of the singing was closed
away, fainter and sadder, and she stepped past the two men and
sat down on the same side as the sergeant, but at a distance
from him. The two soldiers looked at her ankles and legs as she
took her coat off; they watched her take off her fur-lined, good
leather gloves, and fold them and put them into the brown
leather bag that had hung from her shoulder by a strap. Then
the sergeant raised the bottle of cognac to his mouth, his lips
funneling moist and red around the bottle's greenish glass.
When he had drunk, he handed the bottle across to the big soldier with the reddish hair. He sat down again on the opposite
seat, and raised the bottle to his mouth, and as he drank he
swayed with the swaying of the train.

"I see you're married," the sergeant said to the girl. He sat
looking down the length of the bench at her, and he jerked his
chin in the direction of her hand. His chin was deeply cleft, and
a thread of cognac that ran through the cleft and the stubble
shone yellow in the compartment's naked light. "I see you got a
ring on your finger," he said. The cuffs of his shirt hung loose
below the sleeves of his blouse, and as he looked at her he
fumbled a moment at the undone buttons at his wrists.

"Yes, I am. I'm married," the girl said.

The soldier had lowered the bottle now, and he wiped the
mouth of it with the inside of his hand. "Have a drink," he said,
and he shifted down on the bench a little to hold the bottle out
to her.

"No, thanks," said the girl.

"She's a lady," said the sergeant. He gave a sad, loud guffaw of laughter and slapped his thigh.

For the first time, the soldier sitting by the window turned his head and looked at them. "There's enough of them that ain't ladies traveling on this here train tonight," he said in a slow, stubborn voice. His face hung narrow and pale between monumental ears, the features of it nearly poetic in their melancholy. "There's two sleeping-car loads of French war brides traveling right along here with us tonight," he said, and perhaps he should have been speaking of plowing one crop or the other under, or of getting the silos full, instead of talking like this to strangers about women. "I don't envy them none that's getting them dames," he said.

"French war brides lying down in sleeping berths while American war correspondents have to sit up all night. That's rough. That sure is rough," said the sergeant, and the boy from the farm pushed his cap down lower on his brows and turned his face to the dark of the window again.

The big soldier handed the bottle of cognac back to the sergeant, and then he slid farther along on the boards of the seat until he was sitting opposite the girl. "I got a bottle of Martell in my coat there that nobody's ever touched," he said. He leaned forward, his arms leaning on his thick, broad legs, his knees coming close to the girl's knees. "If that's what's keeping you from drinking, I'll get the new bottle out. You won't have to drink after anyone else. It's as pure as the driven snow," he said.

"It's not that," the girl said. She put her soft hair back from her shoulders, talking a little loud above the steady roaring of the train. "I just don't like the taste of it—not straight." For an instant, she saw the booths of the Third Avenue bar where they'd gone in the one winter they had had together, gone six nights a week in the early hours of the morning, after the paper had been put to bed. "My husband's a newspaperman," she heard herself saying, and now that she spoke of him, the tumult and outcry had seemed to cease in the train so that these strangers might listen, the cursing and crying and moaning for another country to come to a halt so that these others might hear more clearly the inimitable sound of love. "So we used to keep funny hours," she said, "and on the way home from work we'd stop in for a drink, at one or two o'clock in the morning, or whenever it happened to be. He needed something strong, and he'd take it straight, but I could never manage to get it down." She could see him in his old blue jacket sitting across a table from her, the first taste of the drink taking the weariness from his face, and giving the gentleness back to his mouth and eyes. "I haven't seen him in eight months," she said. "I've been around newspapers all my life, but I couldn't get over. I simply couldn't get them to send me over." *In thirteen hours now, a little less than thirteen,* she thought, glancing at the watch on her wrist. The distant voices in the train had begun to sing again, and she listened to the faint, far, nostalgic music as she sat smiling blindly at the soldier's swaying face.

The sergeant had been watching her, and now he put the cork back into the bottle of cognac, and pressed it down with the cushion of his thumb. Then he propped the bottle upright in the corner, against the wooden paneling, and he slid unsteadily along the boards until he had come close to the girl. "We're good guys. We're all right guys," he said, and it might have been that the words she had spoken had touched some troubled springhead of emotion in him. "You just got to try and understand us." His tunic was open, and his big, soiled hands were fumbling in his pockets, and after a moment he brought a piece of paper out. "I got this to show the army. I got this to show them I wasn't off somewhere getting drunk, like they might think I was," he said, and his black-rimmed fingers held the creased bit of paper out to her, and she took it in her hand.

There was an English doctor's name and address in Somerset printed out at the top of it, and under this the simple, explicit statement of fact was made: "This is to certify that John Henley White, born January the fifteenth, 1947, died of pulmonary pneumonia on February the nineteenth, 1947, and that his father, Sgt. Harry White, of the United States Army, was present at his funeral. Here witness my Hand and Seal . . ."

Behind the sergeant, the cognac bottle had toppled over, and it rolled back and forth on the wooden seat with the motion of the train. As he reached back for it, he kept his eyes on the girl. She looked slowly up from the words that were written on the piece of paper.

"Surprises you, uh?" he said. He took the cork out of the bottle with his teeth, his head tipped sideways to do it, and still he did not take his eyes from her, and he waited a moment before beginning to drink. "Surprises you to find out I had a son, don't it?" he said. He was almost smiling, as if relishing the wiliness of some trick he had played.

The girl folded the paper where it had been folded before, and he looked at her fingers as she gave it back to him.

"The nineteenth of February. I'm sorry," the girl said in a low voice.

"Sure. Four days ago," said the sergeant. A dribble of cognac was running down his chin. He put the doctor's certificate away in his inside pocket, and he passed the bottle of cognac to the soldier on the other seat. "He was five weeks old, John Henley White. My wife's an English girl, married her two years ago over there when we were stationed in Somerset," he said. "That's where I come from now. She sent me the telegram last week and I flew over. I took one of them big planes, not any of these here little French crates but the big, four-motor jobs you read about in the papers always cracking up." His heavy lips hung open, bright and moist, and his eyes, with a slight glaze on them now, were fixed on her face. "I bet I gave you a surprise. I bet you'd never have taken me for a married man," he said.

"Look," said the big soldier, and he leaned toward the sergeant from the opposite bench. "Does it occur to you that the lady is bored with all this kind of talk? Does it occur to you that beauty incarnate doesn't give a snap of her dainty fingers for your relatives?" He handed the bottle back to the sergeant, and the sergeant lifted it and threw back his head and drank what cognac remained in the bottom of it, and then he dropped the empty bottle on the floor and kicked it under the seat. "You got to make yourself interesting to a lady," the big soldier said. "Tell her about your travels, the countries you been to, the kind of things you seen." He stopped talking, and he sat there looking at the girl, his big, square-boned knees in the khaki cloth almost touching her knees. "In the past three days I've been in Paris, I spent two hundred thousand francs, and I don't regret a penny of it. Not for what I got," he said.

The little farm boy by the window, with the cap tipped low on his brows, turned away from the rushing darkness of the night outside and looked at them bleakly, almost reproachfully, again. "I don't envy you what you got in Paris. I don't envy nobody anything he's got," he said. "I could of had exactly the same as anybody else. I could of had a French war bride traveling right along with me on this here train tonight. I could of been taking her to Bremerhaven the way the rest of them are going, if I'd of been sucker enough to marry her."

The sergeant gave a yipe of laughter. "You sound as if you turned kinda choosy just when you hadn't ought," he said, and he slapped his thigh, and guffawed high and loud.

"I found out too much just in time," said the farm boy, speaking slowly, stubbornly. He looked at them in something like hesitation a moment, as if there were more to say and as if he were about to say it, and then he turned back to the fleeing darkness, to the memory of the fields of home, the valleys and hills and the snowbound roads of home to which his longing gave substance in the foreign night. "Roll me over / In the clover," came the faint, sad chorus of crying down the corridor, and the farm boy rubbed his hand quickly on the pane. "Well, what do you know, it's snowing," he said. The big soldier stood up from his place opposite the girl and began making his way unsteadily toward the corner by the door where the two swaying khaki overcoats hung. "I bet there's a lot of that laying around home now," said the farm boy by the window.

"A lot of what?" said the sergeant, holding his loud, high laughter in.

"Why, snow," said the little soldier, as if surprised that it fell in this foreign country. "Real, winter snow. I bet they're out coasting at home tonight."

The big soldier had reached the overcoats, and he stood there swaying and groping in the pockets of one of them. In a moment he brought out the fresh bottle. "This time you're going to start it off," he said to the girl. He sat down facing her again, and he held the bottle between his knees as he uncorked it. "You're going to have first go at this one, just to sweeten it for the rest of us." He held the bottle toward her. He had spread his big legs wide, one on each side of her silk-clad legs now, ready to close in on them in flagrant embrace.

"No," said the girl. "I'm tired. I want to try to get some sleep."

"Man," said the sergeant, "she just don't like Martell. You can tell that the way she's looking at it. She don't like your brand nohow, boy, so you might as well take it away." He slid back up the seat until he was in the corner by the door where his overcoat hung above him, and he reached up and pulled a bottle out of a pocket. "The brandy of kings," he said with a roar of laughter. "Good old Courvoisier," he said, caressing the bottle in his black-nailed hands.

"You see," the girl began in a quiet voice once his wild, high laughing had ceased, "it's after half past ten at night."

The big soldier opposite her was smiling, his heavy, sloping shoulders hunched forward, and he held the bottle of Martell toward her still. "You'd better try some of this before you drop into the arms of Morpheus," he said.

"No," said the girl again, and, with her coat around her, she moved down the boards of the seat and settled herself by the window. Just across from her now, the little farm boy was asleep with his narrow, tired face against the glass. "I'll take this end," she said, making it sound natural and right above the steady, mechanical rhythm of the train. "You two will have all the room you need up there." But the sergeant's arm had reached out and gone suddenly around her. He brought it tight around her neck, with the back of his soiled hand pressing her throat, and his knuckles forcing hard against her jawbone and her chin.

"Not until I get what I want," he said. She could taste his breath on the little space of air between them as he forced her head and her soft, glossy hair back hard against the side of his face. "I want to get some of that rouge off your mouth. I've been wanting to ever since you walked through that door," he said.

"Would that I might leap to the lady's defense," said the big soldier, "but you outrank me, Sergeant, you outrank me." He had shifted down closer to the farm boy so as to sit nearly opposite to her still, and his legs in their khaki were stretched out now as if in longing toward her. "You take what you're entitled to, Sergeant," he said, and he lifted the bottle of Martell and took a long, deep drink. "You take it first. I'll take what's left."

The girl's heart beat swiftly in impatience and outrage a moment while the back of the sergeant's hand forced up her chin. She was thinking fiercely, *They can't do anything, not a single thing. In a little while he'll walk down the platform, looking in every window for me. . . .*

"Stop being fools," she said in a low, unshaken voice, and she twisted within the crook of the sergeant's arm, and with her two hands she lifted the weight and the abomination of his flesh, and flung his arm away. His will, and his tough physical power, seemed suddenly to have ebbed in weariness, or hopelessness, or in the remembrance of some half-forgotten grief, and his hand, with the sleeve unbuttoned at the wrist, fell soiled and empty on the wooden seat.

"What I need is a drink," he said.

It was then, as he lifted the bottle of Courvoisier to drink, that the compartment door was jerked suddenly back, and a tall, young, blue-eyed corporal stepped in. He wore a battle jacket, with three years of overseas stripes on his sleeves, and his hair was black, and it fell loosely across his forehead, soft and untractable, as if it had just been washed that afternoon. He closed the door behind him, and he stood with his handsome young head lifted, holding to the handle of it still, his grave eyes looking straight toward the corner where the girl sat with her legs drawn up under her and her coat around her in the cold.

"I saw you in the station when you came through the gate," he said. "I thought maybe you had a sleeping berth, and then I just saw you now through the compartment window as I came down the corridor." He did not seem to see the others sitting in the compartment with her, or the sergeant's legs stretched out like a barrier across the aisle. "I've got a seat in the car next door," he said. "I mean a seat with upholstery—second class. You'd be better off in there, if you'd like to take it," he said.

"And you?" said the girl, speaking quickly to him.

"I'll switch with you," he said.

The big soldier had been drinking from his bottle of Martell, and now he wiped his mouth with the side of his hand and held out the bottle to the corporal. "Oh, young Lochinvar, take a drink of this," he said.

But the corporal had not seemed to hear him speak. He was looking straight at the girl as he stepped across the sergeant's outstretched legs. "I'm so sick of looking at Frenchwomen," he said, and he sat down on the wooden seat beside her, sitting sidewise so as to look into her face. "You're American. You're wonderful," he said.

"Take it somewhere else," said the sergeant, who slumped on the bench behind him, but the corporal might have been a deaf man for all that he knew the sergeant was there.

"I haven't been home for eighteen months," said the corporal, his voice eager, his blue eyes in their short, thick fringes of black lashes fixed on her eyes, his ears deaf to everything except what she might say. "Eighteen months is a long time to be away from where you want to be."

Behind him, in the corner, the sergeant straightened up, and slapped his thigh, and roared aloud. "It's rough, it sure is rough them treating you like that," he said, and he lifted the bottle of Courvoisier and drank again.

"I want you to have my seat in the other car," said the corporal. With his long, narrow fingers he combed the loose hair back off his brow. "You're beautiful. You're like all the girls at home who don't come over."

As if the single word "home" had sounded clear as a clarion call above the rushing tumult of the train, the farm boy by the window roused from sleep and raised his head. "You on your way to Bremerhaven?" he asked in his slow, stubborn, perplexed voice. He sat looking across at them, and at the light, in bewilderment a moment, blindly fingering the stuff of his uniform as if it were not khaki but denim or corduroy, perhaps, that he had expected to find there. "You on your way home, too?" he said. But the corporal had not seemed to hear him.

"I haven't anything against the French," said the corporal, looking at the girl still. "But the women aren't like you. Your skin is different, and your hair, and the sound of your voice is different."

"You'd better watch out, Corporal," said the big soldier, and he grinned at them from the other bench. "She's got French blood in her. She's got a drop or two of English, too."

"No," said the corporal, and although he heard the sound of words at last, he did not turn his head from the sight of her. "They don't make them like that over here. They don't know how," he said.

"There're plenty of them there French ones on the train to-night," said the farm boy by the window. "War brides. French war brides," he said, looking at the corporal. "Some fellas don't seem to give a whoop and a holler what they get hold of. Maybe they don't know something I found out just in time about the French," he said.

"Isolationist, are you?" said the big soldier, and he lowered the bottle of Martell.

"Sure," said the farm boy in his slow, stubborn voice. He turned his face back to the darkness of the night. "That's the word I was looking for," he said, and he drifted bleakly into sleep again.

The sergeant had got unsteadily up from his place by the door, and with one hand he held to the baggage rack above him for stability while he took the two or three steps down the compartment to where the corporal sat beside the girl. "I guess ladies and gentlemen don't drink the way the rest of us do?" he said, and he stood there swaying above them. His tunic hung open still, and in the hand that swung by his side he held the half-empty bottle of Courvoisier.

"Sure, I drink," said the corporal, glancing up at him. "I've been drinking for two days in Paris. I don't want to drink any more." He shook the hair back off his forehead, and then his blue eyes looked eagerly, earnestly, through their smudged fringe of lashes at the girl. "I've got a house at home, a house of my own," he said. "My uncle left it to me. I've rented it to a family. They pay me a hundred and twenty-five dollars a month, and I'll get more when the OPA controls are off. But I don't want to live there. I'm just telling you about it so that you'll know. What I want to do is to go up to Alaska," he said, his voice grave, eager, young. "I want to open up some kind of an inn, something with cabins, or maybe bungalows, in the woods around it, up on the Alaskan highway. I've been getting estimates on the price of land up there, and building's cheap once you get your ground cleared. Do you think you'd like Alaska?" he said. "It would be for about three months of the year, the season up there, say the fifteenth of June to the fifteenth of September, and I'd build something really good, something picturesque. Do you think you'd like to take a chance on it?" he said.

The sergeant made another unsteady step, and now he stood between the girl and the corporal, a swaying barrier, holding with one hand still to the baggage rack above his head.

"Perhaps we could talk about it tomorrow," the girl said, and she touched the corporal's sleeve an instant. "I'm tired. If you meant what you said about the seat in the other car, I'd like to take it—"

The sergeant's head swung like a bell between them now, his moist lips open. "You get out of here," he said to the corporal. "Get out quick."

"No," said the corporal. He looked up in almost childlike credence and trust at the sergeant. "I'm twenty-three," he said, and he put the hair back off his forehead. "I swear I've been looking for twenty years for her. I never thought I'd find her overseas." He turned back to the girl again, and he went on, saying, "I'm from Oregon, but that doesn't mean I want to spend my life there. I'd want the woman who married me to have as much say about that as I have myself. But I'd like you to think about Alaska. I'd like you to keep it in mind." He put his hand in his blouse now, and he felt in the inner pocket of it. "I've got some photographs I could show you—just small ones, but they'd give you an idea," he said. "There're trees there that take your breath away, bigger than in California even, and when you get up high enough, it's glacier country."

The sergeant swung, seemingly without muscle or bone, like a hanged man between them. "Go on. Get out of here. Get out," he said.

"Sure," said the big soldier on the other side. "You be a good boy and run along back to Oregon."

"You'd better go," said the girl in a soft voice to the corporal. "You go, and I'll go with you." She had gathered her coat closely around her, and she slid her legs carefully, cautiously down.

"Yes," said the corporal, but he did not get up from the bench. He sat there looking at her. "My God, you're beautiful. I love you. I respect you," he said.

The sergeant held with one hand to the baggage rack still, and although he had scarcely seemed to move, he raised the nearly empty bottle he held in his other hand, and he brought it down, vicious and hard, on the side of the corporal's head. For an instant the corporal's underlip quivered like a child's, but he did not fall at once; he even sought to rise to his feet, with a look of surprise and sickness on his face. And then his eyes closed, and he sloped sidewise, huddled within himself, and the sergeant lurched aside to let him slip to the compartment floor. When he was down, lying full-length as if in sleep, the sergeant leaned over him in silence and hit him again, this time across the forehead where the loose hair fell upon his brow, and what was left of the cognac ran out of the mouth of the bottle and splashed across the front of the corporal's blouse and stained the campaign ribbons on his breast. The girl sat gripping her coat around her with her trembling hands, and her teeth were shaking in her head.

"Let's kick the guts out of Oregon for interfering where he wasn't wanted," said the big soldier. He tried to get up from his seat, but he couldn't stand any longer. Beyond him, the farm boy slept in peace against the cold, dark window glass.

The bottle of Courvoisier had dropped from the sergeant's hand with the force of the last blow he had given, and now he stooped down, grunting, his soiled fingers groping for the bottle as it rolled back and forth across the compartment floor. When he had got hold of it again, he raised the emptied bottle above the corporal's head.

"Don't touch him! Don't you dare to hit him again!" the girl cried out. She had jumped to her feet, she had flung herself forward as if to save from annihilation the actual flesh and bone of all that remained of decency. *There're other people on this train, like people you know, like people you see in the street,* she was thinking in panic. *There're Wacs, and brothers, and sons, and husbands . . . there're people singing.* She could hear their voices, far, unheeding, calling out in nostalgia, as the Germans had called out before them, to a loitering, blond-headed woman named "Lili Marlene." *People who understand words, if I can get to them, if I can say the words to them,* but her legs shook under her as she walked. She had got past the big soldier, who sprawled in stupor on the bench now; she was making her way past the body of the corporal. The sergeant stood upright, his legs straddling the fallen man, the empty bottle hanging from his fingers, swaying, half smiling, before the compartment door. "Get out of my way!" she cried out in fury to him. "Get out of my way!" And he did not speak, but, half smiling still as she flung by him, he lifted his hand and stroked her soft, dark hair.

Outside in the cold of the corridor she began to run past the closed compartment doors, the drawn curtains, the masked lights, running fast, with the tears falling down her face, toward the sound of the sad, sweet, distant voices in the rushing train.

Cabaret

The stage was small; it was no more than a platform improvised at the far end of a long ground-floor room which had been for three centuries a *Gaststube* in a small town in Land Hesse. The *Gaststube* walls, ponderous with ancient wainscoting and large mirrors framed in gilded wood, seemed now to have set aside their own historical significance to converge toward the vanishing point at which the unseen actors were about to play. The curtains were still drawn, and behind them a half dozen of the young players waited in impatience, the grease paint bright and porous on their faces, elated as children are elated with their own wild, nearly incommunicable fervor, taking turns at peering through one or the other of the two holes which pierced the velvet curtains at the height of a man's eye. To the townspeople who had put their good clothes on for an evening of entertainment and taken their places at the tables under the elaborate brass chandeliers, these holes were not perceptible, but to the restless group of players they were like windows opening upon life itself, each containing the exact measure of promise the evening held.

Among them was a girl in pink satin, lace-trimmed underwear, and if she had played Ophelia the night before, that was over and done with, for now she had coarsened into the professional female, with her limbs stripped naked, and her small untrembling breasts revealed as hard as rock within the yellow lace. Perhaps her jaw was too determined and businesslike for love, but still she was turned out in a traditional concept for its diversions, with high-heeled black satin mules on her bare, blue-veined feet, and rhinestone butterflies caught in the dark bush of her hair. And there was a long-necked boy with lank brown locks, in a velveteen jacket and a flowing tie, dressed to play the part of a poet; and a blond-haired youth in white linen shorts, and a T shirt, with the bronze of artificial sunburn glowing on his face and throat and forearms, as well as on his muscular calves and thighs. There was a man with a wealth of black whiskers, perhaps the curled black horsehair of mattress stuffing put to this use, with a fur cap on his head, and a bright red tunic tucked inside his trousers, who stood on tiptoe in his Cossack boots, seeking to see across the shoulders of the others into the *Gaststube*, with the hammer and sickle in metal crossed in the fur of his cap, and worn on his tunic, in the region of his heart. Another young woman stood in the group of them, a girl with narrow hips, and metal-colored hair, and a skin still tawny from the summer sun. From the sullen look of her mouth, and the weariness of her lids, it could be deduced that she had seen Dietrich play a role or two; and it may have been that her legs were as beautiful as Dietrich's, but only her broad shoulders, and her slim arms, and her smoothly knit bare back, were revealed in the long black sheath of satin which she wore.

But there was one dominant figure who stood taller than the

rest of them—a young man in the shabby greatcoat of a Wehr-macht soldier, with the Wehrmacht cap, bearing a swastika, placed jauntily on his head. He was a bold young man, but in spite of the look of insolence in his eye, there was something else to him. There was vigor and drama in his bones, and a chronicle of suffering and deception was written in pride and intrepidity upon his face. On either side of his arrogant, humorous mouth there were scars marked deeply in his flesh, such as mark with bitterness the faces of those who have been disabled young, and who will have none of it.

"Petscher's using the upper half of his wife for a showcase to-night," he whispered sharply. He had shouldered aside whoever was in his way, and put one cold blue eye to a hole in the cur-tain, and he spoke with irony. "Advertising three watches on one side of her bust and a selection of fake gold cuff links on the other, all with the price tags hanging on them. Every article on display may be purchased at Petscher's, Marktplatz 21, open 9 a.m. until 5 p.m., Monday through Saturday," he said, and he stepped aside in impatience to let the poet see.

It was the Wehrmacht soldier who had conceived of the cab-aret show they were about to give, and his was the voice that was ready to roar aloud the others' lines, as well as his own, if their courage failed them now. They were known for their Schiller, and Gorki, and Molière, and their Shakespeare was re-spected; but the performance on which the curtain was about to rise had nothing to do with the classics. It was their own, with the name of no other playwright signed to it; it was their com-mercial venture, for money they had to have. They had talked too long among themselves of Sartre, and Tennessee Williams, of Thornton Wilder, and Pirandello, of Camus, and Borchert, and Saroyan, speaking as intimately of these strangers as if they stood waiting their cues in the wings with them. The cue was money, and their palms were itching for it. They must have money in order to speak aloud with passion not only the lines of the classics, but a lingo contemporary enough to be taken for blasphemy in the hushed and darkened auditorium of a pom-pous country's defeat.

"The Schunk and Fiddemühle garage people have just come

in," said the girl in the tight black satin sheath. Her eye, the lid
of it smeared with blue salve, was fixed to the other hole in the
curtain, and her voice was husky and low. "Frau Schunk in silver fox, and Frau Fiddemühle in ostrich feathers. You can get
the stink of black-market gas on them from here," she said.

The Wehrmacht soldier put his hands on her naked shoulders,
his touch professional, impersonal, as if his palms cupped nothing more living than metal or stone. And it could be seen that
the two middle fingers of his right hand were missing, and that
on the left there remained only the forefinger and thumb.

"Two tables empty still! I want the place filled up!" he whispered sharply, having moved the girl aside so that he might see.
From beyond the curtain could be heard the murmuring of the
spectators' voices, and the chiming of silverware, and china, and
glass.

Below the platform, a pianist, a violinist, and a harpist had
taken their places, and the pianist touched the keys softly, while
the violinist and the harpist lowered their heads and tried their
strings. And then, when the watches marked half past eight, the
lights in the *Gaststube* were extinguished, and the three musicians played the introductory bars. The murmuring of the spectators ceased, the waiters no longer moved from table to table,
but were lost in immobility in the shadows, and behind the curtains, on which the footlights cast their scallops of illumination,
all but the Wehrmacht soldier hastened from the boards. He
stood alone in the center of the stage, his head, with the beaked
cap of the German Army on it, raised, his arms folded high
across the breast of the long gray overcoat, waiting dramatically
there while the sound of casual life was stilled. It was in this
posture that the spotlight found him when the curtains parted—
his hands thrust out of sight beneath his armpits, his brutal
young mouth set, his greased lids masking nothing of the
boldness of his eyes.

"You know my face? You have seen me before?" he asked the
spectators. "You saw me at Stalingrad, you say? Yes, I was
there!" His voice rang out across the *Gaststube* with a sound of
violence, of profound excitement in it, which made a theatre of
the place at once, and his word struck the brass of the chande-

liers and the darkened panes of the mirrors like the flat of a castigating hand. The people to whom he had put the question had no interest left for the goblets of pink and yellow water-ice which the waiters had set before them, or for the flute-shaped glasses of white wine. "It was cold that winter! We were hungry, but there was nothing to put between our teeth except our bitterness! We ate our horses when they fell, and gnawed at the living when the cold had turned their carcasses to stone!" he said, and those at the tables who had taken their wafers up to eat them, put them down upon their plates again, and the Wehrmacht soldier lowered his voice to a whisper, and his eyes were bright and bold as he leaned across the footlights toward the tradespeople who had paid their money out for something advertised as a sensational cabaret. "Three hundred and thirty thousand men defending the frontiers of the Fatherland, defending our frontiers on the Volga!" he said in savage irony. "Do you remember Height 135, the Kasachi Hills, Gumrak, Tulevoy Ravine?" he whispered sharply. "Can you tell me how many hundreds of thousands of us, how many generations of us, died?" And now he freed his maimed hands from his armpits, but with a show of difficulty, as if drawing them from the grip of some powerful encumbrance which held them fast. He ran his right forefinger inside the collar of his coat, his mouth twisted as he gasped audibly for air or sustenance, turning his hand with skill so that no one might see the welt of flesh where the quick prehensile digits once had been. "Defeat!" he shouted in a choking voice. "Defeat! That was the sentence passed on us, and no reprieve! Defeat by cold, hunger, ground by the tread of tanks to rag and rot, screams throttled by the thumbs of death, eyes turned to ice before the tears could fall from them!"; saying it to them as husband, brother, or son, who would never return again might have said it before he died. The spectators sat uneasily upon the ancient straight-backed chairs, for now it was no longer a performer before them who mouthed written lines, but a manifestation of their own reality who spoke their rankling pain aloud. Those who had returned, lamed, broken, no more than stumps of men, had said it to them in words similar to these, so for a moment it seemed this was the voice of Germany itself which spoke to them across the footlights, and, sitting at the tables, they looked into one another's faces, and nodded quietly. And then, without warning, he betrayed them all, baring his teeth and spitting the taste of Germany's defeat across the boards. He stood erect again, his hands thrust into the pockets of his overcoat, his chin flung up. "Bombed out? Lost everything? Don't like the Occupation?" he cried, aping the whine. "Bah, the tune's been played three years too long! The notes are flat!" This was the signal for the musicians who sat below the platform to begin softly to play. "At Stalingrad I took an oath concerning that!" the Wehrmacht soldier said in his contempt for them. The mask of comedy was clapped onto his face now, and he strolled, in time with the music's tempo, back and forth across the stage.

> *"I swore if I survived to mime, to rant,*
> *Lived to shoot boar and roebuck in their*
> *season, study Hegel, Kant,*
> *That I would split my sides with laughing!"*

he said, speaking confidentially to them, and he broke the rhythm of his stanzas to throw his head back and give them a sample of that laughter at its best.

> *"The war that followed cold or hot,*
> *The Germans unified or not,*
> *Stalemate in Berlin, check at Bonn,*
> *The West Mark battle lost or won,*
> *Negotiations mostly black,*
> *If I got back*
> *From Stalingrad, I swore to laugh!"*

And now his violent laughter rang across the *Gaststube* tables, and rattled through the chandeliers. He stood there with his head flung back upon his muscular throat, the white of his teeth and eyes, the bold blue of his lids, and the ochre of his make-up, embellished by the sphere of illumination in which he was contained as if in purest glass. His hands were laid against his belly, adroitly placed so that their mutilation might not be perceived, and the words he tried to speak were lost in the sound of his own loud shameless laughter, and in the spectators' laughter which spread, without their knowing why they laughed, from table to table in the crowded room.

> *"Let Occupation statutes wait*
> *While we enjoy our buffer fate!"*

he managed to roar out at last;

> *"For what's a state if not of mind,*
> *Bi-zone, tri-zone, or any kind?*
> *Whatever comes, there's Garry Davis,*
> *Who's absolutely sure to save us! Let's laugh!"*

he cried, the strength of his voice again drained by his laughter; and, as he bent double, crippled by his mirth, the people at the tables laughed until the tears came into their eyes.

With the laughter at its loudest, the musicians brought their music to its climax, and the curtains were drawn before the townspeople had time to recover and see the look of calculation in the convulsed actor's canny eye. *Twenty-eight tables,* he estimated rapidly, *seating four to eight persons each, makes an average of one hundred and sixty-four times the cover charge of D.M. 2, plus ten per cent of the refreshments, approximating possibly D.M. 1000 per night, if this continues for the two-week run.* The young, he thought savagely, buying our way back to decency again! You'll have Sartre and Camus to choke on when our new season begins! And when the curtains parted again, but an instant later, the Wehrmacht soldier was gone, and the stage was set for a bedroom scene, for things were moving quickly now. On the boards was a shabby divan, which had perhaps served as prop for thirty years or more, refurbished now with fancy lace-covered cushions; and behind the divan was a three-panelled screen of midnight blue, with a pair of black silk stockings flung across it; and beside the divan a night table on which stood a perfume atomizer, and a half-empty bottle of cognac, and an empty liqueur glass. On the divan itself reclined the barelegged, long-jawed young woman in her pink undergarments, the rhinestone butterflies enmeshed in her hair.

The musicians played "Tales of Hoffmann," with a ludicrous

twist to the rendering of it, as if their tongues were in their cheeks, and the young woman lying on the divan stretched her firm white legs and arms and sang her aria of complaint. There were some in the audience who had seen her play Juliet or Ophelia in the weeks before, but all that was left of Juliet now was the look of the flesh designed for love, and all that remained of Ophelia was the repeated gesture of the arm and hand, not strewing flowers, but reaching for the perfume atomizer or the cognac bottle or the glass. For now she was "France," obscene, corrupt, degenerate, and a hazy reproduction of the Eiffel Tower had been painted in the window of the canvas backdrop so that there would be no mistake about her nationality. But she sang in German, spraying her bare chest and shoulders and the dark bush of her hair with perfume as she warbled of the Ruhr. Coal, coke, and steel was what she wanted in payment for her favors, as a lesser tart wanted jewels for her fingers and pelts for her back. She sang in German, but it was in French that she cried out in alarm when the blond young athlete in his white shorts and T shirt sprang through the window frame painted on the backdrop, effacing the Eiffel Tower for an instant as he came. Around his neck hung a string of American canned foods which clattered aloud as, with his jaws chewing steadily at a wad of gum, he hastened to her across the little stage.

"*Mon dieu, c'est toi,* Marshall?" the young woman cried out, and the tradespeople seated at the tables roared with laughter as he sought to take her in his strong bronzed arms. The young woman glanced uneasily toward the door, and at the window behind her, while the young man dropped on his knees before her, and, seeking to press his hand in passion on his heart, his fingers closed instead upon a can of Heinz's spaghetti in tomato sauce.

"Have you tried my Chinese dinner, boxed for four, complete with chopsticks and pigtail?" he pled with her, making this speech in English as he kneeled before her on the boards. "Or my Italian *pasta* which requires no cooking, seasoned with pre-digested Parmesan? Or my Danish eggs, with the tenderness of the hen frozen in? There's another treat in store for you!" he wooed her to the accompaniment of the necklace of cans,

"Golden bananas dehydrated by camel drivers right on the desert and shipped to you with the money-back guarantee of twelve full ounces of desert sunlight sealed in each can, topped by true-to-life skins in a separate package, just add water, stitch the bananas securely inside, and, boy, you'll taste the tropics, you'll hear the throbbing heart of the jungle—"

"But, Marshall, I haven't a can opener!" the young woman cried out, and she poured the liqueur glass full again.

"There's one in every can of Alaskan minced clams!" the young man went on, still talking fast. "In fact, in each can of this superlative fish food, you will find a Shetland pony and cart, a fireless cooker, a 1949 Chevrolet, a television set, Hollywood, and a foreign agent just lifted from a key position in the State Department—" And now he must wait until the uproarious laughter had subsided at the tables before he could hope to be heard again. The spectators rocked on their chairs, or they shouted their laughter aloud, or else they pressed their handkerchiefs to their mouths to staunch it, their delight augmented by their knowledge that he had been a prisoner of war for three years in America and had learned this jargon at first hand, thus, in some fashion, having outwitted, and outwitting still, his captors by aping their idiom so viciously. "Get your atomic energy today the sure way!" he besought her, and he jumped up from his knees.

"Hush!" whispered the young woman, but she let him put his arms around her as she glanced furtively about. "Perhaps we aren't alone, *mein Schatz,*" she said, and, as he snapped the elastic strap of her brassière upon her shoulder, the audience cried again in its exquisite pain.

The snapping of the brassière strap was the bewhiskered man's cue, and he emerged laboriously from under the divan, cursing, irate, shaking not one, but two fists in the air. And while the spectators howled at the sight of the scarlet tunic, and the hammer and sickle in such straits, the girl fled in her high-heeled black satin mules and her pink underwear around the table, with the young man in his shorts bounding after her, the string of cans he wore clattering and jumping as he ran. As he passed the night-table, he reached for the cognac bottle, to seize it up as weapon, but missed it in his panic and got the perfume atomizer instead. And now he raced on with it, spraying its contents at the bearded man who came lumbering behind him in pursuit.

"Veto! Veto!" shouted the man who ran as unwieldy as a bear, the fur cap slipped sideways on his head. It was he who managed to seize the cognac bottle by its neck, and he brandished it at the blond young man who leapt with agility before him a jump behind the half-clothed figure of the whore. "Veto! Veto!" cried the man in the red tunic, and he swung in his tracks to cut off the girl's retreat, and the fur cap flew from his head. At the sight of him standing with his arms wide open, the young woman turned too, and ran, the symbol of a country whose name was pain to every German in the room, but who now pretended as they laughed that France was not the unpaid debt, the unhealed wound, but merely a vulgar woman in her underwear. This they can take, thought the Wehrmacht soldier, standing in the wings, and hearing the laughter in the hall. This they can fool themselves with for a little while, until the rest of it comes!

And so they were off again, the girl on her high heels still in the lead, racing in single file past the reproduction of the Eiffel Tower, the three of them disappearing behind one end of the screen and coming out the other, the tin cans clattering, the atomizer spraying, the musicians below the platform playing faster and faster, neck and neck in tempo with the actors' pace. "Veto! Veto!" spluttered the man in his doused red tunic as the cologne water filled his mouth and eyes and nose. At the height of this pandemonium, with the chandeliers quivering on their antique stems and laughter rocking the place, the velvet curtains were drawn closed.

The next skit was as tranquil as a summer field: three pretty young women with aprons tied around their waists, and their hair worn in shining plaits, stood hand in guileless hand upon the stage, and recited, in childlike trebles, their seemingly naive couplets concerning the monetary reform. One girl in Hessian peasant dress, represented the Reichsmark, another, in Bavarian costume, the Deutschmark, and the third, the East Zone mark, with a beribboned Slavic headdress crowning her serene broad brow. The townspeople could eat and drink at ease to this accompaniment, even signal to the waiters for more wine, laugh circumspectly, and clap with moderation when the curtains closed. But the skit which followed on the heels of this was something else again: the girl in the black satin sheath stood there alone, one languorous hand placed on her slender, sloping hip, as striking as Dietrich herself to them, metallic-haired and glamorous in the clear cone of the spotlight on the darkened stage. The music played softly, with yearning, below her, and her greased lids were heavy, her long emerald eyes seemingly drugged with dreams or memories of love. She sang of this country that was theirs, of the cities that were rubble, and of the people who lived in the cellars and craters that remained. And, as she sang, her low husky voice was bitter, and the words were half crooned, half snarled in passion, while she moved in insolence and indolence, her hips weaving slowly, across the boards.

"Bathtubs hang by their piping from second stories still," she sang in her sultry German to them, "and bedroom doors swing on their hinges, opening forever now upon eternity! Staircases end in space, the last flight gone, and moss upon them, but our hearts run down them still in memory! Out of the débris where once a city stood, a vine writhes upward through a fallen statue's hand, two swallows build their nest on a church altar laid open to the rain, a tree grows tall and flowers through a schoolroom's broken heart, where children played who'll never play again!" Out of these ruins, this rubble, she snarled at the people in the *Gaststube*, love, or some imitation of it, had crawled like a rat, had slithered in hunger and desire from the moonlit stones. "Girls," she drawled huskily, making the word a long vicious caress, "came one by one, came two by two, and walked the streets in search of it," and she moved slowly, sinuously, across the stage. "Girls buttoned their worn jackets tight!" she cried out in grim pity for them. "Girls lingered on street corners like alley cats, accosted the living with their hearts sick for the dead!"

And, as she sang, the girls, almost identically dressed, came one by one and two by two from the wings, and they strolled with lagging steps past the ruins which took tentative shape now on the canvas backdrop. They wore plaid wool skirts, and bright plastic shoulder-strap bags, and saddleback shoes, and nylon stockings, and all they wore was recognizable as that mail-order-house merchandise which had become standard apparel for the *Fräuleins* of the American Zone. There were six or eight of them, moving like shadows against the shadowy ruins which served as background to the single figure in her monocle of light. Their singing began with a drowsy humming in the throat, and, as if following their lead, the musicians below them found the notes upon their instruments, and the young woman, swaying to the rhythm of it, drawled huskily, and with contempt, the words the audience knew well.

"Johnny, *wenn Du'ne Kamel hast,*" she sang, and cigarettes appeared, whether Camels or not, in the hand of every sauntering girl; "*bin ich bei Dir zu Gast,*" it went, and the minute separate wings of illumination fluttered briefly in the darkness as each girl paused, with the music's beat, and struck a match, and bent her head, and drew the first breath in. And then they strolled aimlessly, idly, on again, humming the tune at the same lingering pace at which they walked. "Johnny, *wenn Du'ne Kamel hast,*" went the words as the girl sauntered past the moon-lit ruins, "I'll spend the whole—long—night—with—you!"

The applause was such that they must do a portion of their act again, with the girl who might have been Dietrich speaking their intention as she swayed before them, muscular, savage, slender, in her tight black dress. And then the curtains were drawn closed, the lights came on in the *Gaststube* chandeliers, and the musicians got to their feet and made their way out to the entrance where draughts of cool night air came through the opened doors. This was the intermission, and when the girl, her flesh shining with grease paint and sweat, stepped into the wings, the Wehrmacht soldier, who had discarded his uniform now for the part that was to come, put his quick strong hands upon her naked shoulders, and drew her savagely against him.

"My God, we've put it over!" he said.

"The *Herr Kulturreferent* is giving us two columns in tomorrow's paper!" cried the symbol of France, no longer in her underwear, and she beat the Wehrmacht soldier on the back. "Three tables have ordered the best champagne! The management is trying to get ice!"

"Wait," said the blond girl huskily, her curved, clinging body stirring under the Wehrmacht soldier's hands. "No one sitting out there at the tables has come in for criticism yet."

"What should we wait for? Censure?" the soldier cried out, his whisper loud, and reckless, and gay. He wore a local conception of American democratic dress: gray flannel trousers, which had not recently been cleaned or pressed, striped shirt, striped tie, and a shapeless brown felt hat pushed to the back of his head. And now he dropped his hands from the girl's shoulders, and he turned to manipulate the backdrop depicting the city ruins away across the boards. With him labored the poet, still dressed for the poet's role, and the bearded man, no longer in a tunic or with a fur cap on his head, but wearing an ancient black frock coat, and trousers that tapered to gaiters buttoned over the split leather of his shoes. "Listen to them snapping their fingers for more wine out there, maybe even for beefsteaks!" the Wehrmacht soldier said, speaking of these others as if more than a length of curtain divided actors from audience, and as he and the poet and the bearded man shifted the scenery in the heat, the sweat stood on their brows.

And then the blond young man, no longer in white shorts or with a necklace of tin cans around his neck, maneuvered the backdrop of a stately university building out of the wings and into place.

"*Herr Oberstaatsanwalt* Jauernick has made reservations for twenty-five for Saturday night!" he said, his voice hoarse with effort. He was wearing knee-high boots now, and shirt and trousers of military cut, and of a familiar brown. On his right sleeve could be seen an insignia done in black and white, and circled with red, in size and shape and from a distance deceptively like the one the world had cause to know. But instead of a hooked cross within the circle, there was the head of a sheep, done in white on black, with one ear up and one ear down. "If we want to make money, perhaps we shouldn't go too far," he said.

"Too far?" cried the Wehrmacht soldier, and he straightened up and pushed the American felt hat back further on his head. "We're just halfway! Do you want us to back down now?"

"If they walk out tonight, the whole thing will be off," said the blond young man in his shirt and trousers of military cut, and he looked at the others uneasily.

"When a miser is played on the stage, does the miser in the audience recognize himself?" the Wehrmacht soldier roared in his impatience with them.

"Then what's the use in playing it out?" said the poet, speaking scarcely aloud.

"We could do the one on dying British aristocracy instead," said the bearded man in the frock coat. The vacillation in his voice had nothing to do with his height or his breadth or the show of whiskers on his face, and he set to brushing the dust of the boards from his rusty black in order not to meet the Wehrmacht soldier's eye.

"By God!" he cried out, and he swung on his heel, and he jerked the felt hat forward with his mutilated right hand. "By God!" he said again, and then he made the rest of it sound humorous. "Have you forgotten? We're playing for posterity!"

But the skit which followed immediately after was harmless enough. It was certainly not the one which the evening had been leading up to, word by word, and line by line. It was played by the bearded man in his gaiters and frock coat, and the Wehrmacht soldier in his American clothes, and the poet with his velveteen jacket and his soft silk tie. They disagreed in couplets, and in rhyme as well as song—the typical *Herr Professor* of a provincial town, and the typical poet-philosopher, and the typical collaborationist whose tradition dated since 1945, speaking sometimes in chorus, sometimes separately. The *Herr Professor* maintained that super-learning should be dispensed by super-pedagogues exclusively, and only to super-super-alumni in super-scientific fields. As he stepped a minuet with dignity, holding the tails of his frock coat like a skirt in his two hands, he stated the consensus of academic opinion was that those who were merely the sons or grandsons of college graduates could hardly qualify for entry into university. They must be the great-grandsons of university scholars, or else the super-standards set by super-precedent would suffer, he asserted, and the ideal of super-erudition be lost. The poet-philosopher deplored the infiltration of foreign influence into the national arts, and his voice was languid, weary, as he ran his fingers through his lank hair. He did a turn or two of a swooning waltz, complained of television from America, existentialism from France, and barbarism from the East, then leaned against the backdrop for support, describing himself, and nearly collapsing beneath the weight of it, as the standard bearer of culture for the Western world.

But it was the Wehrmacht soldier in his gray flannel trousers and striped shirt who made them rock with laughter again. He stood with the felt hat pushed to the back of his head, and a chewed cigar in one corner of his mouth, explaining the ethics of collaboration in a rapid, nasal twang. Yes, sure, he worked with the *Amis*, he said; he liked the way they kept their feet on the desk during office hours. It saved shoe leather, and you had to take things like that into consideration, with the price the stores were asking for shoes now.

"Sure, I work with the *Amis*," he sang in a nearly perfect imitation of American, and he jitterbugged expertly to the music, his hands kept out of sight, his teeth still chewing the cigar. "They don't have Coca Cola in the Eastern Zone!" he sang. "They don't have Primadoras in Moscow!"

And then this skit was over, and the stage set for the final scene. For a moment, after the curtains parted, there was silence in the *Gaststube*, for nothing was there before the spectators except the blankness of the backdrop and the empty boards. There was nothing for the eye or mind to fasten on, or for the ear to hearken to, until the cadence of marching began off stage. At first it was a mere light tattooing, as if the feet were coming from a long way off, and then, as the piano and violin and harp began to play the martial music, the volume of its sound increased, coming louder, and even louder now, out of the wings. And, as it grew, the rhythmic pulsating seemed to fill the *Gaststube*, beating not only upon the ears but striking its tempo on the flesh as well, oppressing them, crowding them, like a gigantic throbbing heart closed in the *Gaststube* with them, stopping the air in their nostrils, the speech in their mouths.

Then came the men and women, dressed similarly in brown, wearing knee-boots, and with the deceptive insignia on their sleeves, marching in from both sides of the platform in single

file, and there they about-faced, and came to a halt, their feet
still marking time. There were perhaps no more than five or six
of them on either side, but they appeared to be more numerous
as they stood with chins raised and muscles rigid, in the cramped
space of the stage. They held themselves with singular intensity,
as if the eyes of the entire world were fixed on them; and it may
have been that the eyes of the entire world were on them,
watching in apprehension every gesture these young people
made. Two of the men could be recognized as waiters who had
served at the *Gaststube* tables not ten minutes before, recruited
because of the shortage of male players, and marking time with
the others on the boards. But it was not this which caused the
first titter of laughter to run through the room. The thing which
set it off was the recognition of another figure, one wearing the
brown uniform as well, who came limping down the human corridor of men and women whose boots still marked the time and
temper of an epoch that was past. He wore the official beaked
cap, with the crown exaggeratedly high above the brow, and
under one arm he carried an outsized portfolio. Now that he
paused downstage, before the footlights, his title could be seen
written plainly out in Gothic letters upon the leather, so no mistake could possibly be made concerning his identity. *"Propa-
gandaminister für den Reiksschleisskreitzer,"* it said, and the
spectators glanced at those seated at the other tables before
they tittered at the outrageous name.

"Halt!" barked the poet, cast now in the Propaganda Minister's role, and on the stage the double row of boots ceased instantly to move.

"Baa-aa!" responded the uniformed men and women in a single docile voice. They stood, their eyes upon him, giving him an
incredible salute. It did not consist of the arm raised stiffly as of
old, but of the thumb being pressed to the tip of the nose, and
the fingers of that hand wagged at him in apparent gravity.

And now the tradespeople, dressed up in their best clothes, sat
uneasily at the tables, startled a moment by the shamelessness of
it, but entranced by the very indecency of what they saw. Even
those who had believed in it all once did not rise from their seats
and walk in protest from the room, but instead they resorted to

laughter. And, having laughed, they seemed relieved, as if they had broken a mirror set before them, and now it could no longer bear their completed image, but only fragments of it, on its glass. When the Propaganda Minister made his absurd address, they laughed as people will who have taken a long time to see the point of a story which other people consider funny, and who laugh all the louder to cover their own stupidity. Or perhaps it was because of the amount they had drunk that they were ready to laugh now at whatever took place upon the boards, but, however it was, they roared in anticipation when the Propaganda Minister announced that the *Reiksschleisskreitzer* himself was about to appear, and they laughed the louder when a house-painter, in the traditional paint-bespattered, white cotton suit, balancing a ladder on one shoulder and a bucket of paint hung over his arm, made his way from the wings.

The young men and women in uniform cried "Baa-aa!" in homage to him, and, as he fought his way with difficulty up the corridor they formed, the swinging ends of the ladder walloped first one and then the other, nearly knocking them off their feet, and the onlookers laughed louder in their savage joy. They watched him set the bucket of paint down, and then seek to set the ladder against the backdrop, working with that sidesplitting, clumsy concern with which a clown prepares his act. Once the ladder was upright and wavering uncertainly behind him, he stooped for the bucket of paint again, and it could be seen that there were two fingers missing from his hand. And now he began to mount the ladder, testing its balance step by step, while the men and women on the stage stood at attention, and bleated their exalted "Baa-aa!" When he was at the top, and wavering precariously there, he turned his back upon the audience and began to slap the dripping brushfuls of white paint out. "Slap!" went the brush across the backdrop, and a shower of white paint fell on the men and women and the Propaganda Minister below. "Slap!" went another brushful, and despite the fact that their uniforms were splattered with it, they raised their voices in another fervent "Baa-aa!"

At least, all the voices except one, which suddenly called out: "Boo!"

"Execute him! See that his widow gets no pension and doesn't collect his life insurance!" barked the Propaganda Minister, and the spectators roared anew as hands reached from the wings and jerked the offender from the stage.

The *Reiksschleisskreitzer* swung perilously around now on the ladder, and he began his speech to the uniformed men and women and to the *Gaststube* as he slapped the paint out wildly on the empty air. The spectators were prepared to laugh at all of it; they only asked that the words, and the pitch of the voice, be familiar enough to them so that they could hold their aching sides and writhe upon their seats. For what was he but the point of a colossal joke that history had played upon the world, the burlesque of a man some other people had chosen as their leader once at some other time and in some other place? This was someone they had no use for any longer, for he had deceived them into believing he would succeed in what he had set out to do. There would be another, a better one soon, who would give them back their pride.

"For decades now we have been oppressed, we have been treated like taxpayers!" he cried out, slinging the paint across the stage. "But if today we are allowed only twenty-five thousand housepainters, I tell you by 1951 we shall have fifty thousand housepainters, regardless of whether we have any houses!" he shouted, and he painted the picture of the future in reckless dripping strokes on empty space. "And in 1954, we shall have a hundred and fifty thousand housepainters, and in 1956, one million nine hundred and fifty thousand housepainters!" he cried, his voice rising higher, the words coming faster, the ladder swaying more wildly as the numbers rose. "And in 1958, we shall have five million five hundred and fifty thousand housepainters!" he cried, and the men and women in uniform wiped the paint from their eyes and their mouths, and in one voice shouted "Baa-aa!" "In 1960, we shall have fifteen million housepainters!" he was telling them now, his own voice rising to a scream as they bleated: "Baa-aa, baa-aa, baa-aa!" "In 1962!" the *Reiksschleisskreitzer* shrieked, and then the ladder gave its final oscillation beneath him, and the Propaganda Minister, limping and skipping and jumping to his aid, received the bucket of white paint square upon his head, and the *Gaststube* rocked with laughter as the *Reiksschleisskreitzer* and the ladder fell.

This was the end of the performance, but not of the cabaret, which was obliged to prolong its scheduled three-week run. Ten additional tables were somehow moved onto the *Gaststube* floor, but still there was not place enough for all. Those who had been there once would return a second, and even a third time, reminding one another that this kind of political satire had long been popular with the metropolitan German public, saying, with gratification, that it was too European, too informed, as entertainment to have any place in American night clubs or music halls. They came back, the tradespeople and the professional people of this town, and of the towns near it, to see the take-offs on the *Amis,* and the Russians, and the French, and to hear a German woman sing bitterly of love. And perhaps some of them returned for the last act alone, to close their eyes in the darkness, and drink their wine, and wait for the sound of the voice that cried higher and higher to the rhythmic pulsing of the feet.

The Kill

When they first came to Germany with the Army of Occupation, the boy was six, and all through the first year, and the year that followed, the thought of going hunting was there, casting its shadows of longing like twilight across the bright hours of all that children have to do. He saw his father and the other men go off on Friday nights, or on the eve of an American holiday, wearing their combat boots and their field jackets, and he wanted to put the food he would need, and the ammunition, into the rucksack his mother had bought him to serve the puerile end of picnicking behind the house, and go off with it riding his shoulders as he had seen the others go.

"We get across a lot of country in one evening, John," his fa-

ther said all that first year to him, or else he said nothing when
the boy asked, but went on cleaning the long smooth metal
chambers of the rifle he had shot the wild pig or the roebuck
with the night before. He was partly American Indian, a small,
strong, muscular man with black hair cut close to his wide, long
skull, and copper-colored skin drawn tight across his cheekbones
and the high bridge of his nose. "It's tough on the legs," he
would say, and he would fit a clean white square of muslin into
the eye of the steel cleaning rod, and slip the rod neatly into the
barrel of the gun, and manipulate it quickly in and out.

Or, "You'll have to wait until you're older, John," his mother
said in a dreamy voice to the boy, as if speaking of something as
far as love or combat to him, as she studied her own young, prettily tinted face in the glass.

The father was a master sergeant, and toward six o'clock on
Friday evenings in the spring and summer, the other non-coms he
hunted with would begin coming to the house. They would leave
their Fords, or their Pontiacs, or their Chevrolets parked in the
lane, and they would come up the dirt path and crowd into the
narrow hallway, and set their musette bags and their rifles
against the wall. The boy knew all their faces, and he knew some
of the names as well, but he knew best the tumult of their preparations, the stamping of feet from hall to kitchen, and the talk of
ammunition, and destination, and what the weather might turn
to before dawn. He would wait in the hall, dark-browed, dark-
eyed, and troubled, standing close to the burnished wood and
the metal of their rifles, brushed by the canvas of their jackets as
they passed.

"Look at them," the boy's mother would say when the time
came for them to go. She would stand at the dining-room window with him, watching them in their boots and khaki, their fatigue caps worn casually on the backs of their heads, as they
loaded the two or three cars they would drive away in, leaving
the others parked in the lane before the house. "All going off
and leaving their wives as if they were sick and tired of them!"
she would say, her glossy hair touching her shoulders, her small
voice filled with grief.

"Maybe they're not all married," the boy would say, standing there in his blue jeans and his faded cowboy shirt, watching them go.

"Sure, they're married. But they don't care about that. They go off anyway," his mother would say in bitterness. It was not until after supper, when the stars were out and the cars stood locked and silent before the house, that she would begin to cry.

And then it was the second year, and he was seven, and one morning in June he and his mother walked down a cobbled street of the hillside town together, and he spoke of the boy's-size rifle that could be sent from a stateside store named Roebuck, if his mother would just sit down and write the order out.

"You'll have to wait awhile, John," his mother said. They had come to a toy store as they walked, and she stopped to look at the music boxes, and the farm beasts carved in smooth, white wood, and the cuckoo clocks, and the reflection of woman and boy was there between them and the things behind the show-window glass. The mother was wearing a pale wool sweater, and a rose-colored skirt, and on her feet were suede slippers such as a ballet dancer wears, and she stood there, chewing her gum reflectively. "Look at that darling little fawn," she said, but the boy was looking past the wooden animals to the other things that hung inside. He could see tomahawks, cardboard but painted silver so that they had the vigor of weapons, with Indian horses splashed in savage flight across their ersatz metal; he could see leather-thonged bows, and painted arrows, and the feathered headdresses of Indians, and, beneath these, the world of music boxes abruptly died. "I'd like to buy myself a music box," said the mother, and she turned to go through the shop door, touching her own soft, light, un-Indian hair.

The German who owned the store stood just below the headdresses and the tomahawks, but so far removed from them that he seemed a figure cut from a newspaper tabloid and placed, as colorless as print, under their barbaric reality. He spoke English in a way the mother did not, and had she referred to this, he would doubtless have told her that he spoke a better English, for what was she but an American who had no right to the English tongue? He had been a POW in England, he said, as if this were a distinction to which she could never hope to attain.

"Gosh, those music boxes are cute!" the mother said, and then the boy asked her a question about his father's people.

"What kind of a headdress do you think my grandfather wore?" he said.

"Well, maybe on the reservation he didn't wear a headdress," said the mother, but her mind was on the music boxes with the pretty Alpine scenes done on their lids. "Maybe your grandfather's grandfather, or somebody way back like that, wore a headdress. My husband, he's part American Indian," she said in explanation to the storekeeper, and he looked at her with a bleak, jaundiced eye.

"These come from Munich," he said, and behind the counter he turned to take one down. He held it before them, the ivory-stemmed, many-colored feathers springing thickly from the headband of green leather, and the strings of beads and the raccoon tails swinging shoulder-length on either side. "The Indian was introduced to Germany by the German author, Karl May," he said, permitting the Indian no choice of nationality.

In the end, it was a music box in the shape of a drum and painted mauve, with a mountain chalet done in light and shadow on the cover, that the mother bought. When she lifted the lid of it to take the powder puff out of its circular mauve tray, intricate threads of music were plucked, as if by magic, from within. There were three tunes in it, and the "Blue Danube" was the one that played the longest, and when they were back in their own house in the American community, and the delicate skeins of the tune unwound beneath the powder puff, the mother waltzed slowly through the room, her eyes half closed, her soft hair floating like a young girl's from her shoulders as she danced. No matter how long she lived, she said to the boy, she would never like anything better than listening to the three small tunes the box contained.

"Maybe when you have time, you could look at the Roebuck catalogue and ask about the boy's-size rifle," the boy said tentatively when the "Blue Danube" was done.

"Oh, I wish you had some feeling for music, John, that's what I wish! All this business of shooting and killing, it makes me sick!" his mother said, her voice coming the long way back from enchantment to him. She moved to the table, and picked up the little mauve drum, and she turned the silver key tighter and tighter so that the music would play.

That was a Friday, and in the evening the sergeant neither the boy nor his mother had seen before walked into the house. He was a heavy, big-boned, slow-moving man who, perhaps because he did not raise his voice as did the other non-coms, or because his eyes, which were yellow as a cat's eyes, moved from object to object in retarded motion, appeared to function in a condition of total repose. He came into the front hall, and he leaned against the wall, smoking slowly, his rifle hanging from his shoulder, his bag at his feet. He stood there, immune to the uproar of the others, his eyes looking through the kitchen doorway at the mother in a corn-colored sun dress, making sandwiches at the table, but looking as impersonally at her as he looked at the pictures on the wall or at the thin boy in his dungarees.

"Ain't you coming along with us, son?" he said then, and he stood with his pale eyes holding the boy's eyes motionless while the stream of preparation moved around and past them in the encumbered hall. "When I was your age, I used to go hunting every Saturday night with my old man. You get some kind of coat on you and come along," he said, and the boy hesitated only an instant before turning quickly toward the stairs. "I'll be waiting at the door for you," said the sergeant, and he was there when the boy came back with his mottled calf's-hide jacket on, and they went together down the dirt path to the cars. The father's winterized jeep stood by the curb, and the sergeant opened the door of it as if he had done this many times before, and when the boy was in, he swung his musette bag in over the front seat, and he climbed up, carrying his rifle with him, his back and shoulders stooped within the cramped interior, and he sat down on the rear seat by the boy. "My old man used to call it going to the other side of the moon," the sergeant said. He stretched his heavy, slothful legs across the accumulation of paraphernalia that already cluttered the floor, and his big shoulders pushed against the Plexiglas of the rear window, the surface of which had been rendered opaque by days or weeks, or months, it may have been, of rain and dust and grime.

"My father tells me about a lot of things," the boy said. "He says if my grandfather went hunting with us, well, he'd put his ear to the ground to find out where the roebucks were feeding."

"That was the Indians' telephone," the sergeant said.

"He was a chief, and I guess he wore a headdress," said the boy. "I saw them in the German store today."

And then the father and the others, bearing their variegated equipment, came out of the house and down the path, and the boy's heart went bleak within him, for he knew what was to come. The father was trimly dressed and belted in his khaki, and his step was quick and light as he came toward the jeep. He laid the bag, and the binocular case, and the cigar box of ammunition on the motor's flat, square hood, and, his gun hanging from his shoulder, he leaned in to set these things in place. The muscles twitched in his copper-colored jaw as he worked, but, except for this, there was no sign that he had seen the sergeant and the boy.

"I'm taking this young man out hunting with us tonight," the sergeant said at last from the shadows of the rear seat.

"Only he isn't going hunting," the father said, and he did not lift his head. "You get on back to the house, John," he said. He worked in silence and proficiency, dark-skinned, intent, and, before the boy moved to go, the quality of the conflict altered, for the mother had come on her ballet-dancer slippers through the yard and across the dirt walk to the jeep.

"If I stayed home from the show to make them, maybe you could remember to take them with you," she said, standing incredibly clear-skinned and glossy-haired in the light that had no hint of evening in it, holding out to the father the paper of sandwiches he had left behind. Only when the father turned back from the open door did she see that the boy and the sergeant were seated in the jeep, and the look in her face turned sweet and slightly dazzled in the summery air. "Oh, excuse me! I didn't know there were people already in," she said politely.

"I can't say as he asked me to get in, but I always like a jeep," the sergeant said, and he lifted his hand slowly and took the fatigue cap off his head. "Only if I had a family, a fine little family like he's got, I think I'd buy me a regular car—"

"Oh, his family!" said the mother in derision, and she touched the ends of her soft hair.

"I keep a jeep because it suits me for hunting," said the father, and, having said this, he closed his mouth again.

"Oh, hunting!" the mother cried out; for whatever the time of year, each was possessed by his own complete desire: the mother for the father to dance with her at the Sergeants' Club, or to sit close to her in the darkness of a movie theatre, and the father's longing to move across the fields and through the woods in the twilight of morning or evening, and the boy's longing for the accouterments of man and his activity. "I don't recall having seen you or your wife around the community," the mother said, and smiled at the sergeant who sat in the shadows with the boy.

"Because I ain't got a wife," said the sergeant, stirring gently in his area of quiet. "I'm in barracks, and I tell you it's real lonesome there. I guess that's what led me to take your boy along hunting tonight—"

"Except he isn't going hunting," said the father. He was ready to leave now, and he straightened up, and he had no time to waste.

"Why shouldn't he go?" the mother cried out suddenly. "Why in the world shouldn't he go?" Her slim bare arm in the sleeveless yellow dress moved quickly, and she flung the wax-paper parcel in past the father onto the driver's seat. "If some gentleman comes along who's considerate enough to want to look out for John, why, I think it's simply wonderful! I'm certainly very grateful to the sergeant. You," she said, turning sharply on the father, "won't have to be bothered with him at all. And there's no reason why you should be, is there? You're only his father, and that's really nothing, is it? That's nothing at all when rabbits and deer and boar and things like that are running around asking to be shot. Even a wife's just nothing then," she said.

"Get out now, John," said the father, his voice as low as if he spoke in the quiet of the forest.

"You're hard on him, ain't you, Sarge?" said the other sergeant, but he shifted his heavy legs so that the boy could climb across.

"I'm hard on everybody. You can get out, too," the father said.

The boy and the mother went back into the house, walking a little apart from each other, and the boy went into the dining room, and he stood close to the window, watching the cars from there as, one by one, with the hunters and their paraphernalia in them, they drove away. And the boy remembered another time that could not have been too long ago, for the reality of it had not altered, an evening when he and the father had walked through the woods together, and the silence had parted before them like water parting before a swimmer's hand. The father had carried no gun that time, but had talked of the way the leaves turned with the wind, saying this meant rain would fall before the night was through.

Indian blood, said the father's voice, will tell you to move upwind, and will tell you not to stalk your enemy before a storm, for after rain he can read the record all too well. And then the silence broke, and a babble of bird tongues filled the forest, and there stood the tough-hided monster, the wild, reddish sow, with her forefeet spread, and her eyes of golden glass. "That's what the birds were talking about," the father whispered, and his hand touched the boy's shoulder, and they stood still.

"Anyway, I almost went hunting," the boy said now, but it may have been that he felt the quality of courage disintegrating in him, for he walked out of the dining room, and up the stairs.

The lights were lit in the windows of the houses of the American community, and in the windows of the German houses across the valley, but he had not slept yet when his mother called him to come and eat.

"I made some peanut-butter sandwiches," she said. They were there on a plate on the oilcloth of the kitchen table, and beside them stood two glasses of milk. She did not wind up the music box, but instead she took out a pack of cards, and she and the boy began playing slapjack as they sat there eating the sandwiches, with their hands slapping hard at the faces of the knaves whenever they played them out. After a little while they heard the front door open, and they turned their heads, and they saw the sergeant who was a stranger to them standing there. He had closed the door behind him, and he stood in the hall with the hunting equipment still slung from his shoulder, holding his fatigue cap in his hand. "Oh, Lord, I must have forgot to lock it!" the mother cried softly, and the cards fell from her hands.

"If you let me come in, I wouldn't stay long," the sergeant said in a low voice.

"Well, it's getting late for callers," the mother said, and the boy watched her shake her hair back like a lovely movie star.

"I wouldn't take up much of your time," said the sergeant, moving down the hall. "If I could sit down for just five minutes, I'd tell you what I been thinking about ever since I met you, and then I'd go away."

"My husband, he doesn't care for late callers," said the mother, but she looked with singular pleasure at the sergeant, her chin lifted, her eyes half closed, as the boy had seen her look into the glass. "What kept you from going hunting with the rest of them?" she said.

"A woman," the sergeant said, and now he had ceased to move again, and he waited in the narrow hall. "If you asked me to sit down, I'd tell you about her," he said, speaking very humbly.

"There's an alarm clock on the kitchen dresser," the mother said, turning her head to look at it. "You can come in and sit down with John and me five minutes, and then you'll have to go."

"Thank you kindly, ma'am," said the sergeant. He began to move again, reaching dreamily, lazily, to lay his cap on the coatrack shelf above his head, slipping the bag and the rifle from his shoulder and hanging them below the cap, moving carefully, deliberately. Then he came down the hall toward the woman and the boy who sat in the bright, square box of kitchen light. "This is like coming home," he said. He drew the third chair out from under the table, and he sat down and folded his arms in the khaki sleeves of his jacket on the oilcloth cover, and he looked at the mother's face.

"Get him a Coke, John," said the mother. As she picked up the scattered playing cards to lay them straight, the sergeant kept his eyes on her narrow, white-skinned hands.

"I don't want to drink nothing. I just want to sit here dwelling on things," said the sergeant gently. But still, once the boy had opened the bottle and set it down before him, he lifted it and drank. "Thank you, son," he said, and he looked at the mother's face again. She was straightening the cards in her fingers, and petals of color lay warm under her eyes. "Sometimes a man'll go so blind he won't see the treasures he has right under his own roof," he said.

"Get the sergeant an ash tray, John. Maybe he'd like to smoke," the mother said.

"I don't want to smoke," the sergeant said, but still he took out a cigarette, and lit it, and then he broke the match in two, and dropped it into the ash tray the boy had put down on the cloth. "I wanted to know one thing. I wanted to know the name and the location of the German store in town where they got them Indian feathers. I want to buy them, that headdress, for the boy." He took the cigarette from his mouth, and his yellow eyes were on the mother's face as he held it out to her across the oilcloth, and across the bits of peanut-butter sandwiches still left on the plate. "I lit it for you. You take it," he said in a low voice to her.

When the mother reached out for it, her hand was trembling, and her eyes were held by the sergeant's eyes as she put it in her mouth. She drew a deep breath of the smoke in, and then she turned her head and spoke to the boy, and her voice was trembling and light.

"You'd better go upstairs to bed, John. It's getting late," she said.

The boy waited a moment, still hoping she might say the store's name where the feathers might be bought, but she did not say it. She was looking in weakness and helplessness at the sergeant, and the boy went down the hall, his eyes on the sergeant's rifle on the coat rack, and he went up the stairs.

That was Friday night, and on Saturday the shabbily garbed offspring of the American Army of Occupation played their wild games in the yards and streets of the community. The heels of their cowboy boots were worn, but nailhead-studded holsters hung at their hips, and the imitation ivory revolvers these encased were bejeweled in emerald and ruby and topaz. Dogs raced behind the fences of the individual yards, yelping for freedom, and others ran with the children—boxers, and wire-haired terriers, poodles, spaniels, dachshunds, or schaeferhunds, each dog in itself the emblem of the temperament of the humans with which it lived. Little girls, wearing blue jeans only a few sizes smaller than those their mothers wore, followed, the shifting center of agitation, pushing their burdened doll coaches and whispering together, forever lingering on the outskirts of the games the cowboys played.

The boy was out with these others in the tide of sun, ready to lash or be lashed to the stake for burning, or to draw his jewel-studded pistol from its holster and menace the girls from ambush as they came. The mothers were down the hill at the commissary, getting the weekend groceries in, and the fathers were gone —they were off in the wilderness, hunting still, exempted for a little longer from daily liability. The German housemaids had ceased their work, and they leaned their strong, bare arms on the window-sills, and, wooed by sunlight, they called their own language out above the midwestern or the southern sound of the children's voices, and the barking of the dogs.

"Lise! Helga! Erika!" the maids called to one another, and the German delivery men on the American milk truck that had halted at the end of the lane called out: "Lise! Helga! Erika!" in falsetto mimicry. The milk truck was khaki-colored like an army truck, and its windows were barred like the windows of a prison van, but on the rear door of it was painted a pink-legged stork, better than life-size, with its eye cocked, half in sagacity, half in humor, and in its beak it held the four ends of a folded diaper in which were borne bottles of milk for the children of the American community. "Helga! Lise! Erika!" called the male voices in mockery, and the men jumped onto the truck and slammed the barred doors closed. The motor throbbed, the gears changed slowly, and as the truck jerked into motion, and the big wheels turned, a wild, stricken cry was heard on the bright air, a cry so alien to the medley of other sounds, so wounded in its anguish, that the truck ground to a halt again, and the men jumped down.

The thing that had cried out in fierce reproach lived still. It was a wire-haired terrier, part white, part black, which must, a little while before, have tired of playing and flung itself down, panting, in the truck's area of shade. And now, still panting, it made its way across the lane, and its entrails followed, writhing with their own hot life as they whitened in the dust. The first sharp note of terror had ceased, but a wail of indescribable mourning came now from the bright-tongued, dripping mouth, a long, outraged lament for all that was lost forever, all that must be traded in for death with this breath or the next because of one fatal instant of immobility.

The German maids were fixed like images of women in the open windows in the sun, and the three men from the milk truck stood mute before the spectacle, their hands fumbling in their pockets for cigarettes, while the dog sought to sit on the soiled, flattened rags of its hind legs, and could not, and turned, snarling and snapping in frenzy, seeking to tear the dusty strings of its own vitals away. Even the little girl whose property he had once been watched tearless and in silence, as the cowboys watched. But it was the children who knew what there was to do. They held the dogs back by their collars, striking the muzzles of boxers, or poodles, or schaeferhunds when the high whining of curiosity whistled too loudly through the eager snouts, and they spoke cautiously together, as if in church, and then the boy turned to the men.

"If I got my father's pistol, would you shoot him so he'll die?" he said.

For a moment the three Germans did not speak, and the dog turned its head again and snapped at its own disemboweled and living substance, its eyes glazed sightless with pain. Then the tallest man, wearing glasses, opened his mouth as if he had an answer to give, but instead he straightened a cigarette out in his fingers, and put it between his lips. The driver of the truck smoothed his brass-bright hair back with the palm of his hand, and ran his tongue along his lip, and looked at the other men, but he too did not speak. The third man was dark, with a slender, sunburned neck and square brown hands, and he wore the anciently but snappily cut black breeches and the high military boots, now cracked with wear, that father or uncle or history had bequeathed to him. Having no military decorations to embellish what he wore, he had stuck two daisies, with a length of the coarse stalk and green buds, behind his ear.

"Okay, I'll shoot him," he said, his accent as good as an American's, and the boy turned swiftly, and ran through the sunlight toward the locked, silent cars that waited still at the far end of the street, swerved between the last two, and then raced through the gate of his front yard, and up the path, taking the corner to the back door fast.

The Walther pistol was kept in his mother's and father's room, on the top shelf on the clothes closet, strapped in a leather holster and concealed, for safety, under a pile of folded khaki handkerchiefs. He knew he could reach it by standing on a chair. Twice his father had taken it out before him and cleaned it, and showed him how to handle it. It would be loaded, for the father kept it loaded ever since burglars had broken into the house, but the magazine safety would be on, and no cartridge in the chamber yet. The boy stood on the straw seat of the chair and reached into the corner of the shelf for it, and he could feel the blood pounding in his eardrums as he touched the smooth leather of the belt and holster with his groping hands.

Then he was out again in the sunlit lane, and nothing had altered. The maids waited motionless at the windows still; the knot of children had not unraveled; the shadow cast by the halted truck, the Germans smoking their cigarettes, the residue of the dog's life staining the dust were all unchanged. The dog lay propped on its front legs, its wild tongue panting, its lips drawn back from its white teeth as if preparing to laugh aloud.

"You'll have to release the safety," the boy said as he took the pistol out of the stiff, tan, leather pocket that strapped it fast.

"Okay," said the dark-haired German in the knee-high boots.

When he cocked the pistol, the children did not move. It did not occur to any of them to turn their heads or go. The German held the pistol at arm's length and took careful aim while the cowboys stood, holding their own dogs by the collars as they watched, or holding to their scooter or bicycle handle bars, and the girls to their doll buggies in which their soft-skinned, life-size infants rode. And the terrier looked with his unhinged, frenzied eyes at the disaster which seemed scarcely to be his as it lay discarded in the dust behind him, and his bright, young mouth was still ready to laugh. The boy put his hands deep into the pockets of his blue jeans, and he closed his fingers tightly in his palms as he waited for the sound to come. But the German did not fire. Instead, he lowered the pistol, and he turned toward the boy.

"If the MPs come along, I'll get into trouble," he said, the cigarette jerking on his lip.

"But they won't see you. They're not around here," the boy said, and the German gestured with his chin toward the row of houses where the maids leaned eagerly from the kitchen windows in the sun.

"There's too many people watching. They'd all tell who done it when the MPs asked," he said, and he took the stub of the cigarette from his lip, and let it fall.

"But you've got to shoot him. You've got to do it," the boy said, his voice gone high.

"And if I don't get him the first time, then I'll have to shoot again," said the German, and he gave a short laugh. "That'll be giving the MPs two chances to hear. Or maybe the shot goes wild and hits the street, or hits a rock, and bounces back, and one of the kids gets hit instead."

When he lifted his hand to draw the back of it across the sunburned square of his forehead, the two daisies on their tough, green stalk fell from behind his ear into the dust, but he did not see them fall.

"That's right," said the tall German who wore glasses.

"It's *verboten* for any Cherman to have a firearm," the blond one said.

"Okay, then let me have the pistol," said the boy.

He held it in his right hand, at arm's length from him, and

there was no color left in his face, but his arm, his hand, were steady as he aimed.

"Does he know how to shoot?" the tall German asked, looking anxiously through his glasses at the other children.

"Sure, he knows how to shoot. His grandfather was an Indian once," a cowboy said.

And then the blast of it came. The boy heard the snarl in the terrier's throat, and he lowered the pistol, and he saw that the dog lay on its side, and the panting had ceased, and the shape of laughter was stiffening on its mouth.

"You got him right between the eyes," said the dark-haired German, and he lit another cigarette, and stooped in his ancient military boots to see.

On Saturday evening, at suppertime, the doorbell rang, and the sergeant whose face they were beginning to know walked in as he had done the night before, and hung his cap on the clothes rack in the hall.

"You shouldn't have come back," the mother said, standing bare-limbed, her feet in gilded sandals, bare-armed, in a pink summer dress, holding to the kitchen table for support.

"I had to come back," said the sergeant. "I've been thinking about it all day."

"About what?" the mother whispered, and her eyes moved on his face.

"About last night," he said, standing big and indolent before her.

"I know, I know," whispered the mother, and the sound of her voice died.

And on Sunday evening he came back again, and, as had happened before, when they had eaten they had a game of slapjack, and then the mother sent the boy upstairs.

"The sergeant has to get to bed early too, so he'll be leaving any minute now," she said.

But on Sunday night it was different, for the hunters returned late from the woods, and the tumult of voices as they started their cars in the lane outside and called out to each other woke the boy from sleep. Once they had gone, he lay listening to his father's voice, speaking from the jeep, or from the hall, and he knew that at least one man had stayed with him. And then he heard the drag of bodies as the dead beasts were carried in, hearing even that intermission in their work when his father and the other man paused to open a bottle in the kitchen, and the sound of the sliding panel of the dresser as his father took the glasses out. Twice he heard the slamming of the refrigerator door, and then the whine of the spigot as they ran the water over the ice trays. After this interval, they came out into the hall again, his father and the other man, and, with his head raised from the pillow, the boy could identify each move they made. Now they were lashing the four feet of the roebuck together so that it might be hung in the cellar from a ceiling hook, and the boy heard the grunt of their breathing as they stooped, the scrape of their shoes on the stone of the cellar stairs as they bore the roebuck down. They made the journey twice, stopping to drink again in the kitchen after they had brought the second body in from the car and laid it on the floor. So it would be a boar and a roebuck, he thought, for two roebucks were not allowed one hunter. And suddenly he did not want to think of the lifted guns, and the animals panting out their lives, and he turned his face to the pillow to keep the sight away.

But still he lay listening, and after this work was done, and the door to the cellar closed, the men went again into the kitchen, and their voices murmured as they drank. In the end the other man went down the hall, and out the door, and the boy got from his bed, and moved in the darkness across the bare boards to the window. He watched the headlights brighten the lane a moment, and the last car go. Now only his father's jeep was left by the curb, and his father moved in the kitchen, and the boy heard the mother stirring in her room, she too having waited perhaps, listening, as he had listened, for the last hunter to go. He heard her seeking her slippers and dressing gown, and then she went softly down the stairs.

"Oh, my God, there's blood all over!" she said, not having reached the last step yet.

"All right," said the father, speaking from the distance of the kitchen to her standing on the stairs. "I'm a hunter, a good hunter," he said, his voice hard, and a little vain. "I'm also a good sergeant. I'll clean up any muck I've made."

"Who came back with you?" the mother said.

"A friend," said the father, and then there was a pause, perhaps as he lifted the glass from the table and drank again. "A friend who doesn't talk out of turn to other men's sons, and doesn't get lonely for other men's wives. Next time he comes, tell him to take his cap with him when he goes."

"Well, I'm sure I don't know what you're talking about," the mother said.

And now the father walked out of the kitchen, and into the hall, and his footsteps halted near the stairs.

"Don't be frightened. The killing's over," he said, and the mother gave a little cry.

"You're hurting me! You're hurting my arm!" she said in a low voice.

"Well, there's the blood on the floor. So maybe there won't be a next time. Maybe we finished him off," said the father, speaking savagely.

"You wouldn't have done that!" the mother cried out, speaking scarcely aloud.

"You'd better not look in the cellar," the father said, and the boy heard him jerk the sound of laughter out.

"Well, that sergeant," said the mother, and her voice was dimmer, farther now, and the boy knew she must have moved down the hall into the kitchen, and had perhaps sat down at the table where the sergeant had eaten with them, perhaps even taken the father's glass up in her hand. "He came back to get the name of the German store where the Indian headdresses are. He wanted to buy John one. That's all he wanted," she said.

"An Indian headdress made in Germany!" said the father. "Did you tell him that having Indian blood in your veins doesn't mean wearing feathers pulled out of a German turkey's tail?"

"He just asked the name of the store, and then he left. He's going to buy it on Monday for John," said the mother, speaking softly, as if in grief, perhaps nursing the glass in her slender, white-skinned hand.

"Let him bring it here. I'll shoot him through the heart as he walks through the door," said the father, and the boy stood in the dark of the upstairs hall, listening to him speak. "Having Indian blood means the country comes to life for you, even this cursed, devil-ridden country, this country of barbarians," he said. "Not the people's faces, or their language, all right, not that, but my blood gives me what's in the grass and sky and trees. As long as men keep quiet, I can remember all the signs, and all the memories that aren't even mine, and not even my father's and grandfather's, but older than that. I can read the stars the way they did, and shoot just once, and kill with that one shot, because my blood remembers that they did." And, *Maybe she'll tell him,* the boy thought, standing in the upstairs hall; *maybe she'll tell him about the dog, and that I couldn't stop crying after she came up the hill. Maybe she'll tell him I kept on seeing him panting,* he thought, but the mother must have been thinking of other things, for she did not speak. "I got a boar and a roebuck this time. The others got zero," the father was saying, but saying it softly, without vanity. "They haven't got forest-sight."

The sound of it paused, and after a moment, the boy heard him set the bottle down on the table, and the water from the spigot running into the glass. "Nobody can take it away, nobody at all," he said. "I go out in the woods, and it's there, and there's nothing else, and the year, the country, and woman, even, they're wiped out. I'm a man alone, and I need to eat, and I'm going to kill in order to eat, and I shoot just once because I know distance, and light and dark, and my hunger's as steady as my eye. And then I come back to this!" He broke it off suddenly, and the laughter jerked out. "To a hall with a sergeant's cap hanging in it! Listen," he said, and his fingers may have closed on the mother's arm again, for she gave a little cry. "I am my father's son, and my son is my father's grandson, and whatever I have, it was given him, too. When he goes hunting, my son, he'll go when he's ready for it, and not with a stranger, but with me. Get that straight," he said.

The boy listened in the dark of the upstairs hall, and he thought: *Maybe when the stain's gone from the dirt out there, I won't see him sitting up panting. Maybe when it starts raining, and there isn't any more dust on the road, I'll stop remembering.*

In the kitchen, there was the sound of water gushing into the pail, and then this ceased, and the father walked out into the hall and set the pail down, and the scrubbing of the boards began. *Maybe this year he'll teach me how to read the stars*, he thought, *and I'll learn that, and maybe next year will be different, and I'll want a gun again.*

"Listen," the mother said from the kitchen. "I bought one of those music boxes. You know, the powder-puff kind. I'll play the 'Blue Danube' for you. It's the prettiest thing you've ever heard."

"All right. Play it," said the father, scrubbing the wood.

As the delicate threads of the tune unwound, the boy went back to his bed again, and he lay down without pulling the covers over him, and lay looking at the dark in the window that was richer and deeper than the bedroom dark. Every now and then the father would halt in his scrubbing of the hall, and the boy could hear the whisper of the mother's feet as she danced across the floor. Her hair would be floating free of her shoulders, and her pale silk dressing gown swinging around her, light and wide, and the boy felt a sense of peace laid like a cover over him. The door downstairs was closed against the night, and against any stranger who might come, and his mother danced, and, because of the whiskey she had drunk, her eyes would be heavy, like a dreamer's eyes.

"Kiss me, kiss me, John, kiss me," she said to the father, and the scrubbing in the hallway ceased.

"Fix me another drink," said the father after a moment, and his voice was not the same voice. "I'll waltz with you, baby, once I've got the barracks clean," he said.

A Disgrace to the Family

This was their first breakfast together, after five months of separation, and, because of what had happened, it was not easy for the father to find the right things to say. They sat in the morning sunlight, with two cups of coffee and a plate of sugared doughnuts before them, at one of the tables which stood on the covered asphalt walk outside the American coffee-shop door. The man was in a suntan uniform, with a gold leaf on each shoulder, a spare, weary-lidded man, with his jowls dyed ruddy, perhaps from the outdoor life he liked to lead or perhaps from a steady, if circumspect, intake of alcohol. He had removed his stiffly visored cap, with the brass insignia weighting it, and laid it on the chair that stood empty between him and the seated boy, and it could be seen that the color of youth was beginning to fade from his closely cut brown hair.

The boy had quite another air about him, a casual, poetic look, with the green eyes and the straight black hair which bespoke Irish blood. His skin was exceptionally white, his nose was short, and his delicate lips seemed drawn and pained, with what may have been for the moment nothing more than bodily fatigue. The gray flannel suit he wore, he had slept the night in, stretched out on the cushions of a first-class compartment bench in the Paris–Frankfurt train.

He and the man had carried their trays out from the cafeteria counter, and now the boy pulled his rumpled flannel jacket off and jerked the black silk shoestring tie from under the soiled white collar of his shirt, and tossed them both across the back of the chair on which the man's army cap rested in the shade.

"Well," said the man. He cleared his throat, keeping his eyes to himself until he had determined how much of censure and how much of love and welcome he should give. "Well, Tar, how does it feel to be fourteen? Only five teens to go before you're twenty," he said, committing himself to nothing yet.

He looked quickly across the cups, and the sugar basin, and the cream jug, and the plate of doughnuts, at the boy, not meeting the clear, fearless eyes, but letting his gaze glance off across the silky eyebrows which converged in a few vagrant hairs above the childish nose.

"I guess I feel sort of responsible," the boy said, and the man felt an abrupt sense of shock that these were the words the boy had chosen to say. At the sound of them, the man looked in discomfort across the well-tended triangle of thin spring grass to the varied and fluctuating tide of men and women, some in uniform, others not, which moved in the sunlight through the open portals of the Post Exchange. "Maybe something like making the grade of corporal when you've been a private for thirteen years," the boy said, not quite making a joke of army ratings, but still with a twist of humor, of irony to it. "How did it feel when you got to be a major?" he asked respectfully then.

He did not look at his father as he said it, but he spooned the sugar into his cup, and stirred it, and picked up a doughnut in his travel-grimed fingers, and, before he took a bite of it, he looked shyly across the table at the man.

"Well, I can't say I remember feeling any added importance when it happened," the man said quietly, and his eyes went narrow as he looked away into the sun. But whatever he said, his mind was on the other thing, and how he would bring himself to speak of it.

His army friends—the bachelors, the couples, on the same post with him a hundred kilometers farther up the Hessian river— knew this much, but nothing beyond it: they knew that his son, the one child he had, was coming from an American boarding school in France to visit him for the first time in the Zone. "Hi, there!" they'd been saying for two weeks now, halting their cars on the country road and calling through the open windows of them to where he sat behind the new car's wheel. "What day's the boy getting in?" they'd say; or the affable couples, in tactful, casual pity for his eternal loneliness, might ask, "Let us know if there's anything in the way of rolling out the red carpet for him you'd like to have us do." And the man had felt his own raw-boned, ruddy, blue-eyed face seek to break its mask of disappointment and bitterness, and give them the grin that they expected, for they had no way of knowing what depths the meeting held of complexity and pain. *In your language and mine*, he could not bring himself to say, *he's been court-martialed. He's been given a dishonorable discharge. He's been sent away.*

"Maybe after a certain age," he went on saying to the boy, who was dunking his second doughnut in the liquid in his cup, "let's say around forty, the pattern for responsibility or irresponsibility's already been set." *But try to keep the moral tone out of it, try to keep from alienating him with that,* he told himself quietly, and he took a swallow of coffee.

"Only you're not forty yet," the boy said, defending him from the unseen adversary of age; and, now that he had spoken out in loyalty, they looked, for a troubled, unexpected moment, with sudden emotion into each other's eyes.

The man may have said then that in a few more weeks he'd be forty, or he may have merely begun eating, with the memories coming to confuse him of the things they had done in other years together, before the name of honor had been impaired. And, as he ate, the fugitive hope came to his mind that now the boy was here with him they might go hunting together, as they had hunted in Maine one season when the boy could hardly lift a rifle; but almost at once the shadow fell across his heart again, as manifest as if someone had halted beside their table and stood in silence between them and the light of spring.

"The people look pretty grim here," the boy said, watching them coming and going through the tall, arched doorway of the Post Exchange.

"It's just possible that nobody gets much pleasure out of an occupation," the man said, eating. "Neither the occupiers nor the occupied. But that's something between you and me."

"After you've seen French faces for a long time, you feel the difference," the boy began saying, but this was the kind of thing the man did not want to hear said.

"Did you pick up much of the lingo over there?" he asked, clearing his throat of the sudden irritation in it.

"Quite a bit," said the boy, with a bite of doughnut big in his cheek. "I like it. I can read it pretty well."

"I thought I noticed a little difference—a kind of accent," the man said, perhaps believing it was like this they might come, cautious step by step, to the threshold of what had taken place. He looked at the thin bleached wooden spoon he held in his hand, his face baffled, looking perhaps blindly at it, and without warning he snapped it in his fingers and dropped the pieces on the asphalt under his feet. "We've got a two-hour drive to the house. We might as well get going," he said.

They walked beside each other, keeping a little apart, along the triangles of grass, past the Quartermaster's Clothing Store and the Beauty Shop and the While-U-Wait Shoe-Repair Salon, to the parking lot.

"As soon as I get home, I'll take this suit off," the boy said, and he might have been speaking of a regulation prison dress. "I'll change into dungarees as quick as I can. You know what I've done? Read all the old books all over again, and stenciled the names of the famous on my dungarees—Pathfinder and Deerslayer and Uncas . . ."

"Look, Tar," the man interrupted, perhaps believing for a deceptive moment that the boy was eight or nine years old again, and that nothing of speech or ease or comprehension had been laid away. "Tar," he said quickly, and in that instant it seemed to him that he would be able to go on with it, and then he heard the voice of the colonel's wife calling out as it had called across the Snack Bar to him the afternoon before. "Hi, there! You see that boy comes right over to us as soon as he gets in, hear now? My bunch of wild Indians wants to put him on their ball team!" she had warbled from the organized, tactful front of pity for one widowed officer's loneliness. "Except that he can't be accepted on equal terms with other kids," was the answer he hadn't given her. "He's forfeited his right to that, my son has," he hadn't said. And "Hi, there!" the voice of the colonel's wife called ever more distantly, ever more faintly, dying to silence at last in the Snack Bar a hundred kilometers away.

They had come to the curb where the long, gleaming cars were parked. The boy drew his open hand along the shining black hood of the impervious car.

"You know, I like her," the boy said, his voice gone cunning again, either with humor or irony. "I like her extra wheel base and her mechanical drive and her air heater," he said, and the man felt the sense of judgment falter in him, for surely it was only the uncovetous who could speak so lightly of a thing which women dreamed of in their beds at night, and which men would strive a lifetime to obtain.

And now the boy rode beside him in the fine new car, with the music from its radio playing to them, and they did not speak their thoughts aloud as they watched the needle quivering higher and higher on the gold-faced dial. The *Autobahn* streamed swiftly under them, and the man drove with a certain pride at first, as if he, too, played some meaningful part in the car's accomplishment, and then he stopped the vanity of this, and he glanced sideways at the reflection of the boy in the windshield mirror, thinking, in sudden irritation, that the boy's hair had been let grow too long. But that was France for you, that was certainly France, he thought, impatient with himself for not having foreseen it; even within the normal, homelike surroundings of an American school, that was the kind of thing France could be counted on to do. And now that the boy's hair was as long as a poet's hair, it seemed to him even more like that of the boy's mother. Here was the blue-black, living hair that had been hers, and the greenish eyes, and the tender mouth, alive still and close, in the glass bay of the car beside him, although it was four years since she had died. And if France could be blamed for the length of the boy's hair, perhaps the other thing could be laid to that alien country, thought the father, and he cleared his throat, as if to begin the words of it at last. But he did not speak, for it was then, with the needle trembling at sixty, that the outlandish object raced across the *Autobahn* before them, and the tires screamed out as the father swerved the car.

"That was a close one," he said, and he sat back, his blood gone weak, behind the wheel. He had brought the car to a halt by the side of the highway, a distance beyond where the dog stood now, incongruous as a scarecrow in the right lane of the streamlined road. The dog's lean legs were propped apart on its outsized paws, spread wide in order to hold its carcass upright, and its bony, lantern-jawed skull was raised so that its nostrils might catch the scent or its eyes might search the faces of the riders who flicked past. The man and the boy turned in their seats to look, and through the back window of the car they saw him moving tentatively toward them, advancing with a cautious, crablike gait.

"He's looking for someone," said the man, and he added, "He's got the blood of a hunting dog in him. He can't walk straight."

"He's a big, thin puppy. He's scared," said the boy, and he opened the door of the car, and stepped down onto the strip of earth that hemmed the road. "Come on, old man, come on," the boy said, but the dog had halted.

It stood quite still now, perhaps ten yards behind the car, with one forefoot lifted, watching the boy with dark, white-rimmed, craven eyes. Its coat was mottled brown and gray, and through this shabby garment thrust the points and angles of its framework.

"He hasn't got a collar on," the boy said now.

"If you put him over a clothesline and beat him, the dust would come out of him like out of a door mat," the man said. His right arm, in the suntan sleeve, was stretched out along the back of the seat where the boy had ridden beside him, and his fingers tapped limberly, quickly, on the linen of the cover, the knuckles showing white beneath his ruddy skin. "What do you intend to do with him?" he said.

"Well, I'd like to take him home with us and feed him up," the boy said, and, turned in his seat, the man sat watching the boy move toward the dog across the concrete surface of the *Autobahn,* the slender boy figure, with his hair long on his neck, and one hand outstretched, and the thin fingers snapping in cajolement to the dog, which sidled slowly, unsteadily away. And, with each step he took in his bagging gray trousers, it seemed to the man that the boy moved further and further from the confines, and from the correction even, of the inflexible system of which he was himself a part.

He watched the curved, vulnerable body moving off through the noontime sun, seeing it so clearly as the dead mother, come alive and tender and wooing again, that he feared if he watched it longer his own belief in the justice of the discipline which must be meted out would be drained forever from his will. Perhaps the boy had her love of poetry, too, and her singing voice, the man thought; and the words of a song she had sung, and that he had long forgotten, returned to him, and he sang the first lines of it, hardly aloud, as he sat alone in the car.

> *"Then put your head, darling, darling, darling,*
> *Your darling black head my heart above,*
> *Oh, mouth of honey, with the thyme for fragrance,*
> *Who with heart in breast could deny you love?"*

And then he closed his fingers tightly into his palm, as if throttling the sound of this, and, turned in the seat still, he watched the dog backing toward the edge of the *Autobahn,* and the boy moving after him with his wooing hand outstretched.

Then the dog whirled suddenly, the loose ears swinging like ribbons come undone, and it fled, in one long, unbroken streak of terror, its half tail clapped in panic between its sloping thighs. And this might have been the last they were to see of the dog—the sight of it skidding into the fern and brambles and brush—except it was perhaps even closer to starvation than its jagged hide betrayed. Just as it left the suave surface of the road, its claws danced sideways as if on ice and, in full flight still, it lurched and fell. The man watched the boy stoop down by the roadside, and pick the dog up, and bear it in his arms—the angular, unyielding head, the bony forelegs, threshing in rigid protest—back to the waiting car.

"I bet he isn't a year old yet," the boy said, breathing a little hard.

"I bet he's over a hundred," the father said grimly. "If they saw him in Spain they'd put blinders on him and send him into the bull ring and let him be gored."

But still the father got out, and he spread an army blanket over the linen covers of the big, softly cushioned seat, and the dog sat upright, as stiff as if shackled by *rigor mortis,* on the army blanket, its front legs braced, its bones thrusting like kindling through its dusty hide.

"He looks as though he'd been walking for a couple of months," the boy said. He had turned in his seat to look at the dog as the car began to move. The blade of its jaw and the pallid gums showed naked within the loose, speckled, hound-like lips, and it watched them with a regard that had gone already beyond human wariness, and beyond surrender, beyond man's valuation of cowardice even, obsessed as it was by the vision of eternal hunger which burned in the reddish caverns of its skull.

"He's probably walked from the Eastern Zone," the man said, and, driving, he could see in the dusky glass of the mirror tipped above the windshield how the sunlight glinted across the dog's narrow shoulders and across its chest and brow. And this glowing copper burnish on the hide, this, like the crab-wise gait, was part of the hunting dog's true heritage, the man knew, handed down untampered with, no matter what quantity of tamer blood had watered the veins of the generations that had intervened. "Put a scythe across his shoulder, and he'd do for the figure of Famine in a pageant depicting European culture," the man said bitterly.

"Well, you know, I might call him that. I might call him 'Famine,'" the boy said. He could not take his eyes from the dog that rode behind them, with the sunlight giving an auburn nimbus to the parched hair of its coat. There it rode, as stiff as a corpse on the gallows, swaying upright with the fluid, easy swaying of the car.

The house they reached an hour or more later stood to itself a little distance outside the American community. It was a worn white stucco house with a flat modern roof, and the terrace that fronted it overhung first the garage that was built into the slope of the wooded hill, and then the walled lane, and, last, the river valley. By the time they had come to it, the man's will seemed to have hardened, for he could not bring himself to say "Here we are, then," or "How do you like the looks of it?" but he drove the car at once, and with savagery even, into the garage beneath the terrace, and closed the double doors of it, so that anyone passing in the lane might not see it standing there and know that they had come. It was as final as if he had said to the curious countryside and to the Occupation forces on its soil that the bachelor friends, and the affable couples, and the colonel's wife, could stew a little longer in their pity, for this was not a homecoming. It had a sterner, more official name.

"Take the bags," the man said sharply, speaking German, and the wizened, bent *Hausmeister*, in his starched white jacket, lifted the boy's two worn, scuffed bags and carried them up the cemented garden steps in deceptive, obsequious alacrity. In the entrance hall, the *Hausmeister* set them down on the clean china tiles while he closed the door, with its burden of clouded bull's-eyed panes and iron fretwork, behind the man in his uniform and the boy in his shirt sleeves and the dog with the bones wearing through its threadbare hide.

When the *Hausmeister* had stooped and picked up the bags again, and borne them away up the polished oak stairs, the man and the boy and the dog stood alone in the silence of the hallway. "Of course, you know, Tar, I've had a letter from the school, sparing no details," was the way the court-martial proceedings began, without benefit of judge or jury. And then the man turned to lead the way into the library of this house which bore the temporary name of home. "You know, the school won't take you back," the man said, once they stood in the room.

To himself he thought, *I need a drink, a stiff drink, or I need to go hunting before I can go through with it. I need to establish myself before him;* and it came to him then that the longing to take the boy hunting had never left his mind.

"You know the charges," he went on saying, and the boy said in a low voice that he knew. He stood there in his soiled, rumpled shirt, the collar of it open, the gray, bagging trousers hanging precariously, it seemed, on the worn leather belt at his hip bones; and the man felt his own hostility rising like a tide within him at the sight of the gentle, brooding look which did not falter in the boy's grave face. In the presence of the antlered deer heads, and the tusked boar heads which looked, with glazed golden eyes, down from the walls, and in the shadow of the towering, national pieces which furnished the room—the massive bookcases, cabinets, sideboards, designed by greater-than-life-sized men, it must have been, in order to contain the outsized German tomes, the super beer mugs, the mighty busts of statesmen and composers—the boy appeared even more frail, more vulnerable, than in the sunlight on the *Autobahn,* and the man ran his finger in irritation inside the collar of his suntan shirt, and undid the button at the neck, and tossed his khaki tie away.

"Look. Before we talk about it I want to get my dog something to eat," the boy said. "You know, the good-officer-taking-care-of-his-men kind of thing. *Proveditor, provedore,*" he said, the ring of irony or mockery nearly as audible as laughter in the lightly spoken words. It was when the boy turned to go, and the carcass of the dog turned on its rigid, rust-colored legs, perhaps not to follow him so much as to try for liberty again, that the man saw the boy as lost to the code to which he himself gave fealty, saw him corrupted by some foreign knowledge, some covert access to poetry or beauty, or to love, which made them strangers because it made light of all the rest.

Once the boy and the dog were gone from the room, the man went to the heaviest of the cabinets on the summit of whose accumulated niches and recesses and shelves a mammoth bust of Bismarck stood, its blind bronze gaze not circumscribed by the library walls, but fixed in rebuke, it seemed, upon an eternal Germany which lay, unaltered and unalterable, beyond. The man took his key ring out and selected a key from among the others on it, and when he stooped to open one of the three richly carved doors which formed the cabinet's base, he saw that fresh scratches defaced the wood around the lock. He opened the cabinet door, and took the half-empty bottle of whiskey out, and before he poured the first drink into the silver goblet which hung, bottom up, over the cork, he set the bottle upright on the library table and satisfied himself that the liquid still stood at the nearly imperceptible pencil mark he had made on the label the night before. And, once assured that the *Hausmeister* had not yet found the way to manipulate the lock, he took the first drink, and then the second, quickly down. And *my son expelled,* he thought, as, for the third time, he poured the silver goblet full. *Expelled from decency, from honor, from confidence, yours, mine, or anybody's. You face a firing squad for the equivalent of that.*

After a moment, he corked the bottle again, and covered the cork of it with the upturned silver cup, and when he leaned over to put it in its place, the heat of his shame for what his son had done poured out of his heart and into the muscles of his lean, bare neck, and he knew that he could never face the women and men of his own kind until the boy in his soiled, casual clothes, with his grave, brooding eyes and his ironic tongue was gone again, and his going been explained away.

"The cook say lunch finished now," the *Hausmeister* said, trying his English out as he stood in the doorway of the library, and the man spun as if he had been caught in the act of murder in broad daylight in the sun-filled room.

"*Ready* . . . not finished!" he shouted aloud, aware that his mouth had gone suddenly dry and that his hands were trembling as he drew his palms in agitation back across his hair.

The shame burned there still, like a sunstroke searing his flesh, as he and the boy began eating lunch together, one at either end of the long table, with the *Hausmeister* in his white jacket serving them quietly, obsequiously. But in the middle of the meal the boy laughed outright.

"I can't help thinking it's funny to have hamburger and canned spaghetti served by a butler," he said.

"I suppose you expected lobster and caviar. I'm afraid I forgot to order it," the man said, and now, drinking the cold beer down, he believed it was some external heat which rendered the air impossible to breathe, and he bade the *Hausmeister* lower the jalousies at the south windows which opened upon the terrace and the sight of the countryside beyond its ivied balustrade.

"Excuse me for saying that. I'm glad to be here," the boy said quietly.

Once the blinds had stemmed the tide of light and heat, and the *Hausmeister* had gone softly down the stairs to the kitchen on the floor below, it seemed to the man that the secret he and the boy shared was closed safely away with them in the cryptlike dimness of the dining room, and that he must keep it here even though it meant that one of them must be done to death in fury and furtiveness, stamped violently and silently from life or else throttled soundlessly into extinction so that no outcry would be made, no passer-by would know. He did not raise his eyes to look the length of the table at the boy, but instead he watched his own limber fingers turning the horn-handled knife that lay beside his empty plate.

"So sixty thousand francs," the man said now, his fingers playing with the knife. "Sixty thousand francs taken out of other boys' rooms at night, stolen out of their pockets, their letters, their desks."

"Yes," said the boy, speaking gravely, but still with a certain dignity and ease. "That's over two hundred dollars. There were some boys there who had too much money to spend, and others who didn't have enough, so it made it a temptation."

"But you didn't need it!" the man cried out, with nothing but grief left in his voice, and at the unequivocal condemnation of these words the clarity and the look of fearlessness ebbed swiftly out of the boy's face.

"No, I didn't need it," he said, his voice coming quiet and far from the other end of the table. "But the boy who took it thought I did."

"The boy who took it—" the man began saying, and his heart moved with hope for an instant, and then he tossed the horn-handled knife impatiently away. "Oh, the one who wanted it for lobster and caviar, you mean?" he said. He had got to his feet, and now he stood, swaying a little, feeling hot and perplexed with ill temper in the close air of the room. "Where's your starving dog?" he said, but this was not what he had intended saying, and he left without hearing the answer the boy had started to give.

In the basement kitchen, the dog had eaten what the boy had put before him, his body arched as if he stood in a high wind, his tail blown forward between his quivering hindquarters, his lean jaws jerking the mouthfuls of raw meat down. But, even though fed, he gave no sign of recognition when the boy went to him, but he sat erect on the folded army blanket, hungering still, and watching for escape. And now, in the boy's room, he did not surrender to the softness of the rug on the floor or the boy's hand stroking his skull. He merely waited, the red coals of his eyes not extinguished, for all their fire was invisible now, but cannily veiled, while the man and the boy, in their separate rooms, seemed to sleep the hours of the afternoon away. But they did not sleep deeply, for, in the broken bits and pieces of their dreams, each told the other the strange but credible story of his life, in which the only experience they shared—except for that of sharing the same family name—was that of remembering the same woman, and of shedding upon her long-dead and long-unheeding breast, one his drunken, and the other his adolescent, tears.

Now twilight had come, and the man opened the library door and ventured out on the terrace, believing that no one would perceive him standing high above the valley in the dusk. He stood watching the evening move up the quiet trough of the

country below him, the bluish spume of it fluxing into darkness
as it reached the poplars and willows on the sloping riverbanks,
and engulfed the river which lay between this delicately wooded
hill and the roofs of the medieval town. He felt soothed and
nearly at peace and he told himself now that if he and the boy
could be left long enough to themselves, if they could keep away
from their countrymen, the look of an identical honor might become apparent to them, unaltered by darkness even, and the contour known exactly, whether the eye that acknowledged it were
that of warrior or poet, or the hand that felt its quality were
bare or gloved or weaponless or closed upon a gun. The thought
of hunting had begun to possess him again, when the boy's voice
spoke out behind him on the terrace, saying the lines of a poem
that he had once known well. The boy's voice recited:

> *"Now with the coming in of the spring the days will*
> *stretch a bit,*
> *And after the Feast of Brigid I shall hoist my flag*
> *and go—"*

"Where did you learn that poem?" the man said, a sense of
sorrow for all that was dead and finished flooding his heart.

"It was written by an Irishman named Stephens. I've been
reading his things," the boy said. "And I remember my mother
singing it to me. I have a friend at school, a boy called Luc," he
went on saying with a certain eagerness. "We've been reading a
good many books together, for we seem to have the same taste in
things. Perhaps we understand each other because his mother is
French and the father and mother are divorced. I mean, Luc's
partly foreign, the way I'm partly foreign," the boy said.

"You're what?" the man said in some surprise, but he felt no
sense of outrage, as he would have felt at any other hour of the
day.

"Well, my mother was Irish," said the boy.

"Irish-American," said the man.

"Well, at any rate, we came to a decision about ourselves.
We've read quite a lot, and we've talked about a number of
things," the boy said, and he came forward to the balustrade, his
moccasins whispering on the gravel, and leaned on the stone of

it, watching the tide of darkness rise. "We knew the school we were in was no good for us . . . no good for either of us," the boy said, "and we knew we had to get out of it and start getting our training for the kind of work we want to do."

"And what kind of work do you want to do?" said the man, hardly knowing the sound of his own voice.

"Well, my friend, this boy called Luc, he wants to be a doctor, a surgeon," the boy said. "He wants to go to the right school to prepare himself for that. Perhaps he feels himself French, because of his mother or perhaps the language comes easier to him now, but, anyway, he's found a French school in Paris where he wants to go."

"And his father's trying to make an American out of him?" said the man.

"Well, his father's a lawyer," the boy said. "He's got a big practice in Chicago. He's going back to Chicago soon, and he wants to take Luc with him. He wants Luc to study for the law. And Luc's afraid of his father, so he'll probably go. He'll give up what he wants to be, and he'll try to be a lawyer." There was silence for a moment before the boy added, "But he might just as well put a bullet through his head."

"And you . . . are you afraid of your father?" said the man, and he seemed to be speaking to a much younger child than the one who stood not far from him on the terrace in the dark.

"No, I am not afraid. I want to be a singer," said the boy. "And for that I want to go to Ireland. I want to take a trip to Ireland to find out about the people who were once my people. I mean, I want to find out about my mother's people. There were minstrels and poets and composers among them, and I know the names of the villages where they lived."

A singer, a ballad singer, thought the man, and for a moment he thought he would not be able to hold the rising laughter back. *My son, the only son I have, expelled from boarding school for theft, will now take up a singing career*, he could hear himself saying to the colonel and the colonel's wife. Or, *My son*, he might say; *you know, the thief—well, now he's a tenor. Can't keep up with the young people these days.*

He might say it to the affable couples or the bachelor friends, and then he knew he would start laughing, he would stand there, shaken with violent laughter before them, laughing painfully, uproariously and hideously, the sound of it like the braying of an ass.

And now the telephone bell rang inside the house, and the man shouted out to the *Hausmeister* to say that he had not returned; and when he faced the darkness of the land again, he saw that a few delicate stars had come into the arch of sky above the hill on which the town and castle stood. Nine links of tawny light, like the lighted windows of a ferryboat moored at a pier or the lighted windows of a train abruptly halted in the countryside, shone now between the castle and the river, and these, the man said when the boy's voice counted them aloud, were the lighted windows of the Sergeants' Club. In a moment the sound of the Saturday-night dance music came sweetly across the water and land to the height at which the man and boy stood on the brink of darkness, the far strains of it rising and swelling and fading, then rising and fading again, with the gentle fanning of the springtime air.

"I've been thinking of military academy for you, Tar," the man said, and he looked across the dark, wide cradle of the valley to the lights where the sergeants danced with women in their arms. "I know enough people, so, in spite of what's happened, I could fix it up. I could get you in military academy. I'm sure of that."

"Except I wouldn't agree to go," the boy said, speaking quietly.

"Well, take the army. Consider it," the man said, striving for patience. "There's enough you can hear said against it, and against the military brain, the military code. But, I tell you, it gives you definitions. Good ones, too . . . perhaps not good enough for the poets," he said, and once he had said it, he did not like the taste of venom it left on his tongue.

"And so, if I went to military school, I could be a sergeant instead of a poet, couldn't I?" the boy said, and through its mockery, the pulse of the music came lightly, rhythmically, like the give and take of a dancing woman's breath.

Could they have fought a duel, each for his own assessment of honor, they would have given definition to their conflict, thought the man, but he knew there was no equal ground for any man or boy to meet on other than the terrain of their own separate determination, and no weapons authorized save each his own bleak, unbending will. But it came to the man that if they turned in early, while the sergeants' music still rose and faded in the warm spring night, then they could be off an hour or more before sunrise, each with his gun, and get in the twilight hunting both of the Sunday morning and the Sunday evening, and whatever happened, either by choice or accident, between them would fall into its destined, chronological place.

"What do you say we get up early and go hunting tomorrow?" the man said, saying it casually, as if the thought of it had come to him for the first time then.

"Okay," said the boy, but there had been an instant of hesitation in it. "Okay. I could take my dog along and try him out," he said.

Before he went to bed the boy ran on his moccasined feet down the stone steps to the basement where he and the *Hausmeister* had closed the dog away. When he had unlocked the laundry door and switched on the light, he saw the folded blanket and the tin dish of water on the floor beside it and the iron-barred window, as they had left it, standing open, on the lane. Except that the dog was gone, nothing had altered, and on the iron bars which were planted deep in the stone frame of the window, and placed scarcely far enough apart for a man's hand to pass, the boy found the wisps of auburn hair attesting that it was through here the dog had fought his savage, desperate way.

This might have been the last they were to see of him. The man said as much that night when the boy came up the stairs again. "When they're foot-loose like that, you can't do anything with them," he said, dismissing mongrels, as if they were poets and singers, from the society of upright men. And he believed it still the next morning when they set out in the early cold.

It was four o'clock of a day raw enough for November, and they had flight jackets on, and their trousers tucked into combat boots, and beaked canvas caps, which had been scarlet once, but which were soiled by wear and weather, pulled down on their heads. Two Mauser rifles were rolled on the floor of the car behind them, and as the man drove out of the garage below the terrace, the headlights flooded across the stones of the lane wall and turned the ivy leaves as emerald green as if seen by the light of day.

They came into mist as soon as they descended to the river road, and the man drove slowly, with the drifting phantoms of vapor writhing and twisting like the damned before them on the opaque screen established by the headlights' glare. But once they had moved out of the valley and into farming country, the mist drew off between the rising hillocks, and the man knew that the wraiths of it would follow the passage of water now, and that in the dawn it would trace the streams, and hang like breath above the springs and marshes, following water, as smoke will mark the covert presence of fire under grass and under forest leaves.

"We ought to see boar, at least," the man said, as he drove with the boy beside him, and then he spoke of the personal and unrewarded honor of the hunt, of the obligation to deer and boars and roebucks, and even foxes, in relation to the cycle of their lives. "The rules are there, but you don't get put in the guardhouse if you don't observe them," he was saying. "Every time, every hunt, it's a choice you make for yourself. Either you shoot the doe with her fawn or else you don't shoot her, although they're pillagers, every one of them. Pigs will root a potato field out overnight; they'll ruin the crops of a whole region, and deer the same. But even with pigs you make your own decision if the pig has young."

"I don't think I'll shoot at all," the boy said, and he gave a jerk of laughter. "I've forgotten everything you taught me up in Maine."

"Keep the wind in mind," the man said, driving quickly. "Don't take for granted the way it's blowing. It often turns tricky at the end of night."

The air was clear, but dark still, as they came through the sleeping villages, past the silent, beam-lashed houses whose theatrical façades swung for an instant chalk-white into the flood of the headlights, the geraniums in the window boxes colored briefly and vividly with light. They could smell cattle now, the odor coming from the courtyards, strong and fresh, through the partially lowered windows of the car; and then this was gone and the scent of the pine woods spread about them like the waters of a wide still lake, as the houses dropped away. Trees pressed close upon one another to the edge of the road, their trunks seen corrugated, their branches intricately meshed, but the channeled lights of the car revealed nothing of the fleet, furtive life which trembled in the forest's heart.

"I remember something about boar charging the hunter, don't I?" the boy said.

"He'll charge you if he's nicked and can still run," the man said, taking the corners fast. "Only he's got to know where you are, so it's up to you to stay downwind. You aren't afraid?" he asked.

"No, I'm not afraid, but I'd like to be good at it," the boy said, his voice earnest, humble. "I'd like to be quick and certain at hunting, the way I know I am about swimming or hockey—"

Or slipping into other boys' rooms at night, without a hitch, without anyone knowing who it was until they found the money in your bag—the man went savagely on with it, but he did not say these words aloud.

"The uncertainty's the good part of it," he said instead, swinging the car along the narrowing road. "There's never any clue given, and no way of knowing until the end whether you've won or whether you haven't, because you never know when or how or from what direction the quarry will come. And there're times when you can't even know what the quarry will be, and what you carry home dead isn't what you set out to kill," he heard himself saying, and he felt a chill of premonition enter his heart.

They had driven due north for half an hour or more when the man said, "In ten minutes we turn off the road," and instantly the headlights picked out a shape which stood foraging in the gutter of still another village street, its thin back curved, its tail drawn close between its legs. Even before the boy's hand had closed on his arm, the man slackened the speed of the car, and, as they approached, the beast in the gutter raised its craven head, and they saw the two fierce blazing points of red which were its eyes.

"That's my dog. That's Famine," the boy said quietly, and just beyond where it stood, the man halted the car.

"You aren't going to do it all over again—" the man began saying, but the seat beside him was already empty and the door hung open above the manure-clogged cobbles of the street. But this time when he returned, the boy was not bearing the dog in his arms, but it walked beside him, the boy's hand holding its head upright by his grip upon the slack skin of its neck.

"He's got a bone," said the boy, and the dog looked in unmanned apology at them, a broad, flat, filth-encrusted bone fixed in its jaws.

"He's been excavating for dinosaurs," the man said grimly, and when the boy opened the back door of the car, they saw the dusty remnant of the dog's tail quiver an instant, as if the heart within the boneyard of the breast were moved by the memory of something akin to welcome which they had conceded it once when the sun was up, and taken away again when darkness fell.

The motor turned softly as the man took the bellied concave glass flask from the inside pocket of his jacket and unscrewed the metal thimble from its mouth, and poured the thimble full. While he drank, the boy stooped to lift the dog in through the open door, and the dog did not relinquish the bone between its jaws, but merely endured as its unyielding legs, its knobbled spine, its whole stiff, unmanageable carcass, were hoisted to the seat.

"For Pete's sake, shut the door! The air's as cold as Christmas!" the man said. He filled the metal thimble to the brim again, and held it an instant between forefinger and thumb before he placed it to his lips. "Here's a drink to the dead, the poor dead game we're going to carry back with us," he said, trying to make it humorous, and he drank the whiskey down.

The boy had closed the back door of the car, and now he came to the front, and he put one foot in the combat boot inside to take his place beside the man who sat with the top of the flask poured full again.

"Well, sixty thousand francs," the man said quietly, as if musing on it, saying it as casually as if he spoke of the time of day. And with one foot on the cobbles and the other in the car, the boy seemed to falter, and then he stepped up and sat down on the cushioned seat and pulled the door closed. "Sixty thousand francs. You damned thief. You damned thief," the man repeated softly, and in the light from the dashboard he saw the boy's face drained of blood.

"You damned drunk," the boy said through his teeth.

"That's a good one!" the man said, beginning to laugh. As he screwed the empty cap back on the flask again, he held his anger in. "What were you going to do with all that money? May I ask you what your plans were?" he said.

"I don't have to answer you," the boy said, his voice squeezed tight within his throat. "We're different kinds of people. We don't use the same kind of words."

"Oh, my lines don't scan, is that it?" the man cried out, and he flung the car into gear in fury, and the back tires spun on the cobbles an instant before they gripped the road. "I'm only an officer in the army! Is that what's the matter with me? I can't sing 'Dark Rosaleen' or 'The Wearin' of the Green,' so you have nothing in common with me! I can't go along with the Irish, is that it?" he shouted aloud.

"You leave the Irish alone," the boy's strange pained voice said in the careening car.

They did not speak again until they had reached their destination, and then they were on foot in the fields, the rifles loaded, the binoculars around their necks, and no bond of speech or love to link them. They were two men walking in hostility, with only the safety catches on their weapons between them and what they had set out to do. Neither the chill rolling country nor the forest ahead had visible boundary or shape yet, but the first was known by the presence of stars, and the second by their absence, the fields and marshes established unmistakably by the mere vastness and stillness of the air which opened wide above. The man led the way, and the boy came behind him, with the dog held in leash by an end of rope which the boy had retrieved from a pocket of the car.

All through the autumn and winter the man had come here with the forester, and he could have taken the direction in his sleep, but because of the drink in his veins he felt another dimension in the familiar substance of the landscape, as palpable as the drop of a precipice or the cold proximity of stone. He moistened his finger for the feel of the wind in the dark, and he and the boy moved on against it, keeping first to the paths between the newly planted fields, and then to the sucking ruts of the wagon road, crossing open country toward the waiting wood. And twice as they advanced through this last brief interval of night, the man seemed to hear the whisper of flight ahead, and he halted, and the boy behind him halted, but if game were there, the dog gave no sign that he had caught its scent.

Later, the stars began to alter. Their color deepened, and they hung isolate and golden and singularly proportioned, the sculptured depth of each seeming to cast a shadow behind it in the lighting sky. And presently the first cold ashen look of morning came behind the forest, giving outline to the assemblage of trees. Now the stars were gone, and the man halted again, and lifted his glasses and slowly, inch by inch, he searched the slowly emerging, mist-threaded sweep of land. And then, without warning, the flickering of life was there, hardly discernible on the rise of furrowed ground, caught once in the glasses, then lost, then caught again, and instantly his hand stood still.

There, on the slope above the area of swamp, was the distant, frantically dancing thing, invisible to the naked eye still, and not of a color with the dawn, as deer or roebuck at this season would have been, but stump-black, and nearly slipping the grasp of vision, a darker, faster-scintillating shadow in ceaseless motion, as both light and shadow of a long-outdated silent film will dance in ceaseless motion on the screen.

"There's a pig up there. It looks like a big one," the man said. As he lowered the glasses, he felt the high, breathless pressure of suspense stifling his heart. He had turned his head slightly and he spoke under his breath, but he might have been blinded to the sight of the boy standing close behind him in the twilight, for nothing was left of past or present except a wild pig which rooted for sustenance two hundred yards away. "We'll have to move in closer before we can get a shot," the man said, and he slipped the rifle from his shoulder, and, with thumb and forefinger, he set the safety catch free. At once they were moving again, but no longer toward the forest, but wading, parallel to it now, through the soft, dawn-bleached marsh grasses, breasting the static lagoons of mist, and then coming clear of them into the channels of translucent air.

The man halted again in the suck of the marsh, and the boy halted behind him, and the man raised his rifle to his shoulder and set the hair trigger, while his eye sought the boar again in the sight fixed to the rifle. And there was the shape of it, grotesque, nearly neckless, sharply defined, and still struggling in frenzy, as if held captive in the gray lens of the sight. "Rooting potatoes out," the man said, and then his shot splintered the absolute quiet of the fields and the marshes, the reverberation returning, like an answering salvo, from the far dark hollow of the trees.

"You hit him," the boy said in a low voice.

"Yes, but that's all. He's running," the man said.

He lowered the rifle, hearing the pig's outraged clamor before his eye quite saw it go. Had the wind borne it the intelligence of where they stood in the wetness of the swamp, it would have swung toward them—snout, twisted tusks and yellowed fangs—in shocked fury, the man knew. He had seen it happen more than once before. It would have given them both, and the dog, the full measure of the fierce, tough-hided power still vested in its flesh. But now it fled like the possessed, galloping, squat, black and bull-like, toward the far refuge of the wood, and the man raised the Mauser again to cover the narrow flanks, the small, speeding, lighter-colored hoofs. Afterward he could not explain to himself what had occurred.

He knew this much: the pig was racing neck and neck with its own annihilation, and then he heard the boy's voice speak to the dog before boy and dog went quickly past him, the dog gasping and crying and choking in its passion as it pulled on the rope. And perhaps, if the hair trigger had not been set or if his finger had stopped in time, the thing would not have happened. But as he shot, he saw the pig plunge down through the vapors of mist, emerge in crystal air, and, as the reverberation of the gunfire died, plunge into mist again. The dog was gone, the boy lay on the grasses, and all sound and motion ceased upon the dawn-bleached land.

"I've shot my son," the man said, but he did not believe it, even when he had said the words aloud. He dropped his gun to the ground and took the hunting cap from his head, and he ran his finger inside the collar of his shirt, his throat reaching for air. Then he walked across the palely lighting marsh to where the boy lay, and he fell on his knees beside him, and his heart had turned to fire in him. "Do not die," he said to the pure white face, as if this order given by an army officer's tongue might have meaning to a poet as well. "Do not die," he said, and he lifted the boy to remove his arms from the sleeves of the jacket that he wore.

With the boy's head fallen, as if in sleep, against his breast, he found the gushing mouth of blood in the right shoulder, and he laid the boy carefully down upon the grasses again. His hands had turned weak as a woman's hands, and they were shaking like a woman's, and he strove to steady their trembling as he took the glass flask from his jacket and unscrewed its top. Then he raised the boy's head on his arm again, and he let the liquid fall, drop by drop, against the barrier of the boy's white teeth. But when he pressed his whiskey-soaked handkerchief upon the wound, the boy whimpered and roused, and looked into his face.

"Where's my dog?" the boy said, and he turned his head toward the comfort of the man's breast and cried.

"I'll find him," the man said. "I swear I'll find him for you." He was trembling still as he lifted the boy in his arms, and walked, carrying him, across the mysteriously brightening land . . .

"Someone else took the money," was the first thing the boy had said when he lay on the back seat of the car. "I wouldn't be saying this now, or ever, if I wasn't shot."

"Stop talking now!" the man had cried out, driving fast toward help through the early day. "For God's sake, stop talking, Tar! You can say it another time to me."

"No, I have to say it now," the boy had said, perhaps thinking there would be just this brief final moment allowed, and the man had known then that the boy, too, believed that he would die. "I had to cover up for somebody else. His father would have been through with him. I thought you wouldn't believe it about me. I told him it would be all right because you wouldn't believe it, no matter what the school wrote to you. I thought you knew I couldn't be bothered doing anything like that," the boy's far voice had said.

"So it was Luc, the one whose father's a Chicago lawyer?" the man had cried out. "He thought you needed it to get to Ireland," he said, with the pain of contrition closing in a vise upon his heart.

"Well, that's my business," was all the boy had said.

Afterward, perhaps three weeks or a month afterward, when the evil, tusked head of the boar was mounted, and hung with the roebuck skulls and horns, and the deer antlers, and the lesser boar heads, on the library walls, the man liked telling his bachelor friends, or the colonel and his wife, or the various others, the story of how the boar was slain. Once the bullet was out, and the boy lay sleeping in the army infirmary bed, the man had gone back to the country again, and, in the light of midday, the recounting of it went, he and the forester had retrieved the rifles, and found and followed the trail of the boar's feet through the mud of the marshland, but the boy's dog was not there. They found the bright, stained grasses where the pig must have floundered a moment in defeat, and the marks of its stampede where it had struggled upright and gone on again, the cloven hoofprints brimming with the liquid of diluted blood. And they had followed the dark, impermeable drops of its bleeding through the forest, the trail of them like the beads of a broken necklace scattered alike on the dead and the living leaves.

After two hours of it in the heat, with no sound but the crash of their boots through the labyrinth, and no sign of the life they sought through the complex weaving of the branches, they lost the trail, and that might have been all there was to the story, if the dog's voice, savage and guttural with menace, had not spoken through the trees. First they perceived the jagged hindquarters, with the copper burnish on the hide, and then the narrow shoulders, and then the emaciated neck, with the end of rope around it still. It stood with its back to them, frozen, one shabby forefoot lifted, and even when it heard them coming, it did not turn its head. Trapped in the underbrush before it, stood the wounded boar, as tall as a calf, it had seemed to the man as he lifted his gun, with its monstrous tusked head lowered, fixing the dog with its evil yellow eyes.

"So for one day I had a first-rate hunting dog," the man would end the story. For, once they had got back to the forester's house, the man and the forester bearing the body of the pig between them, the dog had taken fright at the sight of a woman in peasant dress on a bicycle, and had set off, with his sideways gait, down the country road.

The man and his army friends would sit on the terrace of a summer evening, and while the music playing in the Sergeants' Club came across the valley to them, he would fill the highball glasses up again. And as the *Hausmeister* in his starched jacket passed the canapés from chair to chair, the colonel's wife might ask, "And the boy? How's he getting along in Ireland?"

"He's doing fine, just fine," the man would answer, and he'd take the post cards out. "Here's one I got today, sent from Claremorris, in County Mayo," he'd say, and he'd show the picture of the country to them. "That's where his mother's people always lived," he'd say.

The Lost

The war had scarcely come to a close when an American Relief Team drove up in jeeps through the little hills of Bavaria toward a property which had been, in former times, a baronial farmer's demesne. The place was set back off the country road, a good ten kilometers from any village, and the tree-bordered lane which led to the vast manor house, and its barns and stables and dependent buildings, had long since become a cattle-and-wagon road, deeply rutted in the mud of springtime, and encumbered with stones. The heavy iron gates hung, as derelict as unhinged shutters, from the scarred blocks of granite which had stood for generations at the entrance to the drive. There were wild birds flickering through the branches of the trees, but no other sign of life; and even before the Americans had mounted the cathedral-like steps, and opened the massive door of the stone-winged house, they felt the chill of winter and silence and death that stood like a presence in its feudal halls.

The place had served as a Selection Camp from 1938 to 1945, so that any vestiges of personal effects or of individual life had been eradicated a long time before. But the official records of those who had passed through it, on their way to forced labor or to extermination, were found, neatly and alphabetically filed, in the bookshelves of what had once been the ancestral library. Attached to these records were the photographs, each with a number stencilled across the base of it, and each reproducing the grief and the exhaustion of one human being's unforgettable face —photographs of men with rumpled shirt collars and ties either missing or askew, taken full face as well as in profile, in order that the full measure of their anguish might be known; and photographs of women, some wearing blouses caught by antique brooches at their necks, and others in variously patterned aprons, as if they had come from their kitchens or their housework to this place, without having had the time to do their hair. It was the eyes of these men and women, who were there no longer, which looked now at the Americans, and beyond them, upon some indescribable vista of hopelessness and pain.

But when the Americans came, the nature of the place was altered. It became a Children's Center, and children who had journeyed from factory to factory throughout the war, or drifted from home to temporary home, were brought here from wherever they were found, brought singly, or in couples, or in groups. If they had wandered so long that they could no longer remember their people's names, new names were given them, and they were given Displaced Persons' cards, these children from Poland, or Holland, or Czecho-Slovakia, or Hungary. They were known as Unaccompanied Children, and they were given clothes to wear, and food to eat, and the outline of a plausible future at last. The Americans set up slides and swings on the grass of the lawn that lay between the stables and the manor house, and they made a sandpile for them, and then began the long and painful probing of their memories.

It was these slides and swings which the three boys saw first when they rode up on the American Army truck one morning—the wooden slides with the dew of the spring night still beading them, and the empty swings swaying gently on their ropes in the clear morning air. The soldier at the wheel brought the truck to a halt at the curve of the drive, and the three boys who had ridden in front with him waited a moment, looking out through the window and the windshield, reluctant, it seemed, to leave the Army vehicle and commit themselves to a civilian site and setting, for this was a part of life of which they knew nothing at all. Then the boy sitting next to the door pushed it open and jumped down—a tall, dark-haired boy of fifteen or sixteen maybe—and the other two followed, jumping clear of the step and down onto the gravel drive.

The tall one wore a faded khaki battle jacket, with the length of the sleeves turned back in cuffs, and a strip of German parachute silk, mottled green and tan, and as soft as the wings of a moth, knotted around his long curved neck. The jacket was buckled in tight where the waist of a man was intended to be, but the boy had no hips to hold it up, so it hung down long on the shabby G.I. trousers which had been cut down to his size. The two other boys were younger; they were twelve or fourteen, maybe, but they too were dressed like deserters from the ranks of the same army. They wore khaki, machine-made sweaters their G.I. shirts, and their khaki trousers were thrust inside the mud-caked boots of the U. S. Infantry.

"Thanks for the lift," said the tall boy, speaking as good American as you might hear at home. He stood looking up with a kind of deference at the soldier sitting behind the wheel of the truck, and the soldier looked down at the three of them, and fumbled a package of chewing gum out of one pocket of his khaki pants.

"You guys like a stick of gum?" he said, and each of them reached casually up, and took a stick from the package he held.

And then the soldier slammed the truck door closed, and he started the motor, and the three boys stood there, chewing fiercely, the bits of tin foil and the colored paper lying on the driveway under their feet, as they watched the truck back up and go. They had met for the first time the night before, and even when the truck was gone, they did not look into one another's faces for any of the answers that might be given, each in his own fashion seeking to dissemble his timidity. The tall one, his shoulders slouched in the battle jacket, put his hands into his trouser pockets, and his dark, grave eyes looked across the lawn toward the slides and the swings, and the thickly leafed branches of the trees. The boy who was second in size had a square, tawny-colored face, with a short nose and a humorous mouth, and he stooped at once and picked up a pebble from the driveway, and sent it skimming toward the sandpile where it hit hard against the side of a child's wooden bucket that had been forgotten in the dark, damp sand. The youngest boy's hair was of the texture and color of a pony's shaggy, chestnut hide, his skin was delicate and white, and he had a shy, quiet look of expectancy, of hope even, in his wide, auburn eyes.

"I bet a nickel that's the kitchen over there," he said in a high, bright voice, and he jerked his chin toward the right wing of the house.

"You hurtin' for chow already?" said the second boy. His accent might have come straight from Brooklyn, except that it had come from somewhere else before that, and, as he spoke, he folded his arms upon his breast, and spat casually across the drive.

The tall boy looked back from the trembling leaves in the strong, ancient branches, his eyes sober, his head hanging heavy on his soiled slender neck.

"Let's go on up and sign ourselves in," he said, the drawl of his voice having come, it seemed, from a Southern state. "That's what we come here for," he said.

He led the way up the worn stone steps, and through the panelled door that stood open, having summoned courage, now that there was no other choice before them, to face this that was not an army deal. The youngest boy, his back and shoulders straight, and his hands in his trouser pockets, followed behind him, but the second boy lingered on the driveway, skimming stones across the grass. Because it was early still, there was no murmur of life in the house, and after they had come into the flagstoned hall, the tall boy moved on tiptoe toward the flight of stairs. But, at the foot of it, he stopped, and he jerked the battle jacket he wore up to where his waist should be, and tried to peg it on his hipbones. Then he lifted his thin, big-knuckled hands, and he smoothed back his lank black locks of hair.

"Hey, I smell chow," the other boy whispered behind him, but he did as the tall boy did, and sat down upon the first step of the stairs.

"Where'd you pick up you' outfit?" the tall boy asked, speaking quietly.

"Anzio," said the youngest boy, looking up into his face. "My mom and dad, they was bumped off when we bombed the town. I join up with the Fourth Rangers and done the whole campaign with them," he said.

"My buddy's a mechanic, he's an ignition expert. I been suh-vicing cars with him since 1944," said the tall boy, the words spoken soft and low. "He done tried every way there was to take me back, but they just couldn't see it," he said. He was leaning forward, his elbows on his knees, his long hands dangling. "We wanted to do it legitimate. When they Z.I.'d him last week, he told me to come straight off down here and see what they could do."

And now the second boy came slowly up the outside steps, and crossed the threshold in hostility, wanting none of what might be offered here.

"Why the hell don't we make a break and run for it?" he said, stopping before the two others on the stairs. He stood there, re-calcitrant, resentful, the lids narrowed on his opaque, black eyes, speaking savagely to them through his teeth. "You guys too yellow?" he said.

"Breakin' out won't get us nowhere," said the tall boy quietly.

"It'll get us the hell out of this here kid joint," said the second one. He fumbled a half-empty pack of Lucky Strikes from his trouser pockets, and put a cigarette on his lip. "Christ knows I didn't ask to come here," his Brooklyn accent said.

"None of us done asked," said the tall boy, and the smallest boy raised his head, and looked toward the end of the hallway.

"I bet a nickel it's ham and eggs," he said.

Because he was standing facing the stairs, it was the second boy who saw her first. It was only when the hot sullenness in his eyes had shifted to alarm, and, with the cigarette on his lip still, he had spoken the words of blasphemy under his breath, and turned, and gone out the door again, that the two others knew someone was there. She was big, and gray-haired, and matronly, and she held a flowered cotton dressing gown around her as she looked down from the landing at them through the steel-rimmed spectacles that rode her nose.

"Hello," she said. The two boys had got to their feet, and they stood looking up at her.

"Hello," the tall one and the small one said.

"You men come up to the bathroom and wash your hands," the gray-haired woman said to them. "I'll get some clothes on, and then we'll have breakfast with the rest"; and it might have been mother or aunt, who was saying these things to them, except that neither mother nor aunt, nor the prototype of these, had meaning for them. It was not these names, these words in any tongue, that could stir the memory of anything they knew.

"Maybe you been expecting us, ma'am," the tall boy said.

"We're G.I. mascots from Bremerhaven," said the small boy, saying it with pride.

"You bet," the woman said. She did not say "so you're two more the M.P.s got when you were trying to slip onto the transport," although it may have come into her head. She did not put any of the questions to them until breakfast had been eaten, with the hundred-odd others, at the long tables in the dining hall. Then she took them away, a hand laid on each shoulder, into a room that was furnished with wicker armchairs, with flowered chintz cushions tied in the seats, and she took her place behind a paper-encumbered desk, and she looked at the two boys through the steel-rimmed spectacles on her nose. "Sit down, men," she said, and she watched them sit down on the cushions of the wicker chairs. "If it's easier for you to speak German, we can talk German together," she said.

"I been speaking American three-year now," said the tall boy.

"I learn German working in a munition factory. I done near forget every word of it I knew."

"And before that?" asked the woman, but she still did not write anything down.

"Czech," the tall boy said.

The woman did not seem to hear his answer, for she went on speaking of other things, as if saying these things to herself, speaking of countries and peoples the boys had perhaps known once but which they scarcely remembered, and in whose present and future they no longer had a part.

"It's like a big puzzle, or like the pieces of a big vase somebody dropped and broke here, right on the ground in Europe," she was saying, "and the pieces are jumbled together, and maybe we'll never get it straight, because a lot of the pieces are lost. We're trying to find them and put them together. That's what we're trying to do here, and we're doing it slowly, and maybe we're not even doing it very well," she said, and the sunlight from the window glinted on her glasses as she talked. "Maybe the G.I.s you were with made you promises about going to the States," she went on saying, and the two boys sitting in the wicker armchairs seemed to come alive now as they listened to her, but to the tall boy at least she was neither woman nor American, perhaps not human being even, but a voice—disembodied, quiet, direct—which might be coming now to the words they had been waiting to hear her say. "And probably when the G.I.s made you those promises they thought they would be able to keep them," she said. "I've talked to some of these men, I've had letters from them, and I know they believed they would be able to keep the promises. But there were other kinds too. There were some kinds who didn't care what happened to you men afterward. I've known that kind too. They wanted you to learn how to drink and smoke and gamble and shoot crap and use the kind of language they used—"

"I begin shooting crap in Naples," the small boy said in his high, eager voice. "I clean up seven bucks the first night there."

"Look, kid," the woman said abruptly, "if Italy's your country, perhaps you ought to pack up and go back there. You think it over. Perhaps that's where it's right for you to be."

He was sitting upright on the edge of the wicker chair, the khaki shirt open at his neck, the shaggy pony's chestnut hair growing long at his temples and behind his ears, the cut-down G.I. trousers bagging at his knees. He faced the woman for one more untroubled instant, and then the brightness perished in his flesh, and he looked down in grief at the mud-caked boots of the U. S. Infantry.

"I ain't no Eyetie no more," he said, and he did not raise his eyes to look at her because of the tears that were standing in them. "I'm American. I wanna go home where my outfit's gone," he said.

"Wait," said the woman quietly. "What would happen to you over there? We're an organization, and we make our list of candidates for emigration, and then the American Consul decides. We got thirty-five over last year, sent to adoption centers. But there's one thing we can't do much about changing—if you have anyone left to go back to in your own country, then we've agreed we'll send all you men back," she said.

"But if you ain't got nobody left where you come from?" the tall boy said, leaning forward from his chair.

"How do you know you haven't anyone left?" said the woman.

"My folks was hung in Noverzcimki in '42, when the Germans come in," he said.

"What proof have you got of that?" asked the woman.

"I done saw it," the tall boy said, and as the sunlight struck the woman's glasses, she swiftly lifted her hand, as if warding off a blow.

It was after that that she took out the forms and arranged them on the table, holding the fountain pen in readiness above them as she spoke.

"Tell me your name," she said to the tall boy, not looking at his face.

"Janos—it used to be Janos when I was a kid," he said. "But in the army they called me Johnny Madden." He leaned a little further forward, his thin shoulders hunched, his dark, anxious eyes fixed on her. "He wrote you a letter about me. He wrote it last week. Did you get it yet?" he said.

"Yes—a letter. I got a letter from a man named Madden," said the woman, her fountain pen still moving across the paper. "He's on his way back to Chattanooga. He's got a partnership in a garage."

"Partnership with his brother-in-law," the tall boy said, shifting further forward in his intensity. "Sergeant Charlie Madden. He want me to try to get over legitimate. That's why he tole me to come down here."

"Yes," said the woman again. She stopped writing now, and her middle-aged hands straightened the papers on her desk. "He's colored, isn't he?" she said, and now the gray eyes, that might have been aunt's or mother's eyes behind the spectacles, lost their anonymity, and they looked at him in inexpressible kindliness.

"That's right," said the tall boy. "His wife, she done pass on back in '43, and he ain't got no one left to care for. He's an ignition expert, and I learn how to suhvice cars with him. He's got fifteen hundred dollars put in the bank, so he's able to pay for me to come."

"Yes," said the woman. "He wrote me that." She sat there silent, musing a moment, while the tall boy leaned forward from the chair, his eyes asking the question of her even before the words were spoken out.

"Do you think I got a chance of getting over there, ma'am?" he said.

"We can only recommend," the woman said quietly at last. "We don't have any final say." When she was done with the forms, she told them that they could go; they could go to the foreman in the workshop and find out what there was to do, and in the afternoon they would be processed by the Supply and Medical Corps. "You'll get on to the ropes," she said, and they stood before her, the tall one and the short one, incongruously matched. "The third man who came with you, the one who went out to take a walk," she said, "you tell him he needs a license to go fishing. That's what most of them start in doing when they're uneasy here. And he didn't get any breakfast. Tell him we mess at twelve o'clock," she said.

But all day the others did not see the third boy. Wherever he was, he did not come in at the sound of the mess-hall bell at noontime, and he was not in the empty classrooms or in the workshops, or the dormitories, and he was not outside with the children who played underneath the trees. The boy from Anzio swung on the bars with the others in the afternoon, and had the third boy been there, he could have been seen at a glance, for he would have stood out as a stranger among them, perhaps lingering, handsome and sullen and contemptuous, on the outskirts of their activity. Janos went seeking him through the buildings, through the barns and stables, and down the fields that lay behind the house. As he walked, he unknotted the parachute silk from around his neck in the heat, and he fanned it at the thin young wasps which swam about his head. In the gully below, where it seemed to him that water must pass, he could see an area of pine trees stretched in an isthmus of shadow in the pale, shining sea of grass and flowering bush. And there, at the end of the path, where the fast full stream poured musically from the trees, he found the third boy sitting, his back in the khaki shirt turned against the fields and against the house, as if against the sight and sound of all humanity.

"If you just goes up there and tells her your name and everything, then you got a chance," Janos said to him at once. "You got the same chance as Anzio and me." The boy was sitting on the bank, with the khaki sweater pulled off and lying beside the cast-off combat boots on the freshly trampled grass. He had rolled the legs of his G.I. trousers up, and his strong bare legs were hanging in the stream. "She fills out the papers that you got to have, and if they finds out for sure that you got nobody of you' folks left back where you come from, then you has a chance," said Janos. He stood, tall and stoop-shouldered, beside the other boy, watching the water flow swiftly over his naked feet, and mount high upon his muscular brown calves.

"Nuts," said the Brooklyn accent on this alien air, and the boy moved one foot slowly back and forth in the running water of the stream. The side of his face looked golden in the sunlight, and the dark hair lay thick and glossily dressed upon his shapely head. "I got the whole thing lined up. Have a butt," he said, and he took the crumpled paper of Lucky Strikes from his pocket, and held it out toward Janos. "I been looking around. It couldn't

be sweeter," the boy said. Janos took a cigarette from the boy's
hand, and he straightened it carefully in his fingers. Then the
boy brought a silver lighter out of his pocket, and flicked it with
his thumb, and Janos leaned to light the cigarette at the puny
flame which the boy held shielded in the cup of his smooth hand.
"I been contacting people in the area. Natives," the boy said,
and he lit his own cigarette. As he drew the first breath of it in,
he snapped the lighter closed again. "I got a deal on if you
wanta come in on it. I got it fixed up with a Kraut down the
road," he said.

"What kind of a deal?" asked Janos.

And now he sat down on the grass of the stream bank, folding
his long legs awkwardly, as a young horse will, and settling
down in the shimmering tide of sun.

"I'm going over the hill tonight," said the other boy. "All the
good guys that come here, they don't stay. I got that straight
from the Krauts," he said. He leaned back on his elbows, his eyes
half closed against the smoke of the cigarette hanging on his lip.
"All this here kid stuff. Don't let them give you the run-around,"
he said. "Swings, slides, sandpiles, and standing in line for a
bowl of Grape Nuts. I'm through with that kind of crap. I'm
fourteen. I got tired of hanging my stocking up for Christmas
about ten years ago."

"You going back where you come from?" Janos said.

He sat smoking the cigarette, his shoulders hunched, his long
legs drawn up, and his thin arms clasped around them, looking
away across the flowing stream.

"Do I look like a dope?" the other boy said, and he gave a jerk
of laughter. "I come from Poland once, but that don't mean I'm
going back there. I been two and a half years with the Army,
and I got my campaign ribbons, and my overseas service stripes,
and I know my way around this little continent." The smoke
from his mouth drifted lazily across the sunlit air, and his feet
hung in the clear cool water still. "I'm going where things is
easier. I'm going where all my friends is doing business now," he
said.

"The sergeant I was with," Janos began saying after a moment, "he come from Tennessee. We been working together

since '44. When I get over there, I can start right in working with him again."

"Sure. You bet," said the other boy in irony.

"So I'll stick around here until the papers comes through," said Janos.

"You must be kidding, bud," the other boy said. "I saw action with three different outfits," he said then, and the sound of derision was gone from his voice as he turned his mutinous eyes on Janos's face. "I done everything that every son-of-a-bitch in the Army ever done. I done peter parade, and had my broads, and wrote my own Saturday-night passes out, and, sure, they was all going to take me home with them, the whole God-damn Army was going to see to it poissonnaly that I got Z.I.'d when the rest of them was! Sure, all you had to do was go to Bremerhaven when they went, and walk up the gangplank with them, and nobody'd ever stop you, nobody'd ever have a word to say. Nobody except the M.P.s, the God-damn bastards," he said, and he lay there, looking back at the water again, and calling them the several names. "I got three times to Bremerhaven," he went on saying after that, "but I didn't get no further. The first time it was the colonel who had the uniform issued me in '44 who was going to see that I got shipped back when the others went. Except he forgot to fix the M.P.s, just a little detail like that he forgot!" he said in high, fierce irony. "Sure, they'll wave to you from the deck when the troop ship pulls out, and when they get home they'll send you a postcard of the Statue of Liberty! Up in Bremerhaven, they'll tell you just how it can be done, and the brass hats gives you advice for free. Run along to one of these God-damn kid centers, where they'll fix your immigration papers up! Hell, I ain't asking no favors of nobody! I been two and a half years in the American Army. I'm no emigrant," he said, and he shot the butt of his cigarette away.

Janos sat smoking a little while in silence, watching the water stream quickly, melodiously, past.

"That sergeant I was talking about, Sergeant Charlie Madden," he said after another moment, "he used to tell me a lot of things. He used to tell me how they first started measuring the days and nights," he said.

"You can't measure days and nights," said the other boy, but now the scorn was gone, and his voice seemed inexplicably filled with sorrow.

"Sure; way back in the time of emperors, they started in measuring the days and nights," said Janos. "They started in measuring them by letting water fall. They done took two jars, and when the sun come up in the morning, they let the water start dripping from one jar into the other, and when the last drop fell, the sun was already setting, and that was the end of the day. And to measure the nights, they let the water drip back into the jar it come from first," he went on saying, his legs drawn up and clasped in his arms still, his sober eyes looking at the trees. "And the drops of the water falling for a thousand years was like the ticking of a clock. Charlie Madden said for a thousand years they measured up the nights and days that way."

"Christ, I need a drink," said the other boy, and he sat up abruptly. "Listen, kid, if I let you in on this deal, we could make a break together," he said. He took his feet out of the stream, and he spread his toes in the warmth of the sun, and the beads of water ran off his smooth brown legs and feet and glistened on the grass. "This Kraut down the road, he's doing business with the Army—a nice little racket in jewels and schnapps. There're a lot of big shots in the country around here, and they don't want to contact the Army direct, so this Kraut, he picks up their family jewels and their cases of schnapps, and he does it for them. The Army truck, it comes down from Frankfurt at night, maybe two-three times in the week it comes, with a load of coffee and cocoa they lifted out of the commissary depot stock."

Janos drew in the last deep breath of smoke from his cigarette, and then he threw the end of it away, and his long fingers reached out and pulled at a stalk of grass which grew tall beside the stream.

"And then what are you aiming to do?" he said, and he put the fresh, bleached end of the blade of grass between his teeth.

"I'm going to hop that Army truck back to Frankfurt, maybe tonight, maybe tomorrow night. The Kraut down the road's fixing it up for me," the other boy said.

"And what'll you do once you git to Frankfurt?" asked Janos, chewing slowly at the end of grass.

"The truck drops you off at Rhine-Main," the other boy said quickly. "By that time it's maybe three-four in the morning, and the M.P.s is groggy, and you slip in when they're loading the 'transat' plane. The next stop's Gander, and then New Yoik." He smiled with one side of his humorous mouth at Janos. "Do you get it?" he said.

That night was the first night Janos wrote to Charlie Madden. He wrote him to his home address in Chattanooga, sitting there in the chintz-bedecked, lamplit room where the gray-haired woman had put the questions to them in the day. She had drawn up a wicker chair on the other side of the table from him now, and the lamplight fell on the paper she had given him, and on the knitting in her hands, as she helped him with the words he couldn't spell.

"I just wanted to let Charlie Madden know what the score is," Janos said when he had written the first lines out, and he waited, as if there were some answer to be given.

"Nobody knows the score," said the woman, knitting. "It's like life," she said, as mother or aunt might have said it to him. "You have to wait and see." Mother or aunt, she thought as she knitted, knowing the look of her own face in the glass; knowing it was neither mother nor aunt that any of them wanted, but the other things they had learned how to pronounce the names of— the name of a game of cards, or of a regiment whose insignia they had worn two years now, or the name of a city they had never known; or else the smell of a special beverage, or even the smell of car grease, or the turning motor of an Army car. "The other one, the one who went out for a walk this morning," she said, saying it casually, her needles knitting still.

"He's a little doubtful about coming inside and signing up," said Janos, speaking slowly, softly, his eyes fixed on the words he had written carefully out.

"Sometimes they'll stay out for a week, and then they'll come in," the woman said. "You tell him the food is good. You tell him we're not M.P.s." Or aunts or mothers either, she did not say, still knitting. "You tell him we leave you free."

"Yes, ma'am," said Janos, but it might have been he had not been listening to her. "Please, how does you spell 'ignition'?" he said.

But the other boy didn't leave on the truck that night, and he didn't go the next night. He had settled himself in the hayloft above the empty stables, and only Janos knew that he was there. The second night he said he was getting a bottle of schnapps from the German farmer in exchange for two packs of cigarettes, and Janos said he would carry food out from the mess hall to him. So that was the way it began. All day the boy from Anzio played with the other children on the swings and slides, or else he worked in the classroom, or he went to the vegetable garden with the others and helped pull the radishes and the new lettuce out. He did not wear the cut-down G.I. clothes any more, but boy's short trousers, as the others did, and he did not speak of his outfit any longer. And Janos did what Charlie Madden had taught him to do in the shed behind the house where the drive-way came to an end—all day he cleaned the carburetors, and checked the ignition, and overhauled the motors, of the American Relief Team's cars. But when it grew dark, he went out the back door with his head down, and he passed the shed with the cars standing in it, and he went on toward the stable underneath the trees. He wore his battle jacket still, for they did not have the other things to fit him, and inside his jacket he carried the bread and the cheese and whatever else he had slipped from the mess-hall tables after the evening meal was done. Once inside the stable door, he crossed in the darkness to the thick-runged ladder, and he felt with one hand for the polished wood, and closed his fingers on it, and then he began to climb.

But on the third night, the boy in the loft was still drinking water. For half a carton of cigarettes, he said, the farmer had given the bottle of schnapps to an American Army colonel in-stead of to him, and he lay cursing the farmer. But on the fourth night he had the bottle. He lay stretched in the farthest corner on the hay, with the square of a window standing open in the boards above him, and the stars shining clearly in it, and Janos could hear his voice speaking out across the hay-sweet dark.

"My God-damn lighter's gone dry as a witch's tit," the boy

said, and Janos could hear the rasp of the lighter's stone in his hand. "I got to get me to a P.X. and get me some lighter fluid. I got to find me an American shoe-repair and get some soles put on my shoes. I walked through 'em today, but I got the schnapps," he said. When he sat up in the hay, his head and his neck and his shoulders in the G.I. sweater showed dark against the starry square of night. "Have a swig, kid," he said, and the bottle was more than half empty then when Janos drank from it. He had to tip his head far back, and hold the bottle tilted before the sharp hot trickle of liquid ran into his throat. "I got to get me to a man's-size town where there's a P.X. quick," the boy was saying in the darkness. "I bet I got two weeks' ration of butts coming due."

"Maybe when you hits Frankfurt," Janos said, and he wiped his mouth off, and stood the bottle up carefully in the hay, and now, without warning, the other boy began to laugh. He lay laughing beyond Janos in the darkness, shaking with laughter, as if something had come loose inside him, and was rattling around hard inside his belly and his chest.

"In that hick town?" he said, and he lay there swearing at the name of Frankfurt, and laughing in dry, hard jerks of sound.

"I got hole of a piece of sausage for you tonight," Janos said when the laughing had stopped a little. He had undone the buttons of his battle jacket, and now he laid the bread and the cheese and the sausage on the hay.

"For Christ's sake, pass me the bottle," the other boy said, and when Janos found it in the darkness, he passed it to the unseen, outstretched hand.

"My buddy, that sergeant I was telling you about, he could tell you the names of all the stars there is," he said, and he sat looking at the stars in the open, bluish square of night. "They might be one place in winter, and another place in the summertime," said Janos, "but he'd call them for you. We was in three countries together, and the same stars was usually there."

There was a lingering suck of air as the other boy lowered the bottle from his mouth.

"Oh, Christ," he said, his voice sounding thick and strange and far. "I'm thinking of the brass, the God-damn brass," he said.

"I'm thinking how everything they got—chow, or cartons of butts, or pieces of hide—was always bigger and better than what we got." And then he began to laugh again, and he lay there, shaking as he jerked the laughter out. "Have a drink," he said, handing the bottle across the hay-whispering, hay-fragrant, dark.

Janos closed his fingers around the bottle's neck, and then he drank, and with the second long swallow of the liquor, the promise made was no longer a thing that lay, heavy with longing, in his blood. It had come alive now, and he no longer doubted as he handed the bottle back across the hay.

"I know if I just sticks around here, and works, and waits," he began saying, and then he stopped it to say something else. "He taught me how to write in the two years we been together. I wrote him every night since I been here," he said.

"You listen, kid," said the other boy after he had drunk again. "The cards is stacked against us. We ain't got a chance, not you and me. Frankfurt," he said, in the same far thick voice, "I'm through with Frankfurt. I heard the air strip at Rhine-Main wasn't so good, so I changed the plans I had. I go down to the Kraut's place this morning, and he tells me the M.P.s got the guys that was in the set-up with him, and they puts them in the clink. Bust up a nice little racket because they wasn't getting a big enough slice of it themselves. To hell with Frankfurt. I'm going to work a bigger area, like Munich, or Berlin," he said. He lifted the bottle of schnapps and drank again, and the stars stood sharper and brighter in the open window above his head. After a moment, he lowered the bottle from his mouth. "You got dependents anywheres?" he said.

"I ain't got nobody," said Janos. "That's why I know it's going to be all right, and I won't have to be going back home again."

"My old lady, she must've been fixing chow," the other boy said, his voice muffled now, as if he were holding the laughter in. "Because when I come home from school, there was her arm sticking out the end where the kitchen used to be. A direct hit. Pretty neat for '41," he said. "I couldn't get over the gold bracelet that was hanging on her arm still. Funny as hell how the bracelet wasn't twisted or nothing—"

"Maybe gold don't twist," said Janos.

"Maybe it don't at that," the other boy said across the hay.

That was the last time Janos ever saw him. When he climbed the rungs of the ladder the next evening, the boy was gone, and there was only the empty bottle lying in the hay. But because nobody else had known that he was there, no one else knew that he had gone, and the children stood in line for meals, or swung on the swings, or filed into the classrooms, and even the official memory of him was lost in the endless shuffling of children, effaced by the endlessly changing faces and names and histories. Once the gray-haired woman had said to Janos: "That other one, the one who went out to take a walk, you tell him we're having fried chicken this evening," and then the sound of her voice had perished of itself, as if knowing it had come beyond this, and there was nothing left that any living woman might find to say.

Twice in the next month the repatriation trucks came in through the heavy iron gates, and the children left, twenty or thirty at a time, carrying their string-tied bundles in their hands. As the trucks moved off down the driveway, the children sang in high clear voices of hope, returning now to places and people they did not remember ever having seen; perhaps to people who had been mother or father once, and to countries called France, and Holland, and Poland, and Czecho-Slovakia, and Hungary. And after a while the boy from Anzio left too, and the afternoon he left, the woman of the American team came down to the shed and looked through her steel-rimmed spectacles at Janos working on the Army car.

"He had a grandfather in Naples," she said, and she sat down, in her rose-colored sweater and her old gray skirt, on an empty case marked "Tomato Juice" that stood against the side wall of the shed. "And that grandfather never stopped looking for him, he never stopped giving his name and his description to every G.I. he met." Janos was on his knees by the car, smearing the grease on the wheel nuts with his long thin hands. "And now he's on his way back," she said, "and he'll grow up in Italy where he belongs. I wish you were all as easy as that. Your papers, Janos," she said, and for a moment she did not say any more. She sat pressing the gray stuff of her skirt out under her square, strong palms, and she did not look at Janos. "They've checked back on the records, and the Consul says it's official enough that your people were killed. There's nobody of your family left," she said, but it did not seem easy for her to say.

Janos did not move at once; he crouched by the car a little longer, his shoulders hunched, scarcely daring to hear this thing that she had said. And then he undid himself slowly, the long legs straightening joint by joint, the long bent torso coming erect, until he stood up in the shadow of the shed, wiping the car grease from his hands.

"So I can write Charlie Madden it's all right about my coming over?" he said, and he felt his own mouth shaking as he smiled.

"Well, that's what I wanted to talk to you about," the woman said. She sat there below him on the upturned box, carefully and steadily smoothing the stuff of her gray skirt out. "Over there, back home, in the States, it isn't the same as here about a lot of things—"

"Why, sure, ma'am, I knows that," Janos said, and then the fear closed on his heart again. "If I ain't got nobody left, then I'm all right, ain't I?" he said. "If my folks was all killed off, then I'm eligible to go?"

"Well, Charlie Madden," she said, beginning again, "he's colored. Maybe in a combat outfit you didn't hear much talk about men being colored or men being white, or maybe you didn't pay much attention to it if you did. But over there, back home, in the States, there's the color question."

"There's what?" said Janos.

"There's the color question," she said in a dogged, quiet voice, and she did not lift her head to look at him. "There's the question about people being colored or people being white," she said. "In some parts of the country at home, they don't live in the same part of town that white people live. And they don't always go to the same schools, or to the same doctors when they're sick." Janos stood there listening to the words she said, and, as he listened, the woman again ceased being woman, ceased being human being even, and it was merely a voice in the shed that spoke quietly and bitterly of the separate lives that must be lived by people of different colors, as she had on that first day spoken of the hopes that might never come to anything at all. The voice was troubled as it searched logic or history for justification of the nearly incredible story it told. "I cannot explain to you why it is like this, but it *is* like this," it said, the voice faltering in the telling. "So if you did get to the States, there wouldn't be any way for you to live with Charlie Madden. The Consul's office has talked it over with me, and we thought we'd put it up to you. If we put your name on our list, and if you were cleared for emigration, then it would be better if you went to another family, a white family. We'd explain to them about Charlie Madden, and all he'd done for you over here," she said, "and he could come and see you, and you'd still be able to be friends—" and then the voice came to an end, and there was silence in the shed. The gray-haired, bespectacled woman sat on the wooden box against the wall and looked down at the backs of her hands, and the boy in his khaki clothes stood motionless between her and the dismantled car, seeming not even to breathe.

"I got all Charlie Madden's letters," he said then. "He don't make no mention of anything like that at all."

"The adoption committee might find somebody for you who had a garage himself," said the woman.

"Yes, ma'am," said Janos. "O.K., ma'am," he said.

He did not make the decision at once. He waited another week before he went to her office, and he stood by the desk without speaking until she had finished what she was writing down. Then she looked up at him, the pen still in her fingers, and he cleared his throat and spoke.

"There was a question I wanted to ask you, ma'am," he said, "before I finishes making up my mind. I'd like to know if there wasn't no change yet in that question you was talking about—the colored question over there?" he said.

"No," said the woman, and she looked down at the papers underneath her hand. "I haven't been notified of any change," she said.

It was the morning after that—and Janos was not in the mess hall for breakfast—that she found the envelope, with her name printed on it, lying on her desk. Inside it were the two letters,

written neatly and inaccurately on copy-book paper, and signed
with Janos's name. They were not long—the first one merely four
lines saying thank you and goodbye to her, and asking that she
read the other letter, and send it on to Charlie Madden. The letter to Charlie Madden said:

> Yessitdy I talk to the US consil Charlie and what do ya
> think now? Seems my fammillys jus as good as they
> ever waz so Charlie I make up my mynd sudden to go
> back whar they waz waiting for me Im shure ya thinks
> its for the best Charlie so I says so long

The woman sat there for a long time, holding the two letters
in her hands.

Adam's Death

The village the American car stopped in, one late summer afternoon, was off the highroad, in that part of Germany designated
as Land Hesse. There could not have been more than fifty or
sixty houses in the village, and a square-towered church, which
seemed, in its austerity, vowed to relinquish nothing either to the
grace of the rolling wooded country or to the homage of erring
man. The young woman who drove the car had brought it to a
tentative stop near the church, on a cobbled square at the edge
of a grassy common. From opposite sides of the square, the village road wound off among blocks of strong farmhouses, a road
so still that wisps of hay from wagons that had passed lay unstir-
ring—untrodden, even—on it, as if on the broad boards of a quiet
loft. From where she sat in the car, the young woman could dis-
cern no sign of the living on the village thoroughfare, except for
a line of geese that moved along it, proceeding, as if through alternating shallow and deep water, through the areas of sun and
shade. The birds were tall, and their bodies, their throats,
their wings were a clear, unsullied white. But beauty such as

swans possess they had none of, thought the woman, and she watched them pass from sun to shadow, shadow to sun, in stiff-necked bigotry.

Beside her in the car there sat a boy of four or five, with hair as black as her hair, and eyes set deeply, as her eyes were set, beneath dark, delicate brows. For a moment after they stopped, he did not speak, but sat looking out through the lowered glass of the car door at the green of the common, on which school children played. "There're children here, too," he said then, in his high, eager voice.

"Yes," said his mother quickly. "But if we stayed here, you'd simply have to not play with the children."

"But I like to play with children," he said, not turning his head from the sight of them on the grass.

"I know," said his mother, and she looked down at her hands as she spoke. "We've talked about this before." There was no way to say to him that every morning on waking, in the city they had left, the fear with which one had gone to sleep at night was present still, still unallayed, dissolving the mind with panic. "If you got ill, then perhaps you would never be able to play again," she said. A red suède bag lay in her lap, and in it, with her monogrammed cigarette case, her tasselled lipstick, her expensive compact, was a typed report card from his American nursery school. It was headed "Darmfurt, Germany," and it covered July and a portion of August, and beneath the information dealing with place and time and the boy's identity was noted: "Satisfactory progress, although he is still shy, quiet, and has little to say. He seems to enjoy all our activities in his own way, and is most cooperative." "You see . . ." his mother began to say, but she did not go on with it. Even a first-grade primer had no words simple enough to say to him that in the hospitals of the ruined city they had left children lay stricken, stricken and dying, paralysis turning their arms and their legs and their lungs to stone. She sat looking down at her hands, thinking: You see, if you die, you can't enjoy activities. Death isn't cooperative. It isn't cooperative at all.

For two weeks, she had thought of flight, had talked of it with the boy's father—of flight from the city, leaving the fear, the menace, to other mothers, other children, giving them, as a parting gift to keep forever, the hospital beds, the tortured limbs, the strangling breath; believing, in instants of savagery, that she loved or feared more hopelessly than other mothers loved or feared. And here they were now—out of the city, and away from the river valley and from whatever threat the river water bore. Beyond, farther down the road, a bracketed iron *Gasthaus* sign hung above one of the cobbled-courtyard gates, the single word of refuge done in Gothic script and the harplike strokes of it painted black and gold. The houses were bound by heavy, oil-stained beams, and within this framework strong transverse timbers slashed right and left across the massive whitewashed walls.

"These Germans must have been good Germans. They didn't smash their houses all up, the way the Germans in the city did," the boy said.

"Maybe it will be better here," said the mother. "Maybe it won't be like Germany any more."

She opened the door of the car and pushed aside the books that lay on the big, soft cushions of the seat before she stepped down upon the stones. There were four books. Three of them, in new glazed-paper jackets—*Mrs. Dalloway,* with a special introduction by the author; *The Portable James Joyce;* and *The Portable Faulkner*—could be found on Post Exchange book counters, and usually were left lying there. The fourth book was a child's book, shaped like a Greyhound bus, and the faces of passengers were visible at the painted windows of it, and the wheels were cardboard and actually turned.

At the craftily curtained windows of the village houses, there were no faces to be seen—only potted geraniums, red and pink and white, lending the miniature panes a look of innocence. But still the eyes of the old and of other women must have watched from behind them as the young American woman came down the street, slender, small-featured, alert, with varnish as red as blood on her fingernails, and lipstick brilliant on her mouth. The eyes must have censured the bizarre print dress, the red suède shoes, seeing in peasant outrage or uproarious peasant mirth her tanned, naked legs and her arms bare from the shoulder, and the pagan silver bracelets moving at her wrists—and seen, but with pity for him, because of their abomination of her, the boy in faded corduroys who walked beside her, holding the nameless creature's thin, restless hand. But there was no stir behind the windows; there was no whisper of this other life. The air was still, the doors were closed, and from the lofts that stood open beneath the overhanging eaves came the smell of the new hay.

The woman who opened the door of the *Gasthaus* to them wore the Hessian dress, with the heavy skirt of it reaching below her ankles, and her hair, in the local peasant manner, was wrenched up sharply from her swollen brow. The American woman could speak a little German, and she told the *Gasthaus* keeper's wife that she wanted a room with two beds in it, where she and her little boy could stay for a while. As the woman mounted the dark wood stairs before them, there was a wariness in the set of her narrow shoulders, and when they stood in the big, clean room together, it was there in the side of her face, in the small, close, cautious ear, the guarded eye. The ceiling was white and low, and the posts of the painted bedsteads seemed tall enough for the ceiling to rest upon them. The bedposts were a primal blue in color, with flowers stencilled on them in clear yellow, red, and green. Between the posts billowed the soft, deep feather beds, buttoned into starched envelopes, bloated with plumage, and immaculately white.

"Let's live here," the boy said, but the *Gasthaus* keeper's wife was not at all sure that they would be worth the trouble they would give. She moved across the wide boards of the floor to the doll-sized window, where the midget curtain hung, and with the side of her hand she brushed the crisp little bodies of dead wasps from the window sill.

The American woman laid her handbag down on the white-clothed table, as if accepting this now as the place where they would stay. She said that twice in the week she would drive back to the city for food, for American food bought at the commissary—for coffee and rice and sugar and fat, for meat and flour and cereals—and the *Gasthaus* keeper's wife took this for the terms of an agreement proffered, and she slowly shook her head.

"The payment would have to be in Deutschmarks," she said, the wary eye averted. "We have these other things."

"But for us to eat—for the boy and me to eat—so that we wouldn't take your food from you," the mother said quickly.

"Deutschmarks," said the woman, in her simple Hessian dress. She said that when her husband came in from the fields, the American woman would have to talk with him. It was not for her, who was herself merely woman, to tell them whether to go or stay.

"Would you rather be rich or would you rather be hot?" the little boy asked his mother as they followed her down the *Gasthaus* stairs.

"Well, perhaps rich—rich rather than hot," said his mother, with her mind not on it.

"But if you were rich, then you might be hot, too. If you got into a place where there was fire, then you'd have to be hot," the little boy said, and now that they had followed the woman into the *Gasthaus* kitchen, it might have been the room he was speaking of.

The air was tart to smell there, and the little windowpanes were misted, because of the pots of blue plums cooking on the stove. There were other women there, women older than the *Gasthaus* keeper's wife, sitting working at the table, their skirts as heavy as winter coats, and coarse white kerchiefs tied across their heads. They picked the plums out of the baskets held on their knees, and they split the fruit lengthwise with their knives and cut the flat, brown, pointed stones away. The mother saw that their strong, seamed hands were stained from the flesh of the plums they touched, and she saw, as well, that their wrinkled cheeks were sucked inward, drawn tight as silk across their empty gums, as they looked at the half-clothed stranger who had sat down apart from them on a wooden bench and put her arm around the boy. And then in her uncertain German she put the question to them.

"Perhaps you could tell me," she said, "if there are any children ill here—here in the village?" She looked from one to the other of their faces, asking it of them in fear.

"Ill?" said the *Gasthaus* keeper's wife, glancing up from the vessel of plums she was stirring on the stove. "Any children ill?" she said. Near her, on the kitchen dresser, stood a wide-throated pitcher brimming with milk, and three great wheels of country bread, and butter in a crockery dish. Just behind the pitcher of milk could be seen a carton of Camel cigarettes, and four brightly lettered little tins of G. Washington instant coffee, but the mother was not thinking of these things. She was looking at the women's faces, asking this urgent question of their impervious eyes. "Any children ill here in the village?" the *Gasthaus* keeper's wife repeated, and once the other women had shaken their heads, she said "Nay" to the mother, across the vapor of the cooking plums.

But even after the *Gasthaus* keeper had come and talked to the American woman, on the wood steps in the sun, there was still no satisfactory explanation of why she had come to the village with the boy. She said that her husband was stationed in Darmfurt, but to them, whom the Occupation had scarcely touched, this was almost without meaning. Darmfurt, they had been told, was no more than an agglomeration of ruins now, but whatever it was, it lay two hundred kilometres outside the confines of their curiosity. And currency was what he wanted, currency he had to have, so the mother paid the Deutschmarks to him for the first week they would stay. Like his wife, he set aside the talk of bringing food to them; the potato crop was good this year, he said, standing there squinting into the courtyard's warm summer light, a swarthy, thick-shouldered, straight-backed man, savoring the prosperous flavor of the things he said. A neighbor who had bought a cow from him had paid him partly in cocoa, partly in sugar.

"Jack Frost, granulated," he specified. While the village baker, who owed him for the rent of pasture land, had paid his debt to him in flour. "Gold Medal, much finer grained than German flour," the *Gasthaus* keeper said. "Every week, they'll come past your door with soap and rice and coffee to sell," he went on. "I'll buy when the rice is Carolina glazed and the coffee is in tins, not bags. My wife wants the soap that comes in paper wrappers. Octagon, when they have that," he said.

He said they would kill a pig next week, in a private way, not bringing the government regulations into it, and he said there would be plenty of poppy oil to see them through the winter, and as he talked of it, he reached a bouquet of dried poppy-heads down from where they hung, their parched stems knotted with raffia, from the beam above the open door. Then he stooped, and with his blunt, earth-bitten fingers he made a cup of the boy's hand, and, still stooping, he tapped the indigo poppy seeds into the hollow of it out of the split, papery pod.

"But where do they come from—the rice, the soap, the coffee?" the mother said.

"Well, the *Amis* over here have so much they have to get rid of it. Overproduction in America," the *Gasthaus* keeper said. "If they don't keep it moving around the world, then the selling price will drop below the cost of producing, and then they'll have inflation. That's how it is." He stood up, and he brushed the rest of the poppy seeds from his work-worn hands. "They're full of oil. They'll fatten him up," said the *Gasthaus* keeper, and the boy looked up at his mother before he tried them on his tongue.

The first evening they were there, the mother and boy followed along a deeply rutted wagon road together, leaving the houses of the village and the unrelenting tower of the church behind. The road led away through fields and pastures toward the dark regions of the forest, drawing them onward under the pure, unbroken arch of sky or evening, through the clarity and stillness, toward the equivocal forest, as the lingering afternoon itself had drawn them hour after hour toward the night.

"Why is the sky all around? When will the stars come?" the boy asked, his voice as fragile as glass on the clear, still evening air. But the mother and boy spoke little as they walked, perhaps hushed in trepidation of the myriad life of the woods that lay in mystery before them. "Maybe there'll be wild pigs there," the boy said, remembering that once in the spring his father had left the city to hunt them by moonlight in the hills. "Maybe there'll be elephants," he said.

On one side of the road, a stream ran, its passage muted by the long, fresh grasses that flowed within its bed. And on the other side lay the fields planted with winter turnips, their leaves, thought the mother, like Rousseau's strong, lacquered jungle leaves. Beneath this lustrous emerald foliage, the wax-white turnips shouldered their way out of the soil.

"We may see deer come out of the woods," said the mother, and then she glanced to the side of the road on which the stream ran, and she saw the other, the unexpected, thing that stood there just beyond the wagon ruts, in the beginning of the grass. It was nothing more than a stone—a smooth stone shaped like the head board of a bed—but there could be no mistaking the meaning of it. It was a gravestone, its presence stating that life had ended here.

The boy had picked up a spray of leaves from the foot of a tree they had passed, and now he struck at the weeds with it as he walked ahead. But the mother had halted, and she stepped nearer in the deepening light to read the letters and numbers inscribed on the stone. "*Adam's Tod, 1944,*" it said, and below it the curved delicate blade of a scythe had been engraved.

"Adam's death," the mother said under her breath, and it seemed to her suddenly then that all they had fled from might come this far to reach them, might pursue them and outstrip them here. "Adam's death," she repeated, scarcely aloud, and she shivered as if the cold had touched her. "Darling, come back!" she called out in panic to the boy. "It's getting late! Tomorrow we'll go as far as the forest. We'll start out earlier," she said, and, switching the weeds and flower heads as he came, the boy turned back to her from the engulfing tide of dark.

But the next day it rained, and they did not go out, and the day after that the accident took place. A peasant passed by the *Gasthaus* riding a bicycle slowly, bringing along behind him a strong gray mare on a halter as he rode. And behind the mare, or beside her, or else cavorting ahead, came a slim black colt, the fruit of her loins, without bridle or rope, making a show of freedom but tethered to her by love. He was so shy that when pigeons winged up from a courtyard, his supple neck arched like a hunter's bow and his unshod hoofs stamped on the cobbles, but he had a certain kind of giddy humor in his eyes as he skidded from one side of the village road to the other. From the *Gasthaus* doorway, the boy and the mother saw the colt, with his nostrils lipping the shimmering, rain-washed air and his muscles running swift as water within his hide, and the boy went leaping out the *Gasthaus* gate and followed the colt in speechless pleasure, lowering his head and moving as the young horse moved, thin and awkward and somehow brother to the colt, with one eye on his mother, as the colt's eye was on the mare. And then, just before the turn in the road, the boy fell and struck his mouth upon the stones. The peasant wheeling slowly on the bicycle, the mare, the colt, did not pause, not merely not spectators to it but as if they were not on the same unfolding length of film on which this had occurred. Their own complete procession, in perfected Technicolor, flickered a little longer, until they made the turn, on the screen of alternating sun and shade.

Two of the village women brought the mother a towel to hold to the boy's split mouth, and she held it against the blood, the mud, the dung, the violent screams, in her wild, trembling hands.

"To the doctor, the doctor!" one of the peasant women cried out, and from the doorways and courtyards and lofts other voices shouted it aloud. But the doctor had ridden off on a truckload of plums, to sell them to wholesalers in the Kreis, the postman said, and he looked at the boy and shook his head. "To the dentist, to the dentist, then!" the voices altered it, and one of the women ran ahead to show the mother the way.

It was far; it was nearly half a mile to the dentist's house, for he lived on the outskirts of the village, beyond the last of the strong peasant houses, on the very brink of the sun-drenched open land. And as they mounted the footpath to the dentist's house at last, the sight of the village and the sound of its people were left behind, and now there were larks that sang above them, and it might have been that a door had been flung wide to the freshness of the fields and the clear, bright metal of the shining air. It was perhaps this vision of the expanding country, lustrous with rich grasses and melodious streams, that made the boy cease his choking crying, so that they mounted in silence between the fragrant banks of deep, wet clover to the dentist's door.

It was nothing more than a chicken house that he lived in, with salvaged squares and patches of tin nailed to the boards to spare it from the weather. The roof was flat, and there was a rusted pipe thrust through it to serve as chimney, and the bits of timber that had been used to fashion the window frames had seemingly been split from packing crates for this purpose no longer than a day or two before. But on the home-made door the dentist's shingle hung, the letters stencilled in black on a white ground, professionally, neatly done, like that of a well-established practitioner. "Dr. Eli Jacobi, Zahnarzt, Universität Saarbrücken," the letters said to the trembling silence of the country, and the mother still held the blood-soaked towel to the boy's mouth as she knocked on the door.

When the mother told the story, afterward, she could not explain to herself how the thing that had come to matter then was not what had happened to the boy. The facts themselves were simple enough: the boy had split his two front upper teeth in the fall, and the dentist, once he had sponged the blood and filth away, had done expertly, with decision, what there was to do. But the issue—the crisis, even—was something else, something that dealt with the boy no longer but with strangers, something so alien that one could not put one's finger on its name. The dentist had injected Novocain into the lacerated gum, and the boy had not cried out in protest as the needle slid in; he had not moved in protest or pain when the dentist took out the splintered teeth, shielding the pincers from the boy's sight, as he had the needle, with the back of his long hand.

"You see, the roots seem long—long for a child's first teeth," Dr. Jacobi said, speaking a slow, heavy English to the mother. "That is because the teeth had not made their preparations to come out," he said, and he spread the bits and slivers of them on his palm. Dr. Jacobi was a short, thin, soft-looking man, white as a slug—a man of forty, or even older, the mother decided. His crimped red hair receded from a tenuous point of gold above his forehead, his nose was white and prominent, his nostrils were curved, and he had an anxious, light-lashed eye. "So now he must remain so—three or four years so, namely—without these teeth, until the two new ones come down," he said.

But the heart of the story was not this; it had nothing to do with a boy's courage or a man's precision. It did not reside in the

fact that a piano stood in one corner of the single, unpartitioned
room, or that a framed photograph of an Epstein sculpture hung
above it, at a height at which barnyard fowl must have perched
in sleep in this place once, out of the reach of fox and rat and
weasel, huddled close in terror when the stench of their coming
troubled the dark, stale air. Nor was it the books of music that
lay open—the Gershwin and Stravinsky scores, the yellowing
sheets of Mozart's and Purcell's composing—that gave another
meaning to what had taken place. The story was contained in a
pencil drawing hanging above the covered couch that served Dr.
Jacobi as a bed, and on which he had bidden the boy lie down
and rest. It was a drawing of a rutted wagon road, the wheel and
hoof prints upon it, the grasses that grew long beside it, done
sharply and with artistry. By the side of the road, a stone stood
clear of the grass, and on the stone *"Adam's Tod, 1944"* was
inscribed, and below this a scythe blade was curved.

"Who did that drawing?" the mother asked in a quick, low
voice of wonder. She was seated beside the couch where the boy
lay, nearly asleep.

"I made it. I drew it," Dr. Jacobi said, his bloodless face gone
sharp. He was cleaning his instruments quietly and putting them
away, and now he, too, looked up at the drawing on the boards
of the chicken-house wall. "I came here eight months ago," he
said, and as if this were some kind of explanation, "having graduated a little late from university. I came here, to this village
that had no dentist, to set out in my professional career. A little
late," he repeated, saying it bitterly, ironically. "My studies were
interrupted," he said, and he turned to the cleaning of his instruments again.

"So then you didn't know the man called Adam? You didn't
know who he was?" the mother said. The boy slept now, and she
held his helpless, pliant fingers in her hand.

And then, in amazement, she sensed anger in the dentist's gesture as he flung the instruments aside, and his breath and his
step were quick with impatience as he came to where she sat beside the sleeping boy.

"Ah, yes, I knew him! Don't make any mistake! I knew him!"
he cried out, and she saw the passion that had darkened and

transformed his soft pale face. "I knew him alive, or men so like him that I can say I knew him, even if I came here four years after he died. I knew him in Auschwitz, in Buchenwald; we were together in every ghetto of Europe together—men so like him or so like myself that we could be taken one for the other! Adam!" he cried out, and his yellowish eyes blazed at the seated woman. "Just Adam! No more than that! My brother or your brother, your son or mine, lying dead under a stone by the side of the road!" He ran one long finger inside the collar of his shirt, and he cleared his throat savagely, as if seeking to free his voice of the wild emotion that held it fast. "Everyone knew him here—all the village people," he went on, more quietly, then. "They put up the stone for him. They did that much. But the peasants speak of him to me when they come here with their aching teeth, for he still lies heavy on their conscience, the village conscience. Sometimes it seems to me that they come not because of the pains in their teeth but because of the words they want to speak of him and do not know how to say. Because once they knew a man who did something for them for nothing, one man without a name, a refugee, asking nothing of them except the right to stay alive. Just once!" he said, speaking in irony and bitterness of the peasants who stood strong as oak, as rock, about them, embedded in the soil. "They say he came from Berlin—in 1933 or 1934, it was—but they do not say he was fleeing in terror from what was there. He came and he worked their fields for them, slept with their cattle, ate with their swine. Adam!" Dr. Jacobi cried out, his passion rising again. "One man they didn't have to drive a bargain with!"

"And then he died. He died on the wagon road," the mother said, scarcely aloud.

"Yes, yes, he died," said the dentist, nearly master of himself again, and he drew one shaking hand across his crimpy hair. "They cannot tell you if it was an accident, or if he died by his own or by another man's hand. The peasants found him by the road one evening, dead in a lake of blood, killed by the scythe with which he had been cutting the long grass in their fields all day. It had entered his belly," the dentist said, making the gesture, "and come out through his spine, and when they lifted him, they tell me his body was as light as a little child's. Because he had not eaten well," he said, his tongue tip running along his lip. "I ask them when they come here, and I cannot find a man who ever asked him to sit down at his table. He did not sit down and eat with men and women in the ten years he was here. And perhaps sometimes he lays his hand on their hearts in dreams at night, and that wakes them, for there are days when they come uneasily to me and ask me if he had had more flesh to cover his bones, would he have died so quickly by the roadside, or they ask me if they should put a cross upon his stone."

Dr. Jacobi turned away and finished cleaning his instruments then, and the mother did not speak, and after a while the boy stirred and woke, and then they rose to go. It was not easy to bring herself to speak of money, but she did this as he stood by the chicken-house door, and at the sound of her words the quality of strength or pride or reticence he had was taken from him, as if his manhood were taken from him, and he looked away.

"Not money," he said. "You see, a country dentist cannot ask much—one mark or two. It is never enough to pay for what they have to sell. But if I could ask you—that is, if you could bring me something else, not now, but when it is available. . . ."

The mother looked at the hollow side of his face for an instant before she understood. It was perhaps the nearly perceptible outline of the teeth within the jaw that made it unmistakably clear.

"Food?" she said in a low voice, and when Dr. Jacobi turned his head quickly, she saw the bright, violent light of hope that burned now in his eyes.

"Yes, food," he said. "Whatever you could spare." And there was nothing more to say.

Aufwiedersehen Abend

It would be possible to divide them into two nearly equal categories, the American civilians who came to work in Germany. There were those who came because of the varying ways and means of profit, or the illusion of power, which this Occupation employment offered; and there were those who had returned to what had been their homeland once, American citizens now, but still German enough to believe that they alone could draw near to, and perhaps cure, the country's ailing heart. The odd ones, who fitted under neither of these two heads, might be disposed of as fanatics. Some of them were young men who had left Stateside colleges to fight the war, and who had learned in mud, and blood, and combat, a lesson so violent that they had no patience left for classroom or campus. They had severed themselves from their home towns, and their people, and the girls they would go back and marry in the end, and for a second time they had come to this country, but not as soldiers, not in uniform, but as civilians with a mission, having accepted both war and peace as their responsibility.

One of these men, one of this odd minority, was a young man named Rod Murray, who had come out of the Midwest on the common errand of reorientation, come seeking the look of sincerity in other men's faces, and the sound of truth in their voices when they described the roles that they had played. He had been a bomber pilot once, and now his name, and his title as Information Services Officer, were stencilled on an office door in a building designated as American Military Government in an ancient university town. The town, with its *Schloss*, and its medieval halls of learning, stood solidly and picturesquely, built to outlast all wars, it seemed, and all orientation, upon a Hessian hillside. When the work of the day was over, and the Military Government offices closed, Rod Murray did not go back to his billets to play poker with the others, and he did not sit in a

movie hall with his arm around a *Fräulein,* because this quest
for the freedom-loving and the enlightened could know no respite until it had reached some kind of end. The name of love
might have been given to this search, but it was more dedicated
than any pursuit of woman, this fateful seeking in an alien country for men with whom free men might have affinity. Rod Murray could be seen of an evening in the town hall of one or another of the Kreis villages, sitting among the rural storekeepers,
and the farmers who had come in from the land to hear the
Bürgermeister and the *Landrat* speak. And when the *Bürgermeister* and the *Landrat* would have had their say, and the men
and the few women present begun to leave the hall, Rod Murray
would jump up and seek to make his protest heard, and not succeed, and climb up on a chair to say it, standing tall, and slouch-
shouldered, and a little too heavy, in his gray tweed suit among
them, knowing this was no part of the job for which his government paid him, but simply part of man's commitment to his
fellow man.

"Say, this is an open forum!" he would call out loudly, and
without fear, in his shameless rendering of their traditional
tongue. "Now it's the time when questions are asked!" he would
try to say, as he combed his fingers wildly through his dark,
crisp, wavy hair. And the storekeepers, and the peasants, the
women among them wearing their regional dress, would turn
their heads to stare at him, not in censure, or in ridicule, but
merely stare, their bland eyes vacant even of curiosity. And Rod
Murray would jump down from the chair, and shoulder his way
forward to where the *Bürgermeister* and the *Landrat* would be
putting on their heavy coats. "This is the time for the people to
ask you questions about the local administration!" he would cry
out in his ringing voice. "This is the time for them to air their
views and argue with you!" he would say. And the *Bürgermeister* and the *Landrat* would glance at the massively framed
clock above the platform and one or the other of them, lowering
his voice, might say that this was the way the meetings had always been held. What kind of questions had he had in mind,
they might ask him in quiet, conciliatory voices, saying, as they
buttoned their coats over, that once the official addresses had

been delivered, it was customary for a town meeting to come to a close. And the young man who had been brought up among community chests, and cooperatives in the Midwest, would stand there saying helplessly: "But this is a forum for the people! That's the idea of it," his dark, outraged eyes watching the people who had never asked questions of their administrators, and who could not learn to ask them now, turn quietly and go.

But once in the winter, when the snow was falling thick and fast, Rod Murray undertook with impatience an errand which had nothing to do with the mission on which he had come. It was dusk when he set out, for he had put this off until the final moment of the day, and he walked with his overcoat collar turned up, and the limp brim of his worn, felt hat pulled down, following a narrow, cobbled street which wound up through the archaic houses, begrudging every instant of the time that he must give. But he liked the taste of the winter evening on his lips, and the sight of the crowded, leaning dwelling places, so picturesque that it seemed to him he moved through that miniature scenery, and that facsimile of falling snow, which are contained within a paperweight glass ball. He climbed steadily, his eyes seeking the number of a house he did not know. It had been described in the telephone directory as the *Berufsschule für Bewegungs-Ausdruck-Kunst-Rhythmik und Gesellschaftstanz* but there was no sign to confirm this when he came to it, nor was there a bell to be found in the archway's moist, grooved stone. He lifted the knocker on the heavy oak panel of the door, and let it fall, and the ring of its iron sounded in the narrow, snow-hushed street. When the door had opened just wide enough to let him pass, Rod Murray stepped into the flagstoned corridor, and he waited a moment, wondering at the identifiable sense of stealth, the silence, which dwelt within the dancing school's interior. An oil lamp burned at the end of the long hall, and, to the left, a flight of dilapidated stairs leaned against the massive stones of the wall, its baroque banisters hanging, like a great, warped harp, no longer fit for music, forgotten there in the obscurity. And as the half dark cleared, he saw that a woman stood with her back against the door that she had closed behind him, and for an instant he felt the familiar stir of hope that, not

Kant, or Fichte, or Hegel, but this unknown figure, this still unprobed segment of the national mind, the national experience, might yield some portion of the national mystery.

"I'm Mr. Murray, from Military Government," he said, speaking his imitation German to the faceless and nameless presence of the woman in the hall.

"I am the *Frau Direktor* of this poor little establishment," she said hoarsely and rapidly out of the shadows to him; and at the sound of her voice, defensive, cautious, low, he knew it would not be she who had cupped in her bare hands, and shielded through the years, the small, hot, eager flame of individual intent, keeping it clear of the collective blasphemy. "I used to have a big house in Hamburg, with three fine reception rooms, all good enough for royalty, and now it's come to this," she said, the whine resorted to at once, like an arm already slyly lifted in the darkness to ward off whatever threatened blow might fall. "I lost the house, and two concert grand pianos in the bombings. I used to have a fine selection of pupils, girls from decent families, but since the war ended, everything's changed. The quality's not the same," she said, and when she spoke again the voice was even warier. "Have you come privately, or is this an official visit you're making us?" she said.

"It's like this," said Rod Murray quickly, impatient with her voice, her words, her flesh. "One of our Military Government officers is leaving, and we're giving him a party on Friday night, a sort of *Aufwiedersehen Abend*," he said, inventing the German phrase for it as he went along. "I've been asked to take care of the entertainment for the evening, and I was told you had dancers here, professional dancers—girls, of course. As a professional, you'll have to help me," he said, and he tried to see the hour marked on the watch strapped to his wrist. "This is the first time I've had to do anything in the line of entertainment," he said.

"Ah, girls," said the woman, and she seemed to speak in singular relief. "Sometimes the Army sends someone to investigate, so we have to ask. Will you come upstairs, Mr. Murray?" she said, and she moved out of the dark of the doorwell, saying: "Ah, girls. They're mostly *Flüchtlings* or D.P.s now. We haven't much

else to offer," as she gathered up her hanging garments and
moved swiftly past him to the stairs. He followed her up the
trembling structure, having scarcely glimpsed her face yet, and,
at the top, without warning, her profile was cast in outsized
shadow on the wall. The features he saw were not those of a
woman, but of a lean, lipless courtier from another century, an
aging page boy, the scrawny hireling of knights in armor, with
the hair cut like a casque to fit the bony head. The silhouetted
nose was the beak of a bird of prey, and was perhaps even cor-
neous in substance, Rod Murray thought in revulsion as the outlandish figure stooped, bowed and evil, to fit a key into the lock
of the closed door. "There'll certainly be one or two to interest
you," she said, and then she pushed the door open, and gestured
with one horny wing for him to pass.

The big room they entered was as cold as a cave, and it was lit
by four standing lamps which flanked both sides of an upright
piano, with the coats of arms of the leading German cities
embossed in color on their parchment shades. On the piano top
stood a glass vase of crepe-paper roses, and when Rod Murray
laid his hat down beside the vase, he saw that the rose petals,
which had probably once been red, had faded to lavender beneath a film of dust and age.

"I know exactly what I want," he began to say briskly, while
he sought to avoid the sight of the hostess reflected from every
angle in the long, scarred mirrors which hung on two of the four
moldy walls. "I thought of starting off with a Spanish or Hungarian dancer, if you had the right person and the correct music
for it. Perhaps a fandango," he said, but wherever he looked for
gaiety and beauty, there was the aged woman in her hanging,
fanning clothes. Her brow was covered by a smooth, oiled,
ebony bang which a green silk ribbon held in place, and from
under this fringe, her black eyes watched him narrowly. Two
spots of rouge, as dark as bruises, stood high upon her cheekbones, and within the shadow of the grotesquely hooked nose,
the thin lips of a medieval lackey were painted mauve, and
given a shape that was not theirs, so that they might seem athirst
for sensuality. A green brocaded neckcloth kept the disaster of
her throat from sight, but the fleshless cartilage of her ears was

visible through the dyed black tassels of her hair. "Then perhaps follow this with a *romantisches* number, a *Herzen und Blumen* sort of thing," Rod Murray tried to go on with it as he strolled restlessly from lamp to piano, piano to mirror, mirror to lamp again, in this room which held itself in readiness for some function that he could not name. "You might have some acts to suggest, but I don't want to undertake too much. I'd like to know the price beforehand," he said, not knowing yet that this was the first sentence she had understood in its entirety, and understood by instinct only, with her eyes turned canny as a hawk's eye under the oiled ebony fringe of hair.

"I'll get the girls down, and you can make your arrangements with them," she said. "But I get twenty per cent of every fee. That's customary in the establishment," she said, before she flapped from the room, and closed the door, and locked it from the landing. It was then, without any sense of shock or personal outrage, that he recognized the actual nature of the place, and he began to laugh. In his pocket were the two most recent letters from a college girl he knew at home, and he put his hand inside his overcoat and touched the folded thickness of them now.

While he waited, Rod Murray decided on the things that he was going to say. But he did not say any of them, for when the woman unlocked the door again, there were three girls with her, two of them blond, and the third one dark, and all of them identically dressed in flesh-colored bathing suits, with high-heeled, worn, black slippers on their naked feet. She herded them forward, these three white glutted geese, and, as they moved toward the piano, Rod Murray could see the goose-pimples the cold had raised on their plucked bare backs and on their heavy, undressed limbs. The two blond girls halted beside one of the standing lamps, and laid their arms around each other's waists, and faced Rod Murray, smiling, while the dark young woman sat down before the keyboard, flexed the muscles of her forearms, and began to play. As she played, the three of them chanted "Deep in the Heart of Texas" as casually as if the twang and the drawl, and the broken rhythm, were inherent in their birthright, and this accent from one state of America the flavor of their native speech. The hostess had taken a chair facing the piano, and, while the others sang to its accompaniment, she kept time by tapping her wooden leg, or her cloven hoof, or her broomstick, on the dusty boards.

"But this isn't the kind of thing I'm looking for!" Rod Murray cried out, and he retrieved his hat from the piano top, where it left a ring of melted snow. "I wanted dancers! I didn't come to waste my time with this! I wanted professional entertainers!" he said to them in his fury before he hastened toward the door. When he turned the key in the lock, and jerked the door open, the sound of the *Frau Direktor's* tapping, and the rippling of the music ceased, and the women were left there, motionless, speechless, hearing him shout: "Dancers! *Herr Gott,* can't you understand German?", before he jammed his hat on his head, and went running down the leaning stairs.

That was Thursday, and by Friday morning the snow was two feet deep in the streets of the town, and the gray tiled roofs of the *Schloss* and the university buildings, and the houses on the north side of the hill, were crested and fishboned with white. But although the sky was overcast, the snow had ceased to fall. Rod Murray gave no thought to the dancers as he walked through the snow to the *Rathaus,* where the trial of the former editor of the local newspaper was about to begin, for he had seen the articles the Nazi editor had written in the war years and these were in his mind as he pushed his way into the crowded courtroom, and shouldered his way forward, the only American who had taken the obligation as his own, and come. The defendant, sitting side by side with his lawyer, faced the German judge's raised seat, and the prosecutor strolled back and forth in the space left between the court stenographers and the defendant, rubbing his red-knuckled hands together, for he too had just come in from the streets of freshly fallen snow. The defendant was a lean, distinguished, white-haired gentleman, and at times he turned in his chair to smile discreetly, under his clipped moustaches, at his wife and his three daughters, clad in black, who sat behind him. Around these women, the defendant's friends formed a protective block, for the former editor was a celebrated and respected man.

"The defendant has stated, and maintains, that he was an anti-

Nazi editor," were the words the prosecutor now addressed to
the courtroom, and Rod Murray, wearing his overcoat still,
usurped a place on the fringe of the elite, two rows behind the
defendant's wife, and the chair cried out beneath his weight as
he sat down. "As late as March, 1945, the defendant was still
editing the newspaper in this town," the prosecutor said, and
now a murmuring became audible, a whisper of protest which
seemed to spread from seat to seat, stirring even from those who
stood, packed close, in the back of the hall. "As a part of his defense, he has stated that his editorials were not political, but the-
ological in nature," the prosecutor continued. "For an example,
at Easter, 1945, the defendant wrote and published an editorial
on the rising of the new Messiah from the grave." It was known
that the prosecutor was not a native of the university town, that
he was not a Hessian even, but that he was a *Flüchtlinge* from
Rostock who had taken refuge here less than a year ago among
them, and they did not like his alien accent, or the sharp, sad
features of his face. "Now let us assume," the prosecutor said,
giving half of all he had to say to the grave, young judge who
looked down at them from his raised chair, and half to the peopled courtroom, "that there were certain unmistakable ways in
which an anti-Nazi editor conducted himself so that he should
be known for what he was." And now the prosecutor's dark
glance rested upon the conservatively but expensively accoutred
figure of the white-haired editor, and the spectators, too, turned
toward him, some of them half rising from their seats the better
to see this distinguished man whose printed words had for so
long made plausible, and continued to make plausible even in
defeat, the legend of their own ascendancy. Here he sat like a
common man, and yet so manifestly the gentleman, despite the
circumstances which had brought him here to be humbled in
their eyes. But, although his two sons were prisoners of war in
Russia still, as were the sons of many in the courtroom, and although his house, as was the case with so many of their houses,
was still in the hands of the Americans, they knew that his very
blood forbade that he become as common or as humble as they.
"The question with which we are faced is whether the defendant, at any time, or by any voluntary act, gave evidence of being

an anti-Nazi editor," the prosecutor was saying, and the murmuring now rose louder than before.

"Give us another prosecutor!" a voice called out, but scarcely a single voice, for it seemed to come from all four corners of the hall. "We don't need any *Flüchtlinge* here!" the multiple, disembodied voices called, and the young judge cleared his throat and asked for quiet, while the court guards moved through the assemblage. "We don't want anyone from the Eastern Zone to prosecute our townspeople!" the voices said. The judge had got to his feet, and he glanced uncertainly across the courtroom; but he, like the prosecutor, was a man without legal training, except that acquired in these Occupation-sanctioned courts, and it was little comfort to him now that he had been chosen for his political integrity. He stood up, shabby, provincial-looking, in his brown suit of ersatz, wartime wool, unfitted, to the eyes which had just turned from the defendant, for this or any other role which the Occupation might authorize him to play.

"There is in the courtroom now another newspaper editor!" the prosecutor's voice rang strongly out, and, at the sound of its authority, the uproar abruptly died. "I would like him to tell you his experiences. I am going to put him on the witness stand," he said. "I believe he will tell you that, in his opinion, it was not possible for a man to be both an anti-Nazi and a newspaper editor as late as 1945 in Germany."

The witness in question stood up at once in the front row of seats, a broad, short young man with thick-lensed glasses on his nose, wearing a suit that was too tight for him. And, as he picked his way nearsightedly across the intervening people, a titter of laughter ran through the courtroom, and the people did not draw their legs aside to let the witness pass. Once he had been sworn in by the court, he took his place before them in the isolated witness chair.

"I began publishing a political and literary weekly in Nuremberg in 1930. I was eighteen years old at the time," he began his testimony. He had clasped his childishly dimpled hands across the straining buttons of his vest, and a crescent of flesh, which lay pink and fresh beneath his chin, shrunk and expanded, deflated, inflated, as if made of rubber, while he spoke. "Until

1937, I experienced increasing trouble with the Reich authorities," he said, and his voice was pitched almost ludicrously high. "I had frequently refused to print the *Deutsches Nachrichten Büro* communiqués because of their distortion of the news. Early in 1937, I was informed through the *Gauleiter's* office that an impending paper shortage would necessitate the suspending of a large number of small newspapers, and that only those which served the interests of the nation, and the party, could count on sufficient newsprint to go on. In my editorials, I continued to criticize both the domestic and the foreign policy of the regime," he went on in his absurdly pitched voice, "so that it was only a matter of weeks before my offices were permanently closed. It seemed essential to me that all information concerning the restrictions on freedom of speech and action which were being imposed on the German people by the leaders of the Reich should be made known to the outside world, and I succeeded in passing weekly articles into Holland, and these were printed throughout the country, signed by my initials only," he said, and the rosy crescent which doubled his chin, deflated and then inflated, as he spoke. At this moment, as if roused suddenly to interest, the defendant stirred in his chair, and his flat, naked lips stiffened in a half smile of forbearance beneath his white moustache. Then he leaned a little closer to his lawyer, and dropped his lean, gentlemanly hand upon the other's sleeve. The lawyer listened to the communication that was whispered to him, nodding his round head slowly in agreement, his prominent, blue eyes fixed without expression on the ludicrous figure seated in the witness chair. "In the spring of 1940, when the Wehrmacht overran Holland," the witness continued, "my identity as the author of these articles was revealed in the files of an Amsterdam newspaper, and I was arrested in Nuremberg shortly after that. I was tried, and sentenced to fifteen years at hard labor," he said, and then he ceased to speak.

"Will you give the court some of the details concerning your internment?" the prosecutor said.

"I was interned in Dachau. My windpipe was broken during the beatings I received there," he said, his eyes myopic, undecipherable, behind the thick lenses of his spectacles, and no emotion altered his smooth, fat, fair-skinned face. "I had served nearly a third of my sentence when I was liberated by the Americans," he said, making the statement without drama, but, once it was made, the defense lawyer arose.

"If Your Honor permits," he said, the title given in derision to the judge who wore no judicial robes, "I would like to suggest that we who are gathered here today bow our heads before the witness's martyrdom. It is evident to everyone of us that this young man must have suffered the greatest privations during his confinement as a traitor to his country. Perhaps it would be in order to take up a collection for him in the courtroom today. My client has expressed himself as willing to start off such a subscription with a donation of two Deutschmarks and fifty pfennigs to enable this needy man to buy himself a hearty meal."

The laughter appeared to begin just behind the defendant's chair, and it was echoed here and there throughout the courtroom, until, gaining momentum, it seemed to rise from the throat of every man and woman in the ancient hall. The young judge again called out for quiet, but now that the witness had got to his feet, the spectators only laughed the louder, as if, standing there erect, with his short arms straining in the sleeves of his jacket, he was an even more humorous figure than they had recalled.

"Quiet!" the judge admonished them, but the tumult and the laughter rose, and there was no sign or semblance of quiet. Instead, the multiple voice which had spoken out before now gathered power and articulation, and it cried "Heil Hitler!", and the judge leapt up, his young hands trembling, and ordered that the court be cleared.

It was only Rod Murray who moved against the refluent tide, making his way steadily back through the loquacious groups as they drifted toward the exits, past the defendant's wife, the defendant's daughters, the defendant himself, who stood chatting amiably with the local dentist and the owner of the requisitioned hotel. He shouldered his way, in an overcoat bought four years ago in Chicago, back toward the tables where the court stenographers gathered their papers up, and past them to the judge, and the witness, and the prosecutor, knowing that in making his way to them, he approached the flesh and the blood of men who spoke his tongue. And yet there was nothing he could find to say in shame or in anger or in any language to them, but, until the courtroom cleared, he stood there, taking his place beside them, and then they walked out into the sunless day together. On the steps of the *Rathaus* he turned to them, as if to brothers, and he shook the judge's, and the witness's, and the prosecutor's hands.

He ate lunch alone at the Special Services Club, and, with the taste of coffee in comfort on his tongue still, he came out onto the high, bleak terrace of the club. The terra-cotta flower-boxes stood empty on the balustrades, and across the valley of this foreign land of Hesse, the *Schloss* stood strong as a fortress on its hill. It might have been a picture that Breughel had painted, all this which lay before him, the slate-blue houses of the town descending, roof by snow-traced roof, to the barren trees which bordered the dark waters of the river, with even the single crow set as trademark and signature in the leafless branches, except that the bright, myriad, scattered presence of the living, which was the speech of Breughel's heart, had been deleted from the scene. And in a month like this one, Rod Murray thought as he leaned on the balustrade in the chill, gray light of afternoon, he had flown with the others before dawn up this valley, by-passing the university town, and the others before it, the steel hearts of the engines throbbing northward as they crossed these hills toward Kassel, moving in formation toward what they had come out to do. It was no more than one name recalled out of many destinations, remembered now because of the look of the sky and the river, and because he knew that below, at the bridge which spanned the water, a sign stated that Kassel lay no more than a hundred kilometres ahead. Kassel, he thought, hearing again the pulse of the bombers as they bore such annihilation to that one town that the dust and the débris, and the broken galleries and pilasters of where it once had stood, had no more relation to the present than the hushed, volcanic twilight of Pompeii. And then, without warning, he remembered the dancers, and remembered the farewell party would take place that evening, and he fled quickly down the red sandstone steps of the club terrace to hail the Army bus which passed below.

In his office in the Military Government building, his German secretary was putting fresh varnish on her nails, so she could not look up at once when he came in. But she said that the *Herr Direktor* of the local theatre company was putting on a Zuckmayer play which called for a Luger automatic to be fired on the stage. As long as Germans could not be in possession of firearms, she went on saying as she painted the nail varnish carefully on, the *Herr Direktor* had been trying all morning to get in touch with him to find out what he should do.

"That's something for the Provost Marshal's office," Rod Murray said, dismissing it.

"Oke-doke, but it seems it comes under Art Information," said the secretary, surveying her nails. "The Provost Marshal's office sent him down to us."

There was this to be settled, and it took four telephone calls, and an hour and a half of time, and there followed a conference with the *Führer* of "The Nature Lovers" as to which numbers of their repertoire of marching songs would be authorized, under the relaxing of controls, to be sung at future meetings in the springtime hills. It was five o'clock, it was the end of the day, when the young *Führer* left Rod Murray's office, and there had been no time to think of the entertainment for the evening that lay ahead. And then Rod Murray's secretary came in to comb out her long hair at the mirror before going home, and she said that someone from the *Berufsschule für Bewegungs-Ausdruck-Kunst-Rhythmik und Gesellschaftstanz* had telephoned.

"My God, the dancers! The entertainers for the party tonight!" Rod Murray cried, and he jumped up behind his desk.

"Would you like me to take care of it for you?" said his secretary, and she looked at her own face in the mirror as she combed back her hair.

"I wanted Hungarian, Spanish, dancers—in costume, of course!" Rod Murray cried out. "And musicians with their music! I wanted to make it something good—"

"I can make it good," said his secretary. She had turned away from the glass on the wall, and he saw her hair, as he had seen it countless times before, combed dark and soft to her shoulders, and the lipstick laid smoothly on her mouth. "I've been working

six months for you, and you still don't seem to understand me,"
she said, her eyes on him in stubborn, cold rebuke. "The other
officers I worked for here before were different. They all seemed
to understand me," she said, and she came across the room toward his desk, American nylons pulled tight and sheer upon her
well-shaped legs. Then she picked up the short black arm of
mouthpiece and receiver from the telephone, and she dialled the
numbers with a forefinger on which the nail was varnished as
bright as blood. The conversation took a quarter of an hour, and
while she asked the questions, and gave the answers, her dark,
slow glance moved, without expression, upon the features of his
face. And when it was done, she sat, in the green plaid skirt that
must have been ordered from a Sears, Roebuck catalogue page
by whom, or at what interval in the history of Military Government, or for what compensation, he did not know, and she told
him what the *Frau Direktor* of the *Berufsschule* had said. She
said it was only after he had gone down the stairs the night before that the *Frau Direktor* had understood he had come there
for dancers, professional dancers. "You need someone to take
care of you over here. You have too much faith in people. I saw
that right away, the minute I started working for you," his secretary said, and she threw her head back, and shook out her long
soft hair.

"All right," said Rod Murray in impatience. "What else did
the *Frau Direktor* say?"

"She said that some stars of a well-known troupe of dancers
had arrived from Berlin this afternoon, and she could send you
some very cosmopolitan performers, if you wanted them still,"
she said. She had slipped off the corner of the desk now, and she
looked at him with suddenly baleful eyes. "I told her to send
them to Military Government billets at eight o'clock tonight,
with costumes and musicians."

"How much did you settle for?" Rod Murray said, as he
watched her going, as if in pique, to the door.

"Fifty Deutschmarks, including the music," his secretary said,
"and the money to be paid directly to her. She's afraid they
might hold out on her percentage," and then her voice stretched

lazily into irony. "You should call on me more often. I'm pretty good at making bargains," she said.

It was after eight by the time Rod Murray had eaten, and bathed, and dressed, and he was eager for a sight of the entertainers as he came down the stairs. This requisitioned house in which he and the others were billeted was one of the finest houses in town, richly furnished, and handsomely wainscoted and beamed, without a mark of wartime damage on it. And now the lower floor of it was decked out for the farewell party with paper vines of mauve wisteria, and hanging, cardboard stars. A distant banquet table, framed by the dark wood of the wide arched doorways which opened from room to room, could be seen, laid with white linen, in the farthest chamber which once had been the Nazi owner's library. From the stairs, Rod Murray saw the shining glass goblets placed there in preparation, and the punch bowl, still empty, and the Meissner porcelain waiting, the monogrammed silver laid spoon within gleaming spoon, fork curved to fork, beneath the oscillating shadows of the hanging stars. From the kitchen alone, where the servants prepared the buffet supper, came the sound of the living; for the Senior Military Government Officer, and the Criminal Investigation Agent, and the Legal and University Officers, were dressing in their bedrooms still, and the guests had not yet arrived.

Only when he had reached the last step of the stairs did Rod Murray see there were two people sitting side by side on the carved bench in the entrance hall. He took them at first for children, so slight, so submissive, they seemed as they sat there under the massive, mounted stag heads: a pale-haired boy in an opera cloak, with the velvet collar fastened beneath his pointed chin, and a girl in a long, dark shabby coat, drawn close beside him, her body curved as if in weariness, and a muff of black and white rabbit fur upon her knees. The muff was large enough for a deep-breasted *diva* to have carried in triumph, and the girl kept her hands within it, and a bunch of shrivelled, faded violets, made of cloth, was pinned to its molting hide. They were abandoned children, Rod Murray thought, who had put on these adult clothes to give themselves stature and authority for one evening, but not in any spirit of carnival, for their faces, which were turned toward him, were strangely austere. But once they had got to their feet, and stood before him on the delicately tinted Persian rug, he saw they were doubtless his own age, perhaps in their middle twenties, but so frail that he believed he could have lifted them, one in each arm, with ease, and carried them across the hall like dolls.

"The *Frau Direktor* of the *Berufsschule*," the young man began saying in German in a low voice to Rod Murray.

"Yes, yes," Rod Murray said quickly. He took his cigarettes out, and he passed them first to the girl, the stirring of hope quickening in him again, believing it might be from their mouths that he would learn how it had taken place, and how it had seemed to them when they were children, and how much had been explained away so that the human ear could bear to hear the rest. He stood close to the girl now, and her head reached barely to his shoulder, and her hair was wrenched up from her small, swollen brow, and combed into a pompadour, and the long, faded, golden ends of it pinned high upon her skull. Her fingers came, as sharp as a bird's claws, from the rabbit muff, and she did not speak, she did not smile, but her hand, with the cigarette in the fingers of it, withdrew inside the muff again. Her narrow lips were not so much as touched with red, but her dark eyes were outlined and lashed so lavishly and carelessly with mascara in her white, pointed face, that Rod Murray had the illusion that he viewed them through a magnifying glass. "Yes, of course, I was expecting you," he said, and he passed the cigarettes to the young man, whose bony hand tossed one wing of the opera cloak aside and sought to unhook the worn, velvet collar at his throat, as an actor, beginning his big scene and finding stage fright parching his tongue, might fumble desperately for breath.

"Perhaps the *Frau Direktor* told you that my wife and I come from the eastern sector of Berlin?" he said, and he bowed his head to light his cigarette from the lighter Rod Murray held.

"The food situation is pretty grim there, isn't it?" said Rod Murray, but the young man did not answer, for it was not the role of *Flüchtlinge* which they were here to play.

"We've just had a most successful night-club season there," he said, and now, with a cigarette between his fingers, his tongue seemed eased, and he drew the good, sustaining draughts of the tobacco in.

"We have our costumes with us," the girl said, speaking scarcely aloud, and, with her hand inside the molting muff still, she gestured behind them toward the bench. And there, in the shadows against the panelled wall, Rod Murray saw the trademark of those who wander the autobahns in flight, or who sit beneath the bridges, waiting for nothing but a destination—the split, bulging shape of a suitcase, its material varnished to simulate leather, its bulk supported by various lengths and weights of string. "We like to travel," the girl said, with these words refusing their part in that dogged exodus of women and men who crossed illicitly from one zone to the other for the sake of food, or for the opulent look of counters and store windows, or else for the indescribable quality of freedom, either breathed or spoken, the stragglers coming at the rate of a thousand a month, some said, and others put it at closer to a hundred a day.

"The *Frau Direktor* of the *Berufsschule* is my wife's aunt. That's how we happened to stop off in Hesse," the young man said, and, as he smoked the cigarette, he smiled at the thought of this part of the country's rural ignorance, its archaic monuments, its bigotry. "We'll probably stay a little while with her, although there's not much of interest for us here," he said, and he added: "My wife's aunt is Jewish. My wife and I are neither Jews nor refugees."

"We're planning a foreign tour—France, England, and then America," the girl said.

"Look," said Rod Murray, speaking quickly as he glanced at the time upon his wrist; "before you people begin dancing, maybe you'd like something to eat—some sandwiches and coffee? If you wouldn't mind coming into the kitchen," he began, but they must have sensed the weakness, the perturbation in him, for their eyes were on him in slow, cold calculation, examining this which he had just proposed.

"So you're going to pay us in food and cigarettes, then?" the young man said. The three of them stood motionless in the hall-

way, as hushed as if in the deep heart of a forest, waiting beneath the dead stags' lifted, antlered heads.

"That wasn't the arrangement," the girl said, her thin lips
scarcely seeming to move.

"But, of course not. Of course, you'll get paid the Deutschmarks too," Rod Murray said, and he turned to lead them toward
the kitchen.

"And you'll pay it to us?" the young man said, not moving.
"You won't pay it to the *Frau Direktor?*" he said.

They were almost at the threshold of the kitchen, with the fra-
grance of fresh coffee coming richly on the air, when the young
man remembered the cardboard suitcase, and he walked swiftly
back in his cracked patent-leather dancing pumps to pick it up
and bear it with him before anyone should carry it away.

The next to come were the musicians. There were three of
them—one with a shining bald pate, and a leather music portfolio in his hand, and two studious-looking young men, one carrying a violin in its case, and the other an accordion. They were all
three members of the local symphony orchestra, the violinist told
Rod Murray, giving his classical right profile to the conversation,
with his eyes fixed straight ahead, like the set gaze of the blind.
But he was not blind, for he laid his violin case down on the
bench, and he took off his overcoat, as the others did, and then
the three of them strung their identical white silk scarves
through the sleeves of their overcoats, and they hung them in the
cloakroom, and then they raised their open palms, and even the
bald-pated musician made the gesture of smoothing back his
hair. When this was done, they followed Rod Murray across the
polished bare floor of the first reception room, where the grand
piano stood, the violinist carrying his violin in its case, and the
accordionist his accordion on its plaited leather strap, and the pianist the music portfolio. But it was only the violinist, keeping
one half of his face averted still, who looked up and smiled at
the sight of the wisteria, and the hanging silver cardboard stars.

"It will be spring soon," the violinist said, speaking his carefully enunciated English to Rod Murray, and there was a sound
of happiness in his voice, as if he had recognized in these tokens
that a long, cold season was about to change. He and the accor-

dionist were students at the university, he said; they were medical students, and he still turned his head from Rod Murray as he lifted his instrument from its case. It would begin to be more pleasant now, walking up the paths to the lecture halls, he went on saying, and he asked Rod Murray how well he knew the town, and the *Schloss*, and the short cuts leading through the trees. "There is a quite lonely statue of Schiller. It stands among the lilacs halfway up," he said, and he dropped his head, in seeming solicitude, upon the violin's vibrant wood.

The bald-pated man had sat down in his ancient dinner suit on the concave seat of the piano stool, and now he jumped up, and spun the seat on its swivel, and seated himself again, his short legs reaching for the pedals, his blunt fingers stroking the keys. The accordionist lifted his accordion, ornate in ivory and gold, and cradled it in love in his arms for a moment while he peered across the pianist's shoulder at the open score.

"The dancers are changing into their costumes," Rod Murray said, and now, as the violinist tuned his strings, he saw for the first time, and with an almost convulsive sense of shock, the left side of the violinist's face. The head was a classical, rather noble head, constructed of long, solid bones, and crowned with a mane of lightish, lively hair. But the face he saw now was the face of a broken statue, for a scar ran hideously from the lobe of the left ear, slashed into the shattered temple, and crossed the forehead, a welt that served to seam the cavity where the hinge of jaw and cheekbone had functioned once, but where hinge and cheekbone were no longer, and mounted to stitch the empty temple closed. "They're going to do a tango, a rhumba, and a Viennese waltz," Rod Murray said, with his heart gone sick within him. "Let's go out and have a drink before they start," he said. And so it became the violinist's turn to follow, as had the dancers before him, into the kitchen, and there, in his abomination of this face, Rod Murray filled the two tall glasses with Rhine wine. "So you're medical students?" Rod Murray said, keeping his eyes away.

"*Prosit*," the violinist said before he drank, and he went on saying: "We will be doctors. We will cure humanity," saying it partly in humor to the American. "I know a strange story about doctors, about surgeons," he said, speaking a little shyly of this thing he knew. "In the war, you know, the doctors, the surgeons, did great things with plastic surgery. They could make a man's face new again. They could make it look like something it had not been before. My father was a surgeon, an Army surgeon, and he did this," the violinist said, and Rod Murray stood listening to what he said, his eyes fixed on the label on the slender bottle. "But after a time, he found out that a man's face does not stay the way that surgery makes it. After six months, eight months, a man's face will change back again to what he is like himself, inside. If you are a poet," said the violinist as he lifted his glass of wine and drank, "then an Army surgeon, a good Army surgeon, has his duty to perform, and when he operates he must give you a warrior's face. My father did this. But in six months, eight months, the face he has made becomes a poet's face again."

"That is fantasy," Rod Murray said, but he felt this knowledge chilling his blood.

"No, it is the truth," said the violinist, and he put down his glass so that Rod Murray could fill it with white wine again. "If you do not believe this is true, then there is nothing left to believe," he said. "My face," he said abruptly. "They left it the way it is because by that time they had learned. They knew they could make it look the way they wanted, and then in six months, eight months, it would betray them again. It would look like a musician's face, or a poet's face. It would have the old mark of loneliness on it, and this they could not have."

Their glasses stood empty on the kitchen table when they walked back into the reception room together, and the violinist smiled, as if at some secret which he alone possessed, as he moved the floor lamp a little closer to the piano, and adjusted the shade of it so that the light fell on the tilted rack where the open book of music stood. Above them could be heard the slamming of bedroom doors on the upper floors, and then the good-natured chaffing of the other Military Government officers as they came down the wainscoted stairs. And then the bell at the entrance door rang loudly, and the first guests were ushered into the hallway, the American women in long, half-formal gowns, and the men, in Army uniform or in fancy jackets from the Clothing Store, coming in with a clamor of greeting from the wintry night. Once their wraps had been laid aside, the guests moved on, escorted by the Public Safety Officer, or the Criminal Investigation Agent, or the Legal or University Officers, to the farthest room where the platters were laid with heart-shaped sandwiches, and the punch bowl stood filled now to the brim.

The musicians had begun playing "Don Giovanni," to set the romantic tempo of the evening, but once the dancers appeared dramatically in Spanish costume in the doorway, the piano, the accordion, and the violin, took their cue, and they broke into the triumphant bars of "Toreador." And now that the dancers danced, Rod Murray could scarcely bring himself to look in their direction, for they were far too thin to be making this spectacle of themselves in any public place. It seemed to him that the threads of their necks must snap in two, unable to bear the weight of the fleshless skulls they carried, and that their bones would pierce the carnival lace and tinsel of their disguise, and expose them for the skeletons they were. He could hear the girl's hand striking the tambourine with which she danced, and he could not bring himself to turn his head and see again the bony stalks of her white arms lifted, like the arms of those who have already perished reaching from the grave. And the young man, in his matador's suit and his cracked, black, patent-leather pumps, danced his desperate, intricate steps before her, his legs as brittle and thin as sticks of kindling in his cotton stockings, the brass coins jingling with avarice on his tricorne hat. And no one else looked at them, it seemed to Rod Murray; no one else dared watch them as they danced away across the parquet floor. In the farthest room, the Senior Military Government Officer was urging the guests to drink, and the waiters passed with trays among them, and the men's and women's talk and laughter sounded far, anonymous, without human meaning, under the festoons of Japanese wisteria, and the trembling pasteboard stars.

Then the Spanish number was done, and the dancers were gone, and the faint clapping of hands expired through the rooms, and Rod Murray asked that drinks be brought for the musicians, and he himself drank a goblet of punch quickly down.

"Let's give them a dance number now, so the guests can dance while the entertainers change," Rod Murray said, and he stayed near to the musicians, not wanting to meet the Senior Military Government Officer's offended eyes. "What front were you on when it happened?" he suddenly said, and he stood looking boldly at the violinist's face.

"Oh, that! I wasn't on any front," the violinist said, and he dropped his head, as if in apology, upon the violin's wood. "I lived in a town further up toward the north, a place called Kassel. I didn't have time to get to an air-raid shelter. I hadn't been in the Army long, and I hadn't seen any action yet. That's all there is to it," he said.

"Kassel," Rod Murray repeated. He set the cut-glass goblet down on the top of the grand piano, and he stood there, stunned for a moment, at the sound of the town's name. "Kassel. My God," he said. "You were in Kassel."

Before the musicians began to play, Rod Murray picked up the goblet again, and he finished the punch that was in it. And it seemed to him then that if the others, the Germans and the Americans alike, were to go away and leave them together for a little while, it was possible that something quite simple and comprehensible might still be said.

A Puzzled Race

There was nothing of the bureaucrat, nothing of the acquiescent man, or the bending reed in him, although he walked out of a building that housed government offices with an ease that signified he was familiar with the territory. He was gray-haired, and neither tall nor short, not old or young, with a quality as solid as stone about him, and a vigorous step. The air felt foolishly tender and light on his cheek as it might to a man newly in love, and the delicate leaves of the trees before him, the floating heavens, seemed too ethereal to be a part of Germany. Behind him was the vast, familiar honeycomb of the offices of the United States High Commission, and, as he started down the steps, he thought of his age, and a network of lines diffused in humor around his eyes. *I'm too old to feel this pull at the heart,* he thought, but in spite of the accumulated years of his life—nearly fifty now—and of the political climate of this particular year, the spring all about him seemed almost lovelier than any spring he could recall. It had not been lent this poignancy because of any wild, new attachment either to woman or country, he knew as he waited for the uniformed driver to bring his car up to the curb. His wife was his established love, and he needed no other, and America was his country. No surge of nameless emotion could persuade him now that Germany was better than he had believed merely because its outer texture was transformed by May.

"Home first, and then to the airport," he said to the back of the driver's head as he got in the car and closed the door; the same head, the same set of the cap, the same flushed cartilage of the ear, he had spoken his directions to for two years or more. *And this perhaps the last day I'll ride behind him,* it occurred to him, and he lowered the window glass and looked out in silence on the vineyards they were passing. The vines hung like emerald necklaces on the high, tilted slopes above the swiftly flowing waters of the Rhine. Perhaps he felt this sudden tenderness for the landscape of Germany because he might not see it just like this again, for in a few hours he would be leaving it, and, if he returned, he knew this defenseless moment of its rebirth in spring would be forgotten as the Ice Saints of May came shivering in. He had come to know it as a country in which one iron season followed upon another, because of the iron faces, the iron intentions, the bland, iron aplomb. But as he settled back on the deep cushions of the seat, it seemed to him for just this brief instant that he too had laid down his arms, and that Washington could do exactly as it wished with him. *Just for this second, as I look out,* he thought, *I do not care.*

Within a quarter of an hour, they had reached the housing project, and they drove past the rows of two-story apartment buildings that zigzagged, bright with stucco and nickel and plate glass, among the apple and pear trees of the farming country whose fields and orchards had followed the river here before.

This was the American enclave, with an unfinished look to it still, but the circular flower beds before the Post Exchange and before the Coffee Shop were planted with purple and white hyacinths, and grass was beginning to grow at last on the stretches of tan mud around the commissary and the gas station and the dry-cleaning plant. *One strip of newly broken land along the Rhine seeking with desperation to emulate America,* the man reflected, *but failing because the reason for America was not there.* Except for the bicycles, the kiddie cars, the tricycles of U.S. make, that lay discarded on sidewalks and cement-bound lawns, it was still Germany; and except for the children coming home from school, bands of them in blue jeans and cowboy boots, even a group of Cub Scouts in shirts and caps of blue and gold. From the car, he could hear the children's voices, midwestern, tough, and, at the same time, vulnerable and shrill, stirring in him the memory of other springs.

America, he thought, his arm cradled in the car's brocaded sling, *this time you're going to show me a grim face.*

Beyond the apartment houses were four geometrically angled-and-roofed houses, built closer to the river and given an aura of seclusion in indication of the higher rating of the men who lived in them. The car had entered the drive of the first of these, and the man saw the boy waiting on the path that led to the white stone step and the clouded glass of the front door.

"We should leave at four. I'll have my bag ready by then," he said to the back of the driver's head, and he moved forward on the seat. "Get them to fix you a meal in the kitchen before we go. You'll get back late." The car had stopped, and the man got out, and closed the car door behind him, and he started walking toward the boy. "Isn't it getting too hot for the 'coon skin cap?" he said.

Even before the car had stopped, the boy in his blue jeans and red flannel shirt had begun coming over the flat slabs of the pavings that marked the path. And now, head lowered, he turned on his black and white sneakers and fitted himself against the man, his left shoulder pressing, thin and forlorn, into the hard bones of his ribs. He put his hand on the boy's right shoulder, feeling the brittle, inverted cup within his palm, and the sharp wing of the shoulder blade.

"Can I go to the airport with you?" the boy asked, not looking up. He was watching his own feet and the man's, lengthening his step to walk as the man walked toward the smooth, white step and the ultramodern door.

"It would be better if you stayed here," the man said. "Mother doesn't want to leave Vinnie while she's coughing still. You'd better stay with them."

"I'm going to have lots of trouble with my arithmetic," the boy said. "Are you sure you have to go?"

"Yes, I have to go," said the man, and he looked down at the silvery, brown-tipped hairs of the raccoon cap, and the oval of leather that formed the crown. "They want me to answer some questions," he said.

"How many days will it take?" the boy asked, and now he hung back a little, prolonging the moment before they must go up the step.

"I hope it won't be more than a week," the man said, walking slower too. The striped raccoon tail hung the length of the hollow of the boy's thin neck, and when he raised his hand quickly to look at the man, the tail swung, fat as a caterpillar, to one side.

"What kind of questions will they ask you?" the boy said, scrutinizing the man's face now.

"Oh, about people," said the man, and he looked down into the long-lashed eyes below him. The brows were as black as his own brows, but delicate and silky, and the eyes were clear and gentle and a translucent blue. "Just about people I used to know."

They had come so close to the scrubbed white step that had they moved forward they would have mounted it, and opened the door, and gone into the house together, but the man lingered too, as if reluctant to let this moment go. He felt the perishable bones of the boy's shoulder in his palm, and he thought of the process that turned the softness of a boy's substance to that of a man, the toughening, the hardening, the growing suspicion of one another, and the final dying of belief, until citizen suspected

citizen, and friend looked warily at friend. *When does it begin?
How does it happen?* the man thought, looking down into his
son's face. *When do men begin doubting each other, and fear to
look into each other's eyes?*

"Why can't you answer the questions from here?" the boy
asked, his head tilted back, holding stubbornly to the idea that
the man might still not have to go.

"I answered them from here," the man said. "They want me to
say it over again, out loud."

"Because they didn't believe you?" the boy said, his eye gone
a little shrewd.

"Perhaps some of them didn't," said the man. Looking at his
watch, he thought: *I must get my things together, get the papers
straightened out, the last things said to Mary before I go.* And
then he saw the look in the boy's face, and he turned abruptly,
and drew him with him down the stone path, their backs turned
on the house. "I don't want you to worry about it," he said, his
hand holding the boy's shoulder hard. "It's going to be all right.
Last night I found a book about Daniel Boone on the floor beside your bed. It must have fallen off when you went to sleep. I
picked it up and I read it straight through to the end. Maybe
you haven't come to the part where they didn't believe the answers Boone gave."

"I'm at the part where his son gets killed by the Indians," the
boy said, walking close to the man.

"Well, you'll read the rest," said the man. "You'll read about
how, at one time in his life, his fellow citizens couldn't agree
about him, so there was nothing for it but to have a trial." He
and the boy had left the angularly paved path, and crossed the
drive, and they stopped at the edge of the field that, generation
after generation, before the Americans had come, had been
plowed by German plowshares, drawn by German horses, driven
by German hands. But now the field waited, as if in bewilderment, neither pasture nor orchard, garden nor lawn, and certainly
not fallow land. "Look," said the man. Through the ancient trees
that leaned, lovely with May at the end of the field, could be
seen the swiftly passing Rhine, and great, handsome barges rode
the current, so heavily loaded that only their cabins, as pretty as

cottages, with geraniums blooming in their window boxes, and children playing at their doors, rose above the waterline. Yet, however heavy the cargo that they bore, they sped along with singular festivity, as if to the pace of music rippling fast across the water and the air. "There goes a barge flying the Belgian flag," the man said, and, standing with his son in the delicate, spring light, he suddenly saw the words as clearly as if they were written out across the mud and grass. "Men who in private had questioned Boone's loyalty now doubted it in public," went the grievous legend, and he looked away from it to the pennants of bright, flapping clothes that hung, drying, on the barges' decks. "They were cruel, and they were unjust, but they were very natural, these grave suspicions of Boone's loyalty," the words went on. "Americans were a puzzled race in those years . . . There was nothing for it but a formal trial. That Boone ever really contemplated treason is a ridiculous idea, disproved by all his years of faithful service," went the tape recorder of his memory. "It was not the last time that he was to feel the ingratitude of his friends, but it was the first and perhaps the bitterest . . ." Watching the barges go, the man said: "I'd like to take that book on the plane tonight."

"Sure, you can take it," said the boy, but his mind was on something else now. "If you got on that barge then you wouldn't have to go to Washington. You could go to Belgium instead."

"Except that isn't where they're expecting me," the man said.

When they turned to go, the words that he had not said aloud moved with them, and the man watched them pass, like subtitles on a movie screen, across the macadam of the drive.

"In a week, they're going to have the kite-flying contest like last year," the boy said in a low voice as they went up the path.

"I'll try hard to be back for it," the man said. "I'll do everything I can."

"But in the end," the boy said suddenly when they reached the step; "I mean, this thing about Daniel Boone. Did they believe him in the end?"

"Yes," said the man. "Of course they believed him." He could not say to the silvery hairs of the cap that moved below him: *They acquitted him, but something was altered in him, some-*

thing they hadn't the power to condemn or clear. Boone went to Spanish territory, to Louisiana, in the end, and became a Spanish magistrate. He didn't want to give up his American citizenship and become a Spaniard. But he did. It meant becoming a respected man, and making a living for his family again. "They had a trial, and he was acquitted of the charges. You wouldn't be wearing a raccoon cap today if he hadn't been acquitted. Boone wore that cap for half a century before Crockett came along." He pulled the plump, striped tail as they went up the step together. *"In later years,"* the words moved in silence across the frosted glass of the door, *"his children often repeated Boone's stories and his opinions, but to this episode they seem never to have referred."* "I'll be back in a week, and I'll bring you a kite, and we'll fly it, and perhaps we'll win like last year," the man said. He was thinking of his wife upstairs as he walked into the hall.

▲▲▲▲▲▲▲▲▲▲▲▲▲▲▲▲▲▲▲▲▲▲▲▲▲▲▲▲▲▲▲

American Group
1942–1966

▼▼▼▼▼▼▼▼▼▼▼▼▼▼▼▼▼▼▼▼▼▼▼▼▼▼▼▼▼▼▼

The Canals of Mars

She was sitting on the bench, waiting under the park trees, when he came out of the draft-board office on the other side of Columbus Avenue and made for the curb. He had the whitish raincoat on, and his head was bare, and he started to cross at once, not even looking at the lights, stepping between the cars and the careening taxis, with his eyes fixed on her as he came. The first time she had seen him—five years ago at the other end of the Sacher Bar in Vienna—she had thought at once the same thing of him as she was thinking now: that he couldn't be anything but English. In spite of the purely Austrian blood in his veins, she had kept on thinking it of him in ski huts in the Alps when he would come in and brush the fresh snow from his shoulders, with his eyes looking for her; or in restaurants, or in city swimming pools, or on Mediterranean benches; or when she had waited for him on café terraces, and seen him coming at last down the streets of Geneva or Paris or Marseille. The mustache was clipped short and straight as the English military wear them, the cheekbones were narrow and high with the color of weather on them, and he made his way now through the traffic with the same degree of casual pride as would an Englishman better than six feet tall and with broad, sensitive shoulders and the traditional reticence in his bones. When he reached the bench where she waited, he sat down quickly.

"I've got until half-past three," he said. On the street before them, the rain was just beginning to fall.

"And then where do you go?" she said. She looked at the side of his face, at the hair a little light with sunburn above the ear, and the lean shaved cheek, and the pulse that beat soft and tender in his throat beneath the straight bone of the jaw. Five years, she thought, and I'll never get over it, never. Every time I look at him, I know I wasted twenty years of life because I wasn't sitting somewhere waiting for him to cross a street or a glacier or a mountain and sit down.

"Then I check in at Store Seven at Pennsylvania Station," he said. He looked at his watch. "It's just eleven. That gives us four and a half hours," he said, and he shook the cuff of his raincoat down across his wrist again.

"Perhaps we should do something special. I mean, perhaps we ought to do something rather important," she said. She watched the rain falling fine as mist before them in the street. "I mean, like going up the Statue of Liberty, or something. You've had your two weeks' furlough, and now you're going to be a soldier," she said, "so there we are. If you make a sort of ceremony out of the last hours together, it usually makes it go better." If I just don't look at him, she thought, I can go on forever talking like this. "The time in Marseille you took the boat for Casablanca, there was the night before," she said.

"Yes," he said quietly. "I know."

"There were the perfumed sheets," she said. "There was the orange satin cover on the bed. She wanted transient trade. She didn't like married people at all except for the price they'd pay to have a place to spend the night."

"All the way to Trinidad, whatever wind was blowing, I smelled that violent perfume," he said.

"But still it was something special," she insisted.

"Yes," he said, looking at the rain, "it was something special."

"Can you only go as far as her wrist, or can you go up inside her palm and into the torch?" she said. She looked at his hand with the blue veins and the sunburn on it, lying bleakly on the raincoat's cloth on his knee.

"You mean in the Statue of Liberty?" he said. He turned his face to hers, and, as their eyes met for a moment, she saw the look of despair upon his brow. "Four hours go so quickly. Perhaps we could just sit and have a drink somewhere," he said.

Yes, we could do that, we could have a drink, she thought. We could face each other across the half-dark of a table set in an alcove, and after a Scotch the words would start crying out loud like the drowning to one another. There's certainly nothing to stop us from sitting down and having a drink or two somewhere together, and then simply letting it begin. For a little while we could stave it off by talking about the glass sticks that nobody wants to disturb the heart of his drink, or we could put nickels into the jukebox and talk about last year's tunes. Or else we could stop the travesty of uproariousness at once by starting making the plans together, plotting the precise design to defeat the absolute muting of each other's voices, contriving a way to go on saying the things we haven't said often enough in five years of time.

"Perhaps we ought to try doing something better than that," she said, and she felt the rain on her hair now. "The planetarium's behind us. We could go in and have a look at the stars."

"Yes," he said, but he was watching the two soldiers who were coming toward them, his eyes fixed closely on them as they passed the bench. "They have shoes like mine on," he said, "so perhaps they'll let me keep mine." He thrust one leg out from under his coat and looked down at his shoe with the strap across the tongue of it and the buckle on the side. "I want to keep them. I don't want to have to wear shoes without memories," he said.

"The heels are worn sideways," she said. "That wouldn't be regulation."

"I like them that way," he said, still looking at his shoe. "I like the things we did to wear them sideways."

"All around the edge," she was saying, "you can see the skyline of New York exactly as if it were the skyline, and as if it were early dusk, with no light in the windows yet." He was running one finger along the thinning sole. "And after a while, whichever would be the first star at this time of year, that star comes out, and the sky goes slowly darker the way the sky would go tonight if the rain stopped," she said. And to herself she said in silence: *There isn't going to be any tonight; everything that has been night and day or summer or winter is going to end at half-past three.* "And you sit there in the dark," she said, "and the constellations come out in their proper order."

"All right," he said, and he stood up and looked across the

bright green grass at the back of the museum, his eyes on the planetarium's dome. He turned the whitish coat collar up against the rain, and then he drew her arm through his arm. "It's quite a monument," he said as they started off along the path, with the rain falling on them. He looked ahead at the museum. "It's quite a memorial to my going away," he said.

"We'll see the dead green canals of Mars," she said, and she felt his arm lying in peace and quiet against her.

"They'll be something special to take to Australia or Alaska all right," he said.

"The other times you went away, you didn't have anything half as good to take with you," she said in rebuke to him. "The time you went to concentration camp, you had nothing but the bad coffee in the station at five in the morning."

"I had a waltz," he said. "I had a waltz the night before with you. Perhaps I ought to go out waltzing this time," he said. "The way all good Austrians go."

"Where would they put a waltz in the Pennsylvania Station?" she said. She thought of the people that might be there, the mothers, the wives, the sisters, the girls, with their handkerchiefs held against their mouths. *I'm not just one woman taking it alone,* she said in silence. *I'm a lot of women closing their teeth hard on what they're not going to let make any sound.*

"That time, I had a waltz," he was saying as they walked, "and because they wouldn't let you on the platform, I made up a little group to see me off. I had Héloïse and Abélard," he said, "and King Arthur in tourney dress." There was the dome of the planetarium and the closed glass doors before them. The sign on its pedestal said: "Next performance at 2:30," and they walked away. "I had Aldous Huxley," he said. "I had him walking down the platform, just tipping his hat and smiling slightly through the window at me. But underneath that correct manner there was something else: there was an acute expression of grief in his eyes."

"I don't think he's capable of it," she said as they crossed the street. "How was King Arthur taking it?" she said.

"He had what I should have liked to borrow to go off with," he said. "He had all his nobility showing in his face. When the train started going off with me and the other prisoners and the gendarmes in it, his lips didn't move, but his whole face seemed to alter, you know, the way a statue's does when the light changes on it. Have I told you all this before?" he said.

"No," she said. "You simply went through the gate with the gendarmes. For me, it ended there——"

"I don't know why I wanted Héloïse and Abélard to be there," he said, "but I wanted them badly. I kept watching through the window of the compartment for them, just wanting to see them come, holding arms like we are, maybe as some kind of proof that, in spite of the *Historia Calamitatum,* people do manage to survive. Even as brother and sister, I wanted them, I mean, even with the other feeling gone, and only the tomblike devotion left. But they didn't get there until the last minute," he said. "She came running ahead of him down the platform, looking in the car windows for me. Abélard was terribly nervous; I think he was really annoyed at having to be associated with anyone in my position. He stood back, away from the train, distinguished and embittered-looking, snapping at her from time to time. I didn't have handcuffs on, of course, but still he didn't like the situation." They had turned down Broadway now, and the rain was falling hard. "I thought until the very end that he might forget his pride and look at me for a moment as one doomed man at another, but he was past that, he was even past that. I should have known him in the Notre-Dame period," he said, and then they saw the moving-picture theater before them.

"It's *Pépé le Moko*," she said quickly, and they stopped and looked at the face of Jean Gabin in the frames. "It's in French," she said. "I saw it in Toulon after you went away. It's like walking into a *bistrot* and sitting down and hearing all the right things said. It's something you ought to take to Alaska with you. It's even better than the canals of Mars," she said.

He paid the money out, and they walked abruptly into the dark together, feeling their way into seats at the back; and they sat down with their coats on still and looked at the illuminated screen. They sat there silent a little while, watching the canoe trip through the Adirondacks unfold before them, the waterfalls drop without hope to the sun-dappled basins, the needled branches hang low upon the moss, the rapids pass, the pines stand up in melancholy.

"It's a quarter past twelve," he said, after a little, in a low voice to her, and their shoulders were touching in the dark.

"In just a minute it'll come," she said in a whisper. "When this thing's finished, you'll see. I walked in off the quays at Toulon one afternoon when I didn't know whether the Germans had caught up with you yet or not, and there it was," she said. "The speech and the characters are so good that it couldn't matter when you came in on them—I mean, the same way it doesn't matter when you come into actual peoples' lives, because you always know right away, even if you come into the middle of peoples' lives, exactly what they are and what they've always been."

"This," he said in the darkness, "is a picture about canoe trips."

"In just a minute," she said in a quick whisper, "you'll see. Pépé's the tough guy, the bad egg, the *maquereau* who knows all about love from the beginning. He's out of Montmarte, serving a life term in prison in Algiers. Or perhaps it's Morocco, or perhaps not quite a term for life. But it's the shape of love you get. I don't know how you get it. Perhaps there isn't any love in it, but still something like it is there."

"What if we just went somewhere quietly and had a drink?" he said to the sight of the man and woman stroking the canoe across the sunlit screen.

"In just a minute it will change," she said softly. "It's something you can take away with you and keep under glass wherever they send you to. Pépé escapes, he hides in the Kasbah, and there's one line you can keep forever with you. It's when he's kissing the girl who's come from Paris, and he knows he never can go home. He doesn't tell her that she smells of the lilacs in the Bois," she whispered, "or of the *marroniers* along the boulevards. He says '*Tu sens le Métro*,' and he says it the way no one's ever said anything before."

"It's one o'clock," he said in the dark, "and they haven't reached civilization yet."

"This can't go on forever," she said.

"It can go on until they pitch camp," he said. "It'll have to go

on until she's made the coffee and cooked potatoes in the ash."
He had got to his feet now, and he said: "You wait here while I
ask. I don't want to have to see them paddling into the sunset."
She watched him going, the silhouette tall and somehow vulnerable against the rapids' brilliant summer light. When he came
back, he leaned over her in the darkness. "We'll go to the Pennsylvania Station and have a drink," he said. "Gabin goes on at
half-past two."

The bar there was shaped like a clover leaf, and men were
thick around it, army men and navy men with their packs at
their feet. There was one table left, a small one by the plate-
glass window that looked on the arcade, and they sat down and
ordered sandwiches and Scotch, and their eyes met suddenly,
and he reached over and took her hand.

"I know it's impossible to make any plans ahead," he said,
"but if there's any way to telephone, I will. If you'll just be there
almost all the time, I'll try to get through to you. Maybe they let
visitors come on Sunday," he said, the conniving against silence
and time and distance as they had known it in other countries
beginning stubbornly again. "Maybe it isn't final. Maybe it isn't
any more final than anything else was," he said.

"Don't make yourself write too much," she said, and she
watched the people passing in the arcade. "I mean, the routine
will be hard. Don't feel you have to do it."

The food and drink had come now, and they bit into their
sandwiches and drank the Scotch and soda fast.

"I'll try to telephone or telegraph at once," he said. "Only
don't expect it." It was only when he glanced down for a moment that she could bear to look now at his forehead and his
eyebrows and his hair. "I'll be very clever and try to find out the
ropes at once," he said.

"This isn't like the other times," she said, and the first Scotch
was spreading its weakness in her. "This time you're not just one
man bearing the burden alone of what you've decided to do.
There's a national sanction to it. This time you're not an outcast
any more."

"Two more," he said to the waiter, and he pointed to the
empty glasses.

"This time it's different for me, too," she said. "I'm not just one woman keeping her mouth shut about what her husband's doing. I'm Russian women and Englishwomen and Frenchwomen," she said, and she heard the sound of it rising foolish and high.

"You're the canals of Mars and the Kasbah," he said, and because she could not look at him, she closed her hand tight in her pocket and looked straight at the shaved neck of the sailor who stood drinking at the bar. "I don't know exactly at what age one starts putting the thing together," he had begun saying across the table to her, and now there was something else in his voice, and she knew it was this he had been wanting a long time to say. "Perhaps we began putting it together younger over there," he said, "because over there you had to know it young in order to know by what means you could survive. You decided young, and when you were young still you put that kind of armor on you, link by link—I mean, the sort of contraption of ideals, or dreams, or merely exact distinctions, and once you had it clear, you had it for life, and there was no way to get from under it or to set it aside." The second Scotch came, and he took a swallow of it, and his eyes were fixed, grave and deliberate, on her face. "And then the real trouble began," he said. "I mean, the real struggle was to get it out of the realm of vision or poetry, and give it an act at last. You could write things about what you believed, or dream things about it, and there lay the ideal so pure and remote in you that you could deceive yourself into thinking that it would survive alone. But it can't survive alone, and for a long time you can't find the act to give it for survival. But now suddenly it's happened," he said. "It happened to me the way it happened to everybody else standing up there having a drink in uniform—we were suddenly given the outer trappings for the thing in which we had believed. It's something like kneeling down and being knighted," he said, saying it quietly and soberly, and he ordered two more drinks for them. "It'll be a quarter to three in a minute," he said.

They went down the first flight on the escalator, and the second flight they walked down, and there they saw all the other men with the zipper canvas satchels in their hands. He went through the door of Store 7, and it closed behind him, and through the top pane of glass she could see his head and shoulders moving across the room. Beyond the store, five or six hundred men were closed inside the bars, and in a moment he too was there among them, with his little bag hanging in his hand. He put the bag and his raincoat down, and his glance went quickly over the people, looking for her, and then he walked across to the edge, where some of the others stood already, saying the last words to the families that had come to see them go. He put his hand through the bars and touched her sleeve, and the things the whisky was murmuring in them were the things they did not say.

"I don't see Aldous Huxley around anywhere," she said in a bright, strange voice to him. He stood close, with the bars between them, twisting the ring on her finger and looking at her face.

Behind him, a draftee in a gray, silky, summer suit got up on a bench in the enclosure, wavering uncertainly above the humbly standing or seated others, and began to speak. He was not a young man, and his paunch was large, and the drink was hot and tight in his face, and as he swayed above them, he cried the words of his farewell speech aloud.

"Friends, countrymen, and slackers!" he cried. "There aren't five ways of doing your duty, there aren't even four ways, there's only one way! You take a drink, and then you do it! You take a drink——" he shouted, but now the sergeant had put his hand up and helped him down.

"This time it isn't so final. There'll be furloughs," she said through the bars. "You'll have good food—and then they have musical shows, you know, they have famous actresses and dances and things."

"Yes," he said quietly on the other side. "I know." Behind him in the enclosure now, the men were forming into lines, and he turned his head and looked at them. "This must be it," he said.

He looked for his raincoat and bag again, and he picked them up, and then he set off with the others, walking two by two. The waiting families had not begun to move yet, but the woman pressed close beside her called out in a strong, fearless voice:

"Good-by, Mike! You show them what you're made of!" She turned, with her head up, and looked quickly at the other women. "That's my little brother," she said, and tears were standing in her eyes.

And now the women and men started walking along their side of the iron bars, walking at the same pace the coupled men walked toward departure with their satchels in their hands and their eyes turning back to see. As they rounded the pillar at the corner before the descent, the families ceased to call aloud; there was no sound left but that of the men quickly marching. It was not until they reached the head of the stairs that the three Italian women broke through the line and flung themselves forward —perhaps grandmother, wife, sweetheart, sister, or mother— shouting aloud their pain. They fell upon the little man in the pongee jacket as he passed, short, heavy women in silk dresses and high heels, with no hats, no veils, no gloves to mask their anguish, not whisky but merely the passionate flesh betraying the grief of nights and days they could not and would not bear. The little man flung out his short arms in one ludicrous, despairing gesture to them, and then he went suddenly down the stairs with the others. And perhaps it is like that, she thought as she ran on, dry-eyed among the women, perhaps it is like that that men want their women to roar out their good-by.

He was just ahead now, with his height and the weathered look of his skin singling him out, and the raincoat slung white across his shoulder, and they were going fast. He looked back once, and the lips did not move, and she ran futilely and wildly as the others ran, tripping in haste across their feet. She thought of King Arthur, and the face altering like the face of a statue when the light changes on it. This time it is different, she thought; this time it isn't just one man taking nothing but his own lonely honor with him; and then he too went down the stairs.

The Loneliest Man in the U. S. Army

The three of them had been unloading cases at the railway siding since early-morning chow—the one called O'Mallory, who had been a Park Avenue doorman; and the one called Dryden, a college man with an English accent; and the foreigner whose name they didn't know. The foreigner was dark and slight, with skin as rich and golden as a Spaniard's and eyebrows that met in black silk fury above his delicately nostriled nose. Dryden swung the case of canned food to him, noting that the fatigue jacket hung like a peasant's blouse from his shoulders, and that his mouth was sullen. This they should never have asked of the foreigner, he thought; they should never have asked him to be present here. They should have sent him back to where he belonged, perhaps to the dry, southern slope of an olive grove on Mediterranean waters. They should have let him go on eating ripe figs from the trees in the climate and tempo that was his, instead of asking him to wear an army uniform and swing the alien timber of cases from hand to hand.

"What country's he from?" said O'Mallory from the freight-car door and Dryden said he hadn't asked him. O'Mallory was a big, soft-faced, soft-bellied man who had to wear his civilian trousers still because they didn't have anything in stock that was big enough around. He stood with his hands on his hips now, looking past Dryden at the foreigner swinging the cases up in the sun. "You've had an education," O'Mallory said to Dryden. "Ever try another language on him?" and Dryden said he hadn't. "Perhaps he's the one we ought to give the palm to," O'Mallory said.

"What palm?" asked Dryden with his special accent, a quiet, perfectly good accent which he'd brought back with him from years of studying on English soil. Even in barracks, it was this accent as well as the glasses he wore which saved him from encroachment, as if a special franchise had been granted him, permitting him alone to preserve a little longer his own particular identity.

"Why, the palm for the loneliest man in the U. S. Army," O'Mallory said. "I'm the committee and the donor. I'm endowed. Now that poor guy out there, he can't even speak the language——"

"*Merde*," said the foreigner. He had run a splinter into his thumb, and he dropped the case to the ground.

The place was called a reception center, and it spread across the salt marshes of New Jersey or Long Island, with a flat, dune-like look to it in spite of the little firs that had been recently transplanted there. Fifteen hundred draftees came there a day, it was said, and were there put into khaki, given injections and K.P., mustered at sunset to retreat, and, after two days or two months or any conjectural period of time, were shipped away. The barracks where they slept were new, and the land all around was just newly broken, with roadbeds beginning to take shape in the upturned soil. Freshly seeded grass—the blades of it bright and sparse—was coming up through the wastes of mud that surrounded the military kitchen, and the processing building, and the post office, and the still unfinished canteen. A geranium bed, shaped like a star, lay in the visitors' park, and a rustic log fence and benches did what they could to save its face from desolation. But it was the men themselves, and their uniforms, which had the most tentative look of all.

"Stand up, sit down, fall out, fall in, let's go!" the sergeant might sing aloud morning or evening to them. "Button your coat, what's your name, shut up, stand straight, don't talk back!" he might call out as he lined them up, and O'Mallory in his civilian trousers would say:

"It's all right to talk to us like that, Sarge. We can take it. But to Merde you hadn't ought to. Why, Merde's probably the loneliest man in the——"

"On the ball, let's go!" the sergeant might roar aloud, and as the lot of them went down the road in step, Dryden would search for the words to say to the slight, dark foreigner beside him whom they wouldn't let lie in the grass of an olive grove any more.

"*Il n'est pas méchant, le sergent,*" he would say tentatively to the Frenchman, speaking his own tongue to him. He talks like that, but it's nothing, Dryden might say, and the things that he wished to say lay unspoken in his heart. All this, the discipline, the K.P., the cases, the sergeant, they are only details, he wanted to say; they have nothing to do with the reason that we're here. We are walking down this road in formation now because we are part of the fight for existence of my country, and the liberation of yours—and the Frenchman, tripping over the size of the shoes they had given him to wear, would say "*Merde*" loud enough for everyone to hear.

That was the name they had for him in the fortnight or more they stayed there. Even the sergeant called him that because it was easy to say. The sergeant was a permanent-party man, with a straight red neck and cool blue eye, and in his speech and his gait the tough, blunt way of the regular army.

"On the ball, let's go!" he'd call out to them, and Dryden and O'Mallory and the Frenchman would march in step with the others down the road.

The Frenchman kept the palm for a little while, without knowing that it had been awarded to him, or when it was taken away. He kept it until the end of the third or fourth day, when the Chinese boy came into their barracks with the duffel bag over his shoulder, and lay down on his cot, and did not say a word. He had worked in a Chinese laundry in Brooklyn, they learned after he was gone, but that night he was merely a boy who walked in alone and lay down in the dark, and either slept or did not sleep. At three in the morning, when the lights were flashed on, and the noncom came down the aisle and jerked the covers from the shoulders of the men who hadn't stirred, they all saw the thin little Chinaman sitting there on the side of his bed, with his fragile hands closed tight around its bar.

"You on K.P.?" roared the sergeant, and the Chinese boy stood up and waited humbly. "You on K.P.?" the sergeant said again, and the Chinese boy stared, as if dazzled by the light, and slowly nodded his head. "Then where's your towel?" asked the sergeant steadily enough, but at the sight of the black, blind eyes and the face that comprehended nothing, the sergeant's patience broke.

"Where the hell's your towel on the foot of your bed to show you're on K.P.?" he shouted.

"Towel," Dryden pronounced distinctly under his breath, and the Chinese boy turned blindly to him, and slowly shook his head.

"Towel!" roared the sergeant, and he went through the motions of drying his own face. "Towel!" he shouted, and the Chinese boy turned back to him and watched submissively. And then the thing seemed to become clear to him at last, and he moved at once to his private little bag, and felt in it a moment, and brought the shaving brush out. There he stood in the confusion of the barracks, holding it out to the sergeant in one humble, delicate hand.

O'Mallory had been stooping to tie his shoes, and now he straightened up, short of breath, and let the laces fall.

"Look here, Sergeant, this is terrible," he said. "That boy can't even speak the language——"

"Chink's on the shipping list!" said the sergeant. "Shipping list!" he shouted, with gestures, at the Chinese boy.

"My God," said O'Mallory. "You can't talk to him like that. You just can't do it, Sergeant——"

"Fall out, the lot of you!" the sergeant shouted down the room. "Get downstairs for the shipping list! They've started reading the names out!" he said, and he added a few of his own as he moved with the K.P. noncom down the aisle.

"They can't ship me," said O'Mallory, leaning to his shoes again. "If I'm on it, they'll have to take me off. They can't ship a man in civilian trousers, Sergeant. It's never yet been done."

"You'll have to pack your things," Dryden was saying quietly to the Chinese boy, but the boy had sat down on the bed again, with his shaving brush in his hand. "You're shipped out. You'll have to pack," said Dryden gently to him, but in the end he and O'Mallory did it for him. They stood his new shoes by his feet, and they put his dog tag around his neck again, for he had laid it aside when he lay down to sleep. "Now dress. Now you'll have to dress," Dryden was saying to him in a quiet voice, but in his heart were the other things to say. Except this time there were no *ouis* and *nons* to lend two men a common tongue for a little;

there was nothing to summon out of memory to make the explanations clear. He could not say: These are the things we must take no account of—the shipping lists, the noncoms, the names they call. They are nothing in the total of what we are doing, they have no place in the final scheme of victory. We are fighting for something vast and good, he wanted to say, but he could only insert the Chinese boy's tie between the second and third buttons of his khaki shirt. That is the vision and goal that we must keep, he wanted to say aloud to him, but instead he said, as he pointed to them: "Stairs."

"That kid," said O'Mallory, when they came up to bed again, "I'll bet he's about the loneliest man in the——"; and although they never saw the Chinese boy again, in this way the palm was awarded to him, as if posthumously, to wear in honor for a little while.

It was the following evening that the sergeant came through the barracks and stopped without warning by Dryden's bed.

"I see you've got a nice photograph up there," the sergeant said, and he stood with his hands in his pockets and looked straight into Margaret's eyes. Every morning when he wrote the letter, Dryden would put Margaret up above his cot, and there she would stand, her dark hair combed out, the sleeves of her college-girl sweater pushed up above her elbows, and the trees of the campus showing behind. "Means a lot to have a photograph like that," the sergeant said, and there was something else in his voice now. And then, as if he could keep it to himself no longer, he said: "My girl's coming up from Texas on Saturday," and once he had said it he went on down the barrack room, his shoulders straight, his gait tough, and his neck bright red as always from behind.

It seemed she would drive out from the city on Saturday, the sergeant's girl, the way a lot of visitors did. By Friday night everyone in the barracks had heard in one way or another how it was going to be. The sergeant was having furlough that week, and he and the girl were going to spend it together in Greenwich, or maybe Paterson it was, visiting people they knew. It was said with certainty that she'd won a bathing-beauty contest once, or that she'd been "Miss Texas" just the year before. Per-

haps simply because of the look he bore now in his face, it was
even said by some of the men that he had asked for furlough to
get married to her. But however it was, there was something softened in the sergeant, and the barracks were waiting for Saturday and the hour she would come.

It was only the Frenchman who had nothing to say about the
sergeant's girl, and who listened to nothing that was said. On
Friday night he came in from detail, and he lay down with his
hands folded behind his head, and for any sign he gave he might
have been lying stretched out in an olive grove, with his bare
feet crossed in the short, dry grass, and a broad-brimmed hat
tipped over his face to keep the sun away.

"I'll give a can of beer to any man who can tell me something
that will make me laugh," O'Mallory said, and he sat down on
his bed to eat the ice cream on its stick. "I mean, a real loud
laugh with nothing insinuating in it," he said. When the vanilla
dripped onto the leg of his civilian trousers, he wiped it moodily
away.

"Have you heard the one about the corporal and the colonel's
wife?" a voice asked from farther down the room, and the voice
went on and told it.

"I'm sorry, Margaret," Dryden said gravely, and he reached
up for her photograph and put it away. O'Mallory wasn't laughing at all, and the Frenchman wasn't laughing, and when the
lights went out in the barracks, Dryden spoke to the Frenchman
in his own tongue in the dark. "Are you picking up the language
a little?" he said in a low voice to him.

"Not at all," said the Frenchman from where he lay under the
olive tree.

"What's he saying?" asked O'Mallory, and his shoes dropped,
first one and then the other, to the floor.

"He says he can't pick up the language," said Dryden.

"I've been here since 1940," said the Frenchman in a quick,
bitter voice. "I don't know what they're trying to say. My wife,
she can speak a little. She's going to have a baby. She's on relief," he said.

"Is he saying something funny?" asked O'Mallory, and Dryden
said he wasn't. "If he tells you anything funny, you can translate

it for me. I'd give anyone two cans of beer who could make me laugh," O'Mallory said from the dark.

But the Frenchman was talking about the place where he came from now, and the look of the sea around it, and the fishing, and the wall built out in another century to break the waves in winter before they struck the shore. He talked of the lobster traps, and the nets strung out across the rocks when the fishing fleet was in, and he did not speak of women. And it was like this, thought Dryden, it was lying still like this in the dark that they came to know one another. It was not marching down the road in the sun, or bending to pick up the cigarette stubs, or standing at retreat that each could distinguish what the other was. But like this, with their faces blotted out in the dark, and only their voices left, either speaking of women or else not speaking of them, they came to know one another's hearts.

"Spain was down there," the Frenchman said, as if he were tracing it out on the darkness with one lifted hand. "You could walk it in three quarters of an hour," he said, and he added: "Where I come from, they stuff the olives with anchovies, little dried strips of anchovy, and you don't go hungry. Even the capitalists can't take the olives off the branches or the fish out of the sea."

"Is he saying anything funny?" O'Mallory asked again, and Dryden said no, it wasn't funny.

"But when you see what's happening anywhere, you start to walk," the Frenchman said. "When things smell bad, it's time for you to go."

"Do you go alone?" asked Dryden of the darkness, and the Frenchman stirred a little under the olive tree.

"You take the hand of a comrade," he said, "and you walk like that. When you're young, you walk better together than you walk alone. My comrade had never had shoes on her feet until we found some in a store," he said. "They were red ones, but they hurt her, so we carried them in our hands."

"And if you come to a frontier, what do you do?" Dryden asked.

"You walk across it," said the Frenchman. "She was afraid.

She was sixteen then, and she'd always seen water in front of her. She'd never just seen land before."

"And if they stop you, what do you do?" said Dryden.

"You keep your mouth shut, and you keep your comrade's hand in yours," said the Frenchman, and it might have been that he tipped his hat brim further over his eyes.

"And then?" asked Dryden of the darkness.

"Then maybe they send you back by train," the Frenchman said, "and all night the wheels will talk aloud. They'll talk like a gendarme saying the same thing over to you. '*Je vous ramène, je vous ramène, je vous ramène,*' and there's nothing for you to answer. They're government property, the wheels, and they'll tell that to you. '*Je suis l'état, je suis l'état, je suis l'état,*' they'll say, and you'd better not open your mouth to them. You wait for the sign of day," he said, "and when you see the water is there again, you get out through the window, and you run. She couldn't run now. She's going to have a baby," he said, and he lay there silent a minute. Then he said: "We left the shoes behind."

"And then you're free?" said Dryden, trying to make it right.

"Yes," said the Frenchman's voice. "And then you're free," he said, and the sound of it was acid in the dark.

Dryden waited for the bitterness to perish from the air before he spoke.

"But we're going to be free men when this is over," he said. "I believe we're going to be free. I believe freedom can be redeemed by sacrifice, by sacrificing the lives of men—your life and mine, if necessary——"

"*Merde,*" said the Frenchman wearily.

That was Friday night, and on Saturday night the sergeant got drunk. He got drunker than any man had ever been before. He came into the barracks and kicked the ash can the length of the hall, and they heard what he thought about women. But it wasn't until the next morning that they learned what he had done: that he'd hit an M.P. and laid him out in the road-bed, and that they'd taken his stripes away.

"Because his girl didn't come, he went out and got drunk," O'Mallory said. "He waited all day for her, and she never showed up at all. Say something happened to the car, she could have telephoned, couldn't she? But she didn't. Or she could have sent a telegram, but she never did. He held off until after five," said O'Mallory, "and then he started drinking."

They talked about it in the barracks at night, and the name of the sergeant evoked something singularly like tenderness in them now. These men who, a week before, had been civilians, with separate lives and separate loyalties, shared a common honor when they looked into one another's faces and said: "They've broken the sergeant." It gave them a dignity and an outrage in which each played his part when they said: "He's our sergeant still no matter what they've done to him, or how many stripes they've taken away."

But it was O'Mallory and Dryden who made the final gesture. They put on their black ties, and they went together, O'Mallory in his city trousers still, and Dryden spoke the words which the barracks wanted to say.

"Sergeant, whatever has happened, we are at your orders still," he said, and they both saluted. The man who wasn't a sergeant any longer didn't get up and wring their hands, or grip their shoulders, or thank them in a husky voice. Instead, he said evenly:

"If I was a sergeant still, I'd tell you you don't salute a noncom, and that you don't wear black ties in a reception center, not unless you want to be called down, you don't. Now the two of you get out of here."

Dryden went, but O'Mallory waited a moment.

"Look here, Sarge, you oughtn't to of spoken to Dryden like that," he said. "He shuts up like a clam if you step on his toes. Sometimes when I see him writing letters to that photograph he's got, I think he's the lone——"

"The hell he is," said the man who wasn't a sergeant any more, and he sat there looking straight before him, with his head held in his hands.

The palm may have wavered between Dryden and the sergeant in indecision for a moment then, but in the end it was awarded to the man who wrote out his request for it on the panel of a door. The door swung in and out of the ladies' rest room in the clubhouse, and the day before Dryden shipped out he happened to read it there. It was printed in ink, in small, neat letters, and it was placed near the middle hinge, as if in hope that no officer's eye would fall that low to see. It said:

GIRLS: PLEASE WRITE TO THE LONELIEST MAN IN THE U. S. ARMY:
PVT. ROBERT O'MALLORY, 38613309
COMPANY M
R. C. CAMP FEBRUARY

But because O'Mallory was off unloading cases at the railway siding, Dryden couldn't find him that day to say good-by.

Winter Night

There is a time of apprehension which begins with the beginning of darkness, and to which only the speech of love can lend security. It is there, in abeyance, at the end of every day, not urgent enough to be given the name of fear but rather of concern for how the hours are to be reprieved from fear, and those who have forgotten how it was when they were children can remember nothing of this. It may begin around five o'clock on a winter afternoon when the light outside is dying in the windows. At that hour the New York apartment in which Felicia lived was filled with shadows, and the little girl would wait alone in the living room, looking out at the winter-stripped trees that stood black in the park against the isolated ovals of unclean snow. Now it was January, and the day had been a cold one; the water of the artificial lake was frozen fast, but because of the cold and the coming darkness, the skaters had ceased to move across its surface. The street that lay between the park and the apartment house was wide, and the two-way streams of cars and busses, some with their headlamps already shining, advanced and halted, halted and poured swiftly on to the tempo of the traffic signals' altering lights. The time of apprehension had set in, and

Felicia, who was seven, stood at the window in the evening and waited before she asked the question. When the signals below would change from red to green again, or when the double-decker bus would turn the corner below, she would ask it. The words of it were already there, tentative in her mouth, when the answer came from the far end of the hall.

"Your mother," said the voice among the sound of kitchen things, "she telephoned up before you came in from nursery school. She won't be back in time for supper. I was to tell you a sitter was coming in from the sitting parents' place."

Felicia turned back from the window into the obscurity of the living room, and she looked toward the open door, and into the hall beyond it where the light from the kitchen fell in a clear yellow angle across the wall and onto the strip of carpet. Her hands were cold, and she put them in her jacket pockets as she walked carefully across the living-room rug and stopped at the edge of light.

"Will she be home late?" she said.

For a moment there was the sound of water running in the kitchen, a long way away, and then the sound of the water ceased, and the high, Southern voice went on:

"She'll come home when she gets ready to come home. That's all I have to say. If she wants to spend two dollars and fifty cents and ten cents' carfare on top of that three or four nights out of the week for a sitting parent to come in here and sit, it's her own business. It certainly ain't nothing to do with you or me. She makes her money, just like the rest of us does. She works all day down there in the office, or whatever it is, just like the rest of us works, and she's entitled to spend her money like she wants to spend it. There's no law in the world against buying your own freedom. Your mother and me, we're just buying our own freedom, that's all we're doing. And we're not doing nobody no harm."

"Do you know who she's having supper with?" said Felicia from the edge of dark. There was one more step to take, and then she would be standing in the light that fell on the strip of carpet, but she did not take the step.

"Do I know who she's having supper with?" the voice cried

out in what might have been derision, and there was the sound
of dishes striking the metal ribs of the drainboard by the sink.
"Maybe it's Mr. Van Johnson, or Mr. Frank Sinatra, or maybe it's
just the Duke of Wincers for the evening. All I know is you're
having soft-boiled egg and spinach and applesauce for supper,
and you're going to have it quick now because the time is getting away."

The voice from the kitchen had no name. It was as variable as
the faces and figures of the women who came and sat in the evenings. Month by month the voice in the kitchen altered to another voice, and the sitting parents were no more than lonely
aunts of an evening or two who sometimes returned and sometimes did not to this apartment in which they had sat before.
Nobody stayed anywhere very long any more, Felicia's mother
told her. It was part of the time in which you lived, and part of
the life of the city, but when the fathers came back, all this
would be miraculously changed. Perhaps you would live in a
house again, a small one, with fir trees on either side of the short
brick walk, and Father would drive up every night from the station just after darkness set in. When Felicia thought of this, she
stepped quickly into the clear angle of light, and she left the dark
of the living room behind her and ran softly down the hall.

The drop-leaf table stood in the kitchen between the refrigerator and the sink, and Felicia sat down at the place that was
set. The voice at the sink was speaking still, and while Felicia
ate it did not cease to speak until the bell of the front door rang
abruptly. The girl walked around the table and went down the
hall, wiping her dark palms in her apron, and, from the drop-leaf
table, Felicia watched her step from the angle of light into darkness and open the door.

"You put in an early appearance," the girl said, and the
woman who had rung the bell came into the hall. The door closed
behind her, and the girl showed her into the living room, and lit
the lamp on the bookcase, and the shadows were suddenly
bleached away. But when the girl turned, the woman turned
from the living room too and followed her, humbly and in silence, to the threshold of the kitchen. "Sometimes they keep me
standing around waiting after it's time for me to be getting on

home, the sitting parents do," the girl said, and she picked up the last two dishes from the table and put them in the sink. The woman who stood in the doorway was a small woman, and when she undid the white silk scarf from around her head, Felicia saw that her hair was black. She wore it parted in the middle, and it had not been cut, but was drawn back loosely into a knot behind her head. She had very clean white gloves on, and her face was pale, and there was a look of sorrow in her soft black eyes. "Sometimes I have to stand out there in the hall with my hat and coat on, waiting for the sitting parents to turn up," the girl said, and, as she turned on the water in the sink, the contempt she had for them hung on the kitchen air. "But you're ahead of time," she said, and she held the dishes, first one and then the other, under the flow of steaming water.

The woman in the doorway wore a neat black coat, not a new-looking coat, and it had no fur on it, but it had a smooth velvet collar and velvet lapels. She did not move, or smile, and she gave no sign that she had heard the girl speaking above the sound of water at the sink. She simply stood looking at Felicia, who sat at the table with the milk in her glass not finished yet.

"Are you the child?" she said at last, and her voice was low, and the pronunciation of the words a little strange.

"Yes, this here's Felicia," the girl said, and the dark hands dried the dishes and put them away. "You drink up your milk quick now, Felicia, so's I can rinse your glass."

"I will wash the glass," said the woman. "I would like to wash the glass for her," and Felicia sat looking across the table at the face in the doorway that was filled with such unspoken grief. "I will wash the glass for her and clean off the table," the woman was saying quietly. "When the child is finished, she will show me where her night things are."

"The others, they wouldn't do anything like that," the girl said, and she hung the dishcloth over the rack. "They wouldn't put their hand to housework, the sitting parents. That's where they got the name for them," she said.

Whenever the front door closed behind the girl in the evening, it would usually be that the sitting parent who was there would take up a book of fairy stories and read aloud for a while to

Felicia; or else would settle herself in the big chair in the living room and begin to tell the words of a story in drowsiness to her, while Felicia took off her clothes in the bedroom, and folded them, and put her pajamas on, and brushed her teeth, and did her hair. But this time, that was not the way it happened. Instead, the woman sat down on the other chair at the kitchen table, and she began at once to speak, not of good fairies or bad, or of animals endowed with human speech, but to speak quietly, in spite of the eagerness behind her words, of a thing that seemed of singular importance to her.

"It is strange that I should have been sent here tonight," she said, her eyes moving slowly from feature to feature of Felicia's face, "for you look like a child that I knew once, and this is the anniversary of that child."

"Did she have hair like mine?" Felicia asked quickly, and she did not keep her eyes fixed on the unfinished glass of milk in shyness any more.

"Yes, she did. She had hair like yours," said the woman, and her glance paused for a moment on the locks which fell straight and thick on the shoulders of Felicia's dress. It may have been that she thought to stretch out her hand and touch the ends of Felicia's hair, for her fingers stirred as they lay clasped together on the table, and then they relapsed into passivity again. "But it is not the hair alone, it is the delicacy of your face, too, and your eyes the same, filled with the same spring lilac color," the woman said, pronouncing the words carefully. "She had little coats of golden fur on her arms and legs," she said, "and when we were closed up there, the lot of us in the cold, I used to make her laugh when I told her that the fur that was so pretty, like a little fawn's skin on her arms, would always help to keep her warm."

"And did it keep her warm?" asked Felicia, and she gave a little jerk of laughter as she looked down at her own legs hanging under the table, with the bare calves thin and covered with a down of hair.

"It did not keep her warm enough," the woman said, and now the mask of grief had come back upon her face. "So we used to take everything we could spare from ourselves, and we would sew them into cloaks and other kinds of garments for her and for the other children. . . ."

"Was it a school?" said Felicia when the woman's voice had ceased to speak.

"No," said the woman softly, "it was not a school, but still there were a lot of children there. It was a camp—that was the name the place had; it was a camp. It was a place where they put people until they could decide what was to be done with them." She sat with her hands clasped, silent a moment, looking at Felicia. "That little dress you have on," she said, not saying the words to anybody, scarcely saying them aloud. "Oh, she would have liked that little dress, the little buttons shaped like hearts, and the white collar——"

"I have four school dresses," Felicia said. "I'll show them to you. How many dresses did she have?"

"Well, there, you see, there in the camp," said the woman, "she did not have any dresses except the little skirt and the pullover. That was all she had. She had brought just a handkerchief of her belongings with her, like everybody else—just enough for three days away from home was what they told us, so she did not have enough to last the winter. But she had her ballet slippers," the woman said, and her clasped fingers did not move. "She had brought them because she thought during her three days away from home she would have the time to practice her ballet."

"I've been to the ballet," Felicia said suddenly, and she said it so eagerly that she stuttered a little as the words came out of her mouth. She slipped quickly down from the chair and went around the table to where the woman sat. Then she took one of the woman's hands away from the other that held it fast, and she pulled her toward the door. "Come into the living room and I'll do a pirouette for you," she said, and then she stopped speaking, her eyes halted on the woman's face. "Did she—did the little girl—could she do a pirouette very well?" she said.

"Yes, she could. At first she could," said the woman, and Felicia felt uneasy now at the sound of sorrow in her words. "But after that she was hungry. She was hungry all winter," she said in a low voice. "We were all hungry, but the children were the hungriest. Even now," she said, and her voice went suddenly savage, "when I see milk like that, clean, fresh milk standing in a glass, I want to cry out loud, I want to beat my hands on the table, because it did not have to be . . ." She had drawn her fingers abruptly away from Felicia now, and Felicia stood before her, cast off, forlorn, alone again in the time of apprehension. "That was three years ago," the woman was saying, and one hand was lifted, as in weariness, to shade her face. "It was somewhere else, it was in another country," she said, and behind her hand her eyes were turned upon the substance of a world in which Felicia had played no part.

"Did—did the little girl cry when she was hungry?" Felicia asked, and the woman shook her head.

"Sometimes she cried," she said, "but not very much. She was very quiet. One night when she heard the other children crying, she said to me, 'You know, they are not crying because they want something to eat. They are crying because their mothers have gone away.'"

"Did the mothers have to go out to supper?" Felicia asked, and she watched the woman's face for the answer.

"No," said the woman. She stood up from her chair, and now that she put her hand on the little girl's shoulder, Felicia was taken into the sphere of love and intimacy again. "Shall we go into the other room, and you will do your pirouette for me?" the woman said, and they went from the kitchen and down the strip of carpet on which the clear light fell. In the front room, they paused hand in hand in the glow of the shaded lamp, and the woman looked about her, at the books, the low tables with the magazines and ash trays on them, the vase of roses on the piano, looking with dark, scarcely seeing eyes at these things that had no reality at all. It was only when she saw the little white clock on the mantelpiece that she gave any sign, and then she said quickly: "What time does your mother put you to bed?"

Felicia waited a moment, and in the interval of waiting the woman lifted one hand and, as if in reverence, touched Felicia's hair.

"What time did the little girl you knew in the other place go to bed?" Felicia asked.

"Ah, God, I do not know, I do not remember," the woman said.

"Was she your little girl?" said Felicia softly, stubbornly.

"No," said the woman. "She was not mine. At least, at first she was not mine. She had a mother, a real mother, but the mother had to go away."

"Did she come back late?" asked Felicia.

"No, ah, no, she could not come back, she never came back," the woman said, and now she turned, her arm around Felicia's shoulders, and she sat down in the low soft chair. "Why am I saying all this to you, why am I doing it?" she cried out in grief, and she held Felicia close against her. "I had thought to speak of the anniversary to you, and that was all, and now I am saying these other things to you. Three years ago today, exactly, the little girl became my little girl because her mother went away. That is all there is to it. There is nothing more."

Felicia waited another moment, held close against the woman, and listening to the swift, strong heartbeats in the woman's breast.

"But the mother," she said then in the small, persistent voice, "did she take a taxi when she went?"

"This is the way it used to happen," said the woman, speaking in hopelessness and bitterness in the softly lighted room. "Every week they used to come into the place where we were and they would read a list of names out. Sometimes it would be the names of children they would read out, and then a little later they would have to go away. And sometimes it would be the grown people's names, the names of the mothers or big sisters, or other women's names. The men were not with us. The fathers were somewhere else, in another place."

"Yes," Felicia said. "I know."

"We had been there only a little while, maybe ten days or maybe not so long," the woman went on, holding Felicia against her still, "when they read the name of the little girl's mother out, and that afternoon they took her away."

"What did the little girl do?" Felicia said.

"She wanted to think up the best way of getting out so that she could go find her mother," said the woman, "but she could not think of anything good enough until the third or fourth day. And then she tied her ballet slippers up in the handkerchief again, and she went up to the guard standing at the door." The woman's voice was gentle, controlled now. "She asked the guard please to open the door so that she could go out. 'This is Thursday,' she said, 'and every Tuesday and Thursday I have my ballet lessons. If I miss a ballet lesson, they do not count the money off, so my mother would be just paying for nothing, and she cannot afford to pay for nothing. I missed my ballet lesson on Tuesday,' she said to the guard, 'and I must not miss it again today.'"

Felicia lifted her head from the woman's shoulder, and she shook her hair back and looked in question and wonder at the woman's face.

"And did the man let her go?" she said.

"No, he did not. He could not do that," said the woman. "He was a soldier and he had to do what he was told. So every evening after her mother went, I used to brush the little girl's hair for her," the woman went on saying. "And while I brushed it, I used to tell her the stories of the ballets. Sometimes I would begin with *Narcissus*," the woman said, and she parted Felicia's locks with her fingers, "so if you will go and get your brush now, I will tell it while I brush your hair."

"Oh, yes," said Felicia, and she made two whirls as she went quickly to the bedroom. On the way back, she stopped and held on to the piano with the fingers of one hand while she went up on her toes. "Did you see me? Did you see me standing on my toes?" she called to the woman, and the woman sat smiling in love and contentment at her.

"Yes, wonderful, really wonderful," she said. "I am sure I have never seen anyone do it so well." Felicia came spinning toward her, whirling in pirouette after pirouette, and she flung herself down in the chair close to her, with her thin bones pressed against the woman's soft, wide hip. The woman took the silver-backed, monogrammed brush and the tortoise-shell comb in her hands, and now she began to brush Felicia's hair. "We did not have any soap at all and not very much water to wash in, so I never could fix her as nicely and prettily as I wanted to," she said, and the brush stroked regularly, carefully down, caressing the shape of Felicia's head.

"If there wasn't very much water, then how did she do her teeth?" Felicia said.

"She did not do her teeth," said the woman, and she drew the comb through Felicia's hair. "There were not any toothbrushes or tooth paste, or anything like that."

Felicia waited a moment, constructing the unfamiliar scene of it in silence, and then she asked the tentative question.

"Do I have to do my teeth tonight?" she said.

"No," said the woman, and she was thinking of something else, "you do not have to do your teeth."

"If I am your little girl tonight, can I pretend there isn't enough water to wash?" said Felicia.

"Yes," said the woman, "you can pretend that if you like. You do not have to wash," she said, and the comb passed lightly through Felicia's hair.

"Will you tell me the story of the ballet?" said Felicia, and the rhythm of the brushing was like the soft, slow rocking of sleep.

"Yes," said the woman. "In the first one, the place is a forest glade with little pale birches growing in it, and they have green veils over their faces and green veils drifting from their fingers, because it is the springtime. There is the music of a flute," said the woman's voice softly, softly, "and creatures of the wood are dancing——"

"But the mother," Felicia said as suddenly as if she had been awaked from sleep. "What did the little girl's mother say when she didn't do her teeth and didn't wash at night?"

"The mother was not there, you remember," said the woman, and the brush moved steadily in her hand. "But she did send one little letter back. Sometimes the people who went away were able to do that. The mother wrote it in a train, standing up in a car that had no seats," she said, and she might have been telling the story of the ballet still, for her voice was gentle and the brush did not falter on Felicia's hair. "There were perhaps a great many other people standing up in the train with her, perhaps all trying to write their little letters on the bits of paper they had managed to hide on them, or that they had found in forgotten corners as they traveled. When they had written their letters, then they must try to slip them out through the boards of the car in which they journeyed, standing up," said the woman, "and these letters fell down on the tracks under the train, or they were blown into the fields or onto the country roads, and if it was a kind person who picked them up, he would seal them in envelopes and send them to where they were addressed to go. So a letter came back like this from the little girl's mother," the woman said, and the brush followed the comb, the comb the brush in steady pursuit through Felicia's hair. "It said good-by to the little girl, and it said please to take care of her. It said: 'Whoever reads this letter in the camp, please take good care of my little girl for me, and please have her tonsils looked at by a doctor if this is possible to do.'"

"And then," said Felicia softly, persistently, "what happened to the little girl?"

"I do not know. I cannot say," the woman said. But now the brush and comb had ceased to move, and in the silence Felicia turned her thin, small body on the chair, and she and the woman suddenly put their arms around each other. "They must all be asleep now, all of them," the woman said, and in the silence that fell on them again, they held each other closer. "They must be quietly asleep somewhere, and not crying all night because they are hungry and because they are cold. For three years I have been saying 'They must all be asleep, and the cold and the hunger and the seasons or night or day or nothing matters to them——'"

It was after midnight when Felicia's mother put her key in the lock of the front door, and pushed it open, and stepped into the hallway. She walked quickly to the living room, and just across the threshold she slipped the three blue foxskins from her shoulders and dropped them, with her little velvet bag, upon the chair. The room was quiet, so quiet that she could hear the sound of breathing in it, and no one spoke to her in greeting as she crossed toward the bedroom door. And then, as startling as a slap across her delicately tinted face, she saw the woman lying sleeping on the divan, and Felicia, in her school dress still, asleep within the woman's arms.

Evening at Home

I am writing this in the hope that the young woman who told me her name was Mrs. Daisy Miller will read it and tell me why she never brought my two dollars back. I've waited three months, and because she hasn't come back, I'm going to tell it exactly the way it happened, so that if the girl who called herself Mrs. Daisy Miller reads it, she won't have any trouble recognizing the incident and the parts that both of us played. The place was New York and the time was a July evening, a weekend evening, when everyone who could get away from the city had got away. I was going to be alone for twenty-four hours in the brownstone house I rented in the East Seventies, and because of the work I had been doing all day, and because of the heat, I thought I would stay at home. I ate a cool supper in the garden behind the house, and then I came in, and, perhaps in loneliness, I wandered from room to room, as if seeking the people who were no longer there. It was then that I saw the earth in the window boxes of the front rooms had been parched to dust, and I got the green tin watering can in the butler's pantry and I filled it up with water. I might never have seen the girl, and all this might not have happened, if I had not begun to water the geraniums, which were begging for succor in the burning soil.

As I moved from window to window with the green tin can, the light and the heat were just beginning to fade. Below was the quiet street, and across the street stood a rather elegant little private hospital and, beside the hospital, a gabled, russet-colored church, left over from some other period of this century or forgotten from the century before. But what had altered in the familiar scene was that on the steps, which shaped a crescent of russet stone around the church's portal, the young woman lay asleep. She was wearing a simple brown linen dress with a neat white collar at the modest neck and white cuffs at the elbows, and her slender legs were bare. On her feet were new-looking

white sandals, strapped with a broad white band across the instep
and fitted with platform soles. She lay quite naturally, there on
the third step, her body relaxed, her face turned away from the
street, her fingers loosely interlaced across her breasts. A small
hat of glazed white straw, which she must have removed before
lying down to sleep, was placed, as if with care, upon the step
below her, and one could see the thick reddish hair, worn short,
that fell with luxuriant carelessness back from her brow—the
color of hair, I thought then, that means a chalk-white skin and
freckles on the forearms, and on the shoulders, and on the probably upturned, short, wide-nostriled nose.

When I saw her, I stopped watering the geraniums, and I
stood looking down across the street at her, but without any feeling of surprise. The evening was so warm, and the look of the
church's stone so fresh, that to lie down there seemed a reasonable thing to do, and I wondered why she had been the first one
to think of doing it. After a moment, I saw a trained nurse come
out of the hospital next to the church and walk to where she lay.
The nurse was handsome and young, and she had a silky knot of
smooth black hair pinned just beneath the starched cap that rode
high on her head. Her buttocks swung slowly back and forth inside her skirt as she moved with a singularly leisurely gait to
where the girl lay stretched upon the stone. As I set my watering
can down on the hardwood floor and wiped the drop from its
chin, I saw the nurse place one foot, in its unsullied canvas shoe,
on the first step of the church and lean above the girl, not in solicitude or gentleness, it seemed to me, but in distaste, perhaps
even in disdain. She leaned there, almost startling in her im-
maculacy, and her hand did not touch the brown linen dress for
the beating of a heart within it, and her fingers did not feel for
the pulsing of life in the girl's wrist, but, instead, the hand of the
professional picked up the hat of white transparent straw. It may
have been that she was seeking a label inside it, and, perhaps because she found none, she dropped the hat onto the stone again.
Then she straightened up and dusted her palms clean of whatever they had touched, and she moved back across the sidewalk
to the hospital, her body moving slowly, consciously, the hips as
eloquent as language in the clean white dress.

Now she'll get a couple of interns to help carry the girl in, I thought, and I waited, pinching off in my fingers the big lower leaves of the geraniums, which were scalloped with yellow and as dry as paper fans.

On evenings such as this, the hospital doors stood wide, sometimes until after midnight, and the windows of the rooms were open, with the tawny canvas awnings lowered, hollowing each room into a well of privacy and shade. And on evenings such as this, and whether one chose to or not, one participated in the life of the hospital, for the sound of the patients' radios could be heard across the street, and the patients' voices, or the nurses' voices, answering, like the voices of actors on a stage, the delicate summons of the telephone. But now a profound twilit quiet lay upon the hospital as well as on the street, and no bells sounded, no voices spoke behind the awnings. Everything was still; everything had ceased as the nurse went in through the open hospital door. Almost at once, she reappeared, in the ground-floor window to the left, and I saw her, the cap and uniform blue-white in the dusk, lift the receiver and the mouthpiece from the switchboard and plug the connection in. She did not sit down to dial the numbers that she wanted, but she did it standing, selecting them casually with the end of the pencil she held in her hand.

I do not know why I remember all this so clearly, for I had not spoken to Mrs. Daisy Miller then, or given the two dollars to her, so there is no reason why I should remember the details of it at all. But I know that when the nurse's telephone conversation was done and she had taken her lipstick and pocket mirror out, I still stood waiting. Not having understood yet, I was waiting for the two interns, bearing the stretcher between them, to come down the hall and out the open door. It might be, I thought as the twilight deepened, that the girl had been struck by a car in the street and had dragged herself up across the curbstone and up the stone steps of the church and lain down there to die. I was glad that professional help was near, and I stood awhile watching the trained nurse shaping her nails at the open window by the switchboard, and there was only silence as the curtain of darkness jerked, instant by instant, lower on the scene. After a little, a man in a grayish suit, carrying his hat, came wandering from the direction of Third Avenue, his footsteps seeming to precede him through the silence and then he himself to come after, meandering, quiet, slow. At the sight of the girl lying on the steps, his aimlessness wavered toward intention for a moment, but only for a moment, and then he turned his head away, and he crossed the street, but still without haste, doing it casually, as if he had seen nothing, giving a wide berth to the church and the steps and to what was lying on them, and he wandered to the corner and was gone.

And then, standing there behind the geraniums, I knew, with a sudden sense of shock, that there were no interns hastening down the hospital hall with a stretcher between them, that there was no help coming, and that no one had any intention of doing anything at all. I ran to the desk and I opened the telephone directory, and I found the telephone number of the hospital across the street and I dialed it quickly. From where I stood, with the telephone in my hand, I could see the nurse put the nail file down and turn from the downstairs window to plug in the connection, her uniform in the still-unlighted office as blank and sharply edged as paper in the office's accumulated dark.

"Hello," she said, and I heard the word said twice, as if in double exposure, as I watched her. It was spoken first on the wire, and then the almost simultaneous echo of it followed across the evening air.

"Look," I said, "you know there's a young woman lying on the church steps next door to you. Aren't you going to take her in and find out what's wrong with her?"

"I know what's wrong with her," both the high, nasal voice on the wire and the high, nasal echo of it answered. "She's stinko," the trained nurse said. I could see her, in her blank white dress, lift her hand as if to jerk the connection out, and then stop the gesture in mid-air to study the nails on her lifted hand.

"So you're just going to let her lie out there all night?" I said.

"Listen, lady," said the double recording of the nurse's voice, "we're not running a home for alcoholics. I've put a call in to the police. I told them a woman had passed out on the church steps, and to come along and pick her up. And how did you get into this, anyway?" the two voices asked me sharply. "What's this woman got to do with you?"

Maybe I did not actually say the things I am under the impression I said then. Maybe I did not tell her, with my voice shaking like a weak and foolish woman's, to telephone the police again and tell them that they needn't come, because her heart had just thawed out beneath the starch of the uniform, and human blood was running in her veins. For a long time, I believed that I had said a great many fine and noble things to the nurse, but I could not remember the words I had used to say them. It may be that I simply put the telephone down without saying anything at all, but I don't like to believe this. I must have said quietly to her that to sleep in a police station all night might change a young woman's life forever, and alter the hearts of those who loved her, and turn the faith she had in herself to dust and ashes in her mouth. Perhaps I said no more than that if she did not take the girl into the hospital, then I would take her into my house. I must have said that much, at least, for I know that the two voices of the nurse cried out, "For God's sake, take her, lady," the echo more nasal and more impatient even than the voice itself, drawn high and thin across the wire.

"I'll be down at once," I said, and then I saw the nurse's hand jerk the switchboard connection savagely out, and she turned to the open window again, but she did not pick the nail file up. Instead, she raised her head and looked up at the windows of the brownstone house, and as I looked down at her across the geraniums, the white cap seemed to stiffen, and we looked with recognition across the space of the street, as evil as serpents, into each other's venomous eyes.

I went out through the basement door, taking the key of the iron gate with me, and when I stepped from the curb, I could feel the asphalt warm beneath my feet still, from the heat of the day. The evening had deepened, and the entrance hall of the hospital and the office where the switchboard stood were lighted, but beyond them the church had withdrawn even farther into the darkness and stillness of its own richly colored stone.

And the girl had not moved from where she lay, with her head turned slightly on her slender neck, and the white fingers loosely interlaced across her breasts, rising and falling, rising and falling gently as she breathed. I planted my feet firmly on the first step of the church, and I leaned over and slipped one arm beneath her shoulders, and I raised her, but only a little, for at once her loosely clasped hands slid apart and her arms fell, lifeless and useless, by her sides. I tried holding her head in place with my other hand, but I could not keep it from rolling forward on her chest and swinging there.

I laid her carefully down again, and this time I began with her feet. I took the heels of the white platform-soled sandals in my hands, and I lowered them from the third step to the step below. Then I bent the knees, pulling the skirt of the brown linen dress down over them as I did it, and I brought the two feet down to rest between my own on the first step. Now, had she been aware of it, she was in a position to get up and walk away. But the thighs and the torso, and the arms and the head, would not be a party to it. They rested still in the deep, sweet dream that no stranger could disturb. I remembered the hat then, and I thought I would set it on her head in preparation for the journey we would undertake together, and when I had picked it up, I saw that it was a hat such as a bride might have been wearing, with minuscule orange blossoms, as frail as snowdrops, woven foolishly into the glazed-straw crown.

I lifted her head, and I set the hat as well as I could on it, and then I put her head gently down again upon the stone. I stood two steps below her now, holding her feet between my feet, and I took her hands in mine to pull the reclining portion of her into the sitting position that her lower legs alone maintained. And when I leaned above her to gather her hands up, I saw there were no rings on her fingers, and I saw that weariness and perhaps something like disappointment, only more moving, more profound, lay like a mask across her features, taking the look of beauty and the look of youth away. But her skin was as white as the reddish hair had promised it would be, and there were freckles on her forearms, and some scattered on her short, Irish-looking nose. I drew her up by her long, pliant, ringless hands, and her helpless, seemingly boneless arms followed after, and as her head lolled forward on her breast again, the white straw hat slipped from it and rolled down across the steps. As long as I held her strongly by the hands, like this, she seemed to be a person sitting up, except that the spine was water and the head, with the thick, short reddish hair brushing soft as a veil across her cheeks and forehead, swung lower and lower toward her knees.

"Look, my dear, this is very silly," I said, speaking severely to her. "The police have been called, and they'll be arriving any minute." I remembered reading that if you slapped a person's face, it would rouse him, but I could not bring myself to do it. "You're going to try to walk now," I said. "We don't want the police to find you here."

But, having no interest in anything that might be said, she had begun now to tip slowly sidewise, and I sat quickly down beside her, sitting close and putting one arm around her to keep her from lying down again. Holding her like this, I reached down with my free hand to retrieve the white straw hat again, and as I leaned, the girl swayed perilously forward with me, and when I sat up again, she swayed upward as well. We sat quietly for a little while on the steps together, and her head rolled, a detached and separate object, toward my shoulder and came to rest, like a child's head, upon it, and the tide of night lapped slowly up the steps across our feet. And after a short time had passed, I placed the hat, with its woven wreath of orange blossoms, on her head again, in preparation for the journey on which we must embark together, and then I tightened my arm around her shoulders and I got warily to my feet, and as I rose, I tried to lift her with me, but she would not come.

"Now, listen," I said, sitting down beside her again. "Someone has put in a call for the police. They're on their way here." I hated to be persistent about this, but it seemed to me the only reality that might arouse her from the dream. "Besides, if you sleep out here all night, you'll be so stiff you won't be able to move tomorrow," I said, and I even thought of mentioning her hat to her. I thought of saying, "And you're absolutely ruining your new hat. It won't have any shape left any more."

But it didn't matter what I said, I knew by this time, for she had settled back in such comfort against my shoulder again that the hat slipped from her head before I could catch it, and I saw it jump the curb and float away on the surface of the dark. I knew that I must act with more decision now, and I got to my feet again and maneuvered myself up onto the step above her, holding her up by the force of my two hands placed underneath her arms. And, stooping behind her like this, I sought to lift her, but, instead of the girl's rising, her legs unfolded will-lessly beneath her, and her body slid, without life or protest, down the church steps and came to rest upon the sidewalk, but in a sitting position still, because of my hands, which held to her armpits and had not let her go. It was not until I had begun, in desperation, to wheel her, like a wheelbarrow with a loose, wavering wheel and no handles, across the quiet street that I saw the hat lying a little way beyond us, and I did not dare to set her down. Her legs and her heels were doing their part now in getting us to safety, and I couldn't risk breaking the movement of their advance, for it seemed to me then that I could hear the Black Maria purring down Lexington, its siren not quite wailing, its bell just preparing to ring. And in my distress it may be that I manipulated the girl forward too hastily, for her half-reclining body suddenly outstripped her automatically functioning feet, and her legs twisted under her like a cripple's, and she fell upon her knees. Even the strength of my hands beneath her armpits could not make her rise.

So then I tried the only method that remained, and I turned, holding her under the arms still, and I walked quickly backward, pulling her with effort, like a dead thing, the rest of the way across the street and up the curb and over the sidewalk to the basement gate. I was gasping from the effort as I propped her, sitting, against the brownstone of the house while I found the key and opened the gate. It was then, as I raised her again to drag her in across the threshold, that she suddenly began to laugh.

I could identify Mrs. Daisy Miller at any time and in any place by this singularly beautiful laugh, although it may have seemed to me at that moment a little loud. It was high and clear and, in spite of all we had been through together, marvelously untroubled as she lay there on the floor. After I had switched on the hall light, I half lifted, half pulled her across the downstairs hall to the foot of the stairs, and she kept right on laughing. Her eyes had remained closed, and now they were squeezed up with her laughter, and it seemed to me that they contemplated some extremely funny scene of which I was left in ignorance, that they were fixed on the hilarious action of an incident in which I did not share. I do not know how I got her up the steep flight of stairs or how long a time it took me. I only know that as I manip-ulated her up, step by step, I heard, through the sweet bursts and ripples of her laughter, the muted wailing of a police car's siren in the street outside, and the car must have stopped to seek for her, for after a while I heard the sound of its motor as it drove away.

I had planned to get her onto the divan in the sitting room, and this is what I finally managed to do. I lit the lamp on the table by her head, where the ash tray stood, and the volume of Henry James between the two blue leather bookends, and, even lying on the divan, the girl did not stop laughing at the truly funny, truly uproarious thing that she looked on or listened to in sleep. Her nose wrinkled up in delight as she laughed, and the mask of fatigue was gone, as if a hand had lifted it from her fea-tures, and however vulgar the joke might be that had been told her, or told on her, the laughter was pure, so wonderfully pure that I listened to it with longing, wanting to be included in its absurdity.

I undid the straps of her white sandals and took them off and stood them side by side upon the rug, and still she went on laughing, laughing without hysteria or strain, only breathlessly and foolishly. And as I sponged off her face and washed her long, pliant young hands, she kept on laughing, and I looked at her with envy, knowing that no matter how long I lived I would never be able to laugh like that again, because the time of finding circus clowns funny and finding slapstick funny was finished and done with a long time ago. I covered her over with a flowered cotton counterpane from one of the bedrooms upstairs, and I sat down in an armchair near her and for a while I watched the side of her face, and conjectured on her people and on her work and as to what sort of child or woman she might be.

There was something prim and yet arty about her that suggested she might sell books in a small, good bookshop, perhaps on Madison or Park, but the thick, careless reddish hair and the soft mouth would never have had the patience for it. And there was the hat, the white straw hat that I had not retrieved, and never would retrieve now, which might have come on a honeymoon from the sticks, seen first in the catalogue of a mail-order house. (And I thought in the morning, when I went out to look for it and did not find it, that it was perhaps to the sticks that it had, of its own volition, returned.) The sandals were as new as if bought for a young bride's trousseau, and they must have been chosen to match the hat, and perhaps even the handbag that she wasn't carrying any more. And now, as I watched her, her laughter began to subside into little gasps of childlike amusement, but her eyes were closed in delight still upon the ludicrous spectacle that I could not see.

When she had ceased entirely to laugh, I leaned forward in the armchair, and when I spoke, my voice sounded strange and lonely in the silent room.

"Listen, my child," I said, and I cleared my throat uneasily, "if you could tell me where you lived, I could take you there. I could call a taxi and take you home."

But I might have been sitting alone in the room, talking aloud to myself, for all the attention she paid me, and it made me nervous. I didn't like the feel of things at all. I got up, and I walked into the dining room, and I got out the bottle of Scotch from the sideboard and poured not more than a finger of it into a tall, clean glass that I took down from the shelf. Beyond the dining room was the butler's pantry, and I went quickly through the swinging door, not liking the almost human sigh of it behind me, and I held the glass under the cold-water tap at the sink an instant and splashed some water in. I could have gone down into the kitchen in the basement and got some ice cubes and some soda, but the light was not turned on there, and for some reason I had begun to feel uncertain of the dark.

When I went back into the sitting room, I glanced quickly at the girl, and I saw that she was lying just as she had been when I left the room. Her reddish hair was spread out on the gray silk of the cushion that I had put beneath her head, and her bare, slender arms, with the white cuffs at the elbows, were lying outside on the counterpane. I sat down in the armchair near her again, my glass in my hand, and I thought how disturbing it was to know, as intimately as if she had been a member of the family, the face and the arms and the legs and the laughter of one who was an absolute stranger and with whom one had exchanged no words. I took my drink slowly, watching the side of this stranger's familiar face, watching the counterpane rise as her breath was drawn evenly, rhythmically in and fall as the breath was evenly, rhythmically relinquished, in the silence of the lamp-lit room. After a while, I got up, and I put my empty glass down on the table, and I crossed the room and picked out a record and placed it on the gramophone, and the red jewel glowed minutely as a spark on the panel when I turned on the switch.

"I'm going to play you a little music," I said, my voice unnaturally loud. I held the gramophone's metal arm above the record, as if giving her the time to speak, and I found I was smiling like a nervous, effusive hostess at the girl, who had not moved.

The first record was a Strauss waltz, and I knew that the strains of it must cross the street and drift through the hospital windows, and perhaps be heard above the sound of the radios. And when that record was done, I played two Bach jigs, and the movement of them filled the room with agility and life, but the girl on the divan did not stir and did not open her eyes. I would have played more, and perhaps it would have roused her, in the end, but now it was eleven o'clock, and I wanted to go to bed. I lingered awhile longer, not liking the idea of leaving her sleeping there, and then, having left the lamp lighted on the table near her, I went, humming one of the Bach jigs, perhaps for courage in the empty house, as I mounted the stairs.

By now, I felt an acute uneasiness, because of the presence of the girl and the uncertainty of when she might awake and start wandering from floor to floor. After I had undressed and washed

and got into my bed, I could not sleep. I thought I should have
perhaps called a doctor or perhaps roused her by violent means
from the torpor in which she lay. The hands on the phospho-
rescent face of the leather-framed clock on my bureau had
marked one o'clock the last time I lifted my head and looked at
it, and after that I slept, for when I awoke, with a sense of shock
in the darkness, and looked at it again, it was nearly four. And
on the floor below I could hear the feet moving softly, warily,
and I sat up in bed and felt for my dressing gown and pulled it
around me, and my hands were shaking, for some reason I could
not name. When I had found my slippers beside the bed and put
my feet into them, I moved softly across the room to the lighted
hallway, and there I crept to the banisters and closed my hands
on the varnished wooden railing, and, clinging to it, I peered
down the bright well of the stairs. There, on the landing just
below me, the girl stood, her hair shining like copper, peering
uncertainly into the darkness of the basement floor below.

"Were you looking for something?" I called down in a voice
that startled me by its gay, shrill cordiality, and at the sound of
it the girl jumped like a deer that the shot has just passed by.
Then she turned, and she threw her head back, and the soft hair
brushed across her shoulders as she looked up the well of the
stairs to where I clung to the banisters.

"I'm looking for my hat and bag," she said, and the voice, in
contrast to my own, was cool and composed, and pitched ad-
mirably low.

We did not say much more to each other, although there was a
great deal more that might have been said. When I came down
the stairs, she stood looking at me somewhat critically, and I saw
that her eyes were a light sea green in color and that they were
anxious and proud and shy. She said that her hat was a small
white straw hat and that the bag was straw and white as well,
and she didn't want to lose them. And because there was no way
to explain how things had been, I could only say that the hat
had blown off in the street, and that I had not seen the bag at
all. And then, not having put her sandals on yet, and standing
there barefoot but with dignity before me, she said, "I don't

know what my husband must be thinking. I don't know how I got here at all."

And still it seemed impossible to tell her any of the story, for if I spoke of the police having been called, then I might just as well have let the police car come and take her—the bookshop girl, or the bride from the sticks, or whoever she might be. We had gone back into the sitting room now, and I asked her where she had eaten that evening, thinking perhaps she herself would be able to put it together up to a certain moment. She picked up one sandal from the rug, and she looked at it, considering how much she would say.

"I don't think I had any supper," she said, and she sat down on the divan and started to put her sandals on, but she had some difficulty with the straps. "I came out of work with a girl I know, and it was hot, and we went to a bar and had a drink together." Her voice was gentle, pleasant, low. "It was hot when we came out of the bar, and after we had walked for a while along Lexington Avenue, we went into another bar," she said, and perhaps because of the way she told it, without detail or conviction, I did not believe it had happened that way.

She had got her sandals on now, and she crossed to the mirror that hung above the mantel. She took a comb out of the pocket of her dress and stood there combing out her wavy reddish brush of hair. And as I watched her, the narrow fingers looked suddenly efficient, and strong and relentless, despite the delicacy of their bones.

"It's something that could happen to almost anyone," I said.

"What?" she said quickly, and she looked at me in the mirror, almost startled, and her hands stopped combing her hair.

"Why, just that," I said, trying to find the words not to say it. "Losing one's hat and bag like that."

"Yes," she said, and she jerked the comb through her hair again. "I know."

She did not ask me for the two dollars. It was I who made her take the money when she was ready to go. She said she knew exactly where she was going and that one dollar would be enough, and I said it was better to have the two. She suggested of her own accord that she bring it back about four o'clock the next afternoon. It was Sunday, and she would not be working, and it would be quite easy to come up with it, she said. She asked me to write my name and address down for her, and I got a pencil and paper from the desk and did this, and she folded it over in her supple hand.

"Look," I said, "would you tell me your name, too?"

And then I knew how impassable was the chasm of mistrust or fear or suspicion that lay between us, for now she seemed to be taken off her guard, and her green eyes looked wildly at the desk and the table and then at my face.

"My name is Daisy Miller, Mrs. Daisy Miller," she said, and even before I thought of the volume of Henry James standing between the bookends, I did not believe it was true.

At the door, I remembered how we had crossed the street and come through the basement gate together, and now there was nothing left of the thing that we had done together and the intimacy we had shared. I watched her go down the brownstone steps, walking carefully on her platform soles, as if she felt a weakness in her flesh, and I went back into the sitting room to put out the lamp on the table by the divan, where the counterpane still lay.

I am putting this down in the hope that the girl who told me her name was Daisy Miller will read it, because using the name that wasn't hers doesn't matter, and not bringing the two dollars back doesn't matter, but I just want her to know that, after all the rest of it, I hate the story's ending that way.

The Ballet of Central Park

This is a story about children, and about what happened to two or three of them in New York one summer. It is a story that has to be written quickly before it is too late. "Too late for what?" may be asked at once, and to that there is no answer. It would be dramatic, but scarcely true to say: "Before something happens to all the children in the world." But if you think back far enough, you will remember Dostoyevski saying that whatever pain or martyrdom adults endure is of negligible importance because they have already been granted a certain expanse of life. They have had the time to accumulate courage and wisdom, if those were the qualities they put value on, while children have not yet had their chance. Children are still trying to feel their way, Dostoyevski said (or else are shouldering or elbowing their way, or perhaps shouting or stamping or weeping their way), toward what they want to be if everything turns out right in the end. And there is another writer, the gentlest and most misconstrued of men, a man called Freud, who said that psychoanalysis could be at its best a hand reaching out to children in the dark rooms of their confusion, as a hand had never reached out to them before. To those children who cry themselves blind because they cannot bear the vision of the adult world, it could give their childhood the clarity of mountain water, he said.

The story that must be told as quickly as possible is about a little girl who was baptized Hilary by a mother and father who had no other children. They treated this isolate one as though she were a poet of distinction, an actress of international renown, and a musician as gifted and precocious as Mozart. This kind of acknowledgment had been given her since the day of her birth, and in appreciation of it, she had never ceased trying to become these things. Since the time she was six she wrote ballets and danced them out, and she put on puppet shows of her own invention, in which she spoke in four different voices. At twelve, she composed a number of small and agreeable concertos for strings and winds that the school orchestra played. At her home, somewhere in the far reaches of suburbia, she had ridden for years standing upright on a horse's back, around and around in a grassy paddock, her light hair open like a silk fan on the air behind her, her bare feet holding flexibly to the horse's rippling hide.

It should be stated here that I am no relation to Hilary, except inasmuch as every adult is related to all children. I am as casual and, at the same time, as committed, a stranger to her as any passer-by in Central Park, where Hilary ate her lunch between classes, sitting on a bench, two days a week that summer. I am perhaps that idle lady, twisted out of shape by the foundation undergarment she has chosen to trap the look of youth for a little longer, her feet crippled by the high-heeled sandals that grip her toes like a handful of cocktail sausages, who has strayed over from Fifth Avenue, leading an evil-faced poodle, gray as a wasps' nest and as nervous, on an expensive string. And I am equally the lady with bright orange hair and muscles knotted high in the calves of her shapely, still agile legs, who taught Hilary ballet that summer she was fourteen, or thought she taught her, for actually Hilary needed to be taught nothing, having learned it all sometime, somewhere, before. I am also, being adult, the police officer who apprehended Hilary, except Hilary could never be apprehended. She was beyond arrest or incarceration, for the walls of any prison would disappear if she laid the palm of her hand against the stone.

The story begins on a Thursday, the second day of the summer ballet course, when a wealth of sunshine was poured out hot over the trees and lawns and the asphalt bowers of the playgrounds. Hilary had eaten her sandwich and drunk her milk, and before the ballet would begin again she wanted to get to where the flotillas of sailboats and schooners would be blowing across the waters of the lake. She wore a short blue dress over the black legs of her leotard, and her pink satin toe shoes were slung across her shoulder by their knotted strings. Her light hair was wrenched away from her scalp into a glossy ponytail, and her eyebrows were jet black and seemingly as perishable as the markings on a night-flying moth.

As she ran across the slope below those benches where the old men bend over their chessboards in the sun, the violent and unexpected battle began. Balloons of every color, swollen with water, sped from the bushes toward the benches, and smacked wide open on the players, drenching their clothes, their hair, and their crumpled faces. Under this multicolored barrage, they leapt to their feet, and knights, castles, kings, queens, bishops, and pawns rolled to the sidewalk or were flung into the sewer opening of the inner avenue. The old men shook their fists and whimpered imprecations.

"Where are they? Where are they?" one old man cried out as he spun around, but there was no one to answer. "You never know when they're going to strike! They make fools even out of the police!" cried out another, kneeling to retrieve the chess pieces with his veined and faltering hands.

Except for the old men and the passing traffic and the stirring of squirrels, there was no sign of life. Even Hilary was gone, having seen the bare legs fleeing from ambush, and running with them in surprise. When they had scattered in a dozen different directions, she found herself standing with three boys in the circle of the zoo, and for a moment none of them could speak because of the wild beating of their hearts. They had halted before the bars of the elephants' yard, and Hilary saw that the clothes the boys wore had been worn too long, and their shirts were torn like paper. The three of them were as thin as deer, and the backs of their necks were stained brown either by the sun or by the climate of the place their people had come from. The tallest carried a bootblack box on a strap across one shoulder, and the smallest had longish black hair, and the side of his face was of great delicacy and beauty. It might have been carved from the ivory tusk that man had relieved the elephants of some time before, giving them nothing in recompense except this small enclosure of captivity. Beyond the bars, the elephant hides appeared coarser and drabber than ever in contrast with the smallest boy's pure face.

"Do you prefer elephants to zebras or zebras to elephants?" Hilary asked the three of them when her heart had quieted. But it was only the tallest boy who turned his head to look at her, his chest rising and falling, rising and falling, with the laboring of his breath. He said hooded cobras were better than zebras or elephants, and his accent turned to music these words he spoke. The other two had cautiously locked the doors of themselves and drawn the blinds down as they stood looking through the bars. "I like armadillos best," Hilary went on saying. "I saw a lot in Mexico last summer."

"I don't know what that animal is," said the tallest boy; and the middle-sized boy, fragile as a wasp, with dark, narrow shoulders hunched up around his ears, gave Hilary a quick, sly glance.

"It's a mail-clad mammal. It has a coat of armor all over it," she was explaining, her curved hands shaping the way the armor fitted on.

"That would be good," the tallest boy said. He shifted the strap of the bootblack box on his shoulder. "It would be good to be like that," he said.

"You'd have to feed on roots and reptiles to preserve your armor," Hilary said. Because of the mask of wariness he wore, the features of his face were difficult to determine. His hair was like a thick black cap pulled down to join his eyebrows, and the narrow space left between scalp and brows was deeply engraved with the lines of his concern. It went through Hilary's mind then that he was perhaps twelve years old, and the others younger, but he had been so many things for such a long time that his face would have great trouble being young again. "Would you want to live on nothing but worms and carrion?" she asked him, as if speaking to a child.

"I wouldn't mind what I ate if I could be armored," he said, his voice low, the accent altering the sound of the words on the summer air.

"Let's go look at the camels," Hilary said. She was suddenly uneasy, for there were his eyes, two mortally stricken and savage beasts, crouching in pain in the darkness of their lairs.

They set off together, two by two, passing the fox and the coyote cages, and when they came to the peanut and popcorn stand, the two who had not yet spoken abruptly took on their separate identities.

"This here's Giuseppe!" cried the delicate-boned and beautiful boy, pushing the other one into Hilary's arms as he danced up and down. "He wants peanuts, nothing but peanuts!" His teeth were white in the ivory mask of his face, and his eyes were thickly lashed. "He's got a big hole inside him and all the peanuts in the world can't fill it up!"

"Maybe two bags would, just maybe!" Giuseppe said. He had swollen, golden eyes set far to the sides of his skull, and his voice was high and wasplike when he spoke. "Jorge, he likes popcorn.

He steals it from the pigeons! I seen him stealing it yesterday!" he said, his teeth grown long and venomous.

Hilary took her wallet from the pocket of her dress, and she bought them what they wanted. The seals were barking hoarsely behind them in the pool, and the boy with the shoeshine box walked up the macadamized path alone.

"Are you brothers? Are any of you brothers?" Hilary asked, catching up with him.

"We're none of us brothers," he said. They could smell the camels, like bad butter, on the air ahead. "Jorge there, he's from Puerto Rico. Giuseppe's people, they're from Italy. My father and mother, they were born in Spain." Whatever he said, it was as if he carried within him a small harp on which the sun, and the breeze, and his own sorrow played. "My name's Federico. They named me after a Spanish poet the cops killed back in Spain," he said.

"If you'd like some popcorn," Hilary said, holding the waxed bag out to him, "I haven't touched it yet." But he shook his head.

"I only eat reptiles and carrion," he said.

There was no time left even for the camels, for in twenty minutes the ballet would begin again. The smell of them, and the sound of the seals' voices, grew fainter and fainter as Hilary and Federico climbed the steps toward the traffic of the avenue. Federico shifted the strap of his bootblack box higher on his shoulder, and he might have been speaking of something as casual as the way the grass grew between the trees, or of the tunnel of sidewalk shade that was waiting at the top. But what he was saying was that Giuseppe's brother had drowned in the Bronx two weeks ago. It was a kind of reservoir that he'd fallen into, he said, with a big fence around it, and nobody could get over the fence in time.

"There was a cop there, and even the cop couldn't get off his horse quick enough and get over the fence," Federico said, his voice low, the words he spoke playing like music in the beginning of the leafy shade.

"So what?" Jorge, the beautiful, said, coming behind them up the steps.

"He kept on crying for help for a long time, but nobody could get over the fence," Federico said. "People just stood there looking at him."

"Sometimes people are like an audience," Hilary said, not wanting to hear Giuseppe's brother crying out. "You keep on waiting, and sometimes they don't even applaud," she said, her pale mouth chewing the popcorn fast.

"So what?" Jorge said again.

"And what do you do if they don't applaud?" Federico asked.

But it was Jorge, the delicate-featured, the jet-black-lashed, who answered.

"Then they pull the curtain down on you—quick, like that," he said. He stood beside them on the sidewalk now, making a baseball out of his popcorn bag, and aiming it at a pigeon strolling by. "I saw a kid killed yesterday. A horse was running away with her up near 72nd Street, and she fell off and cracked her head wide open on a rock. She was dead like that," he said, and he snapped his fingers. "I got real close. I touched her hand. It was cold like stone."

"That's nothing," said Giuseppe, his long teeth slyly smiling. He had come so quietly among them that they had not known he was there. The cars passed before them on the avenue, and Hilary waited at the curb, waited either for the light to change from red to green, or else for the terrible story to be told. "There was a kid downstairs from us," he was saying, the waspish shoulders hunched up to his ears. "I guess she was something like six months old. And this man—maybe he was her father, except her name was Angela Talleferico, and he had another, different name—he used to get drunk, and he'd beat her when she cried. And one night she kept on crying, and he picked her up by her feet and smashed her a couple of times against the wall. They had his picture in the paper, resisting arrest."

"They kill rabbits like that where I come from in Puerto Rico," Jorge said, and he did a step or two of his casual, gypsy dance. "It's a quick way to die," he said, and Hilary suddenly cried out:

"Stop saying these things! Stop saying them!" Her face was white, and her teeth were clenched. "I don't want all the children in the world to die!" she cried out above the sound of the heedless traffic.

"Well, they have to just the same," Giuseppe said quietly, and he smiled his venomous, slow smile.

"All of them," Jorge said, walking on the edge of the curb as if balancing on a tightrope. "All of them, except for me," he said.

"The poet they named me after, he died, but they never found his body," said Federico. He did not look at Hilary, as if not to see the tears coming down her face. "He wrote a poem telling he was going to be killed. He said they would never find his body. And it was true," he said.

"Maybe God took it," said Giuseppe, the wasp. With his thin crooked arms, he made the motion of great wings flapping across Fifth Avenue.

"You didn't say what your name is," said Federico after a moment.

When she told him, he said the letters of it over twice. And then the light changed, and she lifted one hand and pointed to where the ballet-school sign hung, halfway up the side street, partly in shadow and partly in sun.

"I have to go there and dance," she said, and she crossed the avenue alone, without looking back at them, wanting never to see any one of them again. Her head was down, and her heart was filled with grief, and the taste of tears was salty in her mouth.

That was Thursday, and on the next Tuesday Hilary came back to the city again to work on the *pas de chat* and the *entrechat* and the *arabesque,* and the rest of the rigmarole that the lady with bright orange hair tried to teach the young. When Hilary walked out of the ballet school for the noontime recess, Federico and Jorge and Giuseppe were waiting there beneath the canopy. In spite of the heat, she wore the tight black leotard, and carried over her shoulder on their knotted strings were the same pink toe slippers, somewhat soiled and frayed. But this time her dress was yellow, and her hair fell open across her shoulders to her waist, and she held her lunch in a small brown paper bag.

"Isn't your hair hot?" was the first thing Jorge said. He was even more delicate-boned, more gazelle-eyed, more ebony-hoofed, than he had been before.

"No, it isn't," Hilary said, and she swung the length of it sideways, as if out of the reach of his hand. She did this without thought or intention, not knowing that the outcry of children who had died by violence would be there forever between them, only not to be mentioned aloud again or acknowledged in any way. If Federico had spoken in warning then, telling her that a shadow hung over the streets, the parks, the avenues, the reservoirs, the bridle paths, even in clearest sunlight, if he could have said this to her in musical words, she might have taken them dancing elsewhere, perhaps back on a train into suburbia, where the grass springs green and fresh in the horse's paddock, and the cricket voices are as bright and separate as stars. But Federico did not speak. So instead Hilary went on saying: "If we're going to talk, let's think of the most interesting possible things to say, not about the weather."

Giuseppe began at once by saying there were coins in the fountain across from the Plaza. Jorge was dancing backward down the street before them as they walked, and he said that people made wishes when they threw the coins in the water, so you could make wishes the same way when you took them out. He said that he and Giuseppe had made two dollars and ninety-five cents that morning in the subway; saying they could walk through maybe ten or twelve subway cars on their hands when it wasn't the rush hour; saying they carried the nickels and dimes and quarters that people gave them in their mouths so they wouldn't fall out of their pockets. He said they stood on their heads on the express-stop platforms, because that way you covered two trains at a time, while they played their mouth organs upside down; saying that when they learned to juggle they'd be in big-time money.

"Where do you keep the nickels and dimes and quarters when you're playing the mouth organs upside down?" Hilary asked.

"In our ears," Jorge said; and how they could laugh with all that lay behind them and all that still lay ahead, it is difficult to say; but, except for Federico, they laughed out loud. Even Hilary laughed as Jorge danced backward down the street, speaking to her of rain and shine, and now and yesterday, and what they did winter and summer. "In winter we keep them in our earmuffs, and in summer in our snorkels," he said.

"We went every day except Sunday to the door of the ballet school and waited," Giuseppe said, his shoulders hunched to his golden ears, his face scarred by his furtive, insect-smiling.

"That's not very interesting. That's like talking about your hair being hot," said Jorge, the supple. But Federico did not speak.

"There's going to be a competition at the ballet school," Hilary said suddenly. "They told us that today."

"For dancing the best?" Jorge asked, and he spun himself three times into the air.

"For the best ballet a student writes," said Hilary. She looked at the side of Federico's face, at the lowered head, and the hair jerked down in a black iron helmet to his brows. He carried the bootblack box on a strap over his shoulder as he had carried it before, but today he seemed a little taller. He might be thirteen, or even fourteen, she thought, and she liked it better that way. "I want to do something like *Petrouchka*. I want to have organ-grinders, and monkeys, and things like that in it, ordinary things, not swans or angels," she said.

Jorge skipped to the right and then to the left in his backward dance to avoid the people passing by.

And now Federico spoke. "Did you ever make up a ballet before?" he said.

"I made one out of a miracle play once," she said, and she wanted to tell him then that she had made up a dance of the forest-trees. Each tree was exactly like the others, swaying and murmuring with leaves, she wanted to say to him, until it stepped out from the others and danced in the spotlight alone. And then you could see that one tree had birds' nests in its hair, and the boughs of another were filled with fruit, and another had honeycombs packed in its trunk, and another had mistletoe at its crest, like a lighted chandelier. "I made it up for first graders to dance," she said.

"I don't know what is a miracle play," Federico said.

"It has something to do with religion," said Hilary, "and it has to have magic come to pass in the end."

Being a prisoner bound hand and foot by his own silence, Federico could not tell her that whoever had come close to the Spanish poet whose name he bore had been baptized in the dark waters of his magic. These were the words in which his father had described him.

"Wherever he went, that poet always found a piano," Federico said. "Even when he was running from the cops, he played."

They had come to the traffic light, and Jorge turned himself the right way around to cross Fifth Avenue. The four of them walked clear of the trees together, past the open carriages halted in a row. The long, bony faces of the horses between the shafts were masked to the eye sockets in their feed bags, and pigeons walked in and out beneath them, pecking swiftly at the grains that fell. The cushioned seats of the carriages were older than time, but neatly brushed and mended, and shiny-handled whips stood upright at the dashboards, alert as antennae for any promises that might be on the air.

"Someday we're going to cut all the horses loose and race them up to 110th Street," Jorge said. "We'll go faster than cars, faster than jets. There's big-time money in horse racing."

They crossed through the surf of heat to the shoreline of the little square, and the shimmering waves ran liquid to the curb with them, but came no farther, for here the trees made their own cool grove of shade, and the fountain waited. Hilary sat down on the curved edge at the brink, and took the squat milk carton and straw and the sandwich from her paper bag. Federico slipped the strap of the bootblack box from his shoulder, and set the box down on the pavings, and he stooped to look into the water held in the crescent of stone.

"I thought of writing a shoeshine ballet," Hilary said, beginning to eat. "We'd have to have ten or twelve more shoeshine boys."

"I could get them," Federico said, looking up quickly. "I have friends. I have enemies, too," he said with pride. "The poet had many friends. One of his friends was a matador. He got killed in the bull ring." For the moment he said this, the javelins were laid aside, and the armor was unbuckled. "He wrote a poem about the death of his friend. My father said the poem many times in Spanish to me. My father said it was the best poem he wrote because it had the most *duende*. The *duende* does not come to a poet unless it knows that death is there." If he could have remembered the exact words his father had said, he would have put them into English for her, saying that all one knows of the *duende* is that it burns the blood like powdered glass. He would have told her that Spaniards have said that the *duende* is not in the fingers, not in the throat, but that it surges up from the soles of the feet. He would have whispered across the trembling water: "For those who have *duende,* it is easier to love and to understand, and also one is certain to be loved and understood." But he could not manage to say these things. "If you put *duende* into the shoeshine ballet, then it would be good. It would not be an ordinary dance," was all he was able to say.

Jorge had already sprung on his dark quick legs into the fountain, and his toes sought out the coins at the bottom and flipped them up into his open palm. Giuseppe, striped yellow and black by sunshine and shade, and drained now of his venom, hovered above the surface like a dragonfly. If there were any adults passing, they did not see them, for their eyes, concerned with the vision of something else, had wiped the sight of children away.

"I wish for all the elephants and foxes and coyotes and camels to get out of their cages, and the eagles and ostriches," Jorge said, with the wishing-coins held in his hand.

"I wish for all the cops and the cops' horses to be turned to stone, and everybody not standing in the fountain," Giuseppe said, his mouth stretched grinning in his face, his long teeth hanging out.

"Jump into the fountain quick and be saved!" Jorge cried to Hilary and Federico, but they gave no sign that they had heard. Federico was watching Hilary's finger trace the plan for the ballet up and down, and back and forth, across the stone.

"It could begin with the bombing of the old men playing chess," she was saying. "It could begin with a hundred balloons of every color being thrown across the stage."

"Maybe we ought to start practicing now," said Jorge, leaping from the fountain.

"That part doesn't need any rehearsal," Hilary said, "and there wouldn't be any water in the balloons, but the old men would shake their fists at us just the same. There'll be a dance for boys standing on their heads," she went on with it, "and a dance for boys walking on their hands through a subway train. We'll need eight or ten more acrobats for that."

"I'll get the acrobats, but they're rivals of the shoeshine boys," Giuseppe said.

"Thursday, I'll stay in town after my classes," said Hilary, "and we can begin to practice. The last dance of a ballet has to be like a climax. We'll find some very dramatic music for it. It will be the dance of the knives, the switch-blade knives," she said. "In the end every boy will lay his knife down on the grass."

As she finished speaking, a sudden hush fell on them, and after a moment Federico put the question softly to her.

"Our knives. What do you mean to say, our knives?" he asked.

"Don't all boys carry knives?" she cried a little wildly, not knowing how the thought had come to her. "You must admit that the ballet has to have some meaning. All ballets do. So the stage will get slowly darker and darker, until it is about like dusk, and the boys will kneel and lay their knives down on the grass."

None of them moved. They remained quite silent, looking at her face. And then a stranger's voice summoned them back from where they were.

"Hey, boy," it called out, "I want a shine!"

Federico got to his feet, and picked up his box by its canvas strap, and Giuseppe and Jorge stepped back into the fountain to get on with what they had to do. The stranger was leaning against a tree, and he fitted the sole of his shoe into the iron foothold as Federico knelt before him. The top of the shoeshine box was open now, and from where she sat Hilary could see on the light wood of the inside of it, the name "Hilary" written in shoe polish black, ineffaceable, and strong.

Hilary was the first to get to the meeting place in the park on Thursday. It was five o'clock, and the members of the ballet troupe had not yet begun to assemble on the slope below the benches where the old men played. But after a moment they began to come up the path, or emerge from under the trees, or else come running down the slope. Some of them carried shoe-shine boxes, and some were Negroes; some were olive-skinned, and some were white as grubs. Three or four of them turned themselves upside down at once and stood on their heads as they waited, and one of them played a harmonica, but not loud enough to attract the attention of anyone passing by. At first there were ten, and then fifteen, and at last there were twenty boys, some chasing each other across the grass on silent feet, some shadowboxing, some simply waiting. It was almost as if it were the wraiths of boys who had drifted, in the beginning of evening, to this appointed place. Even the old men at their chessboards did not interrupt their games to glance down to where they were. But Hilary was uneasy in their muted presence until Federico and Jorge and Giuseppe came up from the iron jungle of the playground, and then she knew there was no reason to fear.

"Have you got the balloons?" Jorge asked at once. His eyes were black-lashed, his delicate bones more pliable, his beauty even more eloquent than before.

"Have you got enough peanuts to go around?" Giuseppe said.

"I didn't bring anything for anyone," Hilary said. "It isn't going to be like that. First we decide on the different roles, and then we practice the ballet steps. In the end, if we win the competition, there'll be prizes and things to eat," she said.

But how to describe the rehearsal that now got under way is not an easy thing to do. However it came about, within a few minutes the lot of them were twisting and turning, and swinging and bopping, with Giuseppe playing on the harmonica the music of *Petrouchka*, playing it over and over as Hilary hummed it aloud. Jorge led the boys who walked on their hands, making them clap their feet together; and Federico danced the steps that a matador dances, his chest thrust out, his shoeshine box hanging from his shoulder, leading the bootblacks like him who, day after day, kneeled before men with shoes to be cleaned. As they followed the pattern he stamped in the grass, their tempers were running hot in their blood, but Hilary, the actress of interna-tional renown, the musical genius of sweet precocity, was not aware that this was taking place. That they had come to dance for peanuts, or the slap of water-filled balloons or for some act of violence as reward, had nothing to do with the music of Mozart or Stravinsky, or with the *duende* of a Spanish poet whose last name Federico could not recall. It was six o'clock when the murmur of their discontent became an orchestration for bass violins, but still Hilary did not recognize the deep-voiced prophecy it made.

They had come to the moment for the final dance, for the climax of renunciation, and Hilary, her high, narrow cheekbones flushed, jumped up from where she had been kneeling on the grass. Her voice could scarcely be heard in the vast auditorium of the park as she called out to them in heedless pleasure:

"It was very good! It was better than any ballet I've ever seen! This is almost the end. This is where I come in for the first time, and you must all stop dancing when I come on the stage!"

But they had already ceased to dance.

"Have you got the balloons with you?" one voice shouted out. "What are we getting out of this?" another asked, as if he had looked down in bewilderment and suddenly seen his empty hands. The sky, like a planetarium cleared for stars, was filled with the blue and lingering dying of the light. "We ain't jumping up and down here for our health!" cried another voice from the receding limbo where they stood, their features wiped away, and their color gone, in the slowly falling dusk.

"This is the final part!" Hilary said. "Don't be impatient! This is where you take your knives out, because the ballerina asks you to, and you lay them down, each making up a separate dance!"

And now the roar of their voices was like a tempest rising, and Federico pushed his way through the wild storm to where Hilary stood. He took the switchblade knife from the back pocket of his chinos, and whatever they may have thought he had in mind, he laid it down, with a sweep of his arm, before her. This was the last gesture he was to be permitted for all eternity, for the leaping, screaming mob closed in on them.

"So the Hooded Cobra dies!" they cried in fury. "The Hooded Cobra dies!"

The sirens of the police cars keened in pain, and the ambulance shrieked out like a mother for him, as his blood ran black across the trampled grass. The park was empty. The old men had folded their chessboards and gone home, and there were no children anywhere. He had been cast off by friend and enemy, by life itself, except for the little girl who sat with the iron helmet of his head held close against her heart. "The knife and the cartwheel, the razor and the prickly beards of shepherds, the bare moon . . . religious images covered with lace work," went the words of the poet whose name he had been given; "in Spain, all these have in them minute grass-blades of death." His knife lay there, with no blood on its blade, as the cops leaned over to take her hands away from him.

"Stop crying," said the one who apprehended her. "If you get mixed up in things like this, it has to end this way."

Seven Say You Can Hear Corn Grow

Dan Minos was a boy who collected all kinds of odd information from the newspapers he read, bits and pieces of things that had already taken place, or were still taking place, here and there in the world; such as the report that an octopus in the zoo in Berlin, Germany, was devouring itself at the rate of a half inch of tentacle per day. One of the aquarium officials had stated that the octopus was suffering from some emotional upset, and that by the end of the month, if the situation continued, it would certainly be dead. The boy read this and looked at his own gnawed fingernails, and then looked quickly at something else.

Once he read about how scientists are trying to dilute the venom in the stings of jellyfish that drift along the eastern seaboard like fringed umbrellas (as the paper put it), pulsing in and out among the bathers with limp curved handles hanging under them, while the tide, or some unseen hand, opens and closes them continuously. This poison, went the story, is stored in cups along the umbrella handles, and it acts in the same way as the stuff South American Indians tip their arrowheads with, causing paralysis, failure of the respiratory organs, and death in the case of small sea animals. Another time there was a half-page report on the remarkable navigating abilities of the green turtle, saying that the U. S. Navy was financing a study of how this large seafarer finds the pinpoint island of his birth.

When Dan's mother came back to their Brooklyn apartment at night, she would bring some newspaper or other with her that a customer had left behind on a table in the restaurant where she worked. One night it might be the *Herald Tribune* or maybe the *New York Times* that she carried with her handbag into the kitchen, and other nights it might be the *Journal-American* or the *Daily News*. But whatever paper it was, Dan would go through the pages of it in his room before he went to sleep, not noticing the name of the paper or the date, but reading the columns eagerly, as if in search of some final communiqué that would tell him how either beast or man had coped with the predicament of circumstances; as if seeking, in the silent doom of animals without precisely knowing what he sought, some indication of what his own vocabulary might one day be.

If you came to the conclusion that Dan Minos speculated on these things he read because the world of newsprint was the only world he functioned in, you would be wrong; for he had as well the daily world of high school, and he had major league baseball to follow, and television to present to him as reality the myths of power by which America lives. It was more that he carried the news items he read like a kind of shield between himself and others, a shield that was never emblazoned with any likeness of himself, but with that of aquarium official, or of scientist isolating the sting of jellyfish, or naval experimenter tagging green turtles at Ascension Island. Once it was the likeness of a German priest he carried, a priest who had been sitting in the front row of the circus when the lion tamer in the enclosed arena clutched at his heart and fell to the floor. The wild beasts had slunk down from their perches, the newspaper item said, and moved stealthily toward the fallen lion tamer while the spectators watched with bated breath for what was absolutely certain to take place. And then the priest had jumped up, pulled open the door of the caged arena, warded off the lions with a chair, and dragged the stricken man to safety. (Whether or not the lion tamer died of his heart attack in the end, the newspaper did not say).

It was only the story of the harness racing horse that went berserk in an airfreighter eight thousand feet above the ocean that Dan couldn't put to any immediate use.

"Sometimes I've thought of being a pilot, a commercial pilot," Dan said to his mother that evening when she came home, "but then I read this thing about the horse in the airplane, and maybe I don't feel the same about pilots any more."

"If my opinion was to be asked," his mother said, "I'd say go ahead and be a commercial pilot and forget about the horse." She worked as a waitress, and she never gave him any real trouble except when he came in so late at night that for hours she'd have been walking her high heels sideways up and down outside on the street. Sometimes it was three o'clock when he'd come home, and she'd be walking back and forth on the Brooklyn street without so much as a Kleenex to stop her crying, complaining about him to anyone passing by. "He doesn't know five o'clock in the afternoon from midnight," she'd say to anyone at all. "I don't know how he gets along. He can't tell good from bad." Or she'd give a description of him in case someone had seen him, saying: "He's nearly six foot tall, and his shoulders are broad, and he's nicely built, the way his father was. He'd be good-looking if he went and got his hair cut every now and then." She got up now from the kitchen table, and crossed the room, and took a can of beer out of the refrigerator, and she swore under her breath as the new-type, built-in-the-can opener tore a piece out of her nail. "But my opinion isn't worth anything to anybody, living or dead," she said.

Dan looked at her dark orange hair, and her face bleached smooth as a china cup, with the various features painted carefully on it.

"There were six horses in the plane," he said, thinking of this thing that had taken place maybe yesterday or the day before, "and this one, this champion, he panicked. He'd been winning harness races everywhere, Australia, New Zealand, all over, the paper said. He was worth seventy-five thousand dollars, and he was kicking and rearing like at a rodeo."

"All they had to do was turn around," the mother said, drinking exquisitely from the can. "Planes can always turn around and go back the way cars can't. You get yourself on a throughway in a car and if you're heading west you have to go to Chicago whether you want to go there or not."

"This plane was going to Montreal," Dan said. "They couldn't go back."

"What's so special about Montreal?" the mother asked, her small, cherry lip mustached with foam.

"The freight engineer, he said they'd tried cutting the sling around his ribs so they could get him to lie down," the boy said. "There were three of them trying to quiet him, but he threw them off, and his front legs were hanging out over the side of the stall. He was smashing against the cockpit, like trying to get to the controls. The other five horses had started acting up, so that's when the pilot told them what to do."

"I don't want to hear what they did," the mother said, taking another swig of beer.

"You can't change it by not listening," Dan said. "It happened. You can't make things different by just looking the other way."

"If you drank a can of beer every now and then, things would look different to you whether they were or not," his mother said. "It would relax you. It would do you good."

"The pilot of the airfreighter said the horse had to be destroyed," Dan said, perhaps not even having heard her speak. "That's the word they use," he explained. "But they didn't have a gun."

"They could have pushed the horse out the hatch," the mother said. She got up from her chair and carried the empty beer can across the kitchen to where it had to go. "For a horse worth seventy-five thousand dollars, they could have afforded a parachute," she said, daintily pressing her foot in a bedroom slipper trimmed with gilded ostrich feathers on the pedal of the garbage pail. When the white lid gaped open, she dropped the beer can inside. "Can't you see that horse parachuting out of the plane, pulling the rip cord and everything?" she said, and she gave a little scream of laughter. Then she took another can of beer from the refrigerator, and walked carefully on her wedge-soled slippers back to the table, and sat down. "So this time maybe you'll open it for me," she said, as she had said it on so many other evenings; and Dan took the can in his narrow fingers and twisted the flat metal tongue from its misted top. "I bought another pair of eyelashes today. Better quality," she went on saying. "Real dark long ones, with a new kind of stickum on them. If I go to the show tomorrow night, maybe you'll help me put them on."

"So when the freight engineer got the word from the pilot about what to do, he grabbed a fire ax," Dan said, and she still might not have spoken. He was seeing it exactly as it must have been.

"Stop it!" his mother cried out in sudden ferocity. "I don't have to hear it! I have a hard enough time working myself to death on my feet all day!"

"You have to hear it," Dan said. He looked at her small bright trembling mouth and her quivering chin, but he did not seem to see her. "If you don't know whether you're on the side of the horse they killed or on the side of the pilot, there's no sense trying to work out your life. You have to decide that first," he said.

"On the side of the horse or the side of the pilot? You're crazy!" she cried out in fury, her hand too agitated now to lift the can of beer.

And then, two nights later, on Christopher Street, in the city itself, Dan made the acquaintance of the girl. It could have been any month and any Saturday, with no extremes of any kind, and only the first beginning of chill in the bluish New York air. It had not yet begun to go dark when Dan saw the old man lying across the curb near the corner of Seventh Avenue, lying flat on his thin back with his legs sticking out into the street so that the passing traffic had to swing around them. His ancient trousers were slashed across as if by a knife, and his shoes were split by the bunions and corns he had carried around with him for half a century or more. His small head lay in a semblance of ease and comfort on the sidewalk paving, economically crowned with a crew cut of the purest white. The same white bristled without hostility along his jaws, and his cheekbones were bright as apples on either side of his short, scarlet nose. Beside him, in a turtle-neck sweater and slacks, the girl squatted, her face masked by a swinging curtain of long, straight, almost tinsel-colored hair. She was trying to raise the old man by his shoulders, and she was trying to push her bracelets and the black sweater sleeves back on her forearms, to get these encumbrances out of the way. "Repeatedly striking with force between the horse's eyes," the newspaper line kept going, for no good reason, through Dan's mind as he stooped down, "the flight engineer brought the frenzied pacer to its knees, and the ordeal of terror for man and beast was over."

"He looks as though he'd been here a week," the girl was saying.

"I'll get his shoulders," Dan said, and the girl shifted on the heels of her loafers out of his way.

The mottled-tweed jacket the man wore was soft and expensive to the touch; but however good it had once been, and whatever tall and elegant stranger had worn it once with grace, frayed wool now hung like feathers from the cuffs and from the jaunty lapels. As Dan drew him up onto the sidewalk, the girl moved on her heels beside them, her knees in the tight black slacks almost touching her chin, her bracelets ringing musically when she laid her palms beneath the old man's head. The three of them might have been quite alone in the crowded street. No one slackened his pace, no one turned to look in their direction, perhaps because of the sad sharp odor of grieving dreams and rotted teeth that lay in an aura around the sleeping man. Dan knew it well. It was there winter and summer, in snow or in rain, in the gutters and alleyways of the downtown streets he wandered. It lay in stupor under the park benches in the early mornings when drunks sobbed aloud to stone and grass the furious accusations of their pain.

"You'd better get that pint out of his hip pocket," Dan said to the silky lengths of the girl's hair, knowing, too, the exact size and shape the flask would be. "Sometimes when they fall, it cuts them up right through their clothes."

"You're sharp, aren't you, kid?" the girl said. For the first time now she looked up at him, and he saw that her eyes were wide and dark and stormy, and her brows and lashes were smudged like charcoal across her face. "I happen to live in this city," she said. "I happen to live right on this street." Dan held the little man under the armpits still, and as he looked down at the girl he thought of the things that might be of interest to say. He might tell her that in Japan a drunk is called *o-tora-san,* which means "Honorable Mr. Tiger," and that there are over a hundred and fifty sobering-up stations over there called "Tiger Boxes." He could give her the statistics even, saying that just last year one hundred and twenty-eight thousand and ninety-seven drunks had been taken to "Tiger Boxes" by the police to sleep it off. But he had got the little old man in a sitting position, with his neat skull fallen forward on his breast, and it did not seem the moment to speak. The girl reached into the little man's back pocket and took out the gold-and-red lettered bottle that had clung so perilously to his hip. "Two houses up there's an alley where he can lie down, where the fuzz won't see him," she said. She slipped the half-empty flask into the depths of her black shoulder bag, her bracelets ringing like sleigh bells as she moved.

They were walking now, the little old man held upright between them, and Dan thought of the Potawatomi Indians on Michigan's Upper Peninsula drinking for solace, as one newspaper had said. The professor who made the report had been drinking two years with them, and he said that alcohol now substituted for the tribal customs and rituals that had disappeared from their lives. Alcohol, the professor stated to the press, had given them the illusions that their ancestral rights had restored to them the high status that Potawatomi men had held until the white man had come upon the scene. "This professor said drinking was a way for them of asking for pity," Dan wanted to say to the girl, but he didn't say it. Nor did he tell her that in Brazil the police let sleeping drunks lie as long as they didn't block the sidewalk. With the little man propelled between them, they had come to the alleyway now, and there seemed no reason to speak of things that were taking place so far away.

"Get him to the end, back there behind the garbage cans," the girl said, and the pigeons who had been pecking at the paving stones hurried aside to let them pass.

The girl lowered her half of the little man to the ground, and Dan could not see the back of her neck because of the window shade of her hair drawn down across her shoulders. But he saw her slender, tightly belted waist, and her narrow hips, and the long, slim tapering legs in the black slacks, and he could not look away.

"I'll put my jacket under his head," he said, once the little man lay flat on his back in comfort.

The girl waited until he had folded it under the neat, impervious head, and then she drew the old man's right hand free of the elegant frayed sleeve and laid it, palm down, on his breast.

"Give me the other one," she said to Dan. It lay as if cast off, as if forgotten, on the alley stone, and Dan lifted it while she took the whiskey flask out of her bag. Then she bent the old man's will-less arm so that his two hands lay upon his heart, and she closed his fingers around the flask so that he, this ancient, malodorous infant in his asphalt crib, would find it there in solace when he awoke. "Regulations," the girl said. "Orders from the top." She stood up now, and Dan saw she was not tall, and that her hair was parted in the middle, and that she had no lipstick on her mouth. "This is my job. I get paid for it," she was saying, and a look of singular shrewdness was in her stormy eyes. "I've got quite an important position. I get paid by the city," she said.

"If they're hiring people, I'd be free to work every night," Dan said. They walked down the alley together, past the last of the pigeons hastening back and forth in the beginning of dusk, their eyes cocked sharply in their smooth, gray-feathered skulls. And every word that he and the girl exchanged seemed as reasonable to him as the story of that other, foreign pigeon who had hopped a hundred and sixty miles across Denmark with its wings bound. The newspaper had said that it crossed two rivers, nobody knew how, to get back to where it came from in the end. "I'd like a job like that," he said.

"You have to be twenty to work for the city," the girl said. "You look too young." As they entered Christopher Street again, the street lights came on in the early evening, and she shifted her black bag higher on her shoulder, walking now with that sort of frenzied dedication that takes people across deserts, across prairies, not caring about food, or drink, or sleep, driven toward some final destination that has no geography or name. "You have to know Spanish and French and Puerto Rican, and a lot about history," she said.

"I know about things like that," Dan said, keeping step beside her. "I read a lot." He thought of the green turtles' knowledge of the currents of the sea, and the Caribbean beaches they came back to, not every year, but whenever they could make it, navigating sometimes more than a thousand miles to reach the hot white sands where they were born. "The green turtles' lives are something like history," he said. "Anyway, Columbus left written records about them. I read about how they come swimming in to these beaches, and dig their holes, and lay their eggs. Columbus and the other explorers, like Leif Ericson and everyone, they used to eat their eggs."

"Did they eat them fried or boiled?" the girl asked sternly. "These are the things you have to know."

"That wasn't in the paper," Dan said, and his voice was troubled. They had come to the corner of Seventh Avenue, and the girl turned left without any hesitation, and Dan followed where she led. "They have something like a compass inside them, the turtles," he went on saying. He and the girl were moving through the electric blue and yellow and red of the café lights, and through the spaces of city dark, and his head was turned to watch the side of her face changing as the lights and the diluted darkness changed. "I think I have something like that, too," Dan said. "I bet I could find New York wherever I was. I could come straight back across the country without needing maps or roads or anything like that."

"What country?" the girl asked, with the sharp edge of something different in her voice. "What country are you talking about?"

"Well, this country. The United States. I mean, America," Dan said, as if not quite certain of the name.

"You're pretty weak on geography," the girl said. She was

stepping down from the curb, over rotting orange peels, over onion tails that had once been green, and flattened grapefruit rinds. "We haven't got a country. Wise up, kid. We've got New York," she said.

They crossed this side street as they had crossed the others, moving through the altering sections of dark and light. Wherever the girl was taking him was of no importance, and the impatience of the words she spoke was transformed to gentleness by the curve of her cheekbone below his shoulder, and the delicacy of her temple and brow when she swung back her hair. They were entering warehouse territory now, and high above the traffic hung the perpendicular letters of a sign not written in neon, but only faintly alight with the dying glow of bulbs set in its frame. "Volunteers of America," the sign read, and Dan knew that a queue of men would be standing beneath it, standing night or day, crippled or upright, sober or drunk, and no matter what time of year it was, waiting to pass through the double doors.

"They're waiting for something to eat," Dan said, and the girl did not take the trouble to turn her head and look at him. But she said:

"They're waiting for me. I make a report on them every night. I'm the only one in the field the city trusts." And even this Dan did not question, believing as he did that everything she said was true. Just this side of the slowly moving queue of men, she slipped without warning into the shadows of a warehouse doorway, and flattened her shoulders and her narrow hips against the wall. "Don't let them see you," she whispered, and Dan stepped in beside her. "If they start running after me, don't move. Stay out of sight. Some of them are still very strong even though they're old. If they once get hold of you, they squeeze you terribly in their arms," she said, her voice still hushed, "and they push their chins into your face."

"About us not having a country," Dan said. He was standing so close to her in the darkness that he could hear the breath running in and out of her mouth. "Did you read that in the paper, that we only have New York?"

"Oh, the paper!" she said in irritation.

"Sometimes there're interesting things in the paper," he said. "Last night I read about the artichoke war they're having in France."

"Do you speak French?" the girl asked quickly. "Sometimes I need it. Some nights there're Frenchmen standing in line, sailors who jumped their ships, and haven't any place to go. I have to get their names. I have to make an official report on them."

Dan waited a moment, thinking of this, and then he said:

"Do you report back on these men? Is that the kind of work you do?"

"You're very handsome," the girl said softly, her breath running gently in the darkness, her voice turned tender and low. "I like your hair, and the way you talk, and everything, but you don't seem to understand things very well. I'm paid by the city to call them back from where they are. I'm the only one that can do it." And this might have been the whispered password, the valid signal given, that would cause the sentries to lower their guns and let the trusted through; for now the girl stepped out of the doorway, and her bracelets rang as she made a megaphone of her hands through which to call the words to the waiting men. "Oh, Daddy, Daddy, Daddy!" she cried out in almost unbearable and strident despair, and some in the slowly advancing queue turned their heads, as if aroused from sleep, and some did not. "Oh, P*a*p*a*, P*a*p*a*, P*a*p*a*!" she cried as a daughter from a foreign country might have cried from the sucking undertow before the final music for the drowning played. "Oh, Daddy, Daddy, Daddy, help me!" she cried. "Oh, Popio, Popio, here I am! I'm here!" And now that she had summoned them four times, a wail of anguish rose from the throats of those who had broken from the line, and stumbled back through the darkness to where she was.

Brenda, or Shirley, or Mary, or Barbara, were the names they called out as they tried to run in other men's castoff shoes, in the outsized bags of other men's trousers, and could not. Jean, or Amy, or Pat, or Ann, the muffled voices sobbed like foghorns, and the men in whose throats the hoarse names rose fumbled their way past utility poles and fire hydrants, felt their way like blind men along the warehouse walls toward the sound and the flesh of all they had mislaid in the desert of their lives.

"We'd better get going," the girl said to Dan. She was standing beside him again in the shelter of the doorway, her breath coming fast. "Just run, just run," she whispered, and she pulled him out onto the sidewalk, her fingers closed tightly around his hand.

They did not stop until they had reached the flight of subway steps, and there she let Dan's hand drop. As she threw back her head to look up at him in the wash of the street light, she shook her bracelets savagely.

"You were faster than any of them," Dan said; and, without warning, the vision of the racing horse gone berserk plunged through his thoughts again. As it reared in terror, hammering the cockpit of the airfreighter with its frantic hoofs, Dan touched the girl's silver hair with uncertain fingers, saying: "But you'll have to stop running soon, before you get too tired."

"No, no!" the girl said, whispering it quickly. She stood close to him, looking up at him with her wild, stormy eyes. "You have to get somewhere, don't you?" she said; and then she did not say anything, but she put her arms in the black sweater sleeves tightly, tightly, around Dan's hips, tightly, as if forever, with her head pressed fiercely against the beating of his heart.

It was only for a minute, and then she was gone, running like crazy across Seventh Avenue. The green light turned to red as Dan got to the curb, and the beams of headlights poured between them, and he waited, understanding now with singular clarity the urgency of the choice to be made between horse and pilot, man and man. He could see the white of the harness pacer's eye, and the features of the airfreighter pilot's face, and he knew what should have been done in that interval when the election of either life or death hung in the balance eight thousand feet above the sea. He could not hear the pilot's voice saying *quiet, quiet,* to the stampeding terror. He could not hear it naming the destination to which they were, man and horse, committed, as the course of turtle and pigeon with its wings bound named it louder and clearer than catastrophe. Instead, the pilot's

voice, not only heard but visible as are the words contair
comic-strip balloons, pronounced *destroy,* thus summoning
as witness to his fear. *We are not turning back. We shal*
plete this flight as scheduled, he might have said, but he (
say it; and, standing waiting at the curb, Dan felt the fai
all men in the pilot's failure, and he whispered, "Quie
quiet," to the horse or the girl or the traffic passing by. W
light changed again and the cars halted, he crossed, run
the direction the girl had fled.

But she was not in the alley off Christopher Street. 7
old man was gone, and only his empty flask and the
pails were there. At the "Volunteers of America" the
gone dark and for once the street was empty. Ther
queue of derelict men waiting at the door. It was grov
but Dan did not think of this as he walked up one
down another, searching among the faces that passed
threes through the lights from the cafés, and search:
the solitary others that lingered in the intervals of dar
not find her tonight, still it would not be the end, he l
to himself, for he could come back to the city every r
ever the weather, and on one of the streets, around
corners, he would hear her bracelets ringing or se
hair. If it was not tonight, it would be the night afte
three nights later, or else at the end of the week; ar
had put the drunks to sleep, they would sit down or
together, and he would say, or try to say, "Don't
men back from where they are. Don't make them re
let them go." He would tell her about things tha
place in other parts of America, beyond New Yo
Middle West, for instance, where seven university
made a tape-recording proving that you can hear co.

It was three o'clock in the morning when he
Brooklyn, and his mother was walking up and dc
complaining loudly enough about him for any nei
were awake to hear.

"Your jacket!" she cried out when she saw him con

street. "You had your good jacket on when you left the house!
Oh, God, oh, God!" she wept.

Above them, as they went into the apartment house together,
the one big planet was fading from the sky.